GREEN DARKNESS

Anya Seton's great new novel, the first for eight years.

By the author of *Katherine* and *Devil Water*, a compelling tale woven round the fascinating theme of reincarnation in Tudor times and the present.

The heroine is Celia de Bohun, a very junior member of Sir Anthony Browne's household. Also in the household is Stephen, a priest who is torn between his love for Celia and his love for God. This is the theme which stamps itself on the novel, which now narrates the life of the Catholic gentry in an unstable and often unfriendly world. We see Edward VI and the brief troubled reign of Mary. We see the cunning, sophisticated Elizabeth resolve the problems for her country's gain.

Green Darkness

Anya Seton

CORONET BOOKS
Hodder Paperbacks Ltd., London

Printed and bound in Great Britain for
Coronet Books,
Hodder Paperbacks Ltd,
St. Paul's House, Warwick Lane,
London, EC4P 4AH
by Hazell Watson & Viney Ltd,
Aylesbury, Bucks

ISBN 0 340 17857 4

Contents

Author's Note

The theme of this book is reincarnation, an attempt to show the interplay — the law of cause and effect, good and evil — for certain individual souls in two English periods.

I happened to be raised to this doctrine in which both my parents believed. Mother was a Theosophist long before I was born; indeed she had my horoscope cast when I was a month old. (It did *not* turn out to be a very accurate forecast of my life!)

As a child I grew fascinated by the multitudinous volumes in our home treating of mysticism, occultism, astrology and the like. In my teens the study of comparative religion engrossed me, nor has that interest ever waned. Reincarnation still seems to me the only logical explanation for life's inequities, and half the world believes in some form of it today.

However, for those who do *not* believe this theory, I would hope that *Green Darkness* may be read for the story and the historical reconstruction, and the theme accepted as a sort of science-fiction convention, like the 'time-drugs' or indeed the intricate flashbacks used throughout the last hundred years by many eminent writers.

Medfield Place (and its 1968 inhabitants and friends) is perforce fictional. Though anyone who knows the countryside near the Cuckmere in East Sussex may be able to guess at the prototype.

On the other hand the Tudor portion, 1552–1559, is solidly rooted in historical fact. Anthony Browne (Viscount Montagu) and Lady Magdalen Dacre are presented in whatever exact chronology I have been able to find during many months in England and three years of research. So, of course, are national affairs during that period, and the Tudor reigns.

Celia and Brother Stephen are naturally harder to document, but they existed. The Italian physician, Giuliano di Ridolfi, *was* an astrologer connected with the Duke of Norfolk's household, as I present him.

The first quiver of interest began for me during a visit to Ightham Mote in 1968, with an offhand mention of the 'walled-up girl' and the viewing of the niche from which she was 'ex-mured' in the 1870s. And here I must tender my gratitude to the American owner of the lovely and mysterious 'mote' in Kent—C. Henry Robinson who welcomed me there many times and permitted free use of private notes and his excellent library.

The Cowdray sections of this book have resulted from long stays at the Spread Eagle in Midhurst, frequent examination of the Cowdray ruins and study of the local literature.

The personal history of the de Bohuns, the Brownes and all their relations has been correlated with the help of Collins' *Complete Peerage* and as always the *Dictionary of National Biography*.

Source books make tedious listing, but for the Tudor period I have tried to consult all the pertinent ones.

Oddly enough recent events are often as elusive as Tudor documentaries. One small example. Though I crossed on her, neither I nor my friends retained any idea of the dates for the *Queen Mary*'s last sailings. I had to check with the Cunard Line. This may have some bearing on the peculiarities of memory in general, and therefore on the book's theme.

My warm thanks to the present Howard family in Cumberland, and particularly to the Earl and Countess of Carlisle who welcomed me at Naworth Castle and were most patient with my endeavours to resurrect the lives of their Dacre ancestors.

Several kindly physicians, British and American, have helped me with the medical aspects for 1968. I am, in fact, indebted to a great many people who have taken an interest in this book, but especially to Geoffrey Ashe, the English writer of greater erudition, who took time from his work to make suggestions and unearth for me specific data which I could not find myself.

In the ancient manor of Medfield Place in Sussex there is a huge vellum-bound book containing entries made by the Marsdon family from A.D. 1430 until September 15, 1967, when the death of Sir Charles Marsdon is noted. All but one of the entries are terse dates of births, marriages and deaths.

The exception takes up the whole fifth page of the chronicle, and is as follows:

All Hallowes Eve. Ye 31. yeare of hir Majesties reine, & a tyme of rejoicingye since our fleete has sunk ye wickede Spaniarde, Englande may now with God His Will live in peace under oure most vertuous Queene.

My selfe Thos. Marsdon Esq. beinge yet quite younge but mortal sicke with a wasting melancholy coffing & sore paine in my chest desire to writ in oure familye cronickle by a byegone tragick matter scamped here by my Father for shame — he tolde me of yt on his dethbedde. I have tryed to discover the bodye of the wretched girle which is for certaine welle hid atte Ightham Mote but Sir Chris: Allen & his vexatious ladye heatedlye denye all knowledg — his aged wittes are addled, but she hath a mad wolfishe eye. I wisht to give the girle a Christian berial since it was bye my unckle Stephen she was brote incontinent to her doome. He too suffered grievous paine and dyed in violence I knowe not how. Which unshriven deeds bringe sorrowe to our house. My little sonne when growne enuf to continue the annales must know the event.

My unckle Stephen was monke of Benedict Order in the troubled reines of King Edward & Queene Marye (God rest their souls) he was house priest first at Cowdraye Castle in West Sussex, after at Ightham in Kent.

A terrible lust was sente him bye the Devil, and he broke his sacred vowes. God punished him & the partner of his downfalle. Yet myselfe havinge known deepe tragical love, can find in me naught but pitye for those tormented souls. My unckle is not at reste. I did question an old sheepherd in the pasture near Ightham after Ladye Allen so cholerickally bade me leave: the sheepherd said that the spectre of a black-habited monke

9

was seen both at Cowdraye & Ightham Mote & that he hadde yt from his granddam the poore girle was put away alive, & quick with childe.

I am feable and can no more. I command my heires on fear of damnation yet God his wille permiting to take measures of layinge the ghoste and to finde the murdered girle for Xtian berial.

Medfeilde—Ann: Dom. 1588

PART ONE
1968

One

Celia Marsdon, young, rich and unhappy, huddled in a lounge chair at the far end of the new swimming pool vaguely listening to the chatter of their weekend guests.

Across the pool, above the privet hedge and the rose-laden pergola, sprawled the cluttered roof line of the Sussex manor house, Medfield Place. Richard's home. Her home, now. 'Lady of the Manor', which had seen centuries of these ladies.

In the 1200s some Marsdon—Ralph, was it?—had built himself a small stone keep close by the River Cuckmere. The stones he used were still incorporated in the walls of what looked to be a Tudor mansion with gables, twisted chimney-pots, blackened oak half-timbering among peach-toned bricks. But there were later touches, too, a Georgian bay window added to the dining room, improbable fan lights cut over door-ways, and most shocking of all to the humourless young architect who had come down from London to supervise repairs—two crassly Victorian additions Sir Thomas Marsdon, the only wealthy one of the baronets, had prospered during Queen Victoria's reign owing to his wife's inheritance of collieries in County Durham. During this brief prosperity Sir Thomas had tacked on a large pseudo-Gothic library wing, and a glass garden room which the young architect had wished removed at once.

Richard had been adamant. No matter the period, every brick and beam of Medfield Place was dear to him, and, indeed, the house triumphed over any architectural incongruity. It nestled placidly as it always had between two spurs of the South Downs—those quiet, awesome hills looming purplish-green against the East Sussex skies.

Celia, who was wearing a discreetly cut turquoise bikini, took off her dark glasses, shut her eyes and tried to relax in the sunlight while fighting off a fresh attack of anxiety.

Why should one be frightened? Why again, as often of late, a lump in her throat which could not be swallowed and a sense of suffocation?

This was one of England's rare perfect June days, fluffy clouds scudding across the blue, a faint breeze riffling the leaves, and, said Celia to herself, You have everything a woman could ask for.

She had been told this a hundred times, especially by her mother, Lily. Celia opened her eyes and glanced along the poolside towards her mother who was rapt in conversation with one of those exotic characters she was always finding.

Yet, this particular find was different. True, he was a Hindu and practised Yoga, but he had firmly refused to be introduced as a 'guru', by Lily, for it appeared that he was a doctor of medicine and wished no other title. He had pleasant, modest manners unlike that dreadful, lecherous swami Lily had briefly lionised in the States. *This* Hindu, whose name was Jiddu Akananda, did not wear bunchy robes; his English clothes were well tailored; he had studied at Oxford and then Guy's Hospital, so long ago that he must be sixty. Yet his brown face was ageless, and his lean, supple body as now revealed by swimming trunks was like that of a young man. Celia had had little chance to talk with Doctor Akananda after his arrival last night at the Manor, but she had noted wise, kindly eyes and a sense of humour.

I rather admire him, Celia thought in astonishment. She had not admired most of her mother's collection of swamis, numerologists, astrologers and mediums. Lily was given to sudden enthusiasms and had a certain naïveté which her daughter regarded with indulgence.

Lily Taylor was past fifty and did not look it. Expert tinting kept her hair blonde, while constant dieting kept her natural plumpness from spreading to fat.

When excited, Lily lost her unconscious attempt at an English accent, and her midwestern voice rose now in emphatic agreement with something the Hindu said. 'But, of course,' Lily cried. 'Every intelligent person believes in reincarnation!'

'Well, *I don't*,' remarked the elegant Duchess of Drewton, fitting a slim cigarette into a white jaded holder. 'Lot of nonsense,' she added with her usual smiling assurance.

Celia felt suddenly chilly. She shivered and pulled on her golden beach robe while examining the Duchess. Dowager Duchess, actually, though Myra was barely thirty, but her old Duke had recently died of a coronary and the title passed to a nephew. Myra often combated anyone's statement, as she had Lily's. It was one of her ways of being provocative. And she *was* provocative, Celia admitted, that long gleaming auburn hair caught back in an amber clasp, and the wide sensual mouth. Celia noted that Myra glanced often towards Richard.

Celia, too, with an indrawn breath looked at her husband. He had just executed a perfect swan dive and was towelling himself while blandly ignoring the guests' applause.

Yet, perhaps, with a side-long glance he did respond to Myra? One never knew with Richard any more. He had stopped showing any emotions, especially towards her. The world and Lily, who had come over on an extended visit, thought Richard, a model of charming courtesy. He also had a beautiful smile. It seemed to occur to nobody else that the smile never reached his long-lashed hazel eyes, which remained aloof, a trifle wary.

I love him so desperately. Celia's hands clenched on the chromium arm-rests. I *think* he still loves me, though something has gone wrong, very wrong.

Her heart gave one of its unpleasant thumps as she forced herself to examine what had happened.

It all seemed to begin with a visit to Midhurst last Fall. Hallowe'en it was; in the woodlands, the leaves had turned yellow and russet—so much quieter than the blaze of American maples—and the roads were dappled with fallen leaves and rolling acorns. A smoky violet haze drifted through the folds of the Downs; there was a tang in the air. She and Richard had been so happy that afternoon as they set forth in the Jaguar to meet old acquaintances of his at the Spread Eagle Inn in Midhurst.

They had made love the night before, with ecstatic fulfilment even more joyous than during their honeymoon in Portugal, where, for all her inexperience, Celia sensed something withheld in Richard, the faintest lack of total involvement. But their mutual love last night had been flawless. Especially the aftermath, when she lay naked in his arms, her head on his shoulders, both of them murmuring contentment and watching the starlight filter through the mullioned window.

The glowing contentment still enclosed them as they left Medfield and started towards Lewes. Richard drove slowly, for him, and after a while remarked lazily, 'I'll be glad to see old Holloway again, friend of my father's, and your romantic little American heart will be charmed by the Spread Eagle Inn.' He swerved into a hedge-lined by-way to avoid the main road. 'It's frightfully ancient, all half-timbering, dim passages and smugglers' hideaways.'

'My romantic heart is charmed by Sussex, by England, and

15

especially by my husband,' Celia said, laughing. She cuddled against him.

He rested his cheek against the top of her curly brown hair for a second. 'Foolish poppet,' he said. 'It's not quite the thing to be in love with a *husband*, not done, my dear.'

'Too bad,' she murmured. 'Oh, look, darling, there's a bon-fire on that hill. Is it for Hallowe'en?'

'I suppose so,' he said, 'though we usually reserve those for Guy Fawkes day. "Pray you remember the fifth of November, with gunpowder, treason and plot; the King and his train were like to be slain. I hope this day'll ne'er be forgot." '

'Who did what to whom?' asked Celia eagerly. 'Was it the "wicked" Catholics again?'

Richard did not speak for a moment, then he said, 'It was. The Papists, led by one Guy Fawkes, tried to blow up Parliament. They were foiled. Then, beheadings and hangings all around. We've been celebrating the happy outcome ever since.'

'You sound a bit ironic,' she looked up at his dark profile.

'Atavism, no doubt.' He lit a cigarette and turned the Jag into another by-way. 'The Marsdons were staunch Roman Catholics in those days. We only became meekly Protestant in the eighteenth century, during the age of reason.'

'And you regret the conversion?'

'Good Lord, no! Who bothers one way or the other now-adays? Though sometimes I've had strange — well, dreams.'

She pounced on this, for he so rarely made a personal admis-sion. 'Dreams? What kind of dreams?'

He withdrew a trifle. 'Lunatic fancies, not worth recalling.'

She sighed, always the door slammed shut before she could quite get inside.

'You make rather a fuss over Hallowe'en in the States,' he continued conversationally. 'It's odd how many of our old customs were exported by the Puritans, and linger on across the water.'

'Yes, I guess so,' Celia answered. 'The kids dress up in costumes; they go trick-or-treating; there are pumpkins carved for Jack-o'-lanterns — cider and apple-bobbings.'

'On All Hallows' Eve,' said Richard slowly, 'when wicked witches ride their broomsticks, and the grave gives forth its wormy dead.'

'Ugh,' she said, 'how gruesome. In the States, we just have fun.'

'Yes, new and careless race.' Richard sighed. Her head was

on his shoulder and she could feel the sigh. 'I envy you. You're almost untouched by the ancient Evil, which yet casts its shadow on us all.'

She was silent, never knowing quite what he meant when he talked this way.

At dusk they drove through the village of Easebourne, and Richard said, 'That building to your left was a nunnery in early Tudor times. The church has some rather good effigies of Cowdray Castle's former owners.'

'Oh,' she said, 'who were *they*?' English history had always interested her, but now that passionate love had made her part of England and its past, she had begun fascinated research, particularly of Sussex, which had become her home.

'Sir Davy Owen,' answered Richard, 'bastard son of Owen Tudor. He married a Bohun, the knightly owners of Midhurst in the fifteenth century. There is also an elegant marble effigy of Anthony Browne, the first Lord Montagu, kneeling above his two wives; one wife I don't remember, but the other was a Lady Magdalen Dacre, who must have been prodigiously tall to judge by her statue.'

'Do you go around like an American tourist exploring churches?' she asked laughing. 'I'd never have guessed it.'

Richard's answering laugh held a shade of constraint. 'In general, *no*. But I've played polo at Cowdray, and it is referred to in the Marsdon Chronicle. I was curious.'

She felt a quiver of delight. After a rootless girlhood, what joy it was to belong to an ancient established family, though this consideration had never occurred to her until after the precipitate marriage, nor had she grown accustomed to being a baronet's Lady; an elevation which happened some weeks ago, when old Sir Charles finally died in a nursing home. Before her marriage she had not even been sure what a baronet was.

'There are the ruins of Cowdray Castle,' observed Richard. 'I think we've time for a quick look.'

They turned left through a gate and down an avenue of horse chestnuts towards the fire-gutted shell of a Tudor castle. They passed a fourteenth-century granary, mounted high on toadstool legs to discourage rats; past a row of cottages where yellow light shone through small windows, to the entrance of the ruin.

'It's getting too dark for seeing much, but do you want to have a look? We've got a torch.' Richard stopped the Jag.

Celia followed her husband into shadowy roofless rooms.

Floorless, too, and they groped their way over lumpy grass.

'The chapel was here to the right, as I remember,' said Richard, leading her by the hand. 'And here, the remnants of the Great Hall. Mind the fallen stones!'

She stepped over a threshold and stood in the ruined Hall looking up at a huge stone window of sixty lights—but the glass had long ago vanished.

Her hand clutched Richard's. 'I feel sort of queer,' she said, 'as though I'd been here before. Is that the minstrels' gallery up there? And see those wooden stags, bucks, I mean, high on the walls?'

He did not answer, while he shifted the torch-beam hastily. There were no figures now on the ruined walls, but during a previous visit the custodian had told him that this used to be called Buck Hall, from the eleven statues of bucks representing Sir Anthony Browne's crest.

Richard spoke reprovingly from the darkness. 'One gets queer feelings from old places. Strong vibrations of the past, or I suppose your mother would say that you *had* been here before, in another life. Actually, the psychologists explain it as something called *déjà vu*—one part of the brain reacting after another.'

She was not listening. 'I've been here before,' she repeated, in a dreamy voice. 'The hall is crowded with people dressed in silks and velvets. There's music from viols and lutes. The smell of flowers, thyme and new green rushes. We are waiting for someone, waiting for the young King.'

'You're too suggestible, Celia,' he said, shaking her arm. 'And you devour too many historical romances. Come along, the Holloways will be wondering.'

'I'm very unhappy because *you* aren't here,' said Celia. 'You're nearby, in hiding. I'm afraid for you.'

Richard made a sharp sound. 'Come *along*!' he cried. 'I don't know what's the matter with you!' He dragged her from the Hall and out to the Jaguar. At once the impression of a dream which was not a dream evaporated. She felt dazed and a little foolish. She settled on the front seat and fished a cigarette out of her handbag.

'That was funny,' she said laughing shakily. 'In there for a moment I felt . . .'

'Never mind,' he snapped. 'Forget it!'

She was puzzled, a trifle hurt by his vehemence which was

18

almost like fear. The odd experience seemed important to her, though she scarcely remembered what she had said.

They entered Midhurst through winding shop-lined streets, crossed the Market Square, and parked in the courtyard of the Spread Eagle Inn. Celia was interested in the polished black oak staircase, the passage with a man-sized armoured knight standing near an entrance; but as she entered the low-beamed bar, and greeted the Holloways, she was again conscious of something. A twitch, a prick of awareness. Nothing as marked as her feelings in the Cowdray ruins, yet she had to give it momentary attention, before shaking hands with John and Bertha Holloway.

'Frightfully sorry we kept you waiting,' said Richard. 'We stopped at Cowdray to show Celia the ruins. She doesn't know this part of Sussex, of course.'

I feel as though I *do*, Celia thought, knowing that even that trite remark would mysteriously annoy Richard.

'Oh, my *dear* Lady Marsdon,' cried Bertha Holloway, her plump, earnest face beaming, 'John and I've been so eager to meet you. I can't tell you'how startled we were when we heard that Sir Richard had married an American.' She gulped, apparently feeling that this remark needed amending. 'I mean . . .' She pushed back a straggling strand of mousy hair. 'I mean, not so surprising that he married an American, lots of people do, but that he married at all, he always seemed a confirmed bachelor, though that's silly since he's still quite young, but so many girls have tried . . .'

Her husband removed his pipe from his mouth, put down his Scotch, and said, 'Bertha . . .' in a tired voice.

She flushed and subsided, her pink silk bosom heaving. John had *told* her not to talk too much. Not in anyway to put her foot in it. Now that Sir Richard had a rich American wife he was gradually buying back the heirlooms old Sir Charles had been forced to sell.

John Holloway was a prosperous antique dealer who had, during the years, acquired several of the Marsdon treasures, and who had also been a friend of the dead baronet's. In the Holloway showrooms on Church Street a splendid Elizabethan court cupboard from Medfield Place still remained unsold. John had sent a tentative letter of enquiry; Sir Richard had replied, showing interest. A thumping big price might be got, particularly as an American museum was angling for the gorgeously carved sideboard.

19

John Holloway glanced at Celia who was gulping her Martini very fast and smiling absently as though she had not heard Bertha.

Not the type one would somehow expect Sir Richard to settle for, John thought. Rather plain little thing. Small and dark, nice eyes of a shining crystal grey, smart rose wool frock but no curves to fill it out. Good ankles, though, like most American women, yet nothing striking nor impressive. Of course, there was the money. John shook his head imperceptibly. His business had made him an excellent judge of character, and he knew that Richard was no fortune hunter.

Marriages were ever inexplicable. His sharp gaze rested a moment on his wife, who had recovered and was chattering away about church bazaars, garden clubs and the Women's Institute to a vaguely attentive Celia.

'Another round before we feed?' John asked Richard, who shook his head, smiling.

Celia started. 'I'd like one,' she said in her low voice with its slight American tinge. 'A *real* martini, *plenty* of gin, after all, it's Hallowe'en, we ought to celebrate or something.'

Richard's heavy black eyebrows rose a trifle as he laughed. 'I assure you that this is unusual,' he said to the Holloways. 'I'm not really wedded to a toss-pot. This round's mine, please.' He went to the bar, and presently returned with the drinks.

'I've taken the liberty of ordering dinner,' remarked John who had not wanted another Scotch. 'Dover sole and Aylesbury duckling. They do them rather well here. I hope that's all right, Lady Marsdon?'

Celia jumped again, her grey eyes slowly focused on her host. 'Oh, of course,' she said. 'I simply adore . . . uh . . . sole and duck.' She drained her glass and lit another cigarette.

What's the girl so nervy about? John thought. Have those two had a row? If so, the time was not auspicious for bargaining about the court cupboard. He prodded Bertha, who obediently rose. They all filed into the dining room where the Italian waiter bowed them to a table and produced a vintage Chablis.

Once out of the bar, Celia's unease began to fade. She listened politely to Bertha's breathless account of a committee on which she had served with Lady Cowdray; she listened to a general discussion of antiques between Richard and Mr. Holloway. Finally, in a lull, she remarked that Midhurst seemed a charming town, obviously of great historical interest.

'Oh, yes, indeed,' agreed Bertha rather blankly. 'I'm a Londoner, myself, but John knows all about the old days here. There's a funny hill, just past the church—the locals think it's haunted, and I admit I shouldn't care to go up there myself on a dark night.'

'A funny haunted hill?' Celia asked. 'That sounds exciting.'

Did she feel or imagine a sudden strangeness in Richard? Across the table he was skilfully dismembering his half duckling, but she thought that the long sensitive hands which she so loved, grew tense. She ignored a faint interior warning and said, 'Oh, do tell me about the haunted hill, Mrs. Holloway!'

Bertha nodded towards her husband. 'John knows all that sort of thing. I'd get it muddled.'

Holloway smiled, pleased that his guest had come to life. 'You Americans *do* love a ghost story, don't you! As a matter of fact, St. Ann's Hill has a rather peculiar atmosphere. I've trudged up and over it many times when I was a boy. The footpath's a short cut from the town, down to the River Rother and thus to Cowdray Castle.'

'Was there once a castle on that hill, too?' Celia asked, involuntarily, still ignoring the prohibition which came partly from inside herself, partly from Richard who kept his intent gaze fixed on the duckling.

'Oh, yes,' answered Holloway, faintly surprised. 'What a clever guess. Though I suppose there's hardly a place in England which hasn't seen human habitation. For centuries, until early Tudor times, an ancient family called the de Bohuns had a stronghold on "Tan's Hill". Nothing left now but rubble and bits of wall. And they say that long before the Romans came there was a Druid temple up there, too.'

'Fascinating,' said Celia, gulping down her Chablis. 'And what about the ghost?'

John Holloway laughed. 'Several have been reported by frightened kids, and credulous old women. The most popular one is a "black monk". My great aunt claimed that when she was a girl she saw the monk gliding down the hill into the town on a midsummer's eve.'

'Why *black* monk?' asked Celia, smiling.

Holloway shrugged. 'The Benedictine habit, I suppose. There's some theory that this ghost was once private chaplain at Cowdray, and got tangled up with a village wench. Sort of scandal folk love to hand down through generations.'

Richard pushed aside his knife and fork. He raised his head

21

and said sharply, 'England abounds in ghostly black monks and grey ladies. They come sixpence to the dozen. Holloway —if I'm to examine the court cupboard, I think that after coffee we should go directly to your showroom.'

*   *   *

Celia lay quietly with eyes closed, in the lounge chair by the swimming pool at Medfield Place, forcing herself to remember what happened next, though it was painful.

I don't know what came over me. I insisted on exploring St. Ann's Hill then and there. The others didn't want me to, but Mr. Holloway, in passing through the Market Square, pointed to where it was. I escaped from the showrooms while Richard was inspecting the court cupboard. I ran down an alley, past the church, and slipped between poles that barred the way to cars. I climbed the muddy footpath, and mist swirled around me. I couldn't see much except big dark trees high against the gloomy sky, yet I knew my way.

On top I turned right and clambered up a sharp rise. The holly pricked me, I was stung by nettles. I reached some moss-grown stones, and knew they had been part of a wall. Something stopped me from climbing over the stones. I *couldn't*. I was frightened yet excited. Then beyond, inside the wall, I saw a wavering yellow light, like a lantern. A tall dark shape stood by the lantern. I cried out to the shape with wild longing. But, it disappeared. I began to cry, and floundered back down the hill. I must have run to the Spread Eagle, for there the others found me in the bar. I was still crying by the great fireplace when Richard and the Holloways rushed in. They had been looking everywhere for me. The Holloways laughed uncomfortably as I stammered out what I'd done.

Richard said nothing, but his face went grim while his eyes blazed with anger I had never seen before, nor guessed possible. He bundled me into the Jag. He said cruel things to me on the way home. That I was drunk, that I was mad. That I had seen nothing on the Hill. And that night he did not sleep with me.

Her heart gave a physical lurch and her mouth went dry. Dear God, it's been seven months of excuses. He said he had a back pain, a slipped disc. He *said* he was going to an osteopath, but wouldn't answer my questions. Lately, I've no longer dared ask. He moved to the dressing room. We never men-

22

tioned Midhurst, yet the night before we had known such bliss in each other.

She opened her eyes at a stirring by the pool-side, and saw that Dodge, their butler, was approaching from the garden door of the manor house. Dodge bore a tray of whisky, pink gins and sherry. He was large, pompous, very correct. Exactly the kind of butler they kept saying here in England that one couldn't find any more. But one *could*. With American dollars. One could find an adequate staff even to run a lovely but inconvenient house in the country. There was Mrs. Dodge for cook. There was a housemaid and dailys from the village. If necessary, and it had not been yet, there was Richard's old nanny who inhabited the empty nurseries.

I *should* have got pregnant right away when Richard wanted me to, Celia thought, and felt a clutch of confused panic. She had been afraid of pregnancy.

'What's the trouble, Lady Marsdon?' asked a fluting faintly malicious voice beside her.

Celia started and turned her head. It was Igor, the new dress designer to whom all London was flocking. He was a beautiful young man with a helmet of golden hair. There was a faint trace of Cockney in his voice.

Igor, thought Celia, thankfully reverting to banality—probably something like Ernie or Bert to begin with. Oh, well.

'No trouble,' she said lightly. 'Have you gone all E.S.P. and fey? I'm sleepy from the swim, is all.'

'You know, I *do* feel things,' said Igor, calmly sitting down on another chair and sipping his pink gin. 'I'm sensitive to mood, and when I see my charming hostess looking absolutely *dire*—like Melpomene, the tragic muse, or whatever she was, or possibly Deirdre of the Sorrows . . .'

'How frightfully intellectual you're getting,' snapped Celia, her usual tolerant fondness for Igor suddenly cracking. 'And *you*, darling, are the quite poisonous product of decadence. You design clothes for women to make them look hideous. Oh, quite subtly I grant you, but that purple tent you made for me —*really*, Igor, I'm not such a fool as you think.'

He rose gracefully and made her a little bow. 'I'll design you something that will *utterly* seduce Richard, I promise.' He spoke with sudden gentleness, almost sympathy.

She quivered inside. Her mouth tightened. 'I think, Igor, that I'm in no need of your assistance in regard to Richard, and that in the possible words of my rich, American, plebeian

23

father—who, by the way, has made all this possible—' she waved a small, tanned hand to include the manor house, the gardens, the trout stream, the acres of well-tended woodlands; her gesture even included Dodge who came back to announce that, 'Luncheon is served, my lady.'

She bent and strapped on her sandals. Her indignation faded, and she felt beaten, helpless. What would Amos B. Taylor have said? The scarcely known father who made millions in synthetic textiles after the war, who had died of cancer seven years ago when she was sixteen—wouldn't he have said, 'Oh, talk to your mother, Baby. I don't know what advice to give a girl. Now, if Lily and me'd only had a son . . .'

He never realised how often he said that, nor how much it hurt her. Celia left Igor, and walking along the pool-side marshalled her guests. 'As you are,' she said, 'in the garden room. Dodge simply won't serve out here. It upsets his dignity.'

The Duchess laughed. 'You're learning fast, my sweet. I live in positive terror of *my* butler, though he isn't nearly as formidable as Dodge!' The laugh displayed flashing white teeth, possibly false, despite Myra's comparative youth. People in England thought nothing of false teeth, even when they got them from the National Health.

Celia smiled gently. Her American teeth were her own—small, pearly and the product of expensive years in braces. She noted that even as Myra spoke, the long green eyes turned again towards Richard.

You'll get no place in that quarter, Myra dear, Celia thought. Nor will *you*—she glanced cynically at Igor who was also staring at her husband. You don't begin to understand Richard, nor do I, but I know *that* much. She swallowed hard against constricture in her throat. Like a lump of food which had stuck. Crazy, she said angrily to herself, and led the way to the garden room.

She paused at the foot of the long glass table to review the seating. There were places laid for ten, seven guests plus Lily and themselves. The usual number for a weekend party. Richard enjoyed hospitality and the use of his ancestral home which had been empty and decaying for so long.

On Richard's right went Myra, of course; next to her, Igor; then Sue Blake, a dazzled little American girl who was a distant cousin from Kentucky. Sue was sixteen, she had long, toffee-coloured hair, a piquant face devoid of make-up, and was inclined to bubble, either from nervousness, or genuine rapture at finding herself living 'like a fairy tale', as she kept saying. She came from a modest suburban home outside of Louisville, and it was her first trip abroad.

Next to Sue, on Celia's left she seated George Simpson. He was Richard's London solicitor, a small, middle-aged man with a squeaky voice which made everything he said slightly ridiculous. Between wrinkled lids his pale eyes shifted anxiously. His legal firm had served the Marsdons for three generations, but George Simpson had never before been invited as a house guest to Medfield Place.

Since Richard disliked London, and had a good deal of lingering business to attend to consequent upon his father's death, Celia had suggested that they ask Mr. and Mrs. Simpson. Richard—more democratic than his father—indifferently assented. 'Though,' he had added, 'I haven't a clue what the wife's like—I suppose Simpson *has* a wife. No matter, this weekend looks to be a mixed bag anyhow.'

Mixed enough, thought Celia, smiling at Lily and the Hindu doctor, while she gestured them to their seats. Then, to balance off Myra there was a divorced knight, Sir Harry Jones, who had once been Conservative M.P. for some place in Shropshire. He was handsome in a ruddy, jovial way and had a bold, admiring stare. Twenty-three years ago he had made a brilliant war record—Celia kept meaning to look him up in one of the stud books—but she was pleased, as were all hostesses, to have secured him as an extra man. He was in great demand. Myra's presence had been the lure, though that he and Myra were lovers, as commonly reported, she felt to be unlikely. Myra treated Sir Harry with light indifference. However, Celia had allotted them adjoining guest rooms, just in case.

Celia started to sit down when she saw Richard's slight enquiring frown, and realised that the seat on his left was vacant. 'Oh, dear,' she said to George Simpson. 'I'm so sorry. I didn't realise Mrs. Simpson wasn't here. Is she still sick?'

George's mouth twitched uncomfortably. 'Edna was better this morning,' he said. 'She told me she'd be down to lunch.'

Celia turned to the hovering Dodge, 'Will you enquire after Mrs. Simpson?'

Dodge said, 'Certainly, my lady,' while managing to convey distaste for his errand.

Celia was amused. She had months ago sensed the ratings given their guests in the servants' hall, and knew that the

Simpsons had not passed muster, though they seemed inoffensive enough.

Edna Simpson had taken to her bed immediately upon arrival last night, pleading a sick headache. Celia's sole impression had been of a stout, big-jawed woman with gold-rimmed spectacles and kinky sheep hair.

They all sat down at the glass table, and Celia waited politely for Dodge's report before lifting her spoon to the chilled consommé.

There was a pause until Dodge reopened the door from the main house. Edna Simpson 'made an entrance'. There was no other phrase for it. With slow and measured steps she preceded the butler, bowed towards Richard and the Duchess, then more casually towards Celia's end of the table.

'Pardon me, I'm sure I had no notion of the taime.'

The men rose and Richard murmured enquiries about Edna's health while he held her chair.

'Quaite, quaite recovered, thank you, Sir Richard. This luvely country air after smoggy Loondon.'

Heavens! Celia thought. Where does *she* come from? She did not recognise, as the English could, the North Country accent, curbed by a genteel effort to disguise it, but she flushed with entirely unnecessary embarrassment for Edna, who had dressed herself as she thought fitting to the occasion.

Edna wore a blue toque on her frizzled hair. Her blue lace gown stopped just below balloon-shape knees. She wore dangling pearl earrings and a pearl choker. The entire outfit had cost George a pretty penny at Harrods, and Edna felt nothing but disdain for the others, lounging around half naked in swimsuits, beach robes and sandals. Drinking, too. The table was studded with glasses. This laxness was precisely what she had expected from the aristocracy. If you could call it that. Her icy blue eyes peered quickly through gold-rimmed spectacles. That *black* man, practically a nigger, seated next to her. Well! The Americans, naturally, wouldn't have wits enough to realise how sensitive Englishwomen would feel about that. She stared at the Americans; at Sue Blake who should have been in the schoolroom instead of making eyes at that young dress designer. She stared at Lily Taylor, a woman of her own age, but bleached, painted and half-naked like the rest of them. All tarted up, thought Edna angrily. What an example to her daughter. She did not, however, look at Celia, nor pause to examine the dislike she had felt for young Lady Marsdon when she first met her in the Hall last night. Edna did not permit herself sudden emotions, she had not noticed that the sick headache came on when she met Celia and Sir Richard. Edna had a tonic for any discomforts which might plague her. It was contained in a plain quart bottle labelled, *Bell's Anodyne Tincture*. That this green fluid, smelling of peppermint, consisted of seventy per cent alcohol was known only to her chemist, and would have horrified Edna who had joined the Temperance League at fourteen. The tincture had done its usual soothing work last night, and a few swigs had been restorative this morning.

Edna daintily finished her consommé, put down her spoon and addressed Myra. 'Such a luvely day, is it not, Your Grace?' She checked herself and quickly added, 'Duchess.'

In anticipation of this visit, she had bought a book of etiquette and studied it with care. It seemed rude to address a duchess so baldly, but the book had been explicit on the point: 'Your Grace' from inferiors, 'Duchess' from equals.

Myra favoured Edna Simpson with a leisurely stare, her full crimson lips quirked. 'Perfect weather,' she agreed. 'Mrs. Simpson, would you come from the North Country, by any chance?'

Edna turned a mottled red. 'I did happen to be born in Yorkshire,' she said quickly. 'My father was the—the rector of a small village on the moors, such a pretty little spot.'

George unfortunately heard and exclaimed, 'But, Edna— you never told me that . . . and I always thought your father was . . .' He wheezed and faded off to silence under the glare his wife gave him.

This by-play and its reasons were obvious. Richard hastened to relieve a guest's discomfiture, even so ludicrous a guest as Edna. 'The Duchess is from the North herself,' he explained kindly. 'You people all seem to recognise each other in some magical way.'

Myra laughed. 'Aye,' she said. 'I'm from Coomberland.'

Edna's ear was not subtle enough to hear the parody of her own speech, and she relaxed as she said brightly, 'Indeed? A charming county—all those pretty lakes.'

Myra inclined her gleaming auburn head, and turned again to Richard. The Simpson female was not worth baiting, while Richard was a fascinating challenge.

The salmon mousse with cucumbers was delicious, yet

Celia could not eat. Besides the recurrent thickness in her throat, her heart was giving those erratic thumps. Must run up to London soon, she thought, see that doctor on Harley Street. She looked down the table to Richard and found that he was watching her. The dark brooding look which she could not interpret. Had it always been there from the beginning?

Sir Harry was booming across her at George Simpson about the iniquities of the Labour Government. She had no need to listen, and her mind slithered backwards to those shimmering wonderful days on the ship. 'Love at first sight', yes it happened. That trite phrase, and yet what actually happened had been more like recognition.

A year ago last May on the *Queen Mary*. That's when it started. Suddenly, violently. Yet the voyage had promised nothing different from dozens of other voyages

All the years with her mother after her father died. Travel, travel. Together Celia and Lily had done most of Europe. They had done the Caribbean and Hawaii. Though there had also been a two-year interval in Paris at a school where Celia learned many things besides French.

From time to time there had, naturally, been tentative flirtations, and three luke-warm proposals. Some of these young men Celia could not even remember, though she had been flattered by their attentions, mildly amused by their kisses. Lily, though generally permissive and a good confidante, had always moved on before anything grew too serious, nor had Celia objected. By twenty-two Celia had decided that she was essentially frigid. Just not sexy.

She discussed this sad state with her girl friends who were all either married or had lovers. They applied glib Freudian interpretations which Celia rather unhappily accepted. That she had a father-complex; that she was ashamed of being a girl because it had disappointed her father; that there must be some forgotten childhood trauma.

She once discussed with Lily her inability to be kindled by men. Lily laughed, 'Oh, child, don't be silly. Just wait until the right man comes along. Besides,' Lily added, 'according to your horoscope you'll be married soon, when Venus moves into your Sun sign. You Aquarians don't fall easily in love like Libras, anyway.'

Ten years ago Lily had commissioned Celia's horoscope from a Persian astrologer, and several, though not all, predictions had come true. Perhaps this might.

So Celia, though popular and social enough, mostly escaped into the world of books. She read incessantly, she scribbled poetry, and tore up the results. Somewhere along the line she developed poise and a sense of irony.

Then, last May, a year ago, Lily decided to visit England again.

'Haven't been there in years, and after all it was our ancestors' homeland. We might have several relations. Your poor dear father, of course—well, there're so many Taylors we could never trace his line, but *my* grandmother was a Peabody. Should be easier. You wouldn't mind, would you, dear?'

Celia did not mind. She loved English history, and there was a strong pull towards England which she remembered from a childhood visit when her father was alive as full of birdsong, castles and magic.

They embarked on the *Queen Mary*—one of her last eastbound voyages. Lily, who always knew how to manage these things, sat as she had requested, at the Staff Captain's table. Celia was allotted a nearby table for four. Two of these were a dull couple from London who had been to the States on business; the other was an Englishman called Richard Marsdon.

And it happened, just like that, Celia thought. The long, startled look they exchanged. The recognition, *and* a bizarre overtone of dismay. We fell in love between the vichysoisse and the guinea hen. Though she was then barely conscious of Richard's handsomeness, except that he was tall and dark, and must be over thirty. She saw only the intense hazel eyes under the heavy black brows.

The first evening after dinner they stayed together, watching the horse races, listening to the orchestra, talking very little, until Richard made one personal remark.

'Your Christian name is Celia,' he said. 'It's a name which has always attracted me, not sure why, since I've never known any. But I once bought a rather—well, I'm afraid, bawdy—record which is a sixteenth-century song about a Celia.'

She gave an excited happy laugh. 'I'm so glad you like it, but I must confess I wasn't christened Celia. My parents named me Henrietta for a grandmother. I always loathed the name, and I guess it didn't fit, because when I was fourteen I had Celia's part when our school put on *As You Like It*, and somehow the name stuck with me. I've used it ever since.'

'Strange,' he said slowly. 'Many of life's little quirks are strange.'

She had never thought much about her name change, it had seemed very natural, and her mother, at the time much interested in numerology, had enthusiastically accepted it, with quotations going back to Pythagoras which proved that the numbers in 'Celia' accorded much better than 'Henrietta' with her daughter's birth date. This aspect seemed too silly for mention, and anyway, Richard had given her his warm quick smile, and said, 'Would you like to dance, Celia?'

The rest of the voyage was a delicious haze during which she gradually learned a few facts about Richard's life, though he was reticent.

Richard Marsdon had been born in a very old house in East Sussex, his family was poor, he had won a scholarship to Balliol at Oxford and graduated, 'positively without any distinction, I assure you, nor particular aptitude for anything but reading; no competitive sports, unless you count Judo which I learned as a hobby to avoid undue introspection.'

Puzzled, she asked why 'undue introspection', and he shrugged. 'I'd a tendency to brood, which I later offset by travel, I hope.'

He had accepted the first job that was offered, as secretary to a famous and lazy journalist, who made Richard do all the leg-work to gather material for the sprightly articles the journalist tossed off regularly. Thus, in the past years, Richard had been sent to cover various London events, and also sent to Australia, South America, and just now, the States. He had expected to fly home as usual, but a telephone call in New York from his solicitor, George Simpson, had told Richard of his father's massive stroke and incapacity, 'and I'm needed at Medfield, at last.'

She understood from the warmth of his tone when he mentioned his home that he loved the place, and also that he had felt exiled from it in some way which had to do with his father. Richard further explained that since he was about to throw up his job, once he'd reported to the journalist, and since his father was in no immediate danger, he'd suddenly decided to return by sea instead of flying.

'On such apparently chance decisions one's future seems to hang,' he said, looking at her sombrely. This was actually the only acknowledgment he made of the attraction between them until the last night out.

They had climbed to the boat deck after dinner and sat down on a locker beneath one of the lifeboats.

The tiny stars pricked through the greyish northern sky.

'Land,' said Richard quietly, 'I can smell it. We'll be nearing the Scilly Isles, and then England.'

She shivered, but not from the damp wind. Richard put his arm around her. She relaxed against him, wanting nothing more, held fast in a timeless moment.

The great ship ploughed steadily through the Atlantic, rolling softly in the ocean swells.

With faint astonishment she felt Richard begin to tremble, or was it only the far-below vibration . . . she did not question, nor move as he drew away. But he spoke suddenly in a harsh voice.

'I want you, Celia. You know I want you. As you want me. But I'm *afraid*. At least, there's a barrier.'

She stiffened, the moment shattered. She tried to speak lightly. 'A barrier? What barrier? I know you've no wife. Have you a mistress then? Or a mother you adore?'

His long flexible hand clenched on his knee, then fell open. 'Nothing like that. I can't explain the trouble, except it goes deep—and far into the past, something I read partly. No that's foolish, but when I saw you, I . . .' He stopped.

Behind them streamed the *Queen Mary*'s foaming, glittering wake. There was faint music from the Verandah Grill, creakings from the ship, laughing voices in the distance.

'I want you,' Richard repeated very low, 'yet I want to be *alone*. Let alone . . . to serve God.'

Celia drew back, incredulous. 'Serve God . . .' she repeated. 'I didn't think, at least, I don't understand . . .'

Richard shook himself, and turned to her. 'Of course you don't. I don't myself.'

She had no time to puzzle over this which seemed jerked out of him against his will. Was he drunk, or had she heard wrong? For he grabbed her against him in a kind of frenzy. He kissed her hair, her cheeks, her neck, and then, with violence, her mouth, which opened to his in total response.

She yielded as he pushed her backwards against the rail, feeling no hurt from the iron bar across her shoulders, feeling nothing but a savage joy in the closeness of their bodies.

'Naow, naow—ye two!' said a stolid voice from the deck beside them. 'No 'anky-panky. Captain 'e don't like fun and games up 'ere!'

Celia and Richard separated slowly. She was confused, but Richard instantly recovered. He got up and gave the night-watchman a slight nod.

'Quite right, officer,' he said in his calm upper-class English voice. 'Though this lady is my fiancée, and we were not exactly indulging in fun and games.'

The watchman was taken aback. He had supposed that these were the usual kids sneaked up from Tourist. 'Well, naow, sir,' he said apologetically, 'I'm only doing me duty.'

'Of course,' said Richard, 'we should all do our duty. The only trick is to find out where it's really due.'

The watchman's jaw dropped. 'N'doubt, sir,' he said hastily, and clomped off.

Richard and Celia walked silently through the nearest door, and he rang for the lift. They descended silently to the main deck where Richard had a single cabin and she shared a suite with her mother.

At her cabin door she pushed back her curly salt-damp hair, her bruised mouth trembled as she looked at him. 'Did you really mean that I was your fiancée? What about the—barrier?'

Beneath the straight brows his eyelids flickered, then steadied. He took her hand and kissed the palm. 'Our marriage is predestined, I think,' he said. 'On the outcome we must take our chances.' He bowed and vanished along the dim, vibrating passageway.

It was only later, as she lay sleepless, that she realised there had been no actual mention of love. Nor did that seem important. It's more than 'love', she thought, that tarnished, insipid little word so readily voiced by any amorous couple, More and deeper than that kind of love. What then?

Outside the sheltered cabin the great ship must have run into fog. Celia heard the long moaning blasts from the horn. That means danger, she thought. She considered this a moment, then no longer heard the blasts as she finally fell asleep and dreamed of Richard.

They landed next day at Southampton in the sunlight, and after that life hustled on like a speeded-up film.

Richard seemed possessed by feverish hurry, and he was ably assisted by the excited Lily.

Celia and her mother stayed a week at Claridge's while rushing through financial arrangements, buying a small trousseau, attending congratulatory parties given by Amos B.

Taylor's erstwhile business acquaintances.

Celia saw Richard only once when he came up from Sussex to give her a beautiful but odd engagement ring. It was made of heavy gold—two hands clasping an amethyst heart. 'And all the Marsdon wives have worn it, back to, oh, Tudor times, at least—I believe it was once a wedding ring.'

She forgot her first dismay, for she had been expecting a conventional American diamond solitaire, and said sincerely, 'I'm very proud, Richard, proud to wear the badge of a Marsdon wife.'

He smiled and said, 'Thing's too big for you. I'll take it to the jeweller's. Yes, that's our betrothal ring, and our family motto is: *Beware*, by the way—but then, being Papists we usually *had* to, except in Bloody Mary's reign.'

'A bit sinister,' she said, wishing that he would sit down and hold her close, that he did not show such haste and urgency. 'I'm somewhat daunted at the prospect of running Medfield Place as my predecessors did. Do you think I can?'

'No fear,' he said gently. 'You can do it, and your money will help.'

Already she had grown used to his frankness about material things, but she bit her underlip and frowned. 'Are you sure that isn't all you want me for?'

Richard laughed. 'You know bloody well it's not. I've met plenty of willing heiresses, Greek, American, Venezuelan. Nor wished ever to fall in love.'

His rejoinder made her happy, and any doubts that she might have had were dispelled by Lily.

The marriage took place in a registry office. Richard said that he had no use for churches and flummery. Celia instantly agreed. Nor did Lily, who was normally a great upholder of etiquette, object for long, though she was disappointed.

'It's practical, I suppose,' she said. 'Sir Charles so sick, of course, and men do hate fuss. My dear child, do you realise how lucky you are! You're madly in love, and it's the sort of marriage I've always prayed you'd find.'

Celia was struck by this because Lily's prayers were often answered. Small pains, illnesses, a law suit when Amos B. Taylor's will was contested by a disgruntled cousin, all had vanished before Lily's serene philosophy. 'We must have faith, and everything will come right.'

Yet, thought Celia, a year later at the luncheon party in the manor's garden room, she doesn't guess how wrong my marriage is going now.

'Yes, *indeed*,' said Celia brightly to Sir Harry, 'I do *so* agree with you.' She searched for a clue, since she hadn't heard the question. Not the shocking assassination of Senator Robert Kennedy last week, they had touched on that. So was it still the iniquities of the Labour Government? The Common Market? The punishing taxes and devaluation of the pound?

'—And alas, we can no longer say Empire but the *Commonwealth* . . . then you do agree, Lady Marsdon?'

'New Zealand, I hear, is most attractive,' Celia murmured. It was enough to divert Sir Harry who had once flown there.

'Marvellous country, mountains, waterfalls and a masculine challenge like Australia—we can't find that here any more.'

Celia maintained a receptive smile and looked down the table to Richard. Myra was now a trifle tight and displaying all her blandishments. The inviting gaze beneath mascara'd lashes, the quick meaningful touches on Richard's hand.

Richard quietly removed his hand. He raised his voice and addressed his wife. "What about this afternoon, Celia? Shall we make a set of tennis, or some bridge perhaps. It looks like rain. Have you any plans for our guests?'

Before she could answer, Lily spoke. 'Couldn't we all rest a while, and *then* an expedition!'

Celia saw her husband's mouth tighten, and knew that he was annoyed at her mother's taking over. She herself was relieved. She had made no special plans for the afternoon. She had failed Richard again. He liked everything to be structured and punctual. Besides, Lily so often took over, not aggressively, but from habit.

It's wonderful to be sure of things, Celia thought. I used to be, didn't I? In the polite pause which followed Lily's suggestion, the Duchess spoke up languidly. 'What expedition, Mrs. Taylor? I certainly don't want to gape at a "stately home", nor to go and see if the bluebells are out in somebody's copse.'

Igor giggled, Sir Harry and George Simpson looked alarmed. Except for little Sue, always eager for anything, Richard, the Hindu and Edna Simpson showed no expressions.

'Oh, no, Duchess,' Lily said, 'not the sort of thing you mean. It's to see a very picturesque place about an hour from here in Kent. Nobody lives in it except *ghosts*. Some of them six hundred years old! I have a friend who knows the American owner who spends most of his time in the States or travelling, but they say one might get in by appointment. I've the phone number.'

Richard made a sharp movement which knocked over his wine-glass. 'Do you by any chance mean Ightham Mote?' He addressed Lily in so cold and dry a tone that she gaped at her son-in-law, while she nodded.

Myra raised her eyebrows, the other guests were suddenly aware of tension, as was Celia, who managed to laugh and say, 'Good Lord, what an odd name! What kind of a moat? What are you talking about, Mother?'

Dr. Akananda looked at her. 'No,' he said involuntarily. 'Please do not pursue this.' But nobody heard him.

Richard transferred his dark gaze from Lily to Celia. 'She is speaking of an old manor house which I visited when I was twelve, and found exceptionally dreary, oppressive.' He stood up and said to Dodge, who was deftly covering the wine stain, 'No doubt her ladyship would like coffee served by the pool, since it's still sunny.'

Myra lifted her chin. 'But Richard, *darling*,' she protested, at once reversing her position, and glad to annoy Richard whom she found tiresomely unresponsive, 'Mrs. Taylor's expedition sounds divine. I mean positively creepy. I simply adored the ghost we had at Drewton Castle. Some sort of white lady in the north wing. Not that I ever saw her, though the Duke claimed he often did. Once I think I heard her gibber, or whatever they do.'

There being no particular answer to this, they all went to the pool for coffee.

Celia poured the coffee; when Richard had drunk his, he glanced at his wristwatch and said that he had suddenly remembered an appointment with his tenant farmer which might take some time. He excused himself with impersonal courtesy.

Celia watched him as he strode into the house. He kept his black hair cropped short, shorter than the other men's, except George Simpson who was bald, but Richard's features needed no softening. Beneath the tanned skin and the shadow of a well-shaven beard lay a bone structure worthy of Greek sculpture; no, not *Greek*, a Renaissance type, with long, rather aquiline nose, full lips and deep eye-sockets under the straight black bars of eyebrows.

'Mine host seems a bit put out,' remarked Myra, shrugging. 'Quite the most mysterious man I know. Very polite lord-of-the-manor, but one feels positively smouldering Heathcliffe somewhere. Or am I wrong, my sweet?' She addressed Celia, while voluptuously stroking sun-lotion on her long, slightly freckled legs.

'Of course Richard's not annoyed,' Celia retorted. 'He simply forgot that he had to see Hawkins today. They're building a new pigsty at the farm.'

Myra yawned. 'How dreary. I should think even ghosts would be preferable. Mrs. Taylor, what time would you like to start your "expedition"? I'll drive my Bentley and take Harry.' She nodded towards that gratified knight whose prominent brown eyes glistened expectantly. 'And will *you* come with us, Mrs. Taylor?' Myra added, giving a little purring laugh at Harry's change of expression.

After eight years of boredom, spent mostly at the Duke's principal seat in Warwickshire, Myra was enjoying her widow-hood. She enjoyed playing amorous games, she enjoyed con-quests, and though she had been a faithful wife to her old arthritic Duke, she had no more moral scruples than the wild border lords from whom she descended. Her hedonism and mischief-making were, however, tempered by careless good nature, and an inborn sense of feudal responsibility. Many a tenant near her father's Cumberland castle, or later at Drew-ton, spoke of her with warm gratitude.

Lily, having received the Duchess's sanction, forgot Richard's odd behaviour, and enthusiastically outlined the afternoon plans. 'If you don't mind, dear?' she asked belatedly of her daughter.

Celia knew that she should say, 'Yes, I do, since Richard is not pleased,' but she smiled acquiescence.

Oh, what is the matter with Richard, she thought. Why did he speak so crossly to Mother? What a fuss about nothing! These weekend parties had become a strain anyway. Yet Richard wanted them. He wanted people around. He wanted, and she faced it fleetingly, not to be alone with her.

Edna Simpson lumbered up from the edge of the lounge chair where she had uncomfortably seated herself. Her square bull-dog face was red, her thick lips compressed. Nobody had consulted *her* preferences. Rude, brazen American women! (The Duchess was exempt from Edna's indignation.) Lily re-ceived a hostile glare, then the spectacles flashed as they turned towards Celia. Stupid little thing, not even pretty. The out-sider, the intruder. Disliked her on sight, I did. And my impressions are never wrong. He'll soon tire of her, if he hasn't already.

'It's hot,' Edna announced. 'My headache's returning. I'll rest this afternoon, if it is quaite convenient to have a tea sent up?'

'Of course,' Celia murmured, and was startled by a malevolent stare. This impression seemed so ridiculous that Celia dismissed it.

They all drifted into the house, and Celia went to find Richard. He had already changed and was not in his dressing room, but Nanny Cameron was there. She was laying out Richard's dinner clothes on the small divan where he had taken to sleeping lately.

Nanny's wrinkled, purple-veined hands patted the black tie, the starched white shirt. 'Ther-re,' she said lovingly, and saw Celia standing in the door. 'He'll not be here, m'lady.' Her quick voice with its Scottish lilt could be cutting when it rebuked a lazy housemaid, it could even be disciplinary towards Richard at times, but for Celia, ever since she curtsied to the bride in the entrance hall at Medfield, there had been a gentleness, an understanding; though Celia seldom saw Nanny, who kept to herself in the nursery wing, and emerged only for certain specified duties, such as checking the laundry, and valeting Richard—a task she allowed nobody to share.

'In the study, do you think?' asked Celia. 'Or has he gone down to the farm already?'

Nanny cocked her robin-head, her bright black eyes considered. 'I doot it, m'lady. Ye might try the library. 'Tis in this mood he at times consults that great ponderous book o' the Marsdons.'

'What book?' said Celia sighing. 'Oh, Nanny . . .' Her pleading eyes showed her trouble, and the old woman made a soft sound in her throat.

'Aye, puir lady, there's a deal he keeps to himself, always has—even as a wee bairn. I mind the day I came her-re to tend him. 'Twas a week after the first Lady Marsden died, and Maister Dick but two years old. I never nursed so solemn and quiet a weanling.'

'Did he mind when his father married again?' About Sir Charles's second marriage Celia knew very little. The old baronet had remarried when Richard was twelve. The second Lady Marsden had been killed in an automobile crash while Richard was still at Eton, Richard had given Celia these facts,

37

dryly, reluctantly, as one who had a right to hear them, though they were distasteful.

'To be sur-re, the young maister minded, when the old maister went so daft over that minx that he wed her. My puir lad shut himself up for days, and times I heard him weeping i' the night, and then . . .' She checked herself abruptly, and added in a subdued voice, 'Starved for love that lad was, and not a body to gi'e it to him but me.'

'His stepmother . . .?' Celia asked softly, and Nanny snorted. 'A flibberty-gibberty hussy, nae mor-re heart than a weasel. She properly diddled the old baronet, who should've blessed the day that lorry smashed into her. Though he took it har-rd, the shock and all.'

Celia was not interested in Sir Charles, who had been a shrunken, mindless gnome the once she saw him in the nursing home just before his death.

'I must find Richard,' she said, half to herself, smiled uncertainly at Nanny and went downstairs.

The library was very large and panelled in fumed oak, as the victorian baronet had left it. Between the stacks light filtered through garish stained glass, supposed to represent episodes from Tennyson's *Idylls of the King*. The room smelt musty, unaired.

Celia found Richard standing in an alcove, by a lectern. The window above him showed Sir Mordred leering evilly at Guinevere and Sir Launcelot. Mordred's pea-green robe cast a jaundiced light over the large open book on the lectern. Richard was frowning down at the book, and from the fixity of his gaze, seemed to be staring only at one word or sentence.

'What *are* you reading, darling?' Celia asked softly. Her husband jumped. He slammed the book shut, and a puff of dust spurted towards the window.

'I thought you'd gone,' he said, 'with the others to Ightham Mote.' As he straightened, the murky blue of Launcelot's helmet shone on Richard's face giving it a sickly pallor, and a strange defencelessness.

'Not yet,' she said. 'And I won't go if you don't want me to, though I don't see . . . Oh, my dearest, if you'd only explain.'

'Nothing to explain. Do as you like. I'm off to the farm.'

She stiffened, her heart began to give its erratic thumps. She glanced at the book. It was huge, bound in thick yellowed vellum, a cockatrice—the Marsdon crest—was embossed in tarnished gold on the cover.

'Could I see the book?' she asked, 'see what interests you so?'

For an instant she thought he was going to refuse, then he laughed curtly. 'By all means. It's the Marsdon Chronicle, it covers over five hundred years of family history.' He made a gesture and stood back.

She opened the book at random and peered with dismay at a page of crabbed antique writing, a maze of hen-scratching and curlicues; here and there a blot. The faded ink alone was hard to see in the wavering, coloured light.

'I can't read this,' she said, squinting at what might be a date. ' "viij jun" . . .?'

'I didn't think you could.' He shut the book and placed it high on a shelf next to a row of squat parchment volumes.

'But *you* can,' she put her hand on his. 'Richard, is there something in that family chronicle which you feel gives the past a bearing on the future?'

There was a silent second, she wasn't sure of his expression, but she thought his pupils widened, then he shrugged.

'It would be rather silly if I did, wouldn't it? Isn't the past finished forever?' He glanced down at her hand on his arm; at the gold wedding band and the heavy Marsdon ring, and though he did not move, she felt a chill, a withdrawal.

'Richard, for God's sake, what *is* wrong? We were so happy in Portugal. So close. And even here when we got back—even after your father died. Life with you was fun. It was heaven. What's happened? I don't think it's another woman, but then wives often are fooled.'

Richard's shoulders twitched as though to shake off a burden. His eyes softened and he spoke with the teasing tenderness she had not heard in all these months. 'No, poppet, no other woman. One's quite enough. You've married a bloody-tempered bloke is all. Nor does he understand himself.' He kissed her hand and quickly, in the old way, his hand gently cupping her left breast. 'Go put some clothes on, you're scandalising this library.'

She looked down and realised that her golden lounging robe was open to expose her turquoise bikini, and a good deal of slim, tanned nakedness.

'Sorry,' she said laughing with a wild note of relief. She snatched the robe together.

'I'm off,' said Richard. 'By the bye, is it the Bent-Warners for dinner tonight?'

39

'Yes, you suggested them. Will they fit?'

'Nobody,' said Richard smiling, 'would fit this extraordinary house party. The Simpson woman is a disaster, and probably a secret toper as well, according to the horrified Dodge, who had it from the new housemaid.'

'Heavens,' said Celia, 'I suppose that explains her baleful glares. Poor woman.'

'You're a nice child,' said Richard. 'Charity for all, but *I* feel that the female is sinister.'

Celia scarcely noted the rather startling adjective, under the rush of hope. She looked up at the Marsdon Chronicle, high on the top shelf in the gloom, and made a face at it.

She ran blithely upstairs to her room, humming 'La Vie en Rose'.

Two

Celia and most of the Marsdon house party set out for Kent at half-past three o'clock.

Edna and George Simpson did not go. Edna had her headache, and she gave George his orders privately.

'You'll stay here, too, of course. Sir Richard might want to look over papers with you when he gets back from the farm, and anyway, we don't have to cater to those American women's every whim.'

George sighed. He had been looking forward to the jaunt, but he knew better than to oppose her when her face was flushed, her eyes glittering and she smelled strongly of peppermint. 'Lady Marsdon seems very pleasant,' he said. 'I can see you don't like her, though can't see why, and a young bride's bound to influence her husband. It would be a pity to threaten the Marsdon business which has been with Simpson's since 1880.'

Edna snorted, and lying down on the bed shut her eyes. 'You're a spineless worm, George, allus have been. I troost I know how to behave civilly, but I'll not toady to vulgar Yanks for anybody, and mind you don't go to that Ightham Mote. I don't laike the sound of it.'

As George went out, shutting the door softly behind him, Edna's annoyance shifted to puzzled question. She was aware that there was no reason to dislike the very name of a place of which she had never heard before lunchtime. She also disliked the name of 'Celia'—let alone the young woman herself. But then, she thought, I've a right to my fancies, should be pampered during the 'change', and George knows it. She reached for the tincture which stood on her bedside table, poured out a quarter cupful, drank it and drifted rapidly into snorting sleep.

Myra, driving her Bentley, led the way towards Kent, Lily Taylor sat beside her with a map; Sir Harry sat on the back seat smoking a briar pipe and watching the Duchess's auburn head. The long hair was now arranged into a gleaming Psyche-knot which nicely balanced her long-nosed, but beautiful profile. From time to time she turned to give him a small enigmatic smile over her shoulder. There was promise, surely, in those green glances, and Harry grew hopeful again.

Maybe tonight? He had noted the tactful juxtaposition of their bedrooms, and blessed Celia Marsdon, who must have heard rumours. I wish they were true, he thought. Haven't felt like this about a woman since Denise de Caron, ten, no twelve, years ago. The others've been too easy. No sport. Which diverted him into wishing it were the hunting season — a good run with the hounds. He puffed on his pipe and resumed watching Myra, though it occurred to him that Mrs. Taylor was not unattractive herself. A bit long in the tooth, about his own age, actually, yet still pretty in a plump, blonde way, but no spark, no sex appeal; something like his ex-wife, Peggy, who was a cosy little woman. She had divorced him without rancour, and still wrote friendly notes to him from their daughter's home in Cornwall.

In the Jaguar which followed the Bentley, Igor was driving. Celia had asked him to, partly because it obviously pleased him, and partly because she had begun to feel nervous when she drove herself — a condition which she understood no more than the other distressing new symptoms. She had been expertly driving since she was sixteen and she had, by now, driven all kinds of cars; until last month she had loved driving the Jag. And now, she didn't. But, Celia thought, still glowing from the relief of Richard's warmth in the library, I'll feel better now, I'll dare tell Richard of my nervous nonsense.

Little Sue Blake sat beside Igor in front and kept up a babble of excitement, directed mostly back to Celia, for Igor was intent on the road.

'Oh, Cousin Celia, England's so sweet, so green, and those thatched cottages, just like a calendar we had in the kitchen at home! I've never seen sheep before; the baby lambs are cute, and *what* are those funny-looking pointed things in the field?'

'Oast-houses,' answered Celia smiling, and explained something about hops and the making of beer.

Celia noticed absently that the Hindu beside her was very quiet, that his eyes were half shut, and that there was an inward listening expression on his lean, bronze face.

'Forgive Sue's raptures, Dr. Akananda,' she said laughing. 'England must be a very old story to you.'

He turned and looked at her with a brief, compassionate gaze. Not exactly compassion, she thought startled, more like pity, which would be as annoying as it was uncalled for.

'Why do you look at me like that?' she cried involuntarily.

Jiddu Akananda smiled apology. 'I'm sorry, Lady Marsdon, I'd like to convey to you my sympathy and what help I can give during the trials that may await you. I tried to stop your going here today, but you didn't hear me.'

'Trials,' she repeated sharply. 'What do you mean?'

He raised his slim hand and touched her forehead between the arched dark brows, a gentle touch like a benediction, yet it was also like an electric charge, a quick shimmer of light through her head.

'You must,' he said calmly, almost conversationally, 'hold fast to your course, with faith, for you may be badly buffeted in the tempest that I fear is brewing.'

Celia lifted her brows and would have questioned further, but Sue had caught Akananda's last words and twisted around to say archly, 'Tempest, Dr. Akananda? You Hindu gentlemen are awfully poetical, I've always heard so. Back in Kaintucky we wouldn't think this sky looked like a storm comin'.'

'I suppose not, my child.' Akananda's eyes held an indulgent twinkle, 'Yet there are many kinds of storms. Outside in nature; inside in the soul.'

Sue giggled and pouted. 'You're positively bafflin', Doctor, or should I say, Mr. Guru? I've always wanted to meet one of you, after Jack—that's my brother—went all committed to the Maharishi and kept doing Yoga an' meditations. Jack was a real hippie for a while,' she explained. 'Mom and Dad were horrified. But, I guess he's got over it. He's cut his hair, stopped smoking pot, and is dating a real nice girl.'

'That is splendid,' said Akananda smiling. Sue turned around to answer some comment of Igor's and the Hindu glanced at Celia. 'Your little cousin is charming, and very young. She's also fortunate. I believe that for her this life will be easy.'

'Do you predict future?' asked Celia with a hint of sarcasm. She had not liked the implied warning in Akananda's speech about tempests, especially as the man attracted her. There came from him a radiation, an effect of light around him. And *that*'s idiotic, too, she thought.

'I'm not a fortune-teller,' Akananda answered quietly. 'But through training and discipline I receive more impressions than most people are able to. Yes, you're right in thinking that I was trying to prepare you for a grave ordeal. That much is permitted. I am also permitted, even commanded, to help you as best I can. Though we must all pay our Karmic debts, the

43

Divinity which is above Karma is ever merciful; through God's help and your own actions you *may* be able to reduce a sword-thrust to a pin-prick. It depends.'

Celia stared through the open window where the rose-studded hedgerows and the buttercup fields slipped by. She had not been really listening but one word startled her.

'God ...?' she said hesitantly. 'I used to believe in Him when I was very little, now He's just what somebody said, just an oblong grey blur. I had a funny religious upbringing.' She turned to Akananda, yet spoke half to herself, 'A year in a Catholic convent as a boarder when I was eleven, while Daddy was travelling on business around the world with Mother.'

'But, your parents weren't Catholics?'

'Oh, no, but Mother's best friend was, and they thought it a safe place to leave me. I was lonely and bored, really miserable . . . Before that,' she added ruefully, 'I was a little Christian Scientist, because my governess was one. I went to First Church Sunday School in Chicago. But the governess left. And Mother took up Theosophy. I devoured all the books she did, and was fascinated by them. But after Daddy died . . .'

'Your father had no interest in religions?'

'None whatsoever, he used to laugh at Mother and say he'd leave all that tomfoolery to the women, common horse sense was enough for him.'

'And you agree?'

'I think so,' Celia said. 'As I grew up I got cynical. I'd see Mother enthusiastic and involved with charlatans. Numerologists and astrologists who charged five hundred dollars for a "reading" which was so vague you could twist the meaning any way you wanted. And faith healers who couldn't seem to heal themselves, and a Yogi in California who preached Purity, Sublimity and Continence, and then tried to seduce me one day when Mother was out. It was awful.'

'Did you tell your mother?'

'Oh, yes, I did.' Celia considered this with slight surprise. 'She's never shocked or fusses. I always told her everything. She was very distressed, she soothed me and wrote the Yogi a blistering letter. We never saw him again, of course.'

'And now you fear that Mrs. Taylor has entangled you with another such Yogi?' Akananda asked, amused.

Celia coloured. 'Oh, I don't mean *that*. I don't know what I mean, and I love Mother, I trust her even when she makes mistakes. She always admits them, and has faith in people just the same.'

'Your mother,' he said slowly, 'is a fine woman. She seeks the truth, and often glimpses it. The bond between you is very strong.'

She nodded, half exasperated. She didn't want to talk about Lily. The whole conversation made her uncomfortable. 'Oh, Mother's all right. My whole *life* should be all right now. Oh, it will be, I'm sure.'

Akananda sighed. 'Yes, there's something you desperately want, and you are *not* sure—to understand your husband. There are from the Past appalling obstacles I'm afraid between you and your desire.' It was an authoritative statement.

Celia started and her jaw tightened, 'That's a ridiculous remark, Doctor! Little tiffs are natural in marriage. I don't know what you're getting at anyway.'

Akananda shook his head. 'Poor child, your deep self knows very well what I mean. Why do you swallow and gasp so often, why are your hands trembling?'

She clenched her hands tight. 'Nerves,' she said angrily. 'Everyone gets nervous symptoms, sometimes. Stop probing. You've no right to, and I don't like it.'

'That's reasonable, and your privilege.' He spoke with patient dignity. 'However, I *am* a physician, trained at the University of Calcutta, then Oxford, and Guy's Hospital, and after that two years of psychiatry at the Maudesley in London. I am also a disciple of a great world teacher who was called Nanak once.'

'Is he *dead?*' she asked, her anger ebbing.

'He no longer inhabits a body,' said Akananda. 'He's passed beyond the disciplinary Karmic need to reincarnate.'

'Oh, *that*—' she said. 'I suppose it makes sense or why are innocent babies born crippled, blind—why horrible injustices? Oh, I know half the world believes in rebirth, and even some things in the Bible seem to point that way. But, why can't we *remember* past lives?'

'Remembrance would usually be an intolerable burden, which *all* Merciful God spares us. For that matter, Lady Marsdon, do you consciously remember the first year or two of *this* life?'

Celia shook her head. 'But what difference does it make?' She was tired, drained, bored with the subject. And there was still resentment towards Akananda who had disrupted her

45

hopeful mood. 'You don't seem to be the sort of man who would bother to come to a silly weekend house party,' she said crossly. 'Especially as you hardly know Mother, and the rest of us not at all.'

He was silent, debating whether to answer her frankly. He read her mood and understood it, but after a moment he spoke what he knew to be truth.

'I don't want to annoy you, my dear child, but I believe I've known you and your mother somewhere before this lifetime, though I don't know where. There's a reason for my presence. Also, you have known some of the people at your house party before this. I'm quite sure of that. The great Karmic Law has now brought you to the brink of a precipice where a battle will take place.'

'Indeed,' said Celia shrugging. 'I hope the good guys win.' She fished in her bag and brought out her pink lipstick, applying it carefully. Her hand did not tremble, her throat was not constricted. She was only tired. 'Sue, look! she touched the girl's shoulder. 'Down there in the hollow, that must be the house we're going to. Why, it really *does* have a moat!'

The girl looked where Celia pointed, and her mouth fell open. 'Fabulous ...' She breathed, and then for once was speechless.

Myra turned her Bentley and drove slowly through the opened gates. The Jaguar followed. The cars stopped by a gravelled path. The occupants got out, and joined forces. They were all quiet a while, gazing at the manor house which was gilded by the afternoon sun into the garnet of bricks and tiles, the topaz of lichen-covered stones, broken here and there by stretches of half-timbering—striped ivory between oak beams. Secluded, solitary, enchanted, Ightham lay dreaming within its encircling moat, and on first sight gave all beholders a sense of romantic peace.

Igor spoke first. 'Marvellous, Mrs. Taylor, utterly *fantastic*! I'd no idea such a place existed—and so near London. It takes the Americans to show us our country! Look at those colours, mellow yet vibrant above that ribbon of liquid emerald. Now if I can possibly get those tones in fabric . . .' He squinted, framed off sections with his hands. 'Good thing I brought my Polaroid.' He sauntered back to the car to fetch his camera.

Sir Harry and Myra also turned to Lily. 'Most picturesque,' Harry said. 'Quite worth seeing, must cost a fortune to keep up, though.'

'Yes, indeed,' agreed Myra, surveying the house, the shaven lawns, the rose and peony gardens with a practised eye. 'Charming. I wonder how the owner gets enough staff. I shouldn't want to live here myself, give me a convenient flat in Eaton Square every time, but this is very pretty.'

Lily was gratified, no longer defensive about her expedition. 'Aren't you glad you came, darling?' she asked Celia, and broke off. 'Oh, this must be the guide, they said one would be waiting.'

A middle-aged woman in a floral print dress came briskly over the stone bridge towards them. 'Mrs. Amos B. Taylor's party?' she enquired smiling. 'As a rule we only show the place on Friday afternoons, but the owner is generous and allows exceptions when he's not in residence. Particularly for Americans, since he is one.'

'It's very kind of you,' Lily smiled back. 'As a matter of fact, we aren't all Americans, this is the Duchess of Drewton, and Sir Harry Jones, and Mr. Igor—they're English, and Dr. Akananda, then Miss Susan Blake and my daughter, Lady Marsdon, *we're* the Americans.'

The guide looked faintly startled, though she knew that Americans were given to elaborate introductions. She glanced with interest at the Duchess, whom she had seen pictured in the *Illustrated London News* and wondered at her presence here. For that matter it seemed a peculiar party, with a Hindu, and a Sir Somebody, and a golden-haired youth with a queer name, and 'my daughter, Lady Marsdon' who had drawn away from the others and was staring at the stone tower with extraordinary intensity.

'Now,' said the guide, shrugging, 'we'll start our tour here on the bridge, while remembering that the original fortified manor house was built by either a Cawne or a deHaut in the reign of Edward the Third, somewhere about 1370, we think. It has not been possible to identify all the early owners, but you will find a list on the back of the leaflet. You might like to look at it before starting the tour.' The guide handed out pamphlets. 'That'll be sixpence each if you wish to keep them,' she said.

Myra declined her pamphlet graciously, 'I'm afraid I'm not all that keen on crawling over old houses,' she said. 'Are you, Harry?' He shook his head. 'Then we'll wait for you outside,' she added to Lily. 'I'm quite fond of *gardens*.' She glanced at her diamond wristwatch. 'The pubs won't be open yet, I could do with a gin and bitters, but we've got the tea flask in the car. Will you fetch it, Harry?'

Myra wandered off with her admirer. Igor also preferred to stay outside, enthusiastically snapping sunlight effects as he pranced around the edge of the moat.

'Well,' said Lily, a trifle disappointed, '*we* want to see everything.' She looked at Dr. Akananda and Sue, then more carefully at Celia. 'What's the matter with *you*, dear?' she said laughing. 'You act moon-struck.'

Celia jumped. She gazed hastily down at the moat. 'I was watching the swans.' Two of them were gliding under the bridge among the flowing green weeds.

'Oh, yes,' said the guide, 'the Queen herself had us sent a pair of the royal ones, after swan-upping day. Now this entrance tower has an interesting feature. You see the zigzag stone slit here, it's really a device for those inside the manor to discover safely who might be trying to get in. Quite ingenious. And now the courtyard, entirely enclosed by the buildings, rather small as these things go. Those stocks over there by the Great Hall were often in use for punishment.'

'Punishment?' repeated Sue, wide-eyed. 'And is there a dungeon too, where they tortured people?'

'There is a dungeon,' answered the guide patiently, 'almost under the entrance tower, but we don't show it, it's too dark and dangerous.'

The guide led her party across the cobblestones to the eastern part of the quadrangle and unlocked a massive oaken door. 'This entrance now leads into the vestibule outside the Great Hall. There were structural changes made in the last century on this side of the Hall, otherwise it has remained much as you see it for five hundred years.'

Lily, Sue, Akananda and Celia filed into the Hall which was suddenly flooded with sunshine through the tall mullioned windows to the left. The guide continued to point out features — the original oak roof timbers, the grotesquely caved fourteenth-century corbels, the Flemish tapestries.

Lily and Sue made delighted exclamations. Akananda watched Celia. Her face had flushed, her mouth opened, and her uneven breathing was audible. The Hindu doctor quietly took her arm, and pushed her down on the cushioned bench below the window, noting that her pulse was pounding.

'That bit of armour over the fireplace,' said the guide impressively, 'was found when they drained the moat many years

ago—a Cromwellian soldier, the experts say. Now we'll proceed to the old crypt, then upstairs. Is there something wrong,
Lady Marsdon?' she asked as she turned. 'You seem unwell—
the heat perhaps?'

Celia heard the question from a vast distance, like a poor
connection over a transatlantic phone. She licked her lips. 'I'm
all right,' she said, 'yes, I guess it's the heat.'

Lily made an impulsive move, frowning concern, and would
have gone to her daughter. She was stopped by a small commanding shake of Akananda's head. 'I'll take care of her, Mrs.
Taylor.'

Lily at once obeyed the prohibition in his eyes. She was
reassured as he wished her to be, and turned back to the guide.
'I can't wait to see the rest of this fascinating place.'

'Me, too,' said Sue. 'What's that little door next to the big
door on that wall? It doesn't go anywhere.'

'Oh, that,' the guide smiled. 'That's a niche where they found
the skeleton of a girl when they reconstructed this south wall
in 1872.'

'Skeleton,' cried Sue rapturously. 'What was she doing in
the wall?'

'I'm afraid she was *put* there. It's rather disagreeable, but
this happened in many old houses, centuries ago.'

'You mean she was walled up *alive*?' Sue gaped at the low
empty niche. 'Where's the skeleton now?'

'Ah, that we don't know,' said the guide, bored with a question she had so often been asked. 'No doubt the bones were
dispersed . . . Now, if you will kindly step this way . . .'

Sue was not yet satisfied. 'But don't they know *when* she
was walled up, or who she was? And doesn't her ghost do some
hauntin'?'

The guide answered a trifle curtly, 'It has been said that the
skeleton might have been Dame Dorothy Selby, who is supposed to have warned the House of Lords about the Gunpowder Plot. The Selbys lived here for three hundred years,
but it can't have been Dame Dorothy of whom we have an
authentic portrait hanging in the stairwell, for *that* shows an
old woman. As for ghosts, I know how you Americans dote on
such tales.'

'Of course we do!' Sue cried. 'They're interestin', aren't
they, Cousin Lily?'

Lily nodded. 'Most people are interested in the psychic.
I'm really sorry that Medfield Place—that's my son-in-law's

manor in East Sussex—doesn't seem to have a ghost. But I've heard there are a lot *here*.'

'I daresay,' said the guide. 'Never seen anything myself, but there was supposed to be a cold presence in the tower room. It was exorcised I believe. There're other legends, armoured knights, ghostly hoofbeats, a black monk with a rope around his neck, that sort of thing, but I never heard mention of the walled-up girl.' She determinedly shooed the two women back into the vestibule.

Celia remained on the window-seat with Akananda. The flush had drained from her face, which was now pale and glistening with sweat drops. She slumped against the doctor's shoulder. 'I feel sick,' she whispered. 'Deathly sick. Can't breathe.'

Akananda put a firm hand on her forehead. Through mists of nausea she felt the sustaining pressure.

She straightened slowly, opening her eyes. 'Where's Mother gone?' she said. 'Mother and Sue?' She spoke in a wondering little-girl voice. Her languid gaze roamed about the Hall, it passed over the niche without pausing. He saw that her pupils were so widely dilated that her eyes seemed as black as his own.

'They have gone with the guide to see the rest of this place,' he said quietly. 'I think you had better come outside with me. We'll go find the Duchess in the garden.'

'This place,' she repeated frowning past him at the wainscoting. When she spoke again he was startled by a different inflection. Her voice sounded higher, there was no trace of American accent, yet the tonal quality was not the English that he knew either. There was an unfamiliar cadence as she said, 'This is a place abhorrent. Yet I cannot flee. For I must see him. My love awaits me in secret. Jesu, forgive us!'

She crossed herself with a wavering uncertain motion.

Akananda shook his head. He guessed something of what was hidden from her or any one of the struggling souls who were blindly meshed in the results of a bygone tragedy. But since these souls had free will, he could not foresee the outcome. His thought sped to the exalted ashram in the Himalayas where he had passed some of his boyhood, under the guidance of several enlightened ones, and especially of Nanak Guru. With the yearning memory went a humble prayer for wisdom.

'Come out into the garden, my child,' he said, putting a

hand on Celia's arm, for she had started up. 'You've had enough. Already the protective veil is torn.'

She shook his hand off. 'Let me be!' she cried angrily. 'Always I must go to him. I must tell him.' She stroked her belly. 'It hath quickened. I felt it move this morn.'

Akananda stared at her and saw a subtle change, as though a different face shed a wavering reflection on that of Celia Marsdon. The contours had become more oval, the lips fuller and more seductive, the brows more arched and the eyes held a passionate wilful glint.

'Lady Marsdon,' he said in a calm cold tone designed to reach through to her, 'do you mean that you are pregnant by Sir Richard?'

She made an impatient gesture. 'Will you mock me?' she said. 'I know not a Sir Richard, Stephen is my dear love . . .'

She whirled around and ran through the door. Akananda followed her close behind. She flew up the heavy Jacobean stairs. On the landing she paused, putting her hand to her lips. 'I hear voices. None must know. *She* found us once.' Celia flattened herself into a corner.

The voices were those of the guide, Lily, and Sue who were examining the window in the solar through which bygone ladies might discreetly watch male revelry in the Great Hall below.

'And now,' said the guide, 'we will proceed through towards the Priest's Room and the Tudor Chapel. That chapel is a gem. It was built in 1521 during the reign of Henry the Eighth; it contains priceless linenfold panelling, a painted barrel roof and some fine stained glass . . .' Her voice died away as the party moved on.

Celia emerged from the corner. 'They are gone,' she murmured.

She walked slowly through the solar and an anteroom, while Akananda followed. She was now totally unaware of him, and talked to herself as she entered a dark passage. 'Where is the door? He would not have locked it against me. Might he be at the altar? Yet not at this hour, so late at night. Though he *does* pray overmuch.'

She entered a small cubicle which contained a fireplace and led into the chapel. 'Stephen . . .' she whispered urgently. ' 'Tis unkind to hide.' Suddenly she raised her head and looked up at a dark beam on the ceiling. 'What's that . . .?' she whispered. 'Black, hanging there . . . what's that?'

51

Akananda stood rooted. Sunlight filtered through the bare empty cubicle from the chapel windows.

Celia moved a step nearer the fireplace. She raised her arms high, her hands fumbled over something in the air. She fell to her knees, and as she did so, gave a scream so piercing, so eerie that it shrilled through the peaceful manor rooms like an air-raid siren.

The guide came running back, with Lily and Sue. They stood for an appalled moment staring at Celia who was crumpled on the floor, with Akananda bending over her, his hand on her wrist.

'Dear Lord, what happened?' cried Lily, kissing her daughter and distractedly smoothing the brown curls.

'She fainted,' said the Hindu, 'but she'll be all right. Perhaps we can carry her to a bed.'

'What was that terrible noise?' cried Lily. 'Surely, not *Celia*!'

Akananda did not hesitate. There would certainly now be no escape from suffering, but he would spare the poor mother what he could. 'Was there some special noise?' he asked. 'I was preoccupied with Lady Marsdon.'

The guide at once showed exasperated relief. 'You can depend on it, it was the plumbing. You'd be surprised at the whistles and bangs we get from the plumbing. These old places were never built for bathrooms.'

She went to help Akananda and the others lift Celia. 'Nearest bed'll be in the owner's private wing,' she said. She stared at Celia, 'Poor thing, does she get these spells often, Mrs. Taylor? I had a cousin used to have fits.'

Lily, though much alarmed, was able to say indignantly, 'Celia doesn't have "fits". I never knew her to faint before. But, of course, you know young wives . . . one might expect . . .' she smiled faintly and shrugged.

The guide accepted this, as did Sue, who instantly reviewed all the things she had heard about pregnancy, and examined the unconscious Celia with awed interest.

In twenty minutes Celia had completely recovered, and felt almost normal. She concealed from everyone that she had no idea of anything that had happened since leaving the Jag by the moat bridge.

The guide showed the party out through the tower entrance, accepted the fees for her tip, then vanished.

They found Igor still snapping pictures; the Duchess and Harry flirting on a bench near the ornamental pool.

As the party gathered by the bridge Myra greeted them amiably. 'Well, was the tour interesting? You've scarcely been gone an hour.'

Sue began, 'Oh, it was fascinatin', but I don't think we saw everything because Cousin Celia ...' She broke off gaping at the lawn beyond the moat. 'What's *that*? It's fabulous!'

They all gazed where Sue's finger pointed.

Myra laughed. 'That, my sweet, is a peacock, and this one's a blasted nuisance. Name of Napoleon, the gardener said, when we had to get help to stop him pecking at his reflection on my car door. Conceited, aggressive bird, like all males.'

She gave Harry a sideways look. He responded with an amorous chuckle, and ran his finger slowly down her bare arm.

'I'll snap Napoleon for you,' offered Igor to Sue, 'but those iridescent blues and greens have been done to death. Too blatant. Still, they might suit *you*, Duchess. Shall I try them in a cocktail frock?'

Myra shrugged. 'Thanks, dear Igor, but I don't pay two hundred guineas for any cocktail frock, blatant or not, save your genius for the film stars and the jet set.' She had almost added, 'the Americans', but even Myra's egotism was penetrated by something odd about Mrs. Taylor and her daughter —their total silence, and on Celia's small face a strained haunted look. Myra received a singular impression—a memory of one of the crofters' wives on her father's estate in Cumberland, a woman Myra's mother always referred to as 'tragic', though Myra had never known why. Anyway, the woman had drowned herself in the River Irthing, and the ten-year-old Myra had heard snatches of the adults' pity and horror. Myra disliked uncomfortable memories and dealt with this one briskly.

'The local pub must be open by now!' she said. 'Let's go and get fortified for the journey back to Medfield!'

They grouped themselves as before in the two cars, and drove to the nearby village of Ivy Hatch.

By seven o'clock they arrived at Medfield Place. Richard came out of the manor to greet them. 'Enjoy yourselves?' he asked cordially. He was already dressed for the evening, and looked very handsome.

Myra instantly forgot Harry and gave Richard her lazy

smile. 'We missed you, darling,' she drawled. 'I hope you built a *divine* pigsty!'

'Quite,' he agreed. 'A sanctuary for super-sows. Celia, you seem a bit fagged, but I'm afraid the Bent-Warners'll be here shortly.'

'Oh, yes,' she answered after a minute. 'I'll go and change.' The Bent-Warners? Who were the Bent-Warners? But, one must please Richard. There was danger in displeasing Richard.

Celia turned and mounted the steps into the house, treading very carefully as though uncertain of her balance.

Richard watched her, frowning; when they entered the house he drew Lily into his study. 'Anything wrong with Celia?' he asked. 'She acts very strange.'

Lily hesitated. 'I don't think so. Not really. She had a kind of fainting spell at Ightham Mote . . . but Dr. Akananda says she's all right. I thought maybe it was . . .' she stopped, a flush sprang up on the plump, slightly rouged cheeks.

Richard's gaze hardened. His eyebrows drew together. 'You thought it was pregnancy? I assure you it's not. Nor do I consider that Hindu an adequate medical opinion. If she's not better when I go up, I'll get old Foster from Lewes.'

'That's a good idea,' Lily murmured, dismayed by his tone, and that he left her so abruptly, standing on the study's faded oriental rug. He acts that way because he loves her, Lily thought, and men can never bear illness. It was stupid to be hurt, or to magnify a fainting spell, stupid to catch some of the confused fear she now felt in her daughter. Lily shut her eyes and strove to clear her thinking. In her many religious questings she had once come across Sir Thomas Browne, and might have summed up her faith by one of his aphorisms, 'Life is a pure flame, and we live by an invisible sun within us'. She stood now, trying to *feel* the interior sunlight, the glowing comfort which had never really failed her, though it did now. And being a woman of action, she mounted the great oaken stairway, and knocked on Akananda's door.

He opened the door instantly, and said without surprise, 'Oh, Mrs. Taylor. Come in.' He was wearing a white silk dressing-gown, and his black hair glistened from a shower. Lily had the impression of extreme order and cleanliness while noting absently that the guest room seemed very bare. He must have removed the knick-knacks, the ashtrays, even the French prints which had hung on the walls. The only ornament was a bowl full of fragrant heliotrope and red roses.

'I just wanted to ... to ask you ... well, Celia ... and Richard was rude to me. Of course that doesn't matter ... but he never was until today, and what *really* made Celia faint? Everything is suddenly so mixed up and queer.' Her blue eyes filled with tears.

Akananda looked at her sadly. But it was not the time to give her what explanations he could. 'We'll both pray,' he said. 'You in your way, I in mine. All heart-prayers are heard. All incense rises towards heaven, no matter the perfume it's composed of.'

'Oh, I believe that,' said Lily, her face clearing. 'I guess I'll go to church tomorrow morning. It always makes me feel better. But you don't believe in Christianity, do you, Dr. Akananda?'

'Of course I do,' he said laughing. 'The Lord Christ was sent from God to show the way, the truth and the life, to the western world. But there have been other enlightened Sons of God. Enlightened Beings who redeem mankind. The Lord Krishna was such a one, and the Lord Buddha. None of their basic teachings are incompatible with each other. Because they come from the same source. You understand this intuitively, Mrs. Taylor. And that's all you need. I'll gladly accompany you to that charming village church tomorrow. One can more easily touch God in appointed places of worship. Christian cathedrals, Hindu temples, in mosques and churches. To many souls beauty of surroundings is helpful, to some essential, and yet for those of a different temperament the spirit may more readily be felt in a bare Quaker Meeting House. It doesn't matter.'

Lily agreed with him, now that she thought about it; as she instinctively agreed with any optimistic philosophy. She smiled and said, 'Yes, you make me feel quite comforted, and I really do know that prayers are answered. I don't know why I got upset in the study.'

'Prayers,' he said gravely, 'are always *heard*. They are *answered* according to Divine Law. Prayers are really desires. And desires, good *or* bad, are fulfilled according to their strength. Good desire reaps good action. Evil also has great strength. Violent desires inevitably set the machinery in motion. This earthly plane is run by passions flaming through, and yet always part of the delusions of Maya. As long as there's violence there will be retribution in this life or succeeding ones. I believe you understand this?'

'Well, yes,' said Lily, 'in a way.' Though she wondered what a grave speech about violence had to do with a little fainting spell, or the unexpected sharpness of a son-in-law. 'I've read somewhere lately,' she said thoughtfully, 'that this generation of hippies, the flower children who want to drop out from the whole social structure, the article said they were all reincarnations of those who were killed young in the last war. Do you think that's possible?'

'Quite possible,' he answered smiling. 'At least in part. And their demonstrations against war, hatred and greed, though often misguided, are signs of spiritual progress. However, dear lady, the forces threatening us here in Medfield Place originated farther back in the past than the last war and are of singular *personal* intensity.' He might have continued trying to prepare and strengthen her, as he had her daughter, but Lily started.

'Heavens!' she said, 'I heard a car on the drive. Must be those Warners. I'll be late.' She smiled at him and hurried to her room.

*   *   *

Celia's vagueness and look of strain had vanished when Richard came upstairs to her bedroom saying, 'I hear you fainted at Ightham Mote. What happened?'

She was sitting at her dressing-table, brushing green iridescent eye-shadow on her lids, brown mascara on her already thick lashes. 'Nothing special happened,' she said with a cool smile. Far away and closed off by an iron door, something stirred. Hostility to Richard. She still had no memory of Ightham Mote, and very little of the ride home; but she was aware of a shift in feeling.

Richard stared. That chill remoteness, instead of her usual eager warmth. 'Well, I'm glad you're all right again,' he said uncertainly. 'You didn't look it when you got back. I was worried.'

She turned around on the stool. Her grey eyes, now made much longer by the make-up, examined him quietly. '*Were* you, Richard? Were you really?' She rouged her lips a deep cherry-red, which further astonished him. She had always worn the fashionably pale lipsticks. She stood up in her brief lacy slip, went to her closet and took out a simple flame-coloured chiffon sheath. She dropped it over her head.

'Zip me up, please!' He obeyed clumsily, and when his

fingers touched her soft tanned back, she shuddered and drew away.

She brushed her curly dark hair into a high pile on her head, clipped on earrings as big as golf balls, made of a mass of crystal chunks. There was a matching heavy crystal bracelet. The crystals had a greyish sparkle, like dull diamonds, and gave her a strange, exotic look.

'I thought you didn't like wearing heavy stuff like that,' he said frowning.

'Not my "image"?' asked Celia sweetly. 'Igor brought them as a guest-gift. He says they represent a "mass of petrified tears". I think that rather suits me.'

'Good God, Celia. What a bloody morbid remark! What *is* the matter with you?'

'Nothing at all,' she said, opening a sealed bottle of *Shalimar* and rubbing some on her wrists and neck. The perfume had been an untouched Christmas present, for she used only the lightest floral scents. 'I think,' she added, 'that I'll seduce Harry. It would be fun to take him from Myra.'

If she had suddenly hit him in the face he could not have been more shocked. Flippancy, though unlike her, might be understood. So might teasing, which had once been part of their love-making when they were close. *Had* been close. His face darkened. Mrs. Taylor had thought Celia pregnant. But he hadn't touched her in—well—a long time. Why not? Because he hadn't wanted to. Because sex had suddenly grown repugnant. *You should not have married!* He heard the words in his head.

'The seating arrangements tonight,' said Celia, pulling a stack of gold-rimmed cards towards her on the desk. 'I'll write them fast. Twelve is a nuisance since it won't come out even. Ah . . .' she added, seeing his face ,'you thought I'd forgotten this little detail, didn't you? Despite my vulgar American background I do occasionally remember my social duties. I shall put Harry beside me, and remove Myra.'

Richard swallowed. 'If you're being so childish as to try and make me jealous, the effort's wasted.'

'Don't flatter yourself,' she said. Their eyes met for a moment in anger. That behind the anger was fear they neither of them perceived.

*   *   *

They all sat down to dinner at nine. Medfield's great dining room was always gloomy, the Victorian baronet had papered it with purple brocade, and painted the original oak wood-work a mud-brown. He had also put in floral carpeting, snaky tendrils and blossoms of what might have been water lilies once but now also merged into mottled mud-brown. It had worn all too well, and Richard did not want it replaced.

Fringed purple plush curtains shut out the evening sunlight. The light of thirty candles on the mahogany table and in sconces wavered over ten ancestral portraits, nine of them garish and ugly. The tenth had been painted by a pupil of Holbein in the reign of Queen Elizabeth and represented a Thomas Marsdon Esq. in doublet and hose. A dark, lean young man, whose delicate hand rested on a greyhound's head, and whose haunting melancholy eyes always seemed to follow the beholder. There was a slight resemblance to Richard in this portrait which always had made Celia vaguely uneasy, even though it was proof of the long established lineage which thrilled her.

The Bent-Warners who had expanded the house party were an ebullient young couple in their thirties. Pamela was a blonde, so pretty that one forgave her constant chatter about either her children or the theatre. Robin Bent-Warner sat on Celia's right, and was most amusing. He looked and acted rather like a P. G. Wodehouse character, and capitalised on this, 'My job being tourism, "Come to Britain and enjoy our quaintness", you know. I don't quite sport a monocle, but I hope that's the general effect.'

Celia laughed. The laugh was high-pitched and shrill. Lily, across the table, inspected her daughter anxiously. What had come over the girl? Her cheeks were flushed, her eyes glittered like those extraordinary crystal hunks she wore on her ears and wrist. The flame-coloured dress clung to her very small breasts as it never had before. Or, could it be the way Celia was holding herself? Arched backwards, almost flaunting. And while she laughed at Robin Bent-Warner, surely her bare shoulder was pressing against Sir Harry's maroon-covered shoulder, for he looked startled and pleased. Lily put down a forkful of crab ravigote and pushed her plate back. Celia could not be tight, she had taken no cocktails, nor yet sipped her wine. Then she was coming down with something. Flu made people act unnatural. Some virus, Lily thought, would, of course, explain the fainting and this change in her. Right after dinner we'll see if she has a temperature.

Other people were also watching Celia. One was her husband. Richard made no pretence of listening to either Pam's
chatter or Myra's husky blandishments until the latter flicked
his cheek with her finger, saying, 'Must you glower, my lad?
It's so tiresome. I've seen a side of you this weekend I never
suspected.'

Richard turned to her slowly and smiled, not with his eyes.
'Men are perhaps more complicated than you quite realise,
dear Myra.' He raised his glass in a mocking toast.

She laughed. 'Well, Harry isn't complicated anyway. He's
just plain susceptible. I might be glowering a bit myself, seeing that he's now giving that heavy-lidded bedroom look to
your Celia, but actually, I think it's funny.' And she did. She
had all the assurance of beauty, position and experience. An
unexpected move in the eternal game was zestful. Imagine
that quiet little mouse of a Celia suddenly acting sexy, and
looking it, too, Myra thought with critical interest. As though
somebody had pressed a switch, and a light-bulb flared on.
That this phenomenon was designed to pique the mysterious
Richard, Myra had no doubt, since she was an adept at that
ploy herself. And that the ploy seemed to be succeeding Myra
thought admirable. She mentally shrugged, retiring for the
moment from the lists. She would deal with Harry later.

She also abandoned Richard and addressed Akananda on
her left. 'Tell me about India, Doctor,' she commanded. 'My
grandfather was stationed there, governing something or
other, but I've never been east of Istanbul. Would I like India?'

Akananda, who had been gravely eating, responded with
smiling courtesy. The other close watcher of Celia was Edna
Simpson. Edna, thanks to the tincture, had slept heavily all
afternoon, not even awakening for the housemaid's knock
when tea was brought up. During the nap she had suffered a
recurrent nightmare. Every time that she roused a little and
angrily heard herself moaning she slipped back again into the
same high-vaulted room. Her host and hostess were in the
nightmare though they did not look like themselves. Sir
Richard had no face, but he had a fat, long black snake twisted
around his waist. The snake kept hissing and darting at her
while she tried to grab it and strangle it. Or sometimes she
wanted to grab the snake and make it bite Celia Marsdon,
who stood spreadeagled against the stone wall.

The dream Celia had very long fair hair which she would
not keep decently bound in a kerchief. That was one of her

crimes. Another was the depth of her laced bodice. It showed pink nipples on the tips of full white breasts. Disgusting. So vile a creature should be destroyed. The crucifix said so. At this point Edna always saw a silver crucifix writhing with snakes, and Sir Richard standing behind it, laughing. He would not laugh when the wench was dead. God said so. God was perched on top of the crucifix and he had little black horns. 'Kill!' he shouted. 'Thou must kill! It is a command-ment!' Then the snakes slithered off the crucifix and glided towards her. They reared their heads ready to strike.

Each time that Edna awoke, she heard herself making the mewing stifled noise. And her fat body was clammy with sweat.

She finally roused herself completely at the sound of the car returning from Ightham Mote. She looked down from her window. She saw Sir Richard run to her car, and saw Celia get out. She stared hard at Celia. While her brain felt thick, fuzzy. Her hands were shaking. She was trying to pour out more tincture as George timidly knocked, then walked in.

'Have a good rest, m'dear?'

The green bottle rattled against the glass rim as Edna rounded on him. 'Ye dumb bustard, creeping about like a cat. Ye've made me slosh me tonic. Wot be ye gawking at? Get oot a her-re!'

George bit his lips, his round jaw trembled. They had been married twenty-six years and he was quite fond of her. He had always coped with her quick tempers by capitulation or flight. But he had never seen her like this, nor heard her for-get her careful diction. He glanced frowning at the bottle of tincture, even though the stuffy room reeked only of pepper-mint. 'Should you take more of that stuff?' His voice faltered and he retreated as Edna raised a massive arm as though to strike him. Instead she seized the glass and gulped down what-ever liquid hadn't spilled.

'I need it for m'nerves,' she said in a more normal tone, 'and my head's splitting.' She belched and then began to hiccup.

'You shouldn't go down for dinner, you're not up to it,' he cried anxiously.

Edna hiccuped again and slumped on the bed. 'Oh, I'm oop to it. Musht, must keep an eye on that mealy-mouthed minx.'

'Please, Edna . . . please . . .'

But her brain cleared, she stopped hiccuping and walked determinedly to the cupboard where the new evening frock from Harrods hung ready. It was of navy-blue satin with white polka dots; it fitted snugly over the foundation garment which moulded her abundant hips and breasts into a thick shapeless column. She ran a comb through her crinkled hair, polished her spectacles and set them squarely on her reddened nose.

'Coom on,' she said with her usual authority.

Edna had sat silent in the drawing room, contemptuously refusing cocktails—'I'm afraid I don't indulge.' At table she was silent, sitting like a monolith between Igor and Sir Harry whose entire attention was devoted to Celia. Celia's altered appearance and actions gave Edna venomous satisfaction. The intruder, the interloper showing her true colours. Little slut, thought Edna. Her glance flickered once towards Richard, then back to Celia where it remained.

After the chocolate soufflé, Celia signalled to the women, rose and led the way to the drawing room. The men remained behind for coffee and port, since Richard continued the old custom.

Celia poured coffee for the ladies. She responded to casual remarks from Myra, and Pam Bent-Warner. She assured little Sue that the weather would probably hold, and there'd be tennis tomorrow. She brightly refused Lily's whispered request that she take her temperature. 'Oh, I'm all right, Mother, never felt better.'

Below these actions she was empty. 'Celia' had gone off somewhere, far away, into a cramped little space. Cold, damp, far away. Someone else was using 'Celia's' body. Someone else who could laugh and talk, who could think how ridiculous that Edna Simpson was, squatting on the gold sofa, her thighs spread wide under their covering of polka dots, the pale eyes looking blank as shutters behind the reflection of the bifocals.

As soon as the men joined them in the drawing room Celia jumped up crying, 'Let's *do* something! It's Saturday night, and we've got to be gay! I know, let's dance! We'll go to Richard's music room.'

'Splendid!' cried Igor, twirling gracefully on his toes and waving his beautiful white hands. Harry laughed, while eyeing Celia with the new startled admiration. Been so taken up with Myra I hardly noticed this gel before. Looks like a gypsy suddenly, and she most certainly leaned hard against me at dinner. Astonishing little beasts—women.

Pam Bent-Warner cried, 'Ooh, what fun! I didn't know you

61

had a music room at Medfield Place, Richard! But then, there were never any parties in Sir Charles's time.'

Everyone looked at Richard, who removed his unfathomable gaze from his wife and said, ' "Music room" is a bit grand for the old schoolroom on the second storey. I do happen to have a stereo there, and a collection of records which appeal to *me*. Nothing modern.'

His decisive tone piqued Myra, who cried, 'Let's go invade the schoolroom, see what Richard *has* got! He so obviously doesn't want us to, I believe the records are naughty. Are they Celia?'

'I don't know,' answered Celia, in a voice as light and brittle as the Duchess's. 'Nothing about my husband would surprise me. I called it the music room because Nanny did once. Actually, I've never been in there. Richard keeps it locked.'

'Thrilling,' said Myra. Her long mocking green eyes turned from Richard's stormy face to Celia's flushed one, and she perceived that the girl was under great tension behind that flamboyant mask. She felt for Celia a sudden flicker of feminine alliance. 'How thrilling,' she repeated. 'Bluebeard's closet with a gaggle of slaughtered wives? Or, perchance a den of iniquity, psychedelic curtains, haze of marijuana, erotic statues. We'll suspect the worse, darling. Unlock the ancient schoolroom door!'

Richard reddened. A furious refusal nearly burst out, but he encountered Akananda's gaze. The anxious look of a distressed parent.

Richard controlled himself, and raising his eyebrows said, with a shrug, 'Your lurid hopes will be disappointed, Myra. But, by all means let's inspect the schoolroom. I lock it simply to keep out officious housemaids who disturb everything.'

This was not quite true. Richard locked the door because he had always locked it since he was twelve, and the abandoned schoolroom represented the only privacy from the stepmother, and later from little Tom. It was situated in a remote part of the house next to the servant's quarters. He had gone there seldom since his marriage, and then only when Celia had been shopping in Lewes, or up to London for the day. He had not known that she knew the room existed, and he resented her idiotic wish to expose it to all these people, as much as he resented her extraordinary behaviour since the return from Ightham Mote. Yet, he was aware of her as he had not been in months. Aware that she was alluring, desirable, that deep within him she was arousing a crude lust like the rare and repulsive seizures which had driven him to whore-houses in his university days.

Richard silently led the party upstairs into the south wing. He unlocked a cheap wooden door, dulled by neglected varnish.

'The Chamber of Horrors,' he said, 'and, if you consider it either sinister or festive I shall be most interested.' He switched on the one electric light which was dangling from a massive old gas chandelier.

The room was quite large because the Victorian baronet had produced nine children, and had thrown together two former servants' rooms to use for the primary education of his brood. There was an empty coal grate opposite the door. Battered desks and stools had been piled against a wall. On a plain deal table stood the stereo phonograph, above a rack of records. The speakers had been placed at either end of a long bookshelf.

There were other objects in the room, but only Akananda saw them.

At the shadowy east end of the schoolroom a cupboard door had been removed, thus forming a shallow alcove. Akananda recognised the outline of a prie-dieu, or kneeling chair, and a wooden ledge behind, supporting two candlesticks, and above them on the wall, a crucifix, so black' that it must be ebony, while the Christ figure seemed to be made of tarnished silver.

Akananda knew at once that the crucifix was very old, and knew with equal certainty that Richard did not wish it to be noticed. Nor did anyone else notice the sketchy little chapel.

The disappointed house party grouped around the stereo, except Edna and George who had remained in the drawing room, Edna from annoyance with this impulsive expedition, George from diffidence.

'Good Lord, Richard,' cried Myra, after a rapid survey. 'You win! I never saw a duller place. We can hardly dance *here* Celia, but let's see what the records are.'

She swooped down over the neatly filed rack and drew out one of the square cardboard albums. She read the title aloud, hesitantly, '"Gregorian Chants—Kyrie Altissime, from the Graduale Romanum"—Heavens, what's all *that* about?'

Richard gave a shrug. He answered with elaborate courtesy, 'It is a plain chant as sung by monks throughout Christendom, and for centuries. That one you picked is a ninefold "Kyrie Eleison" which means "Lord have mercy upon us" and is always appropriate, I should think. Would you care to hear it?'

Myra swallowed. 'I—I suppose so,' she said ruefully, 'I brought it on myself, didn't I?' She glanced at the others who had crowded into the schoolroom, at the young Bent-Warners and Sue, who looked blankly polite; at Igor, who was obviously enjoying what he had instantly perceived to be a scene of sorts; at Lily Taylor who was staring in a nervous way at her son-in-law; at Celia who had seated herself in the window, her head turned so that only one crystal earring glittered in the crude electric light, while Harry bent over her, possessively. Myra was aware of that tension which seemed to arise so often during this interminable day.

'Well, put the thing on—do, Richard,' she said impatiently.

He complied with deliberation, placing the record on the spindle, adjusting the speakers and the volume, flicking the control.

The schoolroom was suddenly filled with male voices, mournful and beseeching. 'Kyrie Eleison, Christe Eleison, Kyrie Eleison,' chanted the voices, over and over, insistently minor and dirge-like.

Various shades of boredom gradually glazed all the faces that Akananda could see, but he also saw Celia's back go rigid, and saw that she grabbed the window latch. Then, in Richard's eyes he caught a strange, fleeting look of anguish, and what seemed to be tears. Poor fellow, I believe he's chanted this himself in the past, Akananda thought, 'Lord have Mercy, Christ have Mercy—' He does not quite *know* it, but he feels it, as I do.

When the record ended in a long-drawn-out wail, Myra sat down on the only stool and lit a cigarette. 'A bit monotonous,' she observed, 'definitely damping to the spirits. Surely you don't listen to this kind of stuff shut up here by yourself? You *are* rather peculiar, darling.'

'No doubt,' said Richard. He carefully removed the record and was replacing it in its case when Igor, who had been squinting at the titles in the rack, gave a pleased cry.

'But, here's something different! "Merry Songs of Love-Sport", I think I've heard it!' He scanned the list of songs. 'Oh ... good and bawdy, you're human after all, Richard! Let's hear these!'

'Yes, let's ...' cried Myra, who had been peering over Igor's shoulder at the sixteenth-century titles, ' "A Lusty Young

64

Smith", "A Maiden Did a-Bathing Go", "A Rampant Cock"—
My, my, they sound promising, and here's one about *you*,
Celia! "Celia, The Wanton and Fair". Didn't Richard ever play
you that?'

Celia slowly turned her head, 'No . . .' she whispered, then
cleared her throat to repeat more clearly, 'No, I've never
heard it.'

'And I'm quite sure those songs are not for mixed company,'
struck in Lily, with decision, glancing at Sue. 'We'll go back
downstairs. There's bound to be something on T.V., or some
of us can play bridge.'

Except for Igor who wanted to hear the songs, everyone
looked relieved. They straggled back down to the drawing
room where Edna sat in glassy silence.

Since Celia at once regained her feverish glow, and began to
flirt with Harry, while Richard uncharacteristically ignored
his duties as host, and at once poured himself a stiff brandy,
Lily continued to try to retrieve the evening. An impossible
feat. There was nothing interesting on television; nobody cared
to play bridge.

Suddenly, Celia put her hand on Harry's arm, and suggested
quite audibly that he might like to see the garden by moonlight. He chuckled, and they disappeared together.

'*Well*—of all the brazen . . .' began Edna loudly, looking
towards Richard who was pouring more brandy. Myra joined
him in a highball.

'Are you the jealous type, my sweet?' she asked softly.
'Because if Celia returns the same chaste wife she left, I don't
know Harry, nor does Celia seem to be in the mood to fight
him off. Maybe she's sexually frustrated . . .' added Myra in a
silken voice.

Her boredom with the evening and desire to provoke
Richard had led her farther than she intended. The look on his
face frightened her. It was murderous, dark blood suffused it,
his body trembled. He said nothing at all.

'Good Lord, Richard,' she said apologetically. 'No need to
go all primitive, this is the 1960s, you know, and I was only
kidding, as the Americans say. What *is* the matter with you?
You used to be *fun*!'

He smiled then, a smile more frightening than the anger.

'All women are whores,' he said in the bland tone of one
saying, 'Please pass the salt.'

Myra started. 'Well, thanks, dear—that's one viewpoint, of

course, though a trifle crude and sweeping. You've hardly considered the modern aspect that sex is fun, and . . .'

Richard turned and walked away from her. Myra thought for a shocked moment that he was going to the garden to fetch his wife, to make a scene, but he did not. He sat down on the sofa beside Edna Simpson who bridled with gratification. Behind the spectacles the look she gave Richard was positively doting.

Good God, Myra thought. This whole party's too damn uncomfortable. It was quite unlike any she had ever attended, but her curiosity was sated. I'll remember an important London date tomorrow morning, she thought. Give Gilbert a ring and we'll go out somewhere. Fed up with Harry anyway, and Richard's impossible, maybe slightly mad.

She glided across the room and joined the others to find Sue choking back yawns, Igor leafing through an old copy of *Queen* magazine, and Lily feebly protesting that it wasn't really late to the Bent-Warners, who were worrying about little Robin's cough, and the stupid au pair Danish nursemaid who never remembered the medicine on time.

Just as the party broke up, Celia and Harry returned from the garden. Lily sighed with deep relief though she was even more disquieted about her daughter, whose voice was still high-pitched and who still looked as though she were dressed for a masquerade. Careless, defiant, seductive as she had never been until this evening.

Yet Celia made polite enough farewells to the Bent-Warners, and as her guests all seemed ready for bed, she said good nights with the same casual brightness, nor was there any perceptible difference in her good night to Harry, though Edna thought there was. Edna was sure she saw a signal, a flicker of understanding between the shameless pair. So *that's* it! Edna thought. There wasn't hardly time in the garden, but they'll get together later when it's safe. That poor Sir Richard. A cuckold she's making outo' him and in his own house. Ye'll not get away with that, my girl!

She lumbered upstairs ahead of the rest, and leaving her bedroom door ajar, took two long pulls from the tincture bottle. As the party came up she watched everyone through the crack in the door. The Duchess went to her room, Sir Harry to his, which was next to the Marsdon suite. Sue Blake down the corridor, that nigger doctor, or whatever he was, murmured something to Mrs. Taylor, then they both dis-

66

appeared into their own rooms. George came in, and gaped at her. 'Aren't you going to undress, my dear?'

'In my own good taime,' she said. 'Go to bed, George. In the dressing room. You snore, and I need my sleep.'

He obeyed without further comment. His thoughts were dismal. Something was wrong with Edna. She'd always been short-tempered, dictatorial, but she'd been a good enough wife, barring she'd borne no children. But, that wasn't anybody's fault, the doctors said. And their mutual disappointment made a bond. She had her soft moments, had Edna, or did, until recently. Not exactly soft, but still, reminders of the handsome, blooming Yorkshire lassie he had found working as a waitress in Soho, twenty-five years ago. She had been grateful for his serious interest in her, awed by becoming a solicitor's wife, and so ashamed of her own origin that she would scarcely mention it. Finally said she was an orphan, and that her father had been a plumber in Manchester. She'd been a devout chapel-goer, too, until lately. He liked that trait, even when her horror of drink, card-playing or swearing was a bit restrictive. Women *should* be strict and uphold morality.

Funny thing about Edna and Sir Richard's photograph, George thought, though the incident had never occurred to him before. It was last autumn, and Edna, in from Clapham for her semi-annual forage at the Army and Navy Stores, dropped by his law offices. Sir Charles Marsdon had just died, and George was working on the contents of the long tin box labelled 'Marsdon Estate'. Edna had been rather surprisingly interested. She had pounced on a newspaper clipping about 'the new baronet—Sir Richard'. It was a chatty little article in the *Sussex County Magazine*, and included a snapshot of Medfield Place, with one of Sir Richard. Edna stared a long time at the latter, which was a good likeness.

'I fancy I've seen him somewhere,' she murmured in explanation. 'Good-looking lad, he takes my fancy.'

George had no use for the clipping, and Edna asked for it, perhaps, he had thought, to boast a bit about her husband's grand client at her Women's Institute meetings. It never occurred to them then, that they might be invited socially to Medfield Place. And I wish we hadn't been, George thought. Whatever's in it, there's been too much of that tincture, and she's quite altered. Really shocking, I don't know what to do. He finally went to sleep.

His wife continued to lurk behind the bedroom door in the dark, and presently saw her host and hostess enter their suite in utter silence. Edna nodded, she had expected this. Now to wait until two doors opened stealthily, Celia Marsdon's and Sir Harry's.

She settled her bulk on the desk chair, leaned her head against the door jamb and watched, dozing, then jerking herself awake.

*   *   *

In the Marsdons' bedroom, the atmosphere was thunderous. Richard stood on the edge of the rose Aubusson carpet staring at Celia with a black intensity which almost penetrated the barrier she had built.

'You aren't,' said Richard without expression, 'the woman I thought I'd married, and never should have done.'

Her spasm of sick fear Celia noted objectively, as a physical happening in mid-air, as it were. She took off the earrings, put them in a drawer; she wiped off her lipstick on a Kleenex. 'No doubt you are quite right, Richard. I'm beginning to agree. Divorce may be a trifle difficult in England, but certainly can be managed.'

He stared. Even without those earrings and the lipstick she was a stranger, a hostile stranger, yet her answer astounded him.

'The Marsdons don't get divorces . . .' he said. 'I didn't mean that, I . . .' He heard the wavering in his own voice and was angered afresh. 'Did you enjoy yourself with Harry Jones in the garden?' he asked. 'Did you also enjoy forcing me to open the schoolroom so as to to show your power?'

She did not answer, and he watched her slide out of her flame-coloured dress, then her slip and panties. She stood naked for a moment in front of the mirror, a tanagra statuette, tanned to bronze except for the tiny ivory breasts with rosy nipples, and the triangle around her hips which the bikini had covered. She began brushing her hair with slow voluptuous strokes, arching her slender back. Richard watched the insolent, taunting, naked woman until the throbbing in his head descended to his loins.

'By God,' he cried hoarsely, '*that's* what you want! But you'll not get it here!'

He grabbed her around the wrist, and turning, jerked her across the carpet. Her wrist bones crunched in his grasp.

'What're you doing?' she cried. The fears so long contained burst through in terror. 'Richard, you hurt me! Let me go! What are you doing!' She slapped his face, then let out a strangled scream as he cut his hand across her windpipe with a quick Karate chop. She went limp, and he picked her up. He threw open their door and carried her through the passages, down a short flight into the old schoolroom. He flung her on the stained drugget where she lay gasping and naked, half-stunned by his blow.

Richard went into the alcove and lit two candles. He then removed his clothes and hung them carefully on the prie-dieu; he arranged his shoes at the base. He went to the phonograph and put on the Tudor 'Merry Songs of Love-Sport'. He turned up the volume. Lute, bass viol and recorder resounded through the schoolroom in a sly, rollicking tune. Celia moaned and put a groping finger on her larynx where he had hit her.

'Hurts ...' she whispered. 'You hate me, Richard!' She stared up at him in the wavering candle-light. 'You're naked —what are we doing here...?'

He clapped his hand roughly over her mouth. 'Listen ...!' Above the instruments a raucous tenor voice was singing.

> Celia the wanton and fair
> Hath now no need to despair
> She hath used shameless art
> To inveigle lust's dart
> And she shall suffer it now
> And she shall suffer it now.

'No!' she cried against his hand, 'not like this, not in hate, please, not like this ...'

But he pinned her down and raped her savagely, while she whimpered and struggled.

Neither of them heard the door open, nor heard Edna's cry, 'God Almighty!' Nor knew that the polka-dotted bulk stood over them, until the song ended, and there was a pause, then Edna's voice rose shrill and shaking. 'So, I've caught you out, you filthy little whore, in the act, the very act! Hanging's too good for you.'

Richard raised his head and turned to look up at her.

'God Almighty ...' gasped Edna again, 'I didn't know it was you, Sir Richard.' She stumbled backwards, muttering and heaving. She backed out of the door, and shut it behind her with a resounding thud.

Celia heard the thud. She lay tight and still on the drugget, waiting for the next thud—the slap of a trowel against mortar. And outside the thuds, in the shadowy candle-lit Hall, that gloating woman's face was watching.

Richard turned off the phonograph, switched on the electric light, put on his trousers and shoes. He blew out the altar candles. He looked down at Celia. 'I'm sorry, my dear,' he whispered. 'Terribly sorry. It was disgusting, all of it. My behaviour and that unspeakable woman's . . .'

Celia did not move. Her transfixed eyes were strained towards the wall on her left. They showed white around the irises as they stared, unblinking. 'How long will it be, Stephen?' she said in a faint, reasonable voice. 'How long must it take one to die?'

'You won't die,' he said sharply. 'I'm sorry I behaved like such a bastard. Here—' He bundled her inert body into his shirt.

'You are going to let me die,' she said. She did not speak again.

Her face grew pinched and bluish around the great staring eyes.

Beneath Richard's guilt and grinding resentment that she had, in a way, precipitated the whole degrading scene and his own loss of control, there was horror. Why did she call me *Stephen?*

He picked her up and carried her back through the passages to their bedroom. She was scarcely breathing as he laid her on the bed. Suddenly, she reached her arms straight up above her head, her fingers curled as though grasping at a ledge. Her face flushed purple, she began to gasp.

'It's all right, now,' he whispered, trying to take her rigid, claw-like hand. 'A beastly happening, but you must forget it. Celia—put your arms down!'

She made no response. There was only the gasping noise, and a bubbling sound from her throat.

'Oh, my God . . .' he cried, and rushed out of the room.

Three

Sunday morning the weather still held fair. Mellow sunlight illumined the garden room as members of the house party straggled in for breakfast. Sue came first, then Sir Harry, Igor, George Simpson and finally Myra who had enjoyed a refreshing sleep and looked vibrant in green jersey lounging pyjamas. Nobody spoke much until the impassive Dodge poured out coffee, and the guests helped themselves from the hot table.

'No host or hostess?' Myra enquired, nibbling a piece of dry toast, 'nor Mrs. Taylor? Harry, you look definitely warmed-over, my pet. Night on the tiles too taxing?'

Harry swallowed a mouthful of kipper and gave her a resentful glance. When he had discovered last night in the garden that there was definitely nothing doing with Celia, his hopes had reverted to Myra. After midnight he had tried her door. There had been only a muffled derisive laugh in answer to his discreet knocks. I'm sick of women, Harry thought. Wasting what's left of my life on them. God, I wish I was back in that other June, twenty-eight years ago. Fighting, struggling, retreating, but too busy surviving to get the wind up. Leading my men down that sand-dune, the one place we could have got through, and that moment when I shot the Jerry when he thought he had *us*. God, I wish it was now, or even later, the blitz, the doodle-bugs—but an enemy you could fight. Purpose—and youth.

Harry got up from the table 'Need some exercise,' he announced 'Think I'll ramble over the Downs. Examine that white horse someone's cut in the hill. Tell the Marsdons when you see them.'

The others finished breakfast and drifted towards the pool where they riffled the Sunday papers, and were silent. Even Myra's energy and Sue's exuberance faded into the general vacuity.

Igor made the only remark as he idly shied a pebble at a clump of iris. 'Is there something absolutely dire in the atmosphere, I wonder, or am I just hyper-sensitive? I mean, it's past eleven, and one might reasonably expect . . .' He broke off; they all stared at each other as they heard an ambulance klaxon blaring from the quiet Sussex lane outside the garden's brick wall.

At the same time, Lily Taylor came rushing from the house towards them. She was still in a blue dressing-gown, her blonde hair bristled with rollers, her glistening face drooped woefully, but she had managed to remember Medfield's guests.

'It's Celia,' she cried, '—dreadfully sick, going to the hospital, and Richard . . .' She choked and bit her lips.

There was a startled pause. Then Myra clasped the older woman's arm. 'I'm so *sorry*, Mrs. Taylor. What can we do—except keep out of the way and go home? How dreadful for you. Could I help with my car?'

She was too well-bred to press for details, but Sue burst out in dismay, 'Oh, Cousin Lily, she's not goin' to lose the baby, is she?'

'Baby?' Lily shook her head distractedly. 'I've got to go now, I just wanted you to know. Dodge will serve lunch, I suppose . . .'

Lily sped back into the house.

'Poor woman,' said Myra, 'and poor Celia. Obviously, we'd better clear out. I'll give you a lift back to town, Igor—and Harry, too, if he turns up. I don't feel responsible for the Simpsons—that ghastly creature, but I do wonder where Richard is. I should think not the sort of man to go to pieces in an emergency, but then, *he's* been acting very odd. Oh well . . .' She shrugged her delicate shoulders and went off to summon a maid.

* * *

Upstairs in the Marsdon bedroom, Akananda was consulting with old Dr. Foster from Lewes, who had arrived an hour ago. The doctor looked and acted like an irritable country squire, beet-faced, clipped grey moustache. He stood frowning down at Celia, and spoke to the Hindu with impatient condescension.

'Appalling sight, she is,' he barked. 'Certainly in shock. Some kind of hysterical seizure, I suppose, but bound to admit I've never seen the like. What's the matter with those arms! And the *eyes*!'

He whipped off the handkerchief with which Akananda had covered Celia's pale, clammy face before her mother saw it. The distended eyes showed white as a terrified mare's, and were transfixed to the left. Foster flicked an eyeball with a corner of the handkerchief, but there was no reaction. Her arms were still raised rigid above her head, the stiffened fingers curled in a clutching position. Both doctors had tried to lower the arms, but they were unyielding as iron.

'Girl's not quite dead, yet,' went on Foster. 'I think I get a pulse around thirty, don't you? And she *is* breathing, after a fashion.'

Akananda nodded. 'I believe she may live,' he said, 'though the adrenalin you injected shows no results. We'll use further procedures in hospital, of course. Possibly strychnine, cortisone? And the E.C.G. will give us heart action.'

'My damn machine's busted again,' Foster said. 'New-fangled gadget anyway!'

He shot an annoyed and puzzled glance at Akananda. The fellow spoke with authority, the sobbing mother who had telephoned said the Hindu was a physician, but there was something fishy. Young woman who looked as though she was dying of fright. And where was the husband?

'Where is Sir Richard:' he asked. 'He ought to be here.'

'He is absent. Nor is his presence needed. Shall we take her at once?'

Foster found himself calling the ambulance attendants. The men lifted Celia on to the stretcher.

'Mind the arms,' said Foster. 'They won't bend, we'll have to be careful in the passages.'

Lily had stayed in her room as Akananda had requested. She was dressed and waiting when he put his head in while the procession passed.

'Come along,' he said gently. 'We're off to hospital in Eastbourne.'

'But where's Richard?' she wailed. 'Where did he *go* after he finally roused you?'

'I don't know,' said Akananda. 'He rushed downstairs, and perhaps out of the house . . . We'll look for him later. *Pray*— Mrs. Taylor, for your daughter and for Sir Richard.'

'Not for *him*,' she said through tight lips. 'He's run away. It's inhuman.' She joined the stretcher and its bearers in the hall.

All *too* human, Akananda thought. That glimpse he had had of Richard as he cried hoarsely, 'Celia . . . go to Celia, I'm frightened.' If there were ever guilt and horror on a face, in a voice . . . And surely nothing which could possibly have happened in a couple of hours last night would have brought on these disasters. His psychiatric service at the Maudesley had accustomed him to the fetid aura of madness and impending suicide, but he had never before been personally involved with the patients, nor felt as helpless.

The sun was rising when Sir Richard had summoned him, then disappeared. During the delay in locating Dr. Foster, who was off on another emergency call, Akananda never left Celia's bedside, but he had no medications with him, and could do nothing but elevate the feet, pile blankets on her, and try to sustain the unconscious girl by the force of his will. The servants were unaware until the ambulance came, and then Dodge kept them under strict discipline, milling and whispering in their hall. However, there was one whom he could not control, and when Lily set foot on the ambulance step, Nanny flew out of the manor.

'Madam,' she cried shrilly, 'what ails her ladyship?' She pushed past Lily and blinked down at the inert body on the stretcher. 'The lass isna *deid*?' she faltered.

'No, no,' said Dr. Foster, who had known the little Scottish nurse for years. 'Go back, Mrs. Cameron. See if you can find Sir Richard.'

'The maister . . . The young maister—what's he done?' Her voice trembled, the bright robin-eyes filmed with anxiety.

'He hasn't done anything that I know of,' said Foster impatiently. 'He simply isn't here. Carry on,' he said to the driver who threw in his clutch and set off the klaxon's raucous hooting.

Nanny Cameron watched the ambulance career down the drive and turn towards Eastbourne. 'Oh, dear-r, dear-r, dear-r,' she whispered, her little mouth working. She straightened her shoulders and drew a difficult breath. As she re-entered the house the Duchess was descending the stairs.

Myra was already dressed in a smart town frock, and carried her alligator handbag. She recognised Nanny at once as an upper servant, though hitherto unseen, and said with kindly authority, 'Is there anyone to bring my car around, and fetch the luggage? The staff seem disorganised. I'm so sorry her ladyship is ill, and we'll all leave at once. But would you know where Sir Richard is?'

'I wouldna, Your Grace.' Nanny had heard descriptions of the Duchess in the servants' hall, and been secretly pleased that Medfield Place housed a high-born aristocrat as it often used to in the past, before the first Lady Marsdon died.

'I'll be sairching for the maister.' She added with pleading,

'He canna be far, and he'd tak' shame if ye left wi'out a fare-weel. The gardener's lad'll look to the car and the luggage, Your Grace, but will ye no bide a wee while?'

Myra considered, then reluctantly acquiesced. She longed to be out of the confused, subtly menacing atmosphere, but she was bred to a sense of obligation. In the absence of host, hostess and Mrs. Taylor, it seemed necessary for someone to take over, at least temporarily.

'I'll wait here,' she said, indicating the drawing room.

Nanny sketched a curtsy and hurried away. The other guests gradually joined Myra, even Sir Harry, who came back from his walk and was thoroughly startled by the news.

'Extraordinary . . . extraordinary,' he kept saying. 'Celia wasn't ill last night. *Ambulance*, you say? What could have happened to her?'

Nobody knew, and Harry was aware of a surprising pang. Pity, almost tenderness. Celia'd behaved like a little strumpet last night, he thought, wondering why he used such an old-fashioned word. 'Prick-teaser' was more accurate—letting him fondle and kiss her in the garden, then pulling back and slapping his face like a barmaid. He had been very angry, but now he wasn't. He felt a pang of protective tenderness, and cer-tainty that whatever her sudden illness was, Richard Marsdon was making the girl miserable. Damn his eyes, Harry thought. I wish I'd never come down for this bloody weekend.

Though all the guests shared Harry's view in varying degrees, George Simpson's regret was the most fervent, while he struggled to rouse his wife to a semblance of normalcy. Edna had finally been wakened from stertorous, twitching sleep by the ambulance siren. Her head pounded and when she tried to raise it, she retched.

'Where's me tonic?' she asked George thickly, when she saw him standing by the bed.

'It's all gone.' He looked at the empty quart bottle in the trash basket. 'Get up, Edna, get dressed. Lady Marsdon's very ill, been taken to hospital.'

Between puffy lids her eyes focused slowly. 'Lady Marsdon . . .? Very ill . . .?'

He nodded, and drew back as she smiled. There was mali-cious triumph in the up-curved lips, the puffy eyes. She mumbled something like, 'Hope she dies.'

George grabbed her thick shoulders, and yanked her up-right.

'Before God, I don't know *how*, but I think you're drunk! Here, get to the bathroom, I'll douse you in cold water!'

She shook off his hands and became the picture of offended dignity.

'How dare you, George! You know very well I've never touched a drop in me life. It's joost a headache. It hurts something cruel.' She sagged back on to the pillow. Her mouth fell open, a trickle of saliva dribbled from the corner.

George gazed down at the bed. What'll I do with her? Can't let anyone see her like this. The servants'll talk. And Sir Richard, what would *he* think . . . respectable firm . . . I *can't've* seen that gloating look she had on her face. He shuddered and sank down on the desk chair, his head in his hands.

*   *   *

Nanny Cameron was searching for her young master. She went first to the library and the alcove with a lectern where the Marsdon Chronicle was kept. The library was empty, and the great vellum book rested in its accustomed place on the top shelf. Nanny took it down and ran a tentative finger over the gold embossed cockatrice on the front cover.

'Beware,' she said aloud, knowing well the motto. 'I doot he's listened sharp enough to the war-rning.' She shook her head, then she had a flash of 'the sight' which was as much a part of her Highland heritage as rugged common sense. Guided by the flash she lugged the heavy book over to the lectern, opened it at random. She squinted at a page near the beginning. It was covered with faded close-set lines, long curly strokes and tiny ripples above what must be letters. She could decipher but a few words.

'All Hallowes Eve . . . unshriven deeds bringe sorrowe to our house . . . terrible lust . . . I command my heires . . . fear of damnation . . . murdered girle . . . Medfeilde . . .'

There was a faint pencil line down the margin beside the entry.

' 'Tis this he reads and moithers over when the mood's on him,' she murmured. 'Evil fra' the lang, lang ago, yet her're again amangst us. The Good Lord ha' mercy.'

She sighed dolefully, shut the Marsdon Chronicle; replaced it on the shelf. She hurried from the library, and started on a systematic search through the great mansion. She had reached the foot of the attic stairs in the west wing when she thought of the 'music room'. Aye, to be *sure*. Along dark passages, up and down steps, she trudged to the old schoolroom.

'Sir Richard . . .' she called softly. 'Maister-r Richard.' There was no sound inside. Nanny tried the door. It was locked. She rapped and called again. 'Maister-r . . . 'tis only Nanny. Open up!'

Her ears were sharp and they caught a faint rustling noise. Her heart thumped heavily in her chest. Twenty years ago she had stood like this rapping at this very door. The bad time when the lad was twelve; the weary care, the trouble and the horrifying memories. She rapped again, harder.

'Open up! Sir Richard!' she cried in the nursery tone of command. ' 'Tis Nanny!'

Still there was no answer, and no more sound. 'I'll get them to break the door-r in!' Her voice shrilled with fear.

After a moment she heard a hoarse response. 'Leave me alone. Leave me *alone*!'

She slumped against the door, steadying herself on the knob.

'Maister, her ladyship is ta'en verra bad, gone to hospital. Your guests await ye. Come doon to them!'

There was another long silence before she heard a thickened shout. 'For Christ's sake, let me *be*!'

Though she stayed a few minutes, pleading and exhorting, there was no further sound from inside the schoolroom.

Nanny plodded back along the passages. She descended the stairs and went to the drawing room. Everyone looked up expectantly.

'Any luck?' asked Myra. 'Have you found Sir Richard?'

'Aye, Your Grace, may I speak private wi' ye?'

Myra rose and followed Nanny into Richard's study. 'Well, where is he?' she asked. 'Will he be here soon?'

Nanny shook her head. 'He's locked himsel' i' the old schoolroom. He willna come oot. Doom hae laid its dreedful hands on the Marsdons.'

'Oh, come, Mrs.— What's your name, by the way?'

'Jeannie Cameron, Your Grace, but ever-r called Nanny. I was nurse to Sir Richard since he was a baby.'

Myra nodded. Her own nanny had been much like this. Sensible, fiercely loyal, but superstitious.

'Well, Nanny,' Myra resumed, smiling, 'I'm sure there's no need to fear doom just because her ladyship is ill, and Sir Richard wishes solitude. We'll leave for London, and you must give our sympathy and farewells to Sir Richard when he appears. That's all.'

Nanny's black eyes looked sadly up at the beautiful, impatient face. 'He will *not* appear-r, Your Grace.'

It was a flat statement, and unpleasantly convincing.

Myra exhaled, sat down on the cushioned Tudor armchair opposite Richard's tidy desk, lit a cigarette, and said, 'Just what do you mean by that? I don't understand.'

'No,' said Nanny. Her rosy cheeks puckered like a withering apple. 'Ye dinna understand.'

Oh, Lord, *must* I? Myra thought. All very sad that Celia was ill, and Richard apparently going round the bend—locking himself in that dreary schoolroom and sulking—distressing behaviour but nothing to do with *me*. She glanced through the open casement window at her Bentley which was now waiting, ready-loaded by the front steps. Will take about two hours to get back in town, then give Gilbert a ring, arrange tonight, something exciting, forget this mess . . .

'Your Grace,' said Nanny quietly, 'I'm sore afeared, and there's nobody else her're I weesh to tell why to.'

The quiet tone, the anxious, honest old face were moving.

Myra sighed and settled back in her chair. 'Sit down then, and tell me.'

It took some time for Myra to comprehend what Nanny was trying to say, not that the old woman rambled, but she was earnest and slow as she tried to give the whole picture of Richard's boyhood. It began with the death of his mother when he was two years old and should have been too small to miss her, and yet it seemed as though he did.

The other servants told Nanny that the baby had used many words, even short sentences before his mother died, but when Nanny came he didn't talk at all, nor for months afterwards. He didn't cry either, he didn't smile, he drank his milk and ate his porridge mechanically like those 'wee dollies that jair-rk when ye tug on a string'. The other servants thought him silly-witted; Sir Charles, his father, who looked into the nursery once a day, 'verra grim, he was, the auld maister', said the boy must be subnormal and taken to a London doctor, which intent Nanny had always fiercely resisted. She loved her charge, and never doubted that he would come right in time.

'An' he did, Your Grace The whilst he was three ye never saw a brighter bairn for-r his years. Kenned a' his letters, and

78

made up tables to tell himsel', he'd lairned to smile too, though never-r romping and feckless like most bairns.'

Myra glanced at her wristwatch. This standard tale of a lonely motherless child, a cold withdrawn father, seemed hardly pertinent. Though, no doubt, a psychoanalyst could make much of it. But Nanny continued tenaciously. Myra half-listening received the impression of a little boy who both talked and walked in his sleep, who seemed convinced that he had lived another life before this one, who sometimes insisted that his name was 'Stephen', and that Stephen had been very wicked in the past. He had always seemed both ashamed and afraid of 'Stephen'. And only Nanny knew about this phase. Anyway, the nightmares and the fancies had stopped after she had sent to her shepherd brother in Argyllshire and got Richard a collie pup.

' 'Twas the making o' Maister Dick, that dog, Your Grace.'

'It was?' said Myra, suddenly realising that dogs were un-accountably lacking in this English country house.

'Aye,' Nanny read her thought. 'There's nae dog here today. When Jock was shot, Maister Dick could never-r bear another-r near him. He's like that. And he never mentioned Jock again, for he loved that dog wi' all his hear-rt, an' he felt that what-ever he loved came to a bad end.'

'The dog was shot?' said Myra with some horror. 'What-ever for?'

'Sir Charles thought it had r-rabies.' Nanny twisted her plump hands on her grey poplin lap. 'He didna wait to mak' sure, nor told the lad why, at the time.'

Myra swallowed. 'Well, I suppose one can't take chances with rabies, but I can see how dreadful it was for Richard. How old was he?'

'Twelve, your grace, the year-r everything happened to him.'

'What else?'

'Sir Charles wed that brassy slut, and that woman tur-rned the old man altogether agin his fairst-born. He'd no been a tender-r faither before, though Maister Dick kept trying to please him, and times they'd fish together, ramble o'er the Doons. After *she* got hold o' him, Sir Charles was brutal. He couldna bear the sight o' Maister Dick, he'd sneer at him an' call him crazy.'

'But surely Richard went to school? He must have got away from all this during term.'

Nanny shook her head. 'Sir Charles didna bother-r wi' schooling. Until afterwards . . . The vicar at St. Andrew's tutored the lad.'

Myra frowned. She clearly saw the pattern, a pathetically neglected childhood, the incomprehensible deaths of a mother and a dog, and the effects on a sensitive little boy. She even realised that Celia's sudden illness might present so great a threat that Richard was driven to escape. But then, Richard must be really mental, which she found hard to believe.

'And after all,' she said aloud, 'Richard's not to blame for the blows he's had.'

Nanny stood up, she looked squarely at Myra. 'That's the whole matter of it, Your Grace. He thinks he *is*. And so do I. 'Tis fra the past. When he lived before at Medfield. When he was Stephen. 'Tis i' the Marsdon Chronicle.'

'*Really*, Mrs. Cameron,' said Myra, so astounded that she laughed. 'Has Mrs. Taylor or Doctor Akananda been corrupting you? You're too sensible to believe in reincarnation!'

Nanny stiffened and spoke with dignity. 'I dinna ken the lang wor-rd. I've spoke to nobody o' this, nor would now, save that Sir Richard is acting as he did near twenty year-rs agone.' Her voice dropped, she added in a whisper, 'I fear for him so, come nightfall, that's when it happened afore.'

'What did?' Myra forced herself to ask.

The old woman raised her head and gazed unseeing at the farm ledgers stacked on the study shelves. 'We broke in just in time . . .' she said dully. 'He was hanging ther-re fra the auld gas fixture.'

Myra's green eyes widened; she blinked. She tamped out her cigarette. There was silence during which she dimly heard the ticking of the hall clock, the cooing of doves from the Medfield dove-cote.

'How frightful . . .' she said. 'But Nanny, that was long ago. Sir Richard isn't a miserable child any more, why, he's the baronet, he's married, and though his wife may be ill, that can't be too serious, there's no parallel at all. I'm afraid you've gone nervy, but you really mustn't imagine . . .'

She stopped as Nanny sighed and let her hands fall open in a despairing little gesture. ' 'Twas the curtain cords afore, Your Grace, they be still ther-re.' Again a flat convincing statement.

Myra shivered, then spoke sharply, 'Well, what do you want *me* to do? If you're so worried get Dodge and the gardener to break in the door.'

'I wouldna want them to guess—the sairvants—canna ye see that?'

Most reluctantly, Myra did see that. She did not believe that the situation was nearly as dramatic as the old nurse thought. Moreover, she had the inborn British distaste for emotionalism, and for interference in anyone's private life. Nevertheless . . .

'You want me to speak to Sir Richard,' she said. 'To see what's up?'

Nanny surprised her. 'No, Your Grace, 'twould do n'good. I want ye to telephone the hospital and summon the Heendu gentleman, he's the pairson to help us. They'd no listen to *me*.'

Myra saw the truth of this. A duchess might cut through the barrage of hospital red tape, as Nanny certainly could not—yet the urgency, the explanations—how embarrassing if Nanny's fears were imaginary, yet the steady piteous gaze touched her.

'Very well,' she said, reaching for the telephone on Richard's desk. 'Where's the number?'

*   *   *

In Celia's hospital room a hushed and anxious group stood around the flat white bed where the unconscious girl lay in her motionless trance. The blood pressure cuff was on her arm, while both doctors, Foster and Akananda, watched for the appearance of the throbbing mercury on the gauge, but it showed only a feeble flicker at the bottom, while Foster, frowning heavily, pressed his stethoscope harder against the ribs below the small left breast.

'I fear she's going . . .' he said to Akananda, removing the ear tubes. 'You try again.'

Lily, at the foot of the bed, gave a sobbing gasp.

The matron and another nurse glanced at each other, then up at a glass jar of glucose which dripped into Celia's left arm vein. There had been hope a few minutes earlier in the operating theatre. Lady Marsdon had responded to the inhalation of oxygen, accompanied by slow, monotonous commands from the foreign doctor.

'Relax, Celia. Relax. Let your arms go. Let them go limp. Shut your eyes. Relax. Go limp.'

After five minutes the patient had suddenly obeyed. She shivered once, then the clutching rigid hands had fallen forward, the eyelids shut. They had been able to lower the now flaccid arms, and both nurses, hardened as they were to unpleasant sights, had been greatly relieved at the disappear-ance of that ghastly pop-eyed stare. But, they shared Doctor Foster's conviction that the patient was dying. The mercury now stopped quivering at all on the blood-pressure gauge; it was evident that neither doctor was sure of any heart beat.

'Get the mother out of here,' Dr. Foster barked, and to Akan-anda he added, 'Cardiac arrest—we might massage. Damn it, there's not a decent heart man short of London, and I've never tried it.'

Matron, silent except for a rustle of starched apron, gently shoved Lily through the door and shut it.

Akananda shook his head. 'Heart massage breaks ribs,' he said. 'Great danger of puncture, and it won't help. She will not die, at least, now. She'll remain like this.'

'You blasted fool,' cried Foster. 'What the hell do you know about it!'

'I have,' said Akananda quietly, 'seen several cases of sus-pended animation in India, some Yogis can do it at will. In old-fashioned western medical terms, this is a form of cata-lepsy.'

'Indeed,' Foster's irritation subsided. 'Sorry, I blew up, but I'm only an overworked G.P. and I've never seen anything like this. If she does recover, how about brain damage? And what the devil do we do with the young woman in the meantime?'

'I don't know the prognosis,' said Akananda sighing. 'We must get a psycho-neurologist down. I recommend Sir Arthur Moore, who should be summoned at once. As to Lady Marsdon, we can only keep her warm, and perhaps try cortisone. Sir Arthur may have other ideas.'

'Yes.' Foster was relieved. Fellow seemed sound enough. Anyway, nothing more to be done at the moment, except get on to Sir Arthur, and get himself back to surgery where he was long overdue.

When Foster and the matron had left, Akananda put his thin bronze hand gently on Celia's forehead which was cold and moist. The remaining nurse stared suspiciously.

Akananda shut his eyes and concentrated on receiving some impression from Celia's brain. At first he felt nothing but a dense, velvety blackness.

'Celia Marsdon,' said Akananda silently, 'where are you now?'

He waited, while enfolding himself with her in the dead blackness, until he suddenly felt a tingle in his hand. The tingle ran up his arm, and a scene, tiny and sharp as a stage setting viewed through the wrong end of binoculars, slid into his mind. He saw a hill-top, crowned by greenery, chestnuts, oak; he saw the distinctive shape of their leaves, and beneath them, the glossy dark green of holly. There was a grey, mossy stone wall encircling the trees, and the ruins of a chapel against the wall. He knew it was a chapel because of the lancet window-frames and the rugged stone cross over the portal. A thatched wooden hut was attached to the chapel's south wall, its door hung slack on leather hinges. Two figures stood just outside on the trampled grass. One was a monk in black robes; there was a knotted scourge around his waist, and his head was bent to show a round shaven tonsure of short dark hair around the circular patch. The monk's arms were around a girl in a blue skirt and laced bodice. The girl's curling, tumbling yellow hair fell to her hips, except where some strands shone golden over the monk's black cloth sleeves. The two were frozen still as a coloured photograph; unlike a photograph the little scene vibrated with emotion—a frenzied longing and desperation. Then the scene disappeared.

'Doctor!' repeated the young nurse, as she had already done twice.

The Hindu opened his eyes to see a pert, disapproving face under a starched white coif. 'Yes, what is it, Sister?' he said.

'There's a phone call from Medfield, the Duchess of Drewton wants to speak to you.'

Akananda nodded, slowly composing himself. 'Very well, where's the telephone—at the desk? Don't touch or disturb her, will you?' He indicated Celia.

The nurse gave him a scornful look. 'No fear,' she said. 'Touching *her*'ll be the undertaker's job next.'

Akananda spoke on the telephone with Myra, then found Lily Taylor waiting miserably in the hall.

'I'm going back to Medfield for a bit,' he said. 'Poor lady,' he exclaimed as he saw her face. 'Come back with me and take some rest. There's nothing to do for your daughter at present.' He hesitated, but knowing that of all the people involved in the crisis, Lily alone would partially understand, he added, 'I think that Lady Marsdon, due to some great shock, has been jerked back into the past, *her* past life, and Sir Richard's, and for that matter, yours and mine. It was *then* that the violent emotions and actions were initiated, those which are inexorably showing their results today.'

83

Lily clutched his arm. 'But how can we *stop* it? Celia's dying. Oh, God, I don't understand . . .' She covered her face with her hands.

'We must stop it, or at least, with divine mercy we may stop it.' He spoke with more assurance than he felt. For now, according to the Duchess's phone call, Sir Richard, too . . . He put his arm around Lily, and hurried her to the car.

The Duchess awaited them on Medfield's doorstep; Nanny Cameron just behind her.

'I'm so relieved to see you, Doctor Akananda,' Myra spoke fervently. During the last half-hour she had come to share the old Scotswoman's anxiety, and also her odd faith in the Hindu. 'Richard's still locked in. I went to the schoolroom door myself. There's no sound. Do hurry!'

Akananda inclined his head. 'But I must be alone. Will you all please wait downstairs.' He indicated the drawing room where there was a murmur of subdued voices. Myra put her arm around Lily who was swaying. Akananda mounted the great staircase to his bedroom, while Nanny respectfully and stubbornly followed him three steps behind. She waited by the closed door while the Hindu, inside, purified his mind for the struggle. He chanted very low, words from the Athrava-Veda.

'As day and night are not afraid, nor ever suffer loss or harm, even so my spirit, fear not thou . . . As what hath been and what shall be fear not, nor suffer loss or harm, even so, my spirit, fear not thou.'

Akananda waited until the quiet English bedroom dissolved around him into golden-white light—the illumination of compassionate wisdom—as he raised his arms with touching palms in the universal gesture of prayer. He arose and opened his bedroom door. He nodded without surprise at Nanny's eager expectant face.

'We will go to the schoolroom,' he said.

The schoolroom door was wide open when they arrived, and Richard was sitting at one of the old desks writing. Nanny gasped and ran to him.

'Oh, Maister-r Dick! Thank God. Ye frighted me.'

Richard looked at her sombrely and shrugged. 'I'm not twelve years old *now*, Nanny, and am better equipped to face unpleasant events. You have come from the hospital?' He addressed Akananda. 'How is Celia?' His tone was coldly detached. 'I presume she's in hospital since I heard an ambulance.'

84

'She is very ill, indeed, Sir Richard—unconscious. You must go to her.'

'Has she asked for me, or indeed, perhaps for *Harry Jones*?' Akananda was as shocked as the old nurse was by the tone and implication.

'Good Lor-rd, lad,' Nanny cried, grasping Richard's arm. 'She's no conscious, she's near deid, ye *mun* see her, 'tis your wife!'

Richard stood up and drew back. 'I've done Celia quite enough harm already. It's better that we never meet again. Her mother will look after her, and will, of course, procure the best medical attention.'

There was silence. Akananda noted that the crucifix and the candles had disappeared from the little alcove, even while he sought for the guidance and wisdom he had felt a few minutes earlier—wisdom to combat the inflexibilities, distortions and cruelties of the human will.

'What do you propose to do, Sir Richard?' he asked quietly.

'Rid my house of people, everyone connected with these past months of my mistaken marriage. I wish to live henceforth quite alone, as long as I *choose* to live.'

'Ye've gone daft,' Nanny whispered, tears spilling down her cheeks. 'M' puir bairn, ye've gone daft. 'Tis the cairse fra the Chronicle ye read sae often i' the library, the auld fearfu' deeds 're come back on ye.'

'Bah!' Richard exploded. 'Morbid clap-trap! I shall never think of the past again. The book is closed.'

'That, Sir Richard,' said Akananda sternly, 'in your case is impossible. Circumstances have reproduced themselves in this life so that you may have a chance to redeem the mistakes of your past one. You and Lady Marsdon both. At present you are compounding the evil.'

Richard raised his chin. 'I don't in the least understand you, Dr. Akananda, nor wish to listen to you further. Nanny, will you direct the servants to make up the red bedroom in the east wing. I'll move there until all of Lady Marsdon's effects have been cleared out and I am alone at Medfield Place.' He walked from the schoolroom and down the passage towards the east wing.

The two disparate beings, a Hindu doctor and a Scottish nanny, looked at each other, helpless and dismayed.

'He's no *truly* heartless and cruel, sir,' she said. 'I've ne'er seen him lak this.' She fished a handkerchief from her pocket

85

and mopped her eyes. 'Ye hear-rd him, "*as lang as I choose to live*"—Oh, Doctor-r.'

'I know,' he answered. 'Will you show me the book you spoke of, the Chronicle?'

'Aye,' she said, and led the way down the back stairs to the library.

Akananda carried the heavy volume to the lectern under the stained-glass window. He studied the entry Nanny pointed out. He traced the Elizabethan writing carefully with his brown index finger, while certainty grew within him. Here was the key, which he was not yet quite able to turn, though while he held himself receptive he caught glimpses of past realities which he had hitherto felt only in flashes of intuition, precognition and hurried waves from Celia's psyche.

'Ightham Mote.' He nodded, then looked sharply again at the reference to its Tudor owners; 'Sir Chris; Allen & his vexatious ladye . . . she hath a mad wolfish eye'—as he stared at this there came to him the image of Edna Simpson, the polka-dotted bulk, as she had sat at dinner last night glaring at Celia—later doting on Sir Richard. That identification seemed probable; somehow the woman had last night echoed her old crime. But how? He shook his head. Gropings and perplexities. Tragedy enough right now, and more to come, unless . . .

He was aware of the anxious bird-eyes watching him. 'Yes,' he sighed, 'here are many clues, if we could relive the whole, see clear, what happened . . .'

'Could ye do that?' asked Nanny eagerly. 'Mak' them see the past?'

Akananda shook his head. 'I don't know. I've no miraculous powers. Yet, there are drugs and, perhaps, hypnosis . . . not Sir Richard, he's closed himself in, but possibly—Lady Marsdon.'

'There was an auld wise woman, lived across the bur-rn from our cot when I was a lass, she could do it, mak' ye see the past i' the smoke o' the tur-rf fire. She stopped Jemmie McCleod from murthering his brother that way, when she showed him he'd done it afore, back i' the time o' the Bruce, an' ended up kicking on the gallows.'

He gave Nanny an appreciative look. The Gaelic blood accepted these things as naturally as did the Indian, and it was the crass blind materialism of the western world in general which it was his hope to penetrate.

'Anither thing Meg did,' Nanny went on breathlessly, 'though the meenister and Mother-r 'd ne'er believe. Ma wee sister Annie was bor-rn blind, 'twas dreedfu' sad to see her gropin' and stumblin', and so bonny in other ways. The meenister said 'twas the will o' God, which I thought verra unjust. But one nicht, Meg, she showed me i' the turf smoke, Annie had been a verra cruel woman once and burr-rned out a man's een wi' a red-hot poker. So now *she* suffered the blindness.'

Akananda gave Nanny a brief smile. 'Yes, sometimes the punishment exactly fits the crime, but mostly we are not able to see such conclusive results. We're dealing with great mysteries, you know.'

'Aye,' said Nanny, 'we are her're in con-fusion, and I'm sore afear-rd.'

'Try not to worry,' he said. 'You had better follow Sir Richard's orders, since there is no reaching through to him now.'

They left the library and Akananda went to the drawing room.

'Sir Richard is quite all right,' he said to the circle of raised faces, 'but he does wish to be alone.'

Igor and Sir Harry murmured conventional banalities— they had become very bored by the wait. Myra jumped up, conscious of anticlimax.

'Well, so much the better. Let's get going,' she said to the two men. 'Goodbye, Mrs. Taylor, I do hope Celia is soon re-covered.' She shook Lily's limp hand. 'Goodbye, little Sue,' she said to the girl who looked disappointed. The house party was ending in such a flat, sad way, and nobody would tell her anything. 'Give me a ring in town before you fly home,' added Myra kindly. 'I'll introduce you to some presentable young men.'

The Duchess, Harry and Igor hurried away. The remaining three in the drawing room heard the departing purr of the Bentley, the diminishing crunch of gravel on the drive.

'I must hurry back to Celia,' Lily murmured, taking a sip of cold coffee, then pushing the cup away. 'Richard will come with me, of course.'

Akananda sat down on an urn-backed Sheraton chair and folded his hands. 'Mrs. Taylor, I must talk to you.'

The weight in Lily's chest grew heavier, but she understood him. She turned to the girl. 'Sue, dear, will you take a message to the vicar, tell him your Cousin Celia's fallen sick and won't be at the Flower Guild meeting tomorrow. They may, however, count on the usual hampers of roses for St. John's Day.'

Sue nodded slowly. 'O.K., Cousin Lily, be glad to.' She trailed disconsolately out of the drawing room.

Lily's anxious blue gaze returned to the Hindu. 'What *is* it with Richard?' she asked, very low. 'He's not *really* all right, is he?'

'No,' said Akananda. 'I must tell you, Mrs. Taylor, that he wants to repudiate his marriage, that he wishes every evidence of it removed from Medfield, which I am afraid includes you and little Sue. He has encased himself in steel. Nothing will alter his decision.'

She gasped. 'But then he's gone crazy.'

'Not technically insane,' said Akananda.

'But he *loved* Celia, I know he did. And she's dying—a husband can't act this way, it's not—it's not *decent*!'

Akananda smiled sadly. 'Violent emotions are never decent, Mrs. Taylor. They're blind forces, often strong enough to carry beyond one lifetime.'

'It couldn't be,' said Lily, putting her hand to her eyes. 'Just because Celia flirted some with Sir Harry, and she *was* strange last night—but nothing makes sense. Oh, I feel so miserably helpless.' She gasped, fishing a handkerchief from her handbag. 'I don't mean to cry, doesn't do any good, but if I could understand what's happened to us.'

Akananda rose and walked to the window. He looked out towards the dark green line of the Downs against the serene blue sky. Mysterious and timeless, as remote from shifting human passions as the blissful state of Samadhi which he had always longed to enter. And could not, for he was not yet liberated from attachment and debt. He too was bound on the wheel of Karma.

He turned back to the weeping woman, and touched her shoulder. 'I'm nearly as much in the dark as you are, but with your permission I'd like to make an experiment on your daughter, after I've conferred with Sir Arthur Moore.' And if she lives, he added to himself.

'Anything,' she whispered. 'Anything you think would help.'

'By the way,' said Akananda quietly, 'what's become of the Simpsons?'

Lily started. 'I don't know. I'd forgotten them. Can they still be here?'

'I think so.' His sensitised perceptions were aware of a black focus inside the house, a sinister vortex like a sluggish whirl-pool in an inky tarn. 'No, you wait,' he said to Lily. 'I'll deal with this.'

He went up to the Simpsons' door and knocked.

'Coom in, then,' said a woman's voice. Akananda obeyed, and paused on the threshold, struck by a scene which would have been ludicrous, if he had not been so conscious of evil.

Edna, red and sweaty-faced, her hair rumpled into little damp horns, was on her feet, struggling to hook her foundation garment, while George helped to tug.

'Lumme!' she cried angrily, 'I thought you were the maid!' She clutched a Japanese kimono around her billowing flesh.

'Sorry, Mrs. Simpson,' Akananda bowed slightly. 'Mrs. Taylor wished me to see how you were doing. Perhaps you didn't know that there've been grave troubles at Medfield today. The other guests have left.'

Except for a dull headache, Edna had largely recovered from the effects of the tincture, and had decided that the dimly remembered events of last night were another of those bad dreams she suffered from. It also now occurred to her that the nigger whom she had hitherto hardly noticed spoke excellent University English, quite B.B.C., and seemed to be on intimate terms with the Marsdons. She arranged the kimono with some dignity and spoke genteelly.

'Lady Marsdon is ill? Yes, Mr. Simpson told me.' She indicated George who had retired behind the bed and was gazing at his wife with a mixture of bewilderment and relief. You'd never believe how Edna'd looked an hour ago. Strong-minded she was, after all, his Edna. Something to be leaned on, even though rough and irritable at times, she gave him strength. These past hours were best forgotten.

'I've been quaite ill m'self,' said Edna. 'So awkward in a strange house, but Ai'm sure I've given no trooble. If Sir Richard and Mrs. Taylor are downhearted, we'll stay on and cheer them up, won't we, George?'

Akananda controlled his face and his exasperation at the incredible strength of blind stupidity and malice. He could see around the woman her muddy, dark aura, with its zigzag flashes of crimson. And he knew that she was as unconscious of the evil forces emanating from her as was her husband, or for that matter, her victims—Celia, Richard and Lily.

'Mrs. Taylor is off to hospital to be with her daughter,' he said repressively, 'and Sir Richard is unwell. We'll look up the train, and someone can drive you into Lewes.'

'Indeed . . .' Edna's stubborn jaw squared, but she found herself unable to protest as she wanted to, or marshal convincing arguments for staying near Sir Richard.

'To be sure, Doctor,' said George. 'We'll be packed in a jiffy, won't we, m'dear?'

Akananda, watching with the clairvoyance which he could sometimes command, saw a change in the little solicitor's aura which had been faint and grey. As Simpson spoke to his wife a rosy tinge suffused it, while more amazing still, the angry reds lightened around Edna. There's actually some love between them! Akananda thought. At the same time he had a shock of precognition about Edna. He saw devouring flames leaping around a bloated, screaming face. He shuddered and spoke in a kinder tone.

'You'll doubtless hear soon from Sir Richard, Mr. Simpson. He and Lady Marsdon would wish to extend their regrets at the abrupt ending to the house party if they could. I'll send the butler up with the train schedule.' He bowed and shut the door behind him.

'*Well*,' said Edna, 'takes a lot on himself, that one, doesn't he! What d'you suppose ails the Marsdons? I wonder, could it be food poisoning? I thought the crab was a bit off, at dinner last night. Come to think of it, I was sick m'self, wasn't I! Ten to one it was the crab!'

'It might be,' agreed George eagerly. 'Glad you're all right now, old girl.'

He bustled into the dressing room and began to pack his bag. Edna, too, began to pack, while her resentment at being ousted from Medfield yielded to a growing desire. She had begun to feel queasy again, and her own chemist would luckily be open this Sunday. The minute they got back to Clapham she could get a new bottle of the tincture. Craving for the tincture soon extinguished every other consideration, but she did not mention this to George.

*   *   *

At the hospital there was no change in Celia. When Akananda entered with Lily, the pert little nurse stood up, her young eyes critical. She watched Akananda in silent contempt as the Hindu doctor examined Celia. She had had three years

90

of training and she knew a corpse when she saw one. Matron had agreed when she popped in from time to time.

'Have to get her out of here,' said Matron. 'We need the bed. There's been a three-car smash on the A27, and we've got 'em lying on stretchers below. Hospital's here to care for the *living*, and this woman isn't. Baronet's lady or not, it's ridiculous.'

During his examination, Akananda came very near to private agreement with the nurses. He could find no vital signs of life, no pulse, breathing or reflexes, the body was chill and pallid, though not quite as cold as might be expected in true death. Nor had any rigor recurred since the oxygen had relaxed her. All Celia's muscles remained limp.

Akananda tried to see her aura, as he had the Simpsons', but his clairvoyance failed and left him with nothing to rely on but stubborn hope. He found this hope very hard to sustain against the hostile nurses.

'Cart the body back home then, Doctor,' Matron snapped, after a few minutes' argument. 'I suppose it'll be buried from there anyway, and aside from wanting the bed, this business is unnatural and upsets the young nurses, let alone patients, if they guess it.' She yanked the sheet up over Celia's face.

Lily, who had been watching, now gave a moan and pulled down the sheet. '*Don't* do that, Matron! Please don't. At least wait until the specialist gets here from London.' She took Celia's hand and held it against her cheek.

Matron tightened her lips. 'Well,' she said, 'Dr. Foster says Sir Arthur Moore may be here tonight, and charmed *he'll* be to waste his time on a fool's errand. I was going to stop him from coming.'

'No,' cried Akananda and Lily together.

Matron shrugged. 'Come along then, Sister,' she said to the young nurse. 'I need you below.' The two white-coiffed figures rustled out.

'Do you think Richard would *let* us bring her home?' whispered Lily, stroking her daughter's hand.

Akananda shook his head. Only if she were really dead, he thought. No doubt the force of breeding and tradition would impel the baronet to hold a funeral suitable to a Lady Marsdon. Though one wasn't even sure of that. Nanny, in a horrified whisper as Akananda left Medfield Place for the hospital, had informed him that Sir Richard was smashing photographs of

Celia, and had cut into ribbons the new oil painting of Celia which hung in the stair-well.

The hours dragged by as Lily and Akananda waited in the hospital beside the sheet-draped mound on the bed.

But it was not yet midnight when Sir Arthur Moore emerged from his chauffeur-driven Daimler and mounted the hospital steps, exuding the confidence and shrewd amiability which had helped earn his fat income and a knighthood. He was short, stout, bald, and looked far more like a prosperous alderman than a neuro-psychiatrist, renowned among the nobility for his discreet treatment of various embarrassing afflictions such as chorea, epilepsy, hysterical manifestations and even alcoholism. He was quite aware that his practice had, of late, begun to bore him, and only slightly surprised at himself for having, two hours ago, quitted Lady Blackwood's dinner party—even before finishing an excellent soufflé Grand Marnier—in response to a relayed summons from an unknown Sussex G.P.

The matron received him at the hospital door and began to dither.

'Oh, Sir Arthur—great honour—frightful to bring you down from London—absolutely useless—that foreign doctor, if he *is* a doctor . . .'

'*What?*' interrupted Sir Arthur, waving a plump, impatient hand. 'Chap who called me in wasn't foreign—name of Foster.'

'Not *that* one,' stammered Matron. 'The other one who won't admit your patient's dead, *was* dead on arrival, I think, though they got a few post-mortem reactions, but that was hours ago, and to me it's perfectly obvious that . . .'

She trailed off as the great man raised his bushy white eyebrows and gave her the chill, speculative look which had silenced volubility in obstreperous royalty, disapproving colleagues and even hospital governors.

'Ring up Dr. Foster to say I've arrived,' he said, 'but, first, show me to the patient.'

Sir Arthur entered Celia's room and went straight to the bed, ignoring the two people who were but dimly illumined in the night light. He clicked the top light on himself, and took Celia's wrist while he peered intently at her face. Presently, he dropped the wrist which flopped down on the motionless chest with a little thud they could all hear in the silent room.

'You may go,' Sir Arthur said to the hovering Matron. He added, 'I have nothing to say until Dr. Foster arrives.' Thereby extinguishing her triumphant smile, and as she vanished he continued, half to himself, 'Tiresome woman, she's right, of course, the girl's certainly dead, but . . .'

He was suddenly aware of the man and woman across the bed from him. 'Sorry,' he said to the anguished yet pretty middle-aged woman. 'You the mother?' As Lily nodded mutely, Sir Arthur turned to the man, and evinced uncharacteristic astonishment. 'Good Lord,' he cried, 'is it Jiddu? Jiddu Akananda?' He stared at the chiselled, unlined dark-brown face, the straight black hair, the slender body in a well-cut country tweed. One of the most brilliant students in their class at Guy's and later at the Maudesley. 'What in blazes are *you* doing here?'

Akananda smiled sadly. 'I am trying to prevent this young woman from totally relinquishing her present body, and to prevent others from forcing her to.'

'Indeed,' said Sir Arthur blandly, walking around the bed and shaking the Hindu's hand. 'Same old visionary, aren't you! You haven't altered a bit. Must be thirty-five years, too, since we swotted together at Guy's. Remember that scrape we got into, shock treatment wasn't it? Against old Murdock's express orders — the grandmother and grandfather of a row! What've you been doing with yourself all these years?'

'Calcutta, London, research — very quiet compared to *your* career, Arthur, and I need your help now.' He glanced towards the bed, and the other physician started. He had forgotten the present situation in the pleasure of meeting an old classmate whom he'd always liked, though most of the students thought the man an odd-ball.

'Yes, tell me *all* about this case,' said Sir Arthur, 'every detail.'

Lily, who had been overlooked by both, felt the forlorn relief of surrender to helplessness while awaiting the verdict of experts. Her misery sank to apathy, and murmuring that there must be a cup of coffee somewhere, she wandered out towards the nurses' desk.

Sir Arthur sat down in one straight chair while Akananda took the other. Sir Arthur pulled out a cigar and carefully clipped the tip.

'Don't usually do this near a patient, of course,' he said, striking a match, 'but it helps me to think, and honestly, my dear fellow, I don't see how we can consider *that* — a patient. However, fire away.'

Akananda talked for ten minutes, starting with medical details and procedures, while his colleague listened carefully, nodding at intervals.

'Clinical death is no longer so simple to establish,' he remarked as Akananda paused. 'The transplant lads are finding that out, though by and large, brain waves may show us. We'll have to get her to a machine to find out, though if it weren't for your determination I'd sign a death certificate on the present condition alone. Still, as soon as true rigor and putrefaction set in, we'll know. I'll hold off the ghouls for you.'

'Thank you,' said Akananda. 'I prayed you would.'

The other man was a trifle embarrassed by the Hindu's shining gratitude. He crossed his fat legs and said, 'Well ... extraordinary case. By the bye, *your* interest seems a bit personal—romantic tinge perhaps? Might be an attractive girl when she's "alive", as it were, or is it the mother? You were quite a lad with the girls as I remember, females swooning over you. I was often jealous.'

'No, no ...' said Akananda smiling. 'Those days are long past. And though I have much sympathy for these two unhappy women, it's not the carnal kind you mean.'

'Still pretty ascetic? No wine, women or red meat?'

Akananda nodded. 'Sounds dreary, doesn't it?'

'Takes all kinds ...' said Sir Arthur absently. He frowned towards the bed, his mind reverting to the present problem. 'The husband, the baronet, sounds a proper stinker from what you tell me.'

'He is behaving like one,' agreed Akananda slowly. 'Pathologically so. But he's acting out evil compulsions from the past, and greatly suffering.'

'Childhood trauma?' asked Sir Arthur, blowing a smoke ring and watching it float towards the white ceiling. 'Oedipus complex and all that Freudian stuff they crammed us with?'

'That, yes, in part perhaps.' Akananda turned his head and gazed out of the dark window into the star-lit night. 'Sir Richard is in a dangerous state of fugue, repudiation of present reality. This poor girl, also,' he jerked his head backwards towards the hospital bed. 'As you see, in even greater danger. Also from the past.'

Sir Arthur nodded dubiously. 'Depth analysis indicated? Tedious business and academic at the moment. Can't analyse a virtual corpse. By the way, Jiddu, that was a funny remark

94

you made that you were trying to prevent others from forcing her to relinquish her body. Sounds like witchcraft, or, for that matter,' he put down his cigar and frowned, 'sounds like murder. You can't mean *that*?'

Akananda exhaled and stood up, clasping his hands behind his back. 'Murder is exactly what I mean,' he said gazing down at his bewildered colleague. 'It was murder before, and will be again, unless . . .'

'You mean the girl's *poisoned*?' Sir Arthur interrupted. 'Never occurred to me. We'll run tests; Brainerd's the man for that. I'll see if I can get on to him now.' He jumped up.

'No, no.' Akananda put a detaining hand on the stout shoulder. 'There's no poison here that one can test by western science, not yet.'

'Well, then, what the hell are you talking about?'

'Therapy,' said Akananda, choosing his words carefully, 'preventive measures, and an abreaction.' He hoped that these sonorous terms would satisfy his friend. 'That is, reconstruction of the original traumata, thereby causing a curative catharsis.'

But Sir Arthur grunted crossly. 'Lot of pretentious gobbledygook for the layman, old boy, I've done it myself when I'm groping. In plain English—if the girl isn't dead yet, you hope to bring her out of this cataleptic trance or whatever it is, by making her unconscious live through and accept the disasters she's suicidally trying to escape from?'

'Something like that . . .' Akananda answered after a moment. He hesitated, longing to clarify, to win his friend's entire co-operation for a venture back into the past. But he knew that frankness might provoke doubt, even hostility. Arthur was an excellent neuro-psychiatrist and a great believer in material methods, such as chemotherapy. From the analytic viewpoint he would accept possible regression into any past, even foetal—of the palpable body in which a patient presented itself to him. Of any life existence before the womb or beyond the grave he was scornfully contemptuous. Young Artie Moore had been thus at medical school, and Sir Arthur, the eminent specialist, had obviously not changed.

'Unconscionable time that G.P.'s taking.' Sir Arthur remarked, then jumped. 'Good God, what was that?'

He whirled round and stared at the bed. He rushed over and put his ear to Celia's chest. The girl's condition was unchanged, no apparent heart beat, no reflexes, no expression either, except the remote secret surprise, in itself common enough on newly-dead faces.

'I thought I heard her speak,' said Sir Arthur. He pulled out his silk handkerchief and wiped his forehead. 'Didn't you hear anything, Jiddu?'

The Hindu had not, and he shook his head. 'What did you hear her say?' he asked quietly.

Sir Arthur tamped out his cigar. 'Perfectly idiotic, of course. I must be hallucinating. Need a holiday. Getting as nervy as my patients!'

'But what did you *think* she said?' insisted Akananda.

'Well, it—it sounded like "Stephen".'

'Ah-h—' said Akananda on a long-drawn breath. 'You heard what she was thinking, Arthur, at least you heard an impassioned cry from her soul.'

'My dear chap!' Sir Arthur exploded. 'This case is peculiar enough without muddling it with your metaphysical, extrasensory, transmigrational and God knows what theories. I remember 'em well. The arguments we had! I *imagined* I heard something, perfectly simple auditory hallucination. Sorry I mentioned it, but I was startled.'

Akananda, seeing that his friend was shaken, dropped the subject except for one temperate remark. 'If you can believe in television, Arthur, you can believe anything, don't you think? Invisible pictures, words, vibrations continually surrounding us, and only made manifest by turning buttons on a receptive box.'

'Rubbish, no parallel at all. And damn it, I'm not a receptive box!' He heard footsteps outside and cried, 'Thank God, this must be Foster. Now we can get going.'

Dr. Foster appeared and Sir Arthur plunged into the directives and practical arrangements at which he was adept.

* * *

By the next morning of another balmy June day, Celia had been transported to London and installed in a luxurious room at the London Clinic. The electroencephalogram, taken immediately, had shown the minimal brain wave function, quivers so feeble and sluggish that they were a marvel not only to the technician, but to all the fascinated staff who examined the graph. The prognosis was black.

Akananda stood by while Sir Arthur himself cautiously administered shock therapy. Celia's brain waves were unaffected.

'This beats me. I've never seen or heard of anything like this,' Sir Arthur finally confessed. 'Living corpse, like that American poet—what's his name—Poe wrote about. Even ten years ago she'd have been embalmed or cremated by now, and that really *would* finish her off. As it is . . . I give up. Jiddu, you have a free hand. What do you want to do?'

'Be entirely alone with her, uninterrupted.'

Sir Arthur sighed. 'Very well. I'll give the orders. I suppose you'll try hypnosis, or some damn-fool Indian trick?'

'Perhaps,' said Akananda smiling. 'I'm going home now to rest, I'll return to my patient later.'

'Home?' Sir Arthur was astonished. The chap seemed so rootless, and so dedicated. 'You don't mean wife, kiddies, grandchildren for that matter. I've got one myself. Grandchild. Poor wife's been dead six years.'

'No—none of that. Mine is a solitary path—in *this* life,' he added deliberately and watched the other's expression which remained affectionately enquiring, for Sir Arthur was deaf to the implication. 'I have a tiny flat in Bloomsbury,' he added.

'Well, good luck,' said Sir Arthur, who had missed both breakfast and lunch while struggling to arouse Celia, and was thinking longingly of his own elegant Mayfair mansion where Cook would immediately produce a kidney omelet. 'Give me a ring if there's any change. And I'll check in tomorrow.' He moved majestically along the corridor, ignoring the flutter of nurses and lesser doctors who had hoped for a word with him.

Akananda went down to the waiting room and found Lily Taylor staring at a closed copy of *Punch*.

'Any news?' she asked hopelessly. Her anxious face without make-up, her bright gold curls hanging limp, the simple heather tweeds which she had flung on at Medfield yesterday when the tragedies began, all made her look young and defenceless.

'Nothing new,' Akananda said gently. 'I'm going to try my experiment later. For that I must be alone, but I know you want to stay near here. Get yourself a room in town—Claridge's?'

'Can't I do *anything*?' she cried. 'It's awful just to wait.'

He nodded. 'Of all the unhappy human stresses, inactive suspense is probably the worst. I suggest that you *do* something.'

'But what?' she cried. 'I don't want to see people, go to a movie, distract myself, can't pray either, I've tried. Celia's dying in some ghastly way nobody understands; Richard has gone crazy, or at least insanely cruel; this nightmare *can't* be real.' She folded the glossy edge of the magazine cover and began to tear off little scraps, staring at the bits of paper as they fluttered to the carpet.

Akananda watched her, frowning. He stepped quickly to the nurse's desk and gave an order. He came back with decision. 'Mrs. Taylor, I want you to take a taxi to some church, some hallowed spiritual place where you will sit quietly for at least one hour. Where do you wish to go? Westminster Abbey perhaps?'

'No, no—' she murmured. 'Too much bustle, too many tourists.'

'St. Paul's then? One of the smaller churches?'

She shook her head, still pleating and tearing at the magazine cover.

'Lily Taylor, look at me!'

She raised her head slowly and met his stern, concentrated eyes, the dark brown irises were focused on her like two beams until the fog of misery and utter weariness was pierced, and an image slipped into her mind.

'There *is* a church,' she whispered, 'I might like to pray in. I was there once years ago on an earlier visit to London.'

'Yes,' he said, 'go on!'

'It's across the river, Southwark—a cathedral. I liked it. They call it St. Saviour's, I think, but that isn't its real name.' She stopped, startled by a shiver down her back, like the shiver from hearing a strain of nostalgic music. She tried to look away from Akananda, but she could not.

'What used to be the cathedral's name, its old name?' he asked. 'Quickly! Don't think!'

Her voice obeyed him without volition. 'St. Mary Overies. Next to the Montagu's Priory.'

'Ah-h—' murmured Akananda on a long breath, 'Montagu.' She had given him a clue he needed to help Celia. During his internship at Guy's Hospital he had lived in Southwark, and had himself been drawn to St. Saviour's and its history. He had been uncertain how to guide Celia in her attempt to penetrate her past life. That Celia had been a part of some Tudor period seemed likely in view of the facts given in the Marsden Chronicle, and the name 'Stephen' so strangely heard or imagined by Sir Arthur, but there was no other lead aside from her behaviour at Ightham Mote. He knew that 'Montagu' provided one, and came from the unhappy mother's own buried memory.

A nurse hurried in with the sedation he had ordered.

'Take this, my dear,' said Akananda, giving Lily a large red capsule. 'It'll calm you. Then go over to Southwark Cathedral which was, indeed, as you say, once called St. Mary Overie. You should be able to pray there.'

Lily nodded mutely. The whole terrible situation had receded; she had entered a state of abeyance where only Akananda and his directives were real. She put on her gloves and rose, giving the Hindu a polite smile. She went out to the cab stand. He followed slowly; saw that she entered a taxi, then got one himself which he directed to the British Museum. There he spent two hours consulting the *Complete Peerage* and the *Dictionary of National Biography*. Considerably enlightened, he walked to his Bloomsbury flat where he settled himself in the Asana position while he gradually immersed himself in profound meditation.

The long June daylight was fading into violet shadow; the myriad lights of London glinted like topazes when he left the flat and returned to the hospital where Celia lay.

The night staff had come on, but Sir Arthur's orders had been relayed and he was received with politeness and veiled curiosity.

'Lady Marsdon's condition seems quite unchanged, Doctor,' said the capable Irish nurse who accompanied him to Celia's room. 'I've kept a sharp eye on her, but not touched her, of course. Sir Arthur said not. Will you be wanting medications? Or glucose? We've the I.V. drip ready.'

'Nothing,' he answered smiling, 'except no interruptions for *any* reason. I shall lock the door and take all responsibility.'

The nurse's sandy eyebrows twitched, but she only said, 'Very well, sir.' Then added in a rush, 'Good luck, Doctor. I pray you can save her, I've seldom seen so sad a case, 'tis worse 'n death, 'tis like her spirit's stifled—gives me the shivers. Uncanny. May the Blessed Lord and His Holy Angels have mercy.' She shut her lips and flushed. 'Sorry, sir,' she went out and shut the door.

Akananda locked it after her. He pulled a chair up to the bedside and took Celia's limp, chilly hand in his. He gazed at her calm upturned profile, an alabaster effigy as remote and passionless as those on medieval church tombs. Her dark curls, gummy and matted from electrodes, looked no more alive than painted hair.

Under the cotton hospital gown her chest did not move. Akananda was dismayed. Had the tiny flicker of life really snuffed out? Was it hopeless? He clasped her hand tightly, trying to propel vital force down his arm through his hand into her body. His firm grasp encountered cold resistant metal, and he saw that she was wearing a heavy amethyst heart-shaped ring over the plain gold wedding band. The Marsdon wives' ring. He had casually admired it on the night of his arrival at Medfield, and Sir Richard had said smiling, 'That's the Lady of the Manor's badge of servitude, complete with baleful cockatrice!' They had all laughed, and surely Richard had thrown his wife a teasing, affectionate glance, yet even then Akananda had noticed tension in Celia, she had swallowed several times and the look in her grey eyes had seemed apprehensive.

Frowning and uncertain, Akananda slipped the ring off the small cold finger and laid it on the bedstand. He was watching intently, and thought he saw a tremor flit across the ashen face. But, he knew how easily intense desire could deceive one. Tentatively he moved the wedding ring. There was no doubt of some reaction this time. The hand quivered under his fingers, and he apprehended a faint resistance, though the quiver vanished at once.

Groping, yet greatly relieved, he spoke to her. 'The Marsdon "badge of servitude" is gone from you, Celia. But you wish to keep the wedding band?'

There was no further quiver under his touch. She had slipped back into her faraway void. He sighed and put his other hand on her forehead.

'Celia . . .' he said as he had before, in the Sussex hospital. 'Celia . . . where are you?' There was no response.

'You must let me in, Celia,' he said very low. 'Take me back to where you are. Trust me.' He thought of one of his Master's teachings. There was no such thing as circumscribed time. Time was a dimension. Even as Einstein had proven to those in the West who could understand him. All time existed *now*. The Master had spoken of the 'Akashic Records' as well, the imperishable etheric recordings of all events, and explained them to his young disciples as vaguely like storage—housing motion-picture film which might be selected and viewed at will by those sufficiently enlightened and instructed to do so. But *how?*

Sweat gathered on Akananda's forehead, as he sat in the hospital room, dimly hearing the sound of London traffic; muffled creakings and voices from the tumultuous hospital life outside this quiet room.

He spoke to Celia again, using the power of the words which he felt must reach her. 'Is *Stephen* with you?' he asked urgently. There was no response. 'Montagu . . .' he said, 'Cowdray . . . Ightham Mote . . . Are you afraid, Celia?'

The skin under his hand grew colder, and he knew again an overwhelming sense of defeat. The many years of his western training gathered themselves together to jeer at him. What a credulous fool Arthur Moore would think him, and their professors at Guy's. The brain surgeon—Mr. Lawrence —'Now, Mr. Akananda, kindly dissect this pineal gland for us, we wait with bated breath to see you disclose that mystical third eye you keep talking about, and maybe you can find the soul, or at least its erstwhile habitation, for I must be *fair* and grant you *this* brain's as dead as mutton.'

How the other students had laughed, taking their cue from the elegant, supercilious professor. And I laughed with them. Fearful of their scorn. Apostate, lickspittle, coward! I made a brilliant mockery of that dissection, repudiating all my teachings and my certainties. Deserting the two students who had believed in me. I remember their startled disappointed eyes. I wanted to curry favour with Lawrence, I wanted him to pass me.

A little thing, a trivial incident, but . . .

'You behaved like that before, and the outcome was not trivial.'

Akananda heard the accusation. And the words were in Bengali. He opened his tight-shut eyes and saw a glow on the yellow-painted hospital wall beyond the patient's bed. Through the glow appeared a luminous white figure. From it flowed pity and authority. Akananda prostrated himself on the bare wooden floor.

The communion now was wordless. A series of questions and commands. When St. Marylebone's bells rang ten o'clock from around the corner, the presence vanished. Akananda raised his head, his face was wet with tears, and he knew with certainty, at last, what he must do to redress the wrongs he had inflicted and help those now again in danger. He could not stand aside from bygone sufferings. He must take part and re-live with them the past.

He must negate his present selfhood and enlightenment. He must watch the transcendent film unroll, in full identification with each character.

Akananda rose to wipe his face and damp hands on his white linen handkerchief. He walked to the water carafe on the night table and drank. Then he returned to the bed and pressed his bunched fingers between Celia's eyebrows.

'Where are you, Celia?' he asked for the third time, but now with assurance. '*Answer me!*'

In a moment she sighed, her bluish lips moved and he heard a faint whisper.

'In the great Buck Hall, we are waiting for the young King. The family is in sorrow, but we must hide this. There's gay music from the minstrels' gallery. I smell thyme and lavender among the new rushes on the floor. I'm afraid for Stephen . . . they've locked him up.'

'Yes . . .' said Akananda. But there was one more question, one more link necessary.

'Who am I, Celia?' he said quietly. 'Am *I* there?'

He felt the faint nodding motion under his hand.

'Then who *am* I?'

He waited a long time while her lips twitched feebly. He exerted no will power, no internal commands. He waited.

At last she spoke. 'You are Julian, Master Julian.'

As she spoke the name he stiffened once. The gap was bridged. He shut his eyes and leaned his head against the wall.

PART TWO
1552—1559

Four

At Cowdray Castle, Monday, July 25 of the Year of Our Lord,
1552, the great Buck Hall was garnished and decorated as it
had never been in the five years since old Sir Anthony Browne
had completed it by erecting the lofty bay window, and ex-
travagantly glazing its sixty lights, then vaingloriously placing
on high brackets the wooden statues of eleven life-size stags
as reminders of the Browne crest. From the buck antlers now
dripped flowery garlands; wreaths of roses encircled their
necks. The entire Hall was fragrant because yesterday the old
rushes had been swept out into a fetid heap behind the cow-
byre, and on the oaken floor planks there was a carpeting of
sun-dried green rushes from the River Rother, strewn with
crumbled lavender and thyme. So fresh was the scent that it
counteracted the usual smells of sweat and musk exuded by the
long-packed Court dresses worn by guests and household
assembled by young Sir Anthony for welcoming their King.

Celia Bohun gloried in a new gown, lovingly made for her
by Lady Ursula Southwell out of old treasured lengths of peacock brocade and cream satin. There was even a small lace
ruff, and a demure heart-shaped cap which framed the soft
shining ripples of Celia's corn-coloured hair. The new finery
was one of Ursula's many kindnesses to the orphan girl who
shared her blood, and also shared her anomalous position at
the castle. Ursula and Celia were de Bohuns. Their family had
lived here for nearly four centuries. The magnificent Brownes,
for all their careless generosities, were upstarts, usurpers at
Cowdray.

It was true that Browne men had great swashbuckling charm,
coupled with loyalty which King Henry had rewarded in the
elder Sir Anthony, who had been a trusted emissary and
Master of the Horse, despite his staunch Catholicism. It was
also true that the Brownes had frequently counteracted their
obscure origins by shrewd marriages with younger daughters
of noble houses, like the present marriage of young Anthony
to Lady Jane Radcliffe. And Anthony's maternal grandfather,
Sir John Gage, was even now Constable of the Tower, a fearsome old man. He had quarrelled bitterly with his son-in-law,

so that though Sir John lived at Firle Place in East Sussex, Cowdray never saw him.

None of these connections outweighed Ursula's hidden hurt at the ousting of her solidly aristocratic line from their ancestral home. But Ursula had long been widowed, and she was nearing sixty. She had learned to hide her feelings, except to Celia, and with true gratitude accepted a small upper chamber in the castle and a seat just above the salt at the long trestled dining table, though when the impoverished Bohuns had been forced to sell all their property to the Browne family, the natural expectation was that Ursula would enter some convent —the usual refuge for superfluous women. Two things prevented; the lack of a dowry, and her own lack of interest in monastic routine. Then, lately, there was Celia, her brother John's forlorn child.

In the minstrels' gallery this noon of the boy King's arrival, the musicians were nervously practising a new French madrigal. Edward disapproved of most music, as he disapproved of dancing or levity. The fifteen-year-old King had strong prejudices, all of which increasingly verged on the puritanical. One must be wary of offence.

Celia stood with her aunt Ursula by the buttery screen in the huge Buck Hall, eagerly savouring her first glimpse of assembled nobility. Her cheeks glowed a bright pink, her long bluish-green eyes sparkled with excitement. Lady Ursula possessed no mirror, but the girl knew that the peacock brocade was becoming. She noted the startled stares of two castle pages who had previously ignored her on her visits to Cowdray. Far more flattering recognition followed.

Sir Anthony and his wife, Lady Jane Radcliffe, daughter to the Earl of Sussex, were circling the Hall to greet important guests, and to make a last tour of inspection. They were both dressed in crimson velvet embroidered with gold and pearls. The splendour suited Anthony who was tall, stoutly built for a man of twenty-five, and had the bearing of a born horseman, added to the assurance of wealth.

Lady Jane was puny and shrinking; she had a desolate mouse face, the eyes, at present, reddened from weeping. Three days ago their infant son had died of a convulsion. The little coffin under its white satin pall stood, not in the chapel as it should have, but in an alcove off their bedchamber. No Masses were being said for the tiny soul, and there must be no mention of the tragedy to cloud the King's visit. 'We'll make other babes,

my lady!' Anthony had cried with his usual hearty optimism.
' 'Tis an easy pleasant task.'

Lady Jane did not think so. She had suffered an agonising childbirth, nor was yet recovered. But she never gainsaid her husband.

Sir Anthony had finished his inspection of the Hall and came near Lady Ursula on his way through the screens to the courtyard. He gave Ursula a quick nod, then caught sight of Celia.

'Halloo-oo!' he exclaimed, his bold blue gaze examining the girl. 'Who may *this* be?'

'Celia Bohun, Sir Anthony,' said Ursula, flushing a little. 'My niece. I trust I've not offended in letting her come today —this glorious day for Cowdray. She has few pleasures.'

Anthony shook his head amiably, uninterested in the connection, or in Ursula, whom he had inherited as a charge from his father and very seldom saw. The girl's from that bastard branch of the Bohuns, he thought, staring at Celia. He had heard there were some around Midhurst.

'So fair a maid is welcome,' he said. 'How old are you, poppet?'

'Fourteen, sir,' answered Celia promptly. 'Last month, on St. Anthony's Day, your own name day, an' it please your grace.' She curtsied.

Anthony chuckled, momentarily forgetting the anxieties attendant upon Edward's arrival, the factions involved—the dangers. Celia's ready pert reply amused him, and he noted the innocent provocativeness of the white cleft between her full breasts, the slight protrusion of her red under-lip and the square up-tilted chin.

'This luscious fruit is ripening fast, eh, lady?' he said to Ursula. 'Wherever you've been keeping her. We must find her a husband. Some lusty yeoman to her taste, or even a squire, if I can spare a few angels for a dowry—though, by God's bones, I doubt it after this royal visit.'

He glanced at his wife whose mournful eyes were fixed patiently on the wall tapestry.

Ursula spoke up quickly, knowing that her patron might soon forget Celia's existence. 'The girl is as apt to learn as she is comely, sir. I've taught her household skills and her letters, and Brother Stephen has given her religious instruction.'

'*What!*' Anthony started. His eyes flashed. 'We do not mention *him*, madam! Not while the King is here. You, and all my household *know* that, madam. You have been warned!'

Ursula's long face which was like a kindly mare's, reddened to the roots of her iron-grey hair. 'Aye, sir, pardon, sir,' she said. 'It was a slip.'

'There must be no slips,' said Sir Anthony who could, on occasion and despite his youth, be quite as formidable as his father had been when striving to keep the precarious favour of old King Harry. An easier task, Anthony thought, than pleasing the son—the earnest, bigoted and autocratic young sprig who was now swayed daily by the real enemy. The real danger. Northumberland—mad for power, slick as a ferret, cruel as a wolf, and virtually the true King of England. Lauded be God and His Blessed Mother that Northumberland was occupied on the Scottish Border at this moment. But he had his spies everywhere near Edward. 'There must *be* no slips,' Anthony repeated in a softer voice, 'and I know my household is loyal. Come, my lady.' He put his hand on Jane's arm.

Ursula curtsied as the couple moved on; she turned to Celia and whispered, 'Let's mount to my chamber and wait. We can see the approaching heralds from my window. 'Tis close down here and I'm shaken by the annoyance I caused Sir Anthony.'

Celia obediently followed her aunt up circular stone stairs to a small comfortable room on the third storey. It was near the servants' attic, and in winter heated only by a brazier, but it contained Ursula's only treasures—the four-posted bed of blackened oak, hung with faded crimson, where she had slept long ago with her husband, and at the bed's foot stood her dower chest carved in linen-fold, her Italian X-shaped chair. Her strip of rich 'Turkey' carpet covered the plain square table, and hanging against the stone wall near the window was the sole remembrance of her dead husband, Sir Robert Southwell—his sword in its gilt, encrusted sheath. On the east wall near the bed hung Ursula's ebony crucifix. There were besides these, two unexpected objects on a shelf: a small ephemeris for computing the daily positions of the stars, and a neat roll of horoscopes tied up with a golden cord. Ursula practised astrology; she had received instruction twenty years ago from the Duke of Norfolk's resident Italian astrologer, when Sir Robert was alive and the Southwells had visited the Norfolks at Kenninghall. Most of the great households consulted astrologers; there were official royal astrologers, too. Cowdray had none. Sir Anthony was a practical man, and felt himself quite able to control his own future.

Had he known of Ursula's hobby he would have laughed or shrugged. But he did not, nor anything else about her.

Celia rushed to the window-seat, peeped through the diamond panes to catch a first glimpse of the King's procession on the highway from Easebourne. There was nothing to be seen and she turned into the room frowning. 'My Lady Aunt, *why* must Brother Stephen be hid? He told me so little.'

The girl did not know how her voice softened and lingered when she spoke the young priest's name, but Ursula felt a twinge of guilty foreboding. She sighed and sat down. 'I've been wrong not to tell you, Celia. Acting heedless as a maiden myself in the joy of dressing you, of presenting you below in a manner worthy of a Bohun, at last. Listen! Three days agone when we knew that the King was at Petworth, and would surely come here, Sir Anthony gathered us all in the Hall, all of us down to the lowliest pot-boy. He stood in the minstrels' gallery and gave his commands. He said that to be sure, we were Catholic, that we were as devout a family of the True Faith as could be found in England. None the less, we owed temporal allegiance to our King, and must respect his heretic views. That during the royal visit there would be no Masses, though there might be an English prayer service read from Archbishop Cranmer's new book. That nobody was to genuflect or cross themselves, nor mention saints. Our chapel would be stripped of its holy statues, even the crucifix! This was done that night, my dear, and oddly forlorn our chapel is now. Empty, barren.'

Celia considered this. 'How strange,' she said. 'Surely a great lord like Sir Anthony may do as he pleases.'

'Obviously not,' answered Ursula tartly. 'Don't you know, child, that a year ago March, Sir Anthony was thrown in the Fleet like a common criminal?'

The girl's eyes widened. 'Prison?' she said. 'For what?'

'For hearing Mass at his mansion in Southwark. It's forbidden. Oh, he stayed in the Fleet but six weeks. He has powerful friends, and the King likes him as his father liked Sir Anthony's father.'

'But he had Masses *here*, until just now,' protested Celia.

'Aye,' said Ursula, 'and will resume them. He's lord on his own manor which is a long way from London. No need for the King or his advisers to know this during their two-day visit.'

'Oh,' repeated Celia, 'how very odd.' And she thought with

increased fear about Stephen. She knew vaguely of the religious storms and violent changes which had shaken England since before her birth, but her childhood had been monotonous, isolated and dreary until last September.

Her father she could scarcely remember. When she was three he had been stabbed in a tavern brawl while defending the Bohun name. Celia had lived thereafter in a garret at the Spread Eagle Inn in Midhurst with her mother who served as barmaid, while Celia ran errands, washed tankards, sanded the floors, and even turned the spit, until her gentle, pretty mother Alice began complaining to Celia of sharp pains in her belly which swelled as though there were a baby inside. Celia soon knew that the other servants at the Inn thought there was; she listened half-comprehending to many a bawdy jest and coarse speculation as to the father. Alice herself bore these jibes in white-faced silence.

But, though the young woman swelled enough to contain twins, none ever came. And at Michaelmas while the Inn was roasting the usual geese, and the parish church bell was ringing for curfew, Alice suddenly gave a scream and fell to the floor of their attic room. In a few minutes her heart stopped beating, and when the terrified Celia had summoned help, Alice was dead.

They were good to Celia at the Inn. Master and Mistress Potts, the innkeepers, set her behind the bar to serve ale in her mother's place, but she was dazed and lost. She upset tankards, she bungled orders, and she wept much in the night. She had nobody to turn to. Her mother had kept to herself in Midhurst. Alice was a Londoner, the daughter of a respectable tavern-keeper at the Golden Fleece, which was well known for its high-toned patronage. The Golden Fleece was proud to welcome visiting gentry from the shires, and it was there that Jack Bohun stayed during his one visit to London in 1537. And though he was a moody, hot-tempered bachelor of forty some years, he fell headlong in love with Alice, the landlord's only daughter.

Jack Bohun was neither a knight nor recognised gentry, yet though he seldom spoke of it, he never forgot his distinguished albeit unofficial lineage. He was a Bohun bastard. But until the Bohuns were forced to sell the patrimony to the Earl of Southampton, who left it to his half-brother, Anthony Browne the elder, Sir John, Jack's father, treated the boy as his legal heir. Sir John despised his fat wife—a producer of daughters but no males, and had felt very much like his liege lord, King Henry, about this matter, though he had none of that monarch's power to substitute wives. Sir John would have liked to legitimate young Jack whose mother was a beautiful Bohun cousin. The liaison was accepted everywhere, yet there could be no marriage while the inconvenient wife lived, and she did—for some years after her husband. The young bastard, however, was taken to the crumbling Bohun stronghold on St. Ann's Hill. He was raised with his half-sisters, the legitimate heiresses, Mary and Ursula. He shared in the brief years of security when Mary married Sir Davy Owen, himself a bastard, but a Tudor one. Jack also shared in the family downfall when Cowdray and Easebourne and large pieces of Midhurst were bought by the Earl of Southampton, and inherited by the Brownes in 1542 when the Earl was killed fighting the Scots.

Jack Bohun was a man of fierce passions, and family loyalty, perhaps all the stronger because he was not legitimate. He had deeply resented the newcomers, and quarrelled with Ursula, his remaining half-sister, for her acceptance of the Brownes' hospitality through the years.

Ursula accepted this break with her own realistic philosophy. But she enquired from time to time about the welfare of his widow. Through the servants at Cowdray she soon heard of Alice's death, and the sorrowful plight of little Celia, her blood-niece.

One day in October Ursula rode from Cowdray into town to the Spread Eagle Inn and asked for the Bohun girl.

Ursula was shown to a small black-beamed chamber off the tap-room, and waited with no more than charitable curiosity until a slender girl with matted golden hair and frightened eyes walked slowly through the door.

'Ye sent for me, m'lady?' said the girl in a breathy, stifled voice.

'If you are Celia de Bohun,' said Ursula. Her voice quivered. At this first glimpse of the downcast face she felt a shock of inexplicable sympathy, a sensation of fulfilment, as though this were her own long-lost child, though Ursula had never borne any.

'Pray sit down, sweeting, pray do,' she said.

'I'm Celia Bohun, true enough . . .' The child twisted her work-chapped hands, and dropped a curtsy, then stood, faintly hostile, in the centre of the sanded floor, scarcely glancing at the elderly lady whose name she had never heard of, and who

111

came from the castle for what mysterious purpose she could not fathom, except that it probably represented another blow from fate.

Ursula looked again at the girl who must be about thirteen, for the bitter quarrel with Jack, and his visit to London and lowly marriage happened fourteen years ago. She saw that once properly cleansed the tousled hair would be of a rich buttercup yellow, that the breasts were rounded and straining against the tight, shoddy brown bodice, that the hands though red were delicately made, that the little face had a nascent beauty—full lips, large turquoise eyes with long dark lashes. There was a promise of vibrancy and allure which Ursula herself had never had.

'Celia,' she said gently, 'you are my niece, and since you have none who belong to you now, nor do I, it's time we knew one another.'

Celia jerked her head up and stared, collecting her sorrow-dazed wits, suspecting some stupid jest—in which the world abounded.

'I'm a Bohun, m'lady,' she said defiantly, 'and landlord, he said your name was Lady Suthell, nor have I aught to do wi' Cowdray.'

'I know, dear,' said Ursula with tenderness. 'But I am a Bohun, too, and your father was my brother.'

Celia then looked with attention at Lady Southwell, at the frayed black velvet cloak, the white gauze widow's cap which perched on top of grizzled hair above a raw-boned, kindly face. She had never seen a lady so close, only from a window at the inn when a cavalcade on the way to the castle might stop to make enquiries.

'Mother—' Celia's voice faltered, and she bit her lip. 'My mother,' she went on carefully, 'ne'er made mention o' any kinfolk at Cowdray. She said the Bohuns 're all gone. Anyways, my father was a bastard, and quarrelled wi' the rest afore I was born.'

'Aye—' said Ursula sighing. 'True enough, and an ancient tale long past. But I am your aunt, and I wish to be your friend.' Ursula reached out her hand and the girl slowly took it feeling at the touch her first comfort in weeks, or indeed, perhaps in years, for her mother, though gentle, had never spoken much nor showed feelings.

So began their association, and so very soon, through

Ursula's ambitious plans, began the association with a different and tragic love for one who became to her a cherished daughter.

Ursula had no means of her own, and her pride forbade her to ask Sir Anthony to take in another dependant, nor did she wish to introduce Celia as a servant at Cowdray, though later, after training, there might be a respectable way to get the girl in the castle as waiting-woman.

In the meantime Celia must continue her duties at the Spread Eagle. 'And never forget, dear,' said Ursula, 'that the Inn was once *ours*, that the spread eagle is the *Bohun* crest, so that you have a right there. I'll speak to the landlord myself.'

Landlord Potts was not much impressed with this logic, but he and his wife were good-tempered people and sorry for the girl whom they had known from babyhood

Celia, therefore, lived at the inn, serving ale and dinners as before, but visiting Ursula at Cowdray quite often. Her aunt soon discovered both the quickness of the girl's wits, her hunger for knowledge, and also her total lack of education. Ursula was not surprised that Celia could neither read nor write, and remedied these to the best of her ability. Celia spent many hours learning, and by mid-January she recognised whole sentences when Ursula wrote them out in plain block letters, but Ursula's ambition for the girl grew as her love did. She began to feel that her rough-cut jewel was capable of great brilliance, and also that the absence of any religious training must be rectified. What better instructor for this than the Brownes' house priest—Brother Stephen?

On last Candlemas Day, February 2, Ursula waited outside the private chapel after Mass, and called the monk into the parlour next to the great Buck Hall.

'Brother Stephen,' said Ursula, 'your duties here are not too arduous? I wonder if you'd help me in a certain matter.'

'Most certainly, lady, if I can,' Stephen smiled, bowing slightly, and waited. He was a tall young man, made taller by the black Benedictine robes. His care for the household of two hundred souls at Cowdray was punctilious and observant. He celebrated the Masses, he administered the sacraments—baptism, marriage, burials, when such were required, otherwise he kept to himself, and lived by preference in a stark cabin near the ruined chapel of St. Ann on top of the hill which had once been the Bohun stronghold. He had some books in his cell, and was reputed quite a scholar, but he had no intimates.

Ursula explained her wishes, and the situation.

'I see,' said Stephen after a moment. 'And it's true that your niece should have religious instruction, yet that I should also teach her some Latin and arithmetic seems to me over-weening. What simple woman has use for learning? What profit in the station where God has placed her?'

He was, as always, courteous, and hid his amusement at the old lady's doting folly. He understood that Lady Ursula was lonely, and had somehow found an object for her famished affections. He liked the woman, and listened to her blameless confessions with sympathy, feeling kinship to one who occasionally rebelled against patronage and whose pride had often been hurt. Humbleness and obedience he knew were the Christian virtues he himself lacked most. The other two Bene-dictine vows, poverty and chastity, had never troubled him.

'I do not, good Brother, expect Celia to *remain* in her pre-sent station,' said Ursula, her faded eyes shining. 'I've cast her horoscope, and she has a Jupiter and Venus in benign aspects, and most auspicious stars.'

Stephen laughed. 'Ah, to be sure, you dabble in astrology,' he said tolerantly. 'It's not considered a sin, and if it gives you comfort . . . none the less, God's will *alone* determines us.'

'To be sure,' Ursula agreed, looking up at the monk. 'But God's will rules the heavenly bodies, too.' It occurred to her that Stephen was a comely man, that his features were regular, his hair around the tonsure black and curly, that there was vital attraction in him. But one did not think of a monk as quite a man, besides this one had dignity and aloofness which made him seem older than the twenty-seven years someone had said that he was. 'At least, *see* the child,' added Ursula softly. 'She's virtually a pagan. She knows nothing about our Dear Lord's Passion, about the Trinity, she barely knows the name of the Blessed Virgin.'

'That's dreadful!' cried Stephen shocked. 'She must *not* fall into the damnable heresies which surround us. Tell her to come to me on St. Ann's Hill at noon tomorrow. I'll be waiting.' He said, '*Benedicite*,' and strode out of the castle to cross the River Rother and climb the hill to his quarters.

The medieval Bohun castle was in ruins because most of its stones had been hauled down to the meadow when Sir David Owen married Mary de Bohun and began to build himself a

114

comfortable Tudor mansion among the hazel tree copse called *La Coudraie* in Norman French.

Sir David's architectural efforts had been hampered by poverty; no poverty hampered the new owners. The Earl of Southampton, and later his brother Anthony Browne had made a veritable palace out of Cowdray.

Stephen disliked the place, not only for its ostentation and extravagance but because of the tainted riches which had produced it. Stolen money. Money which rightly belonged to God. Stephen had had many an anguished struggle with his conscience over his position as chaplain to the Brownes, though that position was the result of humiliation and obedience.

Stephen's thoughts returned to that struggle as he clambered up the frozen, muddy footpath to the top of St. Annn's Hill. He entered his cot, and blowing the smouldering embers, swung the crane with its iron pot of mutton stew over the fire to heat.

His home was spartan, but not uncomfortable. It was made of wood, and of stone from the eastern side of the fallen curtain wall. It was neatly thatched, and had a plank floor. St. Ann's little chapel sheltered it from the north winds, and was used by Stephen for private devotions. His wooden bed was piled with fresh straw, which he frequently renewed, for he was cleanly by nature and abhorred lice and fleas. Since leaving the two abbeys which had raised him, and the company of his brother monks, he had obtained permission from his superior in France to relax the rule against private possession to a limited extent.

He, therefore, owned some vellum-bound books, and besides a black and silver crucifix there hung near the one window an oddly charming and naïve painting—of the Virgin. She was golden-haired and seated in a flowery meadow, smiling mysteriously. This bright sketch by an Italian painter—possibly one Botticelli—was sent to Stephen in France at his ordination.

The French Abbot of Marmoutier was a reasonable man, and on saying a reluctant farewell to Stephen, added, 'Your situation in that barbarous and now heretic country will be difficult enough, my son, without depriving yourself of innocent possessions. I know your true character. You will be tempted to no transgressions of our Rule. You have taken the sacred vows, and are as certain to honour them as any monk I've ever had.'

This was extraordinary praise from the taciturn Abbot, and Stephen, as he knelt to kiss the ring was deeply moved. He returned to his native land in a glow of zeal and passionate dedication. He had not guessed at the rebellions, the angers, the contempts he would have to surmount.

*   *   *

Stephen Marsdon had been born in East Sussex, at Medfield near Alfriston. He was the youngest son and destined to the Church from infancy. Since the days of the Conqueror some Marsdon younger son had been given to the Church, and Stephen accepted his lot without question. When he was nine his father, Robert, had taken him the day's journey to Battle Abbey where he entered Stephen as a sub-novice and pupil. The boy's remaining childhood was happy. He was healthy and excelled at the sports permitted to the boarders —races, stool-ball, wrestling and round games. Since he had never known them, he did not miss the accomplishments taught to worldly young gentlemen, jousting, lute-playing or dancing. Stephen was studious, too. He easily mastered Latin and what classics he was given. He was also popular with the other boys. He knew that the teaching monks favoured him, and one day overheard the Abbot of Battle, John Hammond, saying to the novice-master, 'Keep your eye on Stephen Marsdon, by Our Blessed Lady, I foresee a brilliant future for him in the church. He'll be an abbot himself one day, mark my words!'

This prediction delighted Stephen who was a natural leader, and yet had a mystical and sensitive side which made the plain-chant of the monks, the church festivals, the rituals, candles and incense, all agreeable to him.

In 1536 when Stephen was eleven, the incredible catastrophes began throughout England. The events which caused these scarcely filtered down to the sheltered boys at Battle. The actual *coup de grâce*, two years later, came as a shock so great that Stephen and the other sub-novices at first thought it a hoax.

On May 27, 1538, after vespers, Abbot John assembled all his community in the church and made a speech from the pulpit, during which his voice trembled, slow angry tears dropped down his sagging cheeks, while his thin white hands shook the lectern in helpless rage.

The Abbot said that by royal command His Gracious Majesty, King Henry the Eighth, Defender of the Faith, having decreed that all the monasteries were to be dissolved, that this decree most monstrously now seemed to affect Battle Abbey, too. That perpetual prayer and intercessions had already begun. It was unthinkable that Battle Abbey which had been founded in holy thanksgiving by William the Conqueror on this exact miraculous site should be dissolved like lesser foundations, that St. Martin and the Holy Blessed Virgin would never permit such devilish wickedness. Whereupon Abbot John glared at Richard Layton, the King's commissioner, who was sitting imperturbably in the church.

The boys discussed the extraordinary announcement later in their dorter. They spoke at first in nervous whispers, though the monk who usually kept order was absent, praying with his Brothers.

One of the boys, from the famous Sackville family in Kent, spent more time at home, and had greater knowledge of outside events than the others. His name was Hugh, and he had never intended to take the vows anyway. He spoke jubilantly of the matter, and professed great admiration for the King.

'There's a splendid man who knows what he wants and gets it!' said Hugh. 'Wanted a divorce to wed that black-haired witch Nan Bullen. Wanted a son and wouldn't let the Pope gainsay him. But Nan could offer no better than a girl—the Lady Elizabeth, y'know. So King Harry chopped Nan's head off, and wed our late queen. Now he has his son, but wants something else as well.'

'What's that?' asked Stephen, still unable to grasp what the Abbot had told them.

Hugh noisily rubbed his forefingers and thumb together. 'Gold, m'lad,' he answered. 'Riches. Property, like every other man. Now he'll get 'em.'

'What do you mean . . .' faltered Stephen. 'How will he get them?'

'Why, from the monasteries, you dolt. The abbeys, the convents, where else?'

'But he *can't*,' Stephen cried. 'He can't grab for himself what belongs to God.'

'Oh, can't he just!' Hugh guffawed. 'By cock's muddy bones, you'll soon see, ye poor innocent.'

And Stephen soon did see. The magnificent Battle Abbey was dissolved as inexorably as all the other religious foundations. The monks were evicted. The church and sacristy, the Abbot's lodgings were methodically stripped. Gold and silver plate, furniture, even the marble from the high altar were all carted away. The kitchen and cellars were emptied. Some of the ageing hams, and all flasks of the secret aromatic Benedictine liqueur, so carefully concocted each year by Brother Sebastian the cellarer, ended up in the royal palaces of Greenwich and Windsor.

In November, King Henry bestowed Battle Abbey upon Sir Anthony Browne, his Master of the Horse, member of the Privy Council, Knight of the Garter. This rich grant was all the more infamous because Sir Anthony was a Papist.

Stephen had been sent home like the other boys when the monastery was dissolved, and his father shared in a stunned indignation, but dared not show it. Peers were beheaded, gentlemen and lesser folk were hanged for criticising the King.

But Robert Marsdon was sympathetic to his younger son and agreed on the only course now open to a youth with a true vocation. Stephen should enter the novitiate in France, and they chose the Benedictine Abbey of St. Martin at Marmoutier near Tours.

It happened that Stephen rode back to Battle to say farewell to the old Abbot on the very day that Sir Anthony Browne was holding revels to celebrate his new ownership. Stephen reined in his horse, astonished when he saw that the doors were flung wide open in the noble Gothic gateway, that the courtyard was crammed with horses and lackeys. He heard raucous shouts, screams of laughter, and strident dance music emerging from the great refectory, where even six months ago there had been no sounds but gentle scriptural reading as the assembled monks ate together in seemly silence. Scarlet and gold banners embroidered with the buck crest flaunted from many windows. And as Stephen watched, increasingly pained and indignant, a giggling kitchen wench scuttled towards the cloisters which were filled with hay for the horses. She was tripped up by one of the noblemen's lackeys who threw her down on a pile of hay, and pulled up her skirt in full view of the other servants who cheered and applauded.

Nor could Stephen look away, though his gorge rose in a spasm of disgust. He watched the man's heaving buttocks between the stout, red naked thighs—shameless in their lust as dogs, as pigs.

In three minutes the man finished and got up, wiping himself, while his companions jeered.

'So soon done, weakling?'

'I'll warrant the wench is barely warmed, and we'll not deny her remedy!' Another lackey threw himself down on top of the woman whose lewd excited laugh Stephen plainly heard.

He jerked his horse's bridle, and kicked in the spurs. The startled gelding broke into a gallop and they fled down the Hastings road. In a mile Stephen pulled up his horse and retched. His heart was pounding, sweat trickled on his neck. Every fibre in him was revolted, yet he could not stop seeing those pumping buttocks, those spread fat thighs.

Stephen flung himself off the horse, and doused his head in the wayside brook, then he rode soberly back, avoiding the Abbey, and enquired at a tavern where the erstwhile Abbot might be found. The old man's lodging was in the next street; he had not been willing to leave the town he loved so well and where he had once been supreme. He opened the door himself to Stephen's knock.

'Ah, my son,' he cried and embraced Stephen. 'Benedicite! So there is someone who still cares to see me?'

'Oh, Reverend Father,' Stephen cried, 'I've come for your blessing, since I leave next week for France. Holy Mother of God,' he added, beginning to tremble, 'what that renegade monster, that devil has done to our Abbey, and . . .' Stephen choked, went on in a whisper, 'they were even fornicating in the cloister, I s-saw it.'

'Ah . . .' said John Hammond with a heavy sigh. His wise eyes examined the boy. 'You watched, my son?'

A dark flush ran up to Stephen's curly black hair. 'I could not look away. Give me penance, Father! Harsh penance.'

'Did you wish to do likewise, my son? Did you feel a stirring in that part of *you*, for you're not over-young for that.'

'By God's blessed wounds—*no*,' Stephen cried. 'It was bestial, disgusting.'

'True,' the Abbot nodded, 'unless sanctified by marriage for the procreation of little Christians. I understand you still wish to take the vows?'

'Aye,' said Stephen, 'I was born to be a monk, and I wish no other life but that which I saw you and the brethren leading at Battle. Peaceful, beautiful, each action performed for the Glory of God.'

The old eyes misted; the boy's sincerity gave the Abbot his first gleam of relief in weeks. But he had not risen to his abbacy without knowledge of human nature, as well as the crosses

119

sent to try the most spiritual souls, and he issued a warning.

'You will have struggles, my son—many a battle to wage with the Tempter. These battles may not be against chastity, I think you have not a lascivious nature; certainly not against poverty, during your years here I had no report on you concerning undue selfishness, or attachment to personal possessions, but . . .' He paused.

'Oh,' said Stephen tossing his head, 'I'll never fail in obedience to my superiors, Reverend Father. *Never*.'

The Abbot smiled ruefully. 'The test may come in a form hardest for you to endure.' He paused. 'You hate Sir Anthony Browne, don't you?'

'Why, to be sure, Father. I detest him and all his line. He's a traitor to the Church, to God. An Anti-Christ. A fawning lick-spittle heretic, no matter what he calls himself.'

'Strong words, my child, with which I am inclined to agree. In fact, during my wrath, the day he took possession of the Abbey, I made a direful prophecy to him.'

'What prophecy, Reverend Father?'

'That his line, his house, all his pride would perish. Fire and water will destroy them. I saw this in a vision.'

'May it happen on the morrow, then!' Stephen cried. 'What did he say?'

'He was affrighted, his cheeks went white. His lady fell to her knees and wept.'

'Then they should give back the Abbey,' Stephen said sternly.

'That is not so simple,' said the old man. 'The King gave it to him. And Sir Anthony is a good servant to the King. Also, I believe the knight has found a way to ease his conscience.'

'There can *be* none!' Stephen cried. '*None* but restitution!'

'You may have to change this opinion someday,' said the Abbot with a faint smile, 'when your vow of obedience will be tested.'

*   *   *

Stephen, as he ate his mutton stew in the little hut on St. Ann's Hill, thought ruefully of that day with the Abbot fourteen years ago. He had not suspected what the Abbot meant. Though later in France news filtered across the Channel that the Brownes had taken one of Battle's evicted monks as chaplain or house priest, that they had found positions for as many of the other monks as they could.

Today, Stephen knew that Sir Anthony had long ago thought of Stephen for that position, once the young man should have taken his vows. This choice had been made because of reports passed on to him first from the dispossessed English Abbot, then from the Abbot at Marmoutier. Sir Anthony favoured Sussex men, he knew of the Marsdons who came from long established Saxon blood, as the Brownes did *not*. He admired lineage.

In 1548 Sir Anthony senior died, and his son Anthony inherited a great deal of property which by now included Cowdray.

The new Anthony had great respect for his father who had managed to outlive the unpredictable monarch, and young Anthony carried out all his father's policies and wishes.

It was thus that the horrified Stephen was sent by his Order to Cowdray last summer. And found himself fully as rebellious as Abbot John had foreseen. He had loved the cloisters and the companionship of his fellows, he had loved his recent appointment as precentor in charge of the choir, for he had a fine baritone voice, and a true ear.

He enjoyed the rich ceremonies of the Church Year, the changing festivals with the emotions they engendered, and their colours. The purples of penitence, the reds, or white and golds of celebration.

At his ordination three years ago he had experienced mystical rapture. And in his heart he had always expected to fulfil Abbot John's long ago prophecy of orderly progression up the Church scale, and finally, an abbacy somewhere. In France, just possibly—by now he spoke perfect French. In Scotland, perhaps, or—if the entire Benedictine Order's prayers were finally granted—in a once more Catholic England.

Instead, there was Cowdray, and a half-hearted, half patronising, almost entirely frivolous household to be ministered to as house priest in a family which had so wickedly profited by the dissolution of the monasteries.

It would be a grave sin to pray for the fulfilment of Abbot John's other erroneous prophecy—the destruction of the Brownes by fire and water, and Stephen did not so pray, but he did pray for release if it were God's will. He tried not to realise that he was not only bored but lonely. And there was a further distress, quite unexpected.

Before he took up his duties at Cowdray he had gone to visit his family at Medfield. Both his parents were dead, and his brother Tom had married a charming, gentle Kentish cousin and already fathered a tiny son—little Thomas.

Stephen had forgotten his childhood home, and was startled to discover how dearly he loved it. The medley of warm cluttered rooms, the teeming dove-cote, the duck pond, the view of the Downs, all awakened nostalgic memories. He celebrated Mass for his brother's household in their tiny private chapel, and could scarcely keep his mind on the miracle of transubstantiation because of the warm family glow which filled him. He had never been close to his elder brother, nor did he feel so now. He was amazed at Tom's lack of book-learning, at his Sussex speech. But he saw pleasant resemblances to their father, and admired Tom's open-hearted hospitality, his vivid interest in each happening on his manor. Tom supervised everything, the repair of a leaky thatch on a tenant's cottage; the installation on the pond of an Aylesbury drake to improve the flavour of the ducklings; the erection of a tighter fence to keep out the straying sheep from the Downs; the daily welfare of his three horses, his ox-teams and his kennel of hounds. Tom was every inch the budding squire, strict yet kindly according to his principles. He was also very fond of his young wife Nan and their infant son.

Stephen felt an uncomfortable pang one twilight when Nan suckled the baby, casually unlacing her bodice, as they sat in the Hall after dinner sipping the fragrant mead Nan brewed from Medfield honey.

Stephen saw the full creamy breast, and the erect rosy brown nipple before the baby's mouth covered it with a hungry gulp. He looked hastily down at his mead tankard, and asked Tom an abrupt question about enclosure of common lands.

'Aye . . .' Tom crossed his stout legs, considering. ' 'Tis a bad thing fur poor folk. I've took me a bit o' grazing land here an' there, but I've caused no hardship i' the village. They've plenty o' commons. 'Tis different wi' the great lords, they grab an' grab miles fur their sheep or even pleasure—the stag hunts; they close the rivers so they may glut on fish, which was once plenty for all; they've hanged many an honest wight for snaring a rabbit his fathers could take freely.'

'Unfair,' remarked Stephen bitterly, though his mind was fighting the shamed fascination. He had seen French peasant women suckling babies when they came to the Abbey for alms, and been quite as unmoved as when he saw any female animal giving suck to its young. Why then this disquiet at beholding

122

Nan? Because the *child* is of my own blood, the nearest I can ever have to a son? he thought. And because—to his dismay and accustomed for years to conscience searching, he identified the other emotion—Envy. *Tom* had suffered no sudden wrenches to his life, he was the secure owner of Medfield Place, master of its gentle beauty, its comfort and abundance; a contented husband with a pretty woman to warm and care for him, and a hearty boy to carry on after him.

'Ye look a bit grim, Brother,' said Tom chuckling. 'I'd forgot ye're off to serve the son o' the very lord who turned ye out o' Battle Abbey. Ye must think us simple folk here, after all your travels. Now me—a jaunt to Lewes, market days every six month'll do *me*. Medfield's m' whole setisfaction.'

'I know,' said Stephen, sighing.

Tom looked at him shrewdly. 'Yo doant regret ye're priesting, do ye? Now ye've come back to a mighty unsettled country, where the cat jumps right today and left tomorrow. Mebbe 'twill be better when King Edward takes the reins, but now he's ridding himself o' Seymours, he's got himself a worse master. Dudley! That arse-proud, lick-spittle Dook o' Northumberland as he is now. *He's* no friend to us Catholics, an' ye may have a spot o' trouble where ye're going. I look for none here, we're a quiet lot at Medfield, not worth anyone's bother, though we do follow the old ways and the old religion best we can.'

'I'm not afraid of trouble,' said Stephen stiffly, 'and I *never* could regret my joining the Order. Never.'

Stephen left Medfield for Cowdray two days later, and knew that they were relieved to have him go, though Nan, all smiles, gave him the baby to hold and bless. A Benedictine monk in long black-robes, tonsured, with a knotted scourge around his waist and a wooden crucifix on his chest embarrassed them. Not because of the tenantry or villagers—the Marsdons always did as they pleased and were well liked. But because Stephen struck a discordant note through the Medfield harmony.

They were slightly in awe of him, his learning, his travels, his cultured speech. Tom was a great one for bawdy jokes and rough horse-play, but he felt he must suppress these during his august brother's visit. Nan intuitively knew that in some way she disturbed her brother-in-law. She stopped suckling little Tom in front of him. She stopped leaning on his shoulder when she put down his plate, or giving him the smacking kisses with which one greeted relatives, or even strangers in England. And as both Marsdons had in childhood got out of the habit of daily Mass, they found Stephen's insistence a bore.

Yet he thought back to the warm glowing week at Medfield with longing, and did penance for those moments of envy. A more poignant sorrow discomfited him when he let himself think of the cloistered years at Marmoutier, dream-like sheltered years when, he realised now, he had been completely secure and admired, doing what he most enjoyed.

Stephen finished his mutton and then, because it was Candlemas Day, 'the Feast of the Purification of the Blessed Virgin', he added a daub of honey to his loaf of white wheat bread, and drank a mugful of ale. His provisions came from the Cowdray kitchen; a scullion ran up the hill daily with a hamperful. Stephen might have eaten in the Great Hall had he wished, but he seldom did. He knew that his presence was as constraining as it had been at Medfield. He was not yet accustomed to the ribaldry and gluttony he saw around him, nor the drunkenness, nor the little plots and counter-plots for preference, nor the brawls which often broke out between visiting knights, nor the constant and apprehensive court gossip.

He smarted that the usual Candlemas procession at Vespers was forbidden. King Edward had so decreed. Lighted candles were too Papist, and Sir Anthony, though privately observant of the sacraments, saw no reason to cause unwelcome comment by disobeying the King in a minor ritual.

Stephen performed it alone tonight. He carried his little painting of the Virgin into the crumbling, draughty chapel next door, placed it on the bare stone altar and reverently lit three candles to *Her*.

He knelt for the devotions, and in the wavering light Her mysterious smile widened, there appeared to be a dimple near Her mouth; he thought She looked down on him with tenderness. As he finished the last *Ave* he felt a bursting love in his chest, and an ecstasy of devotion almost like that he had felt during his ordination. His discontent and loneliness dissolved in a flood of healing balm—surrender, and joyous submission.

He lifted the crucifix from his chest and kissed it. He remained for hours on his knees, and without knowing that he did so, he chanted Her hymn of praise—*Salve Regina*—in a voice which filled the chapel and drifted out through the unglazed windows to vibrate among the oak, the holly and the elms on top of St. Ann's Hill.

Stephen was too exalted for sleep that night and was still joyful as he carried his lantern down the hill in the winter blackness and strode to Cowdray for six o'clock Mass. He did not remember warnings from the wise Abbot at Marmoutier that God seemed to have so willed it that ecstatic moments of communion and release were usually followed by rigorous trials. He officiated happily at the Mass, which was attended by all the servants, and in the lords' gallery, a few of the highborn. Four ladies today.

There was little Lady Jane Browne, bride of a year, and five months pregnant. She looked ill. Her plain anxious face was haggard, her eyes dark-circled. Prayers for her safe delivery were always included. Beside Lady Jane there was the haughty young dowager, old Sir Anthony's widow whom Stephen had immediately disliked when he first met her; and also young Sir Anthony's sixteen-year-old sister, Mabel, a fat, slothful girl given to snorts and giggles even at Confession. She snuffled now through the responses since she had a cold, and toyed constantly with a new emerald bracelet.

There was also Ursula, Lady Southwell, who cornered Stephen again as he was leaving to remind him that her niece would go up to his hut at noon. He had forgotten and thanked her for the reminder. As he left he passed the chapel door and saw the 'Dowager' Lady Browne sitting in a pew, and frowning with an odd intense expression on her painted face.

Ordinarily, Stephen would have hurried on—one of the old woodcutters was dying and had sent a request for the last rites.

But, Geraldine Browne glimpsed him and called out imperiously, 'Come here, Brother!'

Stephen entered the chapel and stood by the pew. 'Yes, Lady?'

Geraldine turned up to his face her striking agate-blue eyes. Irish eyes, fringed with thick black lashes, but hard and opaque. The examined Stephen insolently.

'I wish you to deliver a message for me,' she said at last, drawing a sealed letter from the velvet pouch which dangled from her belt. 'You appear more discreet than many of your ilk.'

Stephen flushed. The elder Sir Anthony's widow might be

somewhere in her twenties. She was said to have been scarce sixteen when she married the father. She had brassy hair elaborately curled around her widow's cap. Her skin was fine and very white beneath a coating of rouge and orris powder. Many men would consider her beautiful. She had been born Elizabeth Fitzgerald in Ireland, daughter to the ninth Earl of Kildare, but insisted on the name 'Geraldine'. Her childhood must have been as turbulent as her family's fortunes which rose to preferments and sank to attainders, imprisonment and executions, according to the Irish policies of King Henry and Cardinal Wolsey.

Geraldine's father had died in the Tower, accused of treason. Her half-brother and five uncles had been hanged at Tyburn. Her brother, 'Lord Gerald Fitzgerald', rightful Earl of Kildare, was currently supposed to be lurking on his Irish estates in County Kildare, wondering what King Edward's attitude would be under the Duke of Northumberland's new power.

Stephen had heard some of the story, but had been able to feel neither interest nor sympathy in this woman, whose confessions were arrogant and perfunctory.

'Deliver a letter?' he asked warily. 'And *discreetly*? An odd request, lady. Surely one of the pages . . .'

'No,' she said compressing her lips. 'Pages babble. I ask simply that you take this letter tonight at nine to the Close Walks, where a messenger will be waiting for you.'

Her tone annoyed him. Her demand for a servile act of mysterious complicity in some intrigue repelled him. 'I am here,' said Stephen, 'to fulfil my duties at Cowdray. I cannot see that this errand forms any part of them.'

'God's blood,' Geraldine cried through her teeth, 'you think my commands of no consequence? You will soon see differently. I'm the unconsidered dowager now, my family is ignored and I, too. By the Holy Rood, I vow this condition shall alter!'

'It may be so,' said Stephen shrugging. 'If it be God's will.'

Her stone-blue eyes gave him a look of fury, then the lids dropped. When she spoke her tone had changed, become throaty and coaxing. 'Do you not know why I am called the "Fair Geraldine"? That the poor Earl of Surrey immortalised me in beautiful lovesick sonnets which are famous throughout England?'

She put her white beringed hand on his sleeve, paused, then quoted more softly,

'Fostered she was with milk of Irish breast;
Her sire an earl; her dame of prince's blood
From tender years in Britain she did rest
With King's child where she tasted costly food.
Her beauty of kind, her virtue from above
Happy is he that can obtain her love!

'That poetry and much more Lord Surrey wrote about *me*,' she said smiling.

'Fine verse, no doubt,' said Stephen curtly. 'I have heard that Lord Surrey wrote sonnets to you, but so long ago, lady, that surely you were then a mere child—unless rumour is false.'

Stephen had little knowledge of women, but was able to recognise and recoil from blatant feminine lure; and he touched by instinct on a sensitive spot, for Geraldine had managed to conceal the thirtieth birthday soon approaching, as she hid the premature whitening of her red hair by secret chemical rinses.

'For sooth, I *was* a child,' she said hotly, taking her hand from his arm. 'You have scant manners, Brother Stephen.' Her voice rose higher. 'I hate Cowdray, buried here in Sussex mud among yokels. 'Twas bad enough when I was Lady of the manor, but now—forced to yield place to that little meaching whey-faced Jane! But, no matter, I see remedies. And I *will* apply them.'

Stephen had no idea what she meant, nor cared. 'I must hasten,' he said. 'Old Peter Cobb, a wood-hewer, is dying.' He bowed slightly, and hurrying from the chapel immediately forgot Lady Geraldine.

*   *   *

Down in the valley of the Rother, Cowdray Castle's big bell clanged for noon, as Midhurst parish church followed from the town, one note behind. Stephen, in his hut on St. Ann's Hill, mechanically repeated the office for the hour, then cut himself a slice of bread and cheese.

Peter Cobb had died at once after receiving the rites, and Stephen was thinking of death, its dignity, its awesomeness, as he heard a timid knock on his wooden door.

He opened it and stared at a village girl in a russet wool gown and homespun shawl; though it was confined on her head by a knotted linen kerchief, her yellow hair tumbled down her back to the waist. She looked up at him, and he felt a shock of puzzled recognition, a feeling that he knew, not the face, nor the shy look of the shimmering sea-blue eyes, but the person behind them.

'Lady Southwell, my aunt, said I might come,' she said nervously, twisting her chapped hands as he did not speak. 'I'm Celia Bohun.'

'Aye—' murmured Stephen collecting himself. 'We've met before, I think?'

She shook her head. 'I seen ye once from a distance, crossing the Rother, as I went to Cowdray. I ne'er thought to meet ye, but Aunt Ursula, she told me to come up 'Tan's Hill at noon.'

His attitude disconcerted her, he looked very black and forbidding as he stood with hand on either door jamb, as though to bar the way inside, staring down at her with a frown.

'I can go back agen,' she faltered, blushing. 'I doan't want to pester ye, Father.'

The February wind blew bitter from the Downs, and Stephen saw that she was shivering. 'No, no,' he said brusquely. 'Come in to the fire. I promised Lady Southwell I'd see you. And though I am a priest, Celia, I am also a monk. You should call me Brother Stephen.'

'Oh,' she said, still embarrassed. It seemed strange to call this pillar of dignity and obvious reluctance Brother. She followed him uncomfortably into his hut, where he prodded the burning oak log. He indicated the three-legged stool on the hearth.

'Sit down, child, and we will start with the state of your soul. Can you say the Creed?'

Celia moistened her lips, dismayed by his peremptory tone. 'Not—not well,' she stammered. 'Mother'd only take me to church Christmas an' Easter. I forget . . .'

As he waited without speaking, she began hesitantly, 'I believe in One God, the Father Almighty, Maker of Heaven and Earth, and things vis—vis—'

Stephen shook his head. 'In *English*?' he said sharply. 'Oh, I know 'tis the law of this country at present, and the parish priest obeys, but it's wrong, Celia. You must learn the Latin. Stand up!'

He clasped his hands and bowing towards the crucifix began reverently, 'Credo in unum Deum, Patrem omnipotentem factorem coeli et terrae . . .'

The sonorous words meant nothing to her, but she listened with startled pleasure to his beautiful voice, and joined his 'Amen' in a whisper. He looked at her and suddenly smiled. The smile startled her, the flash of even white teeth, the up-turning of his lips transformed his sombre face.

She smiled back timidly, her eyes wide and rueful. 'I could *never* learn that, B-brother Stephen. It sounds like the organ music we had i' the church when I was liddle. The King's men smashed the pipes.'

'Aye . . .' Stephen sighed and motioned her to sit again.

Though she had been born right after the Dissolution, King Henry's vandalisms and robberies had been concentrated on the great monastic foundations, and he had never been one to suppress music like the new young King who was each year plunging deeper into fanatical Calvinism.

'But, Celia, you *can* and shall learn the true Credo, the Pater Noster and the Ave Maria, and I'll teach you the Cate-chism. We'll have lessons. You can come noon-times.'

'If you like, sir . . .' she said uncertainly. The prospect seemed formidable. 'Most whiles this hour I'm no greatly needed at the Inn, 'twixt breakfast an' dinner.'

'Very well, then.' He seated himself in the arm-chair. 'Today, we'll find out what Lady Southwell has been able to teach you. Recite the alphabet!' Stephen had lost the flash of recognition and intimate knowledge of this child and settled himself into an obvious duty, but he was a good teacher and soon put her at ease. Her feelings of rebellion vanished and she answered readily. Time went fast until Stephen glanced at his hourglass and rose.

'Enough today. You've keen wits for so young a maid. We'll soon astonish your aunt.'

'Thank ye, sir,' she said glowing. 'I wish above all to please Aunt Ursula who's so kind to me.'

Stephen inclined his head, thinking that perhaps Lady South-well's ambitious plans for the girl might yet be justified, and that it was agreeable to have the moulding of a mind, while leading the spirit towards a state of grace.

As Celia turned to go she glimpsed the corner of the hut near the chapel, and cried, 'Oh-h—' when she saw the small painting of the Virgin. She ran over to it, and her pink mouth fell open. 'Who's that?' she cried. 'So beauteous. I ne'er saw

129

a woman so comely. Is't a picture of your mistress, sir? Do ye love her?'

Stephen stiffened. He flushed at the blasphemous implication. Celia looked up at him, puzzled, enquiring, until he suddenly realised the extent of her innocence and smiled.

'I adore Her,' he said quietly. 'My poor child, that is the Blessed Virgin Mary. God's Holy Mother.'

Celia blushed, seeing that she had said something foolish. 'I'm sorry, Brother Stephen. I s'pose you couldn't have a leman, to be sure, a priest couldn't, I *have* heard so. Yet, I didn't know God's Mother'd look like that.'

'Nobody knows how She looked on earth, but many painters have shown Her as they think of Her now—the Queen of Heaven.'

Celia nodded thoughtfully. 'This painter believed She was fair-haired like me? And are Her eyes like mine? I've only seen my eyes once when I crept to the looking-glass i' the red velvet chamber at Cowdray. Aunt Ursula hurried me away.'

'Rightly so. You should never indulge in vanity!' Stephen spoke sharply because Celia's long eyes *did* rather resemble those in the portrait, so did the colour of the hair. He stood in front of the picture as though to shield it from desecration. 'Go now,' he said.

She clutched her shawl around her. 'I'll be here on the morrow?'

He almost denied her, for an instant he wished never to see the girl again, but his duty restrained him. He had never in his life broken his word. 'At noon,' he said, made a perfunctory blessing and turned away.

*   *   *

So began nearly six months ago Celia's noon-time visits to Stephen on the top of St. Ann's Hill. He never admitted to himself that he looked forward to them with increasing fervour, and was disappointed when either his duties at Cowdray, or hers at the Inn prevented. He did not notice that she blossomed during this period, that her figure took on new curves, and her little face grew lovely. He permitted himself to rejoice in the quickness of her spiritual progress. She mastered the Latin creed and prayers he taught her first by rote, earnestly repeating every word after him, then he taught her to recognise many Latin words in his black-letter vellum missals. He also taught her simple arithmetic, and in the teachings gradually corrected her Sussex accent and grammar. Her ear was remarkably quick, and it never occurred to him that her progress was spurred on by anything but innate ability, and possibly her strain of gentle blood. Celia herself did not know why she was eager to please him. She did know that she worked very hard to win his rare warm smile of approval.

And sitting in the window-seat of her aunt's room on July 25, watching for the King to come, beneath the excitement of the occasion, she was acutely aware of Stephen's present humiliation and danger.

Sir Anthony had dared take no risks. The presence at Cowdray of a Benedictine monk as house priest would certainly enrage the King or Northumberland's spies. To leave Stephen on St. Ann's Hill was scarcely safe.

Everyone in the town knew that he lived there, and there were always malcontents whom the hope of silver might cause to tattle.

Sir Anthony had commanded Stephen to betake himself to a certain secret room off the cellars near the latrine pit in the south wing. A damp cubicle which had already served to hide several fugitives from royal wrath, during the past troubled years.

Celia knew with her heart how Stephen had rebelled against the concealment and hypocrisy. She guessed from the few words he had said that he had prayed desperately about the matter and finally agreed because Sir Anthony, smiling but obdurate, asked what the Abbot of Marmoutier would decree if he were there to be consulted.

Stephen knew what the Abbot would say. Obedience. Temporal obedience to his worldly master, when the Papist cause would in no way be helped by defiance. So Stephen was shut up in a cell next an ordure pit, and Celia knew that he was suffering.

Suddenly she heard the blare of trumpets and saw banners waving and horses trotting along the Easebourne road. The Cowdray cannons, primed for days, began to boom.

'They're here, Aunt!' Celia cried, pressing her nose to the pane. 'That must be the King, riding alone, what an odd hat like a plumed pan-cake—he's but a meagre lad,' she added startled.

Ursula joined Celia at the window. 'To be sure, child, he's not full grown, and near died of the measles and pox last spring, God bless and preserve him. He favours the Seymours, I believe—and yet,' Ursula squinted her far-sighted eyes, 'there's a look of his father, too, a swagger—the way he sits the horse.'

The King and his procession disappeared from their view, after turning up the stately avenue of oaks, and the castle bell began a frenzied pealing.

'We'll go down now,' said Ursula, squaring her bony shoulders. 'Hold yourself proud. Bohuns've as much right as any in the land to meet the King.'

Five

The Royal Banquet at Cowdray in the great Buck Hall that July evening continued until the sun dipped behind the western block of buildings across the courtyard, and the castle bell rang out seven strokes.

The young King's conversation flagged; watchful eyes noted that his fair skin grew paler.

The banquet proffered by Sir Anthony Browne—who kept a master cook once trained in France at King Henri's court— was sumptuous. It consisted of exotic dishes Edward had never tasted, for he had been kept to simple fare by order of his careful tutor, John Cheke, and by the posthumous directions of his father, King Henry, who had died rueing his own gluttony. John Cheke, however, had not been able to accompany his charge on the Progress, for he was recovering from desperate illness.

Edward, who since his arrival at Cowdray, had already applauded a masque in his honour, taken part in an archery contest, and watched a stately tennis match, was very hungry when he finally sat in the centre of the dais at the High Table. He had guzzled down beef spiced with cinnamon, a rabbit pasty and a fat capon leg. He also, though accustomed to ale or sack, had politely drunk a large crystal goblet of Muscadine from Sir Anthony's famous cellars.

Yet still, the procession of servers continued their ceremonious entrance from the kitchen quarters bearing golden platters which they offered kneeling for the King's approval. He refused jellied larks, roast peacock and salets of summer greens, but he could not resist the sweets. There were gilded honey-cakes studded with almonds. There were raspberry and blackberry flummeries, swimming in yellow cream and sparkling with the rare and costly white sugar Edward had seldom savoured.

And he could not refuse to taste the cook's masterpiece. It was a marchpane confection six feet high and represented the royal arms in full colour.

Edward brightened with a boyish chuckle as he ate a piece of the lion's tail and the tip of the unicorn's gilded horn.

Then, he gave a resounding belch and turned to his host on his right.

'In truth, Sir Anthony,' Edward said, 'you have marvellously, nay, excessively banqueted me. I shall write so to my poor Barnaby who suffers privations in France on my behalf. Poor chuck, I miss him.'

'I grieve, Your Grace,' answered Anthony smiling, 'that you should lack for anything or anyone. Would I could conjure Master Fitzpatrick to Cowdray this instant!' As he spoke he instantly considered this confirmation of the King's affection for the Irish lad, Barnaby Fitzpatrick, who had been raised with him and once acted as his 'whipping boy'. Anthony decided that the Irish connections might be useful, for Barnaby was related to Elizabeth, the dowager Lady Browne, 'Geraldine' as she preferred to be called. Anthony glanced towards the end of the High Table where his step-mother was murmuring in obvious intimacy to Edward Fiennes, Lord Clinton—a chunky, shrewd, businesslike baron of forty. Clinton had commenced a rising career at court by marrying King Henry's first cast-off-mistress—Betsy Blount Tallboys; then upon that lady's death he had prudently allied himself with the house of Dudley and thus with Northumberland, the all-powerful duke. Then Clinton discovered in himself strong Protestant convictions which led to preferments. He became Knight of the Garter, Ambassador to France whither he had shepherded young Barnaby Fitzpatrick, and now he was Lord High Admiral of England. And a widower again. Could the Lady Geraldine possibly entice Lord Clinton? Anthony thought while examining his stepmother hopefully. Aye, perhaps— He watched her and Clinton exchange sips from each other's goblets. Such an alliance would be extremely helpful, and what a relief for poor Jane (and Mabel, his sister) to be free from that haughty vixen at Cowdray.

Anthony had always ignored Geraldine's advice, but it occurred to him that it might be through her influence over Clinton that her brother Gerald had at least been restored to some of his Irish lands in County Kildare, though not to the earldom, which was attained. Indeed, what Catholic could hope for a peerage under this reign? Anthony sighed. He himself owed the King's visit to Cowdray's location near Petworth and Edward's agreeable memories of Anthony Senior. The young Anthony had been largely ignored by Edward's Court, and the King's phalanx of guardians. Also, that sudden imprisonment in the Fleet had been most sobering. Anthony was neither a timid nor an imaginative man, but he had a composite vision of all the severed necks and spouting blood which followed upon disagreement with kings. The latest spouting neck had been the most shocking, for it was that of the Lord Protector, Somerset — the King's own uncle — yet that was partly Northumberland's doing.

Northumberland — born plain John Dudley, fifty years ago, whose grandfather was said to have been a common Sussex carpenter — had mounted the glittering ladder of titles with firm, implacable tread and reached the Dukedom.

Was his influence on the delicate royal lad the result of witchcraft, as was constantly whispered? Anthony shuddered and forced his mind to less dangerous thoughts while he sugared and drank another goblet of wine.

Edward had turned to Sir Henry Sidney who sat next to him by royal command, for Edward shrank from nearness to strangers. And though he denied it even to himself, he had, since his attack of measles, been troubled by deafness. Henry Sidney had a voice which carried. Sir 'Harry' was nine years older than the King, but his boon companion, gentleman of his Privy Chamber, and official cup-bearer. Harry was clever, amiable, well informed and knew precisely the kind of political or theological talk which interested Edward. Harry, too, had recently allied himself with Northumberland through marriage to the Duke's daughter, Mary Dudley. And the net closes — though what it will snare next only heaven — or hell — knows, Anthony thought, angrily checking his errant mind by considering Edward's other and few close friends. Besides Harry Sidney, and Barnaby Fitzpatrick, and Sir Nicholas Throckmorton — a boisterous merry youth who evoked Edward's rare moments of Tudor gaiety — there was John Cheke, the boy's tutor and mentor whom he greatly revered.

It was known from Sussex to the Scottish Border (as every act of Edward's was promptly known) that during Master Cheke's grave illness in May Edward had imperiously prayed for his tutor's recovery. Prayed to that preposterous Calvinistic God of his who abhorred altars, candles, statues, church music or Latin, chantry prayers for the dead and His Holiness the Pope. A God who even more incredibly forbade invocations to saints or the worship of His Own Divine Mother.

Yet all these aberrations must be endured. Trivial outward compliance mattered little if the spirit were not affected.

Anthony remembered for a second his house priest, hidden now in the stinking cell behind the latrines—but there would be only two more days before Brother Stephen might be released, and the chapel refurnished with its crucifix, sanctuary lamp, statues of the Blessed Virgin and St. Anthony of Padua, his own patron. Patron saint too, of that provocative little wench old Lady Ursula had so surprisingly produced as a niece. Anthony gazed down the Hall and glimpsed the girl's golden hair and bluish gown at the far end. Then he started as Edward suddenly addressed him.

'We're weary of sitting at the table, Sir Anthony,' said Edward, rising. 'What do you propose that we do until evening prayers, after which we retire?'

Anthony jumped to his feet, instantly rejecting all the amusements which would normally pass an evening—cards, dice-playing, dancing—of none did the King approve. More music then? But Edward, though said to be fond of some music, had shown no interest in the dulcet harmonies which had been wafting from the minstrels' gallery. A hundred people rose when Edward did, and waited with their faces turned expectantly.

'There's a Spanish juggler, Your Grace, very apt, and he has a monkey . . .' Anthony blurted out. 'If he would divert you, I'll summon him at once.'

'*Spanish* . . .?' Edward's eyes hardened, his boyish voice deepened to extreme displeasure. 'Do you encourage the natives of Spain, sir?'

Anthony reddened and cursed himself for a heedless fool.

'Certainly not, Your Grace, I mis-spoke, I only meant that he seems dark-visaged like a Spaniard, and speaks that broken sort of English. 'Twas only that the monkey's tricks are laughable.'

Edward continued to frown. 'I've no love for Spain,' he said coldly. ' 'Tis the Spanish half of my sister, the Lady Mary's grace, which hinders my true affection for her, that and her wicked. mule-headed Papacy.' He looked up at Anthony. 'I've not yet spoken to all your guests, sir. I hear there are several so-called Papist nobles among them.'

'Aye,' said Anthony, though he chilled inside. '*Erstwhile* Catholics, but have seen their errors. They have come today to do your homage, Sire, they are utterly and loyally your liege men.'

Sir Henry murmured something, apparently calming, in the King's car.

Edward nodded and said more gently, 'Well, Sir Anthony, my father loved your father, and the *sons* shall be friends. I'll now willingly mingle with your company.' He looked at the cluttered tables. 'There are other rooms where we can be more at ease?'

Anthony bowed and motioned the way to the massive richly-carved new staircase which led up to the private chambers and Long Gallery.

The King ascended alone, though Harry Sidney followed close. Anthony gave his arm to Jane and was perturbed that she dragged up each step with a painful sigh.

'Brace yourself, my lady,' he whispered. 'You must take the presentations!'

Jane knew this, for as an earl's daughter she out-ranked her husband.

'Aye . . .' she breathed.

Anthony noted his stepmother and Lord Clinton, mounting arm in arm. He heard his little sister Mabel's high nervous giggle as she bounced along, twittery as a partridge. Pity the girl was so fat and plain-featured, and so unaccomplished. She had been given music and dancing lessons to scant avail. She had neither ear nor grace. Her passions were for eating, chattering and finery. It would be hard to find her a good husband, though it was true that the girl had lacked a mother's watchful shaping. Geraldine had never made the slightest effort, averring that Mabel was dim-witted and tiresome, calling her 'lump of suet' and 'greedy-guts' in moments of exasperation while always begrudging the gifts Anthony goodnaturedly gave the girl on Feast Days.

They all arrived at the Long Gallery which had been newly wainscoted and furnished with crystal candelabra for the occasion. There were fresh-painted wall hangings and a new Flemish tapestry of unicorns and virgins wandering through a misty forest, which the King affably admired. He stationed himself in front of the tapestry on a velvet covered court chair, and waited.

Lady Jane dutifully came up with a gaunt dignified woman in tow.

'May I present to Your Royal Grace, my former stepmother, the Countess of Arundel,' she said, her tone breathy, and her eyes mournful, for her thoughts dwelt continually on the tiny shrunken corpse in the bedchamber.

The boy frowned uncertainly. Jane's voice was hard to hear. 'Eh . . .?' he said irritably, '*Arundel . . .?*'

The Countess bowed, she advanced unsmiling and sketched a kiss over Edward's hand, not touching it. Edward's eyes narrowed. He knew that Northumberland hated the Earl of Arundel, who, since Norfolk's attainder, headed the Catholic peers, and that the Earl had recently been released from the Tower where he had been confined on evidence so flimsy that even the Duke could not detain him.

'Your noble lord is not here, my lady?' asked Edward.

'No, Your Royal Grace,' answered the Countess in a voice as smooth. 'He is confined to his bed at Arundel. He has fever contracted in a most unhealthy place.'

'Hmm-m . . .' said Edward. 'We are grieved to hear it. God send him quick recovery.' He inclined his head. The Countess curtsied stiffly and withdrew.

There was a small uncomfortable pause. Edward, who was growing tired, struggled between politeness to all his subjects and unwillingness to endure other awkward encounters.

Sir Harry Sidney again murmured in Edward's good ear, and the boy sighed acquiescence.

'My lady,' he said to Jane, 'Harry tells me that yonder near the door there are a clutch of Dacres.' He smiled faintly. 'I know *of* them, to be sure, but have never met any.'

The listening Anthony went to round up the Dacres. There were six of them, from two families—Dacres from the South who lived at Hurstmonceux Castle in East Sussex, and the Dacres from Gilsland who had travelled down from Cumberland to summer with their cousins.

In presenting Dacres to the King, Jane and Anthony who scarcely knew one lot from the other were hesitant on the matter of precedence.

Geraldine Browne had been watching sardonically from beside Lord Clinton and she now glided up. 'Your Majesty . . .' She threw a little contemptuous glance towards her stepson and his sickly wife. '*First*, may I present to you, Lady Dacre of Gilsland and Greystoke who lives at Naworth Castle in Cumberland. Her lord, Warden of the West Marches, is at present engaged in the Border disputes. Lady Dacre has here three of her children—Sir Thomas, Leonard and Magdalen.'

'Ah . . . so?' said the King, grateful for this concise, clear introduction, though somewhat surprised by the brisk authority of the young dowager whom he had scarcely noticed. He extended his hand to Lady Dacre.

She gave the thin young fingers a hearty kiss while she made a clumsy bob and said, 'Much honoured, Your Gr-race—and God gi' ye health! These're ma youngsters.' Lady Dacre thrust forward Sir Thomas, a huge, bulky youth with bristly red hair. Then, a second even taller young man who held one shoulder higher than the other by reason of a broken, badly twisted collar-bone. 'Leonard,' said Lady Dacre, patting him. 'An' her-re's ma braw lass, Maggie.'

Magdalen like her brothers had red hair and was amazingly tall. Though only fourteen, she had little gawkiness, nor self-consciousness. She kissed the King's hand with a smack as hearty as her mother's.

Anthony had drawn back to watch the new presentations and was relieved to see that the King's frown had cleared to amused interest.

The Dacres from the North were an imposing quartette. Lady Dacre and her daughter towered over the company, while the brothers must have stood six foot three at least. Moreover, their homespun clothes appeared very old-fashioned and plain among the jewelled velvets, satins, lace ruffs. Uncouth 'Border Lords', Anthony thought, rough and independent as the wild Scots whom they constantly fought. Yet, there was about them a dignified simplicity. The mother . . . Anthony racked his memory. She had high-born English blood, hadn't she? Was one of the Earl of Shrewsbury's dozen children—though her speech held the Northern burr and her manners were unpolished by court standards. Still, Lady Dacre and her large offspring were rather like lumps of honest sea-coal among a trayful of spangled gewgaws.

The Southern Dacres were still awaiting presentation and Geraldine became less brisk. 'The Fiennes branch, Your Majesty,' she said, glancing towards Lord Clinton who was himself a Fiennes, and from whom she had garnered her information. 'Lady Dacre of Hurstmonceux and her son Gregory. Not the *titular* baroness any more, Sire, since the tragic miscarriage of justice in the lifetime of your royal father . . .'

Edward raised his sleepy eyelids while he submitted his hand to a perspiring matron in black velvet, and a wizened boy with a vacant look who clutched at his mother's skirts.

' "Tragic miscarriage of justice"?' said Edward, strangling

139

a yawn yet alert to any possible criticism of his father's law-making.

Geraldine's assurance wavered. She looked again towards Clinton who stepped forward, having admired Geraldine's spirited performance as she intended him to.

'Your Royal Grace,' said Clinton, his speech whistling a bit from the loss of his upper front teeth, 'Lady Browne refers to the unfortunate hanging of Lord Dacre at Tyburn twelve years agone, whereupon his title and estates were forfeited.'

'The hanging at Tyburn of a *peer*?' said Edward, incredulously. 'How could that be? And for what crime?'

'The shooting of a gamekeeper,' said Clinton shaking his square, grizzling head. ' 'Twas all engineered by enemies who coveted the Dacre estates.'

'Monstrous, indeed,' Edward cried, looking sympathetically at the debased baroness, and interested not so much by the injustice as by the vulgar manner of the punishment.

'Moreover, Your Grace,' pursued Clinton, 'this unhappy lady is daughter to Lord Abergavenny, and her murdered husband was my kin. We dare to hope that your royal generosity and clemency will consider restitution, especially to a family so wholeheartedly dedicated to the Protestant religion—as you know *me* to be, also.' Clinton bowed and gave his sovereign a hopeful, albeit gap-toothed, smile.

So *that's* it! Anthony thought. It explained the presence of the Dacres; it partially explained the presence of the Lord High Admiral, though from what Anthony had been observing, Cupid's darts had also pierced the heart of the middle-aged widower.

'We will consider this matter, my lord,' said Edward, 'after consultation with the Duke when he returns from Berwick.'

Geraldine gave Clinton a quick triumphant glance. *They* knew and Sir Henry Sidney knew that the Duke would be agreeable to this comparatively trivial request, for even Northumberland would need support from every possible quarter to further the extraordinarily daring plan he was formulating. One which would catapult every Dudley connection into supreme power.

'We will proceed to your chapel for evening prayer,' Edward said, taking Sir Harry's arm while he swayed in a moment of giddiness.

'Your Grace is unwell?' Harry whispered anxiously, knowing how Edward hated the transient weaknesses he had never known before the sickness in the spring. 'To bed with you, at once!'

Edward shook his head irritably and straightened. 'Your chaplain is waiting, I presume?' he said to Anthony, who was prepared for this.

'My own chaplain is ill, sire—oh, nothing dangerous, some distemper of the bowels—the Midhurst vicar is here to conduct prayers.' And, by Christ's blood, I hope he doesn't falter, Anthony finished grimly to himself. The vicar was a stupid man and barely literate, but he had been well rehearsed.

The King and his company jammed themselves into the lords' gallery, the rest of the guests packed the chapel below. There was no room tonight for the servants.

Edward, after one satisfied glance around the denuded chapel, was fortunately too tired to heed the mumbling ineptness of the vicar's rendition of the English prayers Edward himself had helped to write. But the evening was not yet over.

*　　　*　　　*

Lady Ursula and Celia had remained in the Hall with the lesser folk while the privileged ones went upstairs. They had known nobody, nobody spoke to them, and Ursula, against all reason, felt hurt and disappointed. She had formed foolish hopes for this first evening of the King's visit; she had expected that in some way her darling would be noticed; that something fortunate would happen to insure Celia's future.

She had anxiously mulled over Celia's horoscope again and decided that this was an extremely favourable day.

Yet, nothing *had* happened except Sir Anthony's brief greeting in the morning. The futility of her hopes was further emphasised by Celia's instinctive behaviour when the blue-liveried servitors were clearing the immense clutter left on the tables. Celia, bred to a life of clearing cluttered tables, jumped up to help.

'*No!*' said Ursula sharply. 'Sit down, child!'

Celia, blushing, sat down beside her aunt on a small oaken chest at the side of the Buck Hall. They sat in silence until the steward announced portentously that the King was in the chapel and everyone must assemble for evensong.

'Evensong . . .?' murmured Celia. 'What's that, Aunt?'

'Vespers, possibly,' snapped Ursula, exasperated. 'But, remember Sir Anthony's warning! . . . Whatever these heretic prayers are, don't listen to them. Say a Pater Noster to yourself, then an Ave.'

In the chapel Celia forgot this admonition, she was so much interested in the girl who stood beside her. They all stood. The prayer seats had been removed, since this strange religion apparently permitted no kneeling.

Celia, though moderately tall herself, looked up in amazement at the head a hand-span higher than her own. She examined the profile, the sprinkling of freckles over a snub nose, the bush of wiry fox-coloured hair which curled loose on the broad shoulders—as befitted a maiden. The girl's simple gown was of russet wool over a white lawn underskirt. The neckline was wide and square. Magdalen wore no fashionable ruff or frills and no jewellery except a necklet of the polished crystal pebbles which were known as 'Scotch diamonds'. The girl's clothes gave out an agreeable woodsy smell which Celia's sensitive nose appreciated but could not identify as peat smoke and heather, since she had never encountered either. The girl felt Celia's gaze, looked around and smiled, showing broad even teeth, white as milk. 'Will there be muckle more of this gobbing?' she whispered, jerking her head towards the vicar. 'I canna hear a word o' it, an' 'tis hot as hell's pit in here.'

'Sh-h,' whispered Celia with a nervous look around, but she giggled, and a dimple showed near her pink mouth.

'I'm Magdalen Dacre,' said the girl, ignoring Celia's 'Sh-h'. 'Who are *you*?' Her smallish eyes were the clear brown of an autumn oak-leaf, and they examined Celia with friendly admiration.

At this fresh disturbance the two people on either side of the girls both moved. Lady Ursula turned to check her niece, and Sir Thomas Dacre craned over his sister to look. 'Yon's a tasty dish next to Maggie,' he said out of the corner of his mouth to his brother Leonard. 'A sight for sore eyes. Have a keek for yoursel'.'

Thomas drew back so that Leonard might examine Celia who reddened under the stares of both men then dropped her lashes modestly.

Magdalen chuckled and said, 'The Dacres admire ye, lass, Have a care, there's na woman bor-rn safe fra those two cock-a-hoop gallants.'

Celia understood the tenor of Magdalen's remarks, and was pleased. She felt the first stirrings of feminine power, a delicious sensation which lasted through the vicar's final drone — 'Grace-of-Our-Lord-Jesus-Christ — love-of-God — Fellowship-of-the-Holy-Ghost-be-wi'-us-all-e'er-more—Amen.'

He turned and scuttled down from the pulpit being thoroughly frightened by the presence of the King and his own lord of the manor—Sir Anthony.

The chapel congregation shuffled around and waited until the King should leave the gallery. The Dacres, like Lady Ursula and Celia, knew nobody among the crowd of councillors, knights and equerries brought by the King, nor the few Sussex gentry, all of whom surged past Celia and her aunt, while Magdalen cried, 'Whew, let us gan oot o' her-re, I'm fair stifled!'

Celia was very willing; the young people drifted out through the elaborately fan-vaulted stone porch to the courtyard and the girls sat down on the rim of the castle fountain. The Dacre men stood over them while they all chatted. Though shy at first, Celia soon gained ease, and readily answered questions, expanding to Magdalen's eager interest, and the admiration in the young men's yellow-brown eyes.

Lady Ursula, meanwhile, made enquiries of Hawks, the castle steward, intent on knowing exactly who the red-headed trio were. The answers pleased her. For all their rustic clothes and strange speech, the Dacres of the North were powerful Border Barons, who constantly intermarried with the Nevilles of Westmorland and had therefore a strain of royal blood through the Nevilles' ancestress, Joan Beaufort, daughter to the Duke of Lancaster and Katherine Swynford. Sir Thomas Dacre, the heir, was himself married to a Neville of Westmorland, though where the lady was now, the steward could not say. Ursula instantly crossed off Sir Thomas; but re-examined Leonard, the second son. A pity his back was slightly awry, and his hair and heavy beard so decidedly sandy in colour. Still, thought Ursula, who was groping her way in the hitherto unknown maze of maternal ambition, the Dacre association was not to be scorned. She walked benevolently out to the courtyard and joined Celia on the fountain's curb.

Thus it was that they all heard the herald's trumpet blast, announcing important visitors at Cowdray's gatehouse.

Upstairs, Edward heard the notes of the trumpet and recognised a special flourish reserved only for the arrival of a King's messenger, and though the boy was already on his way to bed in the octagonal state chamber, he checked himself and went to a window. He looked down at the messenger whose livery was emblazoned with the royal badge. 'Another complaint from that pestilential Spanish ambassador, do you think?' he said to Harry Sidney. 'Or,' he added, brightening, 'could it be a letter from Barnaby?'

At that thought he forgot his weariness and regardless of etiquette ran down the great staircase and into the courtyard. 'What have you brought me, Dickon?' he cried.

The messenger fell to one knee and smiled up at the eager boy.

'Letters from France, sir, and one from the Duke in Berwick.'

Edward nodded happily and took the folded red-sealed squares of parchment. 'Good,' he said. 'We will read them at once in our chamber.'

'Also, sire . . .' said the messenger, still kneeling, 'I have conveyed gentlemen hither, from London.' He indicated two men who stood waiting by the entrance. One was slight and young, dressed as a courtier in a crimson satin slashed doublet, small white ruff and short embroidered cape. He doffed his jaunty plumed hat when the King looked his way, thereby disclosing masses of chestnut curls.

The other man was unmistakably a physician. His scholastic gown with long hanging sleeves, the shape of his fur collar and the square-cornered black hat suggested his profession. His ebony staff engraved with the Aesculapian symbol, the huge leather bag which hung from his arm, and his copper neck-chain from which dangled an orange-red jacinth stone (sovereign preventive of plague) all confirmed it.

Celia, her aunt and the Dacres had hastily left the fountain kerb when the King ran out to meet the messenger with Anthony and Harry Sidney hurrying behind.

Celia had not seen the King close before—only from the other end of the vast Buck Hall—and she stared fascinated at the slight pale boy in violet satin, so encrusted with pearls and brilliants that he shimmered like a candle through the gathering twilight.

She barely glanced at the middle-aged physician who held back quietly in the shadows as the young courtier strode up to the King.

Edward stared hard at the impudent pug-nosed face, and his chin rose slowly in a Tudor gesture of disapproval, while Geraldine Browne suddenly erupted from the porch and came running, then cried in dismay, 'Gerald!—Gerald, what do you here?'

Edward's attitude expressed the same question. He turned to Geraldine, saying coldly, 'So this *is* your brother Gerald Fitzgerald, my lady? I thought him to be in Ireland.'

So had Geraldine, and she was much disturbed at the reckless young man's appearance just as her careful plans were beginning to bear fruit.

'Have you sanction to enter England, Master Fitzgerald?' asked Edward frowning. 'And, by what right do you force yourself into my presence?'

He well knew that the Fitzgeralds were a rambunctious, untrustworthy clan who had produced several traitors to the Crown in his father's reign, and been very properly hanged. In April, Northumberland had advised restitution of a small part of Fitzgerald's estates, with the understanding, Edward had thought, that the young man would stay there. Fitzgerald's tenuous relationship to Sir Anthony Browne, as brother to the Dowager, had been brought forth as reason—that and Lord Clinton's rather surprising reminder that through their mother, Fitzgerald had a drop or so of Plantagenet blood. Edward knew little of the Irish in general except that they were all unruly Papists, and Northumberland distrusted them. Edward had even seen the Duke's distrust of Barnaby, and had, in this one instance, been firm. But Edward never thought of Barnaby as Irish.

He was to be reminded now, for Gerald Fitzgerald smiled apologetically, and spoke in a soft wooing voice.

'I crave your clemency, my liege lord, and happy I am to see you in good health. I'd not've left County Kildare except for a matter of advice needed, and Your Grace's well-known wisdom.'

'Well,' said Edward non-committally.

' 'Tis about Barnaby Fitzpatrick, Your Grace—his old father is gravely ill. We know little in Ireland about Court affairs, and thought Barnaby to be with you, sire. His poor distracted mother, my kinswoman, begged me to find Barnaby and tell him of his father's plight. Pardon me, Your Grace, if I have erred.'

There was contrition in the beguiling voice, charming penitence in the blue eyes, which were like his sister's, but lacked the hardness.

At once, keenly touched by the mention of Barnaby and his father's state, it did not occur to Edward that Gerald's excuse was a trifle lame, that many another messenger could have been found to carry these tidings. He hastened to assure Gerald of forgiveness, and said he would give the matter of Barnaby's recall his immediate concern. That they would talk in the morning and, 'Sir Anthony,' he turned to his host, 'you will see to Master Fitzgerald's board and lodging, of course.'

Anthony bowed, as he glanced at his stepmother's relieved face. She'd have to find room in her apartments for this unforeseen brother, there wasn't an empty bed or pallet in the castle. And whatever's afoot, he thought cynically, they'll have a mort of time to confer with each other.

'Is yonder physician with you, too?' Edward asked, indicating the silent figure in dark robes. He was perturbed for Barnaby, and very tired again, but he had been trained from infancy to deal with all matters in an orderly, comprehensive way, He disliked loose ends.

'Oh, no, Your Grace,' Gerald said airily. 'It's some astrologer or doctor, I believe. He says little.'

'You there!' called Edward beckoning. 'Come here and state your business!'

The man moved forward, removed his hat, bowed once and said in a deep calm voice, very slightly accented, 'I have been sent to you, Your Majesty, by Master John Cheke, since he is still too feeble to travel. My name is Guiliano di Ridolfi, once of Florence. I took my doctorate of medicine at the University of Padua, though I have been long in this country where I am called Master Julian.'

Edward did not catch all of this. He said crossly to Harry, 'What's the fellow saying? *Who* sent him?'

'John Cheke, Your Grace,' said Harry Sidney.

'*Cheke!*' cried Edward with incredulous anger. 'What for? My health is excellent. There are my London physicians-royal if I wanted one, but I certainly don't need a *foreigner*. I don't believe Master John Cheke sent you! 'Tis forward and presuming.' The boy's face crimsoned, furious tears started to his eyes. 'I believe you're a Spanish spy!' he shrilled suddenly, beginning to tremble.

Julian looked at the angry boy with dismay and silently tendered a letter of recommendation from John Cheke.

Edward stamped his foot, and knocked the letter from the physician's hand; it flopped to the dusty flagstones. 'No doubt a forgery,' Edward shouted. 'And you are unwelcome near our person. I bid you leave at once!' He whirled around and stamped back to the castle, while Harry Sidney hurried after him.

Julian Ridolfi stood stiffly alone near the gatehouse. The great mansion was being lit up by hundreds of wax tapers, their light shone in the courtyard. All the onlookers including the Dacres had followed the King inside, but Ursula put her hand on her niece's arm. 'Stay—wait a bit!' she said. 'I think I know that poor doctor. I believe he may be the same astrologer who instructed me years ago at the Duke of Norfolk's.'

Ursula hesitated, peering at the motionless bearded figure, aware of both excitement and reluctance, that she was making an important decision which went deeper than accosting a man who had incurred royal anger.

Julian showed nothing of the effort he was making to master his humiliation. Only his eyes, the dark grey eyes of a North Italian would have disclosed the vehemence of his feelings, but they were hooded by the heavy lids. He was not immoderately ambitious, but he was proud, and had suffered of late years. John Cheke's mission had delighted him. He had expected with certainty that it would lead to appointment as a court physician, Julian knew himself to be far better educated and more able than the bumbling English doctors. He had been totally unprepared for this shameful reception. He had not been able to avail himself of the astrological indications he used for others, since he did not know the exact day of his birth, only that it had happened in November, forty-eight years ago. He might thus have seen the light in Scorpio—the physician's sign, or in Sagittarius, sign of the philosopher and wanderer. Both suited him, but he had felt—without any divinations—that his lean, scruffy years of hardship were to be glitteringly transformed.

He hated the mean rooms over a barber-shop in Cheapside where he had lodged ever since the princely Norfolk family who had employed him were plunged into disgrace. The old Duke was imprisoned in the Tower, and Julian's particular patron, Henry Howard, Earl of Surrey, had been summarily beheaded five years ago.

Julian had eked a living by occasional collaboration with the surgeon-barber in the shop below, by alchemical and philosophical studies and by the casting of horoscopes. It had been by great good fortune that John Cheke had heard of him one day last autumn through Cheke's own manservant who had gone to the barber in a frenzy of fear to be cut for a stone in his bladder. Julian, request by the barber to help hold the struggling patient, had instead brought from his rooms a thick tincture of poppy heads to dull the man's pain and then a secret concoction learned at Padua for disintegrating the stone. The servant, delirious with gratitude, had mentioned this to his master. And one day Cheke summoned Julian to his home. The men had liked each other, they were both learned and shared a deep interest in astrology and alchemy. Their religious differences were not apparent. Julian, though nominally a Catholic, of course, had no convictions, and amiably agreed to Cheke's Protestant tenets. He frequented Cheke's home and there met other astrologer physicians, including the renowned young John Dee, whom Julian considered an agreeable charlatan, an enthusiast whose claim to the title of Doctor had no foundation.

Julian's great chance came in May when John Cheke was smitten with plague in its most lethal form of sweating sickness. King Edward, who was kept far away from his tutor for fear of infection, attributed Cheke's recovery to prayer. But Julian attributed it to his own cool-headed ministrations. He used a remedy well known to the Viennese—it was composed of powdered jacinth stone, and a handful of common garden phlox, dissolved together in a pint of fresh ox-blood. Cheke recovered, and was so grateful that last week when he began to fret about his young King, and the strenuousness of the Progress as reported to him, he dispatched Julian to Cowdray.

Despite compassion for the King's hysterical outburst, which he knew to be a symptom of the very overtaxing which Cheke dreaded, Julian was still unable to repress rage at the public repudiation. He was a member of the great Florentine banking family, Ridolfi de Piazza; one of his uncles had married a Medici, and their son had become a cardinal. His own father had been a Florentine senator, an intimate of the Medicis. Julian's young mother who died at his birth was a daughter of the lesser *nobilitá*, and Julian's childhood in a grim old *palazzo* near the Arno had been lonely but luxurious. At thirteen Julian had been inducted into the hectic Medici court life. He had been a ducal page for five years, during which he did nearly as much drinking, brawling and wenching as the rest of them. Yet, he had been discontented, even bored, until one day his father sent him on a mission to Padua, and Julian chanced to attend a medical lecture by Dr. Fracastorius at the famous University. It was a rousing dissertation on the French pox, which Fracastorius poetically named 'syphilis' and included a revolutionary theory of contagion. Then Julian attended lectures on the teachings of Galen, Avicenna and Pythagoras. They ignited in Julian a hitherto stifled spark. A physician he would be. All the branches of advanced knowledge were exciting to him, as he discovered after enrolment at the University—arithmetic, physics, astrology, alchemy and the concoction of remedies, geography, the science of music. He studied them all with as much enthusiasm as he watched Master Benedotti dissect a cadaver.

Unfortunately, Julian's father had decreed for his son an entirely different career—Ridolfis were always politicians, courtiers, occasionally soldiers, it was unthinkable that one of their number should descend the social scale into the dubious ranks of unprofitable scholarship and doctoring.

Ridolfi considered his own physician as barely on a social par with his major-domo, or his scribe.

Upon finding that Julian could not be persuaded from his preposterous designs and had already enrolled himself at Padua, Ridolfi flew into one of his thundering rages, and disowned the boy. He also disinherited him; though later, his family pride not being quite able to stand the thought of a starving Ridolfi, he sent his son a pouch full of gold florins which enabled Julian to get his doctorate and to travel. After his graduation from Padua, a restless enquiring mind drove him towards new scenes. He visited the universities at Louvain, and at Paris, where in 1533 he met the brash young Henry Howard, Earl of Surrey, who though only sixteen had conceived a passion for translating Petrarch, and was himself writing sonnets in the Italian form. Julian was drawn to the young nobleman who reciprocated the interest, partly because Surrey's rash enthusiasms were at the moment engaged by anything Italian.

These encounters resulted in an invitation to England. Among his household of a hundred retainers at the Castle of Kenninghall in Norfolk, Surrey had thought that an Italian physician—trained at Padua, and also adept at astrology—would be an addition.

The next spring, after further letters, Julian availed himself of this offer, and was installed at Kenninghall as a member of the Norfolk ducal household.

For nearly ten years he was content. The life suited him, and he liked Norfolk county which was seldom colder than northern

Italy, and in that ducal family he was considerably more comfortable than he had been since quitting his father's *palazzo* in Florence.

Then, in 1546 came the disaster. The Earl of Surrey, already known as 'the most foolish proud boy who is in England', incurred the touchy wrath of King Henry the Eighth. Surrey, with astounding bravado, sported his legitimate right to exhibit the royal arms in his quarterings—but he put them in the wrong place; in the heraldic quarter which proclaimed a right to the throne.

The Norfolk family had often enough been chastised for presumption, and had many enemies. Henry's father, the old Duke, was flung in the Tower where he languished even now, while on January 21, 1547, young Henry Howard, Earl of Surrey was beheaded for high treason.

The King's men commandeered Kennnighall and all the Howard property. Julian, with the other retainers, was expelled to shift for himself.

And he *had* made shift, accepting with bitter resignation the sudden changes in fortune resulting from despotism and greed. Julian had seen plenty of that in his youth among the Medici.

Nevertheless, despite his philosophy, this new blow tonight disturbed him profoundly. Nor was the disturbance entirely selfish.

The young King had about him a death look. Julian was sure he could dispel this, at least for a while. And strong in Julian, among many less altruistic traits, was a desire to heal.

During the ten minutes in which Julian stood in Cowdray's courtyard, most of the lights were gradually extinguished in the castle. The King had at last retired, and Sir Henry Sidney had given strict orders that there must be no noise to bother His Majesty.

As the gateward truculently approached the discredited doctor, Ursula made up her mind.

She walked up to Julian, with Celia trailing uncertainly behind her, and said, 'Are you not the Italian astrologer whom I met at Kenninghall some years ago when the Norfolks still lived there?'

Julian started, then collected himself, he stared through the dimness at the elderly widow who addressed him. His long Italian face tightened to wariness. 'I do not understand you, Madam,' he said. Reference to the attainted Norfolks was

150

dangerous. In London he had suppressed all mention of his Norfolk years, even John Cheke did not know of them.

'Yes, yes—I'm *sure* that I've heard you speak,' cried Ursula. 'You taught me some astrology, you were kind, you also physicked my poor husband, Robert Southwell, knight—and you made me a good-health amulet.'

Julian now did vaguely remember among Kenninghall's myriad guests in those days, a feeble old knight and his alert youngish wife who had pestered him with astrological questions. And though her face and voice were pleasant, he did not understand why she was accosting him, nor welcome her indiscreet speech. 'I believe you are mistaken,' he began, but Ursula shook her head. She glanced at the hovering gateward whose itch to do his duty showed by a tapping foot and a clutching of his shoulder-pike.

'You've no place to go, have you?' whispered Ursula. 'They'll not permit you in Cowdray. Come along!'

She put her hand under Julian's elbow and hustled him past the gateward and out to the mounting blocks. It was then that Julian noticed Celia, who was as startled as he, but tagged along with her aunt.

There was a bonfire outside, built by the folk who had gathered around at Cowdray hoping for a glimpse of the King. Sir Anthony's guard and the King's own guard were busily keeping order, while the castle servants lugged out tubs full of broken meats left over from the banquet.

'Here—' said Ursula, shoving Julian to the shadowy side of a large oak. 'We can talk here freely.'

'What about, Madam—' He was increasingly suspicious, while her hurryings and bustling added to his humiliation.

'We saw it all, did we not, Celia?' said the lady putting her arm around the girl whose big wondering eyes he saw fixed on him with sympathy.

'There'll not be a bed in Midhurst tonight,' went on Ursula, 'nor are you one to sleep i' the dew-wet grass like a rustic. But you *should* stay over, the King may alter his mind on the morrow, lads fly into fits of passion, then forget them. And you cannot trudge back to London—a man of your position. 'Twould be shameful. You'll not find a horse in Midhurst, either, at any price.'

Julian sighed. He had only a little loose silver in his purse. His hostile dismay lessened, for Ursula spoke the simple truth. He was wearied by the journey, though he had ridden to Cowdray on one of the King's own horses, commandeered by Master John Cheke. It was, of course, no longer available. Moreover, he had had neither food nor drink since the eleven o'clock dinner at Horsham. The King's messenger had set a gruelling pace, and though it was dry near Cowdray, most of the lanes they traversed had been mired to the horses' hocks.

'It is so, lady,' said Julian, 'I know not where to go.'

'You can have my garret at the Spread Eagle,' said Celia suddenly. 'I may sleep in your bed here, my lady Aunt, may'n't I?'

Celia's impulsive offer was precisely what Ursula had in mind, but she loved her niece all the better for it.

As for Julian, his heritage and experience instilled renewed suspicion. What had this pair to gain by kindness, though after all an attic room in an inn was hardly commensurate with his hopes which had envisioned dignified acceptance in Cowdray Castle.

'You are both most courteous,' he said warily. 'Madam,' he frowned towards Ursula, 'may I ask of you one thing? Will you forbear to speak of our earlier meeting at Kenninghall?—which I do remember. Those years are better effaced. For *both* of us. My former patrons are one of them beheaded, the other still imprisoned in the Tower. You are quite able to see that such a bygone association is perilous in these times.'

'Aye . . .' said Ursula after a moment. 'I see. And will respect your wishes. But . . .' she added in a rush, 'I pray you to cast Celia's horoscope. I feel that I've made errors. It is so difficult, I've scant aptitude at figuring.'

Julian bowed, 'Nihil esse grate animo honestius,' he murmured with an ironic intonation.

'Is that Latin, sir?' asked Celia, thereby astonishing Julian who had been talking to himself. He looked at the girl—abundant fair hair, a lovely little face, a trifle square in the jaw for an Italian's taste, very young, and the voice though low and sweet had a rustic tinge.

'It is Latin, my dear,' he said. 'Seneca—who has a fit saying for every occasion, and it means, "Naught more honourable than a grateful heart", and was my answer to your lady aunt's request.'

'It grows very dark,' said Ursula. 'We must hasten, and we dare not take the Highway—robbers, beggars . . .' She frowned then caught sight of a boy in the Cowdray livery scuttling by with a lantern. 'Simkin!' she called. 'Come here!'

The boy came reluctantly, but he knew Lady Southwell as one of Cowdray's inhabitants, who must therefore be obeyed. He accompanied them with his lantern as they took the short-cut to town, across the footbridge over the Rother, and up St. Ann's Hill.

When they got to the top, and the crumbling walls, Celia stumbled and made a queer sound, half-gasp, half moan.

'Are you hurt?' asked Julian; he could see that she had put her hands to her eyes. 'Did you twist your ankle?'

'No,' whispered Celia, choking. This hill top ... so dark and desolate. She had never been to Stephen at night, but she had several times crept up in secret, to watch the yellow candlelight flickering inside the hut, and sometimes glimpsed his handsome profile bent in prayer. The emptiness now pierced through her chest. While she had forgotten him, had been laughing and bantering with the Dacre family, fasci-nated by the King, absorbed in Master Julian's predicament, Stephen was shut up like a foul beast in a cage. And from the conversations she had overheard, today she had begun to realise the risks for Stephen. A local squire had jestingly told a tale at dinner about a house priest caught hiding in a cup-board not ten miles from Midhurst. And how the sheriff had spitted 'the scurrilous Papist knave' through the belly with his sword, and so carried him through the village streets, howling out 'Misereres' and convulsing the spectators by his blood-spurting contortions and gurgling screams.

Celia had sarcely listened to the tale, but the force of it struck her now, and she ran down the hill ahead of the others. Her heart had scarcely stopped thumping, when they all arrived at the courtyard of the Spread Eagle Inn.

The courtyard, the parlours, the tap-room were jammed with roisterers. There was a constant banging of tankards, the roar of lewd songs, the squeal of whistles and recorders and the monotonous shouts of the extra servitors hired for the occasion in response to the bawling of thirsty customers: 'Anon'—'Anon, your worship!'—'Anon, sir!'—'Ye shall be filled, anon!' while the brown ale splashed from the taps into a continuous file of tankards.

It sounded like Bedlam, Julian thought grimly. He had often visited the new hospital for lunatics in London, out of desire to try his own concoction of soothing hellebore on the inmates.

A dull familiar pain had come on in his cheek-bone, and a hollow ache in his midriff, both exacerbated by the futility of this venture. But he had no alternative. 'Where do I go, maiden?' he said to the girl.

Ursula and Celia were about to guide him through a covered alley to the outside back-stairs which gave access to Celia's garret when there was an outcry and fresh confusion near a parlour door. 'Where's the barber?' someone yelled. 'Where's the leech? He's wanted. Quick!'

A harassed little gentleman also dashed out of the door crying, 'A leech! A leech!' in a high frightened way. The gentleman caught sight of Julian who had drawn back against the wall to escape the jostling, but whose long sleeves, lappetted cap, staff and bag were unmistakable.

'Are you a doctor, sir?' cried the little man wringing his hands. 'My wife is taken bad, she must be bled.'

Julian nodded distastefully. 'I am a physician. What's amiss?'

'M'wife. Mistress Allen. She's taken a fit. Pray come, sir!'

Julian tightened his lips but followed the agitated husband into the small parlour where Ursula had first met Celia.

A stout woman lay twitching on the rushes which were fouled with her vomit. Her face was purple as a plum, she made angry gobbling noises. Someone had unhooked her bodice and the heavy breasts sagged out sideways. The land-lady was fanning her with a pewter trencher. Julian waved the landlady aside, and felt the patient's pounding pulse. He pushed up her eyelids and smelled her sour breath.

'Bring me a basin,' he said, and opening his bag extracted a sharp iron lancet. He nicked the woman's arm vein thinking that he had sunk low indeed. Blood-letting was a barber's work, and the woman was drunk. Those of an obviously choleric humour were prone to fits when they were drunk. 'Put a compress of fresh horse-piss on her brow,' he said to the landlady, and to the husband he added, 'Get her to bed, no need for concern.'

The little man still looked frightened. He put his hand to his mouth and whispered in Julian's ear, ' 'Tis not the plague, sir? God and His Holy Mother save us, we came here through Tunbridge where there was plague.'

'It is *not*,' answered Julian with certainty. He had seen all forms of plague, and knew every symptom, he knew the fancies of a plague victim whether he were infected with the suppurating black boils, or the sweating sickness he had cured John Cheke of.

'God gi' ye grace, sir,' said the skinny little man whose eyes watered with gratitude. 'Take this, if it be enough!' He held out a gold sovereign. 'Christopher Allen, esquire, of Ightham Mote in Kent, will ever be friend to ye.'

Julian accepted the coin with a nod, and said, 'I give you good night, Squire.'

Now that the little drama had ended, the goggling spectators and the landlady all vanished into the boisterous taproom. Ursula and Celia had watched from the doorway, and Julian saw them waiting patiently to show him to his garret room. He felt a quick glow of content, of warmth towards these two women whom he had never set eyes on before this evening. It was a peculiar sensation.

He had known many women. During his youth at the Medici court he had satisfied his rampant lusts with any willing female. He had enjoyed an infatuation with a contessa, and followed through the requisite procedure of love poems, clandestine fondlings, delicious fears of discovery by a jealous husband. He had even, moved by the example of many of his fellow courtiers and also of Leonardo da Vinci whom he greatly admired, embarked on a love affair with another young page, a silken-haired lad from Siena.

This affair had been briefly piquant, and then so dull and demanding—the boy wept like a girl, he pleaded and made scenes like a girl, yet was not a girl—that Julian realised now the decision to become a student at Padua was partly influenced by a desire to break with the dissolute Florentine life.

The passing years and his increasing pleasure in his profession had lessened carnal desires. Such occasional urges as he had were amply satisfied in London by a stupid young woman, the plump daughter of the barber whose upper storey he rented. Her name was Alison and she was a widow. Last year she had borne a son she said was his. Julian had accordingly made her an allowance, and permitted the baby to be christened Julian. But lately, since he had known John Cheke, and dormant ambitions were awakened, he had begun to think in terms of the advantageous marriages which he saw constantly taking place in all layers of society. His thoughts had gone no further than this. He had counted on his introduction to the King.

Bitter disappointment, a face ache and a belly ache were the only result, yet he now felt for the kindly elder lady and the kindly young girl that surge of grateful warmth. It was like opening a shuttered window on to a sunlight garden—bright-spangled with flowerets among the welcoming green, a sensation as sweet as it was inexplicable.

Julian slept well that night on Celia's lumpy straw pallet. Ursula slept well next to her niece in the great testered bed at Cowdray. The other castle inhabitants, including the King, slept heavily from surfeit and exhaustion, or, in the cases of Sir Anthony and Geraldine, from the assurance that their projects were going nicely, hopes were maturing, dangers had been avoided.

Only two were sleepless. Stephen in his noisome cubicle under the south wing, and Celia who loved him and felt his suffering in her own body, yet found her restless mind returning again and again to a scene which had nothing to do with Stephen. A monstrous compulsion reproduced the twitching fat empurpled woman who had lain on the filthy rushes of the Spread Eagle parlour. At the time she had felt only the fascination inspired by any shocking curiosity—like the two-headed babe exhibited at the Midhurst Fair—but in recurrent memory there was a growing fear which reason would not allay.

So uncomfortably fearful did she become that she finally slipped from bed, and kneeling below Ursula's crucifix said an imploring Pater Noster in the melodious Latin which Stephen had taught her.

'Libera nos a malo,' she whispered, over and over, until the words lost meaning. Presently she ceased to implore or even to feel.

She sluiced her face in Ursula's pewter basin, combed her hair and put on yesterday's peacock-brocade gown. The room was stuffy. She opened the casement window and sniffed at the dawn-bright air. It smelled of damask roses, of gilly flowers and stock from the pleasaunce. It smelled of the distant Downs, a mixture of dewy grasses and sheep dung.

Celia inhaled deeply and glided out of the room. She ran down the little privy stairs and out of a side door into the gardens, intent only upon freedom.

Six

The remainder of the King's visit to Cowdray held nothing discomfortable. Edward awakened in high spirits, and Sir Anthony provided the amusements which Edward enjoyed.

There was jousting embellished by an allegory—a contest between the champions of 'Youth' and 'Riches'. Six on each side, thundering up and down the tilting green in their gilded armour, with the plumes waving on their helmets, breaking lances, unhorsing each other and receiving applause from the King who keenly watched the manoeuvres. Once, Edward took a lance himself on the side of 'Youth', and challenged his host. Anthony was so expert at tilting that he managed to break his lance, and fall from his saddle without Edward quite knowing how it happened. The boy crowed with glee.

'See you not,' he cried. 'I shall be as fine a jouster as my Father's Grace! When I've reached his size, there'll not be a knight in the kingdom can best me!'

'True, sir—in troth, you are near so already,' the company shouted. And, indeed, that day they all believed it. The King's lassitude and pettishness had vanished. Nobody thought of doctors, nobody remembered, nor wished to, the intrusion last night of a grave Italian physician reportedly sent by John Cheke.

At Cowdray the sun shone all that July day. The young people romped decorously, they shot at the butts, they played a game of Hoodman Blind through the gardens and the maze, almost as far as the close walks. Edward insisted upon being 'it' for a time, and happened to catch Magdalen Dacre, which caused much merriment in which the King joined, crying that he had snared a lioness and feared she would devour him. There were those who missed dancing and gay music, but even the older folk who remembered King Harry's bacchanalian revels, admitted the charm of youthful simplicity and forgot care in watching their young King. Sir Anthony and the other secret Catholics ceased for that day to worry about their futures, or the sinister Duke and his policies. Even Geraldine and her brother, the jaunty Gerald, laid aside their plottings, while Geraldine applied her entire energies to the further enslavement of Lord Clinton. She succeeded so well that the shrewd Baron forgot his caution, and seizing Geraldine behind a rose trellis, embraced her passionately while murmuring endearments.

Geraldine's inward triumph was masked by pretty confusion and sufficient coyness in exhibiting and then withholding her charms that Clinton was inflamed with a lust he had not felt in years, and finally proposed marriage. He even agreed that they should at once announce their betrothal to the King.

This they did during dinner, when the King was not yet surfeited, and was munching the last morsel of a Southdown baby-lamb chop.

Clinton suddenly appeared at his side, holding Geraldine's hand.

'Your Royal Grace . . .' said Clinton, lisping a little for lack of the teeth, and looking as sheepish as a stout middle-aged courtier could, 'we crave Your Majesty's approval.'

Edward stared at his Lord High Admiral, at the prominent eyes, the network of purple veins above his cheek beard, and was amused by the incongruous lisp and diffident air. 'What is it, my lord?'

'The Lady Elizabeth Browne and I wish to wed, sire, and soon.'

Geraldine curtsied and managed to blush a little beneath her artful face paint. 'It is true love, Your Grace,' she murmured sweetly, then remembering the King's deafness, repeated, louder, '*True Love*,' and simpered.

Edward knew nothing of true love in that sense, though he understood affection. He did know the importance of proper marriage among his nobility, and quickly considered this one. It seemed an unequal match. The dowager Browne had no assets that he knew of, and she seemed to him of a very ripe age—and was Irish, to boot. A Fitzgerald. Still, there was the trickle of royal blood and Clinton was rich enough, and important enough to ignore the other drawbacks. And surely the *Duke* approved of Clinton. Edward wished the Duke were here to advise, then suddenly decided that was silly. He was nearly grown, he need not everlastingly rely on protectors and regents, while underneath ran uneasy realisation that he was afraid of the Duke.

'You have our royal consent,' said Edward grandly. 'You are old enough, my lady, to dispose of your own hand.'

158

Geraldine winced and cried, 'My brother Gerald, he is head of my family, and is in complete accord.'

She looked around for Gerald, but he had unfortunately sneaked off from the banquet to indulge his passion for dicing with a couple of equerries.

Anthony Browne came to her rescue. 'In the absence of Fitzgerald, Your Royal Grace, I take leave to sanction the re-marriage of my father's widow.' He bowed to the King, and clapped Clinton on the back. 'Ring?' he hissed, adding to himself, Give the woman a ring, you old cock. You've been through this business twice before and you act like a moon-struck yokel dithering before an outraged father.

Lord Clinton hastily drew a gold and ruby signet ring from his thumb and put it on Geraldine's outstretched finger. The betrothal was accomplished.

Celia watched the pantomime at the High Table from the other end of the Hall. She could hear nothing at that distance, and the resplendent figures bowing and curtsying meant noth-ing to her. Since her morning escape into the garden she had continued to feel as unreal as the carved wooden buck heads which looked down on them all, eleven pairs of sightless eyes, eternally remote from the glitter and the noise.

Leonard Dacre had found means to sit next to her, though her position was inexorably fixed by the steward, 'below the salt'.

Neither Ursula's commands nor entreaties would improve Celia's seating. No wench from the tavern, be she twenty times niece to a negligible knight's widow, had a right to gentry status. The girl was extremely lucky to be seated at all, even on a lowly bench. That she owed this honour to Sir Anthony's casual direction yesterday, only the steward knew, and was far too busy to speculate about.

Nor did Celia. She listened absently to Leonard's crude love-making, as he hunched his lanky body over her, and put his raw-boned freckled face close to hers.

She ate the collops and mince pies. She drank the ale which was served at the lowest table, she listened to a spate of North Country wooing, most of which she did not understand, until the young man, increasingly fired by both her beauty and her indifference, cried, 'By Christ's blood, lass—will ye no *look* at me? Am I so ill-favoured?'

Then, she turned her golden head in its demure heart-shaped cap, and gave him a small puzzled smile. 'I'm bemused,' she said apologetically.

The smile further undid him. Its charm, its dimple, its mysterious unawareness. He had wenched since he was thirteen. He had never had a rebuff, not *he*, a Dacre of Gilsland. Dacres took women, high or low, when and if they wanted them. He and Tom kept tallies, they notched a certain oak beam, over the cellar door at Naworth Castle. Since their full manhood, Tom had suffered the slight handicap of marriage. The Neville wife was jealous, and her family powerful. To counterbalance, as Tom affectionately pointed out, Leonard had the twisted shoulder—the uglier face. But Leonard had found these no detriment. He knew his real prowess, and there was many a lass along the banks of the Irthing, and even as far afield as Newcastle and Carlisle who received a few groats every New Year's Day for the rearing of his bastards.

'Hark ye, lass—' he shouted, as Celia balanced a chunk of mince pie on her knife, and ate it vaguely. 'Where do ye lodge? It's wi' yonder stravaged lady, your aunt I believe,' he pointed up the table to Ursula who was watching them with wary approval, 'Or at the tavern where they tell me ye're often serving wench?' Leonard, too, had been making enquiries.

'At times the one, at times the other,' answered Celia, mopping her trencher with a piece of bread.

'By the Virgin, will ye play cat and mouse wi' a *Dacre*!' Leonard cried.

'You must not swear by *her*,' Celia said catching her breath. ' 'Tis dangerous. Very dangerous.'

'How's that?' Leonard cried, his hand clutching at his dirk.

Celia shook her head. ' 'Tis dangerous for *all*, but in especial for . . .' She sighed, and to Leonard's astonishment her wide sea-green eyes began to shimmer with tears.

'Ye love a lad who is in danger . . .?' he asked sharply. Intuitions were foreign to him. This one was measure of the emotion this strange, unapproachable lass aroused.

'It is so,' said Celia, bowing her head.

Jealousy was now added to Leonard's ardour. It released the natural instinct to lay hands on a desired possession. He grabbed Celia by the neck, upturned her face and bit her lips while he forced his hand into her bodice. Her response was instant. She clouted his ear with a resounding slap.

The pages and equerries nearest them burst into guffaws. Amorous scuffles were common enough, but the piquancy of this one was enhanced by knowledge that the great red-headed lout had no business sitting among them, anyway. However uncouth and ill-dressed, he *was* a noble.

Leonard darted a furious glance at the laughters, and stalked up the Hall where he squeezed himself in next to Magdalen. He did not look at Celia as he pushed past her, his emotions shuttled between resentful respect for her, and heightened desire. Such complexity was baffling and he received his sister's spirited teasing in sulky silence.

Sir Anthony, whose eyes were hawk-keen, saw and interpreted the bit of by-play, even while he parried a sudden spate of embarassing questions from the King. Had Sir Anthony had to deal with much furtive Papistry on his estates? Or were the tenants of Cowdray, Easebourne, Midhurst, Battle and the rest, properly convinced of the diabolical errors in the old religion?

'Oh, entirely so, Your Grace,' said Anthony quietly, and on guard. But the King's eyes were truly guileless, he had obviously forgotten Anthony's own imprisonment for hearing Mass last year, as he had forgotten much which happened before his illness.

'What is your opinion, Sir Anthony, of our new royal chaplain, the Scottish John Knox?' asked Edward with genuine interest. 'He marvellously expounds the true doctrines of Calvin, does he not? Have you studied Master Knox's tract on the abomination of the Mass, and kindred idolatries?'

'Not yet, Your Grace, I shall procure a tract at once.'

'Although at times,' Edward continued reflectively, 'I find Master Knox a trifle unyielding, he and the Archbishop often do not agree on points in my beloved new Prayer Book. I dislike their squabbles.'

Anthony suppressed a smile. He was touched by the boy's evident pride in the new version of the Church of England Prayer Book and delighted to hear that Knox, the fanatical arch-enemy of Catholicism was subjected to any check, even from one as wishy-washy and opportunist as Archbishop Cranmer seemed to be.

'The Duke will soon join me on the Progress,' Edward went on chatting, half to himself and half to so pleasantly receptive a listener. 'At Salisbury, I believe . . .'

Deo Gratias! Anthony thought, and would it were *farther* from here.

'Your Royal Grace had a letter from the Duke last night?' he enquired.

'Aye, he draws me a plan of the new fortifications at Berwick. Most subtly wrought, and will insure peace on the Border. All my lord Duke's ideas are of surpassing cleverness ... He hath even a new devise for the Succession, which I will profoundly consider.'

Anthony was so startled that first he could not believe his ears, then was betrayed into a thoroughly impolite 'What?'

Edward stiffened, he raised his chin in a gesture like his father's.

'My illusion was indiscreet, Sir Anthony, and you will at once forget it. There is nothing settled.'

Anthony had instantly recovered, he bowed and smiled gravely. 'I shall not refer to the new fort at Berwick, Sire, though mention of it seems *not* indiscreet to me, nevertheless, I quite understand that the Scots being ever slippery, and the Border so ticklish, it is best to ...' He babbled on until Edward was entirely reassured, and doubted he had spoken of the Succession at all.

But, on Anthony a lurid, sinister light had burst. He could guess at no details, but he at last guessed the gist of Northumberland's plot. Somehow, the succession of the Princess Mary, and then the Princess Elizabeth was to be altered, though it had been decreed by King Henry himself. Somehow, those Dudleys were going to seize the throne. *De juro* — Northumberland already had *de facto* regal powers.

And a member of his own household, that precious Geraldine with her newly affianced Clinton were in the plot, one which Anthony had thought of no more consequence than a widow's personal anglings to catch a good marriage and restitute her brother to his earldom.

Perfidy! Anthony thought, disgusted and fearful, too.

He had always felt great pity for the unfortunate Princess Mary whose religion was his own; he had less sympathy for the fiery-tressed Lady Elizabeth who was currently living like a nun in sobriety and neglect at Hatfield, and who though a professed Protestant, and once Edward's dear playmate, was now known to be in his bad graces. Northumberland's doing — of course.

Though the Princesses had been declared in and out of bastardy, according to the old King's whims, yet never had he denied that he *was* their father. They were as royal as Edward

—Mary, indeed, was more so, since her unhappy mother, Catherine of Aragon, had also been royal.

His speculations and forebodings were perforce checked by a restless movement from the King, and the need to provide the next acceptable entertainment.

Anthony had by now gauged his guest's tastes. He had, this very morning, instructed his steward to send for a troupe of mountebanks who were temporarily living in tents on the Highway to Petworth. The mountebanks were unmistakably English (no more errors like that), they tumbled, and they juggled, they also had a dancing bear, and a clever little mongrel which strutted around on its hind legs, dressed in a black monk's habit, and clasped its forepaws at command, then collapsed at intervals before a little wooden altar complete with crucifix, which its master placed before it.

When he viewed this trick the King shrieked with laughter. So did all the company who crowded around in the courtyard. Anthony felt no more compunction for the travesty than he would have at watching the re-enactment of Greek Temple rites, or Babylonian dances. The dog's antics bore no relation to his true religion. Lady Jane felt otherwise. She made a stifled excuse and escaped to the bedchamber, where she knelt sobbing by the unburied corpse of her baby.

Celia—she was jammed into the outer passage by the butteries—also felt otherwise when by craning and peeping over shoulders she saw the little dog in the monk's habit. She had begun by laughing with the others, the dog was comical. Then, the trailing black robes, the sham tonsure—a wig plastered on the dog's head—its shrill yelps when the altar appeared, all suddenly appalled her. She looked sideways to the left, where the south wall stood. Somewhere under that must be Stephen. He could perhaps hear the raucous merriment.

She had passed through diverse torments last night. Her healthy youth rejected more misery. None the less, she could not bear this.

Master Julian was doubtless still occupying her attic. In any case, the Spread Eagle had become distasteful to her. She crept up one of the many old stone staircases, and climbing into Ursula's bed, tried to sleep.

*   *   *

At the Spread Eagle that evening, Julian was enduring the

company of the Allens from Ightham Mote in Kent. Mistress Allen had quite recovered from her attack of illness last night. Squire Christopher Allen was still grateful for Julian's timely appearance and the blood-letting. Julian, though bored by both of them, felt moderate gratitude for the gold sovereign, and willingness to endure anything which would prevent him from wondering where his future lay, or brooding on the shattering of his hopes.

They sat at supper in the back parlour, away from the tap-room which was as noisy as last night. The Kentish squire had ordered the special shepherd's pie, and ale. They chatted. Or rather, Julian and her husband listened, while Emma Allen held forth.

Julian—melancholy, distraught, his moment of glowing warmth for the two women at Cowdray quite dissipated into unbelief that he had ever had it—listened, almost uncomprehending, paying more attention to the pain in his cheek-bone and the extreme stuffiness of his nose than to the woman's talk.

Emma Allen was thirty-eight and quite comely, now that she had recovered from her drunken fit, of which she remembered nothing. She was full-bodied—yet appropriately dressed in a maroon velvet gown, over a buff satin underskirt, her waist constricted by a leather corset, her bust concealed by a gold chain and pendant. She did not look stout.

Her plump cheeks were beet-red, her hair still a glossy black, her mouth full-lipped and shiny, though her teeth were crooked and she smiled seldom. Her eyes were remarkable, not for size nor symmetry—they were set rather too close to her nose-bridge—but for their brilliance, like polished jet beneath a thick, slanting fold of eyelid. They had a reptilian quality—the eyes of a lizard, or an oriental—Julian thought on first seeing Emma today. There had been a slave girl from Cathay at the Medici Court in Julian's youth, whose eyes had been set like that. Odd, in an otherwise English face, exotic.

Emma's manner and speech were not in the least exotic, as she recounted her life history, and the reason for the Allens' presence in Midhurst.

Emma Saxby had been born at Hawkhurst in Kent, just over the Sussex border. The Saxbys were of prosperous yeoman stock, and had relations throughout the two counties. One distant cousin was Thomas Marsdon of Medfield, who had married Emma's younger sister, Nan. A good marriage, Emma

164

said, in her flat Kentish twang, though she complacently indicated that her own had been better. Recently, a matter of inheritance had arisen. Her father—and Nan's—had made an unfair will, certain messuages and holdings were left away from herself, the eldest daughter. Vexing financial questions were further complicated by uncertainty as to the exact disposition of Emma's former dowry at Easebourne Priory, where Emma had been a novice at the time of the Dissolution.

'*Easebourne*, ye know, Master Julian . . .' interjected her husband, placidly assuming that the physician would be as interested in this coil about lost dowries and inheritances as the Allens were. 'Easebourne, t'other side of the river past Cowdray, founded by Bohuns, and though small, one o' the best nunneries in England 'twas considered.'

Julian sighed. He had heard neither of Easebourne, nor Medfield, nor Hawkhurst, nor Marsdons. He moved his legs uncomfortably, and wondered whether sneezewort yarrow grew in some nearby pasture. A few sniffs often cleared the nose and eased the face ache.

Emma continued her tale, which was punctuated by Christopher's approving nods. She had had a vocation, no doubt of that—though the scheming wicked Prioress, Margaret Sackfield, had dared to doubt.

The summer before Emma was to take her vows, the monastic world was shattered by King Henry's thunderbolt. The Priory was dissolved; all its property given to the Browne family; the nuns ejected. The dowries, already sent long ago with the novices, then disappeared. During the confusion, nobody knew where. Dame Margaret, the Prioress, also disappeared.

So, the Allens had decided on a journey of enquiry. They would brave Sir Anthony Browne himself, since he must have his father's records of Easebourne, and on the way they stopped at Medfield to see where the wind blew for demanding the inheritance. The wind blew stormy. Tom Marsdon refused to discuss the fairness of Nan's legacy. Law was law, and wills were wills. Furthermore, he averred that anyone who owned the rich manor and lands at Ightham Mote, should take shame to be so grasping. Relations were strained at parting, but the Allens had gained additional information which might be helpful at Cowdray.

'Tom Marsdon's got a younger brother—Stephen,' said Emma awesomely, as though announcing a miracle. 'He's *house priest* at Cowdray! Fancy the luck of it! We were wondering how to get Sir Anthony's ear—though we're well known in our own county, and Ightham's a goodly manor—but a house priest, close connected by marriage to *us*, and monk o' Bennet's order like Easebourne was—oh, he'll see justice is done me!'

Julian's attention was at last riveted. 'But, my dear Madam—' he protested, 'the Brownes, indeed all of Cowdray, are Protestants!' He knew this from Cheke, from the King's messenger, even from the Irishman who called himself 'Lord Gerald' in private. 'They wouldn't have a Benedictine monk as chaplain. It's preposterous. Besides, the King . . .' he paused, 'the King is at Cowdray *now*.'

'Aye, to be sure . . .' said Allen, looking startled, for he was no deep thinker, and left worldly matters to his wife. 'Mayhap ye spoke too freely, m'dear . . .?'

Emma's black eyes took on an opaque look. 'I'm no fool,' she said contemptuously. 'I've been speaking wi' landlord, here. He was mealymouthed, wouldna say this nor that, but *I* trapped him. They've a priest, all right, but he's hid for the nonce. We must wait 'till the King's gone. It's simple.' She took a deep breath and squared her jaw. 'When *I* intend a thing, 'tis good as done. And when *I* want a thing, I'll get it. Soon or late. I have means. God heeds me when I speak.'

Julian looked at her sharply. His perceptions quivered. The arrogance was not so surprising, nor the apparent piety in a woman who had almost become a nun. The abnormal flavour came more from a sudden ruthless note in her flat voice, the flexing of her large hands with their thick doubled-back thumbs. And the narrowing of those slanted eyes. Whatever it was, he was reminded, not this time of the oriental slave girl, but of a lunatic he had seen chained to the wall in Bedlam.

The impression passed at once, for Emma got up, smoothing her skirts.

'Now that we happen here, whilst the King does, we must try to get a glimpse of him,' she said chuckling. 'That'll be something to tell our little Charles, won't it, Kit?' She touched her husband's arm.

'Our son—' she explained to Julian, 'five years old, come Christmastide, and the apple of our eyes, since he looks to be the only one!'

So natural and maternal a remark convinced Julian that his own predicament was inspiring him to overwrought fancies.

Mistress Allen was only an ordinary provincial manor lady, bent on nothing more sinister than retrieving money of which she felt defrauded, and in the process either of quarrelling with or using people. He had met hundreds just like her.

He bade them 'Goodbye,' thanked them for the meal and went out to the inn stables to confer with the ostler, who asserted with conviction that there was not a horse for hire today in the whole of Sussex.

'Furdermore,' said the ostler gloomily, 'King's train 'as et up all the fodder an' pasture fur miles, ye'll no find an ox-cart eider to carry ye to Lunnon, marster.'

Julian went upstairs to Celia's hot attic room, and took from his bag the book he had carried with him. It was the *Meditations of Marcus Aurelius* and his favourite non-medical reading, but today the Roman emperor's practical aphorisms did little to lift his despondency.

*   *   *

On the next morning the King left Cowdray, bound south to Lord de la Warre's Halnaker House, near Chichester. The Allens were among the hordes lining the highway to watch the King go by at the end of an hour's file of laden carts and mules, of mounted knights and equerries.

Edward responded gallantly to the cheers and huzzahs of his people. He waved and he smiled. He caught a bouquet of roses a little girl threw to him, and tucked it on his pommel.

Only Harry Sidney and the yeoman of the privy chamber knew that Edward had been sick in the night with belly gripes, which kept him for an hour straining on the close-stool, and that when he finally lay in bed exhausted, he had begun a queer little hacking cough, and spat a trace of blood into a silk handkerchief. Later, when Edward suddenly began to sweat, Harry had been sufficiently alarmed to mention the Italian physician.

'He may yet be near, Your Grace, since there is no way, I believe, of leaving Midhurst, at present.'

But Edward, like his father, took obstinate whims. He cried out that the fellow was a Spanish spy, that he hated foreigners, that Harry was no true friend to harass his King by outrageous suggestions.

So distraught and tearful did Edward become that Harry spoke no further, and was relieved to see the boy fall into natural sleep. Edward had recovered by morning. Harry again

167

forgot his fears, yet determined to restrict the excessive entertainment and wearisome banquets during the rest of the Progress.

At Cowdray, the tension gave way to general laxness. Even the steward ceased his anxious supervisions, and retiring to his room, ignored the appalling mess which the servants must be chivvied into cleaning up.

Anthony and Lady Jane waited by the gatehouse until the last flourish of trumpets faded after the turn into the Highway, then he put his arm around her and crossed himself. 'Blessed St. Mary,' he said softly, 'it went well, my dear, and is over.'

She gave a sob, leaning her face on his shoulder. 'Now our babe — can be brought down to the chapel . . .'

Anthony nodded 'And that wretched monk released. I vow I scarce thought of him, or the child, during this visit — for which God forgive me.' He gave a gigantic yawn, and said, 'but, we've still got the Dacres. And *Clinton*. I'm not sure of the latter. He might go preaching to Northumberland — and by cock's bones I'm so weary I'd forgot the plot! I *daren't* release the priest until I sound out Clinton!'

Jane did not comprehend, except that here were more unnatural delays. She looked piteously at her husband, said, 'Anthony, I can bear no more . . .' and fainted on the flagstones.

Anthony, though concerned while Jane lay on their bed in a half-swoon, inert, refusing food, praying in snatches, was none the less grateful for a respite.

Lord Clinton and his retinue left the next day en route to Greenwich, where the Lord High Admiral had urgent business.

Geraldine produced floods of tears on parting with her betrothed, but the wedding was planned for September. She had the betrothal ring on her finger — held on with thread — and she was so content with her good fortune that she became kinder to everyone, and took immediate charge of Cowdray as she used to do. Anthony was constrained to admire her aptitude, as she roused the steward and bullied the servants. Her every act proclaimed that she was no longer the neglected dowager, a knight's widow, she was the future Baroness Clinton, and would — when the Dudley plans matured, be one of the first peeresses in the realm.

On the day after Clinton's departure she directed Anthony to release the house priest. 'Let him bury the babe,' she said, 'then, get rid of him. I dislike the man and do not wish him in a house I am associated with. I think him bigoted and dangerously pig-headed. You can find someone else more comfortable.'

Anthony had been dazed by Geraldine's sudden emergence. But he took exception to this command, and his baffled irritations exploded.

'My lady,' he said coldly, 'I'm grateful for your interest, since my wife is ailing. I rejoice in your changed prospects, and wish you well. There are many matters I don't fully understand. Nor perhaps wish to. Whatever your secrets may be with my Lord Clinton, I wish no part of them.'

Geraldine's eyes widened, she tilted her brassy curled head, and looked up at him. 'Are *you certain* you don't, Anthony?' she asked softly. 'I know you well, you're ambitious, I think a coronet would please you. You would like to be called "My Lord", to receive the Garter. You might enjoy a place in the Privy Council . . .'

'*Whose* Privy Council?' said Anthony roughly. 'And by what hugger-muggery? There's *one* I'll never bend to, I despise him. *And* his so-called religion.'

'So *virtuous* . . .' murmured Geraldine, her lips quirking 'so upright, so honourable . . . yet you plunged Cowdray into shame these last days, you toadied the King!'

'I respect the King's known views and wishes,' Anthony cried, furious at the partial truth and her sardonically raised brows. 'But, I'll make no further concessions, and I'll *not* discharge my chaplain.'

Geraldine shrugged. 'As long as I am under your roof—and bear your name . . . I, too, must make concessions . . . *later* . . .' She let the word hang in the air, fraught with meaning and subtle threat.

Damn the bitch, Anthony thought as his stepmother glided from the privy parlour where they had been talking.

He started through passages towards one of the old stone stairs in the south wing, bent on releasing the priest at once. His route took him past lesser chambers and storerooms where he seldom penetrated. He paused at the sound of laughter coming from a room he knew vaguely to be Lady Ursula's. The door was ajar, and he looked in.

He saw first two red-headed Dacres, Magdalen and her brother Leonard. Their size, their fox-coloured hair, dominated the room. Then he saw the cocky little Fitzgerald, Geraldine's brother. The two young men were playing Primero, slapping down the cards, throwing half-crowns on the table, while

Magdalen egged them on impartially. Magdalen was a handsome wench, Anthony thought, as he watched for a moment unseen. Healthy and wholesome as an oak. What an armful in bed, though—she was as tall as he, and his height was more than most men.

Anthony dismissed quickly the contrast with his sickly little wife, moaning in their bedchamber. Then he caught sight of Celia.

The girl was sitting on a stool beside her aunt, and looking out of the casement window. There was *beauty*! Innocent springtime, primrose beauty, enhanced by wistfulness. The large sad eyes were the colour of the sea when sunlight caught it in a rocky pool.

Her brows and lashes were as brown as seaweed, her rich tumbling hair could match the colour of the antique gold chain he had not yet put off after the King's visit. She was like the dream-light virgins who caressed the unicorn in his new tapestry.

Magdalen looked around, suddenly feeling a watcher at the door.

'Ho! Sir Anthony!' she cried, laughing, while she put a warning hand on Leonard's shoulder. 'Have ye coom to chide the gamesters? Ye maun do so, for I vow they cheat!'

Leonard and Gerald sprang to their feet. So did Ursula and Celia. Anthony felt constraint. The men were of his own age, but they made him feel old, that he was the powerful host—the intruder.

'Nay,' he said smiling, 'I've no wish to stop the gaming, nor to judge it. I passed by on an errand.' He waved them to sit down.

' 'Tis snug here,' he said pleasantly to Ursula. 'I trust you've all you need, my lady?'

'Indeed so, sir.' She was much startled by his appearance. He had never honoured her by a visit before, and for days during and after the King's visit she had seen him only from a distance. 'Lady Jane is better, I trust?' Ursula had heard whisperings and dark surmises among the servants.

'No worse . . .' said Anthony curtly, reminded of his errand. He looked at the men—Dacre and Fitzgerald. Especially Fitzgerald, Geraldine's brother, hand in glove with Geraldine.

Well, one could but find out. He was tired of dissembling and nearly ashamed of the role he had played before the King.

He looked up at Lady Ursula's crucifix, he looked at it so long that they all grew puzzled, then Anthony crossed himself.

'This is a Catholic house,' said Anthony harshly. 'We will go to Mass, all those who are *in* and *of* my house, tomorrow morn at six.'

Leonard and Gerald were puzzled by the note of defiance in their host's voice. And, that he was staring so hard at Gerald.

'Why, to be sure, sir,' said Gerald, his eyebrows quirking like his sister's. 'Why not? We're all Catholics—though one must sway a bit wi' the breeze, now and then . . . Eh, sir Anthony?'

Magdalen gave her hearty laugh. ' 'Twill do us good! I've heard no Mass since we left Coomberland, an' the gobblin prayers we've been duling, morn an' night, they're mortal tedious. Where will ye hold Mass, sir—ye're chapel's empty as a tun.'

'It will be refurnished tonight,' said Anthony.

Celia's heart was beating fast. The King had been gone over two days, but Stephen had not reappeared. She had been imagining all sorts of disasters—the King's men had found Stephen and spitted him on a sword—or more likely, Sir Anthony had turned Protestant in truth, and never meant to release his priest, or Stephen had escaped and fled back to France. She had asked a friendly page; he knew nothing. She finally asked Ursula, but her aunt was unwontedly sharp, she indicated that such concern for the house priest was unseemly, and at once began to talk of Leonard Dacre, saying that he was a fine upstanding young lord, that Celia should not be so indifferent to his attentions. Celia had been hurt. She did not comprehend that Ursula's anxious love produced the sharpness, she only knew that the world had grown shadowy and un-moulded. She had no real place at Cowdray with Ursula—enquiry had divulged that the foreign physician still occupied her attic at the Spread Eagle. She had been mutely forlorn.

Anthony's speech aroused her. She could not be carelessly bold, like Magdalen. She had, however, her own strengths, allied to the recently, tentatively discovered power over men.

She went up to Anthony and said in a low, firm voice, 'For the Mass, sir, will you not need your priest—Brother Stephen?'

Anthony was taken aback. The wistful little beauty who was after all only some relation to the bastard Bohuns, spoke to him as though there were no difference in their rank. There was even accusation in the clear gaze.

Anthony smiled slowly. 'You are right, child. We need Brother Stephen for the Mass. Would you like to come with me when I release him?'

'Aye,' Celia said. She heard Ursula's indrawn breath, she felt the mild astonishment in the Dacres and Gerald. These did not touch her.

'Well, then —' said Anthony, amused and titillated, he motioned her through the door. She went, and he followed.

The young men shrugged and returned to their gaming. Magdalen resumed her teasing comments. Ursula frowned heavily. She glanced at her astrolabe, then, she, too, looked up at her crucifix. There was no help there to allay foreboding. Ave Maria — Holy Mother of God — she thought, as women did when assailed by maternal fears, yet what could the Immaculate Virgin really know of sensual threats or the need to protect a girl from her own waywardness.

Anthony and Celia circled down the old stone staircase to the cellars. They were dank, and dimly lit by small rough slits hewn at intervals between the foundation stones. The stench of the latrine pit was sickening. Anthony led the way among beer casks, kegs of salted pork, rotting wooden coffers filled with rusty ironware from the kitchen, old broken pikes and other disused weapons.

In the darkest corner, Anthony paused at a niche and raised his hand to a heavy iron bolt which was hidden by a jutting of masonry.

Celia gasped. 'He's in *there*?' she cried. 'You've bolted him in. Oh, could you not *trust* him?'

Anthony's hand stayed a moment. 'Aye,' he said with some compunction, 'I gave no order for bolting, must be the steward's carefulness, he's the only one knows the priest is here.' Anthony slid back the bolt, and swung open a little door scarce three feet high. They peered in together and, though one of the foundation slits gave scanty light, at first they could see nobody. 'Brother Stephen!' Anthony said.

There was a stirring on the floor, where they saw a long dark figure lying on a pile of straw. 'I want no food, only water —' muttered a voice from the darkness.

Celia, pushing past Anthony, squeezed herself through the door and ran to kneel by the figure. ' 'Tis not the steward!' she cried. ' 'Tis *me*, Celia, and Sir Anthony himself. You're free, sir, *free*!'

Through fevered mists, when he saw sometimes grinning

red demons, sometimes the anxious faces of his fellow monks at Marmoutier, Stephen heard the girl's beseeching frightened voice.

'Begone . . . Celia . . .' he whispered. 'In your hair are golden snakes, perchance a golden rat hides in the snakes . . .'

His hand raised to cross himself, then fell limp.

'Oh, what ails him!' Celia cried. She snatched the burning hand and held it against her cool cheek.

'Delirium,' said Anthony grimly. 'Wait here.'

She obeyed, crouching beside Stephen, fondling his hand and wetting it with tears.

Anthony returned at once with two stout kitchen varlets. They lifted Stephen to ease him through the door. Celia, in backing off so as not to impede them, stumbled over something soft and squashy. She felt it. Only a dead rat. She had seen hundreds of those, and this one's stink was hardly noticeable among the stinks of human ordure seeping through the wall.

Yet, it was the rat which caused Stephen's present danger. They found the bite on Stephen's right thigh, when they had laid the monk on a long counter in the scullery. The men had forgotten Celia as they stripped off the black habit, and exposed the young man naked. She shrank against the serving-hatch and stared.

She did not know how well made Stephen's body was, with broad shoulders, narrow hips, the muscles rounded, the flushed skin as smooth and without blemishes as her own. Her shocked gaze flickered over the mat of curly black hair on his chest, the black hair farther down which nestled around the large reddish objects which she had vaguely known men to possess, and had seen tiny pale replicas of on boy babies. Her cheeks grew hot, she felt the heat into her scalp, and she looked away troubled, fascinated. Then she heard what Sir Anthony was saying.

'God's nails—look at that!' Anthony poked a finger around a puffy mass of proud-flesh from which yellow-green pus trickled.

Red streaks ran down Stephen's swollen leg; he winced when Anthony touched it, and resumed the incoherent mutters while twitching his head from side to side and shivering with a violent chill.

Anthony had seen few wounds in his twenty-five years, and never serious ones, since he had never been to war, but he knew that rat-bites could be most dangerous. 'I doubt he'll live . . .' said Anthony sadly.

The two scullions shook their heads. They liked the house priest, who never chided them unduly, nor gave long exhortations in the confessional.

'We should send for the barber,' continued Anthony, frowning, 'or the wise-woman—Old Molly o' Whiphill. My Lady Jane has faith in her potions.'

'Sir Anthony!' Celia choked—she cleared her voice which was hoarse as a raven's. 'Sir Anthony! There's a physician at the Inn. Master Julian. The one was sent to the King who would have none of him. Get Master Julian.'

Anthony stared at the girl. So many events had followed on the brief scene some days ago in the courtyard, and so anguished was her pretty face, that he thought her to be babbling.

'The Italian doctor!' Celia cried, shaking Anthony's arm. 'Came from Master Cheke ... Oh ... I'll fetch him myself!'

She darted out from the scullery and through the kitchen courtyard.

Thus it was that Julian was installed at Cowdray, though not in the manner which he had expected and hoped.

* * *

During the week of his struggle for life, Stephen lay in one of the small chambers near Ursula's. That lady did most of the nursing, inspired by true goodness of heart, respect for Master Julian, and pity for the young monk who was certainly, in this condition, no threat to Celia or anyone else. She did not, however, permit Celia access to the sickroom, though she was not so unkind as to send the girl back to the attic room in the Inn, which the August heat rendered stifling.

Celia wandered around Cowdray, as mutely unhappy as she had been before Stephen's release, but with the added anguish of certain anxiety.

Julian used all his skill to save the patient, though he began without hope or anything more than scientific interest. Treating a house priest who had been kept hidden from the King, skulking in some bolt-hole, was, if the thing were known, hardly the way to preferment should there still be any hope of such. Even his friend John Cheke would not have considered *this* life worth saving, would indeed have said that the effort was even blasphemous, since Almighty God obviously intended

174

to rid the country of an idolatrous, scheming Papist, one of the creeping worms sent by the Scarlet Woman to bore corruptions through the sound apple of Protestant England.

None the less, Julian applied fomentations of balsam and vinegar to the wound, after he had cleaned and cauterised it carefully. He refused to let blood—to Anthony's great astonishment—and he forced on the young monk great quantities of a febrifuge.

He searched Stephen meticulously twice a day, knowing that the rat's poisoned saliva might reappear in some fresh place as a boil. How such a thing could be, he did not know, but he had seen it happen. No boil appeared. The fever mounted for three days, then suddenly departed, leaving Stephen very weak, but rational. The wound's angry red diminished. The swelling lessened.

On a morning when Julian entered the sickroom, he saw great improvement. He felt Stephen's forehead and arm-pits, they were cool. The pulse was slowed. He looked at the leg which was far less swollen, while the wound was beginning to heal.

'*Benissimo* . . .' said Julian aloud.

Stephen opened his eyes. 'Who are *you*?' he whispered. 'I've thought you to be my Abbot, yet he had no beard!'

Julian chuckled. 'No Abbot I! I'm a physician, and you'll recover, my fine young monk. There *was* grave doubt.'

'Our Lord hath shown infinite mercy, then,' whispered Stephen, after a moment of wonder. He remembered nothing clearly after the first horrible night in his cell, when the rat bit him. 'The Holy Blessed Virgin be praised.'

Julian shrugged. 'Praise Her by all means, if you like, yet I think a more earthly gratitude is fitting.'

Stephen's wan stubbed face looked a question, and Julian proceeded dryly, 'To little Celia Bohun who summoned *me* —and my own ministrations. Though, 'tis true I was aided by your youthful strength.'

'Celia . . .?' Stephen could not grasp this. His thoughts were woolly and aimless as sheep.

'Also Lady Ursula, who has nursed you devotedly—no matter, rest now.'

Stephen drifted off while Julian changed the dressing on his leg. Lady Ursula came hurrying in with a new cleansed urinal and Julian nodded approvingly. He demanded a fastidiousness which she secretly thought foolish. Fresh sheets daily, the immediate extermination of the usual lice and fleas, a bare swept floor. It was a lot of work, but Julian had explained to her—in one of the serious talks she so much enjoyed—that though disease might spring from stagnant, evil air, or the sudden putrefaction of the body's humours, bile, phlegm, blood, as most people thought, Fracastorius, his master at Padua, had been convinced there was another cause. He felt that diseases were transmitted by moving atoms, particles so tiny the eye could not see them, tinier than motes in a sunbeam, and that these particles might be carried on the legs of vermin, and also lived in filth of any kind.

On August 13, two days before the Feast of the Virgin Mary's Assumption, Stephen had begun to chafe at his confinement. He was able to walk around his room without wobbling, and to savour the good meals sent him from the kitchens. He greeted Julian's morning visit with a warm but determined smile.

'Good day, Doctor. You see I'm nearly well. I must return to my duties. I intend to celebrate Our Blessed Lady's Mass in the chapel for all my Cowdray flock. It grieves me to've deserted them so long.'

'Bene, bene—sed festina lente,' said Julian who found his patient's ready knowledge of Latin one of many agreeable traits. He had grown fond of Stephen, partly from natural sympathy towards one whose life has been saved through personal effort, and partly because he recognised a lonely spirit much like his own.

'They'll be glad to have you back,' Julian continued. 'Lady Jane still weeps because her poor babe was buried by the Midhurst vicar.'

Stephen nodded sadly. 'I have prayed for its soul—Master Julian, how is Celia?'

'Celia? Celia Bohun? Why, I hardly know. I glimpsed her flitting around now and then, with the young Dacres until they all left for Hurstmonceux, and with Mabel Browne. She's still in the castle with her aunt, Lady Ursula.'

'To whom I'm grateful, indeed,' said Stephen. 'She's nursed me as a mother would.'

'A fine woman,' agreed Julian rather absently. 'She pesters me to cast the little Celia's horoscope, and I shall do so today, since I'll soon go back to London.' He sighed, and Stephen was jolted from the self-absorption of illness to consider the doctor. A portly, middle-aged, bearded man, with a long

Italian nose and sharp grey eyes which he knew could be very kind, an air of diffidence curiously mixed with authority.

'Aren't you Sir Anthony's new physician? Don't you live in Midhurst?' Stephen was astonished—and more so when Julian briefly explained the mission which had brought him to Cowdray.

'The King would have none of you?—and none of me either,' said Stephen grimly, 'though for different reasons. I submitted to what my conscience told me was God's will. You must do the same.'

'Bah!' cried Julian. 'Now you speak like a monk. God—if indeed there be one—can have no part in the irritable whims of a foolish, sickly boy! True, that boy has power, and it is also true that as Machiavelli writes, "A prince has need for neither humility nor scruples, nor need he hide the selfishness which forms the true kernel of every heart."'

'That remark is overweening,' said Stephen sharply. 'Those who have found devotion and humble obedience to the Divine Will are not selfish. There are many who sacrifice self when they adore.'

'Because to adore is more pleasurable than *not* for such. Man seeks only pleasing sensations, the gross physical ones if that be his nature, subtle appeasements if he be more refined. . . . *You*, caro Stefano,' Julian's look held affectionate mockery, 'would *you* say prayers, recite offices, invoke saints, worship a female deity, if you did not find it pleasurable?'

Stephen flushed angrily. 'You're too glib. Too near the twistings and specious arguments of heretics. I'm not trained to dialectics, nor wish to be. For that matter, was your motive selfish when you spent all those days in curing me?'

'Undoubtedly,' said Julian smiling. 'I enjoy practising my profession. I enjoy the struggle against the final enemy. I enjoy victory. You enjoy thinking that you save souls. I— bodies. I've never seen a *soul*, have *you*, my friend?'

'No—Credo—et exspecto resurrectionem mortuorum.' Stephen spoke so earnestly that Julian whose mind was both probing and limber, suddenly abandoned the irony which he saw to be unfair. And mentioned a topic which had given him occasional thought.

'Well, then, Stephen, you may *have* your Credo, I allow you the *soul*. Have you read your Plato, Ovid, Virgil, even Cicero on the subject?'

'Of *souls* . . .?' asked Stephen, bewildered by the doctor.

'We had some classics at Marmoutier, but the Abbot naturally did not encourage the study of pagans . . . What do you mean?'

'I mean that the men I mentioned, and countless others beside, believed that our souls return over and over to earth in new bodies, that we have lived before and will again, and that the experience of good or evil, the choices made, the deeds, the *will*—all may determine events of the next embodiment or incarnation.'

'*Incarnation?*' Stephen shook his head gravely. 'Master Julian there is but one incarnation, that of Our Blessed Lord. What you're saying is blasphemous. You can *not* believe it!'

Julian shrugged. '*I* am sure of nothing. I simply point out that many better minds than yours or mine have so believed. It's evident that the followers of Jesus thought so too, or why would they have considered that He was once Elias?'

'They were dogs of Jews!' Stephen cried hotly. 'Infidels!'

'Origen and St. Augustine were not infidels, they were Church Fathers, or St. Jerome—did he not write in his *Epistola and Demetriadem* "The doctrine of transmigration of souls has been secretly taught to small numbers of people, as a traditional truth which was not to be divulged"?'

Stephen with an effort controlled annoyance, thinking that the doctor was teasing him, but increasingly aware of his own duty. Though he was grateful to Julian and slightly in awe of him, Stephen said, 'Do not quibble, sir. You imperil that immortal soul which will go to purgatory to redress its sins; after purgatory through Divine Mercy and the Intercession of Our Lord's Beloved Mother, it may ascend into heavenly bliss. That's all.'

'And the resurrection of the dead, which you just quoted from the Creed, the wormy corpses in their winding sheets, must the soul descend into *that* again, the putrefaction which it gladly left behind?'

'The bodies will be made new,' said Stephen stiffly. 'The *same* bodies.'

'It may be so—' Julian suddenly laughed. 'We won't quarrel about it, Stephen, in fact, I know *nothing* worth quarrelling over. I wasn't born for strife.' He poured a glass of hippocras from a flagon on the table. 'Here, drink this! I've tired you with philosophical delvings. And you still have sweats, I see.' He wiped Stephen's moist forehead with the edge of his long sleeve. 'Lie down for a bit!'

Stephen reluctantly obeyed, ashamed of sudden weakness in his body.

'One would never suspect your priesthood to look at you,' Julian observed with dry amusement, inspecting his patient.

Since he had been able to get out of the bed, Stephen had worn a maroon velvet dressing-gown, lent by Sir Anthony. It was an elegant garment, faced with yellow satin and furred with squirrel. His head was again partly shaven as he had demanded when Ursula began to shave his face, but the tonsure as he lay on the pillow was covered. He looked now to be as darkly virile and fashionable a young courtier as Julian had ever seen. Even among the Medicis. Not the *face*, though, that was unmistakably English, and had an air of innocence, or unawareness, no Italian over sixteen ever had.

'They've taken my habit,' said Stephen apologetically, 'to wash. It'll be back tonight. I've no mind to be decked in this thing.' He plucked disdainfully at the velvet. 'It disgusts me.'

'Ah . . .' said Julian softly. 'You truly enjoy renouncing the sensual . . .' but, he added to himself, I think you have never had strong temptation. Julian paused to wonder if he himself were carnally tempted by Stephen. And decided not.

His one experience had been enough, and during the last week he had been desiring Alison again. She was plump, sentimental, stupid, but she was eagerly receptive to his occasional ardours. She would be balm for the disappointments he had endured at Cowdray.

Alison would ask nothing. He had told her nothing of his hopes. And how ridiculous had been his unformed dreams of an ambitious marriage! Almost the only woman he had seen at Cowdray was Lady Ursula, who had a tenderness for him. This was apparent. That she was older, and skinny, would not have mattered much. Men seldom married from inclination. But her total lack of money or influence, and her obvious position as dependant did. She had good blood, so did he, that was an advantage. During the time of striving together for Stephen's life, he had enjoyed her company, liked her mind. He had even admired her rather feverish devotion to little Celia. These thoughts led him to the Allens.

'By the bye,' he said to Stephen, whose colour was returning, as he lay gazing up at the embroidered tester, 'there's a pair of your kin-folk below in the courtyard, champing around for a sight of you.'

'Kinfolk . . .?' repeated Stephen, frowning. 'I have none

179

except my brother and his wife, they wouldn't come here, surely . . .'

'No, not them, these are the Allens, from Ightham Mote in Kent. Mistress Allen is sister to your brother's wife. She's a forceful woman. I've had trouble keeping her at bay during your illness.'

'Never heard of them,' said Stephen. 'And what can they want of *me*?'

'They want you to influence Sir Anthony, of whom even Mistress Allen is somewhat in awe. Matter of a lost dowry at Easebourne Priory sixteen years ago.'

'Blessed St. Michael—' said Stephen. 'What can I do about that? Sir Anthony has the Priory, no doubt he has the dowry, these matters are wicked, but 'tis the present law of the land.'

'*Da vero*, a ticklish situation, but I think you should see the Allens, she *is* kin to you. Promise *anything*,' Julian chuckled, 'that'll get the woman out of Midhurst. She's driving the landlord of the Spread Eagle mad, and me, too.'

Stephen sighed. 'I'll see her, but I make no promises I can't redeem. Is she a Catholic?'

'It would certainly seem so,' said Julian wryly. 'Crucifix on her ample breast, crossings and invocation to saints, after all, she *was* a novice, and would rapidly have become prioress—so she says.'

'Indeed,' Stephen felt a stirring of sympathy for anyone who had been forced out of a vocation. He envisioned a pale ascetic —wistful and suffering.

When the doctor ushered the Allens into the sickroom, Stephen was startled. Emma Allen at once forcefully filled the room, she exuded obduracy and will.

'Brother . . .' she cried loudly, 'Brother Stephen! At last! By Our Lady, I thought ye'd never mend, poor man!'

She plopped on her knees to receive his blessing, while looking up at him boldly, a speculative, provocative stare which made Stephen redden, suddenly conscious that the furred dressing-robe exposed some of his chest. He clasped the gown tighter, while he made the sign of the cross, which he repeated for the meagre little man who hovered behind his wife.

'I don't understand how you think I can help you, Mistress Allen,' said Stephen, 'but I pray you deliver my love and salutations to my brother Tom and his Nan, if you return through Medfield.'

'Not us!' Emma jerked her head. 'Your brother Tom's a stiff-necked fellow, 'll not see reason on Nan's inheritance, mayhap ye can help me later there, but 'tis at Cowdray I need ye now.'

'Aye, so indeed,' put in Mr. Allen, nervously smoothing his pointed beard, 'Emma's been diddled out o' a hundred gold sovereigns at Easebourne Priory. Sir Anthony Browne'll know what happened to 'em.'

'Why have you waited so long, and why can't you ask him yourself?' enquired Stephen, sighing again.

Both Allens answered at once; Christopher's murmurs were an echo of his wife's vehement replies. From them Stephen gathered that the matter of the inheritance had re-awakened resentment over the loss of the novice's dowry, that the journey had not seemed imperative until this summer, after a series of misfortunes on their manor. A chance fire had burned acres of their woodland, a blight had killed many of their livestock, and an expensive planting of the newly imported hops had been infected with downy mildew which killed all the young shoots. In addition, it developed that Emma had political ambitions for her husband whose father had once been Lord Mayor of London, though she admitted that any such ambitions were difficult for Catholics.

As to interviewing Sir Anthony direct, Emma had applied to his steward and been curtly refused.

'So, ye see, Brother Stephen, we count on you,' said Emma, showing her crooked teeth in a fleeting smile.

Stephen nodded. The woman oppressed him, but he knew it was his duty to help a fellow Catholic who was, it appeared, devout enough—also brave enough in these times—to house a priest at Ightham.

'We don't call him a priest, to be sure,' said Emma, 'he's an old, near-doddering cousin o' my husband's, glad to find bed and board in return for saying Mass, the Mote's hid in a hollow and we've no near neighbours to spy on us.'

'I'll see that you get audience from Sir Anthony,' said Stephen whose head was beginning to spin, 'and send you word to the Spread Eagle.' He signed the cross in the air for dismissal.

'Whew—*Dio Mio*,' said Julian, as the door swung to behind the Allens. 'That woman—a basilisque, *une force majeure* as the French say. Thundrous effluvia surround her, and she stinks like sulphur. My nose prickles.'

Stephen sank back in his chair and laughed faintly. 'Voyons, mon cher Docteur,' he said, savouring the opportunity to use the French which had so long been his language. 'N'exagérons pas? Hein? Je n'ai rien éprouvé. C'est une femme dominatrice comme mainte d'autres, c'est tout.'

'You felt nothing strange or baleful?' Julian raised his eyebrows. 'Nor noticed the lewd desirous looks she gave you?'

'Certainly not,' Stephen retorted. 'You were once corrupted by the Medici Court, Master Julian, and I grieve to see the lasting effect.'

This speech was not made in admonishment, it was tinged by affectionate banter and reflected an area of Stephen which he had long ignored. The lightness surprised and delighted Julian, who stared, then chuckled. 'Ah, you've had few intimates, caro, I suspect, and I'm pleased to see that you consider me a friend, as I do *you*!'

'Particular friendships are discouraged in a monastery,' agreed Stephen. 'They hinder single-hearted devotion, they cause human attachments which Satan uses for his own purposes.'

Julian gave a forceful Italianate shrug, waving his hands. 'This would not seem to have been the opinion of your Master, Jesu Christo,' he said. 'He showed marked partiality for John the Apostle, and even Mary Magdalene.'

Stephen frowned, startled by this view and certain that there must be a rebuttal.

'Pax! I'll not disturb you, nor your convictions,' said Julian watching him, 'and am perhaps envious since I have *none*.' He rose and poured a ruby liquid into a pewter noggin. 'Time for the electuary,' he said handing it to Stephen. 'Remember to take it after I've gone.'

'What's in it?' asked Stephen, drinking through a pang of regret. He would miss Master Julian.

'Crushed rose hips—I gathered them myself—blood of fresh sheep liver, honey and claret. This must be made on a waxing moon, and I'll teach you how, 'tis simple and most strengthening. Drink it thrice daily. I'll disclose to you another secret remedy,' added Julian, '—mouldy cheese.'

'Mouldy cheese!' Stephen shuddered 'Was that the rank stuff you forced down me when I could barely swallow?'

'*Da vero*. It cures many a distemper, especially those caused by injury. The Arabs always give it on the battle-field; they even plaster it on wounds. We had an Arabian physician at

Padua in my time, the others jeered at his advice, but from curiosity I tried it on a man's amputated thigh. He healed well and fast. As priest here you should know some doctoring. The cheese, any cheese must have turned green, and the more maggoty the better.'

'Faugh!' said Stephen. 'Why?'

'I don't know for certain. It may be some correspondence in sympathy between pus and decay, or similarity of colour. Medicine is full of mysteries, we can only accept. *Quod est demonstrandum.*'

Stephen leaned forward and looked at the bearded middle-aged man who had probably saved his life, and in doing so must have been an instrument of God's will, unbeliever though he professed himself to be. Stephen discovered another disused emotion—gratitude. He put his hand quickly on Julian's arm. 'I thank you, my friend, and shall pray daily for the welfare of your soul.'

Julian grunted, then smiled. 'By all means, Brother Stephen, prayers can do no harm, and that odd invisible vapour you call "soul" is *your* concern, as the body is mine. Hark, there's a knock!'

They both turned and looked at the heavy oak door. Julian started to rise, instinctively sparing exertion for his patient, but Stephen pushed him down. 'You've no longer need to cosset me, sir,' he said with the quick smile which transformed his grave face. He went and opened the door.

Lady Ursula stood in the passage, holding the monk's cleansed habit. 'Well-a-day . . .' she cried, staring, 'so brisk and debonair, good brother? Here's a marvel of recovery!' She spoke brightly while concealing dismay. In that maroon velvet dressing-gown, she, like Julian earlier, thought that the young man looked like a very handsome courtier, and was glad that Celia had not been allowed to see him.

'Your habit,' she said, thrusting out the black woollen robe. 'You'll wish to don it at once, no doubt.'

'Aye, Lady Ursula,' Stephen bowed. 'You've been good to me. I'll hear confessions tomorrow night as usual, in the chapel. Will you tell the others? And do you know where Sir Anthony is? I'd speak with him.' He sent Julian a quizzical resigned glance, knowing that the doctor understood his boredom with the Allen demands.

'He's in the Great Hall,' answered Ursula, 'with the bailiff, collecting the overdue Lammas Day tithes and rent. Lot o'

183

malingering this August, tenants unsettled what with the King's visit and the hiding of our true faith.'

'Ah—' said Stephen frowning, 'he'll not be in the best temper when I add *my* petition, but I wish to be quit of it.'

'You'll be busy a while then,' said Julian laughing. 'Lady Ursula, I'll copy our young priest's energy and cast Celia Bohun's nativity for you.'

Ursula's kind horsey face flushed with pleasure. 'In my chamber, Doctor,' she cried eagerly. 'I've all that's needed.'

Ursula and Julian left Stephen to get dressed and fulfil his mission. They went down the passage and found Celia in her aunt's room, crouched on a stool while doggedly stitching on a strip of tapestry. Ursula was teaching her needlework, as befitted a lady.

She pricked her finger as her elders entered, murmured, 'Curse it!' Then, blushing, put her finger in her mouth in a naïvely childish gesture. She rose and curtsied to her aunt, her sea-green eyes anxious.

'How does *he* do?' she asked fervently of Julian.

'Very well indeed—cured, in fact,' he answered, observing her sudden radiance with surprise. So . . . what's this? he thought. The child's in love with the priest? *Che peccato! La povera* . . . but young hearts mend fast, and this one is *very* young. 'How old are you, carina?' he asked.

'She's scarce fourteen,' put in Ursula. ' 'Tis all down on this parchment I've prepared for you. I've guessed at the hour of her birth, because . . .'

'Oh, it was early morn for sure, my lady Aunt,' Celia interrupted. 'I've remembered something my mother said once. That she laboured all night and I was born just as the red sun come—*came* blinking through the curtains!'

'Very helpful,' Julian smiled. He glanced at the parchment. 'After dawn in the middle of June would be about five o'clock, I suppose.'

'Ye'll tell me a good fortune, sir, won't you?' asked Celia softly, bending near him, unaware that she smelled of the pungent gilly-flowers she had stuck in her bodice, and that her rich golden hair, the wide cleft between her breasts, her dimpling mouth were all provocative.

'I do not tell fortunes, little one,' said Julian, restraining a desire to touch her. 'I only read what the stars foretold at your birth. Naught but good, I'm sure.' Yet, as he spoke he had a foreboding.

'I think that Celia should leave,' he said to Ursula. 'I require solitude, utmost concentration for this task.'

'Oh, to be sure—go then, dear—' said Ursula, considering how to prevent the girl from seeing Stephen, now unfortunately at large. 'Run down to Midhurst for me. 'Tis market day, there'll be a mercer booth, buy me a skein of crimson silk, I've none left.' She fumbled in the purse which hung from her belt, and tendered Celia a sixpence.

The girl's face again grew doleful, her underlip trembled, but there was a rebellious glint in her eyes. 'Oh, Aunt,' she said, 'd'ye need the silk *now*? Must I go to town again? Can't I stop at Cowdray? Y're forever sending me on errands.'

Aha, Julian thought, the mercurial Gemini, her moods shift fast.

'Do as you're told, child!' snapped Ursula, but tempered the command with a quick hug.

Celia slowly smiled and curtsied, 'I owe you all obedience,' she said in a contrite voice. She disappeared clutching the sixpence.

The two older people looked at each other.

'I have guessed what perturbs you,' Julian said to Ursula. 'Believe me, you should not fret. Puppy-love passes, but it *would* be better if there were distance between them. The little one is beautiful.'

'Aye, I've thought of that. Magdalen Dacre asked us north to visit at Naworth, their castle in Cumberland. I think we'll go. Leonard Dacre, Magdalen's brother is enamoured of Celia, and would suit, though I hope for a better match.'

'Possibly,' said Julian. 'Now, I'm *eager* to cast her nativity.' He sat down and pulled the parchment towards him, glancing at Ursula's efforts. 'You have many miscalculations,' he said, 'Evidently I was a poor instructor years ago at Kenninghall. Bring me your astrolabe.'

Ursula anxiously brought it. She sat down in her armchair and waited, breathing hard, while Julian with a goose-quill pen wrote figures and symbols on another piece of parchment. He worked from an ephemeris he always carried in his bag. It showed the changing positions of the planets during the last fifty years. He also drew a careful chart of the twelve houses, and their various predictions for Celia.

From long practice, he worked fast, humming a little and making occasional comments. 'Her ascendant is the fiery lion, which will strengthen the quicksilver Gemini, and make her headstrong, passionate—the moon in Scorpio—Ah, that too will give her purpose and strong carnal interest, but she has healing power, love of the unknown—a decided character, though tempered by the gentle Libra in the fifth house, the house of love—it also gives her beauty—hm-m—the planets—'

Julian fell silent as he studied the position of Celia's planets. The watching Ursula saw him compress his lips. His pen moved slower, she saw his eyebrows draw together.

'What is it?' she said in a quavering voice. 'What have you found?'

Julian did not answer, he examined again the astrolabe and the ephemeris. Made a fresh set of figures. Finally, he looked up and met her anxious eyes. 'There are afflictions,' he said with hesitation, 'the eighth house, the house of Death—the twelfth—the house of self-undoing—'

'Saturn . . .?' whispered Ursula fearingly. 'But I found beneficent Jupiter in *good* position.'

Julian had not. Venus and Jupiter were each in opposition to the baleful Saturn which was the only planet above the horizon at Celia's birth.

Violent early death, he would have decided had this been the horoscope of somebody unknown, but his sympathy for these two women was strong, and predictions were not infallible. He put down his pen, and smiled at Ursula. 'There are afflictions to be surmounted,' he said lightly, 'yet remember that the stars *im*pel but cannot *com*pel. I should like to see the girl's palms when she returns. I've always thought chiromancy a truer guide to the future. Many folk were born after sunrise on this June 13th. And thus share her nativity. But Celia's *hands* are unique. Entirely her own. Come, Lady, look not so doleful. There are indications here to satisfy your ambitions. She will rise in the world, she may even become close to royalty, and there is *hope* of a brilliant marriage.'

Ursula jumped at reassurance. She seized Julian's hand and pressed it. 'Oh, Master Julian,' she cried, 'you make me happy. *Why* is not Celia my own child? Above all things I wish for that. I love her more than does many a natural mother. And *why* am I not rich and powerful? Why must my spirit be chastened by dependence, humiliation I've done nothing to merit?'

'Brother Stephen would have an answer for those heart-

186

felt cries,' said Julian chuckling. 'God's will is inscrutable.' He released her hand gently.

'Aye . . .' she sighed on a long breath. 'God's will.' She cast a distracted glance up at her crucifix. 'Yes, He *will* shield her from all dangers, if I have faith enough, won't He, Master Julian?'

E una cosa bastante incerta, said Julian cynically to himself, thinking of life's disappointments, its tragic cruelties. He also thought of his conversation with Stephen, and the doctrine of many lives, which he had brought forth as an intellectual game, rather than a conviction. 'If evil befalls, there will eventually be redress, perhaps, and the strength of your desires will sometimes bring fulfilment, no doubt.' He said this from a wish to comfort, but also from sudden boredom. He was hungry, the ache in his cheek-bone had reappeared to plague him, and he, too, must seek Sir Anthony and bid his host farewell, since Stephen was cured.

Ursula interpreted Julian's remark as a reference to paradise, patience, penitence—and was deflated. She moved slowly to the open window and looked down through the hot shimmering August air to the courtyard.

'Here's Celia returning,' she announced, then stiffened as she saw Stephen enter the courtyard from the fan-vaulted portal. She watched the two greeting each other, their startled pleasure was obvious. Celia knelt for the blessing, which Ursula thought too lingering, and during the conversation which ensued, she distinctly heard Celia's happy excited laugh, and saw the tall black-robed figure bend nearer the girl.

'God's Holy Wounds—' said Ursula, under her breath; she leaned out of the window and called, 'Celia! Celia! Come at once! I'm waiting!'

The girl looked up and waved acquiescence, then said a few more words to the young monk.

'It is unwise, my lady,' said Julian, 'to show your fears too plain, or to press her unduly. They are both completely innocent, as yet.'

'Aye,' agreed Ursula, 'but we'll set forth for Cumberland as soon as I get leave from Sir Anthony . . .' She paused and added in a rush, 'He, too, gazes at Celia in a way I think unseemly.'

'*Dio Mio!*' Julian raised his hands, then let them fall. 'Any man would, but you must *not* be so fearful. That child has spirit, taste and loyalty. Moreover, though innocent, she was

187

reared in a tavern and cannot be ignorant. It's not loss of virginity I fear for her, it's suffering and heartbreak. Stephen is as chaste as she, and would never touch her—the other men who wish to bed her, and there *will* be many, can never be dangerous, since barring the most brutal of rapes, of course, no woman's maidenhead is pierced without secret consent.'

Ursula was not listening to him, she was straining to hear the light footsteps outside, and the tap on the door which soon came.

Celia rushed in. 'Here's your silk, Aunt!' she waved a crimson skein. 'Mercer's 'prentice wanted fourpence for it, I told him 'twas disgraceful, and I none o' the Castle gentry to be diddled like that! So I got it for thripence.' She put the change in Ursula's hand. 'And, I met Brother Stephen below! I vow he seems better than afore all his sickness, and he says he'll start my lessons next week again!'

Ursula compressed her lips, but her plans were immature. She could not so soon dampen the girl's gaiety.

She accepted the threepenny bit with a fleeting smile, and said, 'Master Julian, pray will you look at Celia's palm?'

He was immensely reluctant to do so. His hunger, and his discomforts had increased. He would have refused except that Celia danced up to him, holding out both her hands. ' 'Tis part o' the fortune?' she asked giggling. 'Last summer at Cowdray Fair, there was an old wise-woman who read palms. I wanted to try but didn't have the silver.'

He took the small, reddened hands in his, he turned them over and gazed briefly at the Mounts of Venus, Jupiter, Saturn and the Life Line. He started and squinted harder, hoping that his eyes were tricking him. He dropped her hands abruptly. The women waited.

'There's little here,' he said at last, shrugging. 'I see little to interpret, and am wary. I bid you good-day, we'll break fast and meet in the morning.' He bowed and hurried away.

Julian went down the passage to his room, where he poured himself a glass of wine, and tried to deny what he had seen. On both of Celia's palms the Life Line was very short and stopped with an 'island' on the Mount of Venus. In the right palm, furthermore, there was the malignant cross on Saturn at the base of the ring finger. Well, he thought, *many* die young and violent deaths, and she *had* a star on Jupiter which is good. Besides, nothing is certain in this world, and I have seen prognostications go awry, or she may have had a childish injury which distorted her right palm. In any case, I can do nothing. Soothsaying is not my forte—I am a physician. He took another glass of wine, and gradually began to feel resentment towards Ursula who had nagged him into sentiments he deplored. He combed his hair and beard, brushed his robes and went off to find Sir Anthony.

*   *   *

At nine o'clock that evening, Anthony—having spent a long day disposing of tenants, a thieving pot-boy, hysterical accusations of witchcraft against Old Molly of Whiphill, the steward's requisitions, and finally, the requests of Stephen, Master Julian, and Lady Ursula—gave a great yawn, and pushing back from the supper table emptied a flagon of mead.

'Excellent,' he remarked to Lord Gerald, the only remaining visitor at Cowdray. 'The butler chills it in the well, and the honey came from Yorkshire—heather, y'know—gives a tang. Old-fangled drink, but I had my bellyful o' fancy clarets and muscadines while the King was here. God's blood, 'tis hot tonight,' he added, loosening his ruff and mopping his face on a yellow silk handkerchief.

Gerald's bright squirrel eyes peered at his host. 'Ye've had a hard day, Nephew,' he said twinkling. 'Niver so conscientious will I be, if I'm Earl on me rightful lands again.'

Anthony laughed. It amused him when this young bantam who was only three years older, addressed him as 'Nephew'. It did not amuse him to think of Geraldine as 'Mother', and he had never done so.

'When and if you get your earldom,' said Anthony, yawning again, 'spare me the plots, I don't want to know 'em . . . 'Tis a night to get drunk and go wenching i' the moonlight. Pity the Midhurst whores 're so unappetising.'

'You've a dairymaid, Peggy Hobson, she's called. I've sampled her and found her wholesome,' said Gerald helpfully. 'Shall we get her?'

Anthony shook his head. 'I do not foul my own nest. A lapse now and again in town, when My Lady Jane is ailing, but I make full confession and do penance.'

'Is your chaplain strict?' asked Gerald idly, munching on a prune comfit. 'Poor fellow near died, I understand.'

'Aye, he did, but mended enough to resume duties, and saddle me with an importunate matron from Kent.' Anthony made a rueful face as he thought of his interview with Emma

Allen. She had been subdued, ingratiating, but very persistent in her claim to the lost dowry. When Anthony, quite truthfully, asserted that he had no idea where it was, round glistening drops had oozed from the corners of her eyes. Finally, she had collapsed on a bench and given two or three sobs, while her husband distractedly patted her shoulder.

Anthony's conscience was sometimes troubled, as had been his father's by the immense benefits they had derived from the Dissolution of the Monasteries, and to be rid of Emma, he finally gave her six gold angels and a slightly flawed diamond ring.

She accepted these avidly, her tears dried, and she hurried her husband away, clearly relieved that she had got anything.

Anthony had also been generous with Master Julian, expressed thanks for his successful doctoring of the house priest, and given him a small purseful of coins, adding kindly that if he ever had influence at Court he would try to temper Edward's antipathy, 'but I walk the edge of a very narrow plank myself, good doctor, as you must see,' he had said shrugging, while Master Julian nodded and they shook hands in a cordial farewell.

The interview with Lady Ursula had been more disquieting. Anthony was startled, even hurt that members of his household might desire a protracted absence from Cowdray. And he thought Ursula's plan of journeying to the Border wilderness both dangerous and foolish.

'At your *age*, lady?' he said sharply, 'and with that—that fair young maid. Impossible.' He felt further discomfort in realising that each day glimpses of the fair young maid—at the foot of his table, or in the garden gathering posies, or playing with the newest litter of puppies—had become pleasing to him.

'Surely Celia doesn't wish to make this outrageous journey?' he said. 'I thought her happy at Cowdray.'

'She does not know yet,' said Ursula. 'There are reasons—' She took a long breath. 'Reasons why she must go. Sir Anthony, I humble myself to ask this of you, but I'm Celia's only relation, and I know what's best for her. I humble myself further to beg of you horses and an escort.'

'*What* reasons?' asked Anthony hotly. 'Explain yourself, lady!'

He saw her face fall, but the eyes met his proudly, steadily until he thought of this woman he had long taken for granted, as almost formidable. He was also reminded of her lineage. The de Bohun pedigree went back five hundred years to the days of the Conqueror; Bohuns had been the owners of Cowdray and Midhurst until 1528, a scant twenty-four years back at the time of the forced sale to Anthony's uncle of the half-blood, Lord Southampton. While *I*, thought Anthony, had lived here but five years, myself.

'I can't give you reasons,' said Ursula quietly, 'except that they have to do with the avoidance of a grave threat to Celia's soul and salvation, I've been praying to St. Anthony—your own saint, sir—that he will intercede in this matter. That he'll give you a sign, as he has me.'

'Sign . . . ?' said Anthony slowly. 'You've had a sign?'

'Aye, last Tuesday, the candle I lit at his feet sent forth a shower of sparks, and flared high, it shone on the face of the Baby Jesus in the saint's arms, and the Little One smiled.'

'Ah . . . indeed . . .' Anthony was shaken. He could not disbelieve her quiet awed voice, and after all, St Anthony was known as the saint of wonders. 'I accede to your request, My Lady Ursula,' he had said after a moment. 'God gi'e you good speed.'

Gerald had been watching his host during Anthony's reflections, and he now spoke airily. 'Ye're uncommon grave, m'lad, 'tis unhealthy to ponder. Since ye'll not wench, let's try our luck at these.' He drew a leather box from his pocket, and rattled the ivory dice.

Seven

The hazy red August sun had scarcely risen above Trotton forest when the Cumberland-bound party set out from Cowdray.

Anthony, always generous by instinct, had made handsome provision for the expedition. Ursula and Celia were mounted on quiet sturdy geldings. There was a stout mule to carry the coffers and bedding, and there were two escorts — a gangling lad of sixteen called Simkin, and his father, Wat Farrier.

Wat was thirty-nine, a powerful, black-bearded man, ruddy-cheeked beneath shrewd little eyes like a bear's. He had been born near the stables, and raised among them, but from childhood shown so much quick wit and skill at any odd jobs old Sir Anthony wanted done that the elder knight sent Wat to Midhurst dame school for a year.

So, Wat could figure and knew his letters. He was adept at falconry, and supervised the gamekeepers. He was also Cowdray's Keeper of the Horse, and could tilt at the quintain as well as any knight. During old Sir Anthony's lifetime Wat had seen a bit of the world when he accompanied his master on diplomatic or military missions. He had been north to the Border in 1543 during one of the sporadic attempts to subdue the Scots. He had fought at the siege of Boulogne; he had gone to Cleves with Sir Anthony Browne to bring home Anne, 'The Flemish Mare', whose person so displeased old King Hal that there were many ticklish moments for Sir Anthony before the marriage was annulled.

During the last five years Wat had chafed at the restricted life of Cowdray, fond as he was of young Anthony to whom he had taught riding and falconry.

Wat, was therefore, delighted with this mission to the North, and delighted to be free of his wife for a while. Joan, the fair buxom dairymaid of eighteen years past had somehow turned into a frowzy scold. She had grown bony as a rake, and her tongue sharp as a needle.

Wat had often thought of de-camping. There was the war in France which might be joined, or one might enlist in Sebastian Cabot's expedition which was even now recruiting 'men for the three ships which were to search for a north-east passage to India. The western voyages had discovered a new continent, but not, after all, the precious Spice Islands.

Loyalty to the Browne family, inherited down the generations, had curbed Wat's errant wishes. He had solaced himself by galloping off on Feast Days to Portsmouth where he could watch ships loading, and swill down tankards with sailors in The Dolphin.

The escortage of two women on what would certainly be a tedious journey was not quite his fancy, yet there was a secret mission involved which might liven the trip.

Wat turned a minatory eye on Simkin, who was shambling along beside the mule, and for a moment doing nothing to warrant a father's censure; then he glanced at his charges. The Lady Ursula for all her years, rode easily, her back erect, swaying in rhythm to the bay gelding's brisk walk, her gloved hands loose on the reins.

The girl was another matter. She gripped the pommel, her left foot was turned wrong in the stirrup. She'd take a deal of schooling, Wat thought, being, after all, but a bastard Bohun and a tavern wench. Pretty lass, though, or would be if she didn't look so stiff and solemn—ill-tempered, like as not. Women, thought Wat, of all ages, they were strange kittle-cattle, you never knew, and better not find out what was irking them. He glanced ahead towards a ridge of dun-coloured clouds lying low over the Weald to the North. The ways'd likely be muddy after Petworth.

He shrugged his shoulders inside the leather jerkin which was blazoned on the sleeve with the red buck's head, and humming a 'Hey Nonny Nonny', flicked a horse-fly from his stallion's neck.

They plodded through Easebourne, past the Priory, and Ursula looked again at Celia who maintained the silence she had held since leaving Cowdray's gatehouse, when she had responded to Anthony's farewells with a muffled, 'Thank ye, sir.' Blessed St. Mary, Ursula thought, the child looks blasted! But 'twill pass. Lauded be St. Anthony I've got her away. New sights, new people will soon dispel the gloom—a childish wan hope which could have no real basis, since even last night Celia had been gay, laughing at her own mistakes while young Mabel tried to teach her lute-playing, and parrying Lord Gerald's banter with a light coquetry

Nothing could possibly have happened since, to produce

the fixed stony silence. The girl did not even turn her head for a last glimpse of the castle, nor beyond it St. Ann's Hill where a plume of blue smoke showed that Brother Stephen must be cooking his breakfast.

Ursula reached across between the horses and put her hand on Celia's shoulder. 'Only think, sweeting!' she said brightly, 'London tomorrow night, or next—you'll see the Bridge, the Tower, the palaces—we'll go to the bull-ring if you like—ah, 'twill be wondrous exciting!'

Celia answered nothing at all, her strained eyes stared at her gelding's ears.

'Are you queasy, dear? The motion of the horse when you're not accustomed . . . ?'

'No, Aunt,' said Celia, at length, turning her head away.

A pox on it, thought Ursula. Sulky children should be chastised. Her own mother had raised her with nips and slaps when she transgressed. But Celia had not transgressed, and she did not seem a child, her little face showed a chill detachment.

Except for the clop-clop of hooves on the dusty highway to Petworth, and the barking of farmhouse dogs there was no further sound for some miles.

Celia had scant awareness of the others, or the road. The tiny fraction of her mind which had responded to her aunt's question did not ripple the surface of the deep black pond into which she had sunk last night. In her chest she felt the black hollowness. Desolation as an active force, replacing the anger she had felt for a while. The anger was far less miserable, and she willed it to return. I hate him, she thought. I said so, I meant it. I mean it now. But there was the bleak hollowness, sharpened to hurt by little rat-nibbles of humiliation.

Celia had gone to Stephen on Tan's Hill last evening. Were it not for that interview, she would not have been riding to London with Ursula today on the way to exile.

Celia had laid careful plans for escape. For the last three days she had secreted bread, cheese, salted fish in a cache under a yew near the close walks, and she had arranged to hide in Molly o'Whipple's garret until the hue and cry died down. Old Molly, 'the wise-woman', though esteemed by Lady Jane for her herbal remedies, was generally held to be a witch. All the countryside feared her, they would never have looked for Celia at Molly's. Thus had been Celia's plans, formed by the frantic desire to remain near Stephen, and the certainty that he wished her to.

After the moment of official farewell in Cowdray chapel yester-morn when she had knelt for his blessing, it seemed to her that he had asked her to stay. Amidst the shock of sudden bliss when he touched her hair, her neck, she thought she heard him murmur, 'Don't leave me, beloved.' Ursula swept her out of the chapel before she could respond to Stephen, but she had no doubts as to their complete understanding.

Her secret had sustained her through the afternoon and supper. She had been laughing, airy, until they rose from the table after Sir Anthony's kindly toasts to the voyagers. Then Celia excused herself to her aunt, saying that she wished to bid farewell to Mab's litter.

Ursula, harassed by a dozen last-minute travel details, only smiled tolerantly. Celia's passion for the new beagle puppies was well known.

Yet once outside in the barnyard Celia paused only a second at the kennel where the puppies were squealing and tumbling over their mother. She sped past the granary, darted around the row of cottages and down to the meadow. It was near dusk, the cotters were inside getting ready for bed. Nobody saw Celia as she ran across the footbridge over the Rother, plunged into the hillside forest of oaks and elms and up the rough path to the top. She clambered over the mossy remnants of the old wall, and saw without surprise that Stephen was standing a few yards away from his hut. She expected him to be waiting for her.

He had been digging a garden plot, where he would sow the herbs Master Julian had listed for him. His habit was kirtled high, looped under his knotted scourge at the waist. His legs were streaked with earth. His face was flushed and glistening. He had taken off the dangling crucifix which knocked against the spade handle. He looked younger, less monk-like than she had ever seen him, and Celia called out a joyous, 'Stephen! I'm here, at last!'

She ran to him laughing.

Stephen dropped the spade, turning on her a startled face. The girl was wearing the moss green woollen travelling dress Anthony had provided and a russet velveteen cloak. The hood had fallen back from her bright hair. Her face shone white in the gloaming, and her appearance to him was so eerie, like a dryad flitting from the forest, that his hand rose to cross himself. The pagans, he thought in confusion, they held rites on this hill top. Before the True Faith came to England.

'Ye stare so, love—' cried Celia, still laughing, 'but ye knew I'd come to thee.'

Stephen's intake of breath was clear above the chittering of squirrels and the rustling leaves.

'No,' he said.

He pulled down his habit, and became the tall, black forbidding figure she knew too well. 'Celia, why are you here? I said goodbye to you this morning.'

'It was a sham,' she said smiling. 'D'ye think I'd leave thee? Go off a thousand miles from thee? I saw the look in your eyes. You touched my neck, you *asked* me to bide here.'

His flush deepened, and his voice was cutting. 'I said *naught* to you, but the "Benedicite".' Nor had he, yet all day he had been appalled by the realisation that his hand of its own will had caressed her hair, and stroked the petal-smooth white neck while she knelt before him. 'To be sure you're leaving— at sunrise tomorrow—for Cumberland. What else?'

She heard the weakness in the question and laughed again gently.

'Oh, 'tis very simple,' she whispered, bending close to him. 'I've it well planned. I've saved food. I'll hide a while at Molly o'Whipple's and can come to you nights up here. 'Tisn't far. Molly'll not gab.'

'Celia . . .' Stephen knew that the girl was not aware of the full purport of her plan, that her innocence was real, yet he quickly found the needed cold and reasonable words. 'This is folly, child! Disobedient and ungrateful folly. You've no more wits than a titmouse. How long do you think to hide at Molly's? What would you do after?'

'Why—' she said, faltering, 'after a bit I'd go back to Cowdray. And you'd win them over—Aunt Ursula, Sir Anthony. They'll listen to *you*—and we'd be nigh each other.'

'What for?' said Stephen clipping the words. 'I don't want you near.'

She gasped, twisting her hands on a fold of her cloak. 'That's a lie, Stephen,' she whispered, staring up at him. 'You *do* want me nigh!' She rushed forward and threw her arms around his neck. He felt the soft pressure of her body, and his own body's shameful response as she kissed him. Her lips were hot and sweet. The dizzy flame they lit, he had felt before only in wicked dreams from which he awoke shivering and disgusted. He jerked back from her.

'Slut!' he cried, and pushed her so hard that her foot caught on the fallen spade and she fell to the turf. She lay there, her face covered by her hands.

'You're a little fool, Celia Bohun,' he said, 'and by Our Lady, I believe I hate you!'

She did not move, and he stared down with savage joy at her abasement. Stared at the curve of her hips, and the slender naked leg exposed by her rumpled skirt. His chest constricted with a furious pain. '*Misericorde*,' he said beneath his breath. 'These are whorish tricks, Satan's tricks.'

The eight o'clock curfew bell rang out from Midhurst church, a sheep bleated in the pasture by the Rother. Two elm branches creaked together as the twilight breeze freshened.

Suddenly Celia leapt to her feet. She confronted him with arms akimbo, her chin high, and spoke with the vulgar intonation of her tavern childhood. 'Aye—meaching house priest! Ye're roight. I'm a fool. I've been a love-sick moon-calf. I too can hate. 'Tis a far simpler lesson than tothers ye dinned me with. Never fear, I'm off to Cumberland. There're men there'll be joyed to see me, forsooth no doubt there'll be many. I bid ye farewell, Brother Stephen!'

She made him a slow sweeping curtsy, smoothed down her skirts and tossed back her hair. She vanished as she had come, melting into the forest.

'Blessed Jesu—' Stephen whispered. He stood a long time, staring down at the spade. His eyes stung and watered. He walked slowly into the little chapel and knelt on the stone altar slab. 'Ave Maria in gratia plena . . .' The words were dry as the rustling leaves 'Pater Noster—libera nos ab malo . . .' —the meaningless chittering of squirrels.

He went into his hut, and sat on his stool, his eyes went as always to his picture of the Virgin. The benign, the loving look had gone. It seemed to him that the beautiful face smirked at him with leering reproof. He gazed at it a moment. He got up and covered the picture with the purple linen pall which shrouded Her in Lent. Then he strode out of his hut, and down the hill's western slope towards the town, away from Cowdray. He walked all night on Midhurst Common.

*   *   *

Wat Farrier, two days later, guided his charges along the Borough High Street into Southwark, while a clamour of church bells rang out for noon.

'Blessed Mary, what a din!' remarked Ursula smiling. 'I'd forgot the town was so noisy.'

Below the ding-dongs from parish churches on both sides of the Thames, there was a constant rumbling of carts, horses' whinnies, barking dogs, shouted orders to porters and the melodious street cries. 'Who'll buy? Who'll buy?' 'What d'ye lack?' 'Milk—Country milk . . .!' 'Scissors and knives, to grind —to grind!'

The street narrowed, and grew shadowy beneath the over-hanging windows, from which came periodic shouts—'Un-guard below!' While someone flung out the contents of a chamber pot into the gutters. They jogged past the old Tabard Inn, and heard pleasanter sounds through the paved courtyard. The plunking of a lute, accompanied by a penny whistle, and someone singing, 'Back and side go bare, go bare.'

'Used to be vastly *more* noise,' remarked Wat, adjusting his felt hat, and winking at a pretty barrow-maid who was trundling baskets full of peaches and apricots. 'We had the monastery bells *too*. Often I thought my ears'd split. Bigod, I did.'

'Aye,' agreed Ursula thoughtfully. She had not been to London in many years, nor ever lodged on the South Bank before. They were to stay in Southwark in Sir Anthony's town house which was the former Priory of St. Mary Overie. Along with Battle Abbey in Sussex, King Henry had presented this ancient Augustinian Priory to the elder Browne. Ursula had, so far, no particular scruples about dispossessed monks, nor sacred places turned secular, yet as they neared the great Priory Church, now the parish one, rechristened St. Saviour's, and therefore spared destruction, she was dismayed by the raffish state of the adjoining chapels. Both had been boarded up, the fair Gothic stonework daubed with plaster, the stained glass splintered, then replaced by tattered paper. The smaller chapel had become a bakehouse, with an oven built on the site of the altar—the Lady Chapel housed a drove of squeal-ing, malodorous pigs.

Wat, who shared these startled discoveries, gave his deep chuckle, and said, 'Well-a-day, lady—times do change—pigs and bread be more useful to a man than a gaggle o' droning monks, though me old master never've permitted this. Young master he don't pay heed to the property here. Forever stuck down at Cowdray.'

Ursula did not answer, even valued servants must be repressed when they spoke too freely, but it occurred to her that in avoiding his London home, Anthony might be showing proper caution. It was from here that he had been hauled off to gaol for hearing Mass. And Stephen Gardiner, the Bishop of Winchester, once all-powerful favourite, was now disgraced and imprisoned in the Tower. She glanced at the Bishop's Palace close by them. The windows were shuttered; the huge pile had a forlorn neglected look.

It *was* a dangerous time for Catholics, Ursula thought. At Cowdray she had scarcely realised this, and obeyed Anthony's orders during the King's visit simply from fear of displeasing her patron. Larger perils had not seemed real, and, thought Ursula, with an uncomfortable flash of honesty, had she not been secretly relieved when Brother Stephen was shut up in the cellars? Relieved even by the rat-bite sickness later?

They approached the river, and Ursula glanced at Celia. 'Oh, look, sweeting,' she cried, 'there's London Bridge!'

The girl looked eagerly. During the last days of travelling, as they plodded through heavily mired ways, up and down the Weald, entered and left a score of villages, spent the nights at two inns far more luxurious than the Spread Eagle, Celia's gnawing black hurt had receded. She had walled it off in a secret cell. She knew it was there, but she could ignore it.

She stared at the Bridge. Her mother had told her about it many times, and taught her the childish singing game.

'But, it's all *houses*, Aunt,' Celia said frowning. 'It looks like a street. I pictured it of marble, like the chimney piece in the great Hall at Cowdray!'

'Aye, maiden,' said Wat, laughing, 'dreams 're seldom like the truth. Ye'll learn that in time.'

'No doubt!' answered Celia pertly, with a slight toss of her head which tickled Wat. He was delighted that the girl had recovered from the dumpish sulks with which she had started the journey. He was amused that his son, young Simkin, had taken to reddening and goggling when he helped Celia down from the saddle. Might be a match one day, Wat thought. When the lad grows up a bit. He'll not be a stable-boy long. I'll see to that. If I send him a-soldiering he might rise fast i' the world. Wat understood that Lady Ursula had ambitions for her niece, but he thought they were foolish. Celia was only a tavern wench, with a bastard father from an extinct stock. Steward wouldn't even seat the girl above the salt. That showed her station! And Lady Ursula herself—her equivocal position at Cowdray was obvious to all.

' 'Tis here, lady,' he said to Ursula, pointing and nudging her horse. 'Sir Anthony's lodging. I trust the caretaker'll be about since they've had no notice.'

Wat showed his party into the erstwhile cloisters. The central garth was planted now with turnips and pot greens. Four of the Priory rooms had been sparsely furnished with bedsteads, tables, stools and cupboards, but they were dusty and airless. The caretaker, a doddering monk kept on from charity by old Sir Anthony, was finally discovered snoring on a straw pallet.

'Wake up, Brother!' cried Wat, shaking the skinny shoulder. 'We've come from the master at Cowdray!'

The old man jumped. He clutched his tattered habit around him, and peered up with frightened eyes. 'I've done naught wrong,' he whispered. 'There's been no Masses here. Ye can look for yourselves—there's naught Papist here . . .'

'Nay, nay—' said Wat impatiently. 'We be'ent King's proctors. We come from Cowdray, from Sir Anthony Browne. We'll stop here a bit. Bestir yourself, ye old trout.'

Under the combined reassurances of Wat and Ursula, Brother Anselm lost his fears and brightened into garrulity. He had been alone in the Priory room for months, suffering from a leg playfully injured by one of the King's men when they came to arrest Sir Anthony. 'Tripped me up wi' his pike-staff, did the blackguard,' Brother Anselm explained. 'Same one who took an axe to our little altar and crucifix we thought well hid i' the old cupboard.'

Celia kept her eyes away from the monk as he rambled on. Here was no reminder of the secret blow except the habit, and that being Augustinian as well as filthy bore scant resemblance to Stephen's, but she whisked into practical matters—laying their bedding on the steads, helping Simkin kindle a fire to cook dinner. Food and action keep miseries at bay—this she had learned in childhood.

The next two days were spent in seeing London. Ursula was as excited as Celia when they rode through the city from the sinister Tower to Temple Bar, then gaped at the palaces along the Thames until they reached Westminster. Agog as any country folk they gazed at the Abbey, and set foot in the portal. But Ursula would not attend a service there. Her Catholicism she had taken for granted in Sussex; in London she began to realise how destructive the new religion was. As they rode the streets they constantly encountered ruins. Priories, convents, hospitals and churches — (those not rededicated for a parish) — all had been torn down and the stones carted off to build Protestant mansions. The streets seemed very odd without the friars, the monks, the priests, the pairs of nuns who used to throng them. Their place was taken by starving beggars who lay moaning near the doorsteps, hopeless and without asylum.

' 'Tis horrible,' said Ursula, one morning on the Strand, as a tattered scabrous woman suddenly screamed, vomited blood and died before their eyes. 'Nobody cares for them now. Nobody cares for the old, the sick, the poor.' She had doled out all she dared from the purse Anthony had given her for expenses, but it did so little good. And the prices had risen double since she was in London years ago.

Celia was naturally less appalled. She was not mature enough to understand human suffering in which she had no part. But as Ursula continually exclaimed in pity, Celia was forced to recognise the wickedness in the callous transformations. The Crutched Friar's church was now a tennis court where young gallants batted balls. St. Mary's Hospital of near two hundred beds had been razed; nettles grew in the ruins. The Church of the Knights Hospitallers had been blown up with gunpowder. Everywhere they looked they might see jewelled fragments of stained glass, or broken crosses piled in heaps.

'I didn't know it was like this,' said Ursula. 'The Devil has taken London.'

'Yet, dear Aunt,' Celia ventured as they returned from a ride through the city, 'Wat says King Edward is founding a new hospital; that he's not unmindful of the commons' good.'

Ursula shook her head. 'I doubt that pale spineless lad can help his people, nor will live to do so.'

They were approaching London Bridge, bound back to Southwark when Ursula made this remark in a clear indignant tone. The sudden result of it was like a thunderbolt.

A rough hand clamped down on Ursula's shoulder, twisting her in the saddle. A sardonic bearded face thrust close to hers. 'Back ye go!' said the man who wore a brass helmet and padded doublet. He yanked the gelding's bridle. 'Thou too, maiden,' he said to Celia. 'Both of ye!' He carried a pike-staff, and had a dagger at his belt. 'I heard ye plain, mistress,' he growled, prodding Ursula on the leg with his pike-staff. 'An' ye'll answer fur it.'

'Heard what? Answer for what?' cried Ursula, though her heart beat fast. 'Don't you *dare* touch me!'

'Treason, that's wot.' The guard spat on the pavingstones. 'An' ye'll answer fur it to the Dook. He's at Durham House the nonce.' He seized the bridles of both geldings, turned them around with a smart blow on their rumps. The Bridge traffic had paused, a knot of apprentices and housewives gathered close, gaping, murmuring.

'What is it, Aunt?' Celia whispered. 'What's the man want?'

Ursula heard some of the murmurs — 'Duke's man ... Northumberland,' while the thickening crowd edged farther away from them peering curiously, but afraid.

'Holy St. Mary,' cried Ursula, 'I'm the Lady Southwell, this is my niece, we are but passing through London, on the way to the North. We are lodging in Southwark where our supper awaits.'

The guard shrugged contemptuously. 'Ye may be Queen o' Spain fur all I care — an' calling on the saints, too! I smell a Papist. Come along!'

Ursula met Celia's uncomprehending gaze. 'It seems we must go with this knave, my dear,' she said slowly. ' 'Tis some foolish blunder he's made.'

The girl nodded, more exhilarated than frightened, and entirely confused. She had never heard the word 'treason' and did not know its meaning. She thought vaguely that they must have transgressed some mysterious London law; perhaps they should not have picked the wallflowers which bloomed at the edge of a nobleman's gate on the Strand. She *did* understand property rights. The Duke's henchman herded them back along the Strand to Durham House, where the courtyard was thronged with petitioners and miscreants like themselves, under guard. The Duke's steward in maroon velvet cap and gown walked pompously from group to group enquiring the reason for each one's presence. His little eyes gleamed, his pursy mouth tightened when he had talked to Ursula's guard. 'Well done, Carson,' they heard him say. 'Aye, His Grace'll want a look at these.'

There was a further delay in the courtyard, until one of the household guard appeared, told the women roughly to dismount and hurried them inside the Palace. He shoved them along corridors into a Presence Chamber which was actually grander and more luxurious than any of Edward's. John Dudley, recently become Duke of Northumberland, sat on a canopied throne, under an immense shield which he had devised for himself. Even the College of Heralds was not immune to expediency, and since the King had not objected, Dudley annexed the quarterings of the titles he had accumulated. The Warwick bear and staff, the Percy lions acted as supporters, pending Dudley's present endeavour to establish a more authentic pedigree for himself.

The Presence Chamber was filled with sycophants—newly made knights, aspirants to favour, several noblemen who had cannily attached themselves to England's virtual ruler. A clerk sat at a desk below the dais, his goose-quill pen poised over parchment, in readiness for the next entry. Few even looked around as Ursula and Celia were hustled in, but the Duke straightened and stared keenly at the two women.

The Duke was an ugly man of fifty. His baldness was partly concealed by a discreetly plumped cap. He was, indeed, soberly dressed, as became an exponent of Calvinism. His dark forked beard, lip tuft and drooping moustaches were profuse, around a small, pouting red mouth. His eyes, like smoky glass, could be merry on occasion—for Edward they always gleamed with paternal affection. They were often coldly appraising, and ruthless—as they were now.

'Good day, lady,' he said to Ursula; he waved her towards him and waited until she had curtsied. 'My guard reports wicked, aye, treasonable speech from you.'

The clerk wrote busily on the parchment. Ursula stood tall and quiet for a moment. 'I remember no such thing, Your Grace, eavesdroppers and spies oft hear wrong.'

The Duke's lids fell, and hooded his eyes, for he knew this to be true, and he thought that an elderly provincial widow and a green girl were hardly worth his time. 'You made derogations anent the King's Grace and his health. You spoke of the Devil,' said the Duke, 'and you swore by a saint.'

Ursula hesitated, ignored the first accusation, and hurriedly answered the last. '	'Twas a slip, Your Grace. I'm an old lady, and was so startled at disrespectful treatment to one of my rank that I may have forgot and used some words from the old religion.'

Northumberland stiffened, perfectly aware that she had evaded him. He peered harder at her. 'What's that chain around your neck?' he suddenly shouted. 'The pendant's hidden! Pull it out!'

Ursula's thin cheeks flushed, her lips quivered and she bit them. The clerk raised his head while several of the chatting knights turned to watch. Celia, for the first time, felt danger.

The Duke made a gesture to his guard who jerked up Ursula's neck chain, revealing a small ivory crucifix on its end.

'Ah ...' said the Duke, smiling gently, and gestured again. The guard, bowing, handed over the gold chain. The Duke with precise deliberation, twisted off the crucifix, broke it in two, then leaning over dropped the pieces in the clerk's wooden trash bucket.

'You are *indeed* forgetful, lady,' he said to Ursula. 'Forgetful of royal decree, of English law.' He suddenly turned on Celia. 'And you, too, maiden—have you hid on you these prohibited, idolatrous trinkets?'

She shook her head, her luminous eyes staring blankly, 'No, sir ...'

The Duke absently hung Ursula's chain over his knee. He smoothed his forked beard, separating the tufts while he appraised the girl. Honest, he thought. He had not risen to power without intuitions. It was near the supper hour, his stomach growled and he felt that a thorough fright was perhaps enough for these insignificant sprats. A week's imprisonment in the Marshalsea would certainly curb seditious speech or disobedience of law.

'Where do you live in Southwark, maiden?' He continued to address Celia, because the old lady's face was angry and mulish. Carson had reported their residence as Southwark, a lowly suburb, and his question was purely formal.

'Sir Anthony Browne's, in St. Mary Overie's old Priory, just now, my lord,' Celia answered. 'But we come from Cowdray.'

The Duke's nostril indented. *Cowdray!* That undoubted nest of Papacy, though no evidence of such had been reported after the King had stopped there on the Progress. He had vetoed Edward's idea of stopping there, and yet permitted himself to be overridden. Anthony Browne's support would be extraordinarily helpful in the future, if it could be gained. Browne was an uncertain factor. Good-tempered, rich, rather stupid, erstwhile Papist, of course, but he might be converted like so many others. The Duke peered past Celia towards the far door.

'My Lord Clinton!' The Duke suddenly raised his voice and bawled down the Chamber to a fat grizzled nobleman who had just entered.

The crowd made way for Clinton who thought that Northumberland wished again to consult on naval matters, since Clinton had arrived from Deptford's royal dockyards. He stopped, astonished when he saw the two women.

'Aye,' said the Duke, watching, 'd'ye know them? Claim they come from Cowdray.'

'Well, I've seen them there,' said Clinton, perplexed. He had exchanged a few courtesies with Lady Ursula at table, and certainly noted Celia, as any man would. 'What's amiss? They in trouble?'

'It may be . . .' answered the Duke slowly. 'The old lady's a Papist, and was heard speaking very indiscreetly about the King's Grace She may be a bit soft i' the head, and I'll let her go if you vouch for her.'

Here the Duke was treading warily. He had but recently gained Lord Clinton to his cause. Clinton, obstinately in love and indecently vocal about it, was to marry Anthony Browne's stepmother next week in Lincolnshire. The Lord High Admiral was not a man one cared to offend.

'Bah!' said Clinton. 'By cock, Northumberland, you waste our time on them, there's weightier matters—when d'ye join the King at Salisbury?'

Despite the lisp occasioned by his missing teeth, the Admiral spoke with force, and none of the fawning timidity the Duke was used to.

'Next week,' said the Duke. 'But Cheke's with him now. There's much business for me here.'

'Aye,' said Clinton impatiently, 'much.' He indicated with a shrug while he sent a reassuring smile to Celia's anxious, lovely face, just how niggling, he thought, was the detention of the women.

But the Duke, ever cautious, had a new suspicion.

'D'you soon return to Cowdray?' he asked Celia, who flushed, aware of mysterious tensions. But she could not refuse to answer, and could see no harm in doing so.

'Not soon—' she faltered. 'We are bound north.'

'Where to?' said the Duke, and waited, fondling his beard.

'The—the Dacres, in Cumberland.'

The Duke glanced at Clinton. Here was a surprise! He had just returned from conferences with Lord Dacre at Berwick. Dacre was the feudal overlord of the Western Marches. His Barony was essential to the strength of the Border. He was also an entrenched Catholic, but practicality required turning a blind eye to religious differences in the wild north where military strength was the only essential.

'Some Dacres o' Gilsland were at Cowdray when the King was,' Clinton snapped. 'The King's Grace liked them. A pox on it, John Dudley—there's Paul's bells ringing four o'clock—ye've grown picky as an old crone!'

The Duke's lids hid his anger. He resented the use of his actual name; he resented Clinton's words, and later, the Admiral would rue them. He acceded, however, except for one more question, smoothly put.

'Do you call, perchance, at Hunsdon on your way north, maiden?' He looked from the young face to the old one, and saw genuine bewilderment on both.

'What's Hunsdon, Your Grace . . .?' asked Celia. 'I've never left Midhurst before, I know not where we stop on the journey.'

'You, lady—' he finally turned to Ursula. 'You *know* who resides now at Hunsdon?'

'No, Your Grace,' said Ursula, with complete truth, 'I do not.'

Clinton suddenly guffawed, and slapped the Duke on the arm. 'We've coils enough, I warrant, wi'out your inventing 'em. Have done, have done!'

The Duke nodded. 'You may go—lady,' he tossed the chain towards her, 'but guard your tongue in future, mind the trinkets that you wear and have no truck wi' the wicked Bishop o' Rome—or ye'll end behind bars, as you would've today, had not My Lord Clinton seen fit to speak for you.'

Celia gasped and clutched at Ursula's hand. 'Behind bars . . .' They both made a silent curtsy, and now there were many curious stares as they walked down the Presence Chamber. A page guided them out to the courtyard. They mounted their horses, and rode again on the Strand to London Bridge. They did not speak until they were back at Southwark in the little Priory lodgings.

Wat Farrier received them anxiously. 'I'd begun to fear fur ye two, ye should've ta'en Simkin—traipsin' London streets alone is not seemly, ye might run into trouble.'

'We did,' said Celia, sitting down with a plop on a bench. 'Oh, Wat . . .' she clasped her hands tight, and began to cry like a frightened child.

Wat stared at her, then at Lady Ursula, whose face was drawn and very pale. Brother Anselm crouched over the fire, stirring a rabbit stew for their supper. Simkin was flinging knives, trenchers, pewter spoons and mugs on the oak table.

'Naow, naow, lass,' said Wat, putting his arm around Celia's shoulders. 'Wot's ado—wot 'appened?'

'We'll sup first,' said Ursula, 'then I'll tell you.' She had passed the age of easy tears, and could find no relief like Celia's, but her hands trembled as she forced herself to eat, and she fought the panic she had not recognised during the ordeal.

They finished restorative mugs of ale, white bread and stew, then together told Wat their story. He was more dismayed than the women, since he knew many factors of which they had no inkling.

Wat gathered that Ursula's chief resentment was that the Duke had broken her crucifix, and that she had been treated with rude disrespect like any common wench. Celia, the shock having dissipated, began to look on the episode as an adventure. 'That Duke—' she said, 'he wasn't really fearsome, he did say he might've put us "behind bars", but no doubt he didn't mean it.'

'He meant it,' said Wat grimly. 'Fleet, King's Bench or Marshalsea, that's where ye'd have gone, save for Lord Clinton.'

'Well, it didn't happen,' said Celia. 'Jesu, but that ugly little man lives in a fine palace, such gildings, tapestries, carpets and glass. It's even grander than Cowdray. Wat . . . where's Hunsdon?'

'Hunsdon,' Wat repeated in a startled voice. 'Was there mention o' Hunsdon?'

'Aye,' said Ursula, pushing back her plate. 'His Grace asked if we were to stop at Hunsdon on the way North. I've never heard of the place.'

Wat sighed. Despite the King's visit—after all a glittering interlude in which these women took scant part—the two lived at Cowdray as sequestered and innocent as in a nunnery. More so, thought Wat, remembering the worldly frivolities at Easebourne. Their ignorance was obviously becoming dangerous to themselves, and to the interests of his master. He wiped his mouth on his leather sleeve, and spoke firmly. 'The Lady Mary's Grace is at Hunsdon. 'Tis in Hertfordshire, and her favourite seat. We *are* stopping there on the way north.'

Ursula swallowed. 'The Princess Mary?' she said incredulously.

Wat shook his head. 'Not so called now, another thing ye better remember, or ye'll get the lot of us hanged at Tyburn yet, m'lady.'

This morning Ursula would have rebuked such a speech, now she merely said, 'What have we to do with the Lady Mary?'

Wat hesitated. He glanced at the old monk who was swabbing the stewpot with bread, and mumbling the savoury morsels between toothless gums. He glanced at his son who leaned against the plaster wall making calf's eyes at the unconscious Celia, who was listening intently for his answer.

'Message from Sir Anthony,' said Wat briefly. 'Natural to pay our respects. She's still heir to the throne.'

'*Still?*' cried Ursula, pouncing. 'There's no question about it. 'Twas in the late King's will. Everyone knows that!'

'Ah . . .' said Wat, 'knowledge's one thing, wot happens is another. The Lady Mary's a stubborn Catholic, the saints preserve her!'

'And Princess Elizabeth is *not* . . .' said Ursula frowning.

'The Lady Elizabeth is not. By all accounts she's a mealy-mouthed little piece, dresses in sad colours, forever given to swoons and megrims, wouldn't say "boo" to a goose. I'd not speak thus, m'self, except the King's Grace now dislikes both his sisters. Won't see 'em.'

'None the less,' said Ursula anxiously. 'He *can't* alter his father's will.'

'A King may do as e' pleases.' Wat clamped down his lips, then mentioned a bear-baiting they might go to and distract their minds from the day's event. He was no surer of the vague conspiracy afoot than was Sir Anthony who had confided in him a little. But rumours ran fast underground. Servants knew more than their masters ever guessed, and during the King's visit Wat had enjoyed a drinking bout with Lord Clinton's valet. The fellow hinted that the Duke of Northumberland had terrifying ambitions. Though what they could be, nobody knew.

'You may take Mistress Celia to the bear-baiting,' said Ursula. 'I wish to be quiet. Guard her well.'

'Ye'll bide here?' asked Wat, well pleased. 'Aye, rest, lady, we'll be off to 'unsdon by sunrise.'

Ursula nodded absently. She wanted to be alone. She watched the excited Celia go off to the bear-baiting between Wat and Simkin. She glanced at Anselm who had collapsed by the fire.

Ursula pulled the broken gold chain from her waist-pouch, and stared at the twisted link which had held the crucifix. Her eyes watered, she blinked them rapidly, then began to pace the stone floor in unhappy confusion. A longing for guidance seized her, for a priest—but she knew not where to find a priest—for sanctuary then, some hallowed place where she might see the dear familiar symbols which had ever been channels towards prayer and spiration. She looked out of the window to St. Saviour's four little spires, put on her mantle, went downstairs into the old cloister garth and so entered the church.

Its bleakness confounded her. The painted windows had all been smashed, a dull greyish glass replaced some of them. Below the Gothic vaulting the fluted pillars had been scribbled on, names and a few obscene sketches drawn with coal. There was no rood screen before the chancel and no altar. A bare oak communion table stood on the altar steps. On the left, the statue of the Holy Virgin was gone, and somebody, a charwoman, no doubt, had left there a faggot broom and cleaning rags. Ursula's slow footsteps echoed in the empty nave.

There was no place to sit, but Ursula knelt on the medieval tiles in the chancel and began to tell her beads on the rosary her mother had given her fifty years ago at her first communion. Except during the King's visit it always dangled from her belt—a plain little chaplet of onyx and crystal ending in a tiny silver cross. Her mantle had hidden it at Durham Place, or it would obviously have been destroyed like the ivory crucifix. As it was, she looked around warily before she began the 'Ave Marias', and hated the need to be furtive, as she hated the ugly impersonality of the desecrated church which rendered the prayers meaningless.

She murmured on, doggedly, seeking a kind of reassurance she had never sought before. There was none. A door slammed somewhere far off and she jumped, hiding the rosary in her pouch. The world has gone mad, she thought. I'm an old woman, and I don't know what to do. They could have put us in prison. They're strong—strong and evil. Our Dear Lord and His Blessed Mother have fled this land. Yet, if Celia can be safe . . . Her love for the girl was warm, touchable, while all other loves were not.

She got up, noting with remote surprise how agile she was, and still aimless, still uncomforted, walked out of the south door.

The sun was lowering. She glimpsed it misty red, reflected on the Thames where swans glided imperturbably among the wherries and barges of the river traffic.

Ursula wandered along the Bankside to the region of brothels and frowsty ale-houses, called the Clink, unaware of the curiosity she aroused among the whores who lolled in their doorways waiting for trade. They stared at the tall elderly lady in black velvet who moved past them with utter indifference. Nobody molested her. She was protected by her dignity, and something in her quite handsome face which they were able to recognise as dolefulness. Sorrow and bereavement were respected in the Clink.

Ursula continued to walk. She returned through fetid alleys to Borough High Street where she turned north once more towards the Thames. Near the George she was impeded by a jostling pack train of laden mules carrying woven goods into the South Country. She drew against a wall, and heard her name called. So deep was her abstraction that she scarcely heeded, and thought to have mistaken one of the peddlers' continuous hoarse cries.

She started when a hand fell on her arm, and a voice repeated, 'Lady Southwell!' Ursula looked around and saw Master Julian smiling at her.

'No more astonished than I,' he said, chuckling at her expression. 'To meet again in *Southwark*!'

Ursula, after a startled second felt pleasure and a mysterious relief. Her face lit up. 'How happy this is,' she exclaimed, seizing his hand. 'I was in sore distress!'

'I grieve to hear it,' said Julian, amused, a little touched at the warmth of her greeting. He knew love-light in a woman's eye, and was far too wise to disdain it from any source. Besides, he liked Ursula, and found her unexpected appearance agreeable.

They walked along together towards the Priory. Julian had just been to inspect a baffling case at St. Thomas's Hospital hard-by—a flaxen-haired girl called Bessie. Her fair face and

neck were turning brown as a chestnut, and were further disfigured by inky patches. Moreover, the patient retained no
food and was dwindling to monkey-size. Bessie was a cousin of
Julian's mistress, Alison, who attributed the repulsive condition to witchcraft, since the girl had ensnared the husband of
a notorious and brutal fish-wife who cast spells for a sixpence.

Julian was uncertain. Witchcraft might be possible, yet he
suspected that the cause lay somewhere inside the scarlet
secret body. The girl was obviously dying, and Julian itched
to anatomise the corpse later, as he had seen Vesalius and his
own master Fracastorius dissect cadavers at Padua. In England
it was legally impossible to procure a corpse. He had been
trying to bribe the hospital porter to save him the body of
the mottled brown girl when she expired, but had scant hope
of success. Julian, still impoverished, could offer only half a
crown, which was not sufficient to inveigle the porter into
crime.

He temporarily forgot the subject in listening to Ursula's
troubles. She poured them out to him, after they reached the
cloister garth and sat down on a stone bench.

Julian understood that it was not so much the fright of the
arrest by Northumberland's guard which disquieted Ursula
now as a new apprehension in general, and the collapse of
values she had thought to be the foundations of living. It was,
Julian realised, the first time in Ursula's sheltered life that
she had encountered ruthlessness.

'And that poor church . . .' she said gesturing, 'St. Mary
Overie—I'll *not* use its new name—what they've *done* to it.
Why didn't God and Our Lady protect their own?'

'One wonders . . .' said Julian, half to himself. 'Yet, throughout history evil often triumphs. Or what seems to us evil, how
can we be sure?'

She stared. 'Not sure what's evil? You jest, Master Julian!
Or the Devil's hot breath is corrupting you too, in this wicked
town.'

Julian shrugged. 'Possibly. I've never seen him, but then
I've never seen an angel either.' His grey eyes twinkled, and
Ursula gave him an uncertain answering smile before reverting
to her worries.

'Will there be more dangers on the way north, d'you think?
I mistrust our stop at Hunsdon to see the Princess Mary.
Why didn't Sir Anthony tell me! And that man—the Duke—
he sits on his throne like a huge spider spinning webs.'

'*Da vero*—' agreed Julian, as it occurred to him that present association with Ursula might prejudice his own interests. The impulsive woman had made herself conspicuous in dangerous quarters. John Cheke had joined the King's progress at Portsmouth, but Julian had first had one encouraging interview with his friend. There was still hope of a Court preferment. Northumberland would also soon join the King. If discovered—any intimacy with a known Catholic was scarcely wise.

Julian got up from the bench, picking up his medical staff. 'Well, Cara Donna,' he said pleasantly, 'I must return to Alison who awaits news of her sick cousin. May good fortune be yours!'

Ursula started. 'You're not *leaving*!' Her cry was so woeful that Julian took her hand and kissed it in a courtly manner.

'I regret, but I must. At least . . .' he added smiling, 'you've got the little Celia away from the entanglement you feared at Cowdray. That is gained.'

'Aye,' said Ursula swallowing. 'And my Celia is destined for a brilliant future. You said so . . . her nativity, her palms!'

Julian bowed, concealing an interior chill. He had seen other things in Celia's future, but there were no certainties in the fuzzy realms of prognostication, and of late he refused to explore them.

'Master Julian!' Ursula cried involuntarily, 'will you marry your leman—that Alison?' Her thin cheeks flushed.

'*Per Bacco, no!*' Julian was outraged. 'A Ridolfi di Piazza wed a barber's daughter! You insult me, lady!'

Ursula's flush deepened, but her eyes showed relief. 'I'm sorry, Master—to be sure you can find a much better match, if you so incline.'

His frown cleared, he gave her a kind look, far more aware than she of the attraction he held for her. Had she been rich, had she lofty position, her ten years or so of seniority would not have deterred him. She was healthy, and she loved him—besides, all cats are grey at night. As it was, he bowed, said, 'Goodbye, Lady Southwell, no doubt we'll meet when you return,' strode from the cloister garth and forgot Ursula as he regained the High Street. That girl in St. Thomas's, she might be dead by now. If I could have a look at the liver, he thought. It *must* be the liver, or that little bladder above it which makes gall . . . yet though we often see jaundice, what could turn the skin to bronze—to black?—except the plague. He glanced

212

down at the hyacinth he wore around his neck in deference to custom, rather than belief. The girl did *not* have the plague, she had none of the symptoms, but if he told the porter she had? *Then* he'd give me the body, shovel it out dead or alive. Fool not to think of it sooner! Julian hurried back to St. Thomas's.

Ursula, left alone on the bench under the cloister, and even more dispirited than before she met Julian, sighed, and wandered upstairs to await Celia's return from the bear-baiting.

* * *

On the following afternoon when Ursula's party reached Hunsdon in Hertfordshire, they were soaked from a steady downpour, and very hungry. Yet it was a long while before they were admitted to the rambling brick mansion. Unknown visitors were rare at Hunsdon, and always viewed with anxious suspicion. The guard left them standing by the gatehouse while he scurried off to consult higher authorities.

Finally Princess Mary's steward, Sir Thomas Wharton, appeared.

'State your business to *me*,' he barked at Ursula, who by her dress and bearing must be the most important one of the wet bedraggled party. 'Her Royal Grace is unwell, and cannot be bothered by petitioners.'

Wat stepped forward authoritatively. 'We come, sir, from Cowdray. I've a message from Sir Anthony Browne, he wants it delivered *in person*.'

Sir Thomas frowned, noting the buck-head badge. Sir Anthony had been Catholic, but now obviously turned heretic, like so many other scoundrels, or the King would not have visited him. Moreover, there was the alliance between Browne's stepmother and Lord Clinton, a notorious Dudleyite.

'Give *me* the message, fellow . . .' said Sir Thomas. 'If I think it meet, I'll relay it.'

Wat's little bear eyes hardened, his under-lip thrust out. 'Message's in me head—Master wants it delivered in person.'

'That you'll not *do*,' cried Sir Thomas, angered by the varlet's tone. 'I told you her Royal Grace is unwell. Be off with ye . . .' He gestured towards the guard, then froze, startled as they all were by a deep mannish voice calling from a window across the courtyard. 'What's ado, Sir Thomas? Who is it?'

They looked up and saw a woman's head in a jewelled coif lean out the window. 'Bring them in!' the voice called.

Sir Thomas made an exasperated gesture, but he dared not disobey.

When they entered the Hall, Princess Mary stood by a great snapping fire awaiting them.

How small the royal lady was, Celia thought, as she copied Ursula's curtsy—small and pinched-looking under a glitter of jewels and gold-threaded brocade. You'd never look at her twice, if you dressed her in jersey. Her hair, once the true Castilian gold, had faded to drab. Her thin mouth was stubborn. Her eyes sunken and set in a frown of pain.

Though Mary was but thirty-five, Celia thought her old and negligible. She thought the whole visit tiresomely uncomfortable, since she was cold and hungry, nor had much curiosity about the mysterious message. She stood aside and idly counted the panes in the latticed windows, while Mary questioned Sir Thomas in her harsh, deep voice. Wat was seething impatiently, but dared not speak. Ursula watched the Princess's sharp little face grow increasingly suspicious; she saw that Sir Thomas's attitude would prevail and they would all be packed off into the cold drizzle again. She then perceived the elaborate gold crucifix among the other jewels on Mary's flat chest.

Ursula reached in her pouch and drew out her own shabby rosary. She waited until the gesture caught Mary's eye, then slowly kissed the silver cross.

The Princess started, her face was transfigured, her thin lips relaxed into a singularly sweet smile. 'Ahh . . . so . . .' she murmured while touching her crucifix. 'You are welcome to Hunsdon,' she said, 'in the name of Our Blessed Lord.'

She gave orders to the reluctant Sir Thomas, and commanded that Ursula should sup with her. 'You shall tell me, Lady Southwell, about my brother, the King's Grace—how he looked, what he said, at Cowdray. 'Tis long since I've seen him, and never alone any more. He loved me once,' she added beneath her breath. 'Holy Virgin, he can *not* have grown to hate me. He can *not*!'

Thus it was that they were all invited to spend the night at Hunsdon.

Mary had for weeks been both anxious and bored, a condition which increased her nagging ill health. She had headaches, and toothaches besides a frequent dull throbbing in her woman's parts. The memory of her miserable girlhood with her adored, repudiated Spanish mother—the fears, the dangers—never left her, though she seldom mentioned them. She prayed for forgiveness when hatreds overpowered her, especially hatred of the heartless magnificent father who had replaced his legal wife by Nan Bullen, the whore. And hatred of Elizabeth, the innocent result of that sham marriage.

Mary had schooled herself to docility, to semi-exile, to patience. On one point only she had been adamant. She would alter no form nor observance of her religion—her mother's religion—she would have her confessor and her Mass. To retain these against fierce opposition from Edward and his Council, she had invoked her cousin, the Holy Roman Emperor Charles, whose threats of armed intervention had for long protected Mary—until lately. The war in France was ended, the Emperor, a world-weary man, had cooled off from defending a nearly friendless and aging woman who would probably not live to ascend England's throne.

Mary was now forced to celebrate Mass in secret, her ex-postulary and affectionate letters to Edward remained unanswered. She who was well-trained to recognise the scent of danger, smelled vague whiffs of it around her, but she had never doubted her position as present heir to the throne. This was her father's royal decree, it was also manifest Divine Decree. She loved her brother and made excuses for his unkindness because of his youth—in hopeful moments she felt sure that after she managed to see him when he had returned to London, she would somehow regain his affection, and her position at Court. Her prayers, and all the Catholic prayers in Christendom, headed by those of His Holiness the Pope, would soon reclaim Edward from his morass of error. Of this Mary felt certain, and all the more so after hearing Ursula's account at supper of the visit to Cowdray. Mary deplored but understood the temporary need for hiding the Benedictine monk, for denuding the chapel in deference to Edward's temporary madness.

'Tis vile!' Mary cried, slamming down her ale tankard. 'The anti-christs surrounding my poor brother! And the mere chits who are taught these preposterous heresies. Lady Jane Grey is another. Scarce sixteen and as wickedly deluded as his Royal Grace. Imagine what she said when she entered my chapel last May!'

Celia, whose thoughts had been wandering while her aunt

talked with the Princess, pricked up her ears. She had never heard of a Lady Jane Grey, but the girl's age interested her—so near to her own.

Ursula looked expectant. Lady Wharton who was the other member of the supper party shook her head and sighed.

' 'Twas dreadful,' she murmured.

'That girl . . .' said Mary, 'when my Lady Wharton knelt before the Host—we were still permitted to keep it on the altar then—she asked, "Why do you curtsy? The chapel is empty." Lady Wharton replied that she knelt before Him who had made her. And Jane Grey said insolently, "Nay, how foolish, for the *baker* made that sliver of bread up there!" '

Ursula gave a shocked sound, while Celia was disappointed. The baker *did* make the bread, didn't he? Nor had she ever been taught of the miracle of transubstantiation. Stephen had never thought to mention it. What crime is this? Celia wondered, though she was woman enough to understand another allegation against Jane Grey, who apparently eschewed all finery, and had insolently refused a richly embroidered gown Mary presented to her, saying that all ornament was vain, and the Princess by adorning herself was one grown deaf to God's word.

'Wicked impertinence,' said Mary angrily. 'And a sign of these fearsome times which have come upon us. My royal father would have had her whipped, at least.'

The three elder ladies continued their scandalised comments while Celia sat below them at the table, silent as Ursula had taught her to be, unwilling to think of the past, unable to imagine the coming journey, absorbed in slaking her hunger with a surprisingly tough and rancid hunk of pork. She had grown accustomed to the Cowdray fare—always delicious—and missed it.

After supper Mary remembered Wat Ferrier and his insistence on delivering a message. Ursula's confidence had made it plain that Sir Anthony Browne might still be trusted, and Mary had her share of curiosity.

She therefore retired to her privy chamber, which at Hunsdon was no more than a curtained alcove at the end of the gallery, and she summoned Wat.

'Are we surely alone, Your Royal Grace?' Wat asked, first kneeling, then standing with his leathern cap held in his hand.

'Aye,' said Mary, kind but wary. 'What is the message you

so press on me? I trust they've fed you well as can be in the servants' hall?'

He nodded. 'Thank ye, Your Grace . . .' and was silent a moment covertly taking her measure.

He had never seen her close before today, and like Celia, was startled by her meagreness in contrast to the deep voice. She had no sensuous appeal for a man, yet now he recognised in her smile, and the set of her head a likeness to her father. An aura of royalty, dim and tenuous, and she was not the poor little wisp he had thought.

He fumbled inside his jacket where his wife had sewn a tiny pocket. He drew out a small tarnished gold signet ring, and tendered it to her.

' 'Tis this, Your Grace—and pray will ye examine it close?'

Mary took the ring, saw a faint carving of a buck's head at-gaze, and the scroll of a motto—*Suivez raison*—blurred by use.

'Aye . . .' she said. 'What's this for?'

'Will ye know it again?' asked Wat anxiously.

She nodded, knitting her sparse sandy brows.

'If it come to ye again, by *any* hand,' said Wat gravely, 'Your Grace must beware of aught else ye've heard. Of *any* summons.'

She frowned harder. 'You speak in riddles, my good fellow. Forsooth, the message was not so obscure as this? *What* summons?'

Wat did not know. Sir Anthony had made him memorise only these words.

'I mislike this,' she said with a flash of anger. ' 'Tis meant as a warning, I suppose, well meant, I hope. Did Sir Anthony give it you himself?'

Wat was silent, mindful of his master's words. 'Show the ring to Her Grace, say nothing but what I tell you to.'

'May I go, Your Royal Grace,' asked Wat. 'I've a hard ride ahead tonight.'

Mary bit her lips, uncertain, annoyed, and yet knowing that the man would explain no further. 'How so?' she said sharply. 'You can't leave for Cumberland *now*!'

He shook his head. 'London, Your Grace. I'll come back fur my ladies tomorrow.'

He reached his hand respectfully out for the ring. Mary gave it to him, impressed as she always was by male strength and obduracy, even in a servant. Her head ached again, she

217

lost interest in the little episode, lost interest in Lady South-well and her pretty young niece. Though it was barely dark, she could think only of rest, of the soothing mithridate Lady Wharton would give her, and oblivion—were she lucky—for part of the restless night.

It did occur to Mary that Lady Southwell should be secretly apprised of the Mass which would be celebrated in the Prin-cess's bedchamber at seven in the morning. The priest, a Spaniard, now disguised in the Hunsdon household as Mary's secretary, advised against this when he came to bestow the nightly benediction. And Mary wearily let the matter slide. By morning her headache had given way to excruciating twinges in a back molar. While the barber was summoned, and Mary fortified herself with a mug of sack for the inevitable tooth-pulling, she had no further thought for her guests.

Wat returned from a hurried trip back to London where he had deposited the signet ring with a taciturn goldsmith on Lombard Street according to Sir Anthony's instructions.

By noon, having dined alone, and skimpily—the Princess Mary's larder was kept as straitened as her purse—the Cow-dray party set forth again for the North.

None of them had the slightest premonition that they would ever see Mary again. Even Ursula, who had enjoyed their talk at supper, saw the Princess as a cipher who would end her days in confinement and neglect, forlornly shuttling from one to the other of her rustic manors.

Eight

By the time they reached Cumberland ten days later, Ursula was as sated by travel as Celia was enlivened. Neither of them had guessed what a different world they would gradually enter after they crossed the Trent. And for both, the crimson-heather moors, the flaming bracken and now the mountains—rocky, purple, misty-topped, were astounding. Ursula felt only the loneliness as they plodded miles without seeing a human, or even a shepherd's little stone cot. What houses there were had all turned grey and forbidding. There were no more luxurious inns—no accommodations except dearly bought garret floor space in farmsteads. The language became incomprehensible, the food altered. Instead of bread, they were given dry oatcakes, and messes of entrails for meat; instead of good ale or even beer, there was nothing to drink but water, or a white liquid so fiery it burned their throats.

Ursula's spirits flagged even lower as they reached Ulls-water and gaped at the stark brooding mountains, the dark sinuous nut-brown lake. Few South-countrymen had liking for scenery so startling. It was too primitive, too grotesque, and their minds were not aware of any romantic beauty in wilderness.

'I doubt we should have come . . .' said Ursula, for the first time voicing her dismay.

'Oh, but yes, Aunt!' cried Celia. 'I never guessed any place could look like this! Mysterious, grand—one can breathe deep . . .' She did so while her cheeks glowed, though she could not explain a glad yet awed response in her own heart to match the blackish mountains, the grey implacable crags, the orange bracken patches. She thought the lake itself a marvel of enchantment, more incredible than Windermere, even. She who had heretofore seen no body of still water larger than the Midhurst millpond.

Wat came back grumbling from a cottage near Patterdale where he had gone back for directions. He observed Celia's raptures with an even sourer eye than did Ursula.

'Clutch o' mush-mouthed ruffians—these dalesmen,' he growled, jerking his head back towards the stone cot. 'Can't speak the King's English, doubt they know they *have* a King.'

'Did you not get directions?' asked Ursula anxiously. 'We *must* be near.'

Wat shrugged. 'They gobble an' they point up yonder.' His own dirty forefinger jabbed towards the western part of the lake. 'But not 'till I said "Dacre"—when they seemed afeared.'

Ursula sighed. 'Then we must go that way. For sure it'll be Naworth Castle at last,' she added to Celia, 'and I trust they welcome us, sweeting.'

Her plan of escape now seemed as stupid as its reasons. Cowdray and the Benedictine monk had receded to insignificance. This menacing country seemed as far from Cowdray as Venice, as the Spice Islands, of which she had heard talk at Sir Anthony's table. The Dacres's casual invitation given during the King's visit, and her own later impulsive decision to accept it—Oh, I'm a foolish woman, she thought, looking down at the lake, then up at some black storm clouds which had massed in a corner of the northern sky, while slanting sunrays still shone to the west. 'There's too *much* sky,' she said crossly, guiding her horse around a pot-hole.

Celia laughed. Her eyes met Simkin's. He shambled along beside the pack mule, prodding or thwacking its rump when the beast dozed. Celia had become aware of the lad's infatuation for her, and found it agreeable. She had become used to his pitted face, and the droop of his left eyelid. Simkin spoke little except to curse the mule; he blushed and stammered when Celia addressed him directly, but there had grown between them a natural alliance against the elders. A bond of youth and adventurousness.

'There'll be pharisees up here, won't there, Simkin?' asked Celia mischievously. 'Not little Sussex elves but great handsome ones wi' eyes o' burning coal, and black hair streaming in the mountain wind?'

'For sure, m-maiden—' answered Simkin, grinning, while his father said, 'Faugh!' expressing contempt for idiot chat about fairies, and the general tiresomeness of the young. Wat was becoming seriously worried about their safety. He was almost sure he had been directed amiss in Kendal where he had finally unearthed a blacksmith who spoke a recognisable language. The blacksmith, while reshoeing the horses, was vague and taciturn in his directions. There had been no mention of lakes, yet they had now seen two. These Cumbrians didn't seem to call them lakes, they called them meres—maybe the blacksmith *had* said 'mere'. Wat kicked his horse's flank and barked at his son.

'Look to the rope on the bedding-pack, ye chucklehead. 'Tis not fast, mule's lop-sided, ye'll lame it next!'

Simkin silently tightened the rope and rebalanced the packs. It gave him an excuse to pass near Celia and brush against her leg as it dangled in the stirrup. She dimpled and pulled her horse away.

'Lane's narrow,' she remarked, looking down at the youth through her long curly lashes.

Simkin shivered with a thrill of anticipation and fear. Her beauty reminded him of the rose mallows, blue speedwells and marsh marigolds he used to bring to his mother. He wanted to touch Celia and he thought that he would certainly find a way to kiss her tonight. His shyness had been waning with every mile that they struggled into this wild strange country. Yet every time he looked at her she reminded him of Roland. The moments with Roland were before the smallpox made Simkin ugly. Nearly two years ago. Roland had been one of the mummers who came to Cowdray at Christmastide. They played in the Buck Hall before Sir Anthony and his family. The servants had been allowed to crowd in by the buttery screens. The play was about St. George and the Dragon and a beautiful maiden whom St. George rescued. The maiden's part was played by Roland. He was very fair like Celia, and he had her provocative innocent manner. He, too, was beautiful, and Simkin at first sight had yearned for the boy. It happened that after the performance Sir Anthony invited the mummers to spend the night in one of the hay barns, so that Simkin had found it easy to meet Roland by the watering trough, and talk with him. Later, after they had all had much wassail, he had lain with him, too. Lain with Roland in the fragrant hay barn, and discovered a dark rich joy. But in the morning when the mumming troupe left for Chichester, Simkin had hidden himself. He did not understand what had happened to him and soon managed to forget it. He did not now think of that night, except for a fleeting recognition that something about Celia reminded him of Roland.

'Holy Jesu,' cried Ursula, peering apprehensively at the

huge mountain to the west. 'Can that be *snow*? At Michael-mas!'

' 'Tis snow,' agreed Wat. And the least o' our troubles, he added to himself. His charges must reach safety before night-fall, not only because of the weather, but the danger of rob-bery. The shepherd in the cot at Patterdale had stared long at Wat's pouch, then peered through the door at the three horses and the laden mule. Wat fingered his dagger and his match-lock. Bloody-fool jaunt this was. And they could go no faster through the ruts and little brooks full of slippery stones.

By twilight they reached the end of the lake, and a fork where they paused uncertainly beside a ramshackle bridge. There was nothing living in sight but some scraggy sheep.

'O-o-oh, look!' Celia cried. Her keen young eyes spied a battlemented tower through the trees. 'Naworth!'

They turned up a path and scrambled to higher ground.

'There's a church, too,' Ursula cried in relief. 'But what a formidable keep. 'Tis a very fortress!'

'Needs to be on the Borders,' said Wat. 'I wonder where they're lurking.'

The keep was silent and had a grim deserted air. No smoke rising, no lights in the slit windows.

Wat dismounted, crossed to the drawbridge and pounded on the heavy iron-bound portal. He yanked the bell-rope. Nothing happened though they could hear distant jangling from within the courtyard.

'God's nails!' Wat growled. 'What ails 'em in there!'

Border strongholds, Wat knew, always contained guards, and usually cattle—often 'lifted' from the other country. He yanked the bell-rope again.

'Somebody's coming over yonder,' said Celia, pointing up the lane. 'It's a *priest*!'

They all turned and saw an untidy old man in a cassock, waddling out of his grey stone vicarage next to the small church.

'What d'ye want?' he shouted, wagging his tonsured pate at them. 'There's nowt in ther-re but them whull na be dis-turr-bed.'

'But, Sir Priest!' cried Ursula, 'we've come to Naworth by invitation. Lady Dacre *asked* us. We've travelled a long way—' Her voice wavered as the priest scowled at her through the gloaming.

'Her-res not Na'orth,' he said contemptuously. 'Here's

Dacre. Na'orth's thirty guid mile to the nor-th, past Brampton.'

Wat shared Ursula's startled dismay, and struck in forcefully. 'Is't so? Well, bigod, we can go no farther tonight. If this be Dacre, Dacres must own it, and his lordship'd want us welcomed.'

The priest waggled his head again. His stupid face grew stubborn. 'Mebbe so, mebbe so, forbye we dinnent welcome Southrons. Keep's bolted an' shut, so 'twill bide.'

'Where can we sleep?' cried Ursula. 'We're hungry, cold. We can pay . . .' She drew a shilling from her pouch. The pudgy hand went out for it; the priest bit the coin suspiciously.

'Ye can lie i' the kirk,' he said. 'Ther-re's water to drink i' the beck.' He turned and waddled away to his tiny vicarage. He slammed the door and they heard bolts grind into place.

'At least they've a priest up here,' said Ursula ruefully, breaking the silence, 'and a cross on the church.'

'Lot o' good *they* be,' said Wat. 'Can't eat 'em. We might lie i' the church, except our bedding's soaked.' He frowned at the mule who had fallen in the last beck they had floundered through.

They could smell peat smoke from the priest's chimney-hole and a whiff of roasting goose. Nobody had eaten since dawn before they climbed Kirkstone Pass, and the farmstead near Windermere which had sheltered them last night would furnish them no breakfast but mouldy clap-bread.

'That old lump o' suet has a fire, an' I'll make him let us in if I have to beat his door down!' Wat suddenly shouted.

But Wat had no weapon which would budge the barred vicarage door, nor reach the windows which were high up and shuttered fast. He and Simkin pounded and shouted to no avail. A bitter wind rose, whistling from the mountains, bringing with it silver needles of sleet. They crowded together inside the church, shivering, too cold for speech. Wat eyed the sanctuary lamp glimmering above the altar. From the candle inside they might start a fire, but there was nothing flammable in the church except two wooden prayer seats.

'Bigod, Goddamn—' Wat muttered, while his own teeth began to chatter.

The women huddled in each other's arms, striving for

warmth. Simkin stamped up and down the one aisle, his feet numb.

Ursula thought how dreary a death this would make, to starve from cold and hunger in the savage uncaring North. She had begun to burn inside, and knew that an ague was upon her. Her knees wobbled so that she could no longer stand, and she slumped down on the dank paving. From instinct she looked towards the little wooden crucifix on the altar and began to pray.

Her aunt's collapse frightened Celia out of the exhilaration she had been feeling. She chafed Ursula's wrists distractedly.

Wat glanced at them both with exasperated pity while he thought of desperate plans. There must be some cot, some hamlet near by, even in this forsaken country, which he could ride to. The priest had mentioned Brampton, whatever that was, it must be nearer than Naworth. He thought of returning to the shepherd's hut at Patterdale, but that would take all night, and scant hope of help there anyway. And how to leave the women. Lady Southwell was ill already. That he could hear from her moans and prayers through the darkness.

'Sim!' he said to his son, 'stay here wi' 'em. I'll have another go at the keep.'

Wat strode out into the sleet, spurred by the need for action of any kind. He shook his fist at the vicarage, and groped his way back to the great looming fortress. He again found the bell-rope, and listened to the jangling clamour inside with impotent fury. There was no response from the keep. As his arm dropped he felt a touch on his elbow.

Wat started, then crossed himself, for he saw a pale shape beside him. It seemed to be a woman's shape, with long dark hair and a light robe.

'Whyfore d'ye make such a din?' it asked in a plaintive voice. 'Is't the Scots? Are the moss-troopers raiding tonight?'

Wat's scalp ceased prickling, he forgot even his physical cold in relief that the apparition spoke good English.

'No, lady,' he said, 'there's no raid, we're but a party of Southerners bound for the Dacres at Na'orth. We're frozen, starving, benighted.'

'I'm a Dacre,' said the woman in a sad murmurous voice. 'Bluidy Bess, they call me here, though I was born a Neville, and ha' lived in London town. My mother was half Southron.

224

I like Southrons.' Her voice trailed off, and she seemed to be turning away.

Wat grabbed her by the long woollen sleeve. 'I'm a Southerner,' he cried sharply. 'We all are, we need help. Where do ye live, lady?'

'In there . . .' she answered as though astonished. He felt her arm raise as it pointed to the fortress. 'Wi blind Janet.'

'Take us in!' commanded Wat, wondering if she were truly feeble-witted. 'How'd ye get out—not through that portal.'

'Nay . . .' she shrank from his detaining hand. 'My own secret way—when the three kings don't watch me too close.'

'Oh . . .' said Wat, and pondered a second. 'Well, it so happens, lady, them three kings 're friends o' mine, they *want* ye to take me inside.'

There was a long pause, while Wat tried to control his fretting. If she slipped off into the darkness, or if he held her forcibly, there would be no further hope.

' 'Tis very cold out here,' he added, 'the kings don't want ye to get cold.'

'Don't they?' she asked with child-like surprise. 'Yet *they're* cowld, you know, Oswin in particular, King o' Strathclyde. He's cowlder than the snows on Blencathra. For here is his own kingdom.'

'Aye, no doubt—' said Wat, swallowing, 'and I'm a guest in his kingdom, he longs to welcome me!'

He released his breath as he felt her sudden acquiescence. She began to edge around the fortress on a narrow strip of ground between it and the moat. Wat grabbed her flowing sleeve and followed. She began to go down steps just where the moat joined the rushing beck. Wat accurately judged that she had turned into some passage to the dungeon. The air became foul, the stone walls slimy as he guided himself by one hand and held her sleeve with the other. Suddenly they mounted again, and Wat with a spasm of relief saw the distant light of a fire. They crossed a dark chamber, and she stopped at the doorway to the inner firelit room.

'I don't see the kings,' she said on a note of irritation. 'You said they'd welcome you. You mustn't lie to me . . .' There was something threatening in her change of tone as she added the last words, while Wat had his first good look at her.

She was slender, she was probably about thirty, she would

have been beautiful except for the vacant look on her pale oval face and the fixed half-smile on her little mouth.

'The kings must've gone to bed,' said Wat. ' 'Tis late . . . Ah, who's this?'

A stout, aproned woman arose from a velvet-covered chair, and groped towards them. Her eyes were shut, and she cried, 'Lady Bess, Lady—who's wi' ye?' in an anxious voice.

'A *friend*, good dame!' cried Wat heartily. 'No Scot. I vow it on the cross, but friend from the South, bound for Na'orth and in sore need of shelter.'

He muttered, 'By your leave,' and grabbed a fistful of oatcakes which were warming near the hearth. 'Glory be to Christ,' he continued between avid gulps, 'I see ye've a red deer roasting on the spit!'

Bess Dacre watched him sombrely as she stood with one hand on her chest tugging at the grey woollen neck of her gown as though to expose her left breast. 'The blood'll go here,' she said softly, tapping her breast. 'Bring the blood, Janet!' She gestured towards the roasting venison.

'Anon, anon—Lady Bess,' said Janet. ' 'Tis not yet hot enow. Wull ye explain ye're beesiness—' she cried in the direction of Wat. 'I maun hear-r ye speak again. I'm blind.'

'God bless ye, poor woman,' said Wat with sympathy. The oatcakes relieved his light-headedness, and he became practical. It did not occur to him to speculate on the presence of a mad woman and a blind woman as the inhabitants of Dacre fortress, he saw them only as a means of salvation.

*   *   *

Half an hour later Wat had rescued his charges from the church and assembled them by the fireside of the keep's inner room.

Ursula lay drowsing on a pallet which Janet had found. Her violent shaking ceased after Janet gave her a noggin of the fiery liquid which they called 'whiskybaugh'. Celia and Simkin devoured hunks of the steaming venison, drank noggins until Celia's exhilaration returned, tinctured by a dream quality. Nothing seemed strange to her now, she was warm at last, she was fed, she watched with languid interest as the tall woman in grey wool came over to Janet and ceremoniously offered her breast, a white round breast with a raspberry nipple. Janet marked it with venison blood. The mark was a cross, with wavy lines around it; from the familiar offhand

226

way that Janet drew the markings with her reddened finger, nobody could doubt that this was an established custom.

'It quietens m' puir lady,' said Janet with composure, from her velvet seat by the fire. 'This was one o' her bad days— an' a' that wranglin' an' janglin' o' the courtyard bell!' She directed a reproachful look in the direction of Wat who had now regained all his strength, and become curious.

He asked questions, and Janet answered him placidly. This was Lady Elizabeth Dacre, wife of Sir Thomas of Naworth Castle. She had often been a bit daft, but so were all the Neville family. Her brother, the Earl of Westmorland, had been imprisoned in London for trying to murder his father and wife, though this was unproven. He had also been accused of invoking angels to assist in his throwing of dice. But these moments of folly were past. The Earl regretted them; he had repented. Janet obviously believed that any aberrations should be overlooked in so famous and powerful a family. She had grown up at Raby Castle in County Durham with Lady Bess; she had always known how to treat her, so it was natural that when the lady's bad fits came on her, they were both sent to Dacre for a while.

'The three kings 'll mend her agen,' said Janet. 'She's descended fra a' o' them. An' lang time ago she was King Oswin's dotter!'

Celia's interest had been growing in this narrative, even though she fought sleep and was conscious that Simkin had settled himself on the floor beside her. She glanced at Lady Bess who was now seated in the other chair, her chin in her hand gazing idly at the fire.

'What three kings, Dame Janet?' Celia asked. 'And when was My Lady Dacre King Oswin's daughter?'

'Och—' said Janet, turning her pleasant rosy face towards Celia's voice. ' 'Twas hunnereds o' years past—while the Norsemen harried us.'

This was no clarification for Celia nor any of the listeners. But the girl whispered with a glance at the motionless figure in grey. 'They're ... no alive then ...?'

Janet hunched her shoulders. '*She* sees them, and I feel their chill when they coom.'

So, the three kings were ghosts! Celia thought. She was quite tipsy and this struck her as funny. She gave a sudden little laugh.

Bess Dacre turned her long white neck and looked at the

girl. 'There'll be blood on *your* pap, too, my pretty lass,' she said. 'And 'twill do you no good to lie wi' my lord, let ye lust as ye will, and no matter his promises. You'll come to grief like a' his lemans.'

Celia did not understand. Wat and Simkin, both half-drunk, paid no attention to this remark, but Ursula was roused by the sinister tone directed towards her niece. She remembered the offhand remark of the Cowdray steward. That the Neville wife was known to be jealous. Ursula raised her head and spoke to Lady Bess.

'My niece is a child, lady—she comes north for no reason but to visit your mother-in-law with me. She has barely met Sir Thomas. There is naught between them.'

Bess listened and seemed to consider. She gazed at the pallet where Ursula lay, her large black eyes grew vague. Suddenly she rose in one lithe cat-like motion. Ursula shrank and cried, 'Jesu,' under her breath. She thought the woman was darting at her.

But Lady Bess glided past to the wall where a small harp hung on a wooden peg. Bess took the harp and returned to her seat.

'We must sing . . .' she said, nodding graciously towards the dim-lit other room. 'The kings wish music.'

She strummed the little harp and smiled the fixed half-smile again. Bess's voice was low, it held no expression and it sent new shivers through Ursula.

> O! cauld and bare his bed will be
> When winter storms sing in the tree;
> At his head a turf, at his feet a stone,
> He will sleep, nor hear the maiden's moan
> O'er his white bones the birds s'all fly
> The wild deer bound, and foxes cry . . .

'Nay, nay, m'lady—' cried Janet suddenly jumping up and groping towards her mistress. 'Not *that* one, luik ye, we've guests this neet, they're a-weary, we mun rest. Coom, hinny, coom . . .' She took the harp and put it back on the wall. 'Here's ye're neet-cap,' she said in crisp firm tones. They were all dazed, only Ursula, aware of pity and some fear, held her breath while Janet poured red venison blood from a dripping pan into a silver noggin and put it in Bess's hand. The woman drank slowly, savouring each sip. Then she allowed

Janet to propel her to a small adjacent bedchamber, curtained off by a tattered mildewed length of tapestry. In a moment Janet stuck her head around the tapestry. 'Guid neet,' she said. 'Keep the fire oop—there be turves i' the basket, iffen the wood fails.'

Wat was snoring, his head resting on a sack of oats from which he had previously fed the horses, then left them by the courtyard water trough.

Ursula, too, slipped back into an uneasy slumber. The young people lay under their cloaks on the other side of the hearth.

' 'Tis not cold now,' Celia murmured, 'I hope those three kings don't come.'

Simkin was not interested in the three kings. He rolled closer to Celia, then suddenly heaved himself on top of her and covered her mouth with his.

The girl jumped and opened her eyes. She gave the bony young chest a push. 'Oh, leave me be,' she said without rancour, 'I'm too weary for games.'

The kiss meant no more to her than her aunt's would have. It did not even awaken any memory of that other kiss on Tan's Hill.

Simkin rolled off her at once, reddening. He had longed for that kiss. After the food and whisky, while the elders were talking nonsense, he had been growing frantic with anticipation, his loins ached, his head pounded, his manhood throbbed. Yet, when he touched her lips, and even before she shoved him, he had felt disappointment. Almost revulsion. He had never kissed a girl before, though the other stableboys at Cowdray were forever boasting of their bussings and tumblings under hedgerows. He wondered a little about his lack of interest in the dairymaids or the castle chamber wenches the other lads found so exciting. Celia's delicate beauty, her mischief and high station had penetrated his indifference on the first day's journey. He was pleased to find himself in love. Yet he hadn't liked the feel of her soft breasts beneath his chest, nor her moist warm mouth. It had been different with Roland. Simkin gave an unhappy grunt, turned far away from Celia and began to snore as loud as his father.

The Dacre keep settled at last into sombre quiet.

* * *

On the next morning they set out north again. Janet directed them carefully, through the town of Penrith, on up to Brampton, but stop at Kirkoswald Castle on the way. Old Sir William Dacre might be there, he seemed to favour it above all his seats. There'd be a steward anyway who would give them news and shelter if they were benighted.

'We couldn't be,' said Wat laughing, 'if 'tis only thirty mile to Na'orth.'

Janet snorted. 'Ye speak lak a fule Southron, a mile her-re's not like the saft easy ones doon ther-re, an' our debatable land 's ne'er free fra danger.'

'What sort of danger?' asked Ursula, who still felt very weak, though her ague fit had not recurred.

Janet looked towards her kindly. 'The ways'll be clarty,' she said, 'your horses mought fall, the brigs out o'er the becks, an' evil men abroad. 'Ware the moss-troopers! The Maxwells 're riding I hear-r—ye'd be ripe plums for 'em. Your horses, your gold, yon young lass to be ravished, you too, lady, iffen they be fu' o' whiskybaugh, as they'll be for sure.'

'Wat and Simkin will protect us—the Blessed Saints'll protect us,' cried Ursula, crossing herself.

'Havers!' said Janet. '. . . Luik ye, lady. Stop by to see Lang Meg an' her dotters ar'ter ye pass Penrith. Gi'e her a posy o' the rowanberries, it'll please her. She'll guard ye better'n a bushels o' crosses an' Paters—she was her-re afore they a' coom to Cummerland. Iffen ye can count Lang Meg's dotters a-reet ye'll get ye're heart's secret weesh.'

'She's as mad as Lady Bess,' whispered Wat behind his hand to Ursula. 'Hasten, lady, we've no time for this drivel.'

Ursula nodded. They had breakfasted on oatcakes and the remainder of the venison. Though it rained again, they were all fed, including the beasts, and she longed to be quit of the gloomy Dacre keep.

'Give our thanks to Lady Bess.' said Ursula, while mounting her horse. 'I trust she'll soon be better.'

Janet nodded in Ursula's direction. 'Ar'ter the fu' moon,' she said calmly, 'I gi'e her the bluid to drink—we've a pig for today, 'tis more like the bluid she hankers for. Time was when she tasted the other-r.'

'The other . . .?' asked Celia who had been listening with fascinated incomprehension, though aware chiefly of a headache, and that Simkin had not spoken to her nor even looked at her this morning.

'Aye,' said Janet, 'once 'twas her babby's—puir wee bairnie —she loved it well. It died natural, mind ye, and she got a taste o' the bluid while she tried to save it.'

'Blessed Jesu—' whispered Ursula. Her weakness vanished. She slapped her horse with the reins. 'Come on, Celia—all of you—out of here!'

They hurried from Dacre, and cantered through the hamlet past the vicarage where the old priest stood in the doorway of his house and stared at them impassively.

Wat scowled and shouted, 'No thanks to *you*, old turdy-gut, ye've not got a church full o' corpses this morn, may the devil fry ye fur dinner!'

The priest hastily backed into his house, and slammed the door.

'They be'ent human up here . . .' Wat muttered, itching for revenge, but he urged his charges along the muddy lane towards Penrith, which it took them an hour to reach. In the small grey market town they paused only long enough to buy food at a cook-shop—a blood pudding the natives called 'Haggis', more oatcakes—and to confirm, mostly by signs, Janet's directions towards the bridge over the Eden at Langwathby.

They continued in silence. The rain turned to drizzle. Ursula staunchly ignored a new fit of shivering and gave thanks that the mountains had receded, the going was nearly level. They crossed the Eden by noon and continued north until they came suddenly upon a huge cluster of standing stones, many stones grouped near a huge pointed one eighteen feet tall.

'What's that?' asked Celia, her voice uncertain, for an instant she had thought that the stones were people as they loomed through the mist.

'Long Meg, no doubt,' said Wat briskly. 'I've seen them things other places, there's a mort o' 'em on Salisbury Plain. Hurry on, Miss, they're evil, left o'er from heathen times!'

Celia shook her head. 'Wait, wait a moment!' she said. 'Janet told us what to do—if we'd be safe!'

'Tcha!' cried Wat. 'Rantings an' ravings, besides there's no rowan.'

Celia looked around, sure enough there was no sign of the witching-tree and its red berries, though they had passed many such trees in the mountains. The girl thought rapidly. She rummaged in her pouch and found a bit of scarlet yarn she used at night to tie her long hair back against tangles. She had already slid off her horse, and now darted up to the great standing stone. She stuck the red yarn as high as she could up the stone where the roughened surface held it.

'Long Meg, Long Meg—' she whispered, 'keep us safe.' She turned quickly for the part of the rite which had really caught her attention. She must count Long Meg's daughters, because the secret wish in her heart had welled up and exploded into one word, even as Janet spoke. 'Stephen,' was the word. She did not feel surprise, nor any emotion. The word was there, an entity, sharp, solitary. She ran among the stones counting. Fifty-nine, sixty—no, she had counted that one. Try again, slower. Sixty-three. No, start to the right, going widdershins, the four big ones near Long Meg, then carefully, zigzag, touching each one ... sixty-five, but had she counted those two half-covered ones near the hummock? They'd make sixty-seven. She was panting, and her round white forehead glistened with sweat when Simkin came up to her.

'Have done, maiden,' he said in a muffled tone. 'Me dad's vexed at the wait, Lady Ursula's dithering.' He did not look at her. He glanced at the red yarn stuck high on the stone menhir, then stared at the rough grass.

'I can't *count* them!' Celia cried on a note of hysteria. 'Oh, Simkin, will you try?'

'Nay,' he said. 'Come along—do.'

Celia abstractedly obeyed. As they left the circle of stones her disappointment was replaced by astonishment. During all the journey Simkin had been so eager to please her. 'Sim ...' she said with hesitation, putting her hand on his leather-clad arm, 'I wasn't angry last night ... you know, in the keep—when you k-kissed me. I was only so sleepy.'

She felt his arm flinch away from her hand, and saw dark colour flood up his neck to his coarse pitted face. 'Best forgot ...' he said, 'it'll not happen again.'

Celia was puzzled and piqued. She did not want it to happen again, but surely *he* should wish for it.

'I don't mind ...' she said looking at him through her lashes and showing her dimple in the way which had always caused him to respond—other men, too—she had seen the kindling in many male eyes.

Simkin did not kindle, he glanced at her sideways, saw the moist pink mouth, the half-exposed globes of her breasts under her neckerchief. He was upset that she no longer attracted him, upset and confused.

'Best forgot . . .' he repeated stolidly.

When they reached the others he gave her a leg-up to mount her horse, but he did not touch her elbow as he usually did, nor arrange her cloak over the cantle. They proceeded on a trail by the river bank until they reached Kirkoswald. The large castle with its turrets and high tower had been in sight almost since they left Long Meg behind. Wat was heartily glad to see it.

He realised that hopes of reaching Naworth this night were unreasonable. His stallion had gone lame in the off-hind hoof, and Wat was now on foot, cursing the blacksmith in Kendal, as well as the extraordinary lengths of space they called miles up here. He saw by the empty staff on top the turret that Lord Dacre was not there, or his pennant would be flying. But, as Janet had said, at least there must be servants and the steward. Yet Wat's hail at the porter's lodge, and then his tugging of the courtyard bell-rope produced no answer for some time. At last a grill slid back in the iron-bolted door and a young frightened voice cried, 'Gan awa' . . . Leave us be . . . or I'll rouse t' guards! '

'Pray *do*, youngster,' Wat cried. 'Rouse the whole shitten castle, we be Dacre guests an' we demand shelter! '

There was a pause, then they heard the bolts draw back, and the portal swung open cautiously. A round-eyed youth in a filthy plaid cape peered through the crack. He brandished a dirk with a trembling hand.

'Laird Dacre sent ye?' the boy quavered doubtfully.

'By the Mass—yes,' shouted Wat. He pushed wide the door, shooed the women past the protesting boy.

'Naow then—' Wat rounded on the boy, 'where's everybody? Do they hide another madwoman here? Bigod, I begin to think all the Dacres 're mad.'

It gradually developed that this castle was nearly empty, too, though the reason was not so peculiar as the emptiness of the Dacre keep. Lord Dacre had withdrawn every able-bodied guard and put them on the Border to repulse the Maxwells.

The steward here and three scullions were all abed with sickness.

'Na, not the plague . . .' said the boy in response to Ursula's worried question. 'Burnin's an' harplin' coughs an' pains i' their heids.'

Kirkoswald was, however, well provisioned, and the steward presently tottered into the Great Hall to make them welcome when the boy had reported their arrival. He was a sick man, his voice was hoarse, he was racked by coughings, but he poked up the fires, lit rushes, fed them on jugged hare, bacon and claret from his lordship's private cellar.

And so passed the last night of their long journey to Naworth.

By ten next morning they reached Brampton, a town built of sandstone as red as the Dacre bull on the flag which fluttered over the Guild Hall. They had been delayed at Kirkoswald while Wat drew on his expert knowledge, and finally extracted the stone from his stallion's hoof. Two miles beyond Brampton they sighted Naworth Castle, crouching in a forest near the banks of the Irthing.

'Naught but another Border keep,' said Wat in disgust, examining the castle which seemed smaller than Kirkoswald, or Dacre, yet even more forbidding than the latter.

Ursula's heart sank, too. She thought of the luxurious elegance of Cowdray, the myriad sparkling windows, the carvings, the cushioned bays and her own snug room with its turkey carpet and comfortable bed. Her bones ached, another fit of the ague had come upon her, and she sat her horse dejectedly while Wat went off to beg admission at still another bolted portal. If they'll not receive us, Ursula thought ... what then?

Celia glanced anxiously at her aunt whose teeth were chattering; she glanced at Simkin who stood by the mule gazing northward towards a ridge of hilly moors. He had not spoken to her since yesterday at Long Meg's circle of stones. Celia, too, thought of Cowdray. It seemed very far away in time and place. She would not let herself think of Tan's Hill and its inhabitant.

Wat came striding back to them, smiling. Behind him walked a very tall girl in russet cloth who waved her arms and rushed up to them.

'Welcoome, welcoome—ye puir things. Sech a journey!'

It was Magdalen. She looked the bedraggled party over, bestowed a kiss on Celia and helped Ursula down from the saddle.

Lady Dacre herself came out to greet them. During the next hour the forceful Dacre women took charge of the weary Southerners; Ursula was fed whisky and put to bed between homespun blankets. Celia was given a stool near the Hall fire. Wat and Simkin disappeared to the servants' wing. The animals were stabled in the stone byres next to the living quarters. Those stables were empty at present, Magdalen explained, since their own mounts were on the Border suppressing the Scots. All her brothers, Magdalen added, had gone on the raid, though not her father, Lord William, who besides being gouty, was English warden of the Western Marches, and Governor of Carlisle, and therefore deemed it expedient to remain home this time.

'But ma brothern, they'll be back,' said Magdalen laughing, 'on the morrow, or next. Leonard'll be glad to see ye, hinny.' She kissed Celia again. 'We all are, dinnet doot it. In especial Leonard—the rogue!'

Celia blushed, delighted with the welcome, prepared to enjoy herself now that they were safe at Naworth.

She was happy that night, which she spent in Magdalen's bed, curled close and warm, savouring the scent of peat smoke and heather, listening to Magdalen's even breaths and to the lowing of distant cattle.

Nine

A fortnight later Celia longed to leave Naworth, and had, of course, no means of doing so. Wat departed for the South the day after bringing them here. He had left Simkin in charge of the Cowdray horses. But Celia never saw Simkin. Their intimacy had vanished on that night at Dacre. Celia soon ceased to puzzle over this since there was so much else to discomfort her.

The Dacre men came back from harrying the Scots. They brought with them fine milch cows and a bullock, which were immediately driven to Kirkoswald by the cowherd. From the roars of male laughter in the Hall at dinner, Celia understood that the 'lifting' of Scottish cattle was considered a fine feat. So was the routing of the Maxwells—who had been forced back to the Hermitage castle in Liddesdale.

Though a couple of Dacre men had been killed, the Maxwells had lost seven or more, and would keep quiet now until winter was past. The Dacres had burned many farmsteads in Roxburghshire, and had got the cattle. All in all a satisfying foray.

Young Sir Thomas gave his father a vociferous account of it in the Hall, while the men clashed tankards of slightly watered whisky, and the Dacre piper skirled triumphantly in the doorway.

'The Max'ells—they shivered 'n' shook when we charged 'em at Bewcastle,' cried Tom, brandishing the Dacre crimson pennant with its three silver cockle shells. 'A Dacre! A Dacre! A reid bull, a reid bull!' He roared out their war cry while his brothers and father joined in.

Celia shrank as Magdalen next to her bellowed, too. The Dacres were so large, so noisy and so numerous. Besides Tom and Leonard, there were four younger boys. They all had wiry red hair; they stank of sweat, horse dung and whisky. The Hall was not large, the smoke from its central fire was suffocating to Celia, who was used to chimneys, while an assortment of hounds, yelping and scrabbling for bones tossed down in the filthy rushes, increased her confusion.

She longed to get out of it, but was afraid of hurting Magdalen's feelings and the rowdy celebration quietened as the Dacre men got drunk. It was then that Celia noticed one of the brothers who seemed different from the rest. His hair was of a darker red and sleeker; he was more slightly built; and if any Dacre might have been called languid, this one seemed to be.

'Which one's that?' whispered Celia to Magdalen. 'He keeps apart?'

The other girl glanced up the table. 'Och, *him*,' she said laughing. ' 'Tis Geordie. He's ever been a bit saft. Na stomach fur a guid fight. The others 're toughening him. He's over much the pretty-boy, but he's scarce eighteen. He'll learn. Leonard's not reetly seen ye yet,' she added consolingly. 'He's still high flung wi' drink and fighting. Wait 'till the morrow.'

Celia glanced at Leonard hopefully, trying to imagine him as a husband. Magdalen had made it obvious that she had this possibility in mind. Nor were Ursula's hopes unknown to Celia, who realised that she should be flattered. The second son and heir to some of the powerful Dacre inheritance would be a wonderful match for a penniless orphan. Celia had seen enough of the world lately to understand that her wishes had no bearing on marriage. Leonard was big, rough, crude. His shoulder was a trifle crooked, but no matter. There's nobody else for me, Celia thought. An eon of spinsterhood stretched ahead of her, and the deep walled-off hurt quivered.

Yet, when Leonard's attentions did indeed begin on the morrow, they made Celia shrink. He pawed her, he pinched her buttocks, he called her his bonny, but there was never a word of love. Celia felt besieged, and began to avoid him, which was hard in the cramped castle.

In early October, Naworth had unexpected guests. These were a party of two Scottish couriers, an interpreter and an Italian physician. They were bound from Edinburgh to London whither the doctor, whose name was Jerome Cardano, had been summoned by no less a person than the Duke of Northumberland to examine King Edward.

Their arrival caused a great stir at Naworth where important guests were as rare as Border warfare was common.

Lord and Lady Dacre bristled with hospitality. They opened their best barrels of sack, they roasted a precious bullock in the courtyard, they commanded their piper to appear at every meal and perform on the northern smallpipes.

'*Como* — laike-Scotland,' observed Dr. Cardano sighing.

This observation delivered in thick stammering speech pleased none of the Dacres — though it was true, Cardano was a bandy-legged man of fifty-one. He was nearly bald, and at first glance appeared insignificant. Yet he had the assurance born of fame — and a rather sweet smile.

Ursula had conquered her ague, and was present in the Hall at dinner for Cardano and his escorts. She asked eagerly if he knew Dr. Julian Ridolfi.

Cardino's face showed surprise 'Ah-h, si, Dona —' He then turned to his interpreter, saying, 'Guiliano Ridolfi ...' and spoke for some time. The interpreter explained. Doctor Cardano had known Ridolfi at Padua; he was looking forward to seeing him in London. Perhaps Ridolfi had already examined the young King. It would be an honour to consult with him.

'We dinnet knaw His Royal Gr-race was ill,' said Lady Dacre anxiously. 'He was bonny enow at Cowdray. What's gan wrong?'

When this was interpreted, Cardano's watery eyes went blank. He had been warned not to mention the King's condition, and actually knew little about it. He indicated this by shrugs, and a flow of lisping Italian.

'Messer Cardano is only going to re-cast the King's horoscope,' said the interpreter, 'and talk with him on an aspect of astronomy the doctor wrote of in *Practica Arithmeticae Generalis*. He is a famous scholar as well as physician.'

Cardano gave a deprecating smile and gingerly sipped the sack which he thought vile.

He had been invited to Scotland by John Hamilton, Archbishop of St. Andrews, who suffered from coughs, wheezings and sleepless nights spent gasping for air. Everyone thought the Archbishop had lung consumption, but his personal physician, a Spaniard called Cassanate, remembered Cardano who had performed so many miraculous cures in Italy. Fifty gold crowns and a courier were sent to tempt the physician to leave his native land for the raw savage country. He resisted a while but eventually sailed for Edinburgh. He soon diagnosed the Archbishop's trouble as asthma, not consumption, and with secret herbs and inhalations restored the old man to health. This news spread fast southward. There were many

English spies at the court of the dowager queen, Mary of Guise. The doctor's success resulted in the Duke of Northumberland's summons. And a safe-conduct. Cardano himself suffered from pains in the joints which a succession of bleak, draughty, dank castles did nothing to alleviate. He thought this keep even danker and draughtier than those in Scotland, if possible. Moreover, the inhabitants all seemed enamoured of the eldritch squealing noises they produced on their crazy bagpipes.

'E barbaro,' he murmured, 'sono pazzi, tutti.' And settled himself to endurance for another night.

He brightened when Leonard brought out the dice box, and seized it eagerly. This game needed no translation, and before long Cardano had badly beaten the Dacres and gathered up his groats and pennies with weary aplomb.

Leonard was sure that the Italian cheated somehow. He growled this to his brother, Sir Thomas, but their father's eye was on them, they dared not protest. Leonard, baffled and disgusted, turned to a game he felt sure of winning. He sought out Celia and grabbed her around the waist. 'Coom outside, hinny—' he cried, 'the neet's war-rm for October. We'll walk a bit i' the gloaming.'

'I don't want to,' she said. 'I'll stay here.'

The last days had shattered any lingering romantic notions she had about Leonard. Her disillusionment had been reinforced by a warning from Ursula.

'I thought he'd be a good match for you, sweeting,' said Ursula, 'I confess it. But now I fear that all he wants is your maidenhead. You must keep that at all costs. That and your fair beauty is all your dowry. Don't ever be alone wi' Leonard, no matter his promises. I wish,' she added sighing, 'I'd never brought you up here. 'Ware of Sir Thomas, too. There's lust in his eye, and I begin to think that poor wife at Dacre's not as mad as we thought.'

'I'll stay here wi' the others,' repeated Celia to Leonard, her pink mouth tightening. The Hall being crowded as usual with noisy, restless Dacres—and now Cardano's party—she had withdrawn to a stool near the door of the spiral stone stairs. Bored with Leonard, wishing for bed, yet constrained by courtesy to tell Magdalen she was going, she glanced up at the four gaudily painted wooden beasts which stood on a bracket above the High Table. The effigies were all man-sized and comical— a red bull, a griffin, a fish, a sheep. What a barnyard, Celia thought, though she knew from Magdalen that they represented the family's heraldic beasts and were often carried into battle. From this angle they seemed to be peeping down at her, while the sheep and the fish exchanged sly glances. Celia, quite forgetful of Leonard, suddenly chuckled.

The young man started. His face flushed as red as his hair. 'God's bones!' he shouted, 'ye dare laugh at *me*! I'll teach ye not to play the coy Miss!'

He clutched her around the waist, lifting her from the stool. As she struggled he grabbed her wrists in one hand, plunged the other down her bodice, tearing the blue velvet and wrenching her right breast with such violence that she screamed, whereupon he loosed her breast and twisted her neck, forcing her head around until he could cover her mouth with a savage bite.

Even through her fury and panic Celia was conscious of something hard butting against her stomach, of his fetid breath and that he crunched her so cruelly against the stone wall that her shoulder bones cracked.

'*Have done*, Len!' Celia heard the angry cry, though he did not, but he reeled, losing his hold at a resounding blow on his cheek.

He turned, momentarily dazed, and saw his sister standing by him, her amber eyes sparking with fury.

'Let her be, ye randy pup,' Magdalen cried. 'Ye shame us a'!'

Celia's knees gave way as Leonard released her and confronted his sister who was nearly as tall as he—and twice as brave.

'She laughed at me,' he muttered. 'She wouldna coom out wi' me.'

'Bah!' said Magdalen, and shoved him through the door. 'Gan awa'—ye'll not add Celia to your tally o' ruttings.'

Leonard wavered, he could think of no more to say. Despite her youth, Magdalen had always daunted him. He hunched his shoulders and slunk down the spiral steps.

'Did he hur-rt ye, lass?' Magdalen turned to raise Celia who was giving dry little sobs. 'Aye, I see he's tor-rn your bodice, the scurvy wenchster.' She made a sound of pity as she saw the blue marks on Celia's breast. 'We'll suin fix that oop—I've marigold salve i' ma coffer.' She put her arm around Celia and raised her gently. 'Na har-rm 's done, nawbody saw

240

but me as I was passin' on ma way doon to the privy—they're a' too droonk i' there.'

She drew Celia along with her up a short flight to their room. Celia presently fell asleep despite the throbbing in her injured breast, her bruised mouth and a pain in her back. She was assuaged by the other girl's tenderness.

'Len'll maybe askin' your aunt for ye arfter this, he's a dolt to think he'd get ye otherwise, but the Dacre men 're dim-witted.'

'I'll not *have* him, Maggie—' cried Celia. 'I can't abide him, he's vile.'

Magdalen did not answer, but she thought to herself that poor Celia had no choice, if Leonard *did* proffer honourable wedlock. Girls did not decide these matters for themselves. She had come to understand how rootless and unprotected Celia was. Nobody but old Lady Southwell to fend for her. Any husband would be better, and Len would be no worse than most. As for me ... Magdalen thought, ruefully. She knew some of the negotiations her parents had embarked on for their daughter who would turn fifteen in January. It might be a Neville—and pray he was not touched by the family madness—or Jock Graham of Netherby Hall who was a sickly puling youth with a lank-haired pate which barely reached her shoulder. Either husband would come cheap, in view of the Dacre position and Magdalen's own abounding health. Nevilles and Grahams both needed to replenish their stock, and would demand little dowry.

The Dacre choice was further limited by their staunch Catholicism. As the wicked preachings of Master John Knox and other so-called reformers invaded the Border, many of the noble families had submitted to England's official beliefs. Lord Dacre ignored these, and continued in the old way on all his estates, yet even he had not been able to prevent the Dissolution of Lanercost Priory at Naworth's gate, nor the eviction of its Augustinian canons. Though the outrage increased his Catholic fervour.

He and his own—wife, children, guards, servants, tenants—attended Mass, invoked the Saints, celebrated Feast Days as openly and regularly as they had before King Harry's edict sixteen years ago.

A Protestant husband was unthinkable to Magdalen as well as to her parents. And yet, while she lay beside the exhausted Celia, Magdalen had her moment of rebellion. She loved

Naworth, she was a child of the Border, but last summer in the South had shown her how differently one *might* live—that there were graces and elegances she had never guessed. She, too, thought wistfully of Cowdray. Her stay there had unsettled her. Part of her love for Celia was because the soft, beautiful girl reminded her of the South. When Magdalen too slept she had a wistful dream full of vague yearnings which were dispelled by sunlight slanting through the one slit window. Magdalen shook herself awake and to common sense. She was a Dacre. Her lot was irrevocably thrown among the hurly-burly of the Border and guided by her parents' wishes, which also naturally represented God's will. These were facts, and she accepted them.

*　　　*　　　*

Jerome Cardano and his party left the next day for the long journey south. Naworth Castle settled back into the seasonal routine imposed by dwindling daylight and consequent lessening of either outdoor tasks or the chance of Border warfare.

In Cumberland they called it the 'Back End' of the year. Brown leaves carpeted the woods, the young folk gathered mast and acorns, they scoured the ditches for rushes to peel and make into lights. Tenants and cottagers brought their winnowed oats to the manor mills for grinding; shepherds enfolded their flocks; and by Hallowe'en there was much snow on the fells—rimy iron frost along the valley of the Irthing.

On All Hallows' Eve, the last day of October, Leonard's thwarted passion for Celia finally overcame his caution. This happened in the Hall, the only gathering place, while the sky outside was lurid with bonfires lit to ward off bogles, witches and other evils which had licence to roam that night.

Since Leonard's assault, Celia had managed to avoid seeing him except at dinner-time when she clung to Magdalen and tried to efface herself. She could not prevent Leonard from staring at her down the table—long intent glowers from beneath his bristling red brows. These did not intimidate her for long. After some days she found them ridiculous, annoying, and showed it by the tilt of her head and increased fervour in chatting with the younger children, particularly George.

George amused her, and she thought him handsome. His

242

features were fine-drawn, he was slighter than his brothers, his Dacre hair was so dark that except in sunlight it seemed to be chestnut. It curled around his pink cheeks and was remarkably glossy and clean.

She was sometimes puzzled by his rather malicious banter, but she enjoyed his company.

This Hallowe'en some of the young folk took part in the age-old rites. They touched the rowan twig crosses which had been fastened to windows and doors, they threw nuts on the fire having named each one secretly for a possible sweetheart.

'Who'd ye name, Celia?' asked George, as the girl flung hers among the glowing peat.

'Nobody,' she said with truth, laughing. 'I didn't think. Who'd *you* name?'

George's eyelids fell, she was startled by a peculiar expression on his face. 'Nawbody,' he said, 'but there's one lad I knaw'd be content if ye named him.'

For a second Celia thought that he meant himself, and was not displeased, but George jerked his chin down the table towards Leonard who was watching as usual.

'Jesu!' cried Celia, 'he's the last man in England . . .!'

George laughed and shrugged. 'Riddle me ree, riddle me ree, wha's ta tell bull fra cow i' the North Countree . . .' he chanted.

Celia laughed uncertainly. Everybody knew how to tell a bull from a cow and the look on George's boyish face disconcerted her.

She did not notice when Leonard rose and joined his parents who were playing a game of draughts by the light of one of the rare candles reserved for special occasions. She barely noted it when Ursula left the other side of the table at a summons from one of the younger children. There was always much coming and going in the Hall.

George was entertaining her with a tale of a bogle he'd seen last Hallowe'en. ' 'Twas a Roman soldier, I vow,' said George. 'He was walking by the wall, ye knaw the wall, lass?'

Celia nodded. On a fine day after her arrival at Naworth, she and Magdalen had gone rambling to the north. They had crossed the Irthing on a footbridge and tramped a mile to a heap of rubble and huge grooved stones much overgrown with weed. Magdalen spoke of it with respect as the 'Ould Wall', and said that her parents thought some people called Romans had made it to keep the Scots out long before the Dacres came to Naworth.'

'Oh?' said Celia to George. 'What did the ghost do?'

'Naught,' George said. 'Naught but saunterin' and mutterin'. To an' fra, to an' fra, a-saunterin' an' mutterin'. He had a shiny head, an' shiny bits o' something on his legs, but whilst I went nigh t' look close . . . he vanished.'

'You must be very brave, George,' said Celia. 'I'd have been scared.'

'Na,' said George, 'I'm no afrighted by bogles, nor witches neither, though they'll be flying this neet on their ould broomsticks.'

'Past the bonfires?' asked Celia, giving a delighted shudder. 'How dare they?'

'The deevil their master gi'es 'em courage,' said George. 'Ould Horny gi'es courage t' his own.' He sent Celia a quick, sly glance from the corner of his eyes, as though he meant more than was apparent by this remark, but she had no time to question him as she might have for Magdalen touched her on the shoulder.

'M'lord an' lady want ye, hinny,' said Magdalen in a pleased portentous voice. 'Doon there . . .' she gestured to the group at the far end of the Hall.

Celia was somewhat bewildered, but she rose and came with Magdalen.

Lord and Lady Dacre had put away the draught board; they sat motionless, frowning slightly in their carved oak armchairs. Leonard stood behind them, staring down at the hay-strewn floor. Ursula completed the group. She was seated in a lesser arm-chair, and gave Celia a quick excited smile.

'Well, sweeting—' she said to the girl, 'well . . .' and paused, swallowing. 'We've—we've something to tell you.' She glanced at the Dacres.

The old Baron nodded, he clenched his hairy paw, then suddenly relaxing it, spoke solemnly. 'Aye, lass—Leonard wants ta wed ye—I'm no saying 'tis not a bit o' shock. M'lady an' I, we'd thought ta put him back in *her* family, one o' the Talbot clutch, Lady Dorothy, she has rich manors i' Derbyshire, but she's no bonny lak ye, an' I'm bound ta admit, the Talbots 're a wambling lot, they've gan Protestant, and sence Leonard wants ye sa bad, we'll no deny him.'

Lady Dacre nodded, her large kind face so like Magdalen's,

broke into an encouraging smile as Celia looked not only blank but frightened.

'Coom, coom, dear,' she said. 'We'll treat ye roight, we'll welcoom ye like ony ither dotter. Have no fear.'

Celia moistened her lips, she glanced at Leonard who continued to stare scarlet-faced at the floor. She looked at Ursula, and accurately read a mixture of triumph and concern in her aunt's eyes.

'I don't want to,' said Celia on a long frightened breath.

Magdalen grabbed her hand and squeezed it. 'Hush, luv,' she whispered. ' 'Tis what we all wanted. 'Tis best fur ye.' She turned to her parents. 'Leonard's been too rough i' his wooing. Celia's a delicate lass, he mun 'mend his way. Ye great booby—' she cried to her brother with a sharp nudge. 'Tak' her hand, kiss her pure, ye clod.'

Leonard moved slowly, but he obeyed his sister. He came forward, took Celia's hand, and trembling slightly kissed her on the forehead.

The girl shrank in every fibre.

'I don't want to,' she repeated angrily. 'I'd rather not wed at all.' She snatched her hand from Leonard's.

'Tush . . .' said the Baron, who had no patience with girlish whims, and had already settled the matter in his mind with an agreeable feeling of his kindness in acceding to Leonard's startling request, since a penniless orphan, no matter how prettily pink and white, was hardly a mate for a Dacre, still, there were several other sons, and Leonard the least favoured. The subject was closed and he had an important message from Carlisle to decide on tonight. Scurvy Scots, probably Armstrongs from Liddesdale, had made a riotous foray into the city itself. That heretic Knox was behind it somehow, sowing unrest.

Lady Dacre and even Ursula saw Celia's reluctance as a natural shyness, to be resolved in time. Ursula quelled any misgivings by the realisation that this was what she had hoped for—and despaired of. If the girl was disinclined, particularly if that disinclination had anything to do with the far-off monk at Cowdray—indeed this was no time for softness. Girls must obey. *She* had obeyed her parents' decree that she marry Robert Southwell, a stooped querulous man much older than she. Yet she had grown quite fond of him.

' 'Tis settled, Celia,' said Ursula briskly. 'My lord and lady mentioned marriage after Christmas.'

'Aye . . .' said Lady Dacre smiling, 'we'll wed ye proper i' Lanercost Church, then mak' a braw wassailing gaudy-neet o' it, forbye nawbody wor-rks i' Christmastide anyhow. 'Twill be a gladsome revel.' Her brown eyes sparkled at the thought. Magdalen laughed excitedly.

Leonard suddenly gave one of his incongruous guffaws. He sent Celia a crudely lustful look, and said, 'A merry, merry neet, that we'll have, eh, lass!' He was enjoying a glow of virtue, and nobody heeded Celia's whisper, 'I won't. I'd die first.'

*　　　*　　　*

The days sped on inexorably. Martinmas came with its hiring fairs. Soon Advent—the penitential season—began. Meat disappeared from the devout Dacres' table. They ate pickled herring and salt cod—occasionally the delicious little lake fish called char. They attended daily Mass in their chapel, the piper was banished for four weeks. The long, long evenings were spent by the women in straining eyes over their mending. Magdalen undertook to make wedding clothes for her brother and Celia. She was an inept seamstress, the stitches straggled, but she produced, with Ursula's help, an adequate suit of russet cloth for Leonard, and a creamy brocade gown, cut down from an old court dress of her mother's, for Celia.

During these weeks Celia moped, and did as she was told. She grew thin and white, despite mugs of egg-flip given her by Lady Dacre, and Ursula's exasperated admonitions.

Celia's inner misery settled to apathy. She felt unreal, nor believed that the marriage set for December 29 would actually happen. When she could not avoid Leonard, she answered him dully, never looking at him, grateful that he did not touch her. He had taken Magdalen's advice to heart, and now that Celia was betrothed to him, felt a respect for her which her coolness increased. He spent most of his time with the other men, riding over the fells, drinking, dicing on the sly and overhauling his armour, his horses and their harness. He also found time to slake his sudden lusts with a shepherd's buxom widow who lived near Gilsland in one of the Dacre cottages.

Christmas Day came and its burst of feasting and music. The piper returned; there was a fiddler and a flautist. They sang carols and North Country ballads. They ate a wild boar shot by a lucky arrow in Kershope Forest.

246

And at Naworth, as master of the revels for the twelve days of Christmas, they selected a Lord of Misrule. This was a southern custom brought to Cumberland by Lady Dacre when she arrived as a bride of fifteen. The exuberant Dacres were delighted by it, and the rowdy licence always engendered, offset four weeks of fasting and penitence.

Lord Dacre's enthusiasm was heightened by the knowledge that the Protestants despised the custom, though it was known that King Edward, oddly enough, held by his father's example, and saw no harm in some merrymaking to celebrate the Christ Child's birth.

On this Christmas at Naworth George Dacre was chosen. Celia watched the old Baron place the traditional crown on his son's head—the crown was cut from parchment, gilded and studded with little hunks of shiny quartz—then Lord Dacre boomed, 'We are your subjects, Your Grace. What d'ye decree?'

'Yule! Yule! saith the Lord o' Misrule. Every man to make merry and each play the fool!' George answered promptly. 'Fetch all the servants into the Hall!' His face was flushed, his eyes gleamed, he swallowed a ladleful of the steaming hot wassail which was contained in a silver bowl as big as a cart-wheel.

The younger children darted out to round up the servants who had been expecting the summons. Cooks and scullions, stable-boys, dairymaids, shepherds, swineherds, hunters, archers—they crowded into the Hall and overflowed into the passages. George greeted each one with a nod, but a slight frown appeared between his brows. 'I dinnet see Simkin, the Southron lad,' he said finally. The head stable-boy explained that Simkin, not being part of Naworth's household, had not deemed it fitting that he should join them.

'Bowlderdash!' said George. 'Go fetch him!' He took another drink of the wassail.

When Simkin appeared in his stained leather jacket, his coarse black hair tousled, his pock-marked face truculent, Celia's apathy was pierced. Her own unhappiness recognised unhappiness in him who had for over a fortnight last autumn been her devoted admirer, and with whom she had enjoyed many a laugh until that night at Dacre. She watched the quick uneasy look Simkin gave George, and saw a small tightening around George's mouth before he cried, 'Come drink o' the wassail, all o' ye—there's plenty more, then we'll clear the Hall and dance, each one ta his fancy!'

His orders were obeyed. They stacked the trestle tables and the benches. They drank and they jigged while the piper led them in reels. They shouted and leapt and stamped. Many of the men had tied bells above their knees; the jingling added to the din. And there was a hobby-horse who galloped clumsily, butting the dancers.

There were fewer women than men, and Celia found herself grabbed by the swineherd, then one of the hunters, then a scullion, finally Leonard, whom she scarcely greeted before Sir Thomas himself claimed her and was replaced by his father, laughing uproariously.

Everyone danced, even Lady Dacre and Ursula, while the wassail bowl was often replenished. It so happened that Celia was flung off the end of a line, during a wild leaping flourish, and leaned in a corner to catch her breath. Thus, across the Hall she saw George, whose crown though tipped backward was unmistakable, and noted with astonishment that he held Simkin's hand, and seemed to be expostulating with the boy while the dancers whirled by them, unheeding. Celia had only a glimpse through the medley of arms and legs, yet in that glimpse she received a strange impression of intimacy. She frowned, faintly disturbed, but her hand was caught by Lord Dacre's chief bowman who dragged her back into the reel.

They danced until at dawn they fell into bed, exhausted. Celia had managed to forget the approaching marriage, and just at cock-crow she dreamed of Stephen. The dream repeated the setting of their farewell on Tan's Hill, but its outcome did not. In the dream Stephen clutched her hungrily in his arms, saying, 'You'll never leave me, my love,' and when he kissed her they became one being as when two raindrops merge, and they were lying softly together in a golden boat, lulled by the gentle billows beneath them. Shining contentment which lasted until Celia was awakened by Magdalen shaking her shoulder.

'Och, there, slug-a-bed, 'tis late,' said Magdalen laughing. 'Were ye dreaming o' your bridegroom wi' that daft wee smile on your face?'

'Of Stephen . . .' whispered Celia, half-awake and gripped by a sickening sense of loss.

Magdalen nodded. 'That's apt,' she said, 'sence 'tis his day, he mun be proddin' ye ta Mass for his intention.'

Celia's jaw dropped, she stared at her friend who was dragging a comb through her crackling red hair, sluicing icy water out of a basin on to her face. For a dazed moment Celia thought Magdalen was speaking of Stephen Marsdon, though she knew that the girl had never heard of him. Then she understood. To be sure, this day after Christmas was St. Stephen's Feast Day, St. Stephen, the first martyr, who had been stoned to death outside Jerusalem by the wicked Jews — then it was also *her* Stephen's name day . . .

'Hasten,' cried Magdalen. 'We'll be late, an' ye knaw that fashes Faither, forebye there's a mickle ta do fur your weddin' — there'll be fifty extra ta feed iffen the snaw howlds off, the Musgraves fra Eden Hall an' the Graham clan'll be here, na matter what . . .'

'I can't wed Leonard,' said Celia in a flat voice, her eyes hard as sea-ice.

For a second Magdalen was startled. 'Whist, hinny!' She pulled Celia off the bed. 'Ye're haverin', wake oop!' She sloshed water on Celia, ran the comb through the long yellow tangles, flung a hooded cloak over the girl.

Celia allowed herself to be propelled down the stone stairs to the chapel. She said no more. She listened intently when there were references to St. Stephen in the Mass; she murmured responses with the others but her long apathy had vanished. Whatever happened she would *not* marry Leonard. Two and two made four. Fire burned, snow was cold. The River Irthing flowed south. Cowdray was in Sussex. She could not wed Leonard Dacre.

She glanced down the chapel towards Leonard whose narrow foxy-coloured pate was decorously bowed like his brothers, then at the Baron's box-pew where he and his Lady followed the Mass with brisk devotion while keeping a watchful eye on the younger members of their family.

Celia clenched her hands in a fold of her gown and thought frenziedly of plans. Flat refusal would do no good. The Dacres were kindly, but the Baron never altered his decisions; nor were weddings with unwilling brides unknown in the North. Magdalen had laughed about a Dacre marriage where the bride had been trussed up then carried screaming to the altar and jabbed with a dirk until she panted out the vows.

Feign illness then, thought Celia. But how? Deception

clever enough to fool Magdalen or Ursula was beyond her powers. Ursula had loved her once, but to Celia now her aunt seemed an enemy. There was no confidence between them any more.

The girl's chaotic schemes grew wilder. Escape . . . run north to the Border. Those fearsome Scots . . . the Maxwells, the Lowthers . . . would they shelter her—glad of the excuse to annoy Dacres? But how far was the Border, and how to survive in frozen mountains, through icy becks?

As the Lanercost priest made the benediction and said, 'Ite, Missa est,' Celia's cheeks flamed from another idea. If she told them she was not virgin . . . that she was with child? No, they wouldn't believe that either. She scarcely understood exactly what kind of act produced a child, but Magdalen's robust comments had enlightened her on one point. A woman with child ceased to have the monthly courses and Magdalen naturally knew that Celia had just recovered from hers. This event and its precalculation was indeed why the wedding had been set for the 29th.

Blessed Mother—what *can* I do? Celia's heart began thudding, the chapel walls closed around her like a tomb.

'Coom, lass,' said Magdalen nudging her, 'we'll gan out an' gather fresh greens to mak' garlands fur the Hall and church, an' we mun start gildin' the wheat ears fur your bride-crown. Jesu!' she added sharply, 'ye're white an' wambly as a lamb new-born . . . Leonard!' she called to her brother, 'Celia's gan mazy, can ye not gentle her?'

Leonard who had been hurrying from the chapel intent on a farewell gallop to Gilsland and some pleasant hours of bawdry with the warm widow Dixon, paused and looked around at the two girls.

It struck him that Celia did indeed look mazy—pale, bewildered and yet sullen. She showed none of the sparkle and provocative challenge which had so attracted him, and he wondered if he were not making a bad bargain after all. This pallid childish lass might be a poor bed-mate and breeder, and no dowry neither, but he'd never dare own misgivings to his indomitable father who had often berated him for being a shilly-shallying laggard.

'Oh, I'll gentle her Thursday neet,' he drawled with a half-hearted smirk at his determined sister. ' 'Tis not seemly afore-hand.'

Magdalen snorted then tossed her head. She linked her arm

250

to Celia's and conveyed her into the Hall to break their fast with ale and a manchet of bread.

Ursula was already in the Hall, seated at a table beside Lady Dacre. The two matrons had become cronies. The wedding plans excited them, and they were busily sorting ribbons —the bride-laces which would be attached to Celia's girdle, wrists and ankles, to be yanked off by the young folk after the ceremony. They were also counting the requisite favours to bestow on the guests. Lady Dacre had raided her coffers and unearthed some gloves, bows, silver-gilt trinkets she had been storing against a daughter's marriage.

'We'll send to London fur more when your time cooms, Maggie,' said Lady Dacre smiling at Magdalen as the girls entered. 'Celia's wedding s'all be like a dotter's, an 'll not shame us Dacres.'

Ursula murmured her thanks. She was woefully embarrassed by her poverty, and certain that the Dacre generosity must overwhelm Celia with the grateful rejoicing she herself felt. After years of subservience and loneliness, Ursula was blossoming at Naworth where the servants treated her deferentially and the family included her as an equal. She was unconscious of the mutinous pleading look Celia gave her. She smoothed the last white ribbon and laid it on the pile.

'Should be a-plenty,' Ursula said happily, 'unless . . . I suppose none o' the Nevilles 'll come from Raby, 'tis too far . . . ?'

Lady Dacre shook her head, a shadow crossed her florid face. 'Only Tam's puir wife,' she said sighing. 'He's gan ta fetch her fra Dacre. By the Blessed Saints, I hope there'll be na trooble.'

'Oh, surely not,' said Ursula absently. The strange night at the Dacre keep seemed years past, and she had been so feverish with ague that she barely remembered what had happened. Moreover, it pleased her that young Lady Dacre— wife to the heir—should be brought to Naworth to honour Celia's wedding.

Magdalen and Celia also heard Lady Dacre's remark. Magdalen was always optimistic and practical and scarcely noted it. Celia saw the news as yet another nail in her coffin lid.

By twilight Celia's desperation had induced need for action —any action. She went in search of Simkin, praying that she would find him in the stable. It was not hard to escape from Magdalen who had been called to her parents' bedchamber to confer with the elder ladies about a tally of the Graham youngsters whose name Lady Dacre was not sure of.

In the stable, one of the lads quirked his eyebrows at Celia's question, said that Simkin had watered and curried the Cowdray horses an hour ago, and had probably gone to his loft. Celia nodded, got directions and hurried towards the warren of wooden outbuildings behind the castle's south wall. She entered the third door into a dark cavern of oat-bins and stored threshing implements. She sought Simkin because there had once been sympathy between them, because she felt that he was unhappy and because he came from Cowdray.

She saw that there was candlelight flickering above a ladder, and heard male voices from the loft. She called out, 'Simkin!' but stopped as she heard a harsh despairing laugh, then a crooning sound, like the sound a mother made to her babe, and yet unlike—for this held a cruel taunting note.

Celia was deeply puzzled, but she slowly mounted the ladder until her head cleared the trap-door and she could see. She stared uncomprehending while her eyes strained wide.

In the loft on a pile of sacking there lay two naked men. At once she recognised them. Simkin and George. She was Simkin's shaggy black head lying next to George's finely cut upturned profile. Then Simkin's harsh voice cried out, 'Aye . . . so now ye find me ugly, eh? But where'll yet get another cotquean to be your slave an' do your filthy bidding?'

'Ah . . . but ye luv ma bidding, hinny, m'lad,' George crooned in that wooing taunting voice. She saw George's hand begin to stroke the other youth's hairy thigh.

Celia clung to the edge of the trap-door. Her knees trembled, and she nearly retched.

They had not seen her. She crept down the ladder.

'Christ have mercy . . .' she whispered.

She fumbled her way past the oat-bins into the air where a fine powdery snow was beginning to fall. She wandered back through the side postern of the castle. So there was nobody to help her. Nobody.

'Christ have mercy . . .' she repeated, and leaned on the side of the kitchen wall. Time passed while she stood there in the snow. There was bustle in the kitchens, she heard snatches of laughter and the preparatory squeals of the bag-pipes. Jock the Piper was practising for her wedding. 'The bonny bride fra far awa' '—that was the name of the piece.

Celia stood there in the courtyard while her golden hair

whitened with snow. She did not raise her head when the courtyard bell clanged out. She did not watch when the gates swung in and a party of horsemen came through them.

She dimly heard voices. 'What's that?' 'Why 'tis a lass crouched by the wall!' 'Some kitchen wench.'

Blessed Virgin help me ... Celia prayed with the force of shock and despair, and looking up thought that there had been a miracle. That an angel had come down from heaven to comfort her.

A tall whitish figure stood beside her, the kitchen lights gave it luminescence, and it spoke in a low sweet voice. 'What troubles you, poor maiden?'

Celia gave a long shaking sigh and reached out her hand towards the figure. 'Help me . . .' she whispered. A hand took hers, but its touch startled her—so clammy cold yet thickly soft. Celia stared down and saw that the other hand was encased in a drenched velvet glove.

Sir Thomas, having also dismounted, came peering. 'Why, 'tis little Celia Bohun!' he cried. 'Bess, 'tis the lass who'll wed Leonard. 'Tis the bride!'

'Ah, so . . .' said young Lady Dacre, 'sma' wonder she shivers an' hides. Yet the King, my royal father, told me she'd be here.'

'To be sure, to be sure,' said Thomas sharply. 'Coom inside, Bess—all o' ye!' He waved his arm to the servants who had accompanied him from Dacre; one was leading Blind Janet's horse.

It was cheerful though smoky in the Hall. Pine logs crackled, there were candles lit as well as rush-lights. The Baron and his wife gave Thomas and Bess a hearty welcome, smacked kisses on their daughter-in-law's cold cheeks, determined to think her better, relieved that there was no strange look in her large dark eyes.

With composure she sat beside Lord Dacre while they supped. She smiled at times. In her plain gown of bleached homespun she dominated all the russets, blue and greens. She did nothing untoward, drank sack delicately, showed no interest in the bloodier hunks of roasted mutton, and by her remote courtesy somewhat subdued the others.

'Eh, there, Tam,' grunted the Baron to his son, while downing an extra noggin of whisky, 'I vow Lady Bess'll gi'e ye anither son yet, ye'll tak' a go at it this neet, won't ye, lad?'

'Aye . . .' answered Tom, but his eyes shifted and the quick glance he gave his wife was uncertain.

'She'll no ha'e heard o' your doin's in Carlisle, she couldna . . .' said Lord Dacre very low. 'Not that I blame ye—i' the saircoomstances but ye knaw wot happened afore. Keep ye're snot clean at Na'orth, an' dinnet go near that Jeannie, the woodcutter's wench—aye, I'm no' blind. Her belly's thickenin' —'tis ye, I suppose, 'less 'tis Leonard. Either way we'll ha'e ta gi'e her faither some siller.'

Tom said nothing. Not for worlds would he have admitted that he was afraid of his wife, that the thought of bedding her again gave him gooseflesh, and yet excited him.

'Bess 's a'reet,' he said curtly. 'Janet says she's drunk no bluid nor sung that song the past month.'

Dacre nodded. ' 'Twas only her wild fancy made her blame ye fur the death o' the bairn. She'll be over it noo.' He signalled to his piper and demanded a merry jig.

Tom felt the old flush of guilty anger. The baby's death had naught to do with him. A pinprick on the little chest from the dirk Tom had left unsheathed at his belt. It cut wee Tammie when his father gathered him up in a boisterous embrace. A scratch—but it did not heal. It puffed and reddened. Some days later it burst, dribbling green pus and blood. It was then that Bess began to suck and lick the wound insisting that it was the only way to cure her baby. They hid the child from her, but on the second night she stole in and saw the wet nurse they had found. Bess hit the poor wench on the breasts, she pommelled her, screaming that not content with hurting her baby, Tom had given it to one of his whores. Then she had crouched in a corner and begun to lick the infant's chest wound, like any hound bitch or cat-mother. Before they could restrain her, her mouth was full of blood. And the baby died next day. Bess's hoarse screams resonated through the castle. After a week of this they sent her to Dacre. Nigh to a year ago. Tom thought, and the horror had faded. She was quiet and courteous to him now; despite the coarse white robe she insisted on wearing she looked again like the lovely Neville bride he had been so glad to win.

'A wedding,' said Tom to his father. ' 'll gladden the lot o' us.' He began to bang the table in time with the piper's jig. 'Where's Leonard?' he asked.

'A bit late coomin' heem, but he ha' business i' Gilsland; some complaint o' ma crofters, he's na guid at handlin' 'em. I

254

troost he'll not muck up the manor at Greystoke. I'm sendin'
'em there, ye knaw.'

Tom did know. Lord Dacre had bestowed one of his lesser
estates on the young couple.

'We found the lass huddled i' the courtyard,' said Tom
shrugging. 'Na doot they've had a lovers' tiff.' Both men looked
at Celia who was sitting very quietly beside Magdalen. 'A
bonny beauty,' said Tom appreciatively, 'I'd a bedded her
mysen, 'till she got betrothed to Len, but I'm no the man ta
cuckold ma own kin.'

Dacre nodded again. He and his elder son were always in
agreement. They had their code and lived up to it.

'Ye saw Scrope i' Carlisle?' asked the Baron. 'Gi'e me the
full account, we mun keep better order i' the Marches. Scots'll
want a fresh lesson.'

They drifted happily into talk of raids, the fort at Berwick
and the need for circumventing the upstart Dudley's ill-con-
sidered directives.

Celia went to bed that night stupefied and hopeless, and
yet she dreamed, though not of Stephen.

She dreamed of Master Julian, of whom she had not thought
since leaving Cowdray. It *was* the Italian doctor, but did not
resemble him. His face peering down into hers had become
clean-shaven and lean. He had no four-cornered hat, his hair
was smoothly black, and his brown eyes, intense and pleading, were sending a beam of light into her brain. She felt the
light-beam glowing in her head and heard an urgent voice
say, 'Celia!' Something he wanted her to do, something she
could not do.

She shut her eyes tighter against the command, while she
heard other voices whispering near by. Somebody said, 'I
think there was a quiver there,' and she heard a strange
distant roar like rushing water mixed with honkings or hoot-
ings outside, a noise she did not recognise.

'Celia!' Again she heard Master Julian. 'Open your eyes!'
She struggled this time to obey, but she could not. She woke
up instead at Naworth to find that she was trembling, and
filled with wondering amazement. She sat up in bed, thereby
disturbing Magdalen.

'Wot's ado? Lay doon fur pity's sake— Ye've jairked the
covers off me!'

'Maggie—I'd a dream, it seemed real. Master Julian, that
doctor I told you of, the one who tried to see King Edward,

but he'd altered ... Master Julian, I mean. He was trying to help me, his eyes were brown, not grey, but he was real, as real as *you* ...' She put her hand on Magdalen's shoulder.

'Havers!' Magdalen shoved Celia, and pulled up the blankets. 'Mun ye waken me fur sech bletherin'?' she turned over and slept.

Celia lay staring up at the beams blackened from peat smoke. The sensation of the dream's reality lessened and no longer seemed immediate. It was like a sudden memory from childhood, the day she fell downstairs at the Spread Eagle, twisted her ankle and her mother carried her to the bench in the courtyard and gave her some raisins to comfort her. She had never remembered it before, but now she could taste the sweetness of those raisins, feel the crunchy seeds between her teeth. A memory—and so had been the dream.

In bed with Magdalen, and her prospective marriage two nights away, she could think about it calmly, purged from frenzy and desperation. She made no more plans for escape. There was no need, she had no idea what might happen, she simply knew that the wedding would not take place.

*   *   *

On the next following dawn which was Childermas—that evil, ill-omened day commemorating the slaughter of the Holy Innocents by Herod—Celia's certainty was confirmed.

It was a boisterous night of sea-winds roaring down the Solway through Carlisle and over all the Western Marches. Amidst whistling wind and driving hail nobody but Blind Janet heard the commotion in the bedchamber where Thomas slept with Lady Bess. They did not hear his shout, nor later, Janet's wild scream. When Janet, moaning and staggering, managed to grope her way and arouse the Dacres, it was almost too late to save Thomas. And Bess was dead, lying on the floor in a pool of her own blood. She had fumbled her attack on her husband and only severed a portion of his upper arm, but the dirk which she rammed into her own breast— precisely at the spot on which she always made the blood-cross mark—that had pierced straight to her heart.

Celia and Magdalen learned of the tragedy after they went down to the chapel for Mass. The chapel was empty. Puzzled they went to the Hall where some servants were huddling, frightened, murmuring, crossing themselves.

The girls, aware of bad trouble, grabbed each other's hands.

'Wot can be amiss ...?' Magdalen whispered. 'Wot can it be?'

She saw her brother George come in and make for the whisky keg. 'Geordie!' she cried, 'is somebody deed?'

George drank a noggin and walked to the girls. He was blanched; there was sweat on his forehead. 'Aye—Bess is. Tam near so, but our mother says he'll do. She's stopped the bleeding, forbye we've sent to Brampton for the leech.'

Magdalen gasped. Celia drew herself in, very quiet and still. 'Lady Bess is dead?' She crossed herself, as did Magdalen.

'Aye—she turned Tam's dirk on 'em baith. She fooled us these twa neets, 'tis sickening.' He glanced at Celia with a touch of his usual malice. 'There'll be na wedding fur ye the morrow, m'lass! Funeral instead.'

'Yes,' said Celia. 'Oh, poor, poor thing.'

Magdalen gasped again, gave a sob and threw her arms around Celia. They wept together, but it was Celia who comforted.

Later they broke fast with the appalled family and Ursula. She had been helping Lady Dacre staunch Tom's wound, and decently arranging Lady Bess's body on the bed, and had had no time for thought as yet.

The Brampton leech came, poulticed Tom's wound with cobwebs and approved Lady Dacre's tourniquet. He was given no explanation for the savage cut on the young heir's arm, and nothing was said about Lady Bess except that she had had some fatal attack. The Dacre family knew that there would be speculations and rumours to ignore, and would ignore them.

They had consulted with the priest who was as anxious as they not to consign a Neville–Dacre to a suicide's grave at a crossroads, which even her known madness would not have precluded.

So, by evening, when many shocked wedding guests had arrived, Bess's body lay in state before the altar in Lanercost Church. Above the embroidered black velvet pall her waxen face looked serene and lovely. Tall flickering tapers illumined the faint smile often seen on newly-dead lips. A smile of secret knowledge, of remote compassion. All night and all the next day mourners filed by and knelt by Lady Bess's bier, while the priest intoned prayers for the dead. When Celia's turn came and she knelt on the hard bench, she wept like the others, but unlike the other mourners her pitying sorrow was tinged by gratitude. Awe-ful as the tragedy was, it had been the means of Celia's release, and Bess, so gently asking in the courtyard—'What troubles you, poor maiden?'—was after all the helping angel Celia had mistaken her for.

Ten

At the beginning of June in that Year of Grace 1553, Celia and Ursula, accompanied only by Simkin Farrier, set forth towards Cowdray, as unsure of their welcome as they had been of the welcome at Naworth eight months ago.

In March, Ursula had first written to Sir Anthony Browne, requesting permission to return home. She had outlined the Dacre tragedy, hinted that the continuing visit to Cumberland was becoming awkward and burdensome, and asked if Wat might be sent to fetch them, now that the Spring thaws had begun.

When she received no answer, Ursula decided that the peddler to whom she had consigned her letter was unreliable, and sent another by the official courier bound from Carlisle to London with Lord Dacre's report on the state of the Western Marches.

Still no answer came from Cowdray, nor any return courier to Lord Dacre. There was fearful unrest on the Border, alarums and excursions daily, many panic-stricken rumours. The old Baron mobilised his sons and all his clansmen to combat another attack on Carlisle, leaving Naworth so vulnerable that he sent his remaining household to greater safety at Dacre keep. The warning beacons burned nightly on the hilltops. Provisions ran short, and though Lady Dacre was too kind-hearted to say so, it was obvious that the Southerners were a nuisance. Food became scarce, they slaughtered the cattle; lambing was late this year, moreover many ewes were sickly and dropped malformed little foetuses on the scarcely thawed ground. Tempers grew short, and when George Dacre, racked by fever and a bloody flux, suddenly turned shrilly delirious and cried that Simkin Farrier was really a were-wolf, or a 'barguest', Ursula made up her mind.

She approached Lady Dacre and said that they were leaving. The unhappy Baroness did not protest. Magdalen, too, was relieved. She had much affection for Celia, but she agreed with her mother that the guests had stayed overlong, and brought ill luck.

There was no reason to blame the girl for any of the

troubles which had assailed them after Mad Bess's suicide, yet nothing had gone right since with the Dacres, and it was natural that one should resent dependent aliens.

The girls kissed goodbye outside the great postern at Dacre. 'Matters dinnet tur-rn oot as we hoped, hinny,' said Magdalen, sadly. 'Na doot 'twasn't God's will—I'll send ye a bit o' prayer noo an' agen.' But her eyes were peering over Celia's shoulder to see if that puff of dust of the Graystoke road was made by the eagerly awaited flock from the Newbiggin pasture. Otherwise, there'd be no meat again for dinner.

'Farewell, Maggie dear,' whispered Celia, sighing, yet glad that the last months of sorrow and strain were over. Neither girl expected that they would ever meet again.

Ursula had hoarded ten shillings all during the Cumberland stay. She had meant to give them to Celia as a bridal gift, but after the wedding was so definitely cancelled, she had saved the coins for the journey home, once Sir Anthony had given permission. Since none ever came, they must manage without, and did so. Simkin, though taciturn, his pitted face set in an habitual scowl, proved as good a guide as his father. And they all remembered the way south. Celia kept gazing steadfastly ahead, nor looked back to the mountains and the moors which she had thought so excitingly beautiful last year. She had learned much in those months, learned ugly fearsome things. Lust, madness, violence—all those had touched her close in Cumberland. There was also that other thing, the scene in the stable loft between Simkin and George—part of the chilling strangeness, which the healthy young mind refused to dwell on.

By the time they reached London, and the sun shone on tender green leaves, the hedgerows were dappled with wild roses, healthy lambs frisked in the meadows and birds trilled night and day—Celia had begun to laugh again. Ursula, though worried, smiled sometimes, and even Simkin brightened, and took to playing a willow pipe he had made for himself.

They went straight to Southwark and the Priory of St. Mary Overie where they expected to lodge. But Sir Anthony's town house was shuttered and barred. The cloister garth was filled with rubbish, weeds and a litter of runty piglets.

Simkin banged on the doors, he shinnied up to a window and peered through a broken pane. 'Nobuddy within,' he reported. 'Dust thick as me hand, cobwebs like curtains.'

Ursula looked anxiously at Celia. They had no money left,

and she had been so sure of finding Brother Anselm, at least. 'The neighbours . . .' she murmured.

Simkin nodded and hurried out of the cloister. He came back shortly. 'I found an old besom down the street,' he said. 'She didn't want to talk, but says Brother Anselm's dead—last winter. Sir Anthony's never been here at all. She seemed afraid.'

Ursula frowned, then her face cleared. 'Master Julian!' she cried. 'He'll help us! Simkin, go to St. Thomas's Hospital, they'll know where he lives . . . wait, we'll *all* go!'

They prodded the weary horses, Simkin thwacked the mule while they went down the Borough High Street. As they came up to the hospital's dingy grey pile they saw Julian striding towards the portal, clutching his staff and bag. He turned at Celia's happy cry; gave a grunt of astonishment as he recognised the women.

'*Mirabile!*' he said. 'Where did *you* drop from?' And he frowned.

Ursula and Celia explained their plight together, while Julian listened, his eyes grave.

'Then you know nothing of the news,' he said. 'Times are very bad . . . some plague around, but that's not it . . . other matters . . .' He glanced over his shoulder nervously. 'Can't talk here—you've no money at *all*?'

Ursula shook her head, humiliated by Julian's dismay, by his gruffness.

'Well,' said Julian coldly, 'I can lend you a few pence to get you to Cowdray.' He fumbled in his bag. 'My circumstances are straitened . . . at present. You don't even know of *the* marriage? The King's condition?' he finished very low.

They shook their heads, staring at him.

Julian flushed, again he glanced round and examined Simkin. The boy wore the Browne's buck-head badge on his arm. 'You can water the horses yonder,' Julian said, pointing to the stone trough by the hospital wall. 'And you, m'lady, will not be seen in here.' He shoved the two women through a noisy fetid hall lined with pallets and stretchers where the sick lay waiting for admission to the wards.

'Listen,' said Julian, when they were sheltered by an alcove, 'a fortnight ago, on May 21, the Duke of Northumberland married off his second son, Guilford, to Lady Jane Grey who is King Edward's half-cousin. The King's Grace has altered his will in the Lady Jane's favour. Twenty-six peers have signed Edward's "Devise" for the new succession. Northumberland commanded Anthony Browne to sign, but Sir Anthony sent word that he could not leave Cowdray. Edward is reputed to be furious. And, *I've* been summoned at last to His Majesty,' added Julian with a sudden gleam of triumph. 'John Cheke—Sir John he is now, has prevailed on the royal lad to see me. I go to Greenwich tomorrow, and by Esculapius, I'll cure him yet!'

'By Our Blessed Lady, I'm sure you will,' said Ursula slowly, 'but I don't understand. What has this marriage to do with anything, and what is the "Devise" Sir Anthony would not sign?'

'Sh-h—' said Julian. 'Nobody knows of it yet—I mean the people, the commons, but it's clear enough. If Edward should die, the crown goes to Lady Jane Grey . . . and thus, in effect, to her father-in-law, Northumberland.'

'Impossible,' said Ursula roundly. 'What of the Princesses? What of Mary?'

Julian shrugged. 'The Lady Mary is a Catholic, the Lady Elizabeth's true religion is uncertain, but either one might marry a foreign prince, which would be the ruin of England.'

'You approve this monstrous plan!' Ursula cried, her eyes indignant.

Julian stiffened. 'I am a physician, Lady Southwell, an Italian physician. I've nothing to do with moral judgments. Sir John Cheke is my friend and patron, so I think as he does. I shall most certainly cure the King, whereupon these worldly complications will not arise.'

'Oh dear . . .' whispered Ursula, suddenly wilting. The chill in Julian's voice hurt her. She felt old, confused and weary. She saw why Julian did not want to be seen with those connected to Sir Anthony, and looked unhappily down at the pennies Julian had put in her hand.

'I'm sorry we bothered you,' she said, 'but there's nobody else in London. I can see that you mustn't offend the Duke . . . or the King.'

Julian bowed. 'As you say, madam,' he gave her a faintly apologetic smile. 'Hasten to Cowdray, and as you wish your patron well, talk *submission* to him, for he has totally lost the King's favour.' He turned on his heel and hurried down the hall to enter the wards and leave instructions for the care of certain patients in his absence.

'Whew . . .' said Celia. '*He's* grown very curt. I thought he liked us!' She made little sense of this pother about the King's Devise, signing or not signings, and growing hunger fogged her thoughts. They had bought the last pastry and ale yesterday. 'Well, he loaned us enough to eat on,' she said. 'Aunt, there was a cook-shop across the High!'

Ursula nodded sighing. They retrieved Simkin and the horses, then presently proceeded towards Sussex.

*   *   *

At five the next morning Julian rode down the Thames to the royal palace at Greenwich. John Cheke had left orders, and Julian was at once admitted to the King's Presence Chamber. It was beginning to fill with solemn-faced courtiers, some of whom Julian recognised—Lord Clinton, Lord Bedford, John Ridley—the fanatically Protestant Bishop of London. There were also the watchful ambassadors, the French Theligny, the Spanish one, de Scheyve, sent by King Philip.

'Cock's bones ...' cried Clinton in disgust as Julian was ushered in. 'Yet *another* doctor—we've had quacks enough lately, the Duke had far better get back Owen and Butts!'

John Cheke stepped forward and shook Julian's hand. 'I brought this one,' he said. 'He's a friend of mine and has excellent training at Padua. He cured me of the sweating sickness.'

'Indeed,' said Clinton shrugging. 'That fellow Cardano was Italian, wasn't he? A lot of good *he* was. Said the King's Grace'd be hale in a few days and 'd live to be fifty—hocus-pocus with a horoscope!' Clinton winked and chortled at his own wit.

The French Ambassador laughed politely.

John Cheke gave Lord Clinton a stern look, compressed his lips and drew Julian into a smaller chamber off the sickroom.

'His Grace is worse,' said Cheke rapidly, 'yet there *was* so much improvement last month when the Duke brought in that midwife from Cheapside. She gave him potions which bettered him, but now he vomits incessantly—yet he coughs less.'

Julian nodded. He had followed details of the King's illness as best he could when Cheke had time to recount them, and thought the case very grave, though he had faith in him-

263

self and had brought various substances in his bag which he knew had not been tried. Now that the longed-for examination had arrived, he felt a great surge of hope. He heard already in his ears the murmurs of gratitude, of admiration. He saw himself triumphant and secure, at last.

He followed Cheke into the King's room, and looked down at the bed. Edward lay flaccid, with his cheek on Henry Sidney's hand. The harsh difficult breathing filled the room, and the stench was so unpleasant that even Julian faltered. The firm serene greeting he had intended died unuttered.

Edward's eyes were glazed, the lids were lashless, the chicken-claw hands which plucked incessantly at the velvet coverlet had lost their nails, the finger tips were gangrenous. The boy's belly was so swollen that it humped up like pregnancy. The bloated face was a patchy bronze.

Julian stared down, while all his hopes collapsed and a great anger replaced them. '*Il ragazzo è avellenato*,' he shouted furiously.

Cheke and Sidney both knew Italian, and they both recoiled.

'*Poisoned* . . .?' Cheke cried, then checked himself. 'You're mad, Master Julian, wickedly mad!'

But Sidney bowed his head closer to the pathetic, monstrous body on the bed which was shivering and barely conscious. Sidney's eyes filled with tears. He had suspected this for some days. 'What kind is it?' he formed the question soundlessly, looking up at Julian.

'Arsenicum,' Julian answered curtly, and turned away. He had seen several cases of arsenic poisoning when he lived with the Medicis; Edward's condition was unmistakable, whatever his previous illness had been, and the story of the recent great improvement, the sudden collapse, was explained. That midwife from Cheapside brought in by the Duke, and her magic potions which had given the little King new energy and vigour—for a month—just long enough for Edward to alter his succession and disinherit his sisters.

'Well, what can you do?' John Cheke jerked at Julian's sleeve. 'I'll not believe—what you said—'tis impossible—must *never* be mentioned—'tis too monstrous.' Besides real anxiety for the boy whom he had taught and so long guided, stark personal fear showed in Cheke's eyes.

'I can make him more comfortable,' said Julian tonelessly. 'Fetch hot bricks, well-padded, and there's this.' He untied his bag and brought out a vial containing syrup of mandragora, which he held to Edward's blue lips. The boy obediently tried to swallow, then retched. Suddenly, he raised on his elbow and spoke to the three men in a sharp, stern voice, though his unfocused eyes looked past them at a tapestry.

'Oh, my Lord God,' he said, 'defend this realm from Papistry, and maintain Thy true religion, that I and my people may praise Thy Holy Name . . .'

'Aye, aye—my dearest chuck,' Sydney murmured, stroking the King who had begun to quiver. 'He will. Be sure that He will—'

Edward subsided a moment, he looked from Cheke to Sidney; his wandering gaze lit on Julian. 'That spy!' he cried, jumping half out of bed. 'He's a foreigner—a Papist! What does he *here*! Have I not enough torment—Guard! Ho, the guards!' A convulsion seized him, black froth dribbled on his chin.

Julian quickly picked up his bag and staff; he did not need the dismissing signals from the two men by the bed. He withdrew from the sickroom, nor looked behind him as he left.

He rode slowly back to town along the river bank on the bony hired nag, which he had thought never to see again. He had expected to be mounted in future on one of the royal horses. Now, his situation was far worse than it had been. John Cheke would never forgive that shocked cry he had made. Northumberland would never forgive it when he heard, as he certainly would. There had been varlets hovering near the door of the sickroom. When Edward dies, Julian thought, I'll be in grave danger. I am so now. I do not wish to be hanged, or more likely, assassinated—dagger in the back, a convenient fire at my lodging. As he entered Southwark and made, as usual, for London Bridge, the full blow of his predicament hit him like a bludgeon.

He pulled up the nag, dismounted and walked slowly to the Thames. He gazed unseeing at the darting wherries, the barges, the whirlpool rapids rushing through the arches of the Bridge. He looked across the river at the Tower, thinking of all those it had imprisoned and still imprisoned—those who had in some way offended royalty. He thought of his former patron, the Duke of Norfolk. The old man was still there, but his son, the young, the witty and debonair Surrey —dead, six years, reduced to rotting bones.

I must escape, Julian thought. Where to? Italy, of course.

But how? There was no money to bribe a passage to France. No money. Julian bitterly regretted the pennies he had given Ursula. Tiresome woman with her admiring trusting eyes. And the tiresome niece, albeit beautiful, fair enough to find a man to help her. Why then *me*? Not that a few pennies would buy safety. The ports were guarded, everyone knew that Northumberland was preparing for a crisis—yet, some fishing smack out of Norfolk—he hadn't been to Norfolk since his years at Kenninghall, but among the Duke's own fishermen there'd be a boy whose arm he'd saved from amputation— Toby? Robby?—he'd come from Yarmouth. If I can find him, he might sail me over—it's a chance.

Having made up his mind, Julian acted rapidly. He crossed the Bridge into the city; he went to his lodgings, and while gathering up his few portable effects he told Alison the circumstances. As he expected she had only three groats laid by, and her comely doltish face crumpled into tears.

'Ye'll no be leaving me and the child like this, sir . . .' she wailed. 'Wot'll we *do*?'

'They won't harm *you*,' said Julian impatiently. 'Your father'll look after you.' He glanced down at the child—a slobbery tow-headed little boy who was banging his tin spoon on a pewter mug, and uttering a senseless babble. Not for the first time Julian doubted that it *was* his son, there was no Ridolfi look about him, and he was backward in speech and comprehension.

As Alison saw that she was to be deserted, her under-lip shot out, while her round eyes glinted. 'Good riddance!' she cried. 'You and your pots an' your vials, an' runnin' back and forth to St. Thomas's treating o' charity cases when ye might've been making an honest living at your trade—I've m' bellyful o' ye, *Doctor* Julian. Serves me roight fur takin' up wi' a foreigner—my gossips warned me!'

Julian bowed. 'So now your gossips will be justified,' he said in a silken voice.

She stared at him baffled, then began to blubber again as he took the three groats and put them in his purse.

'If it's truth ye're in danger—and I've ne'er believed in your crazy fancies and talk o' the King—' she said, 'ye'll not be hidden i' them black robes an' four-corner cap.'

'*Da vero*,' answered Julian. 'Unusual intelligence, my dear. So you will bring me that old jersey doublet of your father's, the leather breeches and felt hat. Then you will cut my robes off at the knee, so they can serve me as a cloak. In exchange for your father's generosity, I'll leave here my staff, my retorts and medical stores ... Also—my books.' His voice wavered. He glanced quickly towards his bookshelf, the dear vellum-bound companions of all his wanderings. Books of Greek and Latin philosophy. Dante's *Inferno*, Erasmus's *In Praise of Folly*, Boccaccio's *Decameron*, Paracelsus, besides medical tomes by Avicenna and Vesalius. 'Your father can't read them, but I beg he won't sell them unless you're destitute.'

Alison stared at the handsome bearded man, whom she loved in her fashion, and always rather feared. She saw tears in her eyes, and was touched, since it did not occur to her that a man might weep for books. She threw fat sweaty arms around Julian's neck, crying, 'Well, then, sweeting, don't go? Ye'll be safe here i' the garret.'

'*No!*' interrupted Julian. He detached her arms from his neck, though he gave her a pat on her broad rump. He wondered how he had put up with her so long, and was shamed that it took a threat of danger to force him to make the break —and yet, he thought ruefully, if his early morning hopes had been realised, he would have left her too, though not penniless like this. 'Sell the books, if you must,' he said, 'except . . .'

There were two he could not part with, though they would weigh him down: Ovid's *Metamorphosis*—and Marcus Aurelius. And another—his eye lit on it, with dismay. The famous *Grimoire Verum*, a textbook of necromancy. John Clerk, an acquaintance, had recently been arrested for possession of books on witchcraft and black magic. If they searched this lodging, they must not find such a thing here. Julian's name was in it, and many comments in his writing; moreover, its presence would endanger Alison and her father.

'We'll put this one in the fire,' he said, and did so, under the pot of stew Alison was cooking. The vellum curled and blackened; he prodded the book open until the leaves smouldered and gave forth acrid smoke.

'Why d' ye burn *that* one?' Alison asked, vexed because she had always resented his books but knew that, oddly enough, they were worth money.

He answered her in the way she hated, a cool detached voice that made mockery of his words which, moreover, she did not understand.

'That book, my dear, contains formulae for delving into mysteries which are forbidden. I, too, would like to raise corpses from the dead, or invoke the lustful succubi to pleasure me, also to find eternal youth and the philosopher's stone, then transmute lead into gold—but, it seems I lack the temperament. Or, is it that I've never scraped sufficient moss from a hanged man's skull, nor blood from a virgin's womb, nor yet gathered up a vampire's faeces—?'

Alison gaped at him, scowling.

They both started as they heard banging on the barber-shop door below.

'Look out the window,' cried Julian. 'Quick!'

She obeyed, turned back, her pale blue eyes anxious. 'Guards,' she whispered. 'The Dook's men, by the livery.'

'So soon . . .' Julian murmured. He shook himself, and summoned the cool wits he used for medical emergencies. 'Go down, act simple. If they ask for me say you know not my whereabouts, but likely I'm at St. Thomas's Hospital.'

She nodded, much startled that there really might be danger.

'Here, take the child,' Julian thrust the little boy in her arms, 'it'll distract them. I'll go to the garret.'

He escaped up a ladder into the shadowy space of rafters. He crouched behind the great chimney, annoyed that his heart was pounding, and his mouth had gone dry as tinder.

In a few minutes he heard Alison's muffled call—'They've gone, sir.'

Julian descended to the second storey.

'Aye, they're after ye,' said Alison, round-eyed, 'but they heeded my words and left. Here's father's clothes, I brought 'em up. God's bones—'tis lucky *he's* out.'

Julian nodded. 'You've done well, Alison.'

Between them they hurried through Julian's transformation. She cut the black robes to knee length; the doublet and breeches fitted fairly well, though the points to the hose could barely be tied, for the barber was a shorter man. She hurried below and brought up a razor. He shaved fast, and Alison, staring, cried, 'Ah, but ye look much younger wi'out that beard—a'most a green lad, an' a lusty one, too—sweetheart, must ye go?'

She moistened her red lips and gave him an amorous look.

'Obviously I must go,' said Julian curtly. 'You've just seen the Duke's men after me. Give me that loaf, and wrap the stew—here, in this parchment.' He thrust at her a leaf of vellum he had been saving to write an official report on the King's condition.

'Where *can* ye go?' Alison wailed, again flinging her arms around him. 'When'll I see thee once more?'

He did not answer, he scarcely heard her, for there was a disturbance in the street, men's shouts, the blowing of whistles and a watchman's rattle. Doubtless only an escaping thief, but best not find out. He gathered up his bag, stuffed the books in his doublet, hurried downstairs and let himself out at the back door into an alley which contained nothing but two quarrelling dogs and some chickens.

He strode through a maze of alleys past garden patches until he reached Cheapside near Wall Brook. As he entered Threadneedle Street and forced himself to saunter towards Bishopsgate he realised how much appearance makes the man. In his majestic robes, his imposing doctoral hat, the jacinth stone around his neck, fulsomely bearded, he had always commanded respect from the common people and even some gentry. They would bow as they passed him, and often murmured deferential greetings. Now, dressed like a shabby tradesman, he found himself jostled; an urchin cocked a snoot at him, while a pretty barrow-maid gave him a lewd wink. *Dio*, Julian thought, touching his chin which felt cold and naked, I've become one of the hoi polloi, but I don't feel my forty-eight years either! There was no time for reflection upon these interesting changes. Ahead of him down river loomed the great forbidding bulk of the Tower, and he winced. The Duke's spy system was notably efficient. Look at Lady Ursula's experience last summer! I might be too small a sprat for their net, Julian thought, except for Edward's dislike of me. The King was quite unpredictable in his present state. But Cheke, who had taken a brave chance by introducing Julian to Greenwich Palace today, would now be the first to repudiate any concern for the Italian doctor who had mentioned poison, and then once more displeased the King. No friendship could stand a threat to power or safety. Thus was Julian's experience, nurtured by his years in Italy, confirmed by his observations in England.

In a quarter of an hour Julian quitted London through Bishopsgate and took the highway towards Waltham and Norfolk, wondering very much what was in store for him next.

* * *

Ursula, Celia and Simkin arrived home on the day after Julian started his flight. As they passed through Easebourne they saw Cowdray—the beautiful palace ahead, glinting golden in the sunlight, its myriad windows twinkling like diamonds, and they heard gay music wafting from the meadow by the Rother, which was dotted with booths and coloured pavilions; swarming with gaily dressed folk in crimson, green and crocus yellow.

'Why, 'tis our Cowdray festival time!' Ursula cried gladly. 'I'd quite forgot.'

Every year between St. Anthony's Day, June 13, and Midsummer Eve, the 23rd, the Lord of Cowdray had held merrymaking for Midhurst. There were contests, bowling, shooting at the butts, jousting. There were rustic dances and pageants. Sir Anthony provided mutton pasties, pigeon pies and hampers of strawberries, as well as gingerbread. Good Sussex ale flowed from the kegs set up in three of the booths. Those June days had always been a time of jollity, and the gay scene at once raised the spirits of the disgruntled voyagers from Cumberland. Suspicions, dangers, impoverishment—especially Julian's gloomy announcements, seemed ridiculous. Nothing was changed at Cowdray.

'Blessed Mary, but 'tis good to be home!' cried Ursula. Celia laughed agreement, and squeezed her aunt's hand. She scarcely remembered their differences up North, nor quite believed she had felt them. She and Ursula smiled lovingly at each other. Simkin, too, was excited. He was longing to see his mother, and had whittled her a bodkin as a gift. Moreover, he noted a certain banner fluttering at the corner of the fairground. It was green with a grotesque red masque painted on it—surely the banner of the Winchester mummers—and Roland might be with them. His heart beat at the thought of Roland. The miserable affair with George Dacre seemed as remotely nightmarish as the happenings in Cumberland seemed to the two women. They were home again.

'Why, here comes Mabel,' cried Celia, as they turned up the avenue of great oaks towards Cowdray House.

Anthony's young sister was plumper than ever, and very elegant in a mauve satin riding-suit trimmed with miniver, a rakish feathered hat on her crisped brown curls, but her round face looked gloomy. She reined in her palfrey as she saw the trio. 'God's greeting,' she cried, lisping slightly as always. 'Here's a wonder! We thought you settled for ever in the North!'

'But I wrote Sir Anthony twice,' protested Ursula. 'I—I hope we're welcome.'

'Oh, to be sure.' Mabel drew her scanty brows together. 'There's room enough, no visitors in months, but Cowdray's doleful nowadays. Anthony'll hardly speak, and Jane's ill—worse than last time she neared her term.'

'Lady Jane's with *child* again?' asked Ursula. 'We've had no news since we left.'

'Big as a barrel,' Mabel agreed. 'Yet she still pukes a lot.' The girl's attention was suddenly caught by a looping golden thread on her pearl embroidered gauntlet, she began to work the thread back in place. 'They're fine, are they not?' she said of the gloves. 'Anthony gave them to me on his Saint's Day—but I've no place to show them. We don't go anywhere now. 'Tis dull . . . I was off to have a look at the Fair, though I've been every day, but I'll ride back wi' you.'

Celia glanced across the fairground and the river towards St. Ann's Hill. 'Brother Stephen is well?' she asked in a casual, low tone, glancing at Ursula who did not hear.

'Aye,' Mabel shrugged. 'I never see him 'cept at dinner or the chapel. His penances are over-strict. I wish we had a house priest like the Arundels. *He's* merry as a grig, so Mary told me, but I've not even seen the Arundels since Christmas.' She sighed. 'Anthony *promised* we'd all go to London, once Jane's delivered, but lately he won't talk about it. You didn't see Gerald in London, did you?'

Gerald? Celia cast her mind back to the preceding summer. 'Oh, d'ye mean Lord Fitzgerald, your stepmother's brother?'

'To be sure.' Mabel was surprised. 'She's Lady Clinton now. Didn't you see the Clintons?'

Celia shook her head. 'We only stopped in London a couple of hours.' She perceived that Mabel had no knowledge of affairs outside Cowdray, and that while she herself had altered a great deal during the long absence, the other girl had stagnated. Never unkindly treated now, as she had been by 'the fair Geraldine', but lonely and bored.

They arrived at Cowdray's gatehouse where Lady Ursula was greeted with surprise and cordiality by the porter, whose little son she had once helped nurse through the smallpox, during the epidemic which had disfigured Simkin.

They entered the courtyard, and Guy Hawks, the steward,

came hurrying out. He was not cordial, nor ever had been, since Ursula was always unable to present New Year's gifts which he considered worthy. He accorded her a tepid 'How d'ye do', and gave Celia an annoyed glance—that Bohun tavern wench back again, too! He reluctantly admitted that Sir Anthony might be found in his writing cabinet off the long gallery.

He did not bother to show them upstairs, while Mabel, bored again, wandered off to the pantries in quest of a sweet-meat.

The door to Anthony's cabinet was shut. Ursula knocked more loudly than she meant to, because her heart was sinking.

The gruff 'Who the devil is it?' from the inside scarcely helped.

She looked dismayed at Celia, and called, ' 'Tis Ursula Southwell, Sir Anthony.'

They could hear an exclamation, and the scraping of a chair.

The cabinet door was flung open by Stephen. He stared at Ursula, then at Celia. Clear in the sunlight through the oriel window, they saw him flush, saw the tall figure stiffen under the black habit.

'B-Benedicite—' Stephen stammered. He looked at Celia with a startled flicker of greeting. He compressed his lips, then repeated, 'Benedicite,' in a firm tone, bowing slightly to both women.

The girl, suddenly calm, had an instinct of withdrawal. She sketched a small mocking curtsy, and raised her chin. She had both dreaded and longed for their meeting, but since the night of her blissful dream about him in Cumberland, and the anguishing events of the following St. Stephen's Day, his image had faded. Too, she had matured, had observed from the Dacres' stringent Catholicism and their attitudes towards priests, how wicked, how childish, her behaviour towards Stephen had been. She was not nearly as innocent now.

'Well-a-day—By the blessed saints!' cried Anthony peering around his chaplain. ' 'Tis My Lady Ursula, *and* the fair little niece. Prettier than ever, I vow. A very paragon of beauty . . . Northern roses in the cheeks, sparkle of mountain brooks in the lovely eyes. Come in, come in!'

Anthony was not usually so fulsome—he had been deep in gloomy consultation with Stephen, and was cloaking displeasure at the interruption, as well as the fact that he had completely forgotten the girl's name. 'So you've come back to us, and welcome I'm sure. Though I heard a rumour—' Where had he heard it? One of the Nevilles, no doubt. '—a rumour that the banns were published—that we'd lost you to the Dacres.'

Ursula shook her head. 'I wrote to you twice, explaining. I trust, sir, you'll forgive us for returning without permission. We could stay up North no longer.' She smiled appealingly, though her eyes were anxious. 'We won't be a trouble to you.'

Anthony was touched. He jumped up and kissed Ursula on the cheek. 'My dear lady, this was your home long before it was mine. Only I fear you'd be safer in the North. From day to day I expect to be hauled off to the Tower, and that's putting it clear. Moreover, they hint at confiscating Cowdray, all my estates forfeited. You might as well know.'

Celia gasped. Ursula made a quick motion. 'They couldn't do *that*!' she cried.

Anthony gave a rueful grunt, and pointed to an open letter from which two red seals depended. 'That is precisely the subtle tenor of this missive in Latin. Brother Stephen has verified my not very expert translation. And you observe the seals. This one, the Privy Council—that one is the King's.'

'The King is ill,' Ursula whispered.

'One hears so, therefore others think *for* him. But the King has come to hate me, since I would not sign his "Devise" for the new Succession.'

'Aye . . .' said Ursula on a long breath, 'so Master Julian said—we saw him in London.' She stared appalled at Anthony. 'They don't accuse you of *treason*, surely.'

'Not quite—not yet.' Anthony slumped down in his carved chair. His face fell into heavy lines. He had grown thinner, and a muscle twitched beside his eye. The joyous noises from the fairground came through the open window. Anthony half turned his head. 'Let them make merry while they may, poor wights,' he said. 'Soon there may be nobody to give them festivals.'

Stephen inhaled a sharp breath, his hazel eyes softened as he put his hand on his patron's crimson velvet shoulder.

'Courage, my friend,' he said. 'Our Blessed Lady will protect you, for you're in the right. You've stood up for both Divine and earthly justice!'

'Ah ... Stephen,' answered Anthony warmly, '*your* faith has been a comfort to me these last months!'

The two young men exchanged an affectionate look, and Ursula thought how much she had misjudged Brother Stephen in the past, thinking he might be lecherous, and harbouring ridiculous fears for Celia who was standing demurely by the door, not even looking towards the monk. I'm so often wrong, Ursula thought. I should never have insisted on that Cumberland trip, it's brought my Celia naught but trouble and dreadful memories. As for the future—we must trust in God as does this good monk.

'May I come to confession tonight, Brother?' she asked. 'I'm in sore need.'

'Surely there was a priest at Lanercost?' asked Anthony frowning.

'Aye, but I did not make good confessions, for I did not see my sins.'

'By the Mass ...!' Anthony was momentarily diverted from his troubles, wondering what Lady Ursula could have on her conscience. Surely none of the mortal sins, but the girl—*Celia*, that was her name! A lovely little thing, tempting as a peach, *she* might have a thing or two to confess.

'How old are you now, Celia?' he asked.

'I was fifteen, sir, on St. Anthony's Day. We were nigh Oxford then. There was a great thunderstorm, my mare cast a shoe and a spider ran across my arm. It seemed ill-omened, alack!'

Anthony laughed. He now remembered her amusing pertness, and the dimple near her lips when she smiled. 'Certes, that was no proper celebration,' he said. 'We must make up for it.' He thought of the jolly little dance he might have given for her, invite the local gentry, find her a husband as he remembered he had once promised to do, and his face sobered. The local gentry would not come to Cowdray at present. They were afraid. Moreover, there was Jane's state.

He turned to Ursula. 'I'm very glad you're come, Lady Ursula, for I know that you'll help my wife, she's with child, and most unwell. Worse than last time. She weeps incessantly, and the least noise disturbs her. Molly o'Whipple is here, but her simples do no good. Still,' added Anthony, ever striving for optimism, 'the babe kicks and squirms lively i' the womb. Ye can feel it, and my poor Lady Jane is a delicate breeder.'

'To be sure I'll help!' cried Ursula immensely relieved to be needed. 'And Celia—I'll find ways to make her useful.'

Anthony nodded. He glanced down at the threatening official letter on his writing-table. It must be answered somehow—firmly, diplomatically, and soon. The royal messenger was waiting. He turned to Stephen. 'We'll make copies, when we've thought it out. One to Cecil, of course, and that Cranmer, d'ye think?' Anthony's lip curled. He added, 'My Lord Archbishop Cranmer—who was a good Catholic once, yet like the wind-flower, nay rather like an empty puff-ball, he spurts in every breeze. I remember how my father despised him and his connivances to please King Harry—Queen Catherine's divorce—repudiating His Holiness the Pope, and now *perjury*. Signing Edward's "Devise" is hideous perjury, since Cranmer signed the old King's Will which fixed the Succession. Bah!' Anthony banged his fist on the table. 'What's to be expected from a *married* priest!'

'Very little, sir,' said Stephen calmly. 'Nothing at all in matters of conscience. He is, to be sure, *not* married in God's eyes, and thus a fornicator.'

They had forgotten the two women, who stood together rather awkwardly awaiting dismissal. Fornicator, Celia thought, what an ugly word. And with what chill contempt Brother Stephen speaks it. She looked at the young man's mouth—full, red, flexible—impossible to believe that she had kissed it, or that for a second he had certainly responded.

'Shall I go to Lady Jane?' asked Ursula tentatively.

'Aye, pray do,' Anthony gave her his warm smile. 'And Celia'll companion Mabel who pouts adn sulks and wanders about like a lost pup. She should be wed, of course, and I'm sorry I can't arrange it, *now*!'

Stephen turned and stared full at Celia. His tone was judicial, a little frightening, as it had been when she first came to him for lessons atop St. Ann's Hill. 'No doubt Celia may raise Mistress Mabel's spirits,' he said, 'but I deem she can make herself more useful in other ways, too.'

'*How?*' said Celia involuntarily, while both Anthony and Ursula looked surprised.

'She may repair the altar cloths which are in sad condition, also two of the chasubles. I've asked Mistress Mabel—to no avail.'

'Excellent idea, excellent!' cried Anthony heartily, though still a trifle startled by the young monk's tone which was like

275

that of a reproving elder, and saw a new look in the girl's beautiful eyes—was it resentment?

At this moment when Ursula had totally relinquished the notion that there had ever been anything between Stephen and Celia, the idea first occurred to Anthony, but he was far too harassed for speculation.

'I'm not very skilled wi' the needle,' Celia said slowly, on a faint tone of mutiny. She stared down at the rushes, her cheeks grew pinker.

'I'll help you, sweeting!' cried Ursula.

Stephen nodded in her direction with a slight smile. 'Also—' he went on, 'I think it expedient for Celia to return daily to the Spread Eagle. The Potts can find her some small tasks, they brought her up, and will, I'm sure, be glad to have her back.'

'*Indeed!*' the girl cried, as both Ursula and Anthony stared at the monk's imperturbable face. 'Holy St. Mary,' Celia went on, barely controlling the tremble of anger. 'Ye wish me to become serving-wench in a tavern once more? Have *you* perchance been appointed to direct my future?'

Anthony chuckled, for Celia looked rather like an outraged golden kitten, but he was puzzled, and silenced Ursula's protest with a motion of his hand.

'Come now, Brother Stephen. Poor we may be compared to the past, yet not so straitened that Lady Southwell's niece must go back into service. I find your proposition as odd as they obviously do.' Anthony waited. He had grown very fond of his house priest during the last months, when he had been exiled from other confidants, nor felt that he had quite atoned for the monk's imprisonment during the King's visit, and its consequences which had nearly killed Stephen.

'Celia,' said Stephen, still speaking as though she weren't there, 'has quick intelligence, she may have *learned* some discretion. She can keep her ears open at the Spread Eagle where come many strangers who'd never dream of her connection with Cowdray. Isolated as we have become here ...' He stopped, raising his heavy black brows quizzically.

'Oh-h-h,' cried the girl, understanding faster than the others did, 'you want me to be a kind of spy? I might hear news of danger—to us?'

Stephen smiled. 'The London carters, the sheep-traders, sailors trudging from the capital to board their ships on the coast—they all blab of much *we* never hear.'

Anthony nodded slowly as he saw the possibilities in the monk's idea. Except for royal messengers—like the one waiting in the buttery where the steward would see that he talked to none of the servants, nor heard aught as to Stephen's presence and celebrations of the Mass—Anthony had no access to news. He was under what amounted to informal house arrest. His most trusted servant, Wat Farrier, was lodged in a dingy dockside inn near the royal palace in Greenwich. Wat had his instructions for the moment when and if he heard that the King had died. Then he would hasten back to Cowdray if he could—a risky uncertain arrangement.

'Will you try Brother Stephen's plan, Celia?' Anthony said.

'Need ye ask,' cried the girl, her eyes sparkling. 'I'd do anything for you and Cowdray, and 'tis like a sort of Hoodman Blind—a Christmas game!'

'I wish it were,' said Anthony. He picked up his goosequill pen for the starting of a draft.

*   *   *

Thus passed the next three weeks at Cowdray, while they all, even Mabel, lived in mounting tension and uncertainty. Celia walked daily into Midhurst, where the Potts received her temperately, after some hesitation. She served ale, washed mugs during the dinner hour as she had used to; she parried amorous advances in the broadest Sussex accent—and she listened. Each dusk she returned to Cowdray and reported privily to Sir Anthony (she saw nothing of Stephen except in the chapel), sorry that there was so little to tell. There were rumours a-plenty . . . the King was better, the King was worse. The Princess Mary had seen her brother; no, she had been denied his presence. The Duke was massing forces on Blackheath, or instead, he had taken the bridal pair, his son Lord Guildford and Lady Jane Dudley on a pleasure jaunt to Richmond. Two parsons had been hanged at Tyburn, no, burned at Smithfield singing Mass in the old way, and genuflecting idolatrously despite warnings. All church bell ringing of any kind was now forbidden in London. Good money grew scarcer, a groat's worth of meal now cost sixpence. The shillings grew so red with copper 'twas said they blushed for shame. All the ports were more stringently guarded each day.

Celia garnered these tid-bits, among much local gossip as to the rising prices of mutton and grain; the probable harvest; the scandalous behaviour of the chandler's daughter who had

277

set up for a whore not three doors away in the ancient building which had once belonged to the Knights Hospitallers.

Anthony listened patiently, he thanked Celia, but they both knew that her information was worthless.

On St. John's Eve Cowdray closed the Fair by the traditional bonfire. For days the servants had been laying it, chopping down oaks, amassing deadwood, collecting the pitch in great vats. When it was lit; Anthony led his family out to the mound where the Bohuns and then the Brownes had always built the bonfire. The flames were beginning to leap and crackle, reddening the twilight. The merrymakers deserted the Fair to watch. A roar of triumph burst from them when the wood caught.

Soon, the villagers began to dance around the fire, a wild orgiastic dance, as they shouted and leaped.

Anthony, Ursula, Celia and Mabel stood a little apart from the frenzy while the flames flared up tall as a steeple.

' 'Tis the finest bonfire we've ever had,' said Anthony, laughing grimly. And no doubt the last, he thought. He drew himself up as two horsemen suddenly came trotting across the meadow from the highway, and dismounted. One was the squire of Stedham, a village two miles away, and the other, John Hoby, the King's steward at Petworth. Both were vociferous Protestants, and both, he knew, were enemies.

'Good evening,' said Anthony coolly. 'You've come to watch our bonfire?'

'Aye,' said Hoby, who was a great tub of a man with gimlet eyes between folds of puffy flesh. 'Ye can see it for miles. Squire here and me were riding back to Petworth on a matter of business, an' we thought we'd look in.'

'Right welcome,' said Anthony, his muscles tensing. Petworth, having been wrested from the Percies, was now Crown land technically, but Northumberland had somehow acquired the castle. It was known that he kept there a great number of retainers and armed men. As for the Stedham squire, he was a meagre little toady who had once been glad enough to sit below salt at Anthony's dinners, and even a year back begged Anthony for a loan—never repaid.

'Ye celebrate the vigil of St. John?' asked Hoby in a jolly offhand voice, doffing his plumed hat, then clapping it on again.

Anthony hesitated, but he finally answered with sarcastic caution. 'How can you think so, Master Hoby, since saints are forbidden in England. The bonfire is for midsummer's eve. That's not prohibited yet, I believe?'

Hoby grunted uncertainly. 'Ye jest, Sir Anthony?' He stared around. All these yokels and servants—they were enjoying Sir Anthony's bounty, they were attached to Cowdray and would—most of them—be loyal, yet not over a hundred fighting men in the lot. The rest were women, youngsters and old gaffers. And of the family from the Great House, only three women apparently, which tallied with his information. The oldest one in the widow's coif might be Lady Southwell, though he had heard she was up North with the Dacres of Gilsland. Mistress Mabel, the plump young partridge with a stupid look, was Sir Anthony's sister. The other maiden, slender, modestly dressed in green, golden hair tumbling down her shoulders, he did not know, nor did she signify. The King's messenger, while stopping at Petworth on his way back to Greenwich, had said that there were no men in Sir Anthony's family. Obviously true.

Hoby considered his instructions, which were to watch and wait until he received word to strike. His was to be the honour of arresting Sir Anthony for treason, though, he thought pleasurably, clear evidence of Papistry might hurry the matter, and would greatly add to his acclaim.

In this desire John Hoby was not entirely moved by ambition. He had strong religious convictions. He had been moved by the thunderous preachings of Ridley and Latimer, and three years ago he had been totally converted by John Foxe. There was no doubt of the true interpretation of God's Word as shown in the Bible, which Hoby read nightly. Roman fripperies disgusted him—heathen bowings and scrapings, incense and Latin mumblings, the hypocritical witchcraft which professed to believe that a scrap of ordinary bread dipped in the cowslip wine any good wife had made could be turned by incantations into actual pieces of the Lord Jesus Christ's body —this seemed to him obscene.

'I trust, sir,' he boomed above the roaring of the fire and drunken shouts of the merrymakers, 'the answer ye sent the King's Grace showed a meeker spirit than ye've shown up to now?'

'Pity you didn't break my seal and find out,' said Anthony. 'Or did you?'

Hoby's massive face empurpled; he and the messenger had

tried tampering with the buck's head signet seal, and found it stuck too fast.

'I mislike your tone,' Hoby said. 'I asked a friendly question.'

Anthony bowed. 'And it shall be answered. In my letter I again declined certain proposals and regretted that my lady wife's condition prevents me from leaving Cowdray.'

Hoby was no fool, he knew that he was being suavely cozened and yet—there was something attractive about this recalcitrant owner of Cowdray. The Browne men, father and son, were none of your sly, mealy-mouthed nobles—back three generations their stock had been as plebeian as his own. And this stubborn man's plight was so hopeless, you couldn't help a pang of sympathy.

Hoby drew away from the squire who was trying to kiss Celia, and put his hand on Anthony's arm. 'Ye know there's trouble brewing, sir, ye might not want to go to London, I can see that, but ye might to some other place, Cornwall, say —'tis far enough for safety—but don't make a try for the continent—whole coast is watched day an' night, not the meanest little fishing-tub'll get by unsearched.'

Anthony gave a grunt of surprise. 'My dear fellow, are you suggesting that I bolt? I know the ports are guarded, but I also know that all the approaches to Cowdray are, too. Around the fringes of my land there's been appearing a rare lot o' strange gamekeepers, peddlers and even a few gipsies wi' walnut-stained skins and oddly light hair.'

Hoby shrugged, he glanced about, then spoke softly, 'If ye went Trotten–Petersfield road, past Stedham—tomorrow night—it might so hap ye'd not be noticed.'

Really startled, Anthony examined the fat, bearded face. Flamelight jumped and wavered, he could not see the expression in the puffy-lidded eyes. 'You laying an ambush, Master Hoby? Or are you prepared to wink at my escape?'

'I'm giving ye the chance,' Hoby muttered.

'*Why?* You loathe the true Faith, you're hand in glove with the Duke—and the King.'

'Aye, sir, and I'll do my duty—after this. 'Tis midsummer madness's got to me, I'll warrant. I've done plenty soldiering, but I mislike needless bloodshed, or frightening a houseful o' women.'

'By the Mass . . .' Anthony breathed.

He saw that Hoby was sincere, and thereby how great must

be his own danger if such a man were moved to pity, even momentarily.

'I thank you, Master Hoby,' he said quietly. 'Kind actions are rare, and I'm grateful. But, I'll abide here, in my own home, and take whatever fate God sends me. Will you join me in a flagon?'

'Nay.' Hoby already regretted his impulse, especially when he heard the forbidden and sickening ejaculation—'By the Mass.'

'Squire and I'll be off now,' he said. 'I fear we'll not meet again in amity, Sir Anthony Browne.'

He called to the squire, who fancied he was making headway with that fair smiling little Bohun maiden, and left reluctantly.

The two men mounted and rode off.

'You've made a conquest, Celia,' said Anthony, with a thin smile. ''d be a good match for you, once—but he's gone heretic, the lick-spittle!' Besides—there was not a penny to spare for the girl's dowry, the generous gesture he had once thought of making. Anthony scowled past the great bonfire towards the Fair where the last kegs of ale, the last savoury pies were being consumed. It had been a piece of extravagant folly to give them the Fair this summer. Stephen had protested, and with reason, since Anthony had come to confide in him, and he knew his patron's financial predicament. The expenses of the King's visit a year ago would not have been embarrassing to a man of Anthony's wealth, had the usual revenues continued to appear, but they had not. For months no messenger came from his other manors in Surrey, or from Battle. Letters to his stewards received no answer. He had been quietly relieved of his remunerative office as county sheriff. On the home manor of Cowdray conditions had worsened. Cowdray sheep, Cowdray corn and garden stuff not only brought lower prices than was conceivable, but lately they did not sell at all. Anthony's loyal shepherds' and husbandmen's weekly reports went from gloomy to dire. Even the Midhurst rents were laggard, many tenants had grown impudent, surly. Yet, he had promptly given them their traditional Fair.

He turned suddenly to Ursula. 'Is this as it was in your father's time, lady?' He waved towards the bonfire, then to the cluster of bright-coloured tents and flowery booths. 'Does it remind you of your girlhood?'

She heard the note of appeal, and smiled at him, thinking how much of the boy was left still in this big handsome man. ' 'Tis much *more* lavish, sir,' she said gently. '*We* had no tents and banners, nor much music. *We* fed them only cider and bread.'

She saw that she had pleased him, though he sighed. 'Aye, those were simpler, happier days . . .'

Ursula started to say that the past always seemed simpler and happier, then checked herself. There *had* been nothing in her girlhood to match Anthony's troubles. Both religion and throne had been as fixed as the suns daily swing across the sky.

'The Lady Jane seems better, sir,' she said. 'Since yester e'en she's not puked once. 'Tis perhaps the camomile gruel I give her. D'ye know, I believe your lady wife has a surprise for you! I believe there're two babes i' her womb!'

Anthony jumped. 'Holy St. Mary! *Twins?* By God, what a wondrous thought!' He considered this news excitedly. 'Two heirs at a clip, for me, for Cowdray! 'Tis true, Jane's belly's vast this time, much larger than last year. 'Tis true there've been portents. My best mare dropped two foals last week, and I found two spiders on my pillow yester morn. Ah, lady, I thank you!' He bent quickly and kissed her.

Ursula pressed his hand. 'Better not tell her. It may not be so, and the poor soul is much afeared already. She suffered a great deal last time. Oh, I wish Master Julian were here . . .' added Ursula impulsively.

Anthony raised his eyebrows. 'Surely, the good doctor wouldn't concern himself with midwifery?'

'I presume not, but he knows many potions to relieve pain, and has a tender heart, despite . . .' Her voice trailed off. The last meeting with Julian in Southwark had shaken her. 'I wonder if he *has* cured His Majesty. Master Julian was very confident.'

'We must pray so,' said Anthony, though his spirits plummeted again. Whether or no the King recovered, Anthony's personal plight would continue. May God blast that bugger Northumberland, he thought; turned on his heel and strode back into his mansion.

Eleven

On Thursday, July 6, at dusk, Edward died in Henry Sidney's arms. He died after saying quite clearly, 'Lord have mercy upon me—take my spirit.' His own former royal physician, Dr. Owen, bent over the hideously decayed body, and shaking his head, whispered to Sidney, 'At last, poor royal youth—it is done. I believe I could have saved him, Sir Henry, had I not been banished for months. The Duke was misguided to dismiss me . . .'

'Hush!' Sidney said. Tears ran down his cheeks. He eased Edward's body on to the pillow, tenderly folded the contorted gangrenous hands as best he could on the shrunken chest. He drew up the embroidered coverlet. 'Stay with him,' said Henry, 'I must tell His Grace, who wants the utmost *secrecy* at present. Silence about—' He pointed to the body.

Dr. Owen's mouth thinned. 'Aye—I'd forgot you were the Duke's son-in-law—and though my anti-Papist convictions are strong enough, I mislike this hole-and-corner death. No last rites, nor even prayers—'twas far different when his father died.'

Henry flushed, he started to reply when they heard above the palace a tremendous thunder-clap. Lightning flared into the death-chamber.

' 'Tis a warning, Henry Sidney!' cried the old doctor. 'Tell His Grace to heed it!'

' 'Tis an ordinary July storm,' answered Henry, his voice trembling, and he hurried down to the Council Chamber where the Duke and Sir Nicholas Throckmorton were privately supping.

Wat Farrier guessed at the King's death only ten minutes after the Duke heard of it. Wat was outside the palace's back kitchen, near the wash-house when Betsy, one of the laundry-maids, came scurrying down from the royal apartments bearing a hamper of filthy stinking linen. During these last days her errands of this nature had been frequent, the King was incontinent, and his yeoman of the chamber must continually change the sheets and bed-gown.

Wat had taken the trouble—no unpleasant chore since

Betsy was amorously inclined—of seducing the girl, and she greeted him with a mixture of pleasure and fear. 'He's gone,' she whispered, as she dumped the soiled linen in a vat. 'I heard 'em say so as I lingered be'ind the arras, arter Gib 'anded me these.'

'Ah-h,' Wat breathed. 'Ye certain, m'dear?' She nodded, then jumped at another thunder-clap, followed by a roar of wind through the open passage. Wat gave her a warm kiss. 'Thankee, lass.'

'Ye're not goin' out i' *this*?' she cried.

Wat did not bother to answer. He darted to the servants' courtyard, where his tethered stallion was snorting and shivering in the downpour. He spurred the beast, and galloped towards London. The storm had driven all the citizens indoors, he had the streets to himself. In an hour he reached the goldsmith's shop on Lombard Street.

' 'Tis time!' he shouted through the crack which finally opened to his banging.

The crack widened enough to admit Wat, and the goldsmith spoke from the shadows. 'Tom's waiting,' he said in a thin quavering voice, 'an' I've kept his horse on the ready.'

'Make haste!' Wat cried. 'They sent her a summons yesterday. I saw the messenger go. She's probably left Hunsdon, Tom may meet her anywhere along the London road.'

The goldsmith glided to his safe, and took out a small ebony box. Wat peered over his shoulder, to satisfy himself that it was the buck-crest ring. 'Tom must put it in her *own* hand. Has 'e the wit and nerve?'

'He's my grandson,' snapped the goldsmith. He hobbled to another room. Wat heard the shaky voice giving urgent instructions, and then a horse's whinny, followed by pounding hoofbeats on the cobblestones.

'Bigod,' said Wat as the goldsmith returned, 'I hope he stops her. They've laid a subtle trap—those shitten traitors.'

'No more—I wish to hear no more,' the goldsmith whispered. 'I'll thank ye to leave. If aught goes wrong, I've ne'er set eye on ye in my life. Nor your master. Tell him.'

'Ye'll be glad enow fur the reward if all goes well, old bag o' bones,' said Wat with a snort, but he quitted the shop, and mounting his wet bedraggled stallion returned to Greenwich and the dingy wharf-side inn to await developments.

He had two days to wait, and then the whole of London was rocked by news. King Edward was dead, and Jane Grey Dudley

284

was proclaimed Queen of England, at the Tower, on St. Paul's steps, at Charing Cross and Westminster. The city's few remaining bells were set to pealing. The news was greeted with boisterous huzzahs, and 'Long live Queen Jane!' from the archers the Duke had carefully planted among the crowd. Shocked protests were suppressed by force. On the whole the Londoners were dazed. Rumour and speculation there had been for weeks, but fact was different. Even many of the Protestants were appalled. Who *was* Jane Grey Dudley? An undersized though, it was said, learned chit of sixteen. A half-cousin of Edward's, descended from the daughter of Henry the Seventh. But what of his *sisters*, especially the Lady Mary's Grace? And even the Lady Elizabeth? They were of King Harry's own get. At least *Mary* was certainly born in true wedlock from a royal mother. But she was a Papist, half-Spanish, and the poor young King had set her claim aside by will. The placards all over London announced this. At Paul's Cross Bishop Ridley preached a jubilant sermon lauding Queen Jane.

Of more personal interest to Wat was the information that Sir John Gage, Anthony's aged and eccentric grandfather, had at once been removed as Constable of the Tower, and Lord Clinton substituted for the occasion. Wat, remembering his chats with Clinton's valet, said, 'Aha!' and laughed dourly.

Wat waited around in Greenwich for five more days. Betsy was of no further use to him. She could no longer eavesdrop profitably since all the Court had removed to London or the Tower, to prepare Queen Jane for her coronation. Betsy's only news was dismal. The King's body lay neglected and unwatched in his chamber, where the stink had grown so horrible that the servants would not enter it.

Wat haunted the docks. Sailors and fishermen always brought tidings, and he spent most of the money Anthony had given him loosening tongues with pints of ale. At last, on July 14, he was rewarded. A fishing smack from Yarmouth sailed smartly up river on a following breeze. She was loaded with herring commissioned for the palace, and her master, though wary at first, soon could not contain his excitement. The Princess Mary was at Framlingham Castle in Suffolk! East Anglians of all degree were rallying around her. She had been proclaimed the rightful Queen at Norwich.

'Bigod, has she in truth?' Wat cried, betrayed by relief into a triumphant shout. He lowered his voice. 'How'd she *get* to Framlingham?'

The fisherman sucked ale-foam from his lips and grinned. 'Ah—they say she was *warned* at Hoddesdon. Somebody warned her of a trap. She turned back and went skitterin' north to her palace at Kenninghall, an' Northumberland's men arter her. But she got clear, an' high-tailed it to greater safety at Framlingham—brave as a lion, like her dad. She'll get her roights, that one will. They're all solid for her up Yarmouth way.'

'God bless her,' said Wat on a great sigh of relief. 'I'm off to join her,' he said suddenly. 'She'll need every able man!' He looked around the pot-room defiantly, ready to fight arrest, aware that as matters stood his assertion was treason. Instead, he was cheered. Ale-mugs thumped on tables. Several voices shouted, 'We'll join wi' ye, Wat!'

Wat had a fleeting thought for Sir Anthony, virtually imprisoned at Cowdray. But it was yet too soon. There was nothing to report except the proclamation of Queen Jane, the escape of Mary.

'Ferry me an' me hoss 'cross Thames,' he ordered, 'I'll start now.'

The master nodded slowly. 'I'm no Papist, but I'll take ye. If we must have a woman fur queen, better the roightful one, I say!'

In the end several fishing boats and a horse ferry crossed the Thames that night, eleven men aroused by Wat's enthusiasm elected him leader, and one of these who was Suffolk-born offered himself as guide.

At Chelmsford they found the town in a ferment. The church bell pealed for Queen Jane one hour, and Queen Mary the next as messengers came rushing through with new proclamations. At Chelmsford Wat and his little band learned that the Duke had raised an army of three thousand men, and had proceeded into Norfolk to 'fetch in Lady Mary, captive or dead', that he was burning and pillaging as he went, and rousing increasingly angry opposition as he marched towards Cambridge, the Protestant university town where he might reasonably expect to raise stronger forces.

An hour after Wat's party finally reached the great triple ramparts of Framlingham Castle, and joined the hordes of gentry, yeomen and common people who were milling around shouting allegiance to Mary, a royal herald galloped among them. His horse was lathered, his tabard so askew and fouled by spattered mud one could scarcely see the lilies and leopards. He brandished a roll of parchment, and yelled hoarsely, '*London's* proclaimed Queen Mary! Long may she reign!' He panted a moment, then blew a great blast on his trumpet.

The crowd gave a collective gasp.

Harry Jerningham, a rich Suffolk squire, and Mary's staunch supporter, came running from inside the fortress. 'What's that?' he cried. 'Did I hear a-right? Has the *Council* proclaimed Queen Mary in London?'

'Aye, sir,' answered the herald mopping his face on his sleeve. 'Here's proclamation. An' the order's gone out for Northumberland's arrest.'

'Jesu!' said Jerningham. He fell to his knees, and upholding his sword kissed the cross-hilt. One by one, most of the crowd followed suit.

Wat, exalted and triumphant as any of them, had a momentary pang. 'So there'll be no fight,' he murmured to the Suffolk lad beside him. He fingered his musket, touched his dagger. 'I was itchin' to have at the shitten heretics!'

The boy did not answer for they were all riveted by the appearance on the drawbridge of a small pale woman in violet velvet, riding a white palfrey.

'Long live our good Queen Mary!' the herald shouted as all the men uncovered. 'Queen of England, Ireland and France, Defender of the Faith!'

Her pinched face brightened and coloured rosy. She looked instinctively at Jerningham, who nodded. The myopic blue eyes glistened. She pulled the jewelled crucifix up from her bodice and kissed it. 'A miracle!' she cried. 'Our Blessed Lord and his Saints have then answered my prayers.' In her deep mannish voice she added, 'And I thank you, too, all my loyal followers, from the bottom of my heart.'

There was riotous rejoicing that night outside Framlingham's great curtain wall. The weather was warm as new milk, and Mary's lesser followers settled for sleep on the soft green lawns. Before Wat snored with the rest he had a sharp struggle between duty and inclination. The crews from a fleet of men-o'-war Northumberland had sent out to guard the Channel from possible Spanish intervention had been willingly blown into Yarmouth Harbour, and upon being accosted by Harry Jerningham had at once switched sides and declared for Queen Mary. Many from the crews had come to Framlingham, bearing ship's stores for the castle.

Ever attracted by the sea, Wat joined some of these sailors and listened longingly to their tales of tempests, sea monsters near the Canary Isles, of successful battles with pirates, of the beauties of Venice and Genoa, including succulent descriptions of those cities' brothels. Even more fascinating was a bosun called Jack Tate who had actually set forth with Richard Challoner in May on the adventurous search for a north-east passage to India. He had only got as far as Amsterdam when he took sick. The crew feared it was plague, so they dumped him off. By great good fortune, the *Greyhound* was in port, about to sail along the Channel at Northumberland's orders. It picked him up, and thus he had eventually reached Yarmouth and Framlingham.

Jack Tate's eyes were blood-red, he had purple patches on his face, and an ugly running sore near his mouth. It drew his lip up in a snarl which gave him a sinister look, belied by his doggy eyes and amiable voice.

'I doan't know why I doan't 'eal,' he said ruefully. 'I fear 'tis the King's evil. I wonder would our new Queen touch it fur me—arter she's been crowned, to be sure.'

'N'doubt she will,' said Wat absently. 'Now, about that venture. Ye say they was going round Jutland and north to them icebergs?'

It was then that Wat noticed a middle-aged, shabbily dressed man in a battered felt hat standing above them and staring steadily at Jack Tate. The stranger had a long face with dark stubble on his chin, and torn hose, though his shoes of thick leather were unexpectedly good.

'Sit down,' said Wat, 'don't loom o'er us like that. Ye want to hear about Jack's venture?'

The man started and smiled. '*Da vero,*' he said, 'most interesting, but I was thinking about that imposthume on his face, and those blood-shot eyes. I could cure him.'

Wat and Jack both stared, then burst into guffaws.

'I am a physician—my name is Julian Ridolfi—and 'tis the first time in a fortnight I've dared admit that,' said the stranger, unruffled. 'My good man,' he nodded towards Wat, 'didn't I see you at Cowdray last summer? Aren't you Sir Anthony Browne's horse-master?'

'Aye,' Wat admitted after a moment. His wits were quick but he had not yet quite realised that here was no more need

for secrecy. 'Bigod, and are *ye* the foreign long-beard wot
healed our Brother Stephen o' rat-bite? Ye've got the voice
an' the manner, but ye've come down i' the world, old cock!'

Julian bowed. 'Certain changes in my appearance became
imperative, I intended to stowaway out of Yarmouth to the
continent. Recent events make that unnecessary.' He smiled
suddenly, the pleasant smile always tinged with irony. '*Exitus
acta probat*, as wise old Horace wrote.'

Suspiciously, Wat thought this over, and suddenly grinned.
'Wot's that?'

'The outcome justifies the act,' said Julian chuckling. He
had scarcely spoken to anyone during the past fortnight of
hungry, footsore plodding, and was glad of company.

'Ah-ha,' said Wat, 'well, we're i' the same boat then, an'
it's stopped rocking, thank God. How would ye heal Jack?'
he added curiously.

'Chopped greens, eaten raw—' began Julian.

The sailor who had been listening blankly gave an angry
yelp. 'Ye're mad, ye rogue, or else ye jest. Me teeth wobble in
me jaw loike nine-pins, an' me gums 're rotten.'

Julian nodded. 'You have "scorbuto", my poor fellow. 'Tis
common enough.'

Jack paled, 'The French pox?' he whispered. 'That flea-
bit whore at Calais . . .'

'No,' said Julian. 'I believe your disease is called "scurvy"
in England. Since you can't chew, will you drink milk and
fresh ox-blood? New-pressed cider will also help you, though
it will take some weeks.'

'Faugh!' cried Jack. 'Me belly heaves at the thought.'

'Then you will die before your time,' said Julian.

Jack gulped and crossed himself. His crimsoned eyes stared
fearingly at Julian in whom he recognised authority, despite
the shabby dress and the un-English intonation which he instinctively mistrusted. 'Is it witchcraft?' he whispered after
a moment. 'Should I say a spell, a charm?'

Julian shrugged. 'I've never quite distinguished between
witchcraft and medicine. Why yes, to be sure, you may say
"Abracadabra", each time you drink.'

'Could I say a Pater Noster, too?' Jack asked slyly. Wizards
were known to cringe at the holy words.

'Certainly,' answered Julian, smiling. 'Say what you wish.
But, *drink* as I have told you—milk, ox-blood and the juice of
any fruit.'

'An' how am I ter get that muck aboard ship, I'd like ter know?'

'You must change your calling for a while,' answered Julian. ' 'Tis summer, all the farms hire extra hands.' He saw by Jack's outraged expression how unlikely the sailor was to follow his advice, and giving his Italianate shrug, he turned back to Wat.

'You'll be off to Cowdray now? Your master must be very anxious.'

Wat grunted. He had been indulging disloyal fancies. Ship off now, while the country was still unsettled. Maybe take Jack's place on the *Greyhound*. See the exotic ports he had been hearing of—what a luring contrast to the dullness and monotony of Cowdray as it was when he left it for Greenwich a month ago—no visitors, Sir Anthony too worried even for tilting matches, the stables full of restive horses never exercised, an air of gloom intensified by Joan's naggings and a clutch of squalling children at home.

Julian read Wat's thoughts. 'Conditions have changed now, Wat.' He waved his hand towards Framlingham Castle where Mary's royal standard was billowing. 'Sir Anthony and Cowdray are sure to profit mightily. 'Twould be a foolish time for you to desert your master.'

Wat frowned, then sighed. 'Aye, sir—I'd not thought o' that. I wish Simkin was home,' he added. 'I miss the young knave, but he's stuck i' Cumberland wi' Lady Southell an' little Celia.'

'No—' said Julian. 'They're all back at Cowdray, for I saw them in London.' He frowned at the memory of the interview, and all that followed, the abortive attempt to treat the King, the humiliation of fear and flight.

Wat was astounded. 'Didn't Celia wed young Dacre? We heard so.'

'Apparently not.'

'Bigod!' Wat's little bear eyes lit up. 'Ye may depend on it, she's i' love wi' my Simkin. 'Twould be a fittin' match.'

Julian was seldom surprised, he had observed human folly, and man's capacity for self-deception from his boyhood in the Palazzo Ridolfi, but this piece of parental ambition *was* startling. Moreover, during those moments in St. Thomas's Hospital's courtyard he had received a distinct impression of Simkin from his walk, and the way he held his arms. Pederast, Julian thought. I doubt that youth will ever bed a *woman*.

'May your ambitions prosper,' he said. 'Give my salutations to all at Cowdray.'

'Wot'll *you* do, Doctor?' asked Wat. He'd taken a liking to the man, and the way he'd tried to help Jack, though the simpleton didn't realise it.

'Hitch my wagon to the new star,' answered Julian. He jerked his head towards the castle, adding thoughtfully, 'I hear they've no physician with them.'

'They'll never believe ye *are*—lookin' like that. Wait though, can ye weasel your way in to see the Whartons? Sir Thomas is Queen's Governor, they'd know about Sir Anthony's ring— the one wi' the buck crest sent to warn 'er. Tell 'em ye come from Cowdray, ye was leech to Sir Anthony. Here's me badge to prove it.' Wat dug deep in his pouch for the emblem he normally wore on his sleeve and had had to hide for a month.

'*Santa Maria, e ben trovato*—well found, your idea!' Julian cried, sincerely grateful. Events had moved so fast that he had not really made his plans. He pressed Wat's hand warmly. He straightened his shoulders and strode with confidence towards the castle drawbridge.

Wat, filled with the glow of a good deed, mingling with the glow of having resisted temptation, and being about to return to his feudal lord, wrapped his cloak around him, rested his head on a clump of buttercups and went to sleep.

* * *

On July 20, Cowdray and its inhabitants reached the depths of despair. At nine o'clock of that morning Celia hurried miserably towards the Spread Eagle, only because Ursula had sent her. There was no hope of hearing news there any more. Jane Grey Dudley was Queen of England. The proclamation saying so had, ten days ago, been nailed to the courthouse door by a messenger galloping west towards Hampshire and Somerset. He had shouted out, 'Long live Queen Jane!' at Midhurst market cross, while many of the town folk cheered. It was done; the incredible infamy which would certainly ruin Anthony.

'At least the suspense is over,' said Anthony. 'Hoby's men will be here any time now, and I'll not resist.'

Even Celia saw how useless would be any resistance. Anthony's immediate retinue might be loyal—and get killed. Cowdray was a lovely glass-traceried manor house. It was not a fortress to withstand a siege. Moreover, the town of

Midhurst could no longer be counted on to help its feudal lord as it would have in the old days. Tracts, pamphlets and itinerant preachers had converted many to Protestantism. And, though he was generally liked, Anthony's prohibited religion, and the fact that most of his tenants owed him money, naturally produced disaffection.

Midhurst townsmen were no romantic heroes to fight for a lost cause. They were shrewd, practical Englishmen who had taken Anthony's Fair for granted, and were now making plans for their own municipal celebration on Queen Jane's coronation day.

Even Potts, as owner of the town's principal gathering place, had finally told Celia that if she wished to work for them, she could not return to Cowdray, which was known to be under a ban.

'Your arrangement's unseemly, m'dear, e'en dangerous,' said old Potts briskly. 'Ye're a help i' the tap-room, no denyin', an' a pretty servin' wench is an asset. We was fond o' your mother, an' we're fond o' you, but as things are now ye can't keep a foot on both banks, an' that's a fact.'

'But I *belong* to Cowdray,' cried Celia. 'I've none else of my blood save Aunt Ursula.'

'Aye,' the landlord spoke with some sympathy, 'she's made quite a lady out o' ye, but ye maun fish or cut bait, now.' He hesitated. 'Ye can finish the week out, lass, but that'll do.'

Potts knew that even this concession would displease his wife who had lately turned Protestant, influenced by a fiery Calvinistic 'Hot-Gospeller' who was travelling from Southampton to London, and stopped long enough to hold stirring meetings in the Spread Eagle's upstairs assembly room. Mistress Potts would see her husband's mildness as the effect of Celia's golden hair, her luscious body and provocative long sea-blue eyes — which it was.

So Celia had not wanted to go into Midhurst today, yet she was relieved to escape the agony in the castle. Since breakfast, the Lady Jane had been screaming. Harsh bestial screams you could hear in the courtyard. They terrified Celia, as did Ursula's drawn anxious face.

' 'Tis the birth pangs started,' Ursula snapped, upon finding her niece hovering white-faced, her hands clapped to her ears, outside the state bedchamber. 'No, you can't help. Get away. Go back to the Inn. The pence you'll earn may come in useful. No, wait, child. Get Goody Pearson, the midwife who delivered the Mayor's lady. Mrs. Potts'll know where she lives. Molly o'Whipple's no good, she's gone queasy, she's afraid—and so, by the Blessed Virgin, am I!'

They both shivered as another hoarse shriek tore through the shut door.

'Hasten!' cried Ursula. 'I've sent a page for Brother Stephen. Take a short cut o'er Tan's Hill. If ye meet him, tell him, *hurry*!'

Celia sped off. She had been avoiding the short cut on her trips to Midhurst. Tan's Hill held painful memories, but avoidance of Stephen was unimportant against the sick fear of those gruesome sounds of intolerable pain.

She and Stephen met at the footbridge over the Rother. 'The Lady Jane?' he asked quickly. 'Is't bad?'

'Aye,' she said with a half-sob, 'frightful, horrible screams.' She noted that he held the box containing material for the last rites, covered with a linen napkin. She curtsied to it, crossed herself, while her face crumpled.

Like an arrow shafted to his heart, Stephen suddenly knew from her face and her voice what the girl was feeling. Beyond the natural fear of human agony, he understood how Celia must fear for her own woman's lot—the curse of Eve. He raised her chin and kissed her on the forehead.

'Have faith, my child!' he whispered in a voice so tender that she stood swallowing and gulping as she watched him run across the meadow towards Cowdray.

She continued her own trip into Midhurst, along the footpath on the side of the hill, nor ever looked up at the ruined walls, or at the gable of St. Ann's chapel, next to Stephen's hut. 'The midwife,' she repeated over and over. 'Must fetch the midwife, the midwife . . .' She streaked through the spaced poles which prevented access to horsemen, down the alley past the church, and was stopped by a throng in the market place.

It was so dense, and she so dazed, that she could not understand what was happening. There were horsemen seething, a medley of burgesses, barking dogs, yelling children. The Spread Eagle with its black on white timbering, its swinging sign, was scarce a hundred yards away across the square, but she was prevented from reaching it by a wall of backs.

'What's this!' she said aloud. ' 'Tis not market day,' and tried to shove between two stocky leathern shoulders. The man on the right, a burly bricklayer, elbowed her roughly, then turned and saw her.

'Softly there, maiden,' he said. 'Hold still, pretty one, or ye'll be crushed.' He grabbed her around the waist.

'Leave me be,' she panted. 'Must get to the Inn.' She struggled.

'Nobody there—they're all out here. Wot's the matter wi' ye? We maun hear the news.'

Then she saw what they were all staring at. A large sheet of paper being nailed to the courthouse door. A royal herald stood beside it. There were the same lilies and leopards quartered on his tabard which she had seen ten days before when a herald came through to proclaim that Jane was queen. This herald was stout and stood chatting blandly with the Mayor and two aldermen, but he held his shiny gilt trumpet half-raised.

'*Another* proclamation!' cried Celia angrily. 'A pox on Queen Jane! *Lady* Jane is dying at Cowdray.'

'Hush!' said the bricklayer. 'Listen!' And he shook her.

The fat herald put the trumpet to his lips and blew a melodious stave. Then he spat in a leisurely way and lifted his pudgy hands to still the crowd before booming in a voice as brassy as his trumpet, 'The Lady Mary Tudor is hereby and henceforth proclaimed Queen of England, Ireland and France.' The herald crossed himself pompously, as he intoned the Latin words, 'In nomine Patris, et Filii, et Spiritus Sancti.'

The crowd was struck dumb, though for an hour, ever since the herald's arrival in town, rumours had been flying.

'Blessed Jesu . . .' whispered Celia. During that stunned instant she and many another in the market place were more startled by this public exhibition of the forbidden words and gesture than the reason for them.

The Mayor raised the first voice, 'Long live Queen Mary!' His high quavering was followed by a stir. 'Huzzah! Huzzah!' somebody cried. Then the crowd exploded into a roar. 'Queen Mary! Queen Mary! Long may she reign!'

What'll this mean to Cowdray—to *us*. Celia thought without much comprehension. Suddenly she spied Mrs. Potts standing arms akimbo on the doorstep of the Spread Eagle, and was reminded of her errand. She darted away from the bricklayer, through a rain of falling caps which had been tossed in the air, and reached the landlady, who looked at her glumly.

'So now ye can be Papist as ye wish, m'girl,' said Mrs Potts. 'Ye backed the roight cock, ye did. Wily as a ferret *you* be—'

'No, no,' cried Celia, 'I prithee, mistress, where's Goody Pearson, the midwife? 'Tis for Lady Jane at Cowdray. She's trying to birth her babe, and she can't.'

'Tshah,' cried Mrs. Potts, still too angry to listen. 'Ye mealy-mouthed little slut, I'll thank 'ee not to—' She stopped, at the desperate plea in Celia's eyes. 'Eh . . . wot is't ye want?'

'Goody Pearson for Lady Jane at the castle. She's very bad.'

'Why'nt they send fur 'er sooner. They've got that cursed witch Molly o'Whipple, 'ant they? Let 'er use 'er black arts on m'lady.'

Celia clutched Mrs. Potts' arm. 'My Aunt Ursula wants Goody Pearson. Oh *please*, where does she live?'

Mrs. Potts hesitated. She had no real dislike for Celia except feminine resentment of her recent effect on men, and it occurred to her that in view of this shattering change of queens, practical conditions would be different in Midhurst again. 'Well-a-day,' she said with an exasperated sigh. 'She lives back o' the Angel, 'er cot's new-thatched, ye'll know it— but no tellin' she'll *be* there.'

Celia nodded and hurried back towards the High Street, pushing and darting her way through the milling townsfolk. She arrived at the Angel and found it as full of celebrants as its more popular rival, the Spread Eagle. Enquiry at the Angel pot-room, after finding Goody Pearson's house bolted and empty, elicited a vague theory that the Goody had had a professional summons to Woolbeding village and could hardly return that day.

Celia trudged back disconsolately to Cowdray. As she reached the porter's lodge she saw Sir Anthony standing by the gatehouse. His fists were clenched, his shoulders bowed, he had torn off his ruff, his satin doublet was untied and disclosed the white lawn shirt open across the hairy chest like any ploughman.

He stared past Celia as though he didn't know her. 'Why's the bell ringing like that in Midhurst?' he cried. 'How *dare* they make these riotous peals. God rot them— how dare they?' He drew his sword half out of its scabbard; shoved it back in again.

'The Lady Mary's Grace is now Queen of England,' said Celia gently. 'Haven't you heard?'

Anthony's blue eyes focused slowly on Celia. ' 'Tis not the time for sickly pranks,' he said in a shaking voice. 'God's body, you little jade, where have you been? Deserting doomed Cowdray like the rest of them?'

She shook her head, pitying the haggard face, the swollen eyes. 'I went to Midhurst for Goody Pearson, the midwife. I couldn't find her.'

'Nor ever'll need to—' He drew a ragged breath. 'My wife is dead.'

Celia gave a moan, her arms raised to throw around him in comfort, but he was as forbidding as the stone wall behind them. 'The babe . . .?' she whispered.

Anthony made an angry sound. 'They'll never live. There're two o' them, mingy and shapeless as misbegotten rats. They but prove the curse on my line . . . God blast that infernal heartless racket!' he shouted, for now the courthouse bell joined the jubilant triple peals from Midhurst church. 'They should be tolling for my Lady's passing—I sent word to the vicar—'twouldn't take the sexton long. Jane was only twenty.' He made a grimace like the gargoyles she had seen on a London church.

Celia perceived that, shaken by sorrow and guilt, Anthony had not heard her previous announcements. 'The bells, sir,' she said loudly and clearly, 'are being rung for the Lady Mary's Grace. She is *now* Queen of England!'

Anthony started. He shook his head angrily, then his jaw dropped open. 'Mary is Queen . . .? *Mary?*'

'Yes, sir. I heard the proclamation.'

'Holy Blessed Virgin!' Anthony breathed. He quivered then threw back his head and burst into wild hysterical laughter.

'Will you come to the Hall, sir?' said Celia after watching helplessly for a moment. 'Will you take a cup of mulled wine? Aunt Ursula believes it to be calming.'

She put her hand on his arm and tugged. Anthony stopped laughing. His body slumped again. He did not speak, but allowed Celia to lead him into the Great Hall where the steward and many of Anthony's retainers were silently gathered, their faces set in respectful melancholy. They had just been told of Lady Jane's death.

*　　　*　　　*

Three days later it began to seem possible that the twins would live. Stephen had christened them Anthony and Mary

in the bedchamber, just before he administered the last rites
to Lady Jane while she lay in grey-faced stupor, wallowing in
a pool of her own blood which soaked through the flock mattress, and dripped into the rushes below.

Immediately upon her return to Cowdray and her taking
charge of the lying-in chamber, Ursula had selected a wet-
nurse. This was Peggy Hobson, the dairy-wench whose favours
Lord Gerald had enjoyed during the King's visit. Peggy was
quite unable to name the father of her three-month-old son,
though sternly urged to by Stephen who deplored bastards
among his cure of souls. Ursula's practicality permitted of
no moral scruples. Peggy was rosy-cheeked and placid, her
breasts were blue-veined, not too large, tipped by erect brown
nipples, and ideal for their function.

Peggy was delighted by her promotion. She made no demur
when her own babe was given to the baker's wife for suckling.
Peggy understood that she could hardly nourish *three* infants.
At any rate, after anxious days of prayer and gentle tending,
Anthony's heirs began a fretful bleating, finally accepted
Peggy's breasts and began to look more like babies.

Anthony, during that week, had little time to wonder that
the twins lived, nor even to continue grieving for poor Jane,
so extraordinary was the immediate change in his fortunes.

While Lady Jane still lay in state in the family chapel, Wat
came galloping to Cowdray's gatehouse. His initial dismay
upon seeing that the Browne standard flew at half-mast, that
the lackeys wore black arm-bands and an enormous wreath of
black-painted cypress hung over the portal, was soon miti-
gated.

'Not Sir Anthony?' Wat cried to his old friend the porter.
'Bigod, it can't be *him*.' He snatched off his hat and held it
anxiously to his chest. 'Ah-r-r—well-a-day, poor thing,' Wat
said when the porter explained. 'She was a gentle lady, God
rest her in peace, an' she died a-doin' o' her duty, which is
more'n I could say fur most.'

Wat ran across the courtyard into the great house where he
encountered Stephen emerging from the chapel where he had
been praying for Lady Jane's soul.

'Greetings, Brother,' said Wat gaily. 'Oh, 'tis very sad.'
He jerked his head deferentially towards the chapel. 'I'll pay
me respects to her later, but aside from that ye must be gladsome now—ye can gi'e her a true showy funeral, all the old
pomp—candles, incense, procession, Masses, right open an'

above-board i' our Midhurst church. Ye can even get yourself a priest to help wi' all the doin's—they're comin' out o' hiding!'

Stephen looked much startled. 'I—I hadn't realised,' he said slowly. From the days of his childhood at Battle Abbey, he had lived in a climate of persecution and secrecy in England. The years at Marmoutier seemed but a roseate interlude. 'Are you *sure*, Wat?' Stephen said. 'Sure that the Lady Mary's Grace'll bring back the true religion? Oh, I know she's reputed a good Catholic, but will she *dare*? Moreover, she's not crowned yet. Not even reached London, has she?'

'Ye can rest easy,' said Wat kindly. 'Country's square behind 'er, ye should've seen the bustlin's i' the villages an' towns I've been through. Crucifixes back on the altars, church plate an' vestments dug out—when they hasn't been sold . . .'

'But Northumberland?' said Stephen. 'He has an army—besides all those powerful noblemen who signed Edward's Devise for Jane Dudley.'

'The *Dook*?' Wat threw back his head and guffawed. 'That whore-son cream-faced coward! *He's* fast in the Tower wi' the rest o' 'em. They arrested him at Cambridge—when he saw he was cornered he declared for Queen Mary like a sensible man, but'll not save his head from the block.'

'*Deo Gratias*. Our Lord's Blessed Mother hath wrought a miracle. How could I ever have doubted?' Stephen added in a whisper.

Wat hurried on to find Sir Anthony, while Stephen turned and walked out of Cowdray in a trance. As he went across the daisy-spangled meadows, his face lifted to the hot July sunshine, he felt an ecstasy of hope and wondering gratitude.

He climbed Tan's Hill, and entered his own crumbling little chapel. The altar was bare, except for a modest wooden cross. During the last months of furtive anxiety, knowing how the temper of the townsfolk had altered, and that during his absence each day, any ruffian would feel free to steal what he wished to, Stephen had hidden his candlesticks, altar cloth and the silver-gilt crucifix in an iron-bound locked coffer. He had also hidden his lovely painting of the Virgin, and the purple veil he had covered her with on the evening of Celia's visit and his tumult thereafter.

That evening seemed a century ago. He was sure that he

had achieved towards the girl a true brotherly feeling. Remote, kindly. The shameful twinges and longings were past.

He took the huge iron key from off his knotted scourge and unlocked the coffer. Slowly, joyfully, he replaced the altar furnishings. He unveiled his precious painting, and kissed Her long, tapering hand. He put Her on the altar, and kneeling on the chapel's leafy ground, addressed Her with abounding love. Gentle tears oozed down his cheeks. It was like the exaltation he had felt on Candlemas Day a year and a half ago, but warmer, softer, since this—untinged by the sternness of sacrifice and duty—was all of a melting, honeyed warmth of thankfulness. He remained before the altar until he heard the Angelus ring out from the village church. *The Angelus!* He had not heard the Angelus since he left France. He listened in awe, then sprang up from his knees. 'I can go down to the church for Vespers! I'm free to go into town!' He cried this aloud, so wondrous did it seem. He brushed leaves from his habit, pulled up his cowl and leaped over the ruined wall to the footpath. He strode through the palings on to the market square and paused by the church's lych-gate. Two little blue-coated apprentices gaped at him. A baker's wench put down her tray of hot fresh loaves and stared. 'Wot's him?' she said to the apprentices, as she examined the cowl, the glimpse of white cassock under flowing black robes, the sandalled feet. 'Is't a mummer?' she asked of the air, too timid to address Stephen direct, but he turned and smiled at her. 'No mummery, my child,' he moved his hand in blessing, 'I am a Benedictine monk—a priest,' he added, as she looked blank.

Her eyes widened. 'Ye come down from Tan's Hill,' she whispered. 'That's where the Devil lives, or mebbe an ogre. I'd not dare go up Tan's Hill.' Suddenly she clutched her hands to her throat, shrinking, so that it was easy to read her fear.

Stephen laughed. 'I'm not the Devil, my child—in fact, my whole life is dedicated to fighting him.'

She did not understand his words though she knew he spoke as the gentry did. 'Well, if 'tis not the Devil,' she said obstinately, 'there's ghosties up there, me gran's seen 'em. They shriek an' gibber i' the night.'

Stephen shrugged and walked into the church where the sparse congregation rustled and turned. The stupid old vicar stopped in mid-prayer, his bearded cheeks paling. Only last month he had taken unto himself a plump comfortable widow as wife, and had been much enjoying his last flickers of lust. Only last month married parsons were legal. The black monk's quiet, sardonic appearance in public confirmed the changes which were rumoured. He gave Stephen a nervously apprehensive look, then was so flustered that he skipped several prayers and gabbled into the benediction. He clenched the rim of the pulpit. They'd make him go back to the Latin, and he'd forgotten it. They'd make him put away Margaret—nay—he knew very well what would happen. Ousted entirely from the church, from the snug vicarage. He saw his fate in Brother Stephen's level steady gaze. I wish he'd died o' that rat-bite, or whatever it was, thought the vicar, and slunk away into his sacristy.

There were a few others in Midhurst like Mrs. Potts who would have echoed the vicar's wish, but all of Cowdray and most of the town eagerly returned to the old religion. It was pleasing to celebrate Saints' Feast Days again, to be able to swear by anything one liked to. For all the older folk, the return to church ritual was comforting, and a relief to endure no more confusing nonsense about when to kneel, or whether the Communion wafer was the True Body or not. Moreover, as traffic between castle and town grew as free and constant as it was before the last six years of Edward's uneasy reign, everyone basked in the news of Sir Anthony's growing national importance.

Albeit in deepest mourning for his wife, Sir Anthony had been specially summoned to London to join the Queen's triumphal entrance there, and had held up her train. Sir Anthony deserved special favour from Her Majesty. Wat Farrier carousing merrily at the Spread Eagle made that clear. He thrilled the pot-room nightly with the story of the warning buck-crest ring, which had positively saved the Queen's life, when it turned her away from London and imprisonment. Wat's own part grew with each repetition until the goggling tradesmen and yeomen in from the country could all picture Wat bravely galloping to Hoddesdon through a thunderstorm raised by Satan himself. Or maybe 'twas King Harry sent the lightning bolts to show his wrath towards Edward's wicked Devise.

Wat's listeners nodded solemnly. They clapped Wat on the shoulder, they stood him pint after pint of ale. They consulted him respectfully on all matters pertaining to the Queen, and how best to celebrate her Coronation in Midhurst. Certain banners and streamers left over from the preparation for Queen Jane might be used, but obviously, something far grander was indicated now. There must be fireworks, which were costly, but if they took up a collection—and besides, Sir Anthony was rich again. He'd see that his own manor did him proud. And then there was the morris dance.

'*Three* morris dances!' exuberantly cried the bricklayer who had held Celia during the proclamation. 'Round and round, one arter t'other, that way the streets'll ne'er be empty.' He beamed at the chorus of approval, until someone cried, 'But where'll we get three Maid Marians, tell us that?'

There was a dismayed silence. Maid Marian was always played by a youth, and the role was unpopular. It took heavy bribery to induce a young man to dress in women's clothes, and simper coyly, mincing and wriggling. Mummers' plays always presented men in women's parts, but that was different. Actors were a low breed apart, they'd not care what they did.

'Willy Bowman'd play the Maid again, mebbe,' said the bricklayer, reluctant to give up his splendid idea, 'and Crazy Ned, could we make him learn the steps . . . and . . . er . . .'

'*I'll* play Maid Marian!' It was a harsh voice from the end bench near the door. After they turned to see who had spoken, the pot-room rang with laughter. 'Cotsbody!' cried the bricklayer, slapping Wat on the thigh. ' 'Tis your Simkin. By the Mass, a merry jape! He can be hobby-horse or dragon if he wants to disguise!'

Wat laughed, too, but the laugh was forced. Ever since his return Wat had found his son to be silent, evasive, given to unexplained absences. More disquieting was a coffer he had found in Simkin's room one day, and curiously opened. It contained a tinsel veil, a woman's rose and cream brocaded skirt, a gold satin bodice and a flaxen wig made of long curly human hair. The whole coffer was scented with musk—the dark blatant perfume assailed Wat's disgusted nostrils. Wat had instantly rejected his first horrified thought that Simkin had stolen this woman's gear to sell. The boy had always been honest, and little as Wat knew of such things, he got the impression that the materials were sleazy, the tinselled veil made from butter-cloth.

That night at supper Wat asked his son point-blank why he

kept trumperies in his attic, and was perturbed by the expression on Simkin's ugly pock-marked face. It was very like a sneer, though the wall-eye often gave an odd expression. 'They belong ta' friend o' mine,' said Simkin, and picked his teeth carefully with a bit of straw. He glanced at his mother who was spoon-feeding the three-year-old.

'Ahr-r.' Wat winked at his son. 'Bit of a hussy, your *friend*, eh? She likes fancy garb . . .'

Simkin looked at his father with the opaque sneering look, but his mother's feeding spoon clattered sharply on the table.

'Tell him, Sim!' Joan Farrier cried, her voice shrill. 'Tell your fadder 'oo owns them clothes. *Tell* him!'

Wat stared at his wife whose thin face was distorted, her mouth drawn awry. Joan was a nagger and a bore, but he had never seen her roused, and at once felt masculine sympathy for his son. This sudden behaviour of Joan's could only be jealousy, she'd always tried to molly-coddle the boy.

'Ye needna name your leman, Sim,' said Wat tolerantly. 'Ye're near a man grown, and 'tis natural to want a bit o' bed-sport time to time.'

Simkin did not answer. He looked down at his trencher, and minced his hunk of mutton into tiny pieces.

'Iffen he won't tell ye, I *will*!' said Joan, trembling. 'That gear your son keeps in his coffer belongs t' Roland, the mummer was here for the Fair. A dainty little meacock is Roland, pretty boy Roland.'

Wat frowned, still feeling only irritation at his scraggy wife's anger. 'And wot o' that, woman? So Simkin likes to store his friend's mummeries, do him a favour . . .'

'Ye're a dom thick-skulled fool, Wat Farrier!' cried Joan, then suddenly collapsed, her eyes bleared while they sent her son a beseeching apologetic look. 'Have a bit more pasty, sweeting,' she said to him. 'Here's a crusty edge I saved fur ye.'

Wat remembered this scene while Simkin sat imperturbably in the pot-room ignoring the rowdy jests. 'I'll play Maid Marian,' he repeated as the noise died down, 'an' better nor anyone's ever played her.'

They were puzzled then, they glanced towards Wat who had become so important a man of late; they waited for him to reprove his son, but as he said nothing, the bricklayer cried heartily, 'So that's settled, the others're easy-like. Naow the Robin Hoods. I'll be one m'self,' which diverted the assembly.

Everyone wanted to be Robin Hood, or Friar Tuck, or Little John. They began to wrangle.

Wat did not allow himself to be perturbed by Simkin's behaviour, lads of that age were given to pranks, they were all moody, and besides, Wat had the chance to see a most gratifying encounter between Celia and his son the next day, when Simkin was currying poor Lady Jane's dapple-grey mare, and Wat was supervising the general bustle of polishing harness, the tally of bridles, saddles, and computing the ostrich plumes needed for the cavalcade to London and the Coronation.

Celia came dancing into the stableyard, glowing and excited. She ran up to the mare, and threw her arms around its neck. 'Oh, Simkin!' she cried, 'Juno's *mine* now! Sir Anthony's given her to me! Isn't it kind of him!' She kissed the mare on its mouse-soft nose.

Simkin looked at the girl and smiled. Who could help it? Wat thought. The girl was the embodiment of lovely girl-hood, her hair glinting, her cheeks pink and white as gilly-flowers, exuding a radiance she'd never shown on the long trip north. 'By the Mass, an' has he then?' said Simkin. 'D'ye want to ride? I'll saddle her fur ye.'

'If you'll come too, Sim. She doesn't know me, and I'm a little afraid.'

She looked up at Simkin through her lashes, the dimple dinted beside her mouth, and Wat was well pleased. 'Go, lad, go,' he said. 'I'll not be needin' ye a while.' To Celia he said, 'Me heartiest congratulations, miss. Yon's a good mare, gentle as a dove, but Sim'll school ye a bit. Take her through the Close Walks, Sim,' he added craftily. The mysterious Close Walks with their lofty yews and enticing by-paths were a famous setting for lovers. And Sim looked his best on horse-back. I'll make him a courier next, Wat thought, get him out o' the stables. Sir Anthony'll do whatever I ask, *now*. That pretty lass would knock the nonsense out of Simkin, and was quite willing, to judge by the look she'd given the boy. Whistling cheerily through his teeth, Wat returned to the chivvying of his underlings.

It was fortunate for Wat's peace of mind that he did not hear the conversation between Simkin and Celia, after the girl's raptures over the dainty little mare died down, and her expressions of gratitude.

'Sir Anthony's so good to me, he's ordered one of the

sempstresses to make me a new dress—for the Coronation, you know! I'm going to London wi' the others. Oh, Simkin, I'm so happy!'

Simkin smiled. 'Thou'rt a lucky one, lass,' he said in a softer voice than she had ever heard from him, yet she felt in his tone a tinge of sadness, of reservation.

'But you'll be going too!' she cried. 'Wat'll bring you, I'm sure.'

Simkin shook his head. 'I doan't care t' go,' he said quietly. 'What colour and fashion is your new gown to be?'

Celia turned in the saddle, and looked at the boy in amused astonishment. 'You jest—you mock me,' she said. 'You can't possibly care about my gown.'

'For why not?' Simkin flicked a fly from his gelding's neck. 'Because I'm ugly, because I'm a stable-boy and stink often o' dung?'

'N-no,' she said uncertainly. She felt an echo of the sinister repulsion of that dreadful unexplained scene in Naworth's grain loft.

'Well,' she said, 'Sir Anthony made my aunt Ursula and me free of the coffers in the west attic. There's a length o' red brocade for the skirt, and good yellow velvet from France for the gown. What's ado?' she asked, for Simkin was shaking his head.

'Red an' yellow's no roight fur ye, Celia,' said Simkin sternly. 'They'll douse yer beauty.'

Celia was so startled that she jerked the reins, the mare jumped, and stopped dead, quivering.

'Ye mustn't bounce like that.' Simkin reached over and stroked Juno's withers. 'This is a dainty high-bred beast, no like the nag ye rode to Cumberland . . . Search the coffers agen. Ye shouldn't wear heavy stuff, silk's better, an' keep to the hues o' pink daisies, blue speedwells, leaf green. Wood violets, mebbe.'

Celia stared, then she began to laugh. 'Oh, Simkin . . .' She gave him her provocative, utterly feminine look. 'D'you care so much what I wear? I thought you didn't even like me after . . . after that night at the Dacre keep!'

They had skirted St. Ann's Hill on the west, and entered the Close Walks, which were actually four avenues of magnificent yews growing around a secret central glade where Anthony used sometimes to hold picnics for his guests. The townspeople avoided trespassing on this demesne, no poachers

304

invaded it, for it was known that 'the pharisees' held nightly revel there. Those easily affronted Sussex fairies had selected the inner pleasaunce before even the Bohuns came to Midhurst. Puck himself was reported to stop there frequently.

' 'Tis not a matter o' likin',' said Simkin after a moment. 'Ye remind me o' someone, I want t' see ye clothed i' the finest way.'

Celia looked down at the pommel. It was a damping answer. 'Let's gallop,' she said and spurred the mare with her heel.

They streaked off down the grassy path between the yews and clumps of holly, glossy green, trimmed back by Anthony's gardeners. They slackened pace before they reached the secret glade. The sun disappeared suddenly, and all sparkle with it. A chill little wind blew up from the Downs.

Celia shivered. ' 'Tis coming on wet,' she said.

'Rain'll hold off a bit,' answered Simkin. 'We'll go on t' the glade, I dropped something there liddle while ago. I'll have a look fur it.'

Celia looked at him. It seemed odd that Simkin had been here recently. His manner was odd. A faint tremor of fear brushed her. She would have liked to turn back, yet found that she did not wish to go alone through the avenues of looming black tree trunks. She followed the boy into the clearing, and silently watched as he dismounted. The grass was still long. Throughout all Anthony's anxious exile nobody had bothered to send gardeners to mow the Close Walks.

Simkin went to a spot near a ring of rose-bushes, pinkly blooming and very fragrant. He parted the grasses and searched carefully. Celia heard him give a grunt of relief as he straightened, holding a fawn-coloured shoe of supple leather, not large enough to be Simkin's.

She urged the mare nearer. Simkin did not notice, as he cradled the shoe in his dirty hands. 'Is that what you were looking for?' Celia asked a little nervously. 'Why, it's got stains on it! Looks like—like old blood!'

Simkin tucked the shoe inside his jerkin. ' 'Tis blood,' he said in a dead voice. 'Mine.'

'Your shoe? You hurt yourself . . . but the shoe's too small for you. At least . . .' She looked down at his mucky, cobbled boots. 'I don't understand.'

'Nor ever will,' said Simkin. He looked up at her on the

305

mare, and she saw hatred in his face. 'God rot ye, fur being a woman!' He spoke through his teeth, and so low that for a second she was not sure, then the shock flushed her cheeks scarlet. She lifted her chin and said with dignity, 'Mount your horse, Simkin! We're going home!'

She nudged her mare and set out between the yews, noting from the following hoof-thuds that he had obeyed. The first drops of rain spattered down through the tunnel of green darkness, as Simkin rode up beside her.

'Aye,' he said, 'I'm naught but an ugly servant, an' ye've become a fine lady. Some day 'twill be different. I'll no have to obey nobuddy, I'll do as I please—wi'out shame.'

His bitter voice stirred her to some pity, though she rode on steadily, her chin high. 'Perhaps you'll get your wish,' she said coolly, and spurred the mare faster. She was no longer afraid of Simkin. His peculiarities, even his moment of hatred were a matter of indifference to her. She recognised a gulf between them that was far wider than the growing social one. Though the rain came down thicker as they left the Close Walks, her earlier happy mood returned. She stroked the mare and crooned to it softly, her heart swelling with gratitude to Anthony, to Ursula who had rescued her from the Inn and a drudge's life, even to Mabel who had ceased pouting and whining now that she would have her visit to London, enhanced by the delicious prospect of the Coronation.

Even Stephen was going with them, Celia thought. She had put aside the wicked folly of her erstwhile feeling for him, and ignored his startling sweetness by the Rother the morning Lady Jane died. But it was contentful to know that she would still have him near. And it was strange, marvellous that after all the furtive years he might openly accompany them as Sir Anthony's chaplain. Blessed Mary, but life is good, Celia thought, one has only to wait a while for troubles to cease. She began to hum a gay Sussex tune—'Oh, come ye jolly plough-boys, come listen to my lays'—and was still humming in the stableyard at the mounting block, while Simkin silently took the reins and led the wet mare to her stall.

Twelve

Sir Anthony Browne arrived at Southwark with his family and some thirty retainers on September 28, the day on which Mary moved down Thames from Whitehall Palace to the Tower, from whence an English monarch always proceeded to Westminster Abbey and Coronation.

Anthony's house, the old priory of St. Mary Overie, was transformed. A small army of plasterers and labourers had refurbished all the rooms and cells around the cloisters. The monks' old stables, after sundry vagabonds had been evicted, were as clean as Cowdray's, though perforce more cramped. Besides the furnishings he brought from Sussex, Anthony had, on his earlier visit to greet Queen Mary, ordered several elaborately carved chairs, stools, tables from a master craftsman in Lombard Street. There were new painted hangings for the walls.

Anthony was pleased by his womenfolk's delighted cries, but he dared not tarry for more than a quick welcoming toast with them. He had found a summons from the Duke of Norfolk himself, asking his immediate presence at Whitehall.

'And *that*,' said Anthony, 'is not the least of our miracles. Six years imprisoned in the Tower, that poor Duke, and now back in all his former glory as premier Peer of England, and Earl Marshal in charge of the Queen's Grace's Coronation.' Anthony added with relish, 'While the spurious Duke—' Anthony drew his hand sharply across his throat, 'in hell where he belongs!'

'Hush, sir,' said Stephen. ''Tis not Christian to gloat over the death of an enemy, however much deserved.'

'Poppycock and folderol,' cried Anthony, and gave the young monk's shoulder a resounding thwack. 'Ye can be as pious as you like in chapel, but you're human, too. Come along wi' me today, see a bit o' the world. Moreover, I need your brains—there's still a skein of plots to be unravelled. You can help.'

Stephen hesitated. He looked through the window at St. Saviour's pinnacled spire. There was much to be done to restore the parish church; his hasty survey on arrival had appalled him. The church was still bleakly barren, niches empty of saints, high altar vanished, dog-shit in the chancel.

'Oh,' said Anthony gaily, understanding Stephen's thoughts, 'that'll all wait. Now Bishop Gardiner's out o' gaol and back here at his palace, you can get hold of a chaplain, straighten the mess. Come along with me and get a glimpse o' the *real* world.'

Celia observed this interchange as she sat beside Mabel at the end of the Priory Hall. I wish he wouldn't go, she thought. *Stephen, don't go!* She dared not speak, she knew the feeling of fear was unreasonable. What business of hers whether Stephen accompanied Sir Anthony into London, or stayed here to start restoring the church. Yet, during that moment in which Stephen still hesitated she felt dismay.

'What ails you, Celia?' asked Mabel with mild curiosity. 'You jumped! Someone treading 'cross your grave?' The girl giggled and crammed another sugar comfit in her mouth. 'Anthony,' she cried, 'won't you be seeing Lord Gerald at His Grace of Norfolk's? Tell him I've made a purse for him as I promised.'

'Oh-h?' said Anthony, glancing at his sister while he adjusted his court sword. He had barely noted some flirtation between Mabel and the young Irish bantling during the past summer. 'I'll certainly *not* see Fitzgerald at Whitehall, and you needn't be setting your cap in *that* quarter, my girl. Fitzgerald's cooked his goose along wi' Clinton and my precious stepmother. He signed for Lady Jane Grey, y'know. Or *don't* you?' Anthony made an exasperated sound. He expected little comprehension from women in general, and had no illusions about Mabel's intellect in particular. 'I'll find you a *worthy* husband now there's scope,' he added impatiently, 'but it can't be tomorrow. Come along, Stephen!'

Stephen went. Celia watched through the window while the men mounted their horses in the cloister garth. Stephen's cowl slipped back as he vaulted lightly into the saddle. The sun brought auburn lights to his thick dark hair, and the tilt of his head almost hid the tonsure. He looked as handsome and arrogant as his master, and she heard his rare laugh ring out at something Sir Anthony said. She hoped that he would look up at the window, and she leaned far out through the casement, staring down with confused, unhappy longing. Stephen did not look up. He cantered from the garth with

Anthony. Celia turned slowly back into the Hall where Mabel was pouting crossly, and Ursula was giving orders to the new bevy of London serving-maids Anthony's steward had hired.

*   *   *

Two days later, on Saturday, Wat Farrier guided Ursula with Celia and Mabel to places reserved for them on Gracechurch Street in the City. Wooden stages had been erected against the buildings along the road of Mary's progression from the Tower, and Anthony had picked an excellent site for his womenfolk. This was just below the triumphal arch which the Florentine bankers had constructed from thousands of massed lilies, roses and heliotrope. The arch was topped by a fifteen-foot angel with a trumpet, all made from green canvas.

The flower perfume was enchanting, and did much to offset the smells of massed humanity—particularly of vomit, since the conduits at Cornhill and Cheapside began at noon to run with cheap claret for anyone to guzzle as he pleased.

Though the women had long to wait, and dared not quit their places on the scaffold, Celia was so bedazzled by the excitement that time did not drag. This morning while dressing herself in the splendid new gown of yellow velvet and red brocade she had felt a momentary misgiving when she thought of Simkin's ignored advice. Seen in Ursula's new mirror, the effect did seem a trifle garish, and she had to pinch her cheeks hard to bring up their colour, but out here among the welter of scarlets, greens, golds, festoons and banners decorating the houses, while even the lowliest fish-wife or chimney-sweep had managed to wear a ribbon or cockade—she merged happily with the pageantry.

Ursula and Mabel were not so happy. The hard wooden bench began to hurt Ursula's skinny rump, even through her new black velvet skirts. Her back ached, and a nagging discomfort made certain the imminent necessity of relieving herself in the gutter as shamelessly as did the common people. Mabel's preoccupations were different but equally uncomfortable. Her fashionable steel corset and farthingale were too tight, and she was sweating profusely in the armpits, thus staining her pale lilac gown. She was also smarting from a further lecture delivered by Anthony before he left for the Tower to join the Procession.

309

No one knew yet how Queen Mary would deal with all the traitors who had tried to set aside her claim; everyone expected that they would be imprisoned and thereafter many of them executed. In any case, Fitzgerald had prudently fled, probably to Lincolnshire with his sister and Lord Clinton. 'And I'm fair sick o' your sulks and naggings, Mabel,' said Anthony angrily. 'I've far more important things on my mind than this senseless folly in hankering for a disgraced, lack-land, Irish rebel!' He had characteristically tempered his harshness with another gift—an enamelled gold brooch which had belonged to Lady Jane, but Mabel's heart was sore. Gerald was the only man who had ever kissed her or made pretty speeches to her, and she had fancied herself practically betrothed.

At two-thirty a wind sprang up, tempering the hot sun, but swirling dust into the waiting crowd. Mabel sneezed and Ursula began to cough. The fragrance from the flowery arch blew north away from them, and was replaced by a stink of chicken dung and decaying poultry from the shuttered stalls below. Most of London's poultry was sold in Gracechurch Street.

'You look over-grim, lady, for such a glad occasion,' said a voice behind Ursula, who started. She turned and saw Master Julian wedged into a seat on the tier behind.

'Blessed Jesu!' she cried, at once forgetting her discomforts. 'What do you *here*?'

He wore new doctoral robes, lavishly edged with red squir-rel; his four-square cap was pulled down at a rakish angle to prevent it from blowing; his curly beard was very short; his grey eyes twinkled; and she thought how well he looked.

'I am here, Lady Southwell,' he said smiling, 'because I helped my fellow Florentines draw plans for yonder arch. We'll see how well the angel performs. I tried to remember the mechanism used by Messer Leonardo da Vinci for a de Medici pageant. Good day, Celia, and Mistress Mabel,' he added as the two girls turned.

Celia's face lit up like her aunt's. Despite the coldness of their last meeting, she admired the doctor. Moreover, she had learned during the past months how many stresses and dangers had surrounded them, which no doubt Master Julian had shared.

Mabel, who hoped that the voice behind them might belong to some handsome gallant, gave a disappointed nod, then resumed the surreptitious effort to loosen the strings of her corset.

'Oh, sir,' cried Celia, 'you joined the Queen's Grace at Framlingham, didn't you? Wat was full of the story. And she made you her physician?'

'For a time,' said Julian, 'the queen gave me marks of favour.' He touched a new gold chain from which hung the jacinth stone. 'At least I no longer am fleeing for my life, and again have prospects.' He gave the two women his rather sardonic smile. At Framlingham, Mary had been distraught, though gracious enough when he presented Sir Anthony Browne's buck-head badge. She had sent Julian off to tend a chamber-woman with a twisted ankle, and asked Henry Jerningham to give the doctor the gold chain—as she indeed frantically tried to reward all the new adherents to her cause. On the night they left for London, Mary had suffered from one of her blinding migraines. Julian again summoned by Jerningham had, of course, no remedies with him. He had gone out to the meadow and picked some cowslips which made a sufficiently impressive concoction when mashed with cowurine. He had given this to her, while saying in his deep, commanding voice, 'This will help you, Your Grace. You will be much better. You will feel well.'

Mary's headache soon vanished. She gave Julian a gold sovereign, from which he had bought these new robes on his return to London. Then, harassed by a hundred grave problems, Mary had forgotten him. Julian, unwilling to see Alison, and certain now that the future was really brightening, had boldly knocked on the door of a Florentine merchant in Lombard Street and asked for lodging until after the Coronation, on the grounds of their common nationality. Heretofore he had had nothing to do with the Florentines in London whom he considered a low-born, money-grubbing lot, but he had meticulously repaid his host—while hoping to advance himself—by designing the triumphal arch, and its huge mechanical angel.

'Hark!' he said, jerking his head around to the south. 'There go St. Sepulchre's bells. The Procession must be starting from the Tower.'

Another half-hour passed before the vanguard, consisting of yeomen and court messengers, cleared the street, strewing it with grass and fragrant herbs before the mounted esquires came riding up it. The common folk crammed against the walls, every window was jammed with expectant faces, the air resounded with pealing bells and fanfares. The exalted clerks of the Chancery, the Signet, the Privy Seal, the Council, were followed by the lesser knights—bachelor and banneret—and finally, the Knights of the Bath. Among the latter, Celia was the first to spot Sir Anthony, who turned and waved to them.

'My brother should be among the peers,' said Mabel discontentedly. 'We have some noble blood.'

'*Da vero*,' agreed Julian, 'and in time I'm sure he *will* be. The Queen has cause to reward him and his family. Sir Anthony's grandsire is John Gates, is he not? The Queen has him back as Tower Constable.'

Mabel shrugged. 'I've never met him. Some stupid quarrel before I was born.'

The stately Procession continued to file by. The judges and justices, the Knights of the Garter, the officers of Mary's household and then, between repeated trumpet flourishes, the loyal peers, two by two. The Barons, the Bishops, the Viscounts, the Earls—the Lord Mayor.

Magnificent as these were, Celia, like everyone else, kept straining to look down the street past them, eager to see the focus of all this grandeur. The crowd hushed as Mary's splendid chariot approached borne between six white palfreys. Mary was effulgent in blue velvet and silver cloth, furred with ermine. Her head was covered by a gold caul, diamond and pearl-studded, and so heavy that she constantly stiffened her neck, and sometimes eased the weight with a nervous little gesture. Her small pale face was set, her smiles forced, and Julian saw the haggard lines, the twitching muscles of nearly intolerable stress. She seemed older than her thirty-seven years. She has no stamina, he thought gloomily, she'll not last long—and then what?

The probable answer to his question rode behind the Queen in a crimson velvet chariot. A girl of twenty, chastely dressed in silver-white, her Tudor hair uncovered and blazing, an enigmatic little smile on her thin lips and an expression of gentle demureness which did not change as the populace, suddenly magnetised, burst from its awed hush and began to roar out blessings on the Princess Elizabeth.

'Harry's true daughter!' they cried. 'Look at 'er 'air!' 'And English, through and through ... poor Nan Bullen was English, whate'er sorry end she come to.' 'God Bless Nan Bullen and 'er little Bess!' shouted a drunken voice from a gabled window. Elizabeth looked up slowly to the window, she raised her long delicate hand in a graceful motion of acknowledgment, then resumed her controlled poise.

'So the small moon pales when the sun comes out,' Julian observed, leaning down towards Ursula, who neither quite heard nor understood. She glanced at the sky which had darkened as the wind blew great clouds across it.

'Who can that be next the Princess in the chariot?' she asked. 'Is't some waiting lady?'

'No,' said Julian, tearing his fascinated gaze from Elizabeth to scan the broad stolid face beside her. '*That* is a very fortunate woman. King Henry's only surviving relict, I saw her once at Kenninghall.'

'*Who?*' said Ursula, astonished.

'The Lady Anne of Cleves.' Julian chuckled.

'Holy St. Mary!' Ursula laughed too. 'I'd forgot all about her!'

'As she most wisely wished. The only sensible one of the lot, but she *is* stepmother to the Queen . . . and Princess. Now watch!' Julian added quickly.

Queen Mary had advanced to within a hundred paces of the flowery arch. Julian's Florentine host darted out, and bowing, rapidly gabbled a laudatory speech. The Queen stopped, seemed rather puzzled, as they could all hear the whirring and buzzings of clockwork and the creak of bellows inside the angel. Julian held his breath. The great green arms quivered and slowly raised the trumpet. It never quite reached the angel's gaping mouth, but six deafening blasts of compressed air shrilled through the canvas lips. They made a resounding noise far greater than human lungs could manage, and might be hopefully interpreted as shouting, 'Ma-ri-a Re-gi-na.'

The horses reared and stamped. Mary herself shrank, then laughed delightedly, while on the street and from every window there was thunderous applause.

Like all the Tudors, Mary adored boisterous novelties. They could see her thanking the Florentine, then glance up at the stage to Julian, who smiled and bowed low.

'One sure way to the favour of princes,' he murmured, quoting Machiavelli, 'is to combine amusement with flattery.'

Julian sat back, well-pleased, especially as he knew that the other diversions arranged along the route must be pallid after this. Some jugglers and morris-dancers, a bed of rosemary cunningly grown into the shape of the royal arms, and under a vine in St. Paul's churchyard, John Heywood, the witty poet and jest-maker was waiting to deliver a eulogy to the Catholic Queen he had always admired. The Procession disappeared when it turned left on the Cornhill.

Ursula and the girls thankfully rose; Julian helped them down to the street. Ursula murmured an apology, and darted up an alley to a recessed privy. When she came back she found Julian and the girls standing near the arch talking to a middle-aged couple with a child in tow. She was faintly surprised since they knew nobody in London, and also surprised that her Celia's face looked wary. 'Wary' was the only word for the set of the lovely little features, the watchful gleam in the sea-blue eyes.

'Ah ...' said Julian as Ursula came up to them. 'Here we meet by hazard some acquaintances. Lady Southwell, these are Squire and Mistress Allen from Kent, and their son— Charles, I believe?'

Ursula nodded politely, while Emma Allen curtsied. The squire uncovered and gave a nervous head-jerk.

'Oh, we met at Cowdray,' said Emma in her loud Kentish twang, 'when we were there last summer to see Brother Stephen who is a relation.'

Ursula looked at the woman with more attention. She was handsome in a florid way. Her slanting black eyes were a bit strange. But she seemed a typical and prosperous provincial matron, up from the country to see the goodly show.

'Will ye all sup wi' us?' cried Emma heartily. 'King's Head's not far on Fenchurch, an' they'll have drawn the October ale. There'll be aldermen there we're to meet. M' good husband's father was Lord Mayor some twenty year back. High time we saw something o' London again. We've not come near this sewer o' stinking heresy since Edward's coronation.'

'Your lofty sentiments do you proud, madam,' said Julian, smiling. What's she after *now*, he thought, remembering her tenacity at Cowdray, and her vehement assertion to him at the Spread Eagle 'When I want a thing 'tis good as done ... God heeds me when *I* speak.' He felt an echo of his repulsion then, and he, too, noticed that Celia had turned away, and was absently fingering a lily in the triumphal arch while her profile was stony.

314

'These your daughters, m'lady?' Emma gave Ursula an ingratiating smile. 'Such pretty young maids.'

Ursula realised that the woman had no idea to whom she was speaking, she had heard only the title, and when Ursula explained, an opaque, considering look dulled the black eyes. Mistress Allen had obviously hoped to have netted bigger game, but she repeated her invitation though less ebulliently.

'Well-a-day, ye must drink to the Queen's Grace wi' us — and tell me news o' my brother-in-law at Cowdray.'

'If you mean Brother Stephen,' answered Ursula, 'he's here in London with Sir Anthony, for whom he is acting as secretary. Your invitation is most kind . . .'

Ursula, who had decided to accept it, thinking how flat the evening might be for the girls after all this excitement, was interrupted by Celia. 'My head aches, Aunt,' she said abruptly. 'I see Wat over there. He'll take me back to the Priory.'

'Oh, sweeting,' cried Ursula, instantly apprehensive, 'we'll all go back.'

'No,' cried Mabel flouncing. 'I don't want to be herded to that stuffy hole in Southwark.' Angry tears brimmed over on to her plump cheeks.

'If you will permit it, Lady Southwell,' said Julian with some amusement, 'I'll escort Mistress Mabel, and return her at a proper hour.'

Ursula instantly acquiesced, and sent Julian so warm a look of gratitude that he was half-ashamed of its trivial cause. She's truly *good*, that lady, he thought, and marvelled again at the feeling of protection both Ursula and Celia sometimes aroused in him. Standing there on grass-trampled Gracechurch Street, jostled by the milling Cockneys, he received again as in Midhurst the impression that all this had happened before. That he had been confronted by the baleful force of Emma Allen, and savoured the appealing sweetness of the aunt and niece — in Greece, 'Grecia', the word said itself in his mind. *Ridiculous*, he thought impatiently, and turned his mind to his real interests. Mistress Allen was not the only one who could play the game of power-climbing. That she had a knighthood in mind for her mingy little husband, he did not doubt. There would be aldermen at the King's Head. They had scant influence at Court, but one never knew what coat-tails might be worth perching on. And after the Coronation I'll see Norfolk, Julian thought, I'll remind him of the 'wheel of fortune' I made for him at Kenninghall. There's been a sudden spin to

315

that wheel. And I spin with it. The arrow now points to fame and riches. But one proceeds cautiously, *poco a poco*.

*   *   *

Back at the Priory in Southwark, Ursula was anxious. Celia's whiteness alarmed her. She thought of the sudden pests, plagues, distempers which struck so fast, especially in London. She sent a varlet to the nearest apothecary for camphor and spirits of wine to make a poultice for Celia's forehead. She made the girl drink a whole mug of heather-mead which she always kept by her for emergencies. After that potent drink Celia gained a little colour, and also the use of her tongue which had been silent ever since they left Gracechurch Street.

'I don't think I'm ill, dear aunt . . .' she whispered. 'I was affrighted.'

'Frightened?' said Ursula tenderly. 'By what, my poppet?'

'By that woman . . .' said Celia in a remote listless voice.

Ursula frowned. This seemed very near to the maunderings which accompanied fevers. 'You don't mean Mistress Allen?'

Celia shuddered and nodded. 'I saw an adder last year, 'twas near the footbridge o'er the Rother. It had those eyes. I ran.'

'My dear child,' said Ursula briskly, 'what nonsense. Are your courses due? Women get peculiar fancies . .'

Celia shook her head. 'There's danger,' she said flatly. She put her hand to her throat. 'Stifling . . . Master Julian speaks to me; he says, "Wake up, Celia! Celia, come back!" '

Ursula swallowed, while a chill ran up her spine. She glanced at the silver mug. 'I've given you too much mead,' she said. 'Master Julian is at the King's Head with the Allens and Mabel, don't you remember?'

The girl sighed, her hand fell limply from her throat in a defenceless little gesture. Suddenly she opened her eyes and stared imploringly at Ursula. 'Must it happen, Mother?' she whispered in a piteous voice. 'Can't we stop it? Don't you see, I *love* Stephen! But I'm so afraid. Make Doctor—Doctor —the doctor understands.'

Ursula quivered, while panic clutched at her. But the girl's lids fell, she began to breathe gently, deeply.

'Holy Blessed Mary—' Ursula reached for her rosary. She

held the crucifix tight in her hand. 'Wat!' she called 'Wat! Come here!'

Wat was gaming with the butler in the Hall. He had just thrown the dice, and was considering his chances, but he heard the fear in Ursula's voice. He hurried into the bed-chamber. 'Aye, lady?'

'Mistress Celia—she's taken very ill, get Master Julian—King's Head on Fenchurch. Hasten!'

Wat clucked sympathetically, he glanced at the sleeping girl and thought that she looked entirely healthy, rosy cheeks, soft regular breathing. But he obeyed. He galloped across the Bridge to the King's Head—a superior tavern for the gentry. He found Julian in earnest conversation with a younger man in doctoral robes, and Mabel sitting disconsolately alone, making pictures on the oaken table with a finger dipped in ale.

The Allens were part of a noisy group on the other side of the parlour.

'You're wanted, master,' said Wat, touching Julian on the shoulder.

Julian looked up, annoyed. His companion was Dr. John Dee, alchemist and astrologer, whom he had met at John Cheke's. Dee was a man of shrewd intelligence, with interests like his own, and he was propounding some very shrewd ideas on personal advancement.

Julian listened to Wat's explanation of the summons, and shook his head. 'You say Mistress Celia sleeps sweetly—bah! 'Twas naught but a green girl's attack of megrims. Lady Ursula dotes and frets overmuch. Now you're here, Wat, take Mistress Mabel home. I've important matters to discuss.'

Wat nodded in complete agreement. Women and their sudden alarums were tiresome. He resented this errand himself. 'Come along, mistress,' he said to Mabel, who was snivelling from disappointment. There were young gallants in the tavern pot-room, but none had noticed her. Mistress Allen, flanked by her husband and son, was quaffing ale and dominating a party of boisterous aldermen. Master Julian gave the girl no more than an absent-minded nod of farewell. Upon her dejected return to the Priory she found Celia asleep and Lady Ursula so unstrung by Master Julian's refusal that she flew into a temper.

'How *dared* you come back without him?' she cried furiously to Wat. 'Did you tell him how ill Celia is, and calling

317

for him? You scurvy horse-churl, I see you didn't! May the Saints punish you!'

Wat lifted one eyebrow, and escaped rapidly back to the Hall and his dice game, but Mabel burst into hiccuping sobs.

Ursula turned on her. 'What are *you* blubbering for? There's naught wrong wi' *you*! I vow y' must 'a kept Master Julian from coming!'

At this injustice Mabel stopped in mid-sob, her brown eyes snapped. 'How dare you talk to me in that way! 'Tis only by my brother's charity that you're here, Lady *South-well*. Ye've no more right here than a church mouse, you and your precious meaching Celia you're so besotted over!'

Ursula stiffened, then slapped Mabel's plump cheek. They both stood aghast, staring at each other.

Mabel had been used to her stepmother's tantrums, and had always rather despised Lady Ursula's control which she put down to weakness. Slaps, pinches, even beatings were expected from one's elders, and this slap—so unforeseen—served to jolt her from dejection. She tossed her head slightly, then walked to the centre table where there was a platter full of candied apple-slices. She took one and crunched it greedily.

With Ursula it was different. She found herself trembling, and her eyes were full of scalding tears. 'Forgive me, Mabel,' she said after a moment. 'It's true that we owe everything to Sir Anthony.' She looked down at the bed where Celia still slept. It was useless to explain the terror Celia's incomprehensible ramblings had provoked, especially that one sinister reference to Stephen; useless to explain that Master Julian's refusal to come to them had hurt and frightened her into fury.

This day was all awry, she thought, as her common sense gradually returned. She sat down on a stool, and drank some of the mead. The sweet liquor heartened her tired body. She reached out and put her hand on the sleeping girl's arm. The flesh was warm and softly vibrant. She called me 'Mother', Ursula thought, while love gathered itself into a wave and flowed down to the girl's arm. For the first time Ursula thought about Alice Bohun, the real mother who had borne this child alone in a tiny room in Midhurst. And knew that it was jealousy which had prevented the natural mention of Alice to Celia, and discouraged Celia's few attempts to talk about her mother after Ursula had, last year, brought the girl to Cowdray.

Ursula sat long on the stool, clinging to contrition and guilt to counteract the eeriness of Celia's semi-conscious words. She had said, 'Must it happen? Can't we stop it?'

'Stop what?' Ursula whispered, then shook herself. The ramblings of an overwrought girl after a day of great excitement. Ursula rose and went to the little alcove where crucifix and prie-dieu had been replaced. Tapers which were lit this morning for the intention of Queen Mary had long since burned. Ursula looked at them, then under Mabel's curious eyes brought an ember from the fireplace and lit two fresh candles. She knelt on the prie-dieu and bowed her head. No set words came. No Paters, no Aves ... nothing but a tremendous surge of invocation. She tried with all her strength to draw down some comfort, some assurance. She stared at the tiny silver figure nailed to the cross until it shimmered, blurred and went blank.

While she knelt, St. Saviour's rang out for Compline. Her weary mind listened carefully to the melodious bongs of the old bell.

'I'll go to Mass at six, Ursula thought, I'll find comfort there, but at once the momentary solace was cancelled by dismay. Brother Stephen would be celebrating the first Mass tomorrow. She had heard Sir Anthony suggest it, since the Bishop of Winchester himself had requested Stephen's presence in the Abbey for the Coronation.

I'm going mad, Ursula thought, my brain softens to mush! She got up off the prie-dieu and began to unhook her bodice with firm sharp tugs. She had seen Brother Stephen celebrate Mass a thousand times at Cowdray. That he was now becoming immersed in the great world, and had won instant favour with Bishop Gardiner, the new Chancellor, diminished any threat to Celia. There *was* no threat, it was wicked, blasphemous to think so. Ursula undressed without calling for the chamber-woman, then lay down carefully beside Celia.

*   *   *

Mary was crowned next day, on October 1, by Stephen Gardiner, Bishop of Winchester, since no other loyal Catholic prelate could be found. Cranmer, the Archbishop of Canterbury had been imprisoned for heresy the instant Mary gained control. Nobody blamed the Queen. Old Cranmer had inveigled for her mother's divorce, he had declared the validity of King Henry's marriage to Anne Boleyn—thus bastardising

319

Mary—he had written the Protestant Prayer Book, he had renounced the Pope, and finally, signed Edward's Devise, proclaiming Lady Jane Grey as Queen. He was, forthwith, sent to join Lady Jane and her husband Lord Guilford in the Tower, which was packed with new Protestant faces.

Yet, there were no more executions after Northumberland. Those close to Mary considered her temperate, the people called her 'Merciful Mary' and continued throughout October to give her admiring support. Her first Parliament was a benign sun of clemency and justice. Her father's outrageous penal laws were greatly softened, especially when Mary herself realised that there had been seventy-two thousand executions during his reign and Edward's—hangings and beheadings for offences ranging from an unproven whisper of treason to the stealing of a hawk's egg. Her reign began with festivals and rejoicings. The more fanatical Protestants sailed unhindered for Lutheran or Calvinistic centres on the continent; most of those who remained bowed to the restored regime and waited hopefully for the prosperity Mary promised her country.

She forebore to persecute her enemies. Even the unwilling usurper, Jane Grey, might hope for pardon. She forgave Henry Sidney at once when he penitently rushed to join her at Framlingham; she forgave Lord Clinton his defection, depriving him only of his post as Lord High Admiral.

During this month, the little household at the Priory in Southwark enjoyed itself. Anthony came home nightly from attendance at Court, and he brought company with him. There was music and dancing; his supper tables were almost as lavish as at Cowdray. Ursula and the two girls savoured a gaiety they had never known. Celia had entirely recovered from her attack on the night of the Procession, she did not even remember it. She bloomed, while discovering the delights of airy dalliance. Every man who came to the Priory showed his admiration; Celia was always sought first as a partner in the galliard, the La Volta, though she ignored coarse advances with the ease born from her tavern years.

Mabel might well have been jealous, except that her stars also turned favourable. On the feast of All Saints, November 2, Anthony brought new guests home. Among them was Gerald Fitzgerald. Anthony had the brotherly kindness to warn Ursula before the young Irishman arrived. 'Tell Mabel to wear her best gown, forbear poutings and speak softly. I've invited her young sprig, Lord Fitzgerald, who is no longer disgraced.'

'Mass!' cried Ursula. 'Here's a surprise! I thought he'd fled to Ireland! Didn't he sign for Lady Jane Grey?'

'Aye,' said Anthony, 'but our Gracious Queen is pardoning 'em all, or most. Especially the Catholics. And "the fair Geraldine", having suffered sharp pangs of dread as the result of a wrong guess, is now plotting more astutely on behalf of her brother and husband.'

'Indeed.' Ursula nodded thoughtfully. 'So you no longer oppose Mabel's inclination?'

Anthony laughed. 'I don't oppose the inclination, but I doubt very much that Fitzgerald will rise to *that* lure. If it could be Celia, now — a thousand pities that she's not high-born.'

Ursula flushed. They both looked at the girl who was sitting on a cushioned window-seat, and laughing at her mistakes as the Kentish Knight, Sir Thomas Wyatt, tried to teach her correct fingering on a lute. She wore the lilac gown Mabel had discarded after the Royal Procession. Celia was so much slimmer that the sweat stains had been completely cut out. She wore a new French-style white lace cap, stiffened and dipped in the front. It framed her little square-chinned face. The golden hair waved loose, and she kept tossing it back out of the lute-strings, and also away from Wyatt's caressing fingers.

'Can't you bring some man here who isn't *married*?' Ursula asked irritably, for she noted a narrowing of Sir Anthony's eyes, and heard his indrawn breath. 'Surely Celia's beauty, her sweet nature and her Bohun lineage make her an equal match for some gentleman?'

'Aye, aye,' said Anthony hastily. 'I'll look to the matter. I've not forgot my promise — there are doubtless many esquires could be found. No hurry, is there?'

Celia felt them looking at her from beside the door. She raised her cleft chin in her own pert, half-teasing way, smiled, showing the beautiful small teeth and the dimple beside her rich mouth. She gave them an affectionate wave with a hand no longer roughened and red, but of a velvety whiteness.

Anthony swallowed. 'She grows daily in charms,' he said in a harsh voice which he redeemed by an uncomfortable laugh.

Ursula glanced at him sidewise. Was it *possible*? Widower of four months . . . yet no new wife in contemplation, at least she'd heard none mentioned, and no eligible young women had as yet appeared at his parties. Anthony's attitude, the look he had sent the girl, surely there was love in it—stranger matches *had* been made. After all, Anthony was not a nobleman, he was again rich enough to forgo a dowry.

Ursula's thoughts were ever mirrored on her face; though she dared not speak, her spurt of hope showed itself plain to Anthony who was both touched and vexed at the naïveté. He drew off his gold embroidered gloves, and tossed them to a hovering retainer. He adjusted the set of his jewelled swordbelt. 'The Queen's Grace,' he said gravely, 'has promised me a peerage, to be conferred upon the occasion of her marriage. A Viscountcy, for which I will select the title Montagu, in deference to my paternal grandmother's family. I shall thereafter ponder well before I choose a suitable wife to be Viscountess Montagu, mistress of Cowdray—and mother to my babes.'

Ursula understood that she had been rebuked, but all of Anthony's speech was so startling that she was distracted from its reason. She spoke quickly, 'Aye—should have guessed—Master Julian *said* Her Majesty'd reward you, sir, and you deserve it. But what marriage—the Queen's, I mean—to whom? Is't decided?'

Anthony's face darkened, he bent his head for his servant to adjust the black velvet hat with its sable mourning feather. 'It is decided,' he said, 'though not generally known. Jesu—but there'll be an uproar,' he added to himself. He gave the puzzled Ursula a polite nod, then went to the head of the stairs to meet new arrivals.

The small Priory Hall, which had once been the monks' refectory, was jammed that evening with the assortment of guests Anthony had invited, ostensibly to attend a revel in honour of the Feast Day. He had hired extra minstrels, and commissioned John Heywood to be master of the revel. Heywood's zealous Catholicism had brought him great danger in the last reign. He fled to Europe but was now returned to a warm welcome from Queen Mary who had been delighted by him in her girlhood when he was a sort of court jester to her father. Heywood, a robust man in his fifties, was a wit. He could also sing, write masques or eulogies, and the merry eye, the ready tongue disguised shrewd intelligence. Anthony had selected him for an experiment this night. They had together, most carefully, determined on the method.

Sir Thomas Wyatt remained near Celia as the guests drifted in. He had drunk a great deal of Anthony's best Canary, and was becoming a trifle maudlin, as he took the lute and began to sing madrigals which had been composed by his father. 'Vengeance shall fall on thy disdain, Thou shalt but gain a constant pain,' he sang, and tried to squeeze Celia's waist. Since it was well-armoured with bone stays she merely laughed at him. He was in his thirties and seemed old to her, especially as his fashionable crimson velvet hat could not conceal a receding hairline and the sparseness of his hair. She knew vaguely that he had a wife in Kent and lived in a castle called Allington. She enjoyed his compliments, and kept an eye on her aunt, for Ursula was, however fleetingly, in the position of hostess to Sir Anthony. Celia, anxious to please her, was watching for the signals which meant 'important guests—get up and curtsy!'

'Ah, cruel maiden,' said Wyatt, stroking her arm. 'You'll not listen ... I know another song for you.' He tightened a lute-string and began in a loud tenor, 'Oh Celia, the wanton and fair, hath ne'er the need to despair, she hath used shame-less art, to inveigle Love's dart—' He broke off as Celia stiffened. He saw with annoyance that what little attention she had been according him was now withdrawn. He looked around towards a commotion near the door, bowings and hat-doffings to a very tall youth whose curly blond hair foamed around a violet satin hat, pearl-embroidered in the shape of a coronet.

'Aye, forsooth,' said Wyatt, putting down his lute, 'His "Majesty" deigns to grace our company. We must all make obeisance.'

Celia was not looking at Edward Courtenay, the Earl of Devonshire, she was staring at the Benedictine monk who had suddenly appeared from the chapel and was staring at her enigmatically—in fact, so dark and piercing was his gaze that it was as though he had never seen her before.

Wyatt left Celia to go and greet the Earl. She gave a nervous little laugh as Stephen walked up to her.

'Celia, the wanton and fair?' he said in an acid tone. 'The willing target for Sir Thomas Wyatt's adulterous musical darts? You're learning London ways apace, my dear. Soon you'll paint your mouth scarlet and whiten your paps like the other fine ladies.'

Celia's mouth tightened, the pupils widened in her azure

eyes. 'You look as though you detested me,' she whispered. 'Brother Stephen ...' she added half in plea, half in resentment.

Stephen shook himself, but his dark frown continued. 'Lady Ursula wants you,' he said coldly. 'She's beckoning. There're great folk here tonight and you'll find the revel far merrier than they will.'

'Ah, you *know* them now—the great folk,' cried Celia angrily. 'You've been with them daily since we got here. You, too, have altered, Brother Stephen. You no longer think solely of the offices, and the spiritual care of our household. I note your new gold crucifix. 'Tis a pretty thing.'

Stephen swallowed, his hands itched to shake her. He said stiffly, 'The Bishop of Winchester gave me this.' He indicated the crucifix. 'And has also shown me practical ways by which the True Faith may be presented in the world.'

'No doubt,' said Celia sweetly. She went over and joined Ursula who was greeting Gerald Fitzgerald while trying to dampen Mabel's too obvious rapture. Mabel looked almost pretty, and Gerald with his impish grin seemed glad to see her.

During the elaborate supper Celia was quietly demure. She was seated between a stout elderly knight, Sir John Hutchinson from Lincolnshire, who ate greedily, and Lord Henry Howard, second son to the Duke of Norfolk, a lad of thirteen who also concentrated on devouring the delicacies Anthony had ordered. The jellied capons, the roast quails, the soused lark—marinated in brandy, and traditional for the Feast of All Saints. These followed each other fast. The servers rushed along the thirty-foot table. Silver goblets engraved with the buck's head crest were never left empty of malmsey or claret. Iridescent Venetian glasses bubbled with a fizzy wine from Champagne, into which most of the company spooned quantities of sugar in an endeavour to make the prickly taste palatable.

Edward Courtenay, Earl of Devonshire, headed the table, above Anthony, as another Edward had done at Cowdray barely sixteen months ago. Celia examined the tall pretty youth, his air of vapid complacency, his rather foolish smile, and the boorish way in which he speared his meat, splattering sauce on his elegant doublet. She wondered very much why he sat in the carved Chair of State, and timidly asked the knight beside her.

'What ye say?' said Sir John sipping dubiously at the wine from Champagne. 'Oh, him! Earl o' Devon, just let outa the Tower—royal blood, ye know, goin' to marry the Queen's Grace, so I've heard. A bit callow, but logical choice—aye, logical choice. She's gotta wed a royal Englishman. Woman must have a master.'

Celia subsided. The matter did not concern her, she cared nothing about the wedding of the intense middle-aged little woman she had seen first at Hunsdon, then in the Procession. She toyed with a fragment of lark pasty, and darted a look at Stephen who sat across the table with two other monks, new friends of his who were chaplains to Bishop Gardiner. Sir John suddenly looked full at Celia and followed her gaze.

'Three black crows—out for the pickings! — like they always were,' he said, shoving his glass aside as he glanced across the table. 'Sorry to see 'em back again. Hate Romish trumpery. Bible and a good Englished prayer book's enough for *me*. Don't care who knows it.'

'You're a *Protestant*, sir? cried Celia, so astonished that she dropped her knife. She had never met a Protestant— except Mrs. Potts. 'But they're wicked *heretics*!'

'Fiddle-faddle,' said Sir John, and seeing Celia's horrified expression, suddenly smiled. He craned around Celia and addressed Henry Howard. 'What d'ye think, young sir? *Ye* was raised Protestant. You had that good man, John Foxe, for tutor. Did he teach you *wickedness*?'

Henry started and blushed. Since the accession of Queen Mary and his father's reinstatement as the premier peer of England, Henry had been drilled daily on the iniquitous folly of John Foxe's teachings during the five years that the Howard children had been farmed out on their Protestant aunt.

'I like Master Foxe,' he said cautiously, 'but it seems he's misguided.'

Sir John snorted and returned to his soused pork. He had accepted Sir Anthony's invitation for want of better entertainment that night, and was pleased to find that the food was excellent.

He had also just discovered that the girl on his left was singularly pretty. Fresh and innocent as a primrose, he thought, startled by a flicker of romantic interest such as he had not felt in years.

John Hutchinson was a widower. He had married—long ago—somewhat above his station, a scraggy little cousin of

Lord Clinton's. This connection had abetted his own rugged abilities, and had often been useful in furthering his career as Boston wool-merchant, ship-owner and finally Member of Parliament. He was fifty-nine; he had frequent attacks of gout, and indigestion, and knew that his days might be numbered. Until they were, all his energies had been centred on restoring Boston to the prosperity it once enjoyed, before plague, famine and particularly the effects of King Harry's debased currency, then the general stupidity of Edward's reign had diminished the port's usefulness. Sir John had been knighted by King Henry twenty-five years ago, in a casual gesture of recognition for a substantial loan—never repaid—which he had at that time been able to tender the Crown. Now, he knew that his Protestant convictions would be unpopular under the new regime, but it was not in his nature to disguise them. Nor to consider them very important. The business of commerce, the expedition of Lincolnshire cloth to Antwerp, the constant struggle to best the port of King's Lynn in the matter of customs levy—*these* were important, and no whims of a meagre middle-aged woman, be she suddenly Queen or not, could sway him.

He put down a spoonful of savoury stuffing and suppressed a belch. He suppressed it because of Celia, and wondered that he did so, or felt that nothing gross or earthy must offend her.

'You are related to Sir Anthony?' he asked.

Celia answered after a moment, she had stopped trying to watch Stephen, and was listening to the minstrels as they played a plaintive new madrigal. 'Nay,' she said, looking at him with some sadness. 'I am a Bohun, though I live at Cowdray. The land once belonged to my father's folk, long ago, and Sir Anthony has kindly given shelter to my lady aunt and me.'

'Aye . . . indeed . . .' Sir John nodded. Pensioners, he thought, dependants. Poor child. Several small inchoate feelings flickered in his mind. There was in him a strain of sentiment, long since sternly diverted to commerce, and blocked for ever, he had thought, by the dull weightiness of his body. 'Your mother?' he asked softly.

Celia looked up startled. Nobody ever mentioned her mother. 'She was a Londoner . . .' said Celia slowly, 'daughter to the landlord at the Golden Fleece, I think. She never told me much, nor often spoke.' Celia's delicate brows drew to-

326

gether in puzzled dismay. There was so little to remember about Alice in the last years except silent endurance—a being walled off from everyone, including her child. I doubt she really loved me much, Celia thought. How different from Aunt Ursula who kissed, petted, scolded, could be sharp, and even foolish, but underneath there was always a cherishing.

John Hutchinson watched the changing expressions on Celia's beautiful face, and fell in love, totally, irrevocably. He had fallen in love but once before, forty years ago—Bessie, the baker's daughter, her chestnut curls, her slumbrous dark eyes, her warm soft body and murmuring sweetness—John had been so besotted over Bessie that his father sent him away to Lincoln, and he had not thought of the heartbreak thereafter until now in Sir Anthony's Priory Hall, all the poignancies rushed back into an aging heart which resisted, as it welcomed them. 'Your name, darling?' he whispered. 'Your Christian name?'

'Celia, sir,' she answered with a touch of her natural pertness, amused by his suddenly doting gaze. Yet the elderly knight's shrewd, still bright blue eyes held a tinge of something more than lechery. There was tenderness, there was protection. Nor did he try to touch her. He smiled gently, and said, 'A beautiful name, "Celia"—and one already dear to me.' He turned from her and pushed the wine goblet aside.

She looked at him more attentively. His heavy-jowled ruddy face was clean-shaven in the fashion of his youth, his silvered hair was still thick and dark at his forehead. His mouth was broad and well shaped, since he had had the good fortune to lose no front teeth. He was soberly but expensively dressed in a maroon velvet gown over a plain black velvet doublet. The ruffles around his thick neck were spotless. His large spatulate hands were clean, the nails trimmed, and he had a great ruby ring on his thumb. A heavy gold chain ended in a golden sheep—the emblem of his guild—and rested on his substantial paunch.

Did my father look like that? Celia wondered. She remembered little of her father, except that he was killed in a tavern brawl, and guessed that he could never have exuded this air of solidity and assured worth.

The minstrels finished their madrigal and were quiet as they placed other music sheets on the stands. Courtenay's high whinnying laugh rang out, and all the company looked up the table.

Sir John had no more idea than Celia how shrewdly this revel had been planned to test the wind of opinion as it might be expected to blow from certain quarters. He was no longer mildly speculative about the gathering. His business sense had vanished, though he did not look at her again, his thoughts were entirely on the girl beside him, while Celia, mildly disappointed by the knight's silence, exchanged a few banal remarks with young Lord Henry Howard.

It was fortunate that the Queen was ailing again and, cancelling all Court functions, had retired to St. James's Palace. She would not have approved Anthony's plan, because she was incapable of seeing any flaws in her own passionate intent. Her advisers knew the dangers, though they were uncertain how great these might be. Bishop Gardiner, Mary's new Lord Chancellor, had rather unwillingly acceded to the experiment. He would not come himself tonight but sent the chaplains.

Anthony leaned back in his chair, and quelled uneasiness by trying to forecast his guests' reactions to the land-mine he and Heywood, with Stephen's help, had prepared.

There was Sir Henry Sidney of Penshurst—the poor little King's closest friend—*uncertain*. Sidney was unobtrusively Protestant, he had declared for Jane Grey, the wife of his brother-in-law Guilford Dudley—both these young Pretenders were still in the Tower. True, Queen Mary had forgiven Sidney, who had rushed to her side declaring allegiance after the tide turned at Framlingham, but he had altered from the merry youth who had truly loved Edward. His demeanour had grown solemn, forbidding. He was no longer popular at Court.

Then, there was Gerald Fitzgerald, now whispering to Mabel, a quizzical look on his cocky young face. He was probably *certain*, though the Clintons had politely refused to attend Anthony's revel. Geraldine would be waiting to see where the cat pounced next.

And then—Anthony looked further down the table. Sir Thomas Wyatt. *Extremely uncertain*. Wyatt had been incredibly rash and hot-headed in his youth. He had fought abroad, and was reputed to be a superb soldier. A sojourn in Spain when he was threatened by the Inquisition for heresy had resulted in outspoken hatred for the Spanish. Recent information had come to Bishop Gardiner—via a dismissed stable-boy whose right hand Sir Thomas had ordered cut off for stealing— that the rich Kentish knight had made invidious remarks about the Queen's Spanish mother. Wyatt was also known to have been often closeted with Courtenay.

Dull provincial bell-wethers like Sir John, the undoubted Protestant sitting beside Celia, and other manor lords of either religion who represented England's provincial squirearchy — well, they were most uncertain, but would probably follow the ingrained tradition of loyalty to the Crown.

The two key ambassadors were present, since neither ever let the other out of his sight if possible.

De Noailles of France — aristocratic, debonair, and a far more impressive figure than Charles the Fifth's ambassador, Simon Renard. Renard suited his name. He was a wily, grizzled old fox, small and cunning. He wore an air of smugness tonight from which Anthony guessed that the Ambassador somehow knew the true purpose of the revel.

And on my right, thought Anthony ruefully, glancing up at Courtenay — is the favoured candidate of the English people, may the Blessed Virgin save us! The newly restored Earl of Devon was tall and fair; he showed his royal Plantagenet descent, which ancestry was precisely the reason King Henry had clapped him in the Tower fifteen years ago. From the Tower he had just emerged — uncouth and untutored as a hound puppy — yet vain and prideful as a peacock. Anthony's polite attempts at conversation during supper had been met with vacant stares, or unmanly titters. Courtenay's one contribution had been a lewd anecdote about buggery with a sheep which might have amused a boy of ten. Though much could be excused by the years of confinement, Anthony found him a singularly disagreeable young man.

John Heywood suddenly approached, bowing. 'All is ready, Sir Anthony.' He quirked one grizzled eyebrow. 'Full bellies empty the head, and I've stuffed mine, so I doubt me skill, or *their* understanding.' He patted his paunch, then waved a plump hand towards the guests. 'A bit o' dancing first to liven 'em?'

'No,' said Anthony smiling, 'we'll on wi' the show.' He gave orders to his servants, and rising, said in a loud carrying voice, looking at Courtenay, 'My Lord Devonshire, an' it be your pleasure, I've arranged for you to view a novelty brought to our realm by Master John Heywood.'

'Aye, verily ... to be sure ...' stammered the young Earl, after a bewildered moment. He made a royal gesture recently taught him by the French Ambassador, and caressed his curly golden beard. 'Certes, certes,' he added haughtily, 'it is our pleasure.'

De Noailles sent the young man a look of approval, and a second glance towards Ambassador Renard his opponent in the delicate jockeyings for their respective countries.

'Dere speaks ze future consort,' said Noailles complacently, flicking a lace·bordered handkerchief in his rival's general direction. Renard said nothing. He rose with the others as the table-boards were stacked and the benches arranged across the Hall to view a small stage. The audience re-seated themselves, buzzing, expectant. Heywood disappeared behind a curtained box. Anthony looked for a moment at Stephen. They were the only two in the Hall who knew precisely what Heywood had planned.

Stephen touched his crucifix as invocation. Anthony nodded slightly, thinking how fortunate he was in his house priest. Stephen spoke Latin as well as Gardiner's chaplains, but he also spoke excellent French, an asset Anthony had only discovered when they reached London. Vastly useful, Stephen had become, thought Anthony, and as for the moment at Cowdray when there had been that flash of suspicion about a carnal attraction between Stephen and Celia ... Monstrous! A shameful thought born from the anxieties of that whole period, and never to be repeated.

Three loud knocks behind the curtained box silenced the company. They watched eagerly while the little red velvet draperies drew back to disclose a tiny stage, bare except for twin golden thrones erected on a dais. They laughed and exclaimed as a small wooden figure moved jerkily across the stage. None of the English had ever seen a puppet-show, and it took them several minutes to discover that the marionette represented their Queen. Its dress was blue and silver, furred with bits of ermine, and on its bent head there was a small glittering replica of St. Edward's crown. Heywood gave his audience plenty of time to recognise the little figure's dejection, and to see that it beat its breast at every third step, then clasped its hands in supplication towards the cross painted high between the thrones.

Suddenly, the puppet stiffened, it glided up the dais and flopped into the right-hand throne, while it stretched its arms out imploringly.

The curtains fell together. The audience rustled and murmured.

'What the devil's *that* for?' demanded Courtenay. 'I thought to see real players. That's only a babe's toy on strings.'

'Hold, my lord,' said Anthony, smiling, 'the next scene may be more diverting.'

The curtains parted to disclose a canvas sea with unmistakable waves upon which perched a carved wooden galleon, its square parchment sails were each painted with an oversized coat of arms, which the audience, with two exceptions, did not recognise.

Anthony watched the ambassadors. Renard gave a small snigger, his thin lips parted in a triumphant smile, but de Noailles started, glared and was betrayed into a horrified exclamation. 'Par Dieu!' he exclaimed half-rising. 'Doux Jésu, c'est outrageux!'

The galleon glided slowly back and forth across the stage, until everyone had noticed the small male figure on the bow — and its black sugar-loaf hat, decorated with a golden lion.

The curtains fell again to an uneasy silence, in which Anthony could hear de Noailles' heavy breathing, and saw that his face had gone scarlet.

'Aye—that was more diverting,' remarked Courtenay, in his role of condescension. Actually, he had never seen a sea, and had been interested by the reproduction. 'Yet, nothing *happens*,' he added critically. 'I like to view fights or even love-making.'

Most of the audience agreed with him. This was pretty pallid stuff, one expected better entertainment from Sir Anthony. Celia wondered when the dancing would start, and missed the music which had accompanied them through supper, but was now silent.

The curtains parted once more. There again were the twin thrones with the Queen sitting pensive on one. The prow of the galleon just showed to one side. The figure in the black-coned hat jumped off the ship and advanced, bowing towards the Queen who jerked upright. She held out her miniature arms and flew down the dais. The two figures intertwined. The Queen and the male puppet mounted the dais touching hands. He sat down on the other throne, and a large placard popped up behind them. It depicted in glaring colours England's royal arms, and the alien coat, linked by ribands and cupids. Above these in glittering gold were an M and a P.

The curtains fell slowly for the last time. As they did so Thomas Wyatt jumped to his feet, his sword half-drawn.

'God's body!' he cried shrilly. 'What shitten mummery is this! Browne, you must be mad!' He glared at Anthony.

'Soft, soft—*mon chevalier*—' said de Noailles, gliding dextrously in front of Wyatt. 'Our host has arranged a *petite comédie pour nous amuser, c'était charmante, on doit* . . .' he paused a second and seeing total incomprehension in Courtenay's face reverted to English. 'We thank ze good Sir Anthony, don't ve, milor'?'

Courtenay stared at the Ambassador. 'I thought it dull,' he said. 'What meant that puppet i' the black hat? Is't a jape?'

Anthony had drawn back behind the Earl. His servants, according to instructions, had lit more tapers in the wall-sconces the instant the puppet show finished. He watched the faces. Most of them were blankly puzzled, including those of the three women in his household. Henry Sidney was staring up at the rafters, his look was grim. Renard was smiling a little and carefully picking his teeth. The others all turned to look at Wyatt, for he was trembling so hard that his sword rattled in its scabbard.

His mouth worked. 'You fool!' he cried to Courtenay. 'You doltish bufflehead! The man i' the black hat is Prince Philip o' Spain. Holy Saints, that Browne would dare to insult us all wi' such wickedness. 'Tis demonic. And every true-born Englishman 'll fight against becoming Spain's vassal!'

These heated words, Wyatt's fury, produced startled agitation.

Then Courtenay said, frowning, 'That puppet was Philip o' Spain? Does he wear a hat like that? I thought it comical.'

At the same time Sir John who had discomfort in his belly, and was wondering how soon he could decently leave, said, 'Well-a-day, the Spanish 're *all* comical, m'lord, when they're not vicious, I hear. Let one Spaniard dare knock at m' manor gates an' I'd tell porter to set the hounds on him. Too many foreigners in England already. Dutch, Flemings, Florentines —takin' the bread from mouths o' honest Englishmen.'

The other knights of the shires all murmured, 'Aye, aye—well said.'

Anthony met Stephen's eyes. They both shrugged. It was too soon for insistence. 'Now that we've seen Master Heywood's little novelty,' Anthony announced smoothly, 'shall we have a caper?' He bowed ceremoniously towards Courtenay.

'An' it please you, my lord, the minstrels 've learned the latest La Volta. I warrant you dance well.'

The Earl's face cleared. He did not understand Wyatt's violent behaviour, nor why de Noailles who had befriended him since his release from the Tower should be thunderously silent. His thwarted youth was bubbling. He had been repeatedly assured that he would marry Queen Mary whom he had found gracious, even simpering in several audiences with her. The thought of bedding her was distasteful, but de Noailles had made it clear that the King Consort might easily satisfy his fancies elsewhere.

'Aye, where's the music?' he asked, and looked around for a desirable partner. His eye had just lit on Celia when Wyatt twitched his sleeve angrily. 'My lord, it's not seemly that you remain in this house where you, where all true Englishmen—have suffered a grievous insult!'

'Insult?' Courtenay raised his chin, and stepped back from Wyatt. 'Y' don't mean that little puppet mummery?'

'I mean the warning our good host has given us. Ye think to be King, my long lad? It may appear that the Queen's Grace favours someone else.'

The Earl's jaw dropped. Gradually, he saw Wyatt's meaning. 'But . . . but . . .' he looked instinctively towards de Noailles. The consternation on the foolish handsome face was so evident that one might almost be sorry for him, Anthony thought. ' 'Tis all *arranged!*' Courtenay cried. 'The people cheer me as I go on the London streets. Only today some goodwife cried out to me when I rode through the Cheap—" 'Twill be a happy day for England when we've another King called Edward!" '

De Noailles had by now recovered, and coming to Courtenay's side spoke in his suavest manner. 'I see no insult in Sir Anthony's divertissement. You will ignore it, milor' . . . we'll confer later. Milor' Devonshire's royal choice is not confined to *one* bride, *peutêtre* . . .' He added this so softly that it seemed of no importance. Renard looked up, then resumed picking his teeth. Wyatt and Anthony understood the threat. If not the Queen . . . there was Elizabeth, the young, the enigmatic Princess, the next claimant to the throne.

Anthony signalled to the minstrels, and the Hall was soon filled with gay music. The company livened, many danced. All, Anthony realised, had been somewhat befuddled by the countless wines he had given them, and they soon forgot the puppet show. Sir John fell asleep with his head on a bench. There were other snores from the staid members.

Ursula herself began to nod. Anthony had a private word with Master Heywood when he paid him three nobles for his services. 'By and large our effort was successful, I think,' said Anthony. 'At least we know that Sir Thomas Wyatt must be watched. And de Noailles, of course. Courtenay is only a puppet himself ... d'you think it possible that the Princess Elizabeth *could* be a menace to our cause? Would she dare involve herself in treason?'

'Can't say ...' answered Heywood. 'That flame-haired wench is a canny one, gone to earth at Ashridge. She early learned when to play sick. She don't want to end up wi' her bloody head rolling i' the straw like her mother. The *people* like her.'

'And they shall like *Mary!*' said Anthony fiercely. 'She's rightful Queen, and will marry as she pleases. Her choice is apt. The scion of the Holy Roman Empire—what better luck for England!'

'England don't want to be Spanish,' said Heywood. 'Most o' it don't want to be Papist, but the Queen's Grace can't see that. She fair dotes on a portrait o' Prince Philip. A lady o' her bedchamber says she kisses it each night like a holy saint. What's to be done wi' an old virgin o' thirty-seven? They itch and burn like ordinary women. God grant she gets a son out o' it. Philip's an able stud.'

'We'll drink to the babe as yet unconceived!' Anthony laughed and clinked a stirrup cup with Heywood. He had a fleeting thought for his own infants at Cowdray in the care of Peggy Hobson. Little Anthony would have a title. Little Mary would marry high. Ambitions long dormant had burgeoned during these lost weeks. And they all depended on pleasing the Queen. He had learned to pay her compliments, but sincere ones. He was no fawning courtier. Her features and small body were insignificant, and her harsh manly voice was disconcerting, so he spoke of her intelligence, her clemency, her devoutness. And since she took great pains to dress magnificently like her father, he noticed the set of her Spanish farthingale, and admired the gilt lace ruff, or the lavish jewels she plastered on her person. Like a green girl, she responded with bridlings and blushings. Enmeshed in hopes of love at last, of a marriage which would have so delighted her poor mother, Mary permitted herself no realisation of how insecure still was her tenure on the throne. She knew that God had performed a miracle in placing her there, He would certainly guide her thereafter. It was left for her adherents to do the worrying.

'And it may be that we fret needlessly,' said Anthony to Stephen after all the guests had gone that night. 'The Queen's Grace has total Faith, and so must we.'

'Aye . . .' agreed Stephen slowly. He was about to return to one of the Priory's old cells. It had been untouched by Anthony's restorations. To this austere cubicle Stephen had, however, admitted a wooden bedstead with cross-roped springs to support a flock mattress—far more comfortable than the pallet in his hut on Tan's Hill. A row of wooden pegs in the passage outside had become necessary to hang up his habits —Anthony had given him a new one of the softest black wool, and his chest was filled with linen cassocks and shifts. His crucifix and two tapers were in the niche, and his precious picture of the Holy Virgin hung on the wall where he might greet Her on waking. The servants strewed fresh herbs on his stone floor, as a matter of course, and he found the scent agreeable. They also kept a silver ewer filled with warm water for his ablutions. It stood on a stand with a slop basin, a jar of soft soap and his razor.

There was a charcoal brazier in the cell, always lit on these raw Autumn nights. Stephen enjoyed the warmth, and never questioned the luxuries which made a room in Southwark far more comfortable than a draughty hut in Midhurst.

There *was*, however, a matter of conscience which he brought up tentatively tonight. 'Sir . . .' he said to Anthony, 'Her Grace the Queen has so far not been allowed to acknowledge His Holiness the Pope's supremacy, and is still the titular head of the Church. But she will not remain so. Then will come the restoration of the monasteries. Have you considered what this 'll mean to you?'

Anthony, who was tired, looked at his young chaplain with some exasperation. 'What d'ye mean, Brother Stephen? God's body, haven't we had enough speculations for one night?'

'I mean . . .' said Stephen slowly, 'that when it comes you will lose this Priory. It must return to the Church. You'll lose Easebourne and Battle Abbey. It was at Battle Abbey that I learned to hate your father.'

Anthony jerked his head and frowned. 'Hate my *father*? Oh, aye, but that's long past. I'd clean forgot.'

335

'I was sent to you at Cowdray as a penance,' said Stephen slowly, 'and I—may the Blessed Virgin help me—am in danger of forgetting this, too. Much of your revenue comes from Church lands. When we have a completely Catholic England, they must be restored to God.'

Anthony was angered. It seemed to him that a trusted, valued hound had suddenly nipped him. 'You are brash,' he said coldly. 'You understand nothing yet of the world. I find your remarks irrelevant!'

'They aren't irrelevant,' said Stephen after a moment, and he flushed.

The resentment in his patron's eyes dismayed him, and he tried to recapture the indignation he had felt sixteen years ago at Battle Abbey.

'I—I have to prepare you, sir,' he said unhappily. 'I don't wish to vex you.' He bit his lips and looked down at his sandals.

Anthony suddenly laughed. 'Come, Stephen. There's not a true Catholic of consequence in England but 's got Abbey lands. Ye can't turn the clock back *that* far—'tis not reasonable. His Holiness 'd ne'er ask such a thing, either. Mass! my friend, spare me the owl face—we've need o' rest. Tomorrow I'll take ye to Whitehall again, ye can mingle wi' that French bunch o' de Noailles, keep your ears open since you understand their jabber. We've troubles a-plenty ahead wi'out inventing 'em.' Anthony strode off along the passage to his bedroom.

Stephen walked into his cell. He knelt before the crucifix and mechanically said a Pater Noster. '*Fiat voluntas tua*,' he repeated and shrugged in relief. 'Thy Will, I've done what *I* can!'

Thirteen

On January 6, 1554, Celia awoke in her chamber at the Priory to the sound of sleeting rain and the feel of penetrating chill in the mists off the Thames. She shivered, coughed and dully counted the seven bongs from St. Saviour's outside her lattice window. She noted that Ursula who slept beside her in the great curtained bed had already arisen, either to use the privy, or more likely had gone out to early Mass.

'Tis the Feast of the Three Kings, Celia thought, Epiphany. Twelfth Night—the end of Christmas—and the beginning of what? There was nothing in particular to look forward to. Ever since the All Saints revel and puppet-show, the weather had been bad, Anthony and Stephen were almost never at home, and one of Mabel's frequent colds had seized both Celia and Ursula in a more violent form. They had coughed agonisingly for ten days. Celia still coughed. She lifted her head from the pillow and found that she had the dull throb in her forehead which had plagued her for several mornings. She flopped back and shut her eyes. She opened them again as the bed-curtains were parted and a chambermaid peered down while tendering her a mug of the steaming ale called 'Lamb's Wool', from the apple froth atop it.

'Good morrow, miss,' said the woman in a pleasant country voice. 'Lady Suthell sent me up ter rouse ye.'

Celia sighed, murmured, 'Good morrow,' and added, half to herself, 'Aye, must drag myself to Mass.'

'Ye needn't, then,' said the woman, 'God don't *want* ye to!'

It took a moment for Celia to understand this extraordinary statement. Then she looked up at the chambermaid. She saw a woman of thirty, with a thin freckled face, nondescript except for a sweet, rather stern smile. This maid had been at the Priory only a day, Ursula having had to dismiss their former chamber-woman for sluttishness and thievery. This maid's kerchief and apron were dazzling white, her brown hair neatly coiled.

'What did you say?' exclaimed Celia. 'What *do* you mean?'

'That Our Heavenly Father don't want ye to go to church

an' pretend ye're a-crunchin' on His Son's bones, and a-suckin' up His blood.'

Celia sat up, shocked, yet inclined to laugh. 'That's disgusting!' she cried. 'You must be mad ... You're called Agnes, aren't you?'

'Aye—Agnes Snoth, widow. I've come from Kent inter London town and am now spreading the Gospel according to His Holy Word, an' accordin' ter m'station in life, which be lowly.' Her smile deepened.

'St. Mary, you mustn't say such abominable things,' said Celia. 'They're, why, they are *heresy*! If my lady aunt heard you—how did you *get* here, anyway?'

'Oh, I went to Lady Suthell wi' some writin' from Mistress Allen o' Ightham Mote. I was nurse ter Master Charles, time back.'

Celia's eyes widened. 'But the Allens 're true Catholics. You never said such things *there*.'

'Oh, no, miss. I hadn't seen the Light then. Master Rogers' services at Paul's Cross converted me. An' I thank God fur it. I'm saved from damnation, from the burnin's in hell fire. I wants ter save *thee*, poppet, ye've a sweet lovely face, an' ye doant seem happy, bein' mired deep in idolatry.'

Celia did not know what to answer. The woman's face had a calm glow, there was great certainty in her way of speaking.

Celia looked at the silver mug of hot ale, it smelled of nutmeg and apple, it smelled delicious. 'I can't drink this,' she said, 'not before Communion. Even *you* know that.'

Agnes nodded. '.'Twas why I brung it. There's naught in the Bible about goin' to Mass, or Feast Days, or holy water, or praying to idols made by human hands, or beads, or some man i' a long frock lurkin' in a cupboard can forgive your sins ...'

'There isn't?' said Celia startled. She had never read the Bible, of course, but she knew that in some way all Christianity was based on it. 'How would *you* know, Agnes?' she said impatiently, rather as to a naughty child who has been found out in a lie. She put one bare leg out of bed, and pulled her night-shift tight around her as St. Saviour's rang the half-hour. She'd have to hurry to catch the eight o'clock Mass.

'Because I've read every word o' the Good Book fur m'self,' said Agnes with quiet triumph, as she held out Celia's woollen chamber-robe. 'I read the Scriptures, Englished by Master John

338

Rogers. Sir John Cheke had me taught. Took me a year, but I learned.'

'Sir John Cheke . . .' Celia frowned. She had heard of him, he had been tutor to the deluded little King Edward, he had espoused the usurpation of Lady Jane Grey. 'He's in the Tower for treason, Agnes,' said Celia severely, 'and you've been *badly* taught. I'll have to ask Brother Stephen to set you right, or we can never keep you here!'

'Oh, Miss Celia . . .' Agnes shook her head sadly, she gave the girl a soft pitying smile. 'Ye're so blind, poor sweeting. D'ye think any scoldin's from a skirted young man'd sway me from God's true word. Ye've but ter *read* it. I've got the Book, Sir John gave it me, it'll comfort ye in all tribulation, an' ye won't need that church yonder an' its wicked mummeries. Our Blessed Lord saith, when two or three 're gathered together in His name was church enough.'

The shining in Agnes's plain freckled face, the resolution in her clear voice perturbed Celia. She knew the woman must be wrong, but found no words to refute her. Besides she noted as Agnes went to stir up last night's embers in the fireplace, that the poor thing had a twisted limp. Celia looked down at the left leg and saw that it ended in a lumpy shape, neatly bound with leather strips.

'Club foot,' said Agnes cheerfully. 'I was born wi' it. I can work as well as any wench, but lots don't want ter hire me. They had to turn me away at the Chekes' when he was put in prison.'

'And since then?' asked Celia. Agnes shocked and puzzled her, she might well be simple-minded which would excuse her crazy speech. Yet, there was warmth, staunchness, a quality which Celia felt as wholeheartedness.

'Since then I've trusted in m' Blessed Lord to guide me like He promised that Our Father knoweth what things we have need of, afore we ask, and He would not leave me comfortless. Yet I couldn't find work, a day here, a day there, a crust or two to keep m'belly from cavin' in, but Our Lord ne'er promised we'd have *no* trials, and one night i' a dream, He told me to use the writin' Mistress Allen give me when she sent me off. I had it put by, an' I remembered she used to boast she had a kinsman worked for Sir Anthony Browne. I'd but to ask i' the tavern to find Sir Anthony lived here.'

'The kinsman is Brother Stephen, our chaplain,' said Celia curtly. It did not surprise Celia that Ursula had hired the

339

cripple provisionally, since she came with a reference, and Ursula was always pitiful. But she was made uneasy by the connection with Emma Allen. Celia's intense dislike of the Kentish squire's wife had faded. In fact, she remembered nothing of her own peculiar behaviour after the Queen's procession, except her half-dream that Emma Allen was an adder. None the less, she could not imagine Mistress Allen employing this woman. And she said so.

'Oh,' said Agnes, 'she hated the sight o' me. Many's the clout I got, an' no wages neither. 'Twas just that my babe'd died an' I had milk fur Master Charles. Me husband was blacksmith at Ightham, but he died o' the sweatin' sickness. I was fair beset. I'd no found m'true Heavenly Friend then.'

'She couldn't've hated you if she wrote you a character,' said Celia.

Agnes was silent while she carefully pushed twigs and straw into the smouldering sea-coals. Mistress Allen's reference had been a bribe. It was entirely due to the night Agnes had been up with little Charles who was croupy, and had gone to the kitchen for hot water, and surprised her mistress, drunk and half-naked, panting in the sweaty arms of a lusty young scullion.

'Well . . . no matter why,' said Agnes slowly. 'She gi'e me the writin'.'

Celia drew breath and began to cough. As the spasms lessened she reached for the ale mug and drank it down greedily. It eased her chest. She banished all thoughts of going to Mass. Sickness was a valid excuse, yet would make a venial sin to confess next Saturday. Her confessions of late to the parish priest had been dull and arid anyway—like her life, since Anthony had stopped entertaining.

Agnes watched the pretty downcast face and said quickly, 'The Blessed Lord'll find ye a good husband, Miss—if ye ask Him right, talk to Him straight, not wi' candles an' grovellin', or gabblin' o' Latin words.'

'Oh, Agnes . . .' Celia gave an exasperated sigh. 'I don't know what I want! Leave me be. And quit talk like that or I'll have to tell my lady aunt, at least. We can't harbour Protestants *here*. And don't upset the other servants.'

'I s'all do wot God tells me ter do,' said Agnes gently. 'An' He's allus wi' me—in me heart.' She said no more, while she limped carefully around the room, making the bed, dusting the crannies, retrieving the chamber-pot to empty in the latrine below.

I wish there were *something* in *my* heart, Celia thought, and knew how foolish it was to be envious of a poor club-footed serving-maid. It's the weather—the sleet drove harder against the panes—it's my headache—it was tedium—soon she would practise her needlework with Ursula, then they would go to the still-room where they were concocting various herbal brews, some medicinal such as Balsam salve, or tincture of poppy-head—some cosmetic like cucumber face-wash. Then Celia would go out to the stables and pet Juno—the horse suffered from lack of exercise as much as Celia did. Then there would be dinner, far less lavish than when Anthony were there, but still enough to sate a depressed appetite, and after dinner the short winter afternoon would fade, and Ursula might get out her ephemeris and by candlelight painstakingly cast the horoscope for the next day. Then Celia would spin yarn while Ursula read aloud from *Gesta Romanorum*, an English translation of wondrous deeds in ancient times, or the Ballads of Robin Hood, or even from a slender volume of love sonnets written by Sir Thomas Wyatt's father, and presented to Anthony by young Sir Thomas before the quarrel at the puppet-show.

Ursula did not much like these poems of yearning, of lost love, Celia had heretofore found in them a sour-sweet melan-choly. Today she felt she could not bear to listen.

Precisely at the moment that she finished adjusting her every-day kerchief, and peered absently into her fly-specked little mirror, she became aware of the deeper reasons for her malaise. It was not the weather, low health or tedium which made the days so drear. It was a forlorn envy at the recurrent sight of Mabel's dithering delight in Gerald's attentions—and the fact that Stephen had totally avoided her since his wrathful speech when he had caught her flirting with Sir Thomas.

Celia walked slowly down to the Hall, and stopped in sur-prise at the doorway when she heard her aunt's voice inside raised in excited glad greeting. Now, who could have come? Celia thought without much interest. She entered the Hall, and was smothered in a hearty embrace.

'God's greeting, hinny. By the Mass, 't's been a lang while!'
'Maggie . . .?' said Celia wonder-struck, drawing back to

stare. It was most certainly Magdalen Dacre, but a vastly different Magdalen from the hungry, anxious Border lass she had last seen in Cumberland.

This Magdalen was dressed in green velvet over silver brocade; she had a cloak furred with the finest miniver; her wiry auburn hair was nearly covered by a fur-trimmed hood. Her long reddish neck and freckled bosom were framed by a fashionable flaring ruff. She had a golden belt from which dangled not only her rosary, but a jewelled pomander which gave forth the scent of cloves. And she wore a pair of elaborately embroidered gloves on her large capable hands.

'A bit o' surprise, eh, lass?' asked Magdalen, her leaf-brown eyes twinkling. 'Ye'll niver guess what I'm doing i' London town. Or did Sir Anthony think to tell ye?'

'N-no,' said Celia, 'we've not seen him for days. He's always at Court.'

'So'm I to be!' said Magdalen chuckling. 'I canna believe ma guid fortune.'

'You're married?' asked Celia with a constriction in her chest.

'Na, na . . .' Magdalen laughed. 'None o' that.' She turned to include Ursula in her announcement. 'The Queen's Grace— God bless an' keep her—has appointed me a maid o' honour. Faither's that pleased. He bought me a' this fine gear.'

Magdalen accepted enthusiastic congratulations in her downright way—no trace of deprecation or false modesty. It was not only the effect of the new clothes which gave her big ungainly body a touch of magnificence, for Celia there was also shock at the difference in their station. In Cumberland among the rowdy, violent, earthy Dacres, Celia had never felt inferior, now she was conscious that Magdalen was the child of nobility, of lineage through Barons and Earls stretching back five hundred years to the Conquest—the only historical date except Christ's birth that Celia knew.

'Ye luik a wee bit dozzened, lass,' said Magdalen suddenly. She examined Celia's face. 'Pale an' peaky. 'Tis the heavy London air?'

'She's been ill,' Ursula interjected. 'We both have. Catarrh and cough. But we're mending. 'Twas good of you to visit us, Maggie. We've been dull and house-bound.' She, too, found Magdalen's transformation overpowering, and wished that Celia had not worn her old homespun kirtle, though it was fitting to the domestic duties they must perform.

'I've not forgot ye,' said Magdalen, who comprehended the situation. Her fondness for Celia had perforce been submerged during the last feverish months, and she had come today on kindly impulse as she was not on duty in the Queen's chambers at Whitehall. Now she was shocked by Celia's thinness, by her obvious despondency.

'Coom, hinny,' she said, struck by a sudden idea, 'no reason to mope here, 'tis Twelfth Night, we maun mak' merry. Do ye go tonight, you an' Lady Southwell, to the Queen's Revels at Whitehall?'

'To Court?' asked Ursula, astounded. 'But we don't belong there. Sir Anthony's never mentioned such a thing.'

'He wouldna mind, he's mebbe heedless,' said Magdalen, 'bein' sae caught oop wi' great matters, yet did he think on it, he'd na want ye droopin' lak this. Forebye, the palace's open wide this neet. There'll be a thousand or more. I'll send a groom fur ye, at three. 'Tis settled then—an' no mincing aboot.'

She bestowed another hug on Celia, a smile on Ursula and hurried off.

Mabel, when she finally arose—she customarily slept the morning away quite indifferent to Mass, now that Brother Stephen no longer disciplined his household—was vaguely pleased, though taking Ursula and Celia to Whitehall would never have occurred to *her*. Mabel was out a great deal herself now, had been often to Court where Anthony had presented her to the Queen in November, under the aegis of the Countess of Arundel.

'Fitzgerald'll be there tonight, of course,' said Mabel smugly. 'He's asked me to sup beside him. I'll wear my new Brussels lace ruff. Pray, lady,' she turned to Ursula, 'can you make that Agnes sew the wires more firmly? I wonder you hired her, she's clumsy and mute as a mole. Soon I'll have tiring women of my *own*, though!' Mabel's plump face brightened, she smiled in a way that made her pretty.

'Aye, child, 'twould seem you will,' Ursula tried to keep the tartness from her voice. For Mabel life had grown sweet. She was transformed, like all women, by a successful love affair, a *suitable* one, which Ursula considered that she had done nothing to deserve; except possibly the accident of birth when Jupiter and Venus were both ascendant. But *why* was she born just then? *Why* did her horoscope indicate a long and prosperous life, largely passed in a foreign land? Which

343

destiny was indeed unfolding. It was forbidden to question God's justice, forbidden to a devout woman—yet through Ursula's mind there darted a memory of talks with Master Julian at Cowdray. Speaking in his ironic way, he had seemed to voice an explanation that events surrounding us in this life might be predicated on behaviour in past ones. That events in this life might also influence future lives on earth. He had quoted from the Ancients, from Plato and Cicero and Ovid— names she barely knew, but when she timidly objected that these men were pagans, he had laughed and said, 'Da vero— so you may have Church Fathers then,' and mentioned St. Gregory and Origen, and even the Bible.

Ursula caught herself up. She had no wish to think of Julian and the hurt he had dealt her by refusing to come to Southwark on the night of Celia's strange illness. There was much to be done to prepare Celia's clothes—and her spirits—for the appearance at Whitehall. Perhaps tonight, she thought with the perennial upsurge of hope, *tonight* will bring the change in Celia's fortunes which Julian himself had foretold.

*   *   *

The palace at Whitehall was jammed on that Twelfth Night. Queen Mary was happier than she had ever been in her life. She sat on her throne in the Presence Chamber, graciously nodding to each one of the indeterminate file of faces whose owners dropped to one knee as they were hurried along by the Lord Chamberlain. She glittered with jewels, and her pinched little face, sandy-browed, thin-lipped, was transfigured into comeliness by the same alchemy which improved Mabel.

Close beside her stood Count Egmont, the Spanish emissary who had just brought confirmation from Prince Philip of her heart's desire. The marriage contracts. She giggled and blushed when Lord William Howard, who had replaced Clinton as Admiral of the Fleet, whispered daring remarks in her ear. That soon he would share her throne, and her *bed*—the wonderful young Spanish Prince. Soon, after years of neglect and thwarted virginity she would have someone worthy to love. She loved him already. True, he was over ten years younger than she, but Count Egmont assured her that Philip was grave and sedate, far older than twenty-seven in his ways, and that he doted on her portrait, as she did his.

Mary's rapture infected her myriad guests. They milled through the State Chambers, enjoying a courtly freedom reminiscent of King Henry's best years. It was cold outside, the Thames was partially frozen, the sleet had turned to snow, then to a cracking frost, but the Palace was warm from the sconces, the roaring fires and the heat of so many velvet and fur-clad bodies.

Anthony was standing near the throne conversing warily with the haughty and immensely rich Earl of Pembroke whose views on the Spanish marriage were known to be adverse. Pembroke had been friend to Northumberland, had signed for Queen Jane, then retracted like so many others whom Mary forgave. He was the most powerful peer after the Duke of Norfolk, he was sternly anti-Catholic, and had never been civil to Anthony until the last weeks when Mary's approval of Cowdray's owner had been so marked.

'Disgusting rabble here tonight,' Pembroke observed. 'Our poor young King'd never have permitted such a throng. Some o' these folk are *commoners*! I wonder at Her Majesty!'

Anthony raised his eyebrows and said, 'True, my lord, and did you mean *me* especially?'

The Earl glanced at him, 'Nay, nay, my good knight, I referred to —' he waved a thin veined hand, 'well, to such as those near the doorway.'

Anthony looked and saw Master Julian standing with the Allens and a young man in doctoral robes. 'I know them,' he said. 'All but the youngest man. They're entirely respectable.'

The Earl snorted. 'So is a quarter of England, I warrant — and the youngest man is John Dee whom I do *not* consider respectable, for all he calls himself a doctor, and has set up as Astrologer Royal.'

'Oh?' said Anthony, slightly amused by the Earl's venom. 'I have heard of him.'

'Dangerous fellow,' said the Earl. 'Black magic, alchemy, witchcraft, two-faced as Janus. Can't have that sort of villain at Court!' Pembroke snapped his turtle-mouth shut and walked off to greet young Courtenay, the Earl of Devonshire, who was languidly approaching.

Cotsbody, what a coil! Anthony thought amused. The maligned John Dee had a pleasant intelligent face, and baseless slander was a frequent pastime among the nobility. However, as he was dedicated to the Queen and her welfare, he thought that he had better join the foursome by the doorway and inspect Dee. He was checked by the sight of Magdalen Dacre towering over the crowd and shepherding two women whom he recognised with astonishment as Lady Ursula and Celia. He rushed forward, beaming and contrite.

'Aye, sir,' said Magdalen, seeing the contrition. 'Since ye prove sae neglectful o' your womenfolk, others mun recall your duties this Twelfthneet.'

Anthony laughed, and thumped his breast. *'Mea culpa*, my ladies, I'm glad to see you,' and he was, though he did not know what to do with them. Lady Ursula had her own handsome dignity, Celia was always pretty, yet tonight she seemed small and uncertain next to Magdalen. Fond as he was of them, Anthony perceived that they were both of the class which Pembroke had contemptuously dismissed as 'commoners!' They were no actual kin of his, and by no stretch of etiquette might they be permitted to sup in the Banqueting Hall, much less the High Table where he had been allotted a place near the Queen.

Magdalen quickly saw his dilemma, even though she was, as yet, unused to Court. She herself must eat among the maids of honour, and it was all very unlike the easy ways at Naworth Castle. She exchanged a look of rueful understanding with Anthony and said cheerfully, 'I could show 'em aboot the Palace, then there'll be food i' the back rooms. They'll have a cake ther-re, too, hinny,' she smiled at Celia. 'God-a-mercy, ye maught cut it reet an' get the beat, then ye'd be a queen fur the neet, same lak Her Majesty . . .'

'Thank you, Maggie,' said Ursula briskly, 'Celia and I will fend for ourselves. You were good to bring us.' She put her hand on Celia's arm, understanding the embarrassment Magdalen's invitation had caused, and appreciative of the girl's good heart. She pulled Celia away.

'Not over there,' said Celia in a toneless voice.

Then Ursula saw Julian standing with the Allens.

'Yet, why not?' added Celia suddenly. She raised her chin, her voice hardened. 'No use milling around among the peacocks like a couple o' draggle-tail sparrows, and at least they'll be somebody to talk to.'

Ursula nodded, relieved by a show of spirit, and glad that the girl had conquered her aversion to Mistress Allen.

But when they threaded their way through the horde of chattering strangers, the Allens had drifted off in pursuit of more interesting company, and Julian was left with Dr. Dee.

'*Benvenuto,*' cried Julian, kissing Ursula's hand. 'We meet always by chance, fortunate chance.'

'Evidently,' said Ursula, removing her hand coldly, though the touch of his lips had sent a tingle through her, 'since you do not choose to visit us, even after urgent summons.'

Julian started, then laughed. 'Dear Lady Southwell, my apologies—Wat said there. was no need, and I see that Celia has recovered, a trifle pale and thin, perhaps . . .'

'We might give the young mistress a sample of our *Elixir Vitae*,' interrupted John Dee bowing sedately towards Celia. ' 'Twould be wise before we try it—elsewhere.'

Celia stared, suppressing her first desire to giggle in weeks. She saw a lean man in his late twenties, he had a long hooked nose, gaunt cheek-bones and a straggling sparse beard. He had lost much of his hair, and wore a black skull-cap embroidered with mystical symbols. His eyes were brown, solemn and completely lacked the sardonic twinkle which always lurked behind Julian's gaze.

'*What* do you want to try on me, sir?' she asked. 'It sounds fearsome.'

Julian laughed. '*Elixir Vitae*, little one—"water of life"—Dr. Dee and I have been concocting it, in our spare moments. We now share a laboratory on Pater Noster Row. You and Lady Southwell must visit it, you'd be amazed at the retorts and crucibles, and the "Shew stone" where Master John can see angelic beings floating in the crystal.'

'Magic?' whispered Ursula, her eyes lighting up. 'But surely . . .'

Julian answered her unfinished question. '*White* magic, lady —no hint of witchcraft. Alchemy's but an extended part of medicine.'

'Aye, to be sure,' Ursula agreed quickly. 'Would I knew more of those arts. Can you gentlemen tell me if my brimstone purge should be distilled i' the full o' the moon, and should I put in egg-white? I've no luck with it, 'twon't come clear.'

John Dee answered her thoughtfully. He always gave serious attention to such queries. He was indeed a serious man.

Julian respected him. He was grateful for the new friendship between them, and the invitation to share Dee's lodgings. He had moved in by Christmas, glad to have found a companion who had travelled widely on the continent, whose scholastic background was sound—and more important—a man whom Queen Mary respected for his astrological skills, which Julian admitted were superior to his own. Dee had cast

347

the Queen's horoscope. He had, however, also cast that of the banished Princess Elizabeth who had known him from childhood, since his cousin Blanche Parry had been Elizabeth's nurse, and was now confidential maid of honour to the Princess. Julian had examined the forecasts which confirmed his own opinion that of the two royal sisters, the younger was the one to support. *Not* an opinion to be voiced in any quarter. Neither Dee nor he discussed it even privately. Elizabeth had quickly fallen from favour, and retired to Ashridge. By December, Mary's brief warmth had chilled to suspicion and jealousy of the brilliant, fascinating rival.

Celia listened vaguely to her aunt's animated questions. Her head throbbed again, she wished they had not come. She wished that she had not worn the red and yellow gown. It seemed to bring ill luck. Fleetingly, she wondered what had happened to Simkin. He had disappeared from Cowdray before they came to London, just vanished one night, and Wat turned surly at the mention of his son's name. But I'm *here*, at Court, among the greatest in the land, Celia said to herself. I should be happy. Yet she felt neglected and forlorn.

A man touched her arm, saying, 'Mistress de Bohun?'

She turned and looked up at Sir John Hutchinson. 'Blessed Jesu!' she said. 'By the Mass, sir, you startled me,' and she smiled. Celia's smile with the dimple at one corner of her lips and the little teeth like daisy petals was so radiant that the stout knight inhaled quickly. He thought the gladness was for him, his heart thumped. Whereas Celia smiled only in relief at the sight of a familiar face who approached her with obvious admiration.

'I m-meant to see you sooner,' said Hutchinson, stammering like a lad. 'I've thought o' ye so much, Mistress Celia, but I fell ill after the n-night I met ye . . .' He paused. Actually, he had been laid up with a ferocious attack of gout which had spread from his right great toe to all his joints, but he did not wish to admit to such an elderly disease.

'Did ye think at all o' me?' he added, touching her cheek.

'Once and again,' she said, lying kindly. 'I've been ill, too.' The reminder brought on a brief spasm of coughing.

'Ye shouldn't be abroad in this weather,' cried the knight, instantly alarmed. 'Ye should be cared for, cosseted, your lady aunt's neglectful.' He looked angrily at Ursula who was by now aware of the addition to their group, though quite unable to remember Hutchinson, except that he had been at the Priory.

'My aunt's *not* neglectful,' Celia cried. 'She's kind and careful of me always!'

'What's all this?' Ursula came forward. 'Have you need to defend me, sweeting? Sir, I know we've met, but confess I've not your name.'

'John Hutchinson, Knight, from Boston i' Lincolnshire, widower, clothier, Member o' the Merchant Adventurers' Company, kin by m'late wife to Lord Clinton, worth about ten thousand pounds, even at the present sorry rate if more o' my cargoes to Calais don't sink.'

'Well-a-day . . . God-a-mercy,' said Ursula. 'Whate'er you be, Sir John, you've enough breath in your lungs.'

'I never beat 'round the bush,' he said. 'Waste o' time.' His shrewd blue eyes looked directly into Ursula's, and she had little doubt of his meaning, as she saw him glance at Celia, and the yearning softness in his square heavy-jowled face. She also saw that Celia was unaware. The girl merely looked amused, a bit puzzled.

'Can't talk now, not i' this hurly-burly,' said Sir John. 'I'll stop by the Priory tomorrow morn. Take her home to bed, my lady, mind she keeps out o' draughts.' He bowed and swung away, limping slightly, through the crowd.

Ursula flushed and bit her lips. Her immediate response was anger. How dared a fat, rustic old clothier tell her how to treat Celia! How dared he covet her treasure! The man was nothing but a tradesman and as old as she. He'd not get past the porter when he came straddling up to the Priory.

'Ah, you are perturbed, poor Lady Southwell,' said Julian softly. He had watched all the by-play, and, as had sometimes happened to him in regard to Ursula and Celia, the present slipped out of focus. The noisy courtiers, the music, the bright-lit palace halls wavered and dissolved. It seemed that he stood alone with the women in a place of shadows, and he was tied to them by poignant silvery threads of sympathy—or no, though there was sympathy, it was more that they were all entangled in a cobweb from which he might free them—if— *si voglio veramente*—if I truly want to—yet if that cobweb were not flimsy stuff? If they were all enmeshed in fine steel filaments, what then? And I'm no classic hero with a battle-axe to hack through, Julian thought, sharply derisive. Still, as he looked pityingly at Ursula, her face seemed to alter. The

349

raw-boned Anglo-Saxon features, the wrinkles, the grey hair became transparent, behind them was another younger face with olive skin, and wistful dark eyes, a face he had once loved and grievously hurt—sometime before the bounds of memory began.

He bent near to Ursula. 'You must leave London,' he whispered. 'Take Celia quickly, go home to Cowdray! Tomorrow!'

'*Cowdray!*' Ursula recoiled. 'Why, Master Julian, the ways are frozen, they're hip-deep in snow. Sir Anthony would never permit it. Besides,' she added, her voice trembling, 'he needs me here to regulate the maids, and sometimes be his hostess. There's naught for us at Cowdray.'

'There is *safety*,' said Julian below his breath, 'for Celia, then?'

She stared at him in disbelief and resentment. 'And since when are you so concerned for our safety? You've twice shown us to be a bother.'

Julian sighed. His foreboding vanished. '*Da vero*,' he said shrugging, 'that may be so. I've become infected by Dr. Dee's visions, his necromancies. I, Guiliano di Ridolfi, Master Physician, should not maunder of omens and warnings like a gypsy crone. My apologies, lady—'tis stifling in here. I see that the Queen's Grace and her nobles have left for the Banqueting Hall. Shall we all seek supper, too?'

*   *   *

Ursula had no need to confront Sir John Hutchinson the next morning. He did not come to the Priory, because the impatient and infatuated knight had waylaid Sir Anthony after supper in Whitehall Palace. Anthony told Ursula about it when he summoned her to his privy closet.

'The old clothier is besotted over your Celia,' said Anthony laughing. 'He wishes to wed her at once. He cares naught for dowry, he'd take her in her shift. He seems to think she loves him. What has that maiden been up to?'

'Nothing,' said Ursula sharply. 'Until last night she's not seen him since the puppet-show. Sir Anthony . . . such a match would be preposterous. I hope . . . hope you didn't encourage him.'

'No, I sent him packing. Though, mind you, Hutchinson's a stalwart man and a knight well thought of in merchant circles. Rich, too. To be sure, he's near old enough to be her grandfather, but Celia soon widowed, possessed of respectable estates—even though they *be* in Lincolnshire—would then have wider choice. One must be sensible.'

Ursula caught her breath. Her eyes stung. 'Why then did you send him off?' she whispered.

Anthony was astonished. 'My dear Lady Ursula—the man's a *Protestant*! He's of that stiff-necked canting lot the eastern counties seem to breed. The lot we've just stifled forever—I pray. Oh, I've no doubt in his moon-calf state he'd overlook her faith, but she'd be undermined—a wife obeys her husband.'

'Blessed Jesu . . .' breathed Ursula on a long sigh of relief. 'Then the matter is closed. Sir Anthony . . .' She paused, went on with a rush, 'We're not too much burden for you? Someone has said we should go back to Cowdray. I try . . . we both try to be of use . . .'

Anthony pulled some letters towards him, and began to read. 'You are—you're most useful,' he said absently, frowning at a Latin missive from Ambassador Renard. 'The Devil take it,' he said, 'the man might be writing in cipher for all I understand of his dark hints and allusions—where's Stephen? Pull the bell-rope, lady. Pray *he* can make sense of this. He's an able Latinist. Godsbody, where *is* that monk? He's for ever running over to my lord Bishop's palace, gaggle o' his brethren there. Skimps his duty to *me*, and I fear there's trouble a-coming.'

'Trouble . . .?' said Ursula timidly. 'What trouble could there be, sir, now the rightful Queen's safe on her throne?'

Anthony made an exasperated noise, but his face cleared as Stephen walked in. 'High time,' Anthony said. 'You'd think us plague-ridden here, the way you avoid us. What's this drivel mean?' He pushed Renard's letter at Stephen who scanned it rapidly.

'I gather,' said Stephen, 'that the Ambassador sniffs a serious rebellion; that we must prepare. His spies daily report alarming news. He suspects that the rebels might attack London from here—from Southwark. He asks you to rally and arm all your men.'

Anthony stared at his chaplain. 'I don't believe it . . . oh, we had indications here on All Saints' Day, but that has died down, and that hot-head Thomas Wyatt went home like a lamb to Kent.'

351

'The lamb is mustering an army in Kent,' said Stephen drily. 'We too have our spies reporting at the Bishop's palace, and 'tis not only Wyatt—Courtenay's gathering forces in the south under Sir Peter Carew, and the old Duke of Suffolk—he's up to no good, either. He'd his daughter on the throne for nine days, and no doubt 'd like her back there again. Though I'd say *that* poor little chit isn't apt to rouse the country. The other one may.'

'*What* other one? What rebellion?' cried Ursula, who had been standing bewildered, near the fireplace.

Both young men turned. They had forgotten her. Anthony smiled. 'No need to fret, Lady Ursula,' he said kindly. 'It'll all blow over.'

'*What* will?' asked Ursula, drawing herself up, her eyes stern.

She had never asserted herself with Anthony and he was surprised. His instinct was to put her off with vague phrases, as he would have his late wife. Ladies—unless they were royal, of course—should take no part in men's affairs. Women had their special functions, they might be courteously deferred to if they were of noble blood like Lady Jane, they should be fondled in bed, bear the necessary heirs, they should supervise certain of the servants in domestic matters—but otherwise . . .

'I'm not as stupid as I sometimes seem,' said Ursula. 'If we are to be endangered here in Southwark, I *demand* to know precisely why.'

'And you should, lady,' said Stephen suddenly, as Anthony continued to look startled. 'I'll tuck the answer in a nutshell. Did you not understand the puppet-show we had here in November?'

Ursula hesitated. 'It seemed to mimic the Queen's forthcoming marriage to Prince Philip o' Spain. And what of that? Seems very suitable.'

'Aye,' said Stephen, 'you think like Her Majesty. Most of England does not. They think we'll become a Spanish vassal, they think that we'll be subjects of His Holiness, the Pope. To prevent such an outcome a great many Englishmen are itching to revolt. They are about to do so. Is that clear?'

She nodded, gazing in surprise at the monk. Even in the confessional she had never heard him so forceful.

'Since I know your discretion,' Stephen went on, 'I'll answer your second question. The "other one" who, if she is not active in plotting, is at least the darling hope of the Protestant factions, is the Princess Elizabeth.'

'I see . . .' said Ursula, after a moment. She did not say how much else she saw. How much was at stake for all of them here. Not only the free observance of their religion, but Anthony's future, his revenues, his promised peerage. 'Thank you, Brother Stephen,' she said quietly. 'Thank you, Sir Anthony, for your forbearance—and your handling of Celia's matter.'

Stephen jerked his head up and frowned. 'Celia? What of her?'

'Oh . . .' said Anthony, shrugging, 'she's enchanted that gouty old lobcock from Boston, John Hutchinson—remember? I suppose he wants to beget a son while he can, his wife was barren.'

Stephen made a quick gesture. 'Plenty of girls besides Celia for *that*!' His face flushed, his tone was curiously muffled.

'Aye, to be sure,' said Anthony, dipping his quill pen in the silver inkwell, 'but the fellow wants Celia. He's crazily desirous of her. Autumn lust.'

'It's indecent . . .' said Stephen in the same muffled voice.

'Nay, quite honourable. Sorry for the poor old goat, pity he's a heretic. As I was saying to Lady Ursula, it's hard to find Celia such a good match.'

'Wi' her wanton tricks, she'll find *someone* to bed her,' said Stephen. 'I doubt you can guard her maidenhead long, lady, she has *le diable au corps*.'

'Whatever that means,' Ursula snapped, 'I dislike it! Monk or not, you've no right to slander Celia. You've grown hard, Brother Stephen. I no longer see the gentle godliness you often showed at Cowdray.'

The dark flush deepened on his lean face. His hand went to the golden crucifix given to him by the Bishop of Winchester. 'I serve God better than I did then,' he said angrily.

'I trust *He* thinks so,' Ursula retorted, and swept out, her skirts twitching.

'Tush, tush—costamaree.' Anthony chuckled at the sight of his chaplain's face. 'Ye should know better than insult her jewel, and you spoke undue harsh. Cease glowering, and help me with the list o' my retainers. Pity I've so few here. Must send Wat for those at Cowdray and Battle Abbey. 'Twill take time to get 'em in this bloody weather with all the weapons and armour.'

'What have you in store at Byfleet?' asked Stephen in his normal tone, referring to the neglected little manor house in nearby Surrey, where Anthony's father had died.

'Not much, I fear, a few suits o' rusty mail, some pikes and halberds. The inventories 're in that coffer—will ye fetch 'em?'

'So you believe *now* there'll be a revolt?' said Stephen as he complied.

'Aye . . . Renard's no fool, and I've just remembered Courtenay's behaviour at the palace last night, his meaning whispers behind his hand to Ambassador de Noialles and the Duke o' Suffolk, transparent as a child, so callow and overbearing I can't stomach him. Yet, I see the danger.'

'And welcome it?' asked Stephen, lifting his brows.

Anthony made a rueful sound of assent. He had never known battle, as had his father, old Sir Anthony, who never tired of recounting his exploits against the Scots, and at the sieges of Morlaix and Boulogne under King Henry. Real fighting, not the chivalric games of tournaments and jousts which had amused King Edward. Never consciously, yet deep in Anthony was the awareness that all his inheritance—the manors, the revenues—was entirely due to the various exploits of his powerful father whom he had respected and feared.

'I note,' he said looking at the inventory, 'that there's a falconet by Byfleet. We'll need it to defend the Bridge. Now which of my men'd know enough to prime and fire it?'

'Possibly old Hobson,' said Stephen thoughtfully. 'Wasn't he your father's armourer?'

Anthony nodded. He entered zestfully into preparatory measures with Stephen.

*   *   *

On January 31 the rebel army was seventeeen miles from Southwark at Dartford, and there was no longer any doubt as to a national crisis. Panic flared over London. The citizens were frightened by the threat to their homes, and many of them were sympathetic to the rebels. The monstrous spectre of Spanish rule, and the Spanish Inquisition, outweighed loyalty to Mary's commands. Even the Mayor and Aldermen began to doubt the wisdom of obeying the new-made Queen.

During the two weeks after Twelfth Night, Anthony and Stephen kept trying to evaluate the constant rumours. The rising in the West had collapsed. Sir Peter Carew had fled to

France where he would command an invading army of French soldiers. The Duke of Norfolk had disappeared into the Midlands with a view to rousing central England. Certainly his Southwark palace across the High Street from Anthony's Priory was of a sudden, shuttered and lifeless. A Sir James Croft had started to gather forces in Wales, nobody knew whether he had arrived there. The young Earl of Devonshire had boasted mightily in his cups that soon he would be King, that several armies marched on London in his behalf. Then, he too vanished from Court. The only certainty was the rising in Kent under Sir Thomas Wyatt. He had conquered the city of Rochester and sent a defiant message through emissaries that he meant to imprison the Queen. There were threats against her life made by Wyatt's more incautious adherents.

Anthony galloped across the Bridge from London back to Southwark on February 1. He raced up the Priory stairs, flung his hat on a table and cried to his assembled household, 'The Queen's done it! God save and keep her. Ye should've heard her! Brave as a little lion, beguiling as a dove, she won over all the wavering cowards at the Guildhall. London's arming at last!'

Ursula, Celia and Mabel stared at him with varying degrees of startled alarm. During the last days they had grown accustomed to a small encampment of Anthony's men in the cloister garth, to guards in coat mail and helmets cluttering up the passageways, or cramming the kitchen, grumbling and shivering. Wat's efforts at recruiting had been seriously hampered by the weather, and by a slithery reluctance he had encountered on all Anthony's manors. The able-bodied men to whom he showed Anthony's orders hemmed and hawed, they made excuses or they nodded solemnly and then never showed up at the appointed time for the march to Southwark. Barely a score of them had arrived.

'You mean the Queen's Grace made a speech?' Ursula asked uncertainly. 'I thought she'd fled to Windsor.'

'Not *she*,' cried Anthony. 'She marched herself and her ladies to the Guildhall, I tell you—and she shamed that greasy Mayor and his Aldermen. They'll fight for her now! The City'll fight. It was superb! King Harry'd've been proud of his daughter!'

'Was Maggie there with the Queen?' asked Celia enviously. The three women had been lately mewed up again at the

Priory for safety's sake, as well as by the continuing bad weather.

'That she was,' Anthony turned to smile at the girl. 'Ye can't miss Magdalen Dacre, a goddess o' the Northland, that one. She was praying, too, I could see her lips move. I like piety in a woman. Oh, Wat—' He broke off as his doughty retainer strode in. 'We've action at last! London's in arms!'

'Bigod.' Wat spat contemptuously into the fire. 'High time. I thought they'd never get off their arses. The baker's boy run in ter say that Wyatt has four thousand men at Black'eath, but the lad's gi'en to fits, an' I heard just *now* Wyatt's crossin' Thames at Deptford. Our men 're fair sick o' this shilly-shally waiting about. Many o' them've gone to the Bankside stews, at least the whores give 'em *something* to do.'

'Round them up—and quick!' said Anthony, wolfing down a meat pasty. 'We've got to march 'em over the Bridge before it's blown up, which my Lords Pembroke and Clinton have ordered.'

'*Them* two,' said Wat in disgust. 'Since when're they in charge? Where's the Duke o' Norfolk?'

Anthony rapidly explained the events of the day. The octogenarian Duke of Norfolk having lost Rochester for the Queen had been relieved of command. Bishop Gardiner had counselled the appointments of the Earl of Pembroke and Lord Clinton in his place.

'Slippery as eels, both of 'em,' said Wat. 'And for maziness, bunglings, choppings and changings, this is the stoopidest broil I e'er heard of. Don't even know which side the river Wyatt's attacking—if he is.'

'They do think he'll cross to the North Bank,' said Anthony. 'He has all those boats he commandeered, seems likely he'd try to take the Tower.'

Celia listened with a feeling of unreality. It was like a gory play she had been to see at Blackfriars. The men were excited, they mouthed and they gestured, but you knew that presently, the mummery would end. The players would bow, the candles be extinguished, the stage go blank and one would go home. I wish I were far away, she thought, the Western Isles where the air is soft and warm, where the sands are made of gold, the trees bend low with fruits like peaches, only sweeter—and someone I love holds my hand.

Her reverie was broken by the appearance of Stephen in the Hall. He joined the men, and though quieter than they, she saw that he, too, was intense, that he made sharp comments. She saw that with a rueful gesture he refused the shirt of fine linked mail Anthony offered him. She heard Anthony say, 'Oh, put it on! Those heretics'll not respect the cloth. I hear they've killed a priest in Maidstone. Besides, I want you to stay here and guard the women. I'll leave ye four men. You don't have to bear arms if it's against your sacred conscience, but you can certainly give orders.'

Stephen nodded. He inspected his charges.

Ursula was tight-lipped and composed, most of her thoughts dealt with shortages. Anthony's guard had consumed all their bread. The usual bags of flour had not arrived from Surrey. The ale was gone, too, and the nearby taverns refused to sell anything but small beer which the men detested. Fuel was low, both wood and sea-coal, since the kitchen fires roared constantly. Ursula's foot tapped as she made a mental tally.

Mabel had reverted to doleful dumps. She had not seen Gerald after the crisis started. She crouched yawning by the fire, and poked it listlessly from time to time.

Stephen looked last at Celia and encountered her own brooding meditative gaze full on. It gave him a shock.

Since the night of All Saints when Celia's wanton behaviour had provoked him to angry admonishment, Stephen had been far too busy with Sir Anthony's affairs and his own congenial visits to the Bishop's palace for thoughts of Celia, whom he felt that he rather disliked. A chit of fifteen, a foolish child at best—an example of Satan's fleshly lures at worst. In either case, to be ignored.

The steady enigmatic look she was giving him from those wide eyes was not childish. Nor did it hold any trace of coquetry. There was both intimacy, and something withheld —an ancient wisdom—in her unwavering eyes, and he could not look away while he felt his pulses begin to pound, and heat seemed to sear through his veins. He grabbed his golden crucifix, and jerked around to Anthony.

'Kneel!' he commanded. 'We will say three Paters and three Aves for protection and divine help.'

Anthony started at him, astonished by the harshness in Stephen's voice.

After a moment they all obeyed—Anthony, the women, Wat, the handful of servers and guardsmen who were in the Hall.

357

The men uncovered, they clasped their hands, and gazed up at Stephen. They murmured in unison, echoing the prayers of their fierce young priest who seemed rather to be giving battle commands than invocations to God and the Blessed Virgin.

'Very proper,' said Ursula, suddenly relaxing when Stephen had blessed them with two sharp strokes in the air, 'Hark!' she jumped. 'What's that?'

They listened to three distant booms which rattled the Priory windows.

'Tower guns, lady,' said Anthony. 'They're trying 'em out, unless the rebels've been sighted over there. Wat, for Christ's sake, hasten before they destroy the Bridge—I'll never get us across by water in time.'

*   *   *

Sir Thomas Wyatt's troops marched into Southwark two days later, on Saturday, February 3. Until the Borough citizens actually heard the trampings and hoofbeats on the Bermondsey road, confusion as to Wyatt's plans had continued. An uncertainty shared by Wyatt himself, who had wasted hours precious to his cause at Deptford, while he received one bit of catastrophic news after the other. The ultimate blow was the defection of the Duke of Suffolk, who, instead of rousing the Midlands, had been caught ignominiously hiding in a tree in Warwickshire. Sir Thomas, bereft now of all support but his Kentishmen and some London turncoats, who had joined him at Rochester, nevertheless continued his plans for attack. He held his head high, he rode his horse proudly as he reassured the few frightened faces peering through shutter cracks along the way. 'We'll not harm ye folks! We've no quarrel wi' *you*. Come out! Come out true Englishmen, 'less ye wish to be ground 'neath the iron heel o' Spain!'

But the citizens remained quaking behind their barred doors. Nothing moved on the streets of Southwark but Wyatt's army and a few mangy curs.

Wyatt marched straight for London Bridge, and found the centre drawbridge lying in pieces in the Thames, while on the London side a battery of guns had been mounted. He did not tell his troops who were milling around St. Saviour's precincts, and through the frozen gardens belonging to the Bishop of Winchester's palace. He consulted with his lieutenants, Rudstone and Isley. They decided to repair the Bridge despite the danger of bombardment. There were now no boats on the Surrey bank, no shipping on the Thames, which was, moreover, filled with ice floes. The short winter day faded. The rebels lit torches; by the sudden appearance of a thousand moving lights in Southwark, Anthony, irretrievably stuck on the London side, first discovered the whereabouts of Wyatt's forces and cursed his decision to leave the Priory so ill-guarded. Yet he could do nothing for them over there, so he said a quick prayer and went to his Queen at Whitehall. He found her calm, but all her ladies except Magdalen were in a state of moaning fright. Magdalen was bracing. ' 'Tis mooch lak a Border Raid,' she said gaily, 'yet on a grander scale i' truth, but whimperin's an' whinin's 'll do ye na guid, ladies.' Thus she rallied her fellow maids of honour. 'Ye *can* fight iffen ye must, ye'll find. I've broke the pate o' a scurvy sneakin' Scot mesel' when I had ta.'

Anthony chuckled, and the Queen actually smiled. Mary continued to show the exalted courage which had inspired her to make the Guildhall speech.

On the Southwark bank Wyatt set his men to digging a trench for great safety from bombardment, and he did his best to rally the spirits of his army. He told them that they would be delayed for a day or two in Southwark, and must commit no vandalism. They must pay for food and drink at the taverns, they must mar no property. He hinted at imminent help from French ships which were even now sailing to their aid; he said jauntily that if the Bridge could not soon be repaired, they would move up river to Kingston Bridge and attack London through Westminster. Victory was almost at hand. His men cheered him, a work-force shovelled and banged at the frozen earth to make a trench. Wyatt's sentries patrolled the south end of the broken bridge.

At eleven in the bitter chill night there came the disturbance at the Priory's portal which Stephen had been half-expecting. He had gathered all the women in the Hall, not only Ursula and the two girls, but the laundry, pantry and chambermaids, including little Agnes Snoth, Ursula's crippled serving-woman. Nine of them in all. The women munched the precious raisins Ursula had provided from the locked coffer in the pantry. Stephen sat at one end of the High Table, peering at his Breviary, his lips moving automatically. Celia stood by one of the lancet windows, straining to see the men beneath flickering torches around St. Saviour's porch.

They all heard the thudding of gun butts on the huge oaken door in the Priory portal. A shot crashed through glass, there was a man's anguished yelp.

'What's ado below?' asked Ursula quietly. 'Sounds as though they were trying to get in.'

'Aye,' said Stephen, shutting his Breviary as he rose. 'Stay here, everyone, don't budge.' He went out and barred the Hall door behind him. He walked downstairs to the last step, and saw the entrance filled with armed men. The portal door was wide open. The porter cowed in the alcove. Anthony's guards, though still struggling, had been securely bound with ropes and thrown in a heap by the latrine. The cook and his scullions were herded in the kitchen, one of Wyatt's archers held them at bay with an arquebus.

Thomas Wyatt himself, his sword drawn, advanced to meet Stephen at the stair's foot.

'Well-a-day, good Brother,' he said with a swift ironic look. 'Benedicite! Pray forgive the intrusion, but I have bethought me that Sir Anthony's mansion is admirably situated for my headquarters. Nobody'll be harmed if ye do as I command.'

'And what is that?' said Stephen instinctively, stretching out his arms to guard the staircase. 'You promised no violence, I heard you, yet you've overpowered my guards.'

Wyatt gave a snort. ' 'Twas easy as sucking eggs! Sir Anthony might've left you a braver lot. I saw from the street you've a falconet on the north turret. I've a mind to send up a few o' my best archers, and a gunner to keep the cannon aimed in the proper direction.'

Stephen's hands gripped the stone rails. 'I forbid you to mount these stairs, I forbid you in the Name of God, on peril of eternal damnation!' His voice rang strident and clear.

Wyatt winced, he stared at the tall black figure and its outstretched arms. He saw the golden crucifix. The convictions of his childhood—long forgotten—swayed him for a trice. Then he recovered.

'What, so hot, my pretty priest? Ye've missed your calling, Brother. Weapons may convince, but never angry words. Get out of my way!'

He raised his sword and struck Stephen a fierce blow on the shoulder with the flat of the blade. The monk was thrown off balance and fell to his knees on the stone floor. Wyatt gestured to his men.

'Oh, tie him up. Throw him in with the others! The rest of you come with *me*.'

Wyatt leapt up the staircase followed by some thirty of his men. He unbarred the Hall and went inside. The cowering women stared at him. A laundry maid shrieked. Mabel clutched at a wall-hanging and made snuffling noises. Ursula advanced towards him, followed by Celia.

'Good evening, Sir Thomas,' said Ursula with freezing dignity. 'Your entrance lacks ceremony. What have you done with Brother Stephen and our guards?'

Wyatt bowed, his eyes darting around the Hall which obviously contained no men, then they paused on Celia. 'You've naught to fear, lady,' he said to Ursula. 'Remain here—yet, I need a guide, I believe. This old place is a warren o' passages, *You*, my poppet.' He touched Celia on the arm. 'Some weeks ago I sang you love songs, you may repay them now.'

'And if I will not go?' said Celia with perfect self-possession, while Ursula gave a stifled sound, and the rest of the women gasped.

'Then, I must force you, darling,' answered Wyatt and grabbed her around the waist.

'*Go* with him, Celia!' cried Mabel on a sudden hiccuping wail. 'Do what he says, or we'll all be killed.'

'I doubt that,' said Celia. 'Sir Thomas is a courteous knight, or all his views are misguided. Certes, I'll go, no need to make a pother.'

And she smiled in her most enchanting manner—the dimple, the sideways look between fringed lashes.

Wyatt was as taken aback as the women—and then delighted. Celia's smile promised and lured. After he had attended to deploying his men, to covering the Bridge and the trench from the Priory roof, there would be time before dawn, time for plucking the fair juicy fruit which was offered.

He swept Celia out of the Hall and re-barred the great door. The girl laughed. All her broodings and miseries were eclipsed by giddy excitement. Here was a rebel leader, a man of war and action, and she had him in her power. She liked the feel of his rough grasp around her waist, she liked the cold hardness of his mailed shirt against her arm. 'Celia the wanton and fair,' he had sung to her. As she darted with him through the angled passages, up and down steps towards the north garret, she heard again the wooing tones of the lute as

361

he had played it to her in the autumn, and she felt in these wild thoughtless moments only the joy of being wanted — and of escape.

She led Wyatt to the door leading up to the turret where old Hobson guarded the falconet. Wyatt's men thundered after them. She drew back, waiting among the rafters, protecting the candle as a blast of air from the north rushed through the opened door. It stung her cheeks and cut her breath. She was aware of a scuffle above her, then a triumphant shout from Wyatt.

The men climbed down the stout ladder carrying something. They laid it on the dusty garret planks.

' 'E's still alive. Tough old bastard,' said a voice, 'put up more fight nor all the rest o' them Sussex lily-livers at the portal.'

Celia stared down stupidly. She saw that the bundle was old Hobson, and that a blackish trickle ran from the corner of his lips into his beard. She bent closer with her candle. 'Blood . . .?' she whispered, recoiling. 'You've killed him?' She stared at Wyatt.

'Nay, nay, sweetheart,' said the knight impatiently. 'He'll recover. Look after him, men! Now, Celia, lead me to a warmer chamber, there must be one that o'erlooks the river. Come, maiden, what ails thee? Ye act dazed!'

'There's only my room . . .' she said on a thin whisper, scarcely heeding him. Hobson was a merry old man. Since his arrival from Surrey he had enlivened the entire Priory by his kindly japes, his fund of tunes and catches, his unvarying good humour. And now his face was become as grotesque as the hideous carved bosses in St. Saviour's, his tongue lolled out besides the brownish ooze which stained his beard, his eye-balls showed white between his twitching lids, a rattling sound came from his throat. When one of Wyatt's men picked him up and flung him across his padded shoulder, there was a gurgle and a rush of blood cascading to the floor planks.

Wyatt grabbed the girl's arms and whirled her around so that she could not see Hobson. 'To your chamber,' he cried, annoyed by the unfortunate episode, aware that the atmosphere of amorous sport had been ruptured, that the girl's coquetry had vanished and she would need forcing.

'To your chamber, my dear.' He now made his voice soft and persuasive. ' 'Tis *only* that I may have a view of the river and the Bridge, you know.' He lifted a strand of her rich gold hair and kissed it. 'Here's the shining net which has caught me in its meshes, snared fast, in thrall to love.'

No one had ever talked to Celia like that, and she quivered. She went with him mutely down the back passages, all dark and empty, to the northern front of the Priory and the room she shared with Ursula. It was warmer there, seacoal embers still glowed ruddy in the gate.

'Yonder is the river-side window,' she said pointing.

Wyatt laughed. 'A pox on the window! I see only the bed, sweetheart, and a goodly one, too.' He waved his hand towards the carved oak four-poster, the red brocade curtains drawn back with silken cords to disclose down pillows and a rich counterpane embroidered in a flowery pattern by Ursula.

Wyatt, struggling and cursing beneath his breath, unhooked his chain mail shirt. It fell to the rushes in a slithery heap. He began to untie the points of his hose, unbutton his cod-piece.

'What are you doing ...?' whispered Celia, drawing back against the cupboard.

'Don't act the innocent wi' me ...' said Wyatt, savagely breaking one of the tangled tapes. 'We've not much time. Can't leave my men long.'

'Time ...' breathed Celia. She shrank harder against the cupboard, her arms hugged across her bosom in the im-memorial gesture of threatened virginity.

He looked at her with exasperation which changed swiftly to lust.

'You were warm enough i' the Hall, warm enough last All Saints—I'm not going to play the gallant now. I've not had a woman in weeks—an' ye *brought* me here!' He strode across the room and grabbed her, ripping open her bodice with one violent tear, while he bent and bit her neck. Celia screamed and scratched his face.

'Scream away,' Wyatt panted, 'an it pleasures you. There's nobody to listen. You little bitch, you're a nuisance!'

He pinioned her arms and was dragging her to the bed when the door opened and Stephen stood appalled on the threshold. He had been untied by Wyatt's guards in order to give old Hobson the last rites, and then had searched the Priory when Celia was missing from the Hall.

Wyatt dropped Celia and shouted, 'Get outa here, you piddling eunuch!'

Stephen went white. He yanked off his crucifix; it fell on Wyatt's chain mail shirt. He moved in one lithe motion and

363

hit Wyatt full on the tip of his bearded jaw. The knight grunted, 'Oof,' and collapsed on the rushes. Stephen and Celia both stood frozen, side by side, while St. Saviour's bell clanged out once.

Wyatt sat up slowly, waggling his head to free his brain from the Catherine wheels and shooting stars. He felt his chin gingerly. As his vision cleared he gaped up at the two who stood over him.

''Odsbody,' he said feebly, 'pardee—who'd've guessed it —the monk, the mighty monk an' the maiden, ye bestow your charms in odd quarters, m'dear—yet I'm grateful to ye, Brother Stephen, ye've recalled me to my duty. Procrastination is a grievous fault, one I seldom harbour—'tis *rashness* I've been accused of . . .' He got up carefully, and pulled up his hose. He buttoned his cod-piece. He plucked Stephen's crucifix from atop his mail shirt and tossed the golden cross into the coal-scuttle. He pulled on his armour and sword belt. He went to the embrasured window, opened it and peered out. 'Bigod!' he cried, 'there's a boat down there off the South Bank, she means to shoot the Bridge i' the tide-rip—I forbade it—'tis treachery. Hark! the gunfire—my sentries.'

There was a rumble and white flash. The Priory's old stones vibrated.

' 'Tis the falconet!' Wyatt cried in malice, in triumph. 'Sir Anthony's falconet! Thank ye, m'dear, for showing me to the turret.' He seized his brass helmet from the stool where he had flung it, made Celia a mocking bow and ran out, banging the door behind him.

Still Stephen and the girl did not move. Then they turned with one accord and looked at each other.

Celia saw his face, naked, young, defenceless, as she had never seen it. She drew a sobbing breath. 'Oh, my dear, dear love . . .' she whispered and ran into his arms. He held her close, yet as though she were a sacred chalice. He trembled as with ague, seeing her naked breasts tipped by coral pressed against his black woollen chest.

'Holy Virgin, forgive me,' he whispered and bending his head kissed her soft open lips.

Weakened by a flood of rapture, she staggered and clung.

He lifted her on to the bed.

She moaned as he kissed her breasts, 'Dear love, dear heart—' pressing herself upwards against him, feeling through his habit the hardness of his desperate manhood on her thighs, on her belly.

They did not know that a chill wind rushed through from the opened window, they did not hear the booming of the Tower cannon, nor the cannon balls which splashed in the Thames or thudded beyond the Priory in the Bankside fields.

He spoke only once in a groan so violent it sounded like anger. 'I love thee, Celia, my God forgive me . . .'

'Nay, nay . . .' she whispered, kissing his neck, his ear and the fringe of soft dark hair on his forehead, 'do not think, my love,' and she pulled his head down between her warm white breasts. 'What more than this can God give? Take me, Stephen —only so can we bear it.'

He shuddered, kissed again her breasts and her moist red mouth which smelled of violets. His pounding heart shook her slender body, yet her own heart had slowed to a honey-sweet calm of expectancy.

It was a whispered 'Jesu!' and the noise of stifled weeping which at last they heard. The room was barely lit by dying coals, but the light of a rush-dip glimmered above the bed.

Stephen turned slowly on his back, then rose. Celia looked up into Ursula's face. It was contorted with anguish, tears running down the furrowed cheeks.

'Don't weep, dearest aunt,' Celia spoke from out the honey-sweet calm, the languorous dream.

'Cover your paps, you miserable hussy!' Ursula cried, and threw her head-veil over the girl. 'Jesu! Jesu! That I should live to see—oh, monstrous . . .' Her voice stifled in a sob.

Stephen walked around the bed, and put his hand on Ursula's shoulder. 'Aye, monstrous,' he said in a voice of great sadness. 'But, she is *not* harmed, Lady Ursula. I love the girl more than myself, almost more than my vows. I did not know it 'till now.'

Ursula stared at him despairingly through the gloom. 'You base hypocritical priest! How should I believe you've not ravished my niece, and *she*, avid as a cat in season—Oh, I *know* what I saw!'

Stephen walked slowly past her to the coal-scuttle where the crucifix and its chain gleamed in the sooty shadow. He picked up the cross and held it in his hand. 'I swear by this,' he said quietly. 'By the broken Body of Our Lord.'

'Ah . . .' breathed Ursula, 'so much for *this* time, Stephen

Marsdon, and I'll not call you "Brother". Yet when your lusts return, and hers—nay, don't answer! I know a remedy!'

Stephen bowed his head. 'So do I, lady.' He went out and shut the door.

Fourteen

Sir Thomas Wyatt's rebellion was finished in three more days when Wyatt surrendered at Ludgate outside the City walls. He had marched his men from Southwark up-river to Kingston where he crossed the Thames; he had marched them down the North Bank and through Westminster while gathering defeat hung as heavy as the rain clouds, black as the February mud through which they struggled with their gun carriages.

There were conflicts along the way, a few men shot. Hourly there were deserters who saw that French help would never come in time and that the London citizens were aroused to fight *any* invasion of their liberties and made no exception of Wyatt.

On February 7, Wyatt was taken to the Tower. During the next days his ring-leaders joined him there, including Courtenay, and the doddering old Duke of Suffolk. The Queen had a *Te Deum* sung in Westminster Abbey and St. Paul's. Hysteria died down.

And Anthony, in high spirits, came home to the Priory over the repaired drawbridge. A pack-train of provisions had finally arrived from Cowdray; Ursula had been able to order a suitable dinner for the returning warrior who was mightily pleased by his victory over Wyatt's troops in the skirmish at Charing Cross.

'Not much disturbance here, was there?' he asked Ursula jovially. 'I misliked it when I saw the rebels were camping in Southwark, but they didn't stay long.'

'Long enough,' said Ursula sombrely.

'Ah, yes,' Anthony was at once sympathetic. 'That business of Wyatt's breaking in here must have frightened you, and the wounding o' poor old Hobson—and I'm not proud o' my other guards either. Still, the whole matter came to naught. Only lasted a few hours, I hear. Haven't seen Brother Stephen yet—some of the ruffians ransacked the Bishop's Palace and made a muck o' the library. He left me a note saying he'd be back later.'

Ursula tightened her lips. She was dreading this moment. She had waited until Anthony drank a flagon of his favourite sack and consumed the oyster pie she had supervised herself in the kitchen. Lent had begun, and since there could be no meat, she had anxiously selected the substitute Anthony best liked.

'Sir—' she said and paused, moving her silver trencher, fidgeting with the pewter spoon. 'Sir,' she repeated, 'Celia must wed Sir John Hutchinson.' She brought out the sentence on a single gasp.

'*What?*' said Anthony, adjusting his thoughts with difficulty. They had been running on Queen Mary's continuing problems. How much was the Princess Elizabeth involved in the rebellion? What to do with her? And there could be no more clemency towards the doubly treacherous Suffolks.

The old Duke would go to the block, and with him his daughter Lady Jane Grey and her husband, Guilford Dudley. Harsh measures were imperative now if Mary were to keep her throne, and marry the Spanish Prince.

'Celia must wed Sir John Hutchinson,' Ursula repeated more slowly. 'Pray, will you summon the knight at once?'

Anthony gave her his full, startled attention. 'But my dear Lady Southwell, you were hard set against the match. What sea-change is this? And what does Celia say?'

Ursula flushed. Her eyes grew woeful. 'Celia will obey . . .' she said faintly. 'There's much heart-break in the Priory, Sir Anthony, but we can avoid worse.'

'Worse? What *do* you mean, lady?'

'I mean dishonour, I mean ghastly sin,' Ursula clenched her hands then let them fall limply on the table. 'I don't know how to tell you—'

Anthony leaned forward wondering very much that this composed lady should show so much distress.

He questioned her gently, thinking that she always made a fuss about Celia's affairs or well-being, and that this would prove to be another little cupboard-storm.

His indulgent smile faded as he understood the facts. He breathed hard, anger and shock churned his stomach. That Sir Thomas had tried to rape Celia and been thwarted by Stephen was unpleasant enough. But the ensuing scene as he clearly envisioned it from Ursula's halting, scarce-audible words—the shameless girl and his austere chaplain, tumbling and kissing half-naked in the big four-poster . . . Stephen's brazen avowal of love . . .

'Aye, 'tis *sickening*,' cried Anthony. 'Perfidious! I see why

368

Celia must be married quickly and sped off to Lincolnshire . . .
Christ! She may even be wi' child.'

Ursula shuddered. 'He swore not, swore by the Crucifix
that he hadn't pierced her maidenhead. Yet it seems he holds
his vows lightly, and Celia will not speak at all. She weeps—
and stares at me—with eyes of hate.' Ursula's voice broke.

'I'll send Wat for Sir John at once,' Anthony cried. 'But will
he *take* a sullen contumacious bride who may be deflowered
to boot? God's body, what a coil! I thought that lewd monk
my friend, damn him, he shall be bastinadoed—defrocked!
Harlotry like *this* in mine own house. And your false ungrateful trollop of a niece—you say she actually *guided* Wyatt up
to my falconet?' He banged his fist on the table.

Ursula drooped. 'Bitter shame . . .' she whispered. 'I can
make no excuse . . .' She saw that Anthony was seized by one
of his rare rages, and did not blame him. She left the Hall
with dragging feet.

*　　　*　　　*

Celia was married to John Hutchinson on February 22, in
the church porch of Saint Saviour's by the parish priest. There
were no guests. Her only attendants were Ursula, and the
giggling rather contemptuous, Mabel. Anthony, stiff-lipped
and curt, acted as guardian and gave Celia away.

Sir John had brought across the river a fellow merchant,
elderly as himself, to be groomsman. Since Sir John flatly refused to attend the usual nuptial Mass—there was none. The
little party trailed back into the Priory where Anthony had
ordered a wedding feast to be set forth. His anger waned—
after he had talked to Stephen—while natural generosity and
sense of decorum prompted him to some observances due any
maiden married from his house, even at such a sorry hugger-
mugger wedding as this.

There was, however, cause to rejoice that matters weren't
worse, Anthony thought, as he ceremoniously installed Celia
in the High Chair next to his.

Sir John had accepted Celia's hand with such trembling joy
that it was embarrassing to see. He had asked no questions
and obviously attributed Celia's silence, her blind faraway
look, to maidenly modesty.

Nor had Celia to be forced into the marriage by threats or
actual punishment, as Anthony feared. She had shown indifference, remote acquiescence. 'Aye, sir,' she said when

369

Anthony informed her of the wedding, 'Sir John seems kind, and I shall be glad enough to live in Lincolnshire, 'tis all one to me.'

Anthony suspected, and Ursula knew, that Celia's behaviour resulted from a note Stephen had sent her through one of the Bishop's pages before he left Southwark—for France. Anthony's own interview with Stephen had been brief, but assuaged Anthony who found it impossible to utter the outraged accusations he had meant to. The young monk's face was a granite wall, his eyes were iron-cold. 'I am sailing, sir,' he said, 'from Dover on the morrow. I go to Marmoutier with letters from Bishop Gardiner. The Queen's Grace wishes to reinstate the Benedictines at Westminster Abbey. I shall start arrangements and retire to the cloister.'

'But I *need* you, Stephen,' Anthony cried in dismay, forgetting his wrath and the cause of it. 'You're more than chaplain to me, you've become my secretary, my friend . . . and now that . . . well—'

He had meant to say that now Celia would be safely out of the way, there was no need for Stephen to leave, but against the stony look in Stephen's eyes, he found that he could not speak the girl's name.

'Whether I ever return to you as chaplain or no, will be my Superior's decision,' said Stephen. 'I *have* enjoyed a particular attachment to you—not the least of my many sins. Farewell, sir. May Our Blessed Lord and His Holy Mother have you in Their keeping.' He was gone.

Anthony felt sharp personal loss. It was natural that he should resent Celia and the trouble she had caused, nor could he forgive her frivolous disloyalty in siding with Sir Thomas Wyatt. Old Hobson, after a week of spewing blood, suddenly died. They had buried him yesterday in St. Saviour's churchyard. Anthony had directed that Celia be present at the grave. She obeyed with the same doll-like blankness that she now showed at her wedding feast, though her little face held uncanny beauty, like moonlit marble. She stared down at Hobson's shrouded corpse as though it were no more than a bundle of soiled linen readied for laundering.

'Your niece is wi'out heart or conscience!' Anthony said angrily to Ursula. '*She* caused this poor soul's death!'

'She suffers,' said Ursula, and turned on Anthony in a quick flash. 'And did you think her heartless when *you* suffered last

July when Lady Jane died? I saw how Celia tried to comfort you!'

'Aye,' said Anthony slowly. Jane's death seemed years ago.

He glanced at the silent bride beside him. Celia had no new gown, but Ursula had provided her own yellowed lace bride-veil, and twined a chaplet of ivy and gilded wheat ears—the only coronet possible in February.

Anthony looked down his table at his subdued guests.

Ursula made no pretence of eating, she politely inclined her head towards Master Babcock, Sir John's groomsman, but showed no other response. She had aged these last days, her bony shoulders sagged, her generous mouth was drawn to a tight line. She did not even talk to Master Julian whom she had unexpectedly asked to the feast, saying that she and Celia knew nobody else in London. Anthony suggested Magdalen Dacre, and eagerly wrote the invitation himself. But the girl was on duty with the Queen that day. She had sent back startled congratulations, a hamper full of French sugar-plums and a pair of embroidered gloves for Celia.

Mabel was fidgeting, she expected to meet Gerald at the Earl of Arundel's supper party later. The groom himself did not speak, he stared fixedly at his new wife as though she were an apparition, a beatific vision.

St. Mary! what a celebration! Anthony thought, pushed back his chair with a loud scraping, shouted to his minstrels, and raised his goblet. 'Wassail to the bride, wassail to the groom!' He turned to Celia, bowing deeply. 'Come, my lady, we'll begin the dance. A Coranto? We'll make merry!'

Celia started. She looked around and behind her in astonishment. Anthony understood and laughed. ''Tis *you* are "my lady". You've wed a goodly knight, Celia. Think on it! And now that *I* do—Ho! Sir John! *You* come dance wi' your bride!'

The clothier rose majestically, he came forward and took Celia's hand. The fourth finger now wore a heavy golden ring made of two hands clasping a large amethyst heart.

Sir John pulled Celia tight against his stout velvet chest. He bent and whispered in her ear. 'No need for fear, my dearling. I treasure ye more than all the gold of the Indies, and this is the happiest day o' my life.'

She heard his words as through a torrent of rushing water, and clutched his arm.

'There, there, poppet,' said Sir John. 'Ye've no wish to

dance? I'm not so apt at it myself. We'll drink the loving cup together shall we?'

Her bridegroom hefted the great silver punch bowl filled with mulled claret, and containing many sprigs of rosemary, sovereign herb for virility and always included at bridals.

They drank with arms entwined as was customary, then passed the bowl to the others.

'Long life together—may your union prove fruitful, eh?' cried Anthony. He nudged the groom and winked at Celia from an effort to capture the jovial bawdry weddings should evoke. 'Eat hearty of the oysters, Sir John—they fortify a bridegroom!'

Nobody laughed but Master Babcock. The bridegroom himself seemed to wince. His bright blue eyes shifted, the tiny veins reddened in his cheeks.

'We thank'ee, Sir Anthony, for this splendid wedding feast,' he said bowing. 'My little bride seems a-weary, we'd best be leaving now.'

Anthony protested for politeness' sake, though he was relieved. There was no hope of squeezing merriment from this gathering. His musicians, unheeded, strummed and tootled through the music of a galliard—even a rousing rendition of 'Back and side go bare, go bare' caused nobody to join in the chorus. Besides, Anthony was as eager to attend the Arundels' supper party as was Mabel; it was hoped that the Queen would be there. She might bring Magdalen, but in any case there would be many members of the powerful Catholic nobility, eager to celebrate their escape from the danger of Wyatt's Rebellion.

Sir John Hutchinson had hired a chariot to convey his bride across the river to his London lodgings. 'They're not as fine as I could wish for her,' he said to Ursula, as they all stood in the Priory courtyard, 'but my servants have done their best—and soon she'll have all comforts, at my manor near Boston. You'll visit us some day, lady? I know you've a fondness for her, e'en though she's been scarce two years in your charge.' He smiled kindly, with only a trace of condescension.

He perfectly recognised Ursula's position in Sir Anthony's household, as useful dependant, temporary chatelaine, for which John considered her most suitable. He assumed that she had done her duty by Celia from a belated recognition of the blood-tie and its obligations, and must be relieved to get

the girl so well off her hands. In fact, he did not really see
Ursula at all, and looked on with impatience when his bride
touched her beautiful mouth to the widow's white cheek. He
thought Lady Southwell's response a bit excessive—a desperate clutch, a stifled noise like a sob, but no words were
spoken, and Celia came with him docilely, permitted him to
seat her in the place of honour in the waiting chariot. The
coachman flicked the horses. The heavy vehicle lumbered
through the portal towards Borough High Street and London
Bridge. Master Babcock mounted his horse and rode after
them. The porter clanged shut the great oaken door.

'Il cuore lacerato sempre riparase,' said Julian to Ursula,
who was standing where she was on the flagstones when Celia
kissed her goodbye, staring at the shut portal and pressing her
hand to her left breast. She turned and looked at him.

He had instinctively spoken to her in Italian, now he translated in a brisker tone. 'The lacerated heart always repairs
itself, my poor lady—you will see her again. Come, the marriage is not what you hoped for, yet no tragedy either.'

'You don't know . . .' said Ursula. 'I forced her into it, she
hates me now—and had I been her true mother I would've
had more wisdom. I've tried to pray—I can't. The words click
and rattle like the beads—no meaning. And now she's gone.'

'This happens to real mothers, too,' said Julian. He examined her with a quick professional eye. Her skin looked grey,
bluish around the lips. She pressed on her left breast so hard
that the knuckles stood out. 'Have you pain there?' he asked
quietly. 'Is there pain, too, in your arm?' She looked down
at her arm in surprise.

'Aye, I believe so.'

He put his fingers on her pulse. 'You will lie down,' he said.
'I've no remedy with me, but will get one from the apothecary
on the High.'

Ursula permitted Julian to help her upstairs where she lay
panting a little on a bench in the Great Hall, while the bustling servants were clearing away the wedding feast. Julian
took the cushion from Anthony's arm-chair and put it under
her head. She shut her eyes, feeling very weak. She dozed a
little while empty tankards rattled on trays, and two of Anthony's hounds snapped and snarled over a fish-head which
had fallen in the floor rushes.

Julian came back with a glass vial. 'Swallow!' he com-

373

manded. She obeyed without question, while he kept his finger on her pulse, but she looked her question, which he answered promptly.

'Tincture of foxglove,' he said, 'Digitalin, but clumsily distilled. I've some at Dr. Dee's laboratory and will send it tomorrow.'

'Thank you, Julian,' she said. She put her thin white hand on his sleeve. 'Could you ... could you not bring it yourself?'

He looked down at her hand, its raised veins showed purple, but the well-kept nails were as smooth and rosy as a girl's. He knew that her use of his Christian name had been unconscious, just as she was unaware that her physical heart, responding to the wound dealt to what the poets called 'the heart', had suffered a slight failure of function.

He steeled himself with exasperation against pity and a recurrent sense of guilt. She was gaunt, she was quite old—lying there in her black velvet robes she seemed a very effigy of mourning.

Her faded blue eyes looked into his face, then turned towards the corbel on the rafter. 'Aye,' she said, 'I know I'm not comely.' Her hand fell from his arm.

'*Sancta Maria!*' Julian snapped, rising abruptly. 'You will rest now. I fear I can't come tomorrow, though will try to soon. Turn to your religion, lady—that's what it's for, I suppose? And make yourself useful! I told you earlier to go back to Cowdray! You didn't heed me, though possibly nothing would have prevented this wedding you pushed—and now regret. You may find the satisfaction of duty by caring for the twin babes Sir Anthony seems to forget. He's gnawed by ambition—and so, *per Bacco*, am I!'

'You?' she stiffened and looked at him again.

'Aye. I'm now quite certain of my appointment as a Court physician. Furthermore, I've found favour in the eyes of a young lady. Mistress Gwen Owen, who is a toothsome widow of twenty, and kin to the Earl of Pembroke. She owns bountiful lands in Wales besides a goodly house near St. James's Palace.'

'I see ...' said Ursula after a moment. 'I see clearly, Master Julian. And I congratulate you. It seems you've no cause to search for the Philosopher's Stone or the *Elixir Vitae*. You achieve what you want without them. Or is success foretold by your stars?'

'I don't know my horoscope,' said Julian curtly. 'I'll make

my own destiny, nor ever be hampered by sentiment—that fool's opiate!'

Ursula bent her head. 'Perhaps so. And now, farewell . . .'

'*Addio, ma donna.*' He patted her shoulder, pulled his squirrel-lined robes close around him and left the Hall.

Ursula shut her eyes and remained lying on the bench while the servants finished clearing the tables, extinguished the tapers and left the fire to smoulder into ash.

*   *   *

In Sir John Hutchinson's lodgings on Leadenhall Street, Celia was dismaying her bridegroom by the amount of mead she was drinking. His servants had prepared a festive little supper which included breast of chicken and spicy sausages sent from Lincolnshire. John observed Lenten fasting only because it promoted the fishing industry, and saw no reason to follow any Papist rule on such an evening. His parlour was decorated with holly branches and a vase of Christmas 'roses' to welcome Celia. He had also ordered a flask of vintage claret. Celia shook her head and asked for mead.

'But, sweeting,' John said anxiously, ' 'tis an old-fashioned drink, and very strong, I'll have to send out for it, and not sure which tavern . . .'

'I'd like some mead,' said Celia. She sat down in an armchair near the fire and folded her hands on her lap. Her unbound golden hair rippled over the carved oak arm-rest, the fire-light sparkled on her new wedding ring.

'Well, to be sure,' said John, 'to be sure, if you wish—' He dispatched a servant.

Until the flagon of mead came, Celia said nothing at all, though John tried several topics. He spoke of his manor in Lincolnshire, and assured her that it was not damp. 'The sea-coals from Newcastle are landed at my jetty, and I'm not one to stint fuel . . . nor hospitality neither, I've a mort o' friends in Boston, some wives as young as you. There'll be dancings, fairs, strolling players, ye'll not be dull, I swear it.'

Celia put her chin in her hand and gazed into the fire.

When the mead came she gulped down a cupful, then another. A flush tinged her cheek-bones. She leaned back in the chair and began running her finger round and round a carved spiral on the arm-rest, but she refused the food John awkwardly pressed on her.

He had dismissed all serving-men. Suddenly she poured

herself another noggin of mead, and John's nervousness exploded into exasperation.

'God blast it, Celia, ye've drunk enough for a barrowman!'

'I wish to be sotted,' she said. 'Better so.'

John swallowed, 'Look, my dear, I must speak plain. Ye needn't be bedded tonight, if that's why ye act so odd, we've a lifetime ahead and I'm not so sure o' my prowess as I used to be, 'tis a chancy thing at my age, but I want thee—I've proven how I want thee—and I wish for a son . . . I want thee, but by God, ye frighten me a bit.'

Celia finally turned and looked at him. She saw the square ruddy face, the imploring eyes beneath heavy brows, a face like Cowdray's prize mastiff, Ajax. 'I'm sorry,' she said. 'You're a good man, Sir John.'

'*Not* Sir John,' he cried, 'I'm thy husband!'

'Aye . . .' she said, 'but not in the sight of God.'

He flinched. Her speech was not thick, yet her intonation was strange. He glanced ruefully at the mead flagon. He thought of his other wedding night near forty years ago . . . how had *she* behaved, that scraggy bride he had married for her dowry and connections? He remembered her chicken-wing shoulders, and the token mouse squeaks of protest as he deflowered her. He remembered that she had a sour smell he disliked. But I was young then, and lusty as a ram, it didn't matter, nor with the others—the female bodies which came later, now and again, after it became clear that Margaret had something wrong with her womb and would give him no heirs . . .

'What are ye *doing*, Celia?'

She had suddenly risen, throwing off the cloak. She moved languorously to one of the vases of holly and Christmas roses. She picked out two of the thick-petalled greenish flowers, and tossing back her hair, tucked a flower behind each ear. They gave her an exotic faerie look. Her eyes glittered behind the long dark lashes . . .

'There should be music,' she said with a throaty laugh. 'Music for the bride. Can't you play the lute for me, Sir John? Can you not sing?'

He shook his head, watching her in fascination. There had been a ballad in his childhood, his nurse had sung it to him as they trudged through the misty fenlands—' 'Ware the elf maiden, she'll get thee in thrall, 'ware lest her honey-lips soon taste o' gall . . .'

John shook his head again violently. 'I know no songs. A pox on it, child, you're overwrought, go to bed—'tis in there behind the arras.'

'Ah-h-h,' she breathed and smiled down at him, tilting her head. 'Then, *I'll* sing one—"Celia the wanton and fair", wouldn't you like *that*, Sir John?'

She moved near him, she raised her white arms and made a gesture of supplication, a wavering motion with her hands. Suddenly his fear left him. Beneath this mummery he saw the miserable despairing child, and he knew that though he might never gain her love, she yet had need of him.

'Hush,' he said, for she was still singing "Celia the wanton and fair" in a harsh cracked voice. He lifted her in his arms and carried her behind the arras. He lay down with her on the bed, and she went limp as he undressed her. He kissed the hollow of her neck. He drew her head against his shoulder where she nestled, giving little whimpers like a puppy. She went to sleep at once, but he had no thoughts of sleep. Through the dark he stared up at the ceiling, savouring the closeness of her body, the faint herbal scent of her hair—no doubt she had washed it in camomile for the marriage. Yet this was not the wedding night he had imagined. His thoughts slid hither and yon. The meeting of the clothiers' guild tomorrow—the new excise on Flemish cloth, and insubordinate factor in Boston—cozening and cheating—the Wyberton dyke must be mended at once before the Spring floods.

The bells rang out for midnight and Celia stirred. She flung her right arm across his chest and whispered, 'Stephen.'

John held himself very still. Stephen? And who was Stephen? Some stripling she had met? Some gallant who had caught her fancy? How little he knew of this girl he had wed. And how old he felt.

He withdrew his arm carefully from under her head. She turned away from him on the pillow, breathing deeply. Presently John slept, too. The inexorable bells awakened him at five.

It took him some moments to understand why there was a girl in his bed. Then he ran his hands over her body and felt a welcome flicker and throbbing in his loins. She did not stir, even as he began to kiss her. Except for her body warmth she lay limp as a new corpse. 'Damn it, wake up!' he cried. 'Ye must've been told your duty, e'en though ye've not the inclination!' As she still did not respond, he mounted her clumsily, uncertain, fumbling.

Suddenly, she spoke. 'I know my duty, Sir John. I'm not hindering you.'

Her cool resigned little voice quenched him, though he gritted his teeth and proceeded as best he could until he was certain of failure. Then he flung himself to the other side of the bed with sounds of sobbing anger.

Celia raised herself on one elbow listening to the sounds. 'Poor man . . .' she said in wonder. 'Can all this mean so much to you?' She leaned over and patted his stout shaking shoulders. 'No doubt 'twill come better later. You said so yourself.'

He gave a cry and heaved himself out of bed. She heard his heavy footsteps thudding across the fresh-strewn rushes as he pushed aside the arras and left the bedroom alcove. 'I'll see ye at breakfast,' he said, and she heard the Hall door slam shut.

Thus passed Celia's wedding night.

*   *   *

Four days later the Hutchinsons arrived at Sir John's manor, Skirby Hall, a mile outside of Boston.

Though travel and new sights had worked their usual magic, and Celia's misery lessened with each mile away from London, she found in the flat marshlands none of the exhilaration she had felt among the Cumberland mountains. The brown sedge, the water-threaded fens succeeded each other with a monotony which she accepted as a portent of her future life.

Her only positive pleasure was Juno, her own mare. Sometimes she talked to the horse as they all rode single file along the interminable dykes—John, Celia, two men servants and a pack mule.

She dutifully responded when her husband turned around to show her some sight or landmark. 'That's the Wash, m'dear, part of the North Sea.'

'Oh, aye,' she said, but saw only a distant expanse of grey water merging with grey sky.

'Look ye, my fowlers are out early,' cried John, watching a group of rough-clad men carrying snares and guns. They had now entered his own demesne. 'We'll have snipe tomorrow, or would ye prefer fat roast mallard?'

378

'Either one,' said Celia, and made an effort. 'What's that ahead? Like a big black stump in the sky?'

John chuckled. 'Ye've said it right, 'tis Boston Stump, we *call* it! The church steeple. Ye can go there time and again,' he added smiling, ' 'twill save me paying the fine the Papists've put on for staying away. I've no use m'self for church-going.'

'I know,' said Celia. 'Nor have I . . .' she added softly to the horse. She looked down at the pouch which hung from her girdle. Stephen's last note was in there—a scrap of parchment folded into a wad under her ivory comb, her two handkerchiefs and the last of the gilded sugar-plums Magdalen had sent her.

What use to keep the note? She had not looked at it since the Bishop of Winchester's page delivered it at the Priory, nor would ever forget its wording:

'After you make your confession, as *I* shall—we will pray God to forget what happened, nor think on it ever again ourselves. S.'

'I shall think as I please,' said Celia to the horse, but her voice wavered. She had not gone to confession since the night Wyatt invaded the Priory. On this point she had lied to Ursula. Celia's knowledge of her religion, her entire interest in it had sprung from Stephen.

She thought of her cherished portrait of the Virgin, the Rival. 'I hate her,' Celia whispered. She suddenly fished in her pouch, drew up the bit of parchment and flung it down into the muddy waters of a drain.

'Did ye drop something?' John asked, but before she need answer he said with quiet triumph. 'Ah, we're here! There's Skirby Hall, they've the banner flying fur ye, sweet—and ye'll find a goodly welcome as Sir John brings home his bride.'

Indeed the welcome was overwhelming. John's tenants and servants were lined along the road, the women bobbed curtsies, the men pulled their forelocks. A trumpet blared above the shouted greetings. John's bailiff, a wizened man like an elderly terrier, came forward and kissed Celia's hand respectfully. 'M'lady, m'lady,' she heard the new title whispered all around her. She heard the admiration, 'Sa young—sa fair. Master's the lucky one . . .'

John heard them, too. He laughed and sweeping Celia up in his arms, mounted the steps like a lad and carried her over the threshold while he whispered in her ear. 'We'll make a

379

son yet, darling. Ye'll see—we'll forget London an' all the world but our own homeland!'

She smiled a little and kissed his cheek, while his tenantry cheered. Yet, much later beneath the crimson velvet tester over John's great bed, that which he so desired became impossible when she nestled compliantly against him and whispered, 'Ah . . . this is sweet . . . to be held close like a father. I remember him a bit . . . he was hearty and strong like you . . . Would that you *were* my father, sir, 'twould make me so happy.'

His arms stiffened around her, then fell away. He sighed heavily.

'Have I said wrong?' she asked. 'I didn't mean to—you're so good to me, I'm grateful, I ne'er dreamed to be "my lady"— you'll find me grateful . . .'

'Hush,' he said. 'No more talking. Sleep now, I've much to do on the morrow, I've been away too long.'

After that night John ordered a different chamber readied for himself. He left Celia to occupy the great chamber alone in the sumptuous bed.

He treated her with kindness in private, with the respect due to his wife in public, but beyond a kiss on the cheek night and morning, he did not touch her again. Celia, though aware that she had somehow failed him, was deeply relieved. She very soon learned her duties as lady of the manor, and found that her apprenticeship under Ursula had given her capability.

Once she understood the Lincolnshire dialect, she had no trouble in directing her serving-maids, whether in the house, the laundry, the dairy or the still-room, and they obeyed her with grudging respect.

By the time the days brightened and flowed to Summer Celia had grown accustomed to the watery wastes around the knoll where the small brick manor stood among its guardian willows; she could look from her window and watch their tenantry walking on stilts through the marshes to catch the so profitable geese, plucked several times yearly for their feathers and quills. The former were exported as far as London where they softened the slumbers of countless citizens. The quills made pens for the learned to use. Goose eggs, too, were sold as Boston mart, along with the warm little corpses of duck, teal, snipe and even the rare great bustard when a fowler's arrow managed to shoot one.

Celia often gazed out at the windmills—she had never seen

so many—while the barley, peas and bean crops grew tall on their arable land. She listened for the distant lowing of their cattle, below the shrilling of curlews. At least there would not be another year of famine in Lincolnshire.

As the marshes turned green and leaden skies over the Wash often blazed crimson and gold in the sunrises she began to feel the still and hazy beauty of the fenlands, though she would never have mentioned this to John, who did not share her quietude of spirit.

He rode daily to his counting-house in Boston where he and his colleagues held gloomy discussions. Boston Haven was silting up fast, a hundred years ago Boston had been the second busiest port in England. Now, as he had seen in London, financial or mercantile interest no longer included Lincolnshire. Moreover, foreign markets were being glutted with the clothier's exports. In order to open up new markets he had joined the Merchant Adventurers and eagerly awaited news of the exploratory ships sent out towards Muscovy and the unknown East. Not one of these ships had been heard from yet, while his own last cargo to Calais had fetched distressingly low prices. And he had trouble with his weavers—a succession of mishaps to that portion of the cottage industry which he controlled.

It seemed to him that with the essential failure of his marriage he had lost all the verve and optimism which had hitherto made him successful.

Then he had another attack of gout, during which he shut himself in his room for days, allowing nobody near him but his manservant.

Celia was sorry, she made possets for him and sent them up to his chamber. She continued to take pride in her housewifery but there was plenty of time for riding out on Juno, and gingerly exploring the mysterious fens. She even wheedled one of the fowlers into teaching her how to paddle the narrow cock-boats constantly used by the amphibious population.

Nobody bothered her. The fen-dwellers all knew her to be Lady Hutchinson and a foreigner, who despite her obvious youth and comeliness, kept herself to herself—as was fitting.

Often on a northerly breeze she heard the bells ring out from Boston 'Stump'—St. Botolph's lofty lantern spire—summoning worshippers to Mass, but she never went, nor did her husband question her. He slowly recovered from the gout and reappeared in the Hall for meals. He regained interest in his manor and his business affairs, he even invited some of his Hutchinson relations from Alford to the Michaelmas Feast at Skirby, but his joviality had vanished, he had grown peevish; complaining that the ale was brewed too thin, or the meat was underdone. He often beat off the pedigreed hounds beneath the table when they begged for their usual bones.

Sometimes he sat silent and brooding for hours.

Celia remained dutiful, faintly distressed, yet scarcely noticing these alterations. Juno's sprained fetlock, or the ailments of a little mongrel puppy she had adopted caused her far more concern.

Celia had named the pup 'Taggle', from the contemptuous remark of a stable-boy who was about to drown the shapeless little runt.

'Wot's tha want wi' *this*, lady? Raggle-taggle as a beggar, sickly, an'll not see th' week out, neither.'

But Celia insisted. She hand-fed Taggle on milk-sops, she rubbed salve on his mange spots, she took him to her great bed and let him sleep curled against her stomach. Taggle grew plump, he had a snout under a wiry fringe on his protuberant forehead, and looked rather like a hedgehog. To every eye but Celia's he seemed ludicrous—to John a positive insult, and he said so in one of his rare criticisms of Celia.

'I wish ye'd not fondle that misbegot little monster, it makes me puke—plenty o' true-bred hound pups ye can have.'

'I love Taggle, sir,' said Celia quietly, 'love him as perchance I would a babe . . .?'

John looked sharply at her and saw that she had meant no taunt, was simply stating a fact. 'Well . . . h-m-m,' he said. 'By the bye, m'dear, tell cook to kill the Michaelmas geese *today*. Weren't hung long enough last year—tough as saddle-leather. An' I hope ye've grown plenty of sage i' the herb garden?'

'I believe so,' she said, 'though my Aunt Ursula ne'er touched the herbs at Cowdray, there were so many gardeners.'

John grunted. He disliked any thought of Celia's past life, as he increasingly shrank from the thought of their future together. He observed that with her skin grown rosy and golden from her summer rambles, her eyes even brighter with a sea-lit translucence, she was becoming a woman of great beauty. She seemed unaware of the covert glances cast at her by his serving-men, or by the two merchants he had entertained before his attack of gout.

Yet he remembered the wild allure she had shown him on the night of the wedding . . . his great toe gave a throb, and he said in sudden anger, 'Ye've been running about somewhat free while I've been laid up, ye'll bide home more now, an' the days'll be drawing in. There'll be needlework to keep ye busy.' He noted her stricken startled face and added more gently, 'I'll teach ye draughts an' I'll read to ye from the Bible at times, there's a deal there to interest you.'

'The Bible?' she repeated faintly. 'The Protestant Bible? 'Tis forbidden to my faith. Stephen said . . .' She stopped, pinching her mouth tight. 'If you wish to, sir . . .' She bent over Taggle, squeezing the puppy so hard that he yelped.

'Who the devil is Stephen?' John snapped. 'Ye mentioned him once before!'

Celia put Taggle down on the rushes and stood up, smoothing her skirts. '*Brother* Stephen, a monk—house priest at Cowdray . . . no importance.'

'Oh, indeed,' said John shrugging. 'One o' *them*, the black crows—I warrant ye've forgot a' that nonsense they taught ye. Ye seem to have?'

'Aye,' said Celia after a moment. 'I've forgot it.'

*   *   *

The Michaelmas Feast at Skirby Hall did the Hutchinsons credit. The roast geese were succulent, the game pies as tasty as the apple and ginger tarts. John's claret—newly landed from France—had an exceptional bouquet, and though his cousins from Alford secretly preferred ale, they were impressed by the Hall's new aura of refinement, and the quietly demure manners of the bride.

Soon after their arrival John had indicated that he found her clothes unsuitable, and sent to Lincoln for several fine wool gowns with square-cut necks modestly filled in with white voile, as befitted a matron. Her hair was plaited under white kerchiefs, he gave her a silver chatelaine—from it dangled her household keys, and a clove-scented pomander ball, but the rosary, of course, had been banished. He could not manage to disguise her youthful beauty, as perhaps he had hoped, but he had subdued all hint of coquetry. She appeared older than her sixteen years, and—having accepted her lot—she behaved so.

She rebelled only once, before the feast, when she discovered that there was to be no music of any kind. 'Not even a piper or fiddle, sir?' she asked in dismay.

'Nay,' answered John sharply. 'Who wants twiddles an' tweedles at their meat? Oh, I won't say no at Christmastide, maybe, an' it pleasures ye, and we might sing a catch or two—the good old country rounds—but this isn't London or Cowdray, and ours here be homely ways. Ye must forget the giddy courtiers.'

She had no idea that it hurt him that she never called him 'John' or 'husband', though his practical mind accepted the reasons. Gradually he almost forgot that he had ever wished her to. The last fierce flare of autumn love died into embers. But he was proud of her as his property, and very seldom unkind.

In October, Skirby Hall had a visitor who roused all the memories and feelings Celia had managed to quell.

One misty afternoon Celia wandered out through her walled garden to a grassy knoll on the edge of the fen, Taggle flopping and snuffling at her heels.

There was an old willow stump where she liked to sit and watch the lane along the dyke from Boston. John had gone to town that day, and though he seldom mentioned his affairs, she knew that he was worried about an overdue cargo ship from Calais. They would not sup until he returned, and Celia was hungry. She debated filching a stay-piece, bread or an apple, from the pantry, then decided that the servants would exchange knowing looks. She knew that they constantly hoped for her pregnancy.

She sat down on the stump and looked towards Boston, then beyond it to the sea. Drifts of fog were blowing in, yet the damp air was very still. She felt, as so often, especially at the gloaming time, an infinite hush, as though something were going to happen, and yet it never did. This vast grey monotony oppressed her tonight. Then she saw a horseman on the Boston lane.

Good, she thought, pulling Taggle from the corpse of a dead frog, so now we'll sup. But the horseman did not ride like Sir John, he seemed smaller, he was obviously groping, uncertain of his way.

She watched him idly, any stranger was of interest, until he turned up towards the Hall. She ran back to the garden and through to their gatehouse. There was still light enough to recognise the horseman.

'*Wat!*' she cried, staring at the buck's head badge. 'Wat Farrier—I'm so amazed, confounded . . .' She ran up to him as he dismounted.

'God's greetin', miss—m'lady, I should say—bloody back o' beyond *ye've* landed in. Cotsbody, the nag an' I 'ave been nigh drownded i' ye're shitten drains. Wot a place!'

'I'm sorry,' she said smiling. 'Come in! I'm *glad* to see you!'

Wat grunted. ' 'Tis worse gettin' here than Cumberland. Have ye anyone about'll gi'e me a drink?'

'To be sure,' she spoke with a tinge of pride. 'I've many servants, but you'll not go to the kitchens, come with me to the Hall. Oh, Wat, how *are* they all, how is my lady aunt?'

He glanced at her curiously. 'Ye've not heard from her . . . nor written neither?'

'Nay,' she said flushing, 'you know I can't write well . . . I didn't like to ask Sir John, and I thought she might write to me, except I've not been thinking much on the past—only now when I see you.'

Wat grunted. 'Lady South'll does well enough, ye may be sure she's not forgot ye, 'twas she sent me here—since m'lord bade me go to Sempring'am anyhow wi' a message to the Clintons, now they're doubly related.'

Celia frowned as she poured out a flagon of ale. 'I don't understand you, Wat. Who is "m'lord" and who is doubly related?'

He waggled his head and sighed in a mixture of exasperation and sympathy. 'D'ye get no news at all midst these God-forsook bogs?'

'I know that the Queen's Grace was wed to Philip of Spain on July 25th at Winchester. We had a bonfire here, and Boston church bells pealed for an hour after the royal messenger got there. But soon as he left, I heard no more. They detest the marriage round these parts, and don't speak of it—Sir John neither.'

'Ah-r-r,' said Wat, nodding. 'Lot o' England feels that way, as ye should know, havin' been mixed i' Wyatt's Rebellion—poor toad.' Wat crossed himself.

'He's dead then?' whispered Celia.

'O' course.' Wat wiped his foamy beard on his sleeve. 'All Spring the bleedin' heads was a-rollin' like bowls on Tower Green. Lady Jane Grey an' her husband died, too. Wot ye expect?'

'I didn't think . . .' said Celia. A sick pang darted through the shrouded memories of what seemed a different life. The debonair Sir Thomas Wyatt had sung to her, laughed with her, desired her . . .

'There's been no danger for Sir Anthony?' she asked in sudden fear.

Wat threw back his head and laughed uproariously. 'To the contrary, Chuck! Sir Anthony is now m'lord the Viscount Montagu, he's Master o' the Horse to King Philip, he's the apple o' the royal eyes an' grown merry as a grig.'

'Wedded?' she asked in a low voice, after a moment.

'Not him . . . not yet. Though I'd not wager a groat he won't pick Lady Maggie when the fit comes on him—an' don't ye know the marriage we *did* have at Cowdray in May?'

She shook her head. 'Not Mabel?'

'The very one. Lord Fitzgerald got hisself turned back into Earl o' Kildare, so Mistress Mabel is a Countess an' has gone off to Ireland. Ye' ne'er saw such doin's at Cowdray, e'en when King Edward come.'

Celia was silent. She knew that she should rejoice for her friends, be glad that Mabel had got her heart's desire. In fact, she was swamped by envy and the sense of exile. Mabel might have bade them to the wedding. Ursula might have written.

Wat, mellowed by the ale, and experienced in reading human faces, had no trouble in discerning Celia's thought.

'Look'ee, Mistress Celia,' he said briskly, 'ye're aunt loves ye as she allus did, but she feels ye vexed wi' her. Ye parted cool, an' she's too proud a lady to push in where not wanted. But she asked me to come here an' tell ye that.' Wat looked around the Hall. 'Ye've a nice little manor here, snug. An' ye've risen to a title . . . Wot's more—' He stopped, and she continued quickly.

'Aye, what more could a penniless tavern wench want?'

'I'm certain ye're husband fair dotes on ye,' said Wat a trifle dismayed at her bitter tone. 'An' when ye start breedin', as no doubt'll be soon, the babes'll keep ye content.'

'There'll be no babes,' said Celia. She picked up Taggle who had been nuzzling her feet, and let him lick her cheek.

'Ah-r-r, indeed . . .' said Wat startled, then comprehending. 'So the knight's lance has lost its thrust? Pity, yet not hopeless. I hope ye've not put horns on him—sing "cuckoo"?'

She shook her head decisively.

'Then,' said Wat, 'ye must get ye a charm. I don't hold much wi' such women's fancies, yet am bound ter say, Molly o'Whipple did wonders fur an old gaffer i' Midhurst. He sired a son on the next full moon. Must be *some* wise-woman near by.'

Celia flushed. 'There's the "water witch",' she said very low, glancing over her shoulder. 'I've heard the servants. They're terrified of her. She's not like Molly, she's evil. The devil is her paramour, he swoops nights out o' the sea to her hut, in the shape of a great black heron.'

'Taradiddle,' said Wat. 'Ye've got courage, an' ye've got silver, go buy a philtre wot'll make ye an' Sir John content. 'Tis worth a try.'

Celia swallowed and looked away. The thought of the 'water witch' was repugnant, and yet subtly fascinating. They said the woman could see the future in an iron basin filled with seawater. They said she could summon the tides, and had caused the last devastating Spring floods, being annoyed at the quality of the provisions the fen-dwellers timorously left every Friday night a hundred yards from her door. Her familiar was a grey seal, it had been seen slithering on a flat boulder in the shallows off Frampton marsh, and had been heard barking inside the witch's hut. Nobody at Skirby Hall had ever seen the witch, who was reputed to have green sea-weed hair, but her magical powers were said to be tremendous.

'Ye should try it,' repeated Wat sternly. ' 'Tis ye're wifely duty, an' ye can allus be shriven later, the priest'll understand ye're plight. Happens often.'

'I have seen no priest,' said Celia slowly. 'This is a Protestant household.'

Wat frowned. 'Bigod, I'd forgot that! But ye tell Sir John he'd better change his tune, or he'll no prosper long. England's gone Papist all the way, now it's gone Spanish, too.'

He made a wry face, belched, then suddenly brought out the name Celia would never have mentioned. 'Brother Stephen'd have a fit, did he know ye was turnin' heretic. He's a proper godly young man, a good priest, I'd allus a likin' fur him.'

Celia clenched her hands beneath the table. 'Did he officiate at Mabel's—at Lady Kildare's wedding?' she asked in a cool, off-hand voice.

'Bigod,' said Wat, again startled by her complete ignorance. 'How could he? He left fur France—two, mebbe three days arter the Rebellion. Ye must know that, ye was there at the Priory, still. Afore ye're weddin'.'

'Oh, to be sure,' said Celia. 'It slipped my mind, I knew he'd moved to Winchester Palace.'

Actually, nobody had mentioned Stephen's name to her after the night of Ursula's anguished reproaches. She knew nothing of him but his own note.

'Went to some place called Marmateer, his old abbey. Her Majesty's orders, I believe. She wants St. Bennet's monks back i' Westminster. I'll wager he rises high i' the Church. Bishop, I wouldn't wonder, even . . .' said Wat, high-flown with strong ale and exuberant at all the rank and preferment which had lately gilded everyone near Anthony Browne. 'Even Archbishop o' Canterbury, who knows? Stranger things have happened.'

Celia's heart gave a hurtful bump against her ribs. 'Who knows?' she echoed. She got up and moved jerkily across the rushes to snuff a candle which was guttering. Amidst the pain so long suppressed there was bitter relief. He was far off in a different country, he had taken no part in the glittering festivities at Cowdray. She would never have to think of him again — as he had commanded.

When John finally came home to his supper, Celia greeted him with unusual warmth. She kissed him sweetly on the lips, and presented Wat so tactfully that her husband, at first resentful, soon grew genial and allowed himself an interest in Wat's budget of news. He especially enjoyed Wat's wry description of the royal marriage John so heartily disapproved.

'It rained,' said Wat, 'from the minute the Prince — as was — set foot on Sou'ampton dock, and him a little bandy-legs, green from pukin' his way over. He had a scowl on his face would scare St. James hisself, 'oos Feast Day it was — the Queen's Grace would have it so in compliment to Spain, but that foreign saint couldn't do nothin' 'gainst our St. Swithun an' his downpours. We was all drenched. I was wi' the horses — Lord Montagu bein' royal Master o' them, and I'd a task, bigod — to curry an' groom the dainty genet Her Majesty had ready fur her betrothed. Shiverin' an' steamin' was that poor filly. We had to get a stouter mount fur the Prince who wrapped hisself in a great cloak, an' ne'er spoke except ter those yellow-faced Spaniards he brought. Seems he don't talk no English.'

'But the wedding itself?' asked Celia eagerly. '*That* must've been splendid? How looked the Queen?'

'Like a small tuffet o' gold cloth an' sparklin' gems from where I was perched. The King was in white an' ne'er took off his comical cap, e'en at the Elevation of the Host—must be odd habits in Spain, but the Queen is besotted, can't keep her hands off 'im.'

'Faugh,' said John. 'This poor land o' ours. Run by Spain through a lickerous old bitch. *I'll* not knuckle under.'

'Shush!' said Wat sharply. ' 'Ware such speeches, Sir John. Plenty men in gaol fur less.' He munched thoughtfully on an excellent saddle of hare, while considering the tavern talk he had heard in Boston when he stopped at the Red Lion to ask his way. There was a gaggle of weavers and sheep-owners in the tap-room. They were wary of Wat, but he had gathered that Sir John was heavily in debt, and under a boycott, largely induced by disasters to his shipments of cloth to Calais, by the excessive amounts of foot-rot among his sheep and by his outspoken Protestantism. Wat sensed that Sir John was considered unlucky, and well knew how a prejudice of this kind blighted a man's prosperity. During these hours at Skirby Hall, Wat felt considerable pity for his host, especially in view of Celia's sad admission, and he now brought out a topic which he thought would hearten Sir John.

'Ye must be gladdened, sir, by Richard Chancellor's safe return from Muscovy, an' the opening up o' the Eastern trade.'

John started and flushed. 'He got back? He brought the *Bonaventure* home again? I wasn't sent the news.'

'Well, ye're a bit out o' things here,' said Wat ruefully. 'Chancellor got back last month, an' brought a Russian envoy along from Tsar Ivan, or wotever their king calls hisself. Ye ne'er saw such furs as they brought, too. Bales o' ermine, an' some saints' pictures framed in rubies big as my thumb. The Queen's Grace was well pleased. They're starting a Muscovy company in Lunnon, an' expect to open up trade routes far as Cathay. It'll be one i' the eye fur them Spaniards an' their boasted gold from the West.'

'Aye . . .' said John sighing. 'I'd go back to London, see if I could buy into the new company, only . . .' He stopped. He knew that he no longer had sufficient cash to interest them. 'My health's none too good,' he said, 'been ailing o' late . . . .'

Wat jerked his head sympathetically. 'Ye can be cured, sir, I'll warrant! Ye're clever little ladyship here'll cure ye, she'll make ye a potion or mithridate,' he winked largely at Celia, 'havin' learned much from her lady aunt 'oos most apt i' the still-room.'

Sir John did not notice the wink, nor see Wat's bearded lips forming the words 'water witch', for he was listlessly mopping a morsel of hare in the gravy, but Celia understood, and gave a small excited sound. Why not? It would be an adventure, something to vary the sameness of her days . . . and if the venture might restore Sir John, if at last it brought him the son he had so desperately wanted . . . aye, Wat was right. It was worth a try.

Celia underwent one of her lightning changes of mood, she sparkled and she laughed. She twined her arms around John's neck and coaxed him into singing a nonsense catch with her and Wat who was delighted.

Oh merry are we met, an' merry let us be,
for we'll sing all night i' the low countree.

Hey nonny nonny but care will flee, as we caper and we jest
wi' a riddle me ree, caper and jest i' the low countree.

The sound of their blended voices, the bell-like harmonies they produced on the long notes pleased even John, who had a good voice, though unused since his grammar school days in Boston.

They sang other glees, while the astonished servants listened and giggled behind the buttery screen.

Wat departed dutifully next morning for Sempringham, bearing a warm mesage back to Ursula from Celia. And a more reluctant one from Sir John that Lady Southwell, could she bear the winter journey, was bid to Skirby Hall for Christmastide. Wat's visit had made him realise how little company he had provided for the girl-wife after all, and his conscience awoke.

Though his business worries continued, he took Celia to the Boston mart and bought her pretty fairings, he took her to a bear-baiting and even overnight to Lincoln, where they stopped with more of his Hutchinson cousins who bored her, though she politely admired the honey-coloured minster, and itched to get back so that she might consult the water witch.

She knew that she dare not mention such a visit to John, who had never heard of the woman's existence—the servants did not gossip in *his* presence, but from the nightly Bible readings she had realised his scorn and detestation of witchcraft. He admitted that there was such a thing, the Bible was explicit on the subject, but any such demonic incongruity near his own regulated homelands would never occur to him.

Celia bided her time, and found sudden opportunity when John grimly announced that his over-due ship, *The White Fleece*, had been blown far off course and wrecked on the Yorkshire coast. He would have to travel there, even though there was scant hope of salvage, and would be gone a week.

Though Celia had no awareness of how close to ruin this disaster brought her husband, she used comforting words, and tried to soothe him. He put her aside impatiently, and went into one of his fits of silent brooding.

An hour after John left with a pack-horse and his groom, Celia summoned her chambermaid who was a garrulous woman of forty and had mentioned the water witch in the first place. The maid's name was Kate and she had been born in the fens. She was stupid and slow at her duties, but Celia who had learned higher standards at Cowdray and the Priory was forced to put up with her. Kate had been chambermaid to the deceased Lady Hutchinson, and it never occurred to anyone but Celia that a better servant might be found. Traditional posts were never altered.

Kate showed no curiosity about her mistress's questions, which she accepted as another vagary of the foreign lady's, but she willingly described the water witch's habitat on the edge of Frampton marsh and the sea. Her directions were so confused that Celia knew she would never find the place without guidance, even though it seemed to be only some ten miles away. She asked if Kate knew of a guide.

For the first time Kate's stolid face showed fear. 'Nabody here goos nigh there, nor should.'

'But,' said Celia patiently, 'you say *somebody* brings her food on Fridays, or she might raise the tides and flood us.'

Kate's chapped red hands worked on her apron, her big loose mouth set like a trap, yet her habit of obedience finally prevailed.

' 'Tis Daft Dickon from Frampton parish,' she said sullenly. 'He's too witless for fear.'

'Aye, so—thank you, Kate,' said Celia with her charming smile.

Into the woman's dull little eyes came a spark of feeling.

'Mistress—doant meddle, pray doant meddle,' she said. ' 'Twill bring ill luck on Skirby Hall!'

Celia shook her head. 'Be easy, Kate—'tis *good* luck I'll bring, and you must forget we've spoken of this. Means naught anyhow.'

Kate looked relieved, bobbed a curtsy and left the room.

Celia curled up on her window-seat and began to plan— confidently, excitedly. Through her lattice window the noon-time sun reduced the fens to a vast fawn colour, for the sedges were browning with autumn. They were laced by ribbons of greenish water. In the far distance the sky and sea met—an indeterminate blue, the only landmark in her window view was the nearest manor windmill which still ground out woad for shipping abroad to dye European cloth. The sails were still, the sheep on their pastures were tranquil little blobs re-peated in the sky by a few white cloud puffs. The flat bright landscape held no mystery, the manor itself was soundless, the hounds and horses quiet, the undoubted bustle in the kitchen could not be heard from her chamber. Celia was conscious that only her own excitement jangled the tranquillity and felt obscurely guilty. And then an odd thing happened.

She heard voices. They spoke in accents unfamiliar to her. Yet it was English. There was a woman's voice, clipped, authoritative, scornful. It said, 'Lady Marsdon's getting worse, I doubt she'll last longer, Doctor. *I* think we *must* call back Sir Arthur. I've kept away all night, as were my orders, but Matron's come on duty now, and you'll not find *her* so lax. We don't like 'em to die at the Clinic on account of laxness, and outlandish clap-trap methods—excuse me speaking plain, sir, but I've seen some cases like this, and what *she* needs is proper medical procedure—another electroencephalogram then shock treatment, *I* think.'

There was a male voice answering, but Celia could not quite hear it. It seemed to her that it said, 'Wait!' Then it said, 'She has certainly reached a crossroad, the outcome is in the hands of God.'

Celia sat in Skirby Hall, and briefly considered the voices, which seemed to come neither from her familiar chamber, nor from the quiet sunlit air outside. Some of the words were gibberish, which vexed her 'electroencephalogram'—and why should she fancy a reference to God? It occurred to her that the man's voice reminded her of Master Julian. She wondered vaguely what had happened to him, the whole episode caught

392

her attention for only a moment, then it slid away as Taggle, who had been sitting with his head on her lap, gave a sharp yelp, bounded to the floor and began to shiver, while his neck fur rose.

'What ails *thee*, sweet?' said Celia laughing. She stooped to pat him, but he cringed. He gave a pulsating howl, then hid under her bed, emitting whimpering snarls. He snapped at her when she tried to catch him.

Perhaps he wants a purge, Celia thought, disconcerted. I'll give him some cassia tonight. He's never acted like this. She resumed her plans for finding Daft Dickon.

Two days later Celia had arranged everything, having ridden Juno to Frampton where she easily found Dickon. He was a scrawny little man with a shock of straw-coloured hair, vacant eyes and a foolish grin. His age might have been anything from twenty to forty, and he lived in a cot with his grandmother who snatched at Celia's proffered shilling, then hid it in the bony recesses beneath her shawl. She shrugged her humped shoulders when Celia explained her errand. 'Thou canst goo the morrow, being Friday, wi' Dickon . . .' she mumbled through toothless gums, 'the more fule thee—effen thee looks on *her*, thou'rt lost . . . 'tis a monster—a fish-'oman.'

'A mermaid?' cried Celia, who had been fascinated by the inn sign in London. She plied the crone with questions and from the reluctant mumbling answers got little satisfaction.

The water witch had been there many years. Before Dickon took the offerings, a 'simple' lass from Wyberton parish had brought them.

The dim-witted were naturally selected for the task, since God in his mercy protected such from witchcraft. Throughout the conversation Dickon squatted on a stool, grinning and nodding, while he plaited long reeds into tough withes to be sold locally for halters.

Celia left when the old woman drowsed into the sudden sleep of age, then she spent the ensuing night in a mixture of apprehension and the childish pleasure of undertaking a prank of which nobody approved. Even Wat, she thought, would now have dissuaded her. The water witch, monster or mermaid was so clearly unlike Molly o'Whipple or any wise-woman Wat could have known. At the last moment before mounting Juno, Celia had a rather shamefaced impulse. She ran upstairs to her chamber, opened her coffer and fished her silver beads from the bottom corner where they had lain since her marriage. She barely glanced at the ivory crucifix as she threw the beads in her pouch among an assortment of shillings, ha'pennies and farthings. Sir John was generous with pocket money, in case a peddler came to the Hall with any trinkets she might covet.

The weather held fair, and Dickon was waiting outside his cot in Frampton, a great woven hamper at his feet.

'G'day, mistuss,' he said giggling, and to her surprise, for she had thought him dumb. 'Geese be flyin', winter's nigh-in'.' He jerked his thumb up towards the sky where she saw a long streaming wedge of wild geese, heading south.

'Aye, to be sure,' she said, relieved that Dickon was not entirely witless.

'Mun goo fast, ussen,' he said, 'or Her'll raise th' floods.'

Celia glanced at the hamper of propitiatory offerings, and lifted the lid. There were thirteen eggs nestled in straw, three brown cottage loaves of fresh bread, a little crock of butter and a mammoth pike wiggling feebly on top. The donations came from the entire district and had been packed in the hamper as usual this morning by Dickon's grand-dam.

'What's *that*?' Celia asked, seeing a large brown homespun packet tucked in a corner.

Dickon stared at it vaguely, but his grandmother who had come bustling out, said, 'Hemp leaves. We've a deal o' trouble gettin' 'em each week, they coom from beyond Skirlbeck at the rope walk, but oncet they was forgot we had a tempest. Seven kine an' a milkmaid droonded.'

'What does she want them for?' asked Celia, half-laughing.

The old woman said, 'Witchery,' and snapped her gums shut.

Celia and Dickon started out, she on Juno and he ahead with the hamper slung over his back.

There was no road; there was seldom a discernible path, but Dickon knew his way with the certainty of any primitive. He skirted the worst drains, though they sloshed through others; he avoided the quivering bogs, and finally led her along a sandy ridge until she could hear the lapping of sea-water on the shingle.

'Yon's witch hut,' he said, jerking his thumb over his shoul-der. 'Dickon goos no furder.' He dumped the hamper down by a large clump of samphire.

She stared at the bushes, at the sandy dune beyond them,

then saw a thin trickle of grey smoke. 'The witch lives down there?'

Dickon gave his odd cackle, which meant assent. 'Dickon goos hoom,' he said, 'Gran's a-waitin'. Her got a rasher o' bacon fur me.'

Celia's good sense suddenly asserted itself. 'Look, Dickon,' she said. 'You bide here. Stop *here* until I come back. You're clever—I'm not. I'll be lost in those fens. I *need* you to guide me.'

She saw that she had not reached him.

'Gran's a-cookin' me bacon,' he said, 'an' dumplin's to goo wi' it.'

He turned and began to walk.

Celia was seized by panic. She slid off Juno, and twined the bridle quickly around a hunk of driftwood. She ran after Dickon. 'Halt!' she said grabbing his arm. He looked at her in alarm.

'Have I doon wrang?'

'Aye,' she said. 'Nay, not if you stay here! You shall have bacon, a whole flitch to yourself at Skirby Hall, I vow it. *If* you do as I say.' She saw that this did not reach him either, yet as she stood there holding his arm, pressing against him in her urgency, she saw something flicker in his blank eyes. His lids narrowed, while his nostrils distended. She pulled his head down and kissed him on the lips. 'See, you can have more o' these, if you wait for me!'

He licked his mouth and gaped at her. She kissed him again, uncaring by what method she could force him to stay.

He gave a strangled gasp, and grabbed her, while slobbering on her cheek. She knew that she had won.

'Loose me, Dickon,' she said in a voice of calm control. 'Loose me 'til I return to you. Bide with the horse!'

His grip on her slackened, his arms fell limp. He put a tentative dirty hand on Juno's saddle. 'Dickon bides here?' he said, and when she nodded sternly he gave his mindless giggle and squatted by Juno's browsing head. As Celia stumbled towards the dune she heard him crooning, 'Dickon bides . . . Dickon bides . . .'

She had picked up the hamper to ensure her welcome, nor minded the weight—before the last years of soft living, she had lifted many an ale keg—besides, the bite of the wooden handle under her clenched fingers emboldened her, kept down the edging fear.

She reached the top of the dune and realised that the hut was not immediately below, where every high tide would have swamped it, but set cannily back in an unexpected crevice of brown rock, which was moreover protected from the sea by still another large dune, dotted with scrubby shore bushes. The hut was made of wattle and daub, like all those in the fens, but as Celia neared it, she saw that the hard clay between the wattles was studded with cockle-shells. The smoke rose from a small squat chimney—a refinement which astonished Celia.

She floundered on, then stopped as she saw the plank door open and a grey seal come slithering through it, giving sharp little barks.

'The familiar,' Celia thought, and stifled a spurt of hysterical laughter when a woman's clear voice called out, 'Ne va pas trop loin, chéri!'

Celia didn't understand the words, but the meaning was plain, and just like her own admonitions to Taggle when she let him outdoors.

She walked resolutely up to the shut door and knocked.

There was dead silence inside. She knocked again, crying, 'Good day, mistress, I've got your hamper!'

Again silence, then a muffled, 'Go away!' which held a note of outrage.

'No,' said Celia, 'I'm alone, I came to see you, brought your provisions.'

The door opened a crack, Celia trembled a little for she knew she was being inspected, but could see nothing except a long, billowing, whitish mass.

'Damoiselle . . .' said the voice, 'you are brave . . . Enter, then!' The door was flung wide, and Celia shrank back.

The water witch was naked, except for thick, wavy white hair which fell to her thighs. The nakedness was Celia's first shock; she saw the outline of firm breasts and belly, slightly rounded like a young woman's, and there were certainly two legs—not a mermaid. Shock mingled with disappointment until the woman tossed back her hair, swept it back with a defiant movement of her long arms and advanced a step into the sunlight.

Then Celia saw the scars. The knotted yellow welts on the legs, the distorted feet, where several of the toes were only stubs. And the face—ravaged on one side by livid bumps, the mouth twisted up towards the right ear.

'Holy Jesu ...' Celia whispered. The hamper fell from her limp hand. 'St. Mary—what happened to you?'

'*Le feu*,' said the woman quite casually. '*Ils m'ont brûlé pour une sorcière. Ah, j'oublie* ...' she paused, searching for words. '*Longtemps* ... long time I 'ave not speak Eenglish, no speak to anyone except Odo—my *phoque*—' she gestured towards the shore where the seal had disappeared. 'I was burned for being witch in France,' she said. 'My English lovair save me.'

Celia started, her mouth went dry. 'Horrible,' she whispered. 'The cruelty ...'

'*Cruauté*,' repeated the woman as though examining the word. 'Possibly *justice*,' her large brilliant eyes fixed ironically on Celia, 'since I *am* a witch!'

Celia expelled her breath on a long gasp. This was no prank, no interesting venture, undertaken for a reason she could not remember. She wanted to flee, and yet her feet seemed rooted. She was terrified, fascinated. 'I—I brought your hamper ...' she said feebly.

'Ah-h,' said the woman. 'You came not only for *zat* reason —you wanted my help.' Her twisted mouth could not smile, but her eyes softened into a gleam of amusement. 'You need not fear me,' she said quietly, 'if your heart is pure.' She had beautiful tapering hands, they were unmarred, for they had been tied behind the stake as her burning began. She put one on Celia's arm. 'Enter,' she said softly. 'It is good to talk ... so many years I have not.'

Celia slowly followed her into the hut which smelled of the sea and was very clean; the floor was covered with sand only a trifle yellower than the witch's abundant white hair. There was a wide couch in the corner made of sacking stuffed with crumbled dry kelp. The little fire was burning driftwood, the flames flickered blue and green. On the hard mud hearth there stood an iron pot and skillet. Celia's eye was then caught by the round central table and an X-shaped folding armchair, because both were so incongruous in the isolated little hut. They were exquisitely carved, and had been painted, though gilding and colours were faded now. Even at Cowdray, Celia had seen no furniture so delicate.

The woman watched Celia, and nodded. 'Milor', from love, then pity, tried to give me some comforts. Afterwards, he left. He was *noyé*—drowned ... sailing back.'

'How could you know?' Celia, puzzled, tried to fight a

397

growing sense of helplessness. She understood that the lover who had managed to rescue the woman from the stake was an English lord, that he must have had this hut built for her and then abandoned her.

'I know much, I know much others cannot, I am Melusine,' said the woman with a proud lift to her chin.

Celia thought the name pretty, though she did not comprehend why it was spoken with such meaning. She now saw that the long eyes that were fixed on her—mockingly, tenderly—were not as dark as she had thought. They were green—the yellowish green of a cat's, and the pupils, too, seemed long instead of round.

Again fear touched her, a wish to escape.

'*Nenni, ma belle*—' The tapering hand tapped her arm. 'We will know each other better when we have shared *les fleurs de rêve.*'

Melusine brought the hamper indoors. Celia noticed how she teetered on her deformed feet, lightly touching the wall for balance. This no longer seemed pitiable. The nakedness had ceased to shock her, but Melusine went to a huge oaken coffer which stood in the shadows, and took out a filmy gown. It was grey, and decorated around the neck with little pearls —made, Celia recognised, in a fashion long forgotten, like an old one of Ursula's. The looseness, the flowing sleeves bordered with pearl bands, the demure cut of the bodice. 'This is how I *was*,' said Melusine. 'Many men loved me. *Alone*, I feel better to be *nue*.'

Celia stood tentatively by the table, watching as the woman slipped into the gown, then said, '*Alors, m'amie*—Take and eat!' She opened the hamper and extracted the packet which Dickon's grandmother had said were hemp leaves. They were mixed with dry flowerets. She poured some in Celia's palm. 'Lie down,' said the woman, 'put them in your mouth!'

'I—I don't wish to,' Celia said, but she obeyed. She found her mouth filled by brown morsels. They were little different from the drying sage or thyme she occasionally tasted in her herb garden. One part of her thought, this is ridiculous, the poor woman is mad—so long here alone. And yet she obeyed.

She lay down beside Melusine on the kelp mattress. She chewed and swallowed the hemp leaves. Melusine did the same.

She did not touch Celia.

Presently, a soft dreamy state overcame Celia, she ceased to think at all, she raised her head on an elbow to see the twinkle of coloured flames as they became vivid jewels, more lovely than any she had ever seen. She smelled amidst the fragrance of the sea, what must be perfume from Melusine's gown, a sweet musky smell, sweeter than any rose. She heard Melusine's voice, and knew not in which language the soft languorous tones were speaking. They had become a distant music which needed no translation. She knew that the woman was talking of herself. Melusine de Lusignan, that there had always been a Melusine back and back beyond the reaches of time. Melusine was born of a fountain, but she took mortal lovers. Melusine knew many enchantments, but she had received a mortal soul. She went daily to Mass, she did no harm, she resisted the blandishments of the Devil. Until one day she was tempted—tempted by a promise. There was a duke who wished to be King. If Melusine, using her great powers, would ensure the King's death, then coffers of gold would be hers, and the Duke would raise her to be his *maîtresse en titre*—even, it might be, Queen.

So small a matter it was, she had but to make a waxen image of the King, pierce it through the heart with a needle which had been dipped in the brains of a hanged murderer, then say certain holy words of power backwards. Well, she had done so. And the very next night the King began to sicken.

Melusine's voice ceased. She took another pinch of the dried hemp, chewed on it slowly, voluptuously. Celia stirred a little. It was like hearing the old time romances Ursula used to read her at the Priory. They, too, had kings, and murders and fairy spells, and was there not even a water sprite called Melusine in one of them?

Her languorous gaze moved from the fire and rested on a pattern of seashells on the opposite wall. The shells formed a star, and there was a rosy whelk in the middle. How beautiful it was—the glossy convoluted pink shell! It glowed and pulsated. She stared at it.

Melusine began again to speak. Now the voice had more urgency, the tone disturbed Celia's trance.

The King would have infallibly died, Melusine said. But they caught her with the wax image. That Medici woman caught her, for she, too, was versed in the Black Arts.

'The Medici woman . . .?' said Celia, jolted from her dreams.

'*La reine*,' answered Melusine, 'Catherine . . . the pawnbroker's daughter . . . she had me burned . . . *c'était juste.*'

Celia swallowed hard. Her head cleared. The expanding walls, the rosy shell, the coloured flames all turned dull, ordinary, as her own chamber at Skirby Hall. The woman's story was real, the King was real—he was King Henri who lived in a palace called the Louvre in Paris on the other side of the water which washed the shores below them right now. And this strange woman, mutilated, half-crazed by the horror she had undergone, whether witch or not— Celia jumped up from the couch.

' 'Tis getting late,' she said. 'Dickon's waiting, I didn't mean to stay so long.'

Melusine's eyes widened to their sad, mocking look. 'First —the love philtre you came for! Some gallant who spurns you, even though you are so fair?'

'No, no,' cried Celia, 'not that. My husband . . . he can't . . .'

'Ah-h,' said Melusine. '*L'impuissance* . . . you came to *help* him?'

Celia bowed her head, though at that moment she could not see John's face.

'Do this!' said Melusine. She took a faggot from the hearth and drew a pentacle on the sand. 'Five points like this. Then take this powder—' She drew a tiny vial from a sack near the window. 'Put it in the centre, then say—"Ishtareth, Ishtareth" three times. Place the powder in his drink. He will lust for you . . . *avec tout son corps*, will make a son on you, for this powder is from the mandrake root.'

Celia frowned, she stepped back, staring from the vial to the pentacle. 'It might harm him . . .'

'Ah, you fear *me*, and what I have done,' said Melusine, 'but God has forgiven me, believe me . . . *Voyons, petite*—you have a crucifix in your pouch. Ah, you jump—but I know these things. Take it out!'

Celia, whose heart resumed the hammering she had not felt since entering the hut, slowly did so.

Melusine took the beads reverently in her hand, she bent and touched her deformed mouth to the cross. '*Je jure que si ton coeur est pure*, if you wish only good to your husband . . . there'll be no harm. Now repeat the word of power. "Ishtareth." It is old as Babylon . . . Ishtar was goddess of love.' She put the little vial in Celia's reluctant hand.

'Adieu,' she said, 'we'll nevaire meet again. *Quand vient la grande marée*—the great tide on All Hallows' Eve, I go with it.'

'Melusine!' cried Celia, struck anew by pity, by a momentary yearning which was almost love.

But the woman pushed her through the door. '*Bonne chance, adieu,*' she said inexorably.

Celia walked up the dune. When she turned at the top, she saw Melusine naked again in her doorway, and heard her calling softly to her seal, 'Odo ... Odo, *reviens, mon ami, je t'attends.*'

By the time Celia reached Skirby Hall the whole episode with the water witch had become painful. She was ashamed of it. She started to throw away the little vial of brown powder, then dropped it in her coffer—with the crucifix. She blotted both from her mind.

During the next days before John returned, her servants were amazed at the bustle she instigated, a perfect rage of housekeeping; floor rushes renewed though they were scarcely a month old; furniture polished with bees-wax until brawny arms ached; the brewer and the baker harassed into making ale and loaves enough for a castle.

John came home and she welcomed him warmly. But she never gave him the water witch's powder.

Fifteen

In the summer of the Year of Grace 1558, John Hutchinson died, and Celia returned to Cowdray. The letter which summoned her arrived in August, and was brought by an elegant young equerry named Edwin Ratcliffe, one of several gentlemen ushers now attached to Lord Montagu's enormous household. Like Wat, nearly four years ago, Edwin had other commissions in Lincolnshire—to the Clintons, to the Cecils—and found this side-track among the eastern fens a bore. He was, moreover, upon arrival startled to see that Skirby Hall was a house of mourning.

The windows were draped in black cloth; Sir John's painted hatchment was nailed over the gate until it could be transferred to the parish church where his tomb was being prepared.

A shabby old gardener acted as porter, and when he gave Edwin the dolorous news, Edwin tried to leave the letter, supposing that the sorrowing widow must be in seclusion, and himself anxious to explore the pallid entertainments of Boston before continuing his journey. The gardener gainsaid him, and insisted on ushering Edwin towards the Hall, saying that her poor ladyship wanted company. There'd been only a handful at the funeral—scandalous few considering what Sir John's position used to be—and *they'd* all gone home.

Edwin, a jaunty youth of twenty who had entered the powerful Viscount's service as a stop-gap before assuming his majority, gave an irritated assent. He was thunderstruck when he entered the Hall and the widow rose gravely to meet him.

'Blessed Jesu!' said Edwin, staring.

Celia, in her cheap black robes, the plain black coif frilled with a touch of white, her wan cheeks, her great sombre eyes, reminded him of a nun. There were now a few nuns to be seen in London since Queen Mary was re-establishing the convents. But never a nun so beautiful.

Edwin dropped to his knee, and silently extended the folded parchment with its red seal.

Celia took the letter, and examined the buck's head signet. 'From Lord Montagu?' she said in a quiet, considering voice.

' 'Tis long I've not seen that device. Kind of him to condole with my loss, though I wonder that he heard so soon . . .'

'I b-believe—'tis not *that*, lady.' Edwin blushed to the roots of the curly brown hair on his forehead and the fringe of beard cut in the fashionable Spanish manner. 'I think it is another matter. I have several missives to deliver.'

'Ah, to be sure,' said Celia. The last weeks to her were a shadowy haze. In truth, she thought, John died, *really* died, only ten days ago. He is in his coffin under the pall in the church. There are tapers burning. I bought them, though he didn't want them. He said they were Papist. The last day was Saturday week, when he spoke to me a moment. For so long he didn't speak. I thought of him as dead then. When was that? Yuletide? Nay, before that. Michaelmas? Nay, later. Must have been Martinmas because we slaughtered the ox, the mart ox, and I was stirring the blood puddings when we all heard him give that horrible cry. Even in the kitchen we heard the cry he gave. I thought he would die then, his face was purple as his pall is now. I hoped he would die. But he got better a while. He fretted so over our new war with France, cursing the Spaniards—King Philip—the Queen. It was February when he got the news of the fall of Calais. He wept, poor soul, he said Calais had been *ours* two hundred years; he lost warehouses in Calais. He wept and ranted, and that night he gave another great cry in his sleep. When I rushed in I thought he'd turned to stone. He could not move, except the flicker of one eyelid. He never moved his limbs again.

'Lady . . .' said Edwin, 'will you open my lord's letter?'

She started. She smiled faintly. She looked at him with deliberate effort, and became aware that this was a comely young man whose sword, slashed satin doublet and tall plumed hat betokened a gentleman; that there was a kindling in his round blue eyes—an expression she had not seen for so long.

'But you must have drink!' she cried. 'I've made you no welcome. Forgive me. There's plenty of ale, bread at least . . .' She moved suddenly to the bell-rope and jerked it, listening for the distant jangle. 'There're only two servants now. I can pay no wages. You see, there was nothing left. Naught but debts. Sir John's heir, 'tis the nephew from Alford—he leaves me here on sufferance a while, but he is antry.'

'How *could* he be—the wretch!' Edwin cried, shaken by a surge of feeling so unaccustomed that he did not recognise it as chivalric. He was no bookish man. He had heard nursery tales about King Arthur and his knights rescuing beauty in distress and thought them dull. Hawking, hunting, archery, tennis, a few scuffling romps with willing wenches, these contented him. He had been betrothed since he was thirteen to the daughter of a neighbouring squire at Petworth. Anne would be fifteen and marriageable by the time he reached his majority in November and came into his dead mother's inheritance. There would be a dual celebration, and at the wedding Anne's manor would be joined to his. He had known the girl all his life, and thought her pleasing—when he thought of her at all. She inspired none of the odd sensations evoked by the lovely widow.

He was silent as Kate shuffled in with a flagon of ale, and glanced at him incuriously.

'Yaw rang fur this, lady,' Kate said glumly. 'Nigh bottom o' keg. Yaw'll hove ter wait fur th' bread, not riz yet—butter's gawn tew.'

Celia bit her lips, then said with a gallantry which Edwin thought adorable, 'Lack-a-day, and such it be. As Job said, "We are born to trouble as the sparks fly upward." '

She did not continue the quotation—'I would seek unto God, and unto God commit my cause,' because the whole passage reminded her painfully of John who had often read it to her. Since he preferred the Old Testament, and often read Job, she had come to view God as a fearsome unpredictable deity, alternately warring with Satan, then enlisting him as a superior correction officer. Yet John seemed to find increasing comfort in his readings, and during the endless evenings before his final seizure, while she stitched and listened, she had gradually absorbed most of the Bible.

Edwin, of a Catholic family, had no idea who 'Job' could be, nor cared. He gazed at Celia—moonstruck.

She poured him some ale. 'Wassail—God give you grace,' she said, sitting on the bench and motioning him beside her. 'I know not your name, sir.'

'Edwin Ratcliffe, my lady,' he said thickly.

Her skin was luminous, like a golden pearl. She smelled of beramot and lavender water. He wondered what her slender body was like under all that swathing black, then blushed again to have had such a thought. He did not touch his drink.

She slowly broke the seal on Lord Montagu's missive and gazed at the elaborate Italianate flourishes which had been made by Anthony's new secretary.

404

'I cannot read this—it is too hard,' she pushed it ruefully towards him. 'Can you, sir?'

Edwin could have, since he had suffered through some years of tutoring and an unsatisfactory year at Oxford, but he knew the contents.

'It is addressed to Sir John Hutchinson,' he said, and crossed himself, 'may God rest his soul—and to *you*, lady. It announces the marriage of my lord the Viscount Montagu and Lady Magdalen Dacre at the Chapel Royal on the fifteenth of July. The Queen's Grace was present. As her health is so poor, the wedding was exceeding small, and hurried. My lord and lady present their apologies to all their friends who were on their country estates.'

'Ah-h,' said Celia. She rose from the bench and stopped to pick up Taggle who was giving imploring whines. So Anthony and Maggie were married. Those two who had meant so much to her once, and who had receded into the void of the past years.

'I'm pleased that I—that *we* were remembered,' she said.

'There's an enclosure,' said Edwin. ' 'Tis in a different hand —and signed "Ursula Southwell".'

Celia swallowed. Bitter-sweet pain, resentment, even anger caused her eyes to narrow. 'Let me see it,' and she pulled the piece of vellum towards her. The handwriting was so shaky that though the words were few, she could read it no better than the official missive. 'Can you read *this*?' she demanded. ' 'Tis from my aunt.'

Aunt? thought Edwin. How extraordinary. He did not know that Lady Hutchinson had any relation at Cowdray. He squinted at the note. 'I believe it says "Celia, I implore you, come to me. I pray Sir John will permit. So I may die in peace." '

'She is dying?' Celia whispered.

'I know naught, lady, I've ne'er seen her. She keeps to her chamber at Cowdray. She was not in London for the wedding.'

Celia was silent so long that he saw she had forgotten him.

She leaned against the embrasure of the window. The murky lattice panes permitted flickering sunlight to shine on her face through a slit in the black curtains. She pushed the curtain aside and looked out over the fens. She had shut Ursula from her heart, long ago—as her aunt had seemed to shut hers. Ursula had not come that Yuletide when she was invited to

Skirby Hall. Instead there was a curt note, so casually sent via common carrier to Boston that it had not reached the Hutchinsons by Christmas. The note said only that the Lady Southwell could not be spared from Cowdray, and was signed by an unknown name, as Lord Montagu's secretary.

John was both resentful and relieved, she remembered.

'So much for your great kin and connections, m' girl,' he cried. 'Can't be bothered wi' us. Ye're well rid o' them — two-faced, black-hearted Papist lot. Forget that false aunt. You cleave to your husband like the Book says!'

Aye, she had thought — cleave to the husband who is no husband, and who was forced on me by an aunt who pretended to love me — for thus she by then, saw her marriage. It became a relief to hate Ursula.

Edwin walked timidly up behind Celia, and said, 'Lady ...?'

She let her hand fall from the curtain, the brilliant sea-blue eyes met his imploring look. 'Aye?'

'You'll want to go to her — Lady Southwell. 'Tis a piteous plea and I — I can escort you. Back to Cowdray. It would — would pleasure me. And, in truth,' added Edwin who was fundamentally sensible, 'wi' matters here as they are, what else can you do?'

Celia hesitated only a moment, then she gave him the dimpled smile, though her eyes remained sober. 'You are courteous, sir. I thank you, and I will go with you.'

*   *   *

Celia left Skirby Hall for ever five days later. Edwin came back for her after delivering his other announcements. The heir from Alford did not conceal his relief as he speeded them from the gatehouse.

Celia rode Juno, and carried Taggle in a little basket behind the cantle. Her only other possessions, the contents of her coffer, made a bundle so small that Edwin was able to lash them on his own horse.

Sir John had not meant it so. In his will written immediately after the marriage he had left her the manor, all his chattels, an interest in his ships and property in Calais. These were gone; how completely vanished even his heir-at-law had not realised until the death.

On that Saturday when he died, John had suddenly grown lucid, had looked up at Celia and said thickly, 'Dearling — I've done wrong by ye. By God I didn't mean to. If 'twere in my power, I'd make thee rich—*Money*—' he cried in a strong voice. 'I'd g'ie thee gold enough to glut a hundred o' those damned Spanish ships! .... Kiss me, child—forgive my lacks—stupidities.'

She had kissed him tenderly on the pain-wrinkled forehead. His eyelid fell, his breathing grew stertorous, but he spoke once more.

'Yea, the Almighty shall be my defence, and I shall have plenty of *silver*.'

Celia had shed tears for him, but she left Skirby Hall dry-eyed. At last she let joy come through. She was going home to Midhurst. She was only twenty, and she knew that again she was desirable. Edwin's every glance told her so.

As they passed through straggling Frampton village she looked away from the cot where Dickon had lived with his grandmother. She did not know if they were still there, but beyond the marshes on the rocky dune she knew that the water witch was not. Melusine and her hut had been washed away on the Hallowe'en tide that year, exactly as Melusine had predicted. It was a tremendous tide blown higher by an easterly gale. Celia heard the servants whispering about it. Better so, Celia thought, and kicked Juno into a trot, eager to reach Peterborough for the night.

Edwin had a fat purse at his belt, and brushed aside her embarrassed demurs by saying that My Lord Montagu was always generous, and would certainly not begrudge her travel expenses. Celia agreed; she knew that both Anthony and Maggie were generous—or had been, but it galled her to be once more dependent. She had been her own mistress in Lincolnshire; during the last months of Sir John's utter collapse she was in complete charge and found it sweet, although she had not known the total ruin of her husband's affairs.

By the time Celia and Edwin reached Easebourne and could see Cowdray's crenellated roof looming through the Park trees, Edwin was thoroughly besotted. She did not keep him at a distance during the journey; she had given him smiles, sweet words. She had even allowed him to squeeze her waist as he helped her dismount, responding with a melting quiver against his chest. When they rode through Petworth, Edwin did not look down the road which led to his own home, and he had begun to make feverish plans for breaking his betrothal. The fury of his parents—and Anne's—seemed unimportant. When he reached his majority surely they could not stop his maternal inheritance. They might disown him, Anne's parents might sue—what matter? Once they met Celia they would give in. Nobody could fail to find her irresistible. And she loved him. He was sure she loved him, yet her so recent bereavement kept her shamefast. He should wait a little.

Edwin did not like to wait, and though the frenzy of his feelings had kept him tongue-tied so far, as they reached Cowdray's avenue he realised how soon she would be swallowed up in the castle, and suddenly burst out, 'Lady! I love thee—I want thee, I must have thee!'

Celia reined in Juno and turned in mild astonishment. 'What's this, sir?' she said smiling. 'You ask me to be your leman? I find it froward.'

'Nay, nay, lady,'' cried Edwin, yanking at his horse's bridle so hard that it started and lunged. 'I mean no dishonour. I wish thee for my wife!'

Celia bent her head and fingered Juno's mane. Then she raised her eyes to Edwin's reddened young face. 'You are kind, sir,' she said softly. 'I'm not ungrateful ...' her voice trailed off.

'I did not mean to speak so soon,' Edwin gulped. 'Celia ... Celia, give me hope, plight me thy troth—love like mine *must* breed love.'

'Alack, not always,' Celia said beneath her breath, while she kept her face downcast, nearly hidden by the widow's coif. She liked Edwin, but for all his seven months' seniority, she knew him to be years younger than she in feeling and experience. Calf-love, she thought, and yet ... She had no plans for the future, no certainty of what awaited her in the beautiful tawny-gold palace at the end of the avenue. And was not any love better than none?

'I cannot answer yea or nay,' she said, and touched his gloved hand at the stricken disappointment in his face. 'And we will see one another, since my lord is in residence.' Until Edwin burst out with his declaration, she had been watching the buck's head banner fluttering from Cowdray's flag-pole.

He reached over and bent from his horse, taking her own gloved hand and kissing it. The glove was one of those Magdalen had sent to Celia's wedding, the fine French leather was worn thin, the embroidery darkened and frayed, but Edwin noticed nothing except the whiff of rose petals from the sachet where Celia had stored her few treasures.

He *is* a gallant lad, she thought, moved by the silent kiss—

perhaps—then forgot Edwin as they drew up to the porter's lodge and her heart began to quake.

The porter did not know her—most of Anthony's household had been changed through the years, but he was respectful to a widowed 'Lady Hutchinson', and greeted Edwin jovially. 'Been quite a journey, eh, sir? Is't true the natives in them parts swim e'en afore they suck?' He chortled and said to Celia, 'Ye can wait in the Presence Room, lady. Master Ratcliffe 'ill show ye where, though 'tis like to be a while. M'lord an' lady rode to Arundel three days agone, and not expected back 'til supper.'

' 'Tis Lady *Ursula Southwell* I came to see,' said Celia evenly.

'Aye, indeed?' The porter looked puzzled. He had been at Cowdray only two months. 'Is't the old dame up i' the south wing? I mind the new page was a-bringin' 'er a posset last week. She's bed-rid.'

'Aye,' said Celia, 'and I can find my way. Nay, sir,' she said to Edwin who was hovering, patently unwilling to leave her, 'I must go alone.'

He submitted unhappily, and watched the slender black figure walk lithely across the side of the courtyard.

The porter chuckled again. 'Smitten by Dan Cupid's darts, eh?' He thumped his hand dramatically over his heart. 'By St. Valentine, I don't blame ye, sir, she's a tasty morsel, and no doubt a good in'eritance from her late husband? I'm partial to widows, m'self.'

Edwin gave him a cold look and headed for the noisy Hall which was, as usual, crowded with Anthony's retainers, some dicing, some playing primero and all drinking.

Celia went into the south wing through a turret and up the old winding stone staircase. She found the familiar room. She knocked twice before there was any answer within. A feeble sound. The woman lying propped on pillows in the bed was so altered that Celia stopped dead, clenching her hands.

Ursula was wizened, her determined rugged face had shrunk to a pale wedge from which the hollow eyes looked out sadly, with resignation. Her lips were bluish, and the only colour in the transparent whiteness. Her grizzled hair hung down over the coverlet in a thin plait which gave her a ghastly air of youth—marred.

She stared at Celia, breathing fast, then held out a fleshless hand. 'So you came, my darling, my child,' she whispered.

'I've made six novenas to St. Anthony. You must reward him for me tomorrow.'

Celia ran across the room and knelt by the bed. She put her forehead silently on Ursula's quivering hand which turned to caress the girl's face.

'In black?' said Ursula in a wondering voice as her fingers touched Celia's coif. 'Not Sir John?'

Celia's slight motion gave assent, and she cried—it was half a sob—'Oh, *why* did you send me away? Why did you never come? I thought I hated you.'

'I know ...' Ursula whispered. Through her rapture of re-lief a grey mist swirled—the faintness she had come to know so well. She gestured to the tabouret beside the bed and a glass vial of liquid. 'The drops, sweetheart—the cordial! I must gain strength enough to talk.'

Celia poured drops into the cordial and held a cup to Ursula's mouth. She waited, tears brimming, until she saw a tinge of colour on the pallid cheek-bones and heard the gasping breaths grow softer. The chamber smelt sour; there were cob-webs in the corner; fleas jumped among the mouldy straw on the floor; the bed linen was stained and damp. None of this was unaccustomed—Celia had slept in many a worse room, but there was an aura of neglect and loneliness that smote her.

'Who cares for you, Aunt?' she cried, using indignation as a shield against the crowding sorrow. 'Have you no chamber-woman?'

'Why, they come ... now and again ... the servants.' Ur-sula shook her head with a touch of the old impatience at so trivial a question. 'There used to be Agnes Snoth, d'you re-member her, dear? At the Priory? She was good to me.'

Celia remembered the neat country maid with the club foot who had made sacrilegious statements about the Mass, about the sacraments, one wintry morning long ago. 'Aye, what hap-pened to her?'

'She was burned for heresy,' said Ursula sighing. 'So many burnings—they sickened me, but Sir Anthony—I mean, His Lordship—always agrees with the Queen's Grace. Heretics must burn. I went back once to the Priory whilst I could still travel. The stench of charring flesh from Smithfield reached even across the river. When I ventured into Cheapside I could hear their screams.'

Celia winced. 'Don't,' she said. 'My lady aunt, forget!'

410

'I can't forget,' said Ursula petulantly. 'Don't you *see*—
'tis the reason—the very meaning of—my silence?'

Celia frowned, shaking her head. 'Pray don't excite yourself, dear aunt.' For Ursula had begun to shiver, her hollow
eyes grew intense, the effort she was making obviously exhausted her. She gestured again towards the cordial.

In a few minutes she spoke more quietly, and from what
she said, assisted by Celia's pitying, then appalled efforts to
understand, the girl perceived a situation she had no inkling
of during the isolated years at Skirby Hall.

The Queen had thought herself with child. Her courses
stopped, she swelled up like a keg, but in the end no babe came
forth, naught but a bladderful of wind and putrid matter.
King Philip had contemptuously returned to Spain, and the
Queen saw this as punishment upon her, as clear evidence
of Divine Wrath that she had been too lax with heretics. So
the burnings began. Not only were the great folk burned, the
Bishops Latimer and Ridley, the Archbishop Cranmer, but
much smaller fry in all the southerly counties. Neither age,
blindness, sickness, nor humble station saved anyone so misguided as to utter a word of doubt against any tenet of the
Holy Catholic Faith.

At Cowdray, Agnes Snoth had been caught reading her
Bible, and when brought for questioning before Hawkes, the
horrified steward, had gushed forth a stream of heresy. The
steward had locked her in the old cell off the latrines until
Lord Montagu should deal with this viper in his nest. Anthony,
who was about to embark as a general to Picardy in the new
French war, had wanted no such sordid and dangerous annoyance on his estate. He sent Agnes under armed guard back to
her original home at Smarden in Kent, where he alerted the
authorities. Agnes, Protestant to the end, had been burned
with others at Canterbury.

'After that,' said Ursula, '*I* was shunned. They could not
openly doubt my piety,' she turned her weary eyes towards
the crucifix in her alcove, 'but Agnes had been dear to me,
and there were suspicions—suspicions,' she repeated. Her
head went limp against the pillow.

Celia's mouth tightened, as she wiped Ursula's damp forehead with a corner of the sheet. So Anthony abetted these
burnings, he had virtually sent a crippled serving-maid to the
stake himself.

'How Lord Montagu must have altered,' said Celia. 'And

411

to think he gave me in marriage to a Protestant, even *entertained* them at his table!'

'Aye ...' Ursula found breath again. 'Much altered. But remember, that was all before the Queen's wedding, before King Philip became my lord's master, and England was received back by His Holiness the Pope, before the *Queen* grew fanatic. Celia—at the beginning, when you went to Lincolnshire I did not write to you because I felt you didn't wish it. When Wat brought back your message, Montagu forbade me the slightest communication with you—I was still in charge of the twins—and since the discovery of Agnes's heresy, I've been really a prisoner. *Now* do you forgive me?'

'With all my heart,' the girl said.

'And for your marriage?' asked Ursula wistfully. 'I've been often addle-pated, blundering, rash—I meant for your best, I was so affrighted by—by—the night that Wyatt came.'

Celia turned her head away. 'That night is long past, buried,' she said. 'Aunt, how was it that you might send me word *now*, at last?'

'Maggie,' Ursula answered, 'Lady Magdalen. When she came here as a bride last month she found me like this, and was pitiful. She sent the new chaplain to me, and a leech who bled me—it did no good. They all know I won't see the summer out—nor need to, now.'

Celia made soothing hopeful sounds which they both disbelieved. Death shadowed the comfortless chamber as surely as the sunlight outside gilded the haymakers whose lusty, merry shouts could be heard coming across the bowling green and pleasaunce.

'I've a stain on my soul,' said Ursula suddenly. 'I've not confessed it to our new chaplain, Dr. Langdale, a busy, impatient man who has come to me but once, when Lady Maggie sent him. He scarce listened anyway, teetering me plague-struck.'

'You've a stain on your soul?' interrupted Celia, smiling. 'By the Mass, it can't be very black ...'

'I think it *is*,' said Ursula gravely. 'I've got Agnes Snoth's Bible, and whilst I could still get from my bed, I've *read* in it, a little.'

'How is this possible?' cried Celia astounded. 'How did this happen?'

Ursula mistook her niece's cry for horror. 'You see,' she

412

whispered sadly, 'they were right to doubt my probity. The Blessed Virgin forgive me.'

'But how—?' repeated Celia.

'During the short time after the spiteful housemaid discovered her, Agnes took refuge in my chamber. She hid the Book under that floorboard near the window. It's been there since.'

Celia stared at the shrunken figure on the bed; she looked at the door, then bolted it. She went to the little hidey-hole beside the window where Ursula had used to let her store the pennies and groats she had earned during her service at the Spread Eagle. She brushed away the mouldering sticky rushes, lifted the loose piece of planking. There was a large book beneath.

The vellum cover was mould-stained, mice had nibbled off its corners, but Celia recognised the shape, and saw familiar lettering on the spine. She lifted the book slowly; it fell open at the start of the New Testament, which showed on intricate engraving of God's plan for man's salvation, Adam and Eve, the Tree of Life, the Crucifixion.

' 'Tis "Matthew's" Bible,' Celia said, half whispering. 'Like the one Sir John would read from. I know the pictures.'

'Holy Virgin!' Ursula's voice shook with fear. 'Aye, to be expected, alack, but, Celia, that Bible was translated, printed, and the notes made by Master John Rogers; he *was* "Matthew". *He* gave it to Agnes himself, when she was briefly in his household. Hide it quick!'

Celia hesitated. This dank-smelling, damaged volume held a reminiscent pathos, an appeal she had not felt during the years when she was permitted no other entertainment. She scraped a patch of blue mould from the title page. 'Can it be so great a sin to read this?' she said in a musing voice. 'In here is the story of Our Lord Jesus.'

Ursula started up in the bed. 'It *is* a sin!' she cried. 'It's forbidden by our faith! *Celia!* John Rogers was the first to burn! Bishop Gardiner tried him with some of the others at our own St. Saviour's in Southwark. Rogers was a heretic, a turncoat priest and married, too! The book is an abomination, I was mad to keep it. Hide it under your cloak; throw it privily into the Rother. Blessed Mary—if they knew *you* had read it—that *I* had such a thing here—'

'Hush,' said Celia. Ursula was wringing her hands, the

weak voice shrilled with hysteria. 'Be calm, I'll rid you of the Book when I can.'

Celia placed the Bible gently back in its hiding place, re-arranged the rushes and took Ursula's frail body in her arms.

Ursula soon fell into an exhausted sleep, while Celia tried to assemble her wits. The disposition of the Bible was un-important at present, it could stay where it was. But she had now serious doubts as to her own reception by the lords of Cowdray.

She heard the old familiar thump of cantering horses on the Easebourne road, and looked out of the same window where she had once seen King Edward arriving with his cortège. Now it was undoubtedly the Montagus. Celia saw the flashing plumes and brooches on the conical brimmed hats introduced by King Philip, the crimson, yellow and azure of velvet riding capes. The tall figures ahead must be Anthony and Magdalen, followed by squires, equerries and grooms.

Several yelping hounds bounded along beside the horses, and Celia was reminded of Taggle. He must still be in the basket, along with her bundle, at the porter's lodge.

She murmured apology to the dozing Ursula, ran down the turret stairs and released Taggle before the Montagus had come up the avenue. Celia clutched the reproachful, squirm-ing little dog tight to her breast, and gained a measure of courage. She went to stand, chin high, just within the court-yard, while the lodge bell rang out. There was a trumpet flourish; the porter and his assistant gatewards ran around bowing, and the steward, Mr. Hawkes, waddled majestically from the main wing to greet his returning master.

Having dismounted, Anthony and Magdalen hurried through the portal. Magdalen saw Celia first, and said, 'What's this, my lord?' to Anthony, 'some puir widow inside o' Cowdray? The almoner should 'a dealt wi' her.'

'So he should,' said Anthony irritably. 'The servants 're growing lax. What d'ye want, mistress? Alms 'll be doled on the morrow. If ye be in dire need of a bed tonight, there's always one in Easebourne at the guesthouse.'

Celia moved forward, the afternoon sun shone hazily across the battlements, but left her face in shadow.

'God's greeting, My Lord and Lady Montagu,' she said curtsying, 'I *have* need of a bed, but not at Easebourne. With your permission I will share that of my aunt, Lady Southwell, who is very ill.'

Anthony looked blank. He had slept badly at Arundel Castle; he had ridden hard to get home; he was weary and distressed. The Queen was again sickly, with intermittent chills and fever, after another false pregnancy. She was swollen with dropsy, and her condition had worsened since Anthony and Magdalen's marriage, when Master Julian, now one of the royal physicians, had secretly told Anthony there was scant hope.

This visit to Arundel Castle had been dismal. Instead of the usual summer sports and merriment there was nothing but gloomy conferences among the Fitzalans and Howards. The Queen had definitely named that slyly Protestant sister, Elizabeth, as her successor. The Queen, after a fit of jealous rage at the ever-absent Philip, had slashed his portrait, and thereafter spent all her days on her knees, praying, or crouched and peering through near-blinded eyes at her Missal.

She refused to see either Anthony or Magdalen, sending a message by young Thomas, the new Duke of Norfolk, that she knew the Montagus served her with devotion, but that she had amply rewarded them, and now wished for solitude.

Anthony's heart was heavy, fears for the future weighted it for the first time in five years.

Magdalen, however, recognised Celia after a moment of astonished inspection. 'Begock!' she cried. ' 'Tis Celia Bohun! Weel-a-day—I niver thought ye'd coom. Ah—widow's weeds? That man is deed? Anither o' those crazy Lollards gan to his judgment, God be thanked. He didn't infect ye wi' his wickedness, lass?'

Celia shook her head, gazing up into the stern little leaf-brown eyes which no longer were loving as they used to be. 'Lady Magdalen, you know why I'm here, that my poor aunt sent for me. I don't wish to be a nuisance.'

'Nay, nay, niver think that!' A trace of Magdalen's old warmth softened her gaze, though she hesitated. There had been some scandal about Celia—Anthony had never said what. And then that disastrous marriage! Magdalen remembered how shocked all the Cumberland Dacres had been when they heard of it. 'Ye're welcome back ta Cowdray, for the nonce, is she not, my lord?' Magdalen said slowly.

Anthony roused himself and gazed at the widow. She had been a very pretty girl, she was now a beautiful woman. He had forgotten her during these years, as completely as Celia had guessed, and the last emotions he had felt about her streaked through his preoccupation. She had been a troublemaker ... she had incited Wyatt; shamefully caused Stephen's departure. She had wed a Protestant, though not without his approval *then*—one must be just—but he wished very much that Celia had stayed in Lincolnshire. Still, no call upon his hospitality was ever refused.

'Aye, My Lady Hutchinson,' he said, unsmiling, 'you're welcome, of course. What have you brought with you in the way o' household? Children, no doubt?'

'No babes, my lord,' said Celia. 'I've borne none. And no household—except my little dog, and Juno, the mare you gave me. Sir John died a ruined man.'

'*Misericorde*, I'm sorry for your sake to hear so,' said Anthony coldly. He tossed his plumed hat and riding gloves to a page. 'My lady, you will attend to this?' he said to his wife, and finally acknowledged the bowing steward. 'Hawkes —tell my yeoman of the chamber I want a bath and a drink. By the Mass, I'm parched wi' Sussex dust.'

Magdalen turned majestically to Celia. 'We will gan in, my dear, and tak' some wine. Ha' ye seen Lady Ursula?'

Celia nodded and her control wavered. She could see so little in this Magdalen of the affectionate lass dressed in russet wool, smelling of peat-smoke, who had stood by this very fountain five summers ago, or who had romped with her in Cumberland. During their brief meetings in London, Celia had attributed the change in Magdalen to fashionable attire and the girl's new position at Court. Now, the change went deeper. The Viscountess Montagu appeared formidable. Her great height was extended by the tall green velvet hat. She had grown stouter, under several gold chains her breasts jutted out like melons. Her freckles were hid by powder, her Northern accent had lessened, yet it was not these things which daunted Celia, it was some subtle interior hardness, and an aura of power which Celia—unhappily aware that she was again a beggar—thought that she apprehended.

The impression faded somewhat when they were installed upstairs in Magdalen's parlour off the great octagonal bedchamber she shared with Anthony.

The parlour was a charming apartment, fresh panelled in creamy oak, picked out with touches of gilt. Along the moulding ran a frieze of scarlet animal heads, the Dacres' bull, the Brownes' buck, fantastically entwined by carved ribbons and garlands. Anthony had refurbished Cowdray for his bride. Magdalen's two ladies-in-waiting curtsied as their mistress entered, and stared curiously at Celia, then resumed their occupations at a gesture from Magdalen. The younger one, a squire's daughter, tinkled softly on the virginals—an instrument Celia had never heard. The other, who was the widow of a knight killed in France during Anthony's brief campaign there, was stitching on an altar cloth.

A serving-man hurried in with a tray bearing a flask of sugared claret. He poured out two goblets.

Magdalen frowned slightly and said to Celia, 'You may sit and drink wi' me. We'll chat a bit. I do not weesh to hear of your time wi' that heretic—very unfortunate, but 'tis past. Where's your beads?' she added sharply, looking at Celia's girdle.

'In my bundle,' answered Celia, though her heart jumped. 'They're broken—they just broke.' She could feel herself flush. She had not told her beads in years.

Magdalen nodded. 'The smith'll mend them. What 're your plans, Celia? After your puir aunt goes to God.' She crossed herself.

Celia flushed deeper. 'I—I haven't thought, lady—all so fast.'

'Ye've no money at all? . . . Jesu, that's bad. Still, I believe we can get ye into Syon! Aye, that'll be best.'

'Syon . . .?' repeated Celia faintly.

'The nunnery near Richmond the Queen's Grace has re-established. That'll be best.' Magdalen's sandy brows relaxed, and having found a solution to the unforeseen problem, she became freer. She chuckled suddenly. 'That's a comical wee dog nestling in your skirts. Do they grow lak that in Lincolnshire?'

Celia tried to smile and explain Taggle over a wave of despair. Syon? A convent? Cloistered, shut away for ever. Surely they had not the power to do it against her will. Yet, the alternative? She knew that this same decision had been offered to Ursula many years ago. Ursula refused, and where had the refusal brought her? To eternal dependence on patronage, to dying in a filthy room in a neglected corner of a castle where she had lived on sufferance, her times of past usefulness forgotten.

Celia thought of Edwin Ratcliffe. Aye, that would be better, so much better, and at least I'd not die a virgin, she thought, with a dark flame of contemptuous rage which darted up from a smouldering cavern she had never explored.

'Ye may gan back to your aunt now, Celia,' said Magdalen, tempering the dismissal with a kindly smile. 'In truth, I'm glad for sweet pity's sake, she's got ye her-re. Ye may order what ye like to mak' her passing easier, ask the housekeeper. If Lady Ursula pines to see the twins, ye mun tell me. Though, my lord forbade it when he thought her unfit. There was a coil about a serving-maid—some damned Protestant wretch —two years back. I knaw leetle about it. An' I'd no be har-rd on the puir owld lady. I'll talk Anthony around, if he questions, which I doot. He has much else on his mind!'

This speech was more like the old Maggie, and Celia was slightly relieved. She smiled, curtsied, and gathering up Taggle, left the parlour and entered into another phase of her life.

She slept that night in the big bed next to Ursula, who seemed the better for it. She looked to Ursula's comfort, and greatly improved the condition of their chamber. She dined in the Hall each noon-time, though the Montagus no longer did. They ate separately from their retinue now. And she encouraged Edwin when she infrequently saw him. Anthony, having thrown off his despondency, plunged into a whirlpool of manly sports. Edwin was constantly commandeered for tilting, or shooting at the butts, or tennis. He was sent on errands to the neighbouring manors. *He* was invited to dine privately with the Montagus.

Ursula never asked for the twins, and when Celia finally encountered them playing outside the maze, she did not wonder. Little Anthony and Mary, albeit only five years old, were a surly, snotty-nosed pair of children. Physically, they resembled Lady Jane, their mother, which meant they were meagre, yet little Anthony already was aware of his rank.

In response to Celia's courteous greeting, he stared at her with hostile eyes and addressed her like a servant. 'Get thee gone, thou great black flapping wench! Nobody wants thee here. I'm the heir o' Cowdray and I say, *Begone!*'

Celia saw their new governess sitting on a bench by the privet hedge. The lady was as inimical as her charges. 'Here is private,' she said, rising angrily. 'Intruders 'll be punished.'

Celia found neither wish nor courage to explain. She left. How different those two might be could my aunt have continued to govern them, she wondered. And realised that there was no answer. As there were no real answers in her life. She was in abeyance. Stuck in a pattern of waiting for a future she could not guess.

One night when Ursula slept—as she constantly did—Celia rose and lit a candle at the brazier which was now well supplied with charcoal. Magdalen had kept her word and Celia's requests for the sickroom were promptly met. A bitter November wind blew off the Downs bringing a swish of sleet against the windows, but Ursula had, after all, survived the summer. Celia lit her candle and looked towards the crucifix. Once she had prayed to it, passionately—the time when Stephen was imprisoned in the cell below them. She sat down on Ursula's X-shaped folding chair and considered that far-off pain until it suddenly invaded her again. How strange that there should still be pain. She wrenched herself from it and considered Edwin. He had found means to waylay her today in the Hall, where the steward at dinner always seated her precisely in line with a salt cellar, betokening her present position at Cowdray.

In two months Edwin's passion for her, albeit constantly thwarted, seemed to have grown. But she knew more of his situation than she had on their journey south. Edwin was betrothed. He had not yet dared to break the news of his new intentions to his parents, though he *had* put off the marriage plans with Anne, saying that Yuletide would be more festive. He awaited his majority on November 20, when he might do as he pleased.

Celia gave him kind words; when he drew her into an alcove near the chapel, she let him kiss her mouth which fired him to a stammering ecstasy, unshared by Celia who found the contact merely pleasant.

Her eyes roamed idly around the chamber, and were drawn to the spot under the fresh rushes where the Bible lay. Ursula had forgotten it was there, as increasing weakness dimmed her mind, and Celia thankfully ignored her agreement to get rid of it. She knew that its presence was a danger, yet disinclination to touch it, a superstitious awe mixed with rebellion, had kept her from action.

She went to the window, and pushed up the concealing plank. *John* had found guidance, solace, even predictions in his Bible. Agnes Snoth had found the same, and all those other burned Protestants. What inspiration had they found to give them the courage to endure the most terrible of deaths?

Celia took the dank tome on her lap, and opened it at random. The thick black letter printing was not hard to read like handwriting. She riffled the pages until her eyes lit on the words 'virgin' and 'widow'. She slowly spelled out the seventh chapter of First Corinthians. It left her dismayed. There was no doubt that St. Paul considered virgins and widows who did not remarry, far more blessed than other women. Celia was both virgin and widowed and did not feel blessed at all. She read on a little with growing vexation and puzzlement. There was a lot about Jews and Gentiles. She had never seen a Jew though they seemed to be in God's good graces, while Gentiles wickedly sacrificed to devils.

'Follow after love, and desire spiritual gifts, but rather that ye may prophesy.' What did that mean? 'Love', aye, yet one must find it before one could follow it. As for 'spiritual gifts', they would undoubtedly be agreeable possessions though of limited use if they led only to prophesying. Celia decided that she did not like St. Paul.

She leafed back through the Gospels, and hit upon the blasting of the fig tree. Here was not the suffering gentle Jesus, the Redeemer, the Saviour, her Latin prayers indicated. It seemed to her very like the action of a petulant man who is disappointed of his dinner. She was reminded of her husband in the days before his apoplexy. One evening he had expected a honey-cake of which he was very fond, and through some mishap, it had not been made. John had shouted an oath, and knocked his empty plate off the table. She knew that the comparison must be blasphemy, and was chilled. She put the Bible back in its hiding place, resolved to throw it in the river tomorrow. There was no comfort in it for her, no guidance, and the Catholics were right.

In guilty contrition she went to Ursula's prie-dieu, and kneeling, gabbled off a Pater Noster, but when she came to the last clause, she was struck by it, and paused. *Et ne nos inducas in tentationem. Why* should an all-loving father *lead* his child into temptation? Why must he be implored not to?

At that moment in Ursula's draughty chamber, Celia renounced God. She would cease to worry about religion. She would conform to any outward acts which seemed expedient at the time, and she would guide her own life as she saw fit. Her own will and desires should be her sole criterion. All else was inconsistency or downright lies. And nothing was worth suffering for.

She crept into bed beside Ursula, snuggled her little dog in the hollow of her arm and fell asleep.

* * *

Two days later, on November 17, Queen Mary died at St. James's Palace, and the whole of England shifted balance.

Anthony and Magdalen were roused at midnight by Wat who leapt off his lathered horse, and plunged upstairs into the Montagu bedchamber without ceremony.

'It's happened, my lord,' he panted. 'An' I killed one hoss gettin' here to tell ye.'

Anthony sat up, gaping at his mud-stained courier. 'She's gone?' he whispered. He bowed his head and crossed himself. 'God give her peace, she had little here.'

Magdalen understood more slowly. Her crinkled red hair bushed around her night-cap, she clutched her nightgown across her bosom, for Anthony had disordered her during the bed-sport earlier.

'The Queen is dead,' repeated Wat, 'an' ye best get ye quick to Hatfield—swear allegiance to the new one. They've all be runnin' there the last week. *All* the Court. But ye told me to wait. As I did when poor King Edward died.'

'Aye . . .' said Anthony, on a long-drawn-out note, 'but this is very different. Jesu . . . Holy Virgin . . .'

Magdalen grasped her husband's arm in sympathy, then her eyes watered. 'Did she die peaceful, Wat?'

'She did. Heard Mass at five, like every day, expired at six, raisin' her eyes to the Host—and whisperin' the Miserere.'

'She was a guid woman, a verra model o' piety,' said Magdalen. 'She prayed much in secret, and 'd no lak to be seen. She was true-hearted and so much to thole! The bairns she fancied she carried, whilst that Philip, that renegade hoosband, och, the maids-in-waiting knew what *he* was! The neet at Hampton he put his arm through my window and grabbed me on the bed, I thwacked him hard wi' the fire-tongs.'

'*Maggie!*' said Anthony sharply, 'I pray thee—'

Maggie accepted the rebuke. 'I was but remembering her trials. The puir wee Queen.' Magdalen wiped her eyes on her hand and reverted to her usual practicality. 'Fetch the steward, Wat. Call the yeomen. We mun start the castle bell a-dirging, and my lord to be made ready.'

'For what?' said Anthony dully. He felt empty. Lost. He had been truly fond of the Queen. There was a time when she said he was the only man in England she could trust. She had altered since the French defeats. The loss of Calais preyed on her during her last miserable months; she blamed all her generals; she talked wildly of treachery, yet Anthony knew

421

he had commanded his troops brilliantly in Picardy. As well as even his father could have.

'My lord!' cried Magdalen shaking him. 'Wake up! Ye mun go!'

'Where?' said Anthony. 'Oh, there'll be the funeral . . .'

'Nay, hinny, nay! That comes later. Go to *Hatfield* like the rest! Hasten before she leaves for London.'

'To Elizabeth?' said Anthony with dreary contempt. 'That two-faced little bastard.'

Magdalen got out of bed, regardless of Wat, who had drawn back watching. She stood like a tower—strong, indomitable. 'Elizabeth is now your Queen,' she said, 'like it or not, Anthony Browne, and if you prize being Viscount Montagu, if, in truth, you value your head, you had better swear allegiance quick.'

'Her ladyship's right, my lord,' said Wat softly. He was devoted to his master and understood Anthony's utter dismay. 'Arter all, the commons is wild wi' joy. They've got a true Englishwoman at last—and she's King Harry's daughter too.'

'I wonder—' said Anthony grimly. 'Queen Mary doubted it—she told me so once. Nan Bullen was a whore, she was beheaded for her whoredom. Who's to say the wench at Hatfield has royal blood?'

Magdalen gasped. She glanced at Wat anxiously, but she knew him to be loyal. She pulled Anthony from the bed with her powerful arm. She shook him again. ' 'Tis the shock has crazed him,' she said to Wat. 'Bring mead to His Lordship. 'Twill hearten him fast. My lord, I niver thought ta see *you* wambly when your duty's clear. I'd ride wi' ye, except I'm three months gone—a perilous time, they say. Think o' your bairns—those ye *have*, an' those I'll breed for ye. Would ye orphan them? Mak' them destitute?'

Anthony slowly bowed his head. He let his night-rail slip down around his hairy ankles, and stood up naked before them—a thickly-muscled handsome man of thirty. As his resolve strengthened, the veins swelled in his neck. He reached for his day linen which was neatly folded on a stool. 'But I'll not compromise my Faith to satisfy the b—, the Queen,' he said, his bearded jaw jutting out.

'She'd *niver* ask it!' cried Magdalen with assurance. 'She went to Mass at Richmond. She's a canny lass and the times I've seen her I thought her gentle and most anxious to please. *Ye'll* know how to please her Anthony—ye've the knack,'

422

Magdalen threw her arms around her husband's neck and gave him a hearty kiss.

*　　　*　　　*

Anthony went to Hatfield and was courteously received. The little brick palace teemed with courtiers, and as Wat said, many of them had arrived before Queen Mary's death. Fearing another of the traps she had stepped around in the past, Elizabeth had again acted the innocent maiden until Sir Nicholas Throckmorton himself brought her the enamelled ring from Mary's dead hand.

When Anthony arrived he found his new sovereign suitably dressed in filmy black and deep in converse with Sir William Cecil whom she had immediately appointed her Secretary of State. Behind her arm-chair hovered young Lord Robert Dudley, Nicholas Throckmorton and Sir Francis Knollys, all of them Protestants who had received no favours during Mary's reign.

As Anthony, kneeling, swore his allegiance, Elizabeth placed her incredibly long slender hands on each side of his, as was customary. Her tawny eyes inspected him contemplatively. Her thin lips curved in a sweet enigmatic smile. 'We know how well you served our late sister,' she murmured. 'And have no doubts of your fealty, My Lord Montagu . . .' She spoke with the faintest tinge of question.

'In all *temporal* matters, Your Grace, I will serve *you* with all my heart,' answered Anthony looking her straight in the eye. And he added, more softly, 'What man could resist so fair a mistress?'

He could see that this pleased her. Much as she loved flattery, and courted it, Elizabeth had long ago learned to listen for the underlying ring of truth. She understood and appreciated the courage of Lord Montagu's qualification, knowing that with the possible exception of Cecil, the religious convictions of her new courtiers yielded fast to expediency. Also, Anthony's bold glance told her that he did indeed think her fair—her skin so startling white it seemed translucent, with a wealth of red-gold hair which gleamed down across her mourning bodice, and that he recognised her charm, an impact born of blandishment and regal dignity. He had never seen King Henry, but he relinquished the doubts he had of Elizabeth's paternity. There was the strength and flexibility of Damascene steel in this young woman. No lowly music-master could have sired a being so intelligent and self-possessed—or so subtly ruthless.

Anthony did not find out the latter quality until later. During the evening he spent at crowded Hatfield, the Queen gave him occasional friendly smiles—but he was removed from the Privy Council. Lord Robert Dudley—those damnable Dudleys—was named Master of the Horse. Other men long in eclipse had reappeared. And it was clear that Anthony would hold no official position in the new reign though he still had several doleful duties to perform for his deceased Queen. He was an executor of Mary's Will, he was one of the chief mourners in her funeral procession.

He returned to Cowdray for the Yuletide, in a mood fully as melancholy as he had left there. He was, accordingly, not disposed to be lenient with vexations in his own household.

Magdalen forbore disquieting him until he had rested for a night, and while lying with his head on her bosom listened to all that had passed at Hatfield.

'Well, my lord,' she said stroking his thick hair, ''t might be worse—and if *she* weds Philip o' Spain as rumour has it, ye'll be back to your former consequence, niver doot it.'

'She'll never wed King Philip,' said Anthony glumly, 'nor anyone mayhap—there's something odd about her, fantastical, I felt it. Oh, she'll dally hither and yon, play the coy miss, yet not a natural woman—no paps neither, like a lad—' he chuckled and ran his hand over Magdalen's belly and breasts, all swelling with pregnancy. 'Yet,' he added, frowning into the darkness, 'she appears to dote on young Robert Dudley, lets him whisper in her ear and touch her neck. By God, that Dudley gang! I thought we'd seen the last o' them when we beheaded Northumberland. Could it be *Robert's* set his sights on a throne, too?'

'Och, hinny,' said Magdalen laughing. 'Y're fair cozened. Robert Dudley *has* a young wife, name of Amy. I've heard 'twas a love match.'

'Bah,' said Anthony, 'any such impediment'd never stop a Dudley's connivings.' Still, he felt comforted, and thought how truly Magdalen resembled the sturdy great oak tree he had first likened her to when they met five years ago.

The next day was Christmas Eve, and Magdalen waited until her lord had breakfasted on ale and salt herring before she mentioned any unpleasant home topics.

'The Lady Ursula is deed,' she spoke quietly. 'I've had her

laid out in the chapel, since she was of your household, an'
was bor-rn at Cowdray.'

Anthony crosssed himself, murmured, '*Resquiescat in pace,*'
and said, 'Lack-a-day, 'twas long expected. There's room for
her at Easebourne church, near her brother-at-law, Sir Davy
Owen. She had the last rites?'

Magdalen shook her head, frowning. 'Unless Celia . . .
Neither Dr. Langdale nor Father Morton was summoned 'til
next day though both i' the house. Celia admits there was
time. I canna understand that lass, she's not even prayed beside the bier.'

'Distraught, I suppose,' said Anthony. 'We'll have Masses
said; for sure the poor lady died in a state o' Grace. Cotsbody,
enough o' funerals! Tomorrow Our Lord is born, and we'll
rejoice. Christmas games!' Anthony's eyes sparkled, he saw
through the window that there was a drift of snow in the
night. 'We'll go a-hunting, tracks'll be easy, I've not had a
good bow in my hands for weeks, nor smelled the Downs. At
the feast we'll have mummers, and many a giddy jape. Edwin
was appointed Lord o' Misrule, he'll keep us laughing. Must
see Edwin at once, help me cast off dull care!'

'My lord,' said Magdalen, reluctant to dampen the high
spirits, 'my lord, Edwin Ratcliffe is gone.'

'Gone?' Anthony stared at her. 'I did not send him any
journey.'

'Gone home to his manor where he's battling wi' his faither.
Squire Ratcliffe's been her-re twice. He's savage. He clouted
the pages. Begock, I thought he was aboot to strike *me*.'

Anthony empurpled with anger and amazement. 'Squire
Ratcliffe? What's got into him? What's ado?'

Magdalen gave an exasperated snort. 'Plenty ado. Edwin
has gone daft for Celia. He vows he'll wed her, and none else.'

'But he's betrothed to that little Anne Weston—he's *contracted!*'

'He was. He's broke it. The day he coom of age. The Ratcliffes vow he's gone mad, and on those grounds 're tryin' to
hold back his mother's legacy. Sech a coil!'

Anthony gulped, and gave a snort like his wife. 'Ye may
well say so. That *Celia*! I'll deal wi' her, and stop this wickedness.'

His wife thoughtfully cut herself another trencher of bread,
and slapped a herring on top of it. 'It's na so easy . . . She's
grieving, shut in her room, I didn't like to speak harsh, though

the lass has certain sure encouraged Edwin. Yet, what's ta be done wi' her? I meant to send her to Syon, the nunnery. Now, it'll be suppressed again.'

'Aye . . .' said Anthony frowning heavily. 'It is already.' He choked on a herring bone, and shouted, 'Name o' God, why can't that wench blandish someone suitable. I was rid o' her once.'

Magdalen nodded. 'But, I've still fondness for Celia. I'm sorry for her. We can't cast her out, 'twouldna be Christian. Anthony, did ye talk to Squire Ratcliffe, mightn't ye calm him? He might soften and 'twould solve Celia's future.'

Anthony's scowl deepened. 'I've enough to do wi' solving my own future, lady, an' I'll not have the Yuletide ruined. I've no mind to soothe a justly angry father, nor countenance a crazy love-sick lad. As for Celia—keep her out of my way! For decency's sake she may remain until her aunt is buried. After that I care naught what becomes of her.'

Magdalen said no more. She thankfully relinquished the subject.

The Christmas festivities at Cowdray proceeded without either Celia or Edwin. The latter was kept guarded in his room at his father's manor and ostentatiously treated as the victim of an attack of madness. Celia continued to spend most of her time in Ursula's chamber, though she was laying plans and biding her time.

She could hear the uproar outside, the raucous cheers as they brought in the Yule log, the carolling of the waits in the courtyard, the stridency from the Great Hall where Anthony's minstrels kept up continuous music—trumpets, pipes, rebecs and drums reverberated throughout the castle. She could dimly hear the songs as the traditional wassails were drunk, as the roast peacock was borne before the company, and the Boar's Head. She was not actually a prisoner; Magdalen had told her she was welcome in the Hall, so long as she kept away from Anthony, but the girl had no heart for merriment. Ursula had died in her sleep, her head resting on Celia's shoulder. It wasn't until the corpse grew cold that Celia realised what had happened. And then she felt only dull resignation, followed by repulsion. The thing on the bed was not Ursula Southwell, nor was the body in the chapel. Ursula was gone for ever, and of the soul all the clergy ranted about, Celia felt no certainty. There were prayers for the dead, but she could not remember them. In any case, what was there to pray *to*? An indifferent

426

void. She was glad when they took Ursula's wasted body away. Glad to have the room to herself and Taggle. She had loved Ursula; years ago she had loved her mother. Both were gone now. Love was gone, faded into a reminiscent sadness like the lingering aura of old wood-smoke. So, new fires must be lit, lively fires to give new warmth, before they too died away.

During that Christmas week, Celia became consciously aware of dormant urges in her body. She caressed her thighs, her breasts, and rubbed them with the marigold pomade she found in Ursula's cupboard. Ursula had made the pomade as a moth repellent; Celia used it for the sensuous pleasure it gave her.

In Ursula's coffer and huge court-cupboard, Celia found many items to enhance her beauty and rejoiced that they were hers.

Ursula's brief will left all that she possessed to 'my beloved niece, Celia Bohun, now Lady Hutchinson', and had been dated four years ago, after Celia left for Lincolnshire. The inheritance which seemed so paltry in the eyes of the Montagus was englamoured for Celia by the delight of ownership. She rearranged the chamber completely. She moved the great bed with its frayed crimson hangings to the northern wall. She took down Ursula's crucifix, and hung up on its peg a tarnished mirror Ursula had acquired during the Southwark days. Now, when Celia knelt on the prie-dieu, she was able to gaze into a wavering reflection of her own face.

At the bottom of the store-chest, carefully wrapped in yellowed linen, she found Ursula's wedding gown. It had once been white, a satin over-dress sprigged with tiny bunches of embroidered flowerets, all faded to an indeterminate cream. The long sleeves were banded with tarnished silver cloth, the tasselled belt had once been of silver, too, but was now blackened. Yet the supple satin, woven at Lyons, had not cracked in forty years, Celia discovered as she shook off the lavender sprigs. Celia tried on the gown, peering into her mirror. The gown was too large, Ursula had been a bigger woman, but the old-fashioned skirts were full enough to accommodate a farthingale. The bodice could be adjusted, the neck lowered, the tarnished bands brighted with alum.

I shall wear this at *my* wedding, Celia thought. She had determined to marry Edwin. The immediate procedures towards that end were not yet apparent, she knew that he was incarcerated at home, but she felt certainty that all difficulties

427

would melt under the force of her will. She and Edwin had stolen several meetings while he was still at Cowdray; she had persuaded herself that she loved him. At least, she was slightly stirred by his kisses, and knew that he was her slave.

The two men who were the prime obstacles to the union, Squire Ratcliffe and Anthony, she was sure of being able to manage—when the time came. Never again shall I be baulked of what I want, she thought. Yet her new-found sense of power must be subtly directed. She was no longer a child to be forced mindlessly into situations she could not control. She would wait until after her aunt's funeral, and meanwhile ready herself.

As an interim step, she discarded the cheap woollen widow's garb, and altered Ursula's best black velvet weeds, knowing that the velvet enhanced the beauty of her skin, and glad that she had refused Magdalen's suggestion that Ursula be buried in them, saying with truth that Ursula would never have wanted such wasteful display.

The funeral was held on December 27, and was a hurried affair. Dr. Langdale officiated at the Mass, but delegated his assistant, Father Morton, to conduct the actual burial in Easebourne church, where a slab had been lifted from the paving near Sir Davy Owen's effigy. Anthony and Magdalen hurriedly attended the Mass, but as it was a chill windy day, did not walk in the funeral procession. Celia walked alone, followed by a handful of the retainers who had once known Ursula—and by Wat Farrier.

After the slab was laid in place, the priest scurried off with the others. Wat turned sympathetically to Celia who was gazing down at the slab.

Wat said, 'Ye'll miss her, won't ye, lady. I mind me o' her many kindnesses, an' she loved ye true.' Like Magdalen, he thought Celia strangely dry-eyed and distant. ' 'Twas well ye came to her at the end,' he added.

'Aye,' she said, 'I'm glad o' that. But death *is* the end, Wat. I doubt anything matters except living. I'll fend for myself, and ne'er harken back.'

'But ye'll say prayers for her soul?' asked Wat puzzled. 'Help ye're lady aunt climb outa purgatory?'

'Have ye ever *seen* a soul, Wat?' Celia answered with a small earnest smile. 'Do you know where purgatory *is*?'

Wat was really startled. Such questions! He was not a religious man. Confession, then Mass, Christmas and Easter,

428

satisfied his inherited tradition. But Celia's great eyes were fixed on him as though she expected an answer.

'Never thought on it,' he said, and also looked down at the freshly mortared slab above Ursula. 'We must have souls ... priests all say so. And purgatory—' he chewed his lips, adjusted his leather jerkin. 'Well,' he said uncomfortably, 'I've ne'er seen Jerusalem, nor talked to anyone 'oo has, but I believe it's there.'

'Jerusalem's a place on this earth,' said Celia, 'and beyond this earth or life is too whimsical for me to credit.'

Wat grunted. He was not in the least disturbed by her pronouncement. Women were always twisting reason for their own ends. He simply felt sorry that she seemed to have lost her Faith, and worried about remarks which might be heretic enough to endanger her.

'Woman wasn't made to think,' he said kindly, 'and her tongue has allus been a dangerous weapon. Keep yours i' the scabbard.'

'I shall,' said Celia, 'except when I need it to do battle.'

She turned down the aisle, and out of the church. Wat followed, startled by her tone yet admiring the willowy grace of her carriage, the proud set of her golden head in its starched widow's coif. At the lych-gate she stopped while Wat unlatched it.

'D'ye never hear naught of Simkin?' she asked.

Wat flushed painfully, a sorrowful anger showed in his little bear eyes. 'Nay, not in years. He run off wi' them Winchester mummers. Broke his poor mother's heart—he run off in women's clothes,' added Wat through his teeth. 'Potts saw him as Sim passed through Midhurst a-clingin' to that pretty-boy Roland, the Devil take 'im! I doant like ter think on it ... me own son ...' Wat gulped.

Celia shook her head with grave sympathy. She understood far better than she had long ago, and she remembered Simkin's vehemence in the Close Walks during her first ride on Juno. 'Some day it'll be different, I'll no have to obey nobody, I'll do as I please wi'out shame.' Had he really achieved this? She remembered how he had told her that red and yellow did not suit her, and yet had cried, 'God rot ye fur being a woman!' Still, there had always been a liking between them, poor ugly tormented lad.

'I'm sorry, Wat,' she said gently, 'still, you've other children and grandchildren to content you.'

'Faugh,' he cried. 'A spineless mewling lot, an' I'm no the man to crouch feebly by his fireside—not yet. Bigod, I'd like to ship out. There's a whole western world across the sea, Span'ard an' French 're hoggin' it all now, but there's *more* to the North, a land like England. I've spoke wi' fishermen from the Grand Banks. They know.'

Celia smiled abstractedly. Adventuring to undiscovered lands did not interest her. She was planning, very coolly, the best time and place to approach Anthony as a first step towards her goal. Twelfth Night, she decided, when he was mellowed by the customary festival. He'd not evict her during the Yuletide. I'll send word to Edwin, she thought. She had already exchanged brief messages with Edwin. The page who had waited on Ursula was enamoured of Celia. Little Robin. He was fifteen, undersized, the lowliest of the pages at Cowdray, and dazzled by the mysterious beautiful widow who stroked his neck and kissed him on the cheek. One of Robin's numerous cousins was a servitor on the Ratcliffe's manor. Celia had bribed the servitor through Robin; sent one of the five shillings she had found in Ursula's pouch. Robin gladly loped the seven miles between Cowdray and the Ratcliffe's for the sake of Celia's thanks.

The twelfth and last day of Christmas came in a crisped sparkle of icy tree-limbs. The brief hours of sunlight shed diamonds on the hedgerows, the privets of the maze and pleasaunce. The air was dry and buoyant. It expelled much of the winter dankness throughout Cowdray's multitudinous chambers which were lavishly decorated with holly, trailing ivy festoons, branches of yew and spruce. From the lintels of each public room hung mistletoe bunches tied up with red ribbons. The kissing balls were nearly denuded of their white berries, since one must be plucked for each kiss to ensure good luck, but the evergreens were still fresh and pungent.

Celia rejoiced in the fine weather—a happy omen. She felt exhilarated in a way she had not been since the day at Skirby Hall when she set out to consult the water witch. Good omens continued through the morning—she sneezed hard before Robin appeared with her breakfast ale and bread. Later, when she reached to the top of the cupboard, a spider fell on her face. As mishaps generally come in threes, so—though, alas, more seldom—may *good* portents. Celia looked out her window towards Easebourne and saw a loaded hay-wain coming

430

towards the castle, and the ox-herd who gangled astride a white ox, had hair as red as a radish.

This multiplicity of good omens offset a passing discomfort. Once, she would have prayed to St. Anthony for the success of her project this day. She had only to run down to the chapel and speak a few imploring words to her patron saint, yet she did not. John Hutchinson's contempt for 'graven images' had left its mark, though she had not been able to like his Protestant Bible either. Religion of either kind was a mockery, a toy for angry children to fight over. I'll have none of it, thought Celia, and unpacked the costume smuggled to her by Robin.

On Twelfth Night at Cowdray the Christmas revels climaxed with the 'Dance of Fools'. Every night there had been mummers from Midhurst and the nearby villages cavorting around the courtyard or in the Hall. These were dressed in simple guises, some wearing animal masks, some having only blackened their faces with soot. They had all been given Christmas pies and pennies, as were the accompanying waits bawling out their carols with ear-splitting vigour.

'The Dance of Fools' was more stylised, and had been held, just so, by centuries of de Bohuns, before the Brownes bought Cowdray, and like the Midsummer Fair, the tradition was perpetuated by Anthony.

Celia had watched the dance several times—when her mother had brought her from Midhurst to goggle near the Cowdray gatehouse among other townsfolk, and during her first year with Ursula when she had seen the ceremony from inside the Great Hall. She was confident that she could manage the dance-steps, and hopeful that amidst the carousing the presence of an extra 'fool' would not be noticed. There were always twelve fools—for the months of the year, for the days of Christmas. Their identity was secret. They were youths chosen by 'The Lord of Misrule'—this year a vapid young squire who had been commandeered to replace Edwin. The fools were dressed as court jesters in the days of Edward the Third, and there were stacks of the old costumes in Cowdray's attics.

By dusk, Celia was ready. The long parti-coloured hood came to her waist and covered her bosom. She had stuffed the horns with sawdust and sewed jingling bells on the tips. The motley trunks were fortunately baggy and hid her hips. She had made a mask, like those she remembered, out of parchment, and drawn thereon a sad clown face, making the eye-

holes very large. She must be able to see what was happening.
Robin had got her a dried pig's bladder which she tied to the
end of a stick. On her hands she put old leather gloves to hide
the amethyst wedding ring. She debated removing the ring,
but some delicacy prevented her, a faint sense of tribute to
Sir John who had been so jubilant, so anxious to make her
happy when he put it on her finger. She chided herself for the
weakness. John was dead, and she had vowed never to harken
back. Well-a-day, she thought, soon I'll have a *new* wedding
ring.

She stole downstairs when she could see the first commotion through her courtyard window. They were lighting the
bonfire near the fountain. On every hill, even on top the distant
Downs the ruddy lights of bonfires were springing up against
the darkness.

Celia knew vaguely what they signified. Ursula had told her.
The bonfires and the 'Fool's Dance' were meant to rid them
of witches, demons or the Devil himself who might have been
encouraged by the licence of the Yuletide festivities.

The twelve fools were already milling together by the gatehouse waiting for the starting signal. There were also three
hobby-horses gallumphing around and neighing falsetto,
amidst much smothered laughter behind the masks. Celia
joined herself to the group without anyone noticing. The fools
had their own traditional music, long practised in an empty
tithe-barn. There were bag-pipers and drummers and a regal
worked by bellows.

As was the age-old custom, Anthony himself soon appeared
under the fan-vaulted porch and cried in a great voice, 'Welcome, sir fools! Will ye dance Christmas out for the Lords of
Cowdray?'

The fools all rattled their pig-bladders and cried, 'Aye, that
we will, if ye do *our* bidding tonight!'

Anthony made a sweeping bow. 'Ye shall be masters here
. . . *Gaudeamus igitur!*'

He stood back as the fools, jingling their bells, all leaped in
the air, then formed a jog-trot procession through the porch
and around the screen into the great Buck Hall. Magdalen,
splendid in gold and green brocade, came down from the dais
to greet them. She laughed and curtsied as deeply as her increasing girth permitted.

The Hall had been cleared of tables, the guests and retainers
were jammed against the walls.

Anthony and Magdalen stayed below the dais, where the Lord of Misrule now sat alone. He was costumed as both a king and a bishop. He wore a glittering mitre above a coronet of gilded ivy. His robe was an embroidered chasuble, but he wielded a sceptre, and he was so drunk that the prescribed greeting he should have given the fools came out as an incoherent mumble while he waved his sceptre aimlessly.

Anthony gave an exasperated laugh, clapped his hands and cried, 'Proceed!'

This was the ticklish moment for Celia. The dance began with six couples bowing to each other then gyrating hand in hand, waggling their flopping horns and feinting with the pig-bladders. An odd man would be noticed, and she well knew how closely Anthony watched the ceremony. She managed to hide behind one of the hobby-horses, and though the Hall was lighted by two hundred tapers and the great fire near the dais, she found a patch of shadow.

The next measure was an intricate leaping darting mêlée, and she joined the fools, stumbling occasionally, yet copying their every leap, and swirling with them to the bleating of the drums. Soon began the part of the dance she had counted on. The group dissolved, and each one ran around the audience, tapping now one, now another with the pig-bladder, and crying, muffled through the masks, 'Come hither wretched wight, we'll purge—we'll purge!'

Soon many of the company had been tapped and risen to join the fools who led them, preceded by their musicians, from the Hall into the chapel where they all began to riot. The fools leaped up and down the aisle, one ran across the altar and thumbed his nose at the crucifix. Another thwacked the statue of St. Anthony on the head. Another pissed in the holy water and sprinkled the guests; one scrambled up the pillar to kiss the Blessed Virgin on Her painted wooden mouth, then he made an obscene gesture towards Her, while all the company roared with mirth.

The two house priests and Anthony looked on tolerantly. Anthony had drunk far more than usual, he had forgotten his cares, his foot thumped in rhythm to the wild weird music; he enjoyed the feeling of debasement for that one night when he was *not* Viscount Montagu, and irreverence towards him, as to the chapel, satisfied a need for masquerade, for a momentary freedom from restraints.

He turned towards an ironic voice at his elbow. 'This is

most interesting, my lord, this Saturnalia. You English maintain the pagan customs in a most admirable way.'

Anthony grunted, annoyed by the interruption. He had invited Master Julian to be a Yuletide guest at Cowdray during the mournful banquet after Queen Mary's funeral. And been rather glad to see him when the doctor appeared yesterday. There were already a score of house guests, another one could always be welcomed, but he disliked the intrusive remark. 'Tonight I am *not* my lord,' said Anthony stiffly. 'And the Fool's Dance has been Christian for centuries, the late Queen —God gi'e her peace—highly approved it.'

'*Da vero, da vero*—in truth,' said Julian smiling. 'I was complimenting you, my friend, I'm enchanted by the spectacle!' He drew back tactfully as one of the smallest fools came capering up.

The fool, madly jingling his bells, thumped Anthony on the shoulder with the pig-bladder and hissed, 'Come,' through the mask.

Anthony was delighted, his good humour restored. 'Surely, I'll come wi' thee, good fool,' he cried. 'Where shall we go?'

The fool waved his black-gloved hands and pointed out along the passage.

The chapel dance was finished, the musicians were already trotting towards the kitchens leading the mirthful procession of fools, and the guests they had tapped. Before the evening ended they would troop through every part of the castle, thus purging it from witchcraft in terms the Devil would understand. At midnight, the chaplains would sanctify Cowdray while swinging censers and reciting the prayers appropriate to Epiphany.

The little fool shook his head as Anthony started to follow the others, he tugged at Anthony's arm.

'This one seems importunate,' said Anthony chuckling, 'and I must obey him.' Highly amused he followed the tugging hand up the Grand Staircase and into a small wainscoted chamber which Anthony used for secretarial purposes. It contained a carved desk, two chairs and a niche filled with ledgers and manor records. It had only one door since it was, in fact, but a privy closet cut off from the Long Galley.

The fool pushed Anthony into a chair, then turned the great iron key in the lock.

'What's this, my fool?' said Anthony, laughing but suddenly wary. 'What d'ye want of me?'

'Obedience, as you have sworn,' said the fool, ripping off the horned hood and the mask.

Anthony gaped. 'Cotsbody,' he whispered. ' 'Tis Celia!'

The girl's golden hair tumbled to her waist. Her face was of startling beauty. Knowing that there would be scanty light in this room she had chosen, she had reddened her mouth and darkened her eyelids. The transformation was eerie, Anthony felt a shiver up his spine. For a moment he could not comprehend why one of the fools should turn into an alluring woman.

'Aye—'tis Celia,' she said with a peal of laughter. 'And you've vowed to obey me.' She moved nearer him, he saw her upturned breasts and little pointed nipples through her fine woollen shift.

'What do you want of me?' he muttered thickly. He lunged forward in his chair and grabbed her around the waist 'Is't *this*, my little demon? Aye, 'tis a night for lust.'

'Nay,' she said, slithering from his hold. 'Not that you displease me, Sweet—far from it. But surely you're not the man to dishonour Lady Maggie, nor—to rape a virgin!'

He blinked, his grasping hands fell limp. He shook his head to clear it from the fumes of sack and lechery. '*Virgin*,' he said. 'Madam, you mock me! *Who* is virgin?'

She sighed. 'I am.' Despite the wavering rush-lights he saw clear her rueful smile. 'I am a virgin,' she repeated quietly. 'Sir John was unable.'

Anthony drew back staring, and was slowly convinced, then stricken by remorse. All those years with that old Lincolnshire clothier—a sterile marriage to which he had helped sentence her.

'Poor little lass,' he said in a far gentler voice. 'Aye, put the fool's hood around your shoulders, 'tis cold in here. What would you have me do, Celia?'

'Arrange my marriage to Edwin Ratcliffe,' she said. '*You* can do it, my lord—a word from you to the Squire. You have the power.'

Anthony sat down. He looked from her beseeching face to his own muscular hands as they lay on the desk. Aye, he had the power to control this small matter, whatever the larger powers he had lost with Mary's death. And why not? The match was not so unequal. Celia was a de Bohun, she was the widow of a worthy knight. She was beautiful and the lad obviously adored her. True, she was penniless. Still, Anthony thought in a growing warmth of generosity, she could be dowered. He could spare the rich Whiphill farmlands, and a tract of woods near Kemp's Hill, also a flock of pastured sheep by the Rother. *Then* the Squire would be mollified.

'When you were a capering fool, my pretty,' he said smiling, 'I swore to obey you. I can do no less for a fair woman.'

Celia ran to him, knelt and kissed his hand. 'You're not angered with me for the trick I played?'

Anthony stroked the soft shining hair. ' 'Twas a richly merry jest and proves your wit. Edwin is lucky! Now, Celia, dress yourself properly, join the company i' the Hall. On the morrow you shall see how well I keep my promise.'

Sixteen

Queen Elizabeth was crowned on January 15, a date picked by Dr. John Dee from meticulous calculations in Elizabeth's horoscope. During Mary's reign, Dee had fallen into disfavour; he was even briefly thrown in the Tower for suspected connivance with Princess Elizabeth. But his forecast and Julian's had come true. Mary died, Elizabeth reigned, and rewarded her new astrologer royal with many promises of preferment, few of which materialised. The new Queen was adept at fostering loyalty by hopes alone.

Julian di Ridolfi did not receive the same favours. He and Dee drifted apart after Julian's marriage, and on Mary's death the Italian physician found himself as subtly but firmly ousted from the new Court as Anthony was, though for different reasons.

Elizabeth, who knew that her popularity with her country was based on her straight English blood, copied her little brother and evinced distaste for foreigners. She had learned many a lesson during the Spanish occupation.

Julian's marriage was brief and immediately regretted. Gwen Owen's Welsh properties turned out to be a few acres of barren mountainside; her house near St. James's Palace was not only riddled with dry rot but partly owned by her brother, who installed there a parcel of brawling brats for the Ridolfis to endure. Gwen herself, though young and comely, was a black-browed Celt, given to melancholy. She had long periods of moaning to herself in Welsh, and after a year, Julian was forced to recognise symptoms of true dementia. He tried on her all the remedies he knew, without success. He even consulted Gwen's kinsman, the great Earl of Pembroke, one day at Queen Mary's Court, and received his answer. 'Oh, that branch of the Owens 've always been mad. I seem to remember that your wife's father fancied himself a dog, and lived in a kennel.'

To Julian's great relief Gwen bore no children, and after the Earl's information, he ceased to share the marriage bed. One day in 1556, Gwen caught the virulent smallpox, and died. Julian was left with half a dilapidated house in London, some useless property in Wales and a bitter memory which he sweetened by philosophical readings in Marcus Aurelius and Seneca.

Occasionally he wondered what had happened to Ursula or Celia. When he saw Anthony at Queen Mary's funeral banquet he had been gratified by the invitation to Cowdray. He was saddened to find that Ursula was dead, but pleased that Magdalen invited him to stay on for her confinement in April. They used to meet often at Court, and Julian had once treated Magdalen for a whitlow on her finger. He knew that in the unlikely circumstance that she should have trouble birthing a child, he could supply far more skill than the midwife. He was also pleased to be near Celia, who had grown radiant and assured.

Anthony had eased all the difficulties attendant upon the marriage to Edwin. It was set for Sunday, April 10. Squire Ratcliffe had given in quite easily. Edwin was released and spent most of his time at Cowdray. The wedding would be held in its chapel, a trifle sooner than the conventional year of mourning for a widow, but Magdalen, following her husband's lead, took a warm interest in the proceedings, and wished them put early enough so that she would not be in child-bed and unable to attend.

Spring came fast during the lengthening Lenten days. The first swallows returned to their old nests, mauve wind-flowers bloomed in the copses, tender gold catkins hung from the hazel trees which gave Cowdray its name. The air grew soft and fragrant. A few new-dropped lambs frisked beside the Rother. From the lords of the manor down to the lowliest scullion, the smell of spring released the ancient joy.

Celia lived in exultance. All that she had wished for, willed for, was coming to pass, without any invocations to saints, without prayer. By her own efforts. She attended Mass politely and shut her ears to the Latin dronings. She felt strong, triumphant and apart. She greeted Edwin affectionately when he was there; she vouchsafed him kisses and gentle words. She forgot him when he returned to his manor. She played with Taggle; she hawked on Juno, galloping over the Downs. Edwin was teaching her the rudiments of falconry.

Once he took her to his manor where she dined with his parents. She captivated the Squire as quickly as Edwin had foreseen. Her demure, downcast looks, the poignancy of her black velvet garb, her soft admiration of the mansion's elegance, its size, its deer park—completed the Squire's capitulation. Mistress Ratcliffe was not so beguiled. She was a peaknosed matron, always on the sniff for trouble.

'The woman's *too* fair,' she said irritably to her husband. 'She'll lead Edwin a dance, the besotted clodpole. I'd not trust her far as ye can fling a rat. Oh, I know My Lord Montagu's giving her a piddling dowry, I know she's his protégée, and for why? She's not kin to him. Depend on't. There's more here than meets the eye. 'T'wouldn't be the first time those great lords fob off their lemans when 'tis convenient.'

Her husband was accustomed to her suspicions and grumbling. He ignored them except for a perfunctory, 'Hold your tongue, lady.'

He had decided to reinstate Edwin's full inheritance, and be damned to the Westons. They must find another husband for their whey-faced little Anne.

*   *   *

On the Thursday afternoon before her wedding, it rained. Celia sat with Magdalen and her ladies in the private parlour where Celia was now welcomed. All of the old friendship had returned. Magdalen was near to term and lethargic. She sat heavily in her cushioned chair. Her belly was huge, even on so big a woman, and she caressed it often, pleased by the lively kicks inside. Her younger lady-in-waiting played a plaintive old tune on the virginals; the elder cut swaddling bands. Celia sewed on Ursula's wedding dress lengths of gilt embroidery Magdalen had supplied to replace the tarnished ones. There was contentment. Celia was even aware of it. I'm happy, she thought. All is well.

She was, therefore, dismayed by a tremor, a sense of warning. Like the moment in her Lincolnshire chamber so long ago she heard voices. They seemed to mingle with the gurgling of Cowdray's leaden gutters. There was a woman's voice, choking with grief. It cried, 'Sir Arthur, I can't stand this! She seemed better, now she's losing ground fast. I don't care *what* Akananda says. As for Richard—he's shut up in that room. Won't eat. Nanny's so frightened, she listens at the door and says he raves and mutters about those stupid Simpsons, and mortal sin. What's happened to those two?' The voice broke. 'It's tragic—tragic.' There was some kind of masculine murmuring in response, then silence.

Celia put down her needle and gazed vaguely around Magdalen's parlour, puzzled rather than frightened. The anguished voice did not sound like Ursula, it had a flatter drawling intonation. Yet she thought of Ursula. But all the names in the woman's speech were meaningless.

Magdalen sipped from the cup of dandelion wine Julian had ordered for her. She looked at Celia and laughed. 'What ails ye, hinny? Rabbit run o'er your grave?'

Celia shook herself, and laughed too. 'I must've been dozing, 'tis a sleepy afternoon. I thought I heard a woman's voice most doleful and lamenting.'

'Och,' said Magdalen, 'it'll be a cow down i' the byre, bawling for her calf. The sounds travel up at times.'

'Look at the dogs!' said Celia, catching her breath.

Not only Taggle, but Magdalen's favourite hound had retreated, stiff-legged, to the part of the room farthest from Celia. They both were whimpering.

'Mayhap they've seen a ghaistie,' said Magdalen crossing herself perfunctorily. 'We had plenty at Na'orth. But they meant na har-rm. I've seen none her-re. O' course, ye might, with ye're Bohun blood.' She yawned deeply. 'I'd lay doon a wee bit,' she added, 'but that my lord'll be back this neet fra Lunnon. Sech a broil ther-re with the Parliament, an' all the daft changes the Queen's Grace wants.'

'Changes?' said Celia, glad to see that Taggle had returned to lie at her feet.

'Weel,' said Magdalen, 'she wants t' put us back to King Harry's day. Or Edward's, rather. Englished Mass an' prayerbook, Communion in two kinds. *She* wants to be supreme head o' the Church. *Daft!* 'Tis a lot o' folderol to please the Commons. Though I'm bound ta admit the Queen's a cannier lass than I thought.'

Celia was not much interested. She had renounced religion in any of its forms on the night in Ursula's chamber. Let them squabble! She was unable to see any threat to her new security, whatever the Queen might decree.

The Ratcliffes were Catholic, but they would doubtless conform to compromises, as would Anthony. Celia vividly remembered the deception at Cowdray during King Edward's visit. The denuding of the chapel, the hiding of the priest.

The priest. Brother Stephen. She thought of him calmly, sadly—as one long dead. The feelings she had suffered, even those brief moments of forbidden love in the Priory had hap-

440

pened to another woman. To a foolish child. She picked up her needle, began stitching, and thought resolutely of Edwin. Three more days and she would be his bride. A dear lad. A gay lad, courteous and accomplished—his only fault that he doted on her so excessively that sometimes he wearied her.

This fault, she knew from observation, would soon pass. Then would be comfortable years, babies, residence in a charming manor, one far larger and more impressive than Skirby Hall. And she would be near Magdalen and Anthony. She would be received at Cowdray as an equal. She felt gratitude to Edwin for his infatuation. Her happiness—only momentarily disturbed by the fantastical voice of an Ursula who was not Ursula—rushed back. She had no premonition, no foreboding. When the young lady at the virginals began to sing 'The Hawthorn Tree' in a small weak quaver, Celia sang with her, strong and clear, 'O, She marvelled to see the tree so green, Hi ho—the leaves so fresh and green.' Magdalen hummed a little, and yawned again.

It was Celia's last placid day.

*   *   *

Anthony came home late. Though the rain had stopped, the Sussex spring mud had delayed him. He sat down to supper in silence. They ate in the privy dining room upstairs to which Celia had recently been promoted on occasion. So had Julian, and both were invited tonight.

Magdalen, though too deeply absorbed in her fecundity to be much perturbed, none the less, could not help noticing her lord's dejection.

Anthony ate roast lamb, drank his sack and spoke not a word.

His children were brought in, little Anthony and Mary. They knelt for the paternal blessing. Anthony looked at them sombrely, said, 'God be wi' ye,' patted them on the head and waved them away.

'Soon ye'll have anither one,' said Magdalen, trying to lighten the gloom. 'An' 'll be a laddie fra the way he rampages.'

'Aye?' said Anthony scowling. 'May heaven help him, for he'll have none in this world.'

Julian had been watching; he understood the situation better than the women did, and his curiosity was far greater. 'They passed the Oath of Supremacy, my lord?' he asked softly. 'The Queen is now Head of the Church?'

Anthony lifted his mug and put it down again. He looked at Julian. 'So it be. Queen Elizabeth has transformed herself into His Holiness the Pope.' He shrugged, then gave a sudden bitter laugh. 'I was the only dissenter. I, Viscount Montagu, alone amongst the forty-three lords, gainsaid this monstrous shift.'

Magdalen gasped. 'Ye *alone*,' she whispered. 'Anthony—ye shouldna. What o' the other Catholic peers—Arundel, Norfolk?'

'All voted "aye",' said Anthony through his teeth.

His wife's cheeks paled until the freckles stood out.

'But the Bishops?' interjected Julian, who saw even more danger than Magdalen was beginning to.

Anthony grunted and shrugged again. 'Oh, the *Bishops*! They voted "no", and much good it'll do 'em—in the Tower!'

Magdalen repeated, 'The Tower . . .' in a horrified tone. 'Oh, Anthony, what *made* ye act agyenst the Queen! It marked ye oot sa clear. Could ye na cozen her, or kept *mum*?'

'I could've . . . I meant to . . .' admitted Anthony slowly. ' 'Twas that stiff-necked monk!'

'Who . . . what monk?'

'Brother Stephen. He prayed at me all one night. Like he was ousting the Devil. He exhorted. He prodded my conscience. He told me the curse o' Cowdray would strike us all, fire to burn and water to drown—did I not hold out. He said 'twas the only way I might avert punishment for my father's grievous sin in taking Easebourne, the Priory and Battle Abbey from the Church.'

There was a long stunned silence, broken at last by Julian. 'It would seem our good friend Stephen has grown persuasive as a Jesuit. I congratulate your courage, my lord. Is the Queen very wroth with you?'

Anthony frowned. 'I believe so, though I've not seen her. That smooth-tongued Cecil spoke to me yester-morn. He implied that Her Grace was much displeased, yet for the love her father bore mine, and the esteem in which she held *me*, she would take no harsh measures at present.'

Magdalen expelled her breath on a long relieved sigh. 'I tould ye she had a merciful heart. Also, she's no truly a Protestant.'

'That may be,' said Anthony, 'however, she's sending me

out o' the country. To Spain and King Philip with a trumped-up mission to retrieve his Garter.'

Magdalen paled again, she moistened her lips. She thought of the St. George's Day when Mary had invested Philip with the Order of the Garter as her consort. She looked down at her belly where the babe had given a mighty kick. 'When . . .?' she said. 'When mun ye gan, my lord? Blessed Jesu, not afore this wee one's born!'

'I hope not,' said Anthony shaking his head. 'Cecil gave me a month to prepare. Poor wife, don't look so doleful. This is better than the Tower, from whence so few return.'

Magdalen was unconvinced. The long sea voyage seemed to her as dangerous. Moreover, she perceived that Anthony was not wholly displeased by the venture which promised excitement. Her fears broke out in anger. 'God blast that meddlesome monk, where e'er he be! He'd no reet to sway ye, I wish I'd him her-re—I'd show him what I feel!'

Anthony gave a small tight smile, and said something to the yeoman who hovered behind his chair. The man bowed and disappeared into the passage behind the arras.

'*That* is a wish I can grant, lady,' said Anthony. 'Would other wishes were so facile.'

Celia had been listening in considerable dismay, though relieved that Anthony would not be leaving before her marriage. Suddenly she took the full meaning of his last speech. Her heart gave a great lurch, her hands went clammy. 'Nay . . .' she whispered. 'Nay, I don't *want* . . .' She stiffened, holding on to the table edge as Stephen walked in.

'*Benedicite*,' he said quietly. He looked into Magdalen's startled face and said, 'My lady, I understand why you might have cause to hate me. I trust that with God's help I may soften your displeasure.'

Celia could not look up. His voice, deep, resonant, found a long-forgotten channel, and seemed to race into her breast where it churned up such turmoil that she shuddered. Julian, who sat next to her, glanced at her sidewise, and saw her whitened knuckles gripping the table. *Per Bacco*, he thought, can it still be thus with her? He shook his head and examined Stephen. *Bello, bel uomo!* Tall, broad-shouldered under the black habit. Must be past thirty, yet his dark, lean face had not altered, except perhaps the hazel eyes. They showed more assurance, even a gleam of humour. The mouth would be sensual on another man. The full ruddy lips under a deep cleft

443

to the long straight nose. When the monk smiled, as he did at Magdalen who was obviously thawing, the mouth indented at the corners, the sternness vanished and was replaced by a composed charm. Behind the exterior Julian felt masculine strength. *La virilitá*, he thought, hardness of stone, heat of fires well-banked. This man should never be a monk, none the less . . . Julian paused and chided himself. *Tuttavia e realmente dedicato*. Dedication, a rare and wondrous quality, one he himself had lost during the stultifying years of Court life. He had not been near St. Thomas's Hospital, he had made no experiments after leaving John Dee's. He was getting old, jaded and used to easy berths like this one at Cowdray.

He was roused by his name.

'Ye knaw Doctor Julian, don't ye, Brother?' Magdalen was making introductions.

'Aye,' said Stephen smiling. 'He cured me once of rat-bite. God's greeting, sir. You look hale.'

'And perchance ye've met M'lady Hutchinson?' pursued Magdalen, who began to see why her lord had been convinced by this tall impressive monk.

Celia had shrunk so far back in her chair that Stephen observed only a widow's coif, and assumed that it belonged to one of Lady Montagu's ladies. He started to make a courteous disclaimer. Then Celia raised her face.

Their eyes met in a prolonged fulminating gaze.

Stephen's mouth quivered, his intake of breath was audible to Julian who felt a shattering through the air, like a thunderclap. He saw the tremors which seized Celia. *Dio mio!* he thought. Everyone must notice this, they are drowning in each other's eyes. And Julian quickly upset his goblet of wine.

The small mishap, and hurried mopping by the yeoman, gave Stephen time for control. 'Ah, yes,' he said, sitting down in the chair indicated by Magdalen. 'Mistress Celia and I have met before, when I was chaplain to my lord.'

Celia was incapable of saying anything. She continued to clutch the table edge. She felt sick, bitter fluid rose in her throat.

Magdalen and Anthony were unaware, too much shaken by their own troubles. Anthony's fleeting thought of the Priory scene years ago seemed so trivial and long past that it had no application now to these two. Stephen had spent much time in France, much in Westminster's Benedictine Abbey as Abbot Feckenham's able junior, and was now a man of such suavity and yet rectitude that Anthony had submitted to his judgment. As for Celia, she would be married Sunday to the man of her choice, and showed pleasure at the prospect. It did not even occur to Anthony that this meeting might be embarrassing. Youthful follies came—and went. There were many really pressing matters.

'Stephen,' he said, 'you'll come with me to Spain, as my confessor? I need you. You've the Latin and the French, you'll pick up the Spanish in a trice. 'Tis a dolt's errand. But ye got me into it, and if I acquit myself well the Queen's Grace may be mollified.'

The young monk shook his head. 'Perhaps . . .' he said. ' 'Twould be an agreeable diversion, but there are stauncher ways for me to serve my Faith. And though the abbeys are dissolved again, Abbot Feckenham is still my Superior. He had other plans for me.'

'Bah! Cotsbody!' cried Anthony, annoyed. 'He wants company i' the Tower, where he's surely bound. What good'll that do your Faith?'

'It *may* yet be the Tower,' said Stephen flushing. 'At present he wishes to send me into Kent, to Sir Christopher and Lady Allen who have great need of a chaplain, and applied to him direct.'

Celia shivered. She raised her eyes once more to Stephen's face, then lowered them. She could not stop herself from shivering.

'The *Allens*!' cried Anthony. 'Not that vulgar, wheedling couple who came to Cowdray during Edward's visit. Mass! Did our poor deluded Queen knight him? The Allen woman was odious. Sorry, Stephen, she's some kin o' yours, I believe, but that's no reason to bury yourself in a forgotten rustic hole. Feckenham has no judgment. Why, you can come back *here* if you yearn to be a simple house priest.'

'You have two chaplains already, my lord,' said Stephen. 'They'll suit you far better than I. They're conformable. I know their records. My Superior sends me to a house where there is no trace of compromise or heresy. Such few homes left in England must be supported.'

'The good Brother maught be reet, my lord,' said Magdalen softly. 'An' he mun follow his conscience, lak' he made ye to do.'

'Bosh!' said Anthony, but he nodded reluctantly. 'How

445

long can ye stay wi' us? Help me ready my papers as ye used to. My secretary's a fool.'

'I've a fortnight's leave ...' said Stephen slowly, 'but I wish to see my brother Tom at Medfield.'

'Och, then,' Magdalen cried, 'ye'll assist at Celia's wedding Sunday! That'll please ye, eh, hinny? Since the Brother's an ould friend?'

Stephen spoke quickly before Celia need respond. 'I must leave here *Saturday*, but I wish Lady Hutchinson the greatest happiness.'

Celia made a faint mewing sound, the parlour tapers wavered and blackened around her. She slumped down, and would have fallen if Julian had not caught her.

'Some little faintness,' said Julian in response to Magdalen's cry of concern. 'Transient disorder of the belly. 'Tis warm in here, and I thought she ate the stuffed pork too fast.' He dipped his napkin in the wine and pressed the drenched linen under Celia's nose. 'She wants blood-letting, I'll do it anon.'

'I'm all right,' Celia murmured. ' 'Tis naught.' She sat up straight and looked at Stephen. 'I believe brides are given to vapours,' she said with a choked laugh. 'Haven't you heard that, Brother Stephen?'

He could not answer her, though Magdalen said, 'Verra true. M'sel', I'd a qualm or two afore our marriage! Brother Stephen, ye may tak' the blue chamber whilst ye're wi' us.'

'Most kind of you, my lady, but I've a fancy to go back to my old quarters on St. Ann's Hill, if you permit. A nostalgic wish.'

'They're tumblin' doon,' protested Magdalen. 'No guid shelter for ye. Weel,' she added seeing his determination, 'I'll send a page wi' a new-stuffed pallet, candles an' a jug o' ale, at the least.'

Stephen bowed his thanks and begged to be excused as he wanted to say the prayers for Compline in the deserted chapel of St. Ann—that he would report to Anthony on the morrow. He blessed them all, while avoiding any glance towards Celia.

'Yon's a guidly priest,' cried Magdalen warmly, 'far a' he looks lak Bonnie Black Will, the lustiest man an' best fighter on the Bor-rder ...'

'My Lady Maggie,' interrupted Celia, 'I'm yet queasy, may I go to my chamber?' She darted out even as Magdalen gave sympathetic assent.

No, carina, no mi povera. No! thought Julian looking after

446

Celia. He half rose to follow her. He had *said* she needed a blood-letting. I could stop her, he thought, whatever her mad plan. I *could* detain her. But this thickly cushioned chair was comfortable. He had not finished the delicious marchpane tart, garnished with orange rind—a confection he loved. Besides, Anthony's chief minstrel came in with his lute and began singing 'Da bel contrada', an Italian madrigal Julian had himself introduced at Cowdray. He settled back to enjoy the music.

Celia ran down the great staircase, through the porch and into the courtyard. She saw Stephen striding towards the gatehouse. She ran around in front of him, so that he halted. 'Stephen, I must speak with you. I must. Dear God, I never knew 'twould be like this again. Torment, anguish.'

He raised his chin, staring down at the lovely face dimly seen by the courtyard torches. 'We've naught to say to each other.'

'We *have*. I saw it in your eyes! I must talk to you. Only *talk*—' she stammered. 'I need counsel. I'll come later up Tan's Hill.'

'*Nay!*' he cried in a great voice. 'I forbid it. Leave be, Celia!' He pushed her aside, and strode with rapid, almost running steps through the gatehouse into the darkness.

Celia stood quiet for a moment on the cobbles. 'I must talk with him,' she whispered. 'Only to see him alone again. 'Tis not wrong. Blessed Jesu help me!' She clamped shut her lips at the instinctive supplication. How stupid it was!

Her wits cleared, and the top of her mind thought with cool precision.

She went to the scullery and soon found Robin. She beckoned to him. 'Which page is to carry the requirements to Brother Stephen, the stranger monk, on Tan's Hill tonight?'

Robin looked at her adoringly, and said he would find out. He came back in a few minutes to report that the order had only just come down to the servants. But the yeoman who brought it said that Robin might as well go himself.

'Very good,' said Celia stroking his cheek. 'Bring the tankard of ale to my chamber. I wish to taste of it before it goes to the holy brother. It should not be too sour.'

Robin nodded. He did not dream of questioning. He brought up the tankard brimming with foamy ale, and waited like a good dog in the passage while Celia bolted her door, and ransacked the store coffer. She found the vial the water witch had given her nestled beneath an old linen shift she had brought from Skirby Hall.

Celia, breathing hard, took a brand of dead charcoal from the brazier. She pushed aside the rushes and drew on the wooden planks the five-pointed star as Melusine had showed her. She put the vial in the central pentagon.

'Ishtareth,' she said, three times, staring at the vial. She took it up and poured the brown powder into the ale tankard. She opened the door and said to Robin, 'This will do.'

He bobbed his head and took the tankard. 'Dear Robin,' she said. 'My sweet, pretty lad, you're a great comfort to me.'

He blushed and kissed her cold hand. Even his youthful self-absorption was pierced by her wild look. Her beautiful eyes glittered like the sapphire in Lady Montagu's ring. 'Are ye well, m'lady?' he faltered.

'Aye, aye,' she said impatiently. 'Go!'

She knew that she must wait awhile until the castle quieted down, until Stephen finished his evening office, and might have drunk the ale. She flung off her widow's robes, hurled the frilled coif in a corner and arrayed herself in the bridal dress. She let down her hair, combed it into a cascade of gold. She peered in the mirror, and pinched her pale cheeks to bring up the colour. She opened a little silver bottle Edwin had brought her, among other gifts, saying that he loved the essence of gillyflower, and hoped she would use this on her bridal day. She rubbed the spicy scent on her neck and arms.

'Ishtareth . . .' she said and laughed. The laugh sounded strange to her, as though someone else had made it. For a second she looked at the bed where Ursula had lain. It was empty, its brocaded coverlet as smooth as when the chambermaid had finished this morning, except that Taggle was curled up at the foot, his chin on his paws, his brown eyes staring at her under the fringe of bristles. He did not try to follow her as he always did when she put on her black cloak. He did not move, he stared at her unblinking.

Celia pulled the hood close around her face. She left the chamber, ran down the turret stairs and into the courtyard. She was now beyond caution, and when the porter said uncertainly, 'What ho, Lady! Ye're late abroad,' she did not answer, leaving him to think what he would. She ran through the pasture and over the Rother's footbridge. She climbed the path up Tan's Hill and scrambled across the rubble of the old Bohun stronghold. A candle was lit in the hut—so Robin *had* been there. The door was on the latch, and she went in. Stephen stood by the little chapel door, his head bent, his Breviary in his hand.

She let her cloak slip down, and advanced slowly, holding out her arms to him.

'Celia . . . I forbade this,' he cried. His book dropped to the earthen floor. 'What in the devil's name are your wearing? Don't look at me like that!' He put his hand over his eyes and whispered, *'Maria Beata—Miserere mei.'*

'Ah,' Celia said sweetly, softly. *'She's* not here now.' Celia pointed to the rotting wall where the Virgin's picture used to hang. *'I* am, Stephen. And I wear my bridal gown for you. None but you.'

'Christ!' he cried. 'My God, why did I come back to Cowdray!'

'You've drunk but little of your night ale,' she said quickly looking into the tankard. 'We'll drink together, a loving cup. Here, my dearest.'

She took a sip and held the tankard to his mouth. He pushed it away.

'I don't love thee,' he cried. 'I don't want thee. I quelled that wicked passion long ago. When I went back to Marmoutier and confessed all to the Abbot, I grew content. I wore the hair shirt, I scourged myself. Celia, I've made my vows to God, and to Her—there can be nothing but hell for us, if we should commit so so horrible a sin.'

'Ah, indeed?' she said. 'At least, you'll not refuse to drink to my bridal, you'd not be so discourteous, good Brother Stephen.' She pointed to the pallet. 'Nor will it harm your soul to sit wi' me a short while. I'm a-weary. You know that I felt ill at supper.'

'Aye,' he said after a moment. 'I'm sorry for that. I'd not be churlish to you.' He had achieved a polite, nearly normal tone. He sat down gingerly beside her on the edge of the pallet, and quaffed deep of the ale. 'To your health, and that of your bridegroom. I'll pray for you both.' He stared rigidly at the wall.

'I thank you,' said Celia. 'How good it smells in here. The pallet is new-stuffed with meadow grass and thyme, and do you smell another fragrance that I am wearing?' She leaned near him. ' 'Tis carnation and woos the heart to languorous ease . . . Stephen, look at me!'

He turned slowly, against his will. Her eyes brimmed with

tears. Crystal drops glistened on her cheeks. Her pink lips quivered like a child's. He had resisted her voice, her fragrance, her feminine lure, but her tears astounded him.

'Nay, darling, don't weep,' he whispered. His arms raised of themselves, he pulled her close, kissing her wet face. He kissed her mouth gently. Gently it opened beneath his.

Soon they lay naked together on the pallet, and she spoke but once. 'Love so wondrous sweet can *not* be wrong.'

He did not listen. Through the last shattered barrier came only dark flooding triumph.

The honeyed fire consumed them both, until they lay quiet, her head buried on his shoulder. Outside from the ash tree a lark began his dawn-greeting warble. Wind sprang up and rustled the new beech leaves. Midhurst church bell rang out for six o'clock Mass.

Stephen said, 'My God . . .' He turned away from her and groaned.

'Nay, love, don't turn away,' she said piteously. 'Now that we are one, as it was always meant to be. Stephen, that first day we met, here on Tan's Hill, think how it was even then.'

'I can't think,' he cried, yet he remembered how she had stood beside his picture of the Blessed Virgin, and he had seen resemblance, how it sickened him—and now, the ultimate betrayal of *Her*.

He sprang up from the pallet, yanked his habit around his nakedness and ran outside into the grove of oaks beyond the chapel. Early sunlight shimmered on the dark tree trunks. Mist swirled up from the bed of last year's fallen leaves. He stood, a black figure as stiff as the tree trunks, his unseeing eyes fixed on a clump of green spears which were piercing through the leaves. A song-thrush hopped along a bough near Stephen's head, it chirped tentatively, then thrilled out its melodious little notes in which the country people always heard a question, 'Did he do it? Did he do it? For sure he did.'

Stephen looked up at the bird. 'You may well mock me,' he said, and laughed while he beat his clenched fist against a tree trunk. The thrush flirted its tail and flew away. And so the Devil's familiar jeers at me, Stephen thought. The Devil was in this grove where the Druids used to worship. There, lurking behind a gnarled old oak, something moved. It was black and scarlet, a glimpse of horns, and a hideous leering mouth with fangs. Stephen stared again, and there was nothing there but an elm tree stump, blasted long ago by lightning.

I'm going mad, he thought. He went to the well; though choked by leaves the spring rains had brimmed it. He sluiced his head and neck.

His wits cleared, the horror vanished, leaving behind only dullness encased by the sense of doom.

He went back in the hut. Celia lay as he had left her, huddled and naked, looking up at him with frightened eyes.

'You must go, dear,' he said gently. 'At the castle we'll hope they haven't missed you. Make some excuse. I'll leave today, myself.'

From the anguish of panic she cried, 'You *can't*! You can't leave me again! Not *now*!'

'What else is there?' he asked. 'In time you'll be happy in your new life with Edwin Ratcliffe.'

'And *you*?' she cried. 'You'll be happy in your new life? You can forget this night?'

He shook his head. 'I don't expect happiness. When I dare pray again 'twill be for mercy, forgiveness. Our carnal love . . .'

'*Carnal love!*' she interrupted fiercely. 'Is that all it means to you? All that *I* mean?'

She saw the flicker in his eyes, and that he bit his lips as though to hold back something. He touched the gleaming tendril of hair which partly covered her left breast, then snatched his hand away.

'Go, Celia!'

'Aye,' she said. She sat up and pulled on her shift, then the crumpled bridal gown. 'This can *not* be the end for us. I won't permit it. If I didn't love thee, I could *hate* thee, Stephen Marsdon!'

He did not watch as she slipped out of the hut. He sat on the pallet, his face in his hands, the tonsure gleaming white on his bowed head.

*   *   *

Julian awakened that Friday morning in a very bad mood. All his joints were stiff. It took him several minutes even to reach for the chamber-pot. There was also a darting pain behind his eyes. He had remedies in his coffer, but felt too wretched to try and get them. By the time a servitor came up to his room with the breakfast ale, early sunlight had vanished and an east wind started to blow, bringing with it more rain. Draughts whistled around the window.

'*Clima sporco*,' said Julian crossly to the servant, whose broad Saxon face showed mild surprise.

'Sir?' he asked, 'd'ye lack somep'n?'

'I merely remarked that this was a swinish climate,' said Julian massaging his swollen fingers. ' 'Tis chill as a tomb in here. Make me a fire!'

The man waggled his shock of hair. ' 'Tis April! No orders ta light chamber-fires in April . . . I dunno . . .'

'Bring me wood and tinder, you dolt,' cried Julian. 'I want a small fire, at least.'

'Jest a liddle fire?' The man looked unconvinced. He went out muttering to himself.

Sancta Maria, Julian thought, and he pulled the blankets close around his shoulders, craving Italian sunlight, craving heat with a passion nothing else could rouse in him now. Once Lady Montagu was delivered and he had received the ten gold angels which he expected, he'd try to sell the miserable little properties his wife had left him, and he'd go home. To Florence? No, that too would be chilly. South! South! Calabria, Sicily, what matter if he could find no rich patron there? Lie in the brilliant sunlight and gladly starve, or he could beg. '*Signori, gentile signori—per pietá* . . .'

He looked around hopefully at a knock on his door. So, the simpleton had come with the wood after all. He cried, 'Enter!' and was bitterly disappointed to have Celia walk in.

'F-forgive me, Master Julian,' she said, taken aback by his angry face. 'I asked where your chamber was . . .' She swallowed and paused.

'*Chiaro!* Obviously . . . but *why*?'

'I—I thought—you might—you would—help me. There's nobody else. You've often seemed fond of me. . . .' Her voice trailed off.

Julian crouched in his blankets and looked at her with displeasure. The egotistical arrogance of the young! And of beauty. Some subtle change in that beauty; loss of the plaintive aura of innocence. The long sea-blue eyes were heavy, dark-circled; her mouth looked bruised; there was a red mark on her neck which he very well recognised. He had made many such marks himself on lovely flesh in the long ago.

'The monk, no doubt,' he said with bored contempt. 'Poor fellow—and no use confessing your lechery to me, it's quite useless. I'm not interested.'

She flushed scarlet and stepped back. 'It's *not* like that, not lechery,' she cried. 'It's love, Master Julian, *love*! Can you not understand that?'

'Ah, yes,' he gave his quick shrug, 'an extremely pleasurable sensation, but you'll find it so with young Edwin, too. *He* must have had more practice in the art. Only keep last night's peccadillo to yourself. Women talk too much.'

Celia stared at him with such horror that he forgot his aching body. The deep-buried string reverberated. A hazy, guilty discomfort—this has happened before—under the olive trees —white marble columns—supplication and denial.

'It's *love*, it's torment—I can't live without him!' said Celia in a hoarse whisper. 'And he is leaving me again, Master Julian, I can't bear it—and yet he loves me, he *must* love me, I gave him the water witch's powder.' She suddenly crumpled on a stool, and hid her face in her hands.

'You *what*?' said Julian. 'You did what?'

It came out in muffled broken sentences. The visit to Melusine. The pentacle, the charm, the mandrake root. *Mandragora*, Julian thought, the most powerful of herbs, the Devil's testicles they called it in Arabic, yet, given the look he had seen exchanged between Celia and Stephen, the lightning bolt of violent desire, what herb was needed? Human passion could generate enough black magic without potions.

He had few scruples and only the half-forgotten ethics dictated by his Hippocratic Oath, and yet he felt a touch of fear. For her, for himself. 'What did she say, this witch, when she gave you the powder?' he asked gravely.

Celia raised her head, her unfocused gaze went beyond Julian. 'That if my heart was pure, that if I used it only to— to help my husband—there was no danger.' She spoke in a wooden tone like a child repeating by rote.

'And did you?' he asked.

She shook her head slowly.

'Did you then use this mandragora only to reinforce your own lust? Or did you use it for—for—well, Brother Stephen's *happiness*? Was that your motive?'

He saw her widened eyes go shuttered and blank.

'I love him,' she said. 'Naught else matters.'

Julian sighed. 'If naught else matters—why do you disturb me?'

She clasped and unclasped her hands. 'Send for Stephen. Tell him, show him—we can flee to the continent. We could be wed. In Germany, even a priest can be wed. In Swisserland,

453

too, I've heard. He can even remain a priest there. He need only give up his unnatural Benedictine vows.'

There was silence. Then Julian said, 'You ask too much, Celia. Nor do you understand the man you say you love. You think only of yourself. And I am a-wearied. You'll get over this madness in a day or so, and marry as you should. Go now— and on the way back to your chamber, find somebody to bring me up wood.'

Her straining face took on a hunted look; the great eyes fixed on him with piercing reproach. 'You do not care what happens to me—or Stephen. Nay, why should you? Yet, I thought . . . I felt. I fancied you were trying to help me— dreams—a kind of dream, I was dying—great danger.'

'My dear girl,' said Julian impatiently, 'you're overwrought. You were merry yesterday morning, I heard you laughing with Lady Montagu over the decorations in the chapel for your wedding, the primrose bunches, the streamers of pink ribbon. I assure you that the unfortunate actions you encouraged last night are but a transient frenzy. You'll soon forget.'

'Will I?' said Celia in so harsh and peculiar a tone that Julian blinked. She gathered up her black skirts, sketched a small unsmiling bow. 'I'll give order for the wood,' she said, and left his chamber.

Julian felt dismay, tinged with anger. Unreasonable, childish behaviour. Ridiculous request that he talk to the monk, who, very properly, was leaving. And then the effrontery of trying to embroil him in a particularly sordid affair, which must come to the Montagus' attention—and redound to Julian's own detriment. He needed those gold angels. *Per Bacco*, I hope Lady Montagu delivers soon, he thought. I'll stuff her with mouldy rye bread, hasten the birth . . . No, better— demand to examine her and rupture the membranes. Fortunately, this lady from the rugged North was not prudish, as were so many English women. England, he thought, with a spasm of distaste.

What folly to waste all these years in a place so alien. What had possessed him? Some force he did not understand. A quotation from Plato darted like a spear through his bafflement. 'In every succession of life and death you will do and suffer what like may fitly suffer at the hands of like . . .' Julian had amused himself with Plato's certainty of transmigration once . . . 'how each soul selected its life—a sight at once melancholy, ludicrous, strange. The experience of their former life generally guided the choice . . .'

Was that, in truth, the answer? Julian, considered a moment. Then forgetful of the pains in his joints, he pulled out from his coffer and old notebook, in which he had—during the years at Padua—written down certain precepts which struck his youthful fancy. There was one by Francesco Guicciardini, a Florentine historian attached to the Court of Alessandro de Medici. Julian looked slowly through the pages until he found the excerpt.

'Whatsoever has been in the past or is now, will repeat itself in the future, but the names and surfaces of things so altered that he who has not a quick eye will not recognise them, or know how to guide himself accordingly . . .'

Possible, thought Julian uncomfortably, very possible. He noted farther down the page a Latin excerpt he had also copied; it was by St. Gregory of Nyssa who had written it in the third century. 'It is absolutely necessary that the soul be healed and purified. If this does not take place during its life on earth, it must be accomplished in future lives.'

'Future lives,' Julian thought. What a wearisome prospect. Back on earth again for struggles, disappointments, pain, despair.

'*Cui bono?*' he said aloud, raising his head and staring at the tiny leaded window panes which were clouded by cold mist.

'So that finally purged of self-will, purged of desires, the soul becomes one with God.' Who said that to him almost forty years ago at Padua? Julian remembered a very dark face under a turban. Black eyes like ripe olives fixed in yellowed corneas. An Arab, wasn't he? They had some Arabian students at the University. The Italian youths made fun of them. But this man wasn't a student, he was a visitor. He had come from Mecca, and landed in Venice, but he wasn't a Moslem, or was he?

Suddenly it seemed important to Julian to remember the man's name, and what he had said in a guttural mixture of Latin and barbarous Italian. So important, that Julian sat down on the hard oak chair and scarcely noted the arrival of a sulky servant, or the lighting of a small fire, though he stared into the flames until he saw the man clearer. Small; rough homespun robes; dirty white turban; and those black-olive eyes ringed by saffron, penetrating, yet impersonal. There were other students who had come to laugh at the freak . . . a room in a palazzo . . . some banquet . . . but the man refused wine or meat. His name was *Nanak*! How had they come to hold private converse? Had Nanak singled him out from the others? They had certainly sat alone for a while on a cushioned marble bench, and Nanak used odd foreign words, which he said were Hindian, from the vast continent to the East where Christofero Colombo claimed to have landed from the West. Though, as to that, there were sceptics at Padua — geographers who heatedly denied that the Genovese had found anything more important than a few uncharted islands. No Paduan, no Florentine, no Venetian ever trusted a man from Genoa — nor each other for that matter.

A log snapped in his fire, and Julian pulled himself together with a jerk. He had started to think about Nanak, and his wits had gone rambling. He no longer wanted to remember the little man, yet for a moment he forced himself. Something about 'Karma' or 'Chiurma' as it sounded to Julian, and seemed to be equivalent to the Christian, 'As ye sow so shall ye reap,' though not necessarily applied to this life, nor to the orthodox conceptions of heaven, hell, purgatory, but to a succession of rebirths called 'Sumsara', in which one experienced the result of every act good or bad, every thought, especially every strong desire. 'Be careful what you crave for,' Nanak had said, 'since you will eventually get it.'

The young Julian had been fascinated. He had questioned Nanak eagerly, until the dense black eyes were hooded, only the yellowed whites showed, and the little man said, 'You are not ready . . . leave me alone.'

Julian had persisted, asking why he could not remember past lives, if such he had had, until Nanak, wearily tolerant, smiling a little as to an importunate youngster, said, 'Sometimes *if* it's for the soul's good, one remembers. It may be to prevent further harm to others, or redress old wrongs — you have one toe on the Path, or I would not have spoken with you. How well and fast you climb depends on you. Remember this, though, that for those who have developed even as far as you have — sins of omission will be punished by the Law as certainly as acts of violence.'

Julian was disappointed then. In retrospect he found the admonition wordy and pithless. He remembered that he had been chiefly struck later by the realisation that Nanak's last speeches seemed to have been delivered in a completely foreign tongue, though the man had not moved his lips at all. Such, perhaps, was the power of imagination. Or was I drunk? Julian thought. We had much wine that night. Vexed with himself and the whole memory, he got up and held his veined, swollen hands close to the fire. I desire warmth, sunlight—his mouth took on its ironic lift—nor do I intend to wait for some possible future life to attain them!

He struggled out of his night-robe, and painfully garbed himself for the day, while listening to eleven strokes from the clock tower. Dinner was not far off. Unfortunately, it was Friday and the devout Montagus never served meat. There might, however, be a fat stuffed carp. His mouth watered at the hope.

*   *   *

Celia did not appear in the Hall for dinner. And nobody missed her. Julian assumed that she might be upstairs with the Montagus, and was pleased at her absence. Her hysterical visit to him could be ignored. He chatted pleasantly with a lawyer from Chichester who had stopped to see Anthony about extension of lease on one of the numerous Montagu properties, and been asked to dine by the steward, as a matter of course. Julian had decided to induce labour in Lady Montagu next Monday, after the wedding. His mind was at peace.

Celia did not appear for supper either. The absence would not have been noted, except that Edwin Ratcliffe rode over to see his betrothed.

The Montagus received him cordially, if in a somewhat absentminded way, and sent the nearest page to fetch Celia. The page happened to be Robin, and he came back after a long time, his blond brows furrowed, his beardless face anxious.

'I can't find her, my lord,' he said dropping briefly to one knee, then gulping. 'I've searched everywhere—Juno's gone, too.'

'Her *mare* is gone?' said Anthony, readjusting his mind with difficulty. He and Magdalen had a hundred matters to arrange before he left for Spain. Not the least was the possible betrothal of little Anthony to the Arundel heiress. Also, Magdalen's brother, Leonard, seemed to be causing trouble on the Border. If Anthony were to regain Queen Elizabeth's favour Magdalen Dacre's family must certainly be kept in line.

'I fear she's gone, my lord,' said Robin, swallowing a sob.

'She's cleaned out her coffers, most o' them, and left her little dog. There's a note writ to you.'

Anthony, frowning, took the scrap of parchment which Robin tendered him. He examined the sprawling block letters. They said:

'MILORD—I CAN NOT WED EDWIN RATCLIF PARDON FORGETTE ME—CELIA. ROBIN MUSTE CARE FOR TAGLE.'

Anthony read the note twice then passed it to his wife.

'What i' the name o' Jesu does this mean?' Magdalen read the note with stupefaction. 'The lass is mad,' she said. 'Her wits 're addled. What a bother! Depend on't, 'tis some coy trick. She wants ye to find her, Master Radcliffe.' She handed the note to Edwin.

Edwin read it while a painful flush covered his young face. He could not speak. The scrap of parchment trembled in his hand.

'The little minx,' said Anthony, almost inclined to laugh. He thought of the Fool's Dance on Twelfth Night—the way she had diddled him, and the moment of fierce desire she had roused in him. The remembrance sent heat to his loins even now. 'I'll find your bride for you, Edwin,' he chuckled, 'if ye've not the guts for hunting.'

Magdalen gave her lord a long speculative stare. Since she had grown so swollen and unwieldy, Anthony had made several unexplained absences from their bed. Last night he had vanished for two hours, murmuring about belly gripes and the latrine. Like a wise and realistic wife she had not questioned, though she had kept a sharp eye on a particularly toothsome dairymaid. The stab of a brand-new suspicion brought immediate collapse of her affection for Celia. 'Master Ratcliffe can seek his br-ride himsel',' she said coldly, her russet eyes glinting at Anthony in such a way that he said hastily, 'No doubt. To be sure, he must.' He resented Magdalen's obvious suspicion, and felt injured since it had no basis in regard to Celia. There *was*, however, the gateward's daughter . . .

'I'll search for her,' said Edwin in a cold tone. 'I can not understand . . . She seemed to love me, though I was never sure.'

'Coom, coom,' said Magdalen briskly, 'ye mauna be chickenhearted. Ye'll find the naughty lass. An' lucky she be to 've won ye! Quick! She'll not 've gan far 'i the rain.'

Edwin bowed and went off with dragging feet. Beneath his crushing humiliation was a certainty. Celia had gone from his

458

life as suddenly as she had entered it, seven months ago. Like the rockets which had flared across the sky at the Queen's Coronation. Brilliance, then nothing but a charred stick left in the hand. His infatuation extinguished itself almost as completely, when he thought of his mother's warnings, and the sweet doleful face of little Anne Weston whom he had so callously jilted.

Edwin mounted his horse outside the Lodge. He debated a moment—Celia might have fled in any direction, there was no guessing. He had never been sure of her inward thought. He slapped the reins, pricked his horse, directed it towards the Petworth road and his own manor.

In Cowdray's privy chamber the Montagus looked at each other. Anthony responded to his wife's sardonic questioning gaze with an exasperated shrug, then he smiled and put his hand gently on her freckled arm. 'I've naught to do with Celia's whimsies, my dear, I swear it by God's Precious Blood.'

Magdalen's eyes softened, she leaned over and kissed his cheek. 'Then why has she fled—if indeed she has?'

'Whyfore does the wind blow north today, and south to-morrow? We've done our best for her, and 'tis not the first time the girl has caused me embarrassment.' He started at a sudden thought. Stephen had left this morning, after spending an hour efficiently helping the secretary with some of Anthony's old papers. The monk had been composed and urbane; he had even said that he might reconsider acceptance of Anthony's invitation to Spain, that he wished to leave early to consult with Abbot Feckenham again. Nay, Anthony thought, there could be no connection between Stephen and Celia now. A pox on Celia! He reverted to the more interesting subject of little Anthony's betrothal.

As for Magdalen, since she knew nothing of any past connections years ago, she was spared any such disquietude at all.

Seventeen

On Lammas Day, August 1, Celia trudged into the village of Ightham in Kent. She had spent nearly four months in flight from Cowdray and their passage was blurred. She had existed in limbo since the drastic action she had taken after Master Julian refused any help.

She headed instinctively towards London, and got to Surrey before her shillings were gone. Then she slept in a field with Juno, and been arrested by an angry bailiff. 'Trespassing, vagrancy, stealing pasturage.' They threatened her with the pillory, but released her in return for Juno — an obviously valuable mare. Celia did not protest, she had no means of feeding Juno. She kissed the horse farewell on its soft muzzle, and walked through Southwark, never pausing to glance towards the Priory. She wandered to the King's Head on Fenchurch Street, the only tavern she remembered because it was the one Emma Allen had invited her to on the night of Queen Mary's procession.

She applied for work, and was hired. She returned to her girlhood duties — drawing ale, serving customers. She endured without hope or plan though she was often awakened by a clutch of panic in her chest, and nausea which made her retch. By morning she had forgotten, and listlessly performed her chores. Her routine had continued until three nights ago — a Saturday.

The King's Head was jammed with riotous tipplers. Celia incurred first the lust, and then the fury of an alderman who grabbed her as she came up from the cellars with a flask of malmsey. His hot bearded mouth and foul breath as he kissed her roused such a rage of disgust that she scratched his face and banged the flask upwards at his crotch. The alderman was momentarily felled. When he reappeared his face was bleeding from four savage nail wounds, and he went straight to the landlord, complaining violently of Celia. The alderman was influential and also the King's Head's best customer. He brought his friends to the Inn and spent there nightly many crowns. He now threatened to take his coterie elsewhere, and the landlord coldly dismissed Celia. There were more complaisant tavern wenches to be hired, and this one, though she did her duties, was not popular with the other servants. She was too pretty, too fine of speech, too aloof. Also, there was some mystery about her. Mysteries were dangerous.

Celia accepted her dismissal in silence. She had earned a few pence besides her keep, and as though the alderman's attack were the key, overwhelming desire rushed through an open door. She packed her few possessions in a cloth bundle, and set out for Kent.

The village of Ightham swarmed with visitors. It was Lammas quarter day, and rents due. Farmers, cottagers and shepherds were clustered before the George and Dragon.

The neighbourhood rustics munched on Lammas Day white loaves. A troup of tumblers was performing on the village green. Warm August sun drew luscious scents from the barrows of cherries and apricots set out for sale.

Nobody noticed Celia who was dressed in the simple costume she had adapted from Ursula's clothes and her own before she left Cowdray. She wore a laced bodice, cut-off skirts, a kerchief on her head. Her bare feet were dusty and not yet toughened. She had discarded her leathern shoes, to be saved for some occasion she could not yet imagine. They were in her pack. Around her neck she wore a tiny pouch which contained her wedding ring. She went into the George among the lowlier customers, and asked for ale and a bit of bread. The barmaid said, 'Take wot ye like, chuck—a ha'penny fur the ale, but Lammas Bread's free. They allus send loaves from the Mote.'

'Ah-h,' said Celia, 'you mean from the Allens at Ightham Mote?'

The barmaid nodded. 'Sir Christopher keeps up the old ways, I'll say that fur 'em, though there's rumours they don't conform to our new Queen Bess. Wot be ye a-doin' 'i these parts? Come for the hop-pickin'?'

Celia was grateful to find simple friendliness—so unlike London. She smiled at the apple-cheeked Kentish maid, and her smile, long unused, felt rusty, but the dimple appeared next her mouth. The barmaid stared. 'Why, chuck,' she said, 'ye be fair as a blossom was ye not so thin. H'ant ye some brave lad to care fur 'ee? Ye don't look a worker.'

'No lad,' said Celia, 'and I *am* a worker. I'll pick hops if I must, but I'd like something steady. Any posts you know of around here?'

'I'll think on't,' said the barmaid. 'Me name's Nancy. Wait i' the kitchen whilst I carry the trays outdoors. Folk be clamouring.' She went out to the garden where trestle tables were set to accommodate the holidaymakers.

Celia crouched on a stool by the hearth. She drank her ale and ate a loaf of the fine white Lammas bread. These relieved the dizzy fatigue. She found a clout and dipped it in the kettle, then washed a cut on her sore foot. She waited.

Nancy did not forget her, and came back in a while. 'I've heard o' somep'n,' she said. 'There was stable-boys at one table, they come from the Mote. Maught be a post *there*— scullery-maid. M'lady Allen 'as just thrown out the last one, give her a sound beating, too. Found she'd a big belly and couldn't name the father. Very strict is m'lady, harsh they say, when she's in her cups, which be often.'

Celia held herself very still. 'Is't a large household at the Mote?' she asked. 'Is't heavy work?'

'As to that I'm not sartain,' said Nancy. 'But ye maught gi'e it a try.'

'I mean,' Celia said carefully, 'are there many to wait on? Grown children . . . the steward . . . a chaplain, for instance?'

'Of childern, only the heir, little Charles. The steward's a wee rabbit of a man, Will Larkin, he'd no be hard on ye, and aye—'tis said they've a new chaplain 'oo tutors Master Charles, but we've not seen him in the village.'

'I'd like to get the job,' said Celia. 'Good Nancy, how shall I apply?'

'Why, 'tis easy.' Nancy gave a happy grin. 'Master Larkin's out there now on the Green, watching the tumblers. I saw him. He'll soon be here for his pot. Ye can arsk him then.'

'I've no references,' said Celia, and to Nancy's expression of startled dismay, she gave a vague lot of reasons. She came from Sussex, but had not there been a servant; she had been married and widowed in Lincolnshire. The King's Head episode she touched on quickly.

'Aye,' said Nancy nodding. 'Barmaid's first lesson is keep temper, ye don' have to go a-bangin' at their cods!' She exploded into hearty laughter. 'I've wanted to g'ie one or two the knee m'self, but 'twon't do. Look now, chuck—what's yer name, by the bye?'

'Cissy,' said Celia after a moment. 'Cissy Boone.'

'Well, Cissy, ye speak ladylike, I believe—unless'n it's

462

Sussex speech. Ye can't write I suppose? Write yer own reference?'

'I must try,' said Celia slowly.

'Pen and ink i' the parlour,' said Nancy. 'I mum get on wi' the work.'

Celia went to the empty parlour and tried. She finally achieved the best note she could.

'CISSY BOONE IS A TRUSTY SERVENTE. LYVED FORE YEAR WITH ME IN LINCS. I COMMEND HIR. LADYE HUTCHINSON,'

Nancy, who had not even learned the alphabet, was delighted with this effort when Celia read it to her.

The rest was simple. Steward Larkin was no scholar himself, and the note impressed him. So did Celia whom he saw through a blur of cataracts, He was also quite deaf, and did not notice the manner of speech which puzzled Nancy. Lady Allen had ordered him to hire a scullery-maid on trial, a mason and chimney-sweep, the last sweep having died most foully of a great sore on his privy parts. Larkin acquired all three servants during the Lammas celebrations and herded them into his cart.

The distance between Ightham village and The Mote was about two miles and took the sluggish oxen an hour to cover, but Celia was so relieved to be off her bruised feet, and now so nervous about her decision, that she wished the time far longer.

The road ran through hop-fields, nearly ripe for picking, between oast-houses and lush orchards. There were some gleaners in the hay fields despite the holiday, for heavy purple cloud banks to the east signalled rain. The cart rumbled downhill and came suddenly on The Mote snugly nestled in the hollow.

To Celia, after Cowdray, Ightham Mote seemed small and unimpressive. A typical old-fashioned fortified manor house, of which she had seen dozens. The encircling moat was also evidence of an earlier age. She looked again, and suddenly The Mote seemed not old-fashioned but sinister, like a beast crouching in its lair. Celia shifted her gaze to the range of windows facing her and saw a woman's face glimmering from a corner of the upper storey—a white face, subtly luminous.

'Who's *that*?' Celia said involuntarily. 'She looks frenzied.'

The steward turned and said, 'Eh? ... What say, m'dear?'

'That!' cried Celia, pointing. 'That woman, she's flapping

something out of the window—something like swaddling bands!'

'Oh, *her*,' said the steward. 'That'll be Isabel. She "walks" sometimes. Around dusk. I can't see her. They say she mourns a babe was killed i' those nurseries, back when the De Hauts lived here, mebbe two hunnerd year agone.'

Celia said 'Jesu . . .' on a long shocked tone. She looked again, but the face had disappeared.

'Lot o' ghosts at Ightham,' said the steward cheerfully. 'Only thing I don't like m'self is the "Cold Room".' He pointed to the chamber in the entrance tower above the portal. 'I go in there and find m'self shivering and shaking in a trice.'

'What happened there?' said Celia, then had to repeat the question louder.

'Damme if I know,' said the steward. 'Murder, no doubt. These old places 've seen a lot o' murders. Don't do to dwell on 'em.'

He gave the ox-herd an order and the cart lumbered to the range of buildings—stables, brewery, dairy and forge—across the lawn from the manor. Here they all scrambled down. Larkin consigned the mason and sweep to the blacksmith, but knew that he must present the new scullery-maid to Lady Allen herself. She was very particular about the house servants.

Celia's heart beat fast enough to suffocate her as she accompanied the steward across the bridge over the moat, then through the tower to the courtyard.

There was still light enough to see that the courtyard was small and paved by cobblestones. These hurt her feet even through the shoes she had donned in the cart.

'If they're i' the Hall,' Larkin said, 'ye'll have to wait. Milady don't like disturbings at her food, an' don't 'ee dare set foot outside the servants' quarters *ever*.'

'Aye, sir,' said Celia faintly. She stood on the doorstep, her kerchiefed head bowed, her body tingling with the sense of Stephen's nearness.

It so happened that Emma was in good humour tonight. They had broached the March beer and found it excellent. Her husband was his usual absentminded amiable self, and little Charles had made them all smile by his comical rendition of a counting song which Brother Stephen had taught him. Charles was blossoming under the new Chaplain's instructions. So, though not aware of it, was Emma. She looked forward to Mass and confessions now, pleasure augmented by the know-

464

ledge that despite the Queen they maintained the old religion. That Mass was again forbidden increased her ardour. She was, moreover, gratified by an invitation from the new Lord Cobham to ride over to Cobham Hall for dinner next month. It had been disappointing that even after Christopher's knighthood they had received little recognition from the County.

She accepted the steward's report affably. 'Good, good. D'ye hear, husband? Larkin's bagged three servants today at Ightham.'

Sir Christopher nodded and echoed his wife. 'Good. Well done. I'll see the mason myself i' the morning. Chimney piece wants mending in the upstairs parlour, and be he skilled, I might build a new oast-house by Wilmot hill.'

'Then there's the cupboard I want in the Hall,' Emma said. 'The safe we sadly need—that'll come first. Where's the new wench?' she turned to Larkin. 'I'll see her in the buttery.'

Celia was as silent as she dared be during the interview.

Emma glanced at the reference, and found it convincing. She noted it was signed by a 'ladyship'. Celia's thin, downcast face certainly did not remind her of the beautiful girl in scarlet and yellow satin at Queen Mary's procession. Celia's 'Yes, m'lady,' and 'No, m'lady' sounded merely well-trained.

'So that's settled,' Emma said. 'All found and a shilling every quarter day. Attend Mass each morning.' She looked sharply at Celia. 'You said you were raised a Catholic?'

'Aye, m'lady.'

'That's a miracle in itself, coming from Lincolnshire,' said Emma with her tight smile. 'And no fooling about wi' the men!' she added, though she thought with satisfaction that this scrawny, sparkless bit of womanhood was not likely to be tempting. 'Ye can bed i' the far attic wi' the other maids, an' I don't expect to see you again until my Gaudy Day.'

'Aye, m'lady,' said Celia.

Before her dismissal she raised her eyes once towards her new mistress. Lady Allen at forty-three was still handsome in a stout, full-blown way. Her heavy face was scarlet on the cheek-bones—by the buttery rush-light one did not see the tiny broken veins. Her black hair gleamed like a rook's back under a green velvet cap. Her slanted dark eyes, glittery as jet under thick lids, might be considered attractive. I was a fool to be afraid of her, Celia thought. I believe she's stupid, for all she's so overbearing.

That night Celia ate a snack with her fellow servants at

Ightham Mote, and slept dreamlessly in the maids' attic. She had arrived where she wanted to be. Stephen was somewhere under the same roof, and her love for him, so long pent, flooded her in warm luxurious waters.

During the next two days she obeyed orders exactly, and did not venture from the servants' wing except for Mass. There was a great deal to do — hauling water in buckets from the moat, washing a constant litter of pots, mugs, tankards, dishes and spoons on the cramped stone counter. She also ran errands to the larder and buttery for Tom the cook, a portly, middle-aged Londoner who grumbled about the dampness from the moat, the faulty kitchen flue or the quality of the meat he was required to roast.

The indoor staff was small, because Emma was a penny-pincher. She made do with three maids and one servitor to wait on table. His name was Dickon Coxe, and he was the son of the Allens' principal hop-grower. Dickon had thought to better himself by working in the manor house, but since he was also made to serve as butler, and valet to Sir Christopher, he felt himself ill-used.

It became clear to Celia, after two days of hard work, that The Mote was badly run. Emma Allen took but spasmodic interest in housekeeping, yet none the less fiercely criticised anything which discommoded her. If she had the fancy for pigeon pie, she expected it to appear for supper, though nobody had been told to raid the dove-cote. She kept the pantry keys dangling at her girdle, but neglected to unlock the pantry, though the dishes she ordered through the steward called for spices and sugar.

She slept most of the morning, to arise bleary-eyed barely in time for the ten-thirty Mass. The staff went to a six o'clock Mass.

The services were held in what was still called the 'new' chapel, though it had been built forty years ago by a Richard Clement, one of The Mote's numerous owners. The old chapel which had served the early manor lords for four centuries had been deconsecrated and become a passageway and storeroom.

The new chapel, which Celia entered with great trepidation, glowed with the richness of linenfold panelling and carved gothic pews. The wood, despite many coats of beeswax, was still a pale beige which only time would darken. The windows held saints' pictures in Flemish glass.

Celia had tied her kerchief so as almost to hide her face,

and sidled into the back pew between a dairymaid and the new mason. The sight of Stephen at the altar, magnificent in a green and gold chasuble, cut her breath. She felt that her love was so tangible that he *must* notice her, though he never looked her way. She stayed huddled in her seat like several others who had not been shriven lately and therefore might not take Communion.

At the conclusion of Mass Stephen vanished into the priest's room behind the altar. Celia returned to the servants' quarters, and a great jumble of pots and skillets to be cleaned.

' 'Tis man's work, that,' said Dickon, passing the scullery on the way to the buttery to fetch Sir Christopher's morning ale. 'Had I time, Cissy, I'd gi'e ye a hand. Ye seem over-delicate.'

'I'll make do . . .' said Celia, though her back ached from lifting iron pots, and her hands were raw from the scouring sand.

'We used to have a scullion,' said Dickon, 'but *she* found maids come cheaper. I'll tell 'ee something. If ye've need, don't ask steward, he's scared of his own shadow, let alone m'lady's. Try Sir Christopher, can ye ever find him alone. *She* listens to *him*, at times.'

'Thank you, Dickon,' Celia said quietly. 'I'll make do.' She thought that Dickon—a small man with sleek russet hair, a long nose and pointed chin—looked rather like a fox, while instinct told her not to trust him. He might feel kindly towards a pretty kitchen wench just then, but anything he did would be to Dickon's interest. He confirmed this by a sudden sly leer.

'There be ways to get on in this house, if ye're clever.'

'Aye?' said Celia, reaching for another pewter dish.

'When ye're sent to pantry or larder there'll be a bit o' sugar loaf or nutmegs ye can slip i' a pouch under yer skirts. Then slip 'em to me, I can sell 'em in Ightham, we'll split profit.'

'I see,' said Celia.

'Oh, ye won't get catched,' continued Dickon. 'Tom Cook, *he* don't notice, an' m'lady's so fuddled wi' drink mostly she'd never know—only mind her temper if ye cross her straight. She near broke the back o' that scullery-maid we had last. And a month agone she killed one o' the hound pups.'

'Killed a puppy,' whispered Celia staring at Dickon. 'Whatever for?'

' 'Cause she stumbled over it on her way to bed. Then she wrung its neck. Aye, she's a devil w'en the fit takes her.'

Celia shivered. She thought of Taggle with an ache of yearning, but nothing could sway her now.

'How's the new chaplain do?' she asked, sluicing dirty water down the drain hole.

Dickon shrugged. '*She* dotes on him. Sits next him at table, touches his arm whilst they talk, and "Oh, Brother Stephen, d'ye think this? Or that?" ' Dickon put on a high falsetto, ' "Pray, sir, don't eat so dainty, ye fast overmuch," and in truth he does. I ne'er met a monk before—this 'un wears a hair shirt under his habit. I saw it when *she* sent a message to his room. Horrid itchy it must be too, all a-bristle wi' clipped horse tail.'

'Oh,' said Celia. She had no doubt what the hair shirt penance was for, and the thought made her angry. Why must he repudiate the happiest moment of his life, and hers? Why must he punish himself for it—as he had punished her by desertion? Could a loving God, or His loving Mother require this of humans? The Bible reported Christ as saying that a father would not give his son a stone when asked for bread. And *I'll* not accept a stone now, Celia thought. I'll fight for the new life inside me, as I didn't for my own. She compressed her lips, and mopped the last of the dishes.

A bell jangled on the board set high in the passage outside the scullery. Celia glanced up. 'That'll be for you, Dickon?'

'Nay,' he answered. ' 'Tis for Master Charles's nursery-maid, Alice, and be she dandling about wi' cook again. She's a stupid wench. Soon or late, *she'll* find out.'

Celia laughed thinly. 'I believe you're afraid of Lady Allen!'

Dickon jerked his head. ' 'Tis best to do her bidding. She talks poor-mouth, but she've a share o' gold sovereigns in a strongbox, an' I aim to get some for me own.'

'How can you?' asked Celia.

'Fur keeping me mouth shut about the Papist practices here. County sheriff'd be interested to hear we've Mass in Latin, crucifix and candles, wi' a black monk for chaplain to boot.'

'Ah . . . I see . . .' Celia frowned. She had not realised that Stephen might be in danger again now Queen Elizabeth reigned, that there might be a repetition of the situation at Cowdray when King Edward came.

'Can you not just filch from the strong-box?' she asked in

so casual a tone that Dickon was completely fooled. He thought the new scullery-wench receptive, and had just discovered that she was pretty. He was proud of his wits, and enjoyed boasting to so agreeable a listener.

He chuckled. 'I see ye're a girl after m' own heart. The coffer's too strong for me, and *she* keeps the key around her neck. Besides, she's building a wall cupboard for it i' the Hall. That'll be bolted and double locked, ye may be sure. Nay, there be easier ways to get at the gold.'

He trotted off whistling, towards the buttery.

That evening just before dusk, after the kitchen supper of pease porridge and small beer, Celia violated rules and left the servants' wing.

First she went out to the garden and searched among the roses and lilies until she found a clump of gillyflowers. She picked two of the fragrant flowers. Then she crept up the back stairs and into a room called The Solar, which had been the fourteenth-century withdrawing room. It had a squint or window into the old chapel so that bygone invalids might see the altar. The Solar also had another small interior window which looked down into the Hall below. Celia pressed close to the grille and stared.

Emma and Christopher Allen sat side by side in two armchairs at the head of the table; little Charles was next to his father; Stephen sat on a stool beside Emma, while Larkin, the steward, ate in isolation below the salt cellar.

Though Stephen had not noticed her in chapel, when his every thought was on the celebration of the Mass, this time Celia's concentrated yearning gaze disquieted him. She heard him say to Emma, 'I've the odd feeling that someone's watching us.'

'What nonsense,' cried Emma with her grating laugh. 'I'd never think *you* one for fancies, Brother Stephen.' She prodded him playfully in the ribs and bestowed on him a look which could only be called languishing.

Stephen drew away and changed the subject. 'I see the mason's making progress with the niche for your new safe.' He pointed to a spot below the upstairs grille where Celia stood.

'Aye,' said Emma, 'but the old wall's three foot thick, and he's a mortal slow worker. Moreover, he's stupid as a sheep. Ye'll have to find a better journeyman than him, Larkin,' Emma

469

suddenly addressed the steward who choked, and said, 'To be sure, lady, I'll seek one on Monday.'

Then Charles, as black-haired and florid as his mother, gave vent to his desire for more sugar plums, since he had finished the last of those his indulgent father had brought from London. There was no means of gratifying him, and his frustrated roars were ear-splitting.

'He wants a good caning, sir,' said Stephen. 'Spare the rod and spoil the child.'

But the Allens shook their heads. Disparate in most other ways, they were yet united in spoiling their heir.

Celia left the grille and wandered through to a chamber with an oriel window. At the end of it her anxious surveys of The Mote's topography were rewarded. She opened two doors and went into what was certainly Stephen's room. There was a wooden cot made up with unbleached linen. There was a chest and his missal lying on it. There was his picture of the Virgin, so pretty, so calm, and a candle burning beneath her in a sconce.

Celia paused beside the image. 'What do you know of love?' she said. The vapid passionless face looked back at her with a faint superior smile. 'I'll win him yet,' said Celia, 'and be damned to you!' She heard her own angry voice with a prick of fear. Gross blasphemy—and the Devil lay in wait for blasphemers. She had the two gillyflowers clutched in her hand, their clove-like scent pervaded the priest's little room.

Celia plucked a dozen golden hairs from her head and entwined them around the gillyflowers. She tied the ends in a bow-knot, and put the offering on Stephen's flat pillow. She slipped away, and regained the kitchen quarters. Would he guess? She wasn't sure, but she felt at peace, a great lifting of the spirits. She had begun the needful measures.

She was not even disturbed later when Emma Allen entered the kitchen like a whirlwind and whacked the cook with an iron ladle because he had burned the Banbury tarts. Emma was further incensed when she realised that Alice had been sitting on the cook's lap.

'Whoremonger!' Emma shouted. 'Fornicator! And *you*, ye little trollop—get out o' here. I'll put ye in the stocks come morning.'

Celia, from a corner, observed that Emma was almost white with rage; her face was grotesque; she lurched and swayed as she delivered her tongue-lashing. She was obviously drunk, and her antics affected Celia no more nearly than a mummers' show.

* * *

Stephen found the gillyflowers tied with golden hair on his pillow that night and was perturbed. He could think of nobody who might have put them there, though the first suspicion was Emma Allen, and induced loathing. He had come unwillingly to realise that the woman was infatuated with him. She touched him often. In the confessional she leaned against his knee, and confessed transgressions so minor he had trouble not smiling. She seemed unaware of her graver sins, and his tactful injunctions resulted only in smiling nods and the slanting look of desire in her black eyes. He wished he had gone to Spain with Anthony, yet at the time only drudgery and obedience seemed the proper penance for that night of dreadful guilt on St. Ann's Hill. Stephen took up the gillyflowers and their bow of golden hair and stared at them again. There was no hair that colour at Ightham Mote. Burnished gold. It isn't possible, he thought. She's married to Edwin Ratcliffe and has forgot me as she must. He looked up at the Virgin and said with great feeling, '*Salve Regina, mater misericordiae, vita dulcedo, et spes nostra —*'

The picture retained its calm remote look. Stephen went to bed, but before he did so he removed the hair shirt. The skin of his belly and back was an angry red dotted with little pustules. The Abbot, his confessor, had only commanded the hair shirt for three months. Now four had passed, and Stephen had scourged himself also, every day with his knotted girdle. Worse than these penances had been Abbot Feckenham's weary disappointment. 'I never expected *this* of you, my son, not lewd sins of the flesh, you have seemed to me so chaste, so upright a monk that I thought you immune to that devil's bait.'

'Aye, Father ... I'm not as strong as I thought.' Thus he had answered, and suppressed the memory of that night, though it returned in shameful dreams.

His hand trembled as it held the gillyflowers. He wanted to throw them out the window into the moat, and yet could not. The scent troubled him, and he put them inside his coffer. There were mysteries surrounding him and the sensation of rushing towards a precipice which could not be there.

He sat down on his cot and thought determinedly of pleasant things. The week he had spent at Medfield with Tom and his family. They had made him very welcome, and Stephen rejoiced to see his brother so prosperous. Tom had risen to be virtually Squire of Medfield, while Nan kept pace with him, wore velvet on Sundays and had silver dishes on her table. Nan resembled her sister, Emma, only in colouring, otherwise she was a sweet placid woman. She had given Tom two more babies after little Tom, who was a bright sensitive five-year-old, a trifle shy with his black-robed uncle. Tom Marsdon, the father, had grown proud of his lineage as he grew to be a considerable landowner, and showed Stephen one evening a large vellum-bound book in which he wished his learned brother to write down all the Marsdon names, their births and deaths, which they could remember.

'Ye know, Stephen,' said Tom laughing a little, 'we've got a *crest*, us Marsdons, leastways there's a thing like a winged snake and some words on the old siller goblet belonged to our great-granfer.'

Stephen was interested in anything which kept his thoughts from straying back to the poisonously sweet night on St. Ann's Hill, and he examined the great cup carefully, though in his childhood he had seen it a score of times when it appeared for Christmas and other ceremonial occasions.

'Sure enough, Tom,' he said, 'that bit of carving is a cock-atrice and the words beneath,' he squinted at the rubbed letters, 'I believe they're French, *En garde*, that is to say, "Beware". Aye, Tom, that's not a bad motto, we must ever beware of temptation—or of *pride*,' he added suddenly, smiling at his brother.

'Well, I *be* proud,' said Tom grinning, 'proud o' the Marsdon stock what's been at Medfield hunnerds o' years, an' never a word o' blame against 'em, proud that liddle Tom'll own greater lands, more livestock, an' a finer manor house than m'father left *me*. But will ye write down i' the chronicle?'

Stephen complied. Between them, even after inspection of the tombs in Medfield church, they could go no further back than their grandfather who had been born in 1430. Stephen entered his dates then continued the chronicle up to the birth of little Tom and his sisters.

Nan watched his labours and the elegant calligraphy in awed silence. She blushed with pleasure when he showed her her own name—Thomas Marsdon married Anne Saxby, Martin-mas A.D. 1550.

'And that'll be the last marriage in the book, Nan,' he said, smiling at her, 'until your children grow up.'

Nan looked at him with troubled eyes. 'Oh, I wish ye weren't a monk, Brother,' she said sadly. 'I know that's wicked o' me, but I warrant ye'd be a fine husband and father and now everyone's leavin' the old religion agen.'

'Which is no reason for me to, or *you*,' said Stephen sternly.

Nan sighed. 'Nay, o' course you're right. The times are so confusing. When I was a girl we had Mass one way, then come King Edward we couldn't have it at all. Then we went back, under Queen Mary, and I liked it, I knew what I was doing. But now under Queen Bess there's no telling what to believe. Medfield church is stripped agen. Bare as an eggshell, and no candles or chanting neither.'

'I know, Nan,' Stephen echoed her sigh. 'But God will prevail. The True Faith will prevail.'

'Aye . . .' she said dubiously, 'but I wish ye weren't going as house priest to Emma . . .'

'Why so?' asked Stephen.

Nan frowned, she picked thoughtfully at a loose thread on the Turkey carpet which covered the table. 'Emma's m'own sister . . . an' I shouldn't . . . but there was allus something odd about her, something . . . awry. I was afraid o' her—when she was sent back from Easebourne Priory at the Dissolution, I was a little girl . . . She used to snare birds—thrushes, larks—wi' bird lime, she'd twist their necks, and keep the corpses a long time in her chamber, never minding the stench. Still, these be foolish words, she's well married to old Kit—Sir Christopher, that is—and I know she's devout, she cleaves to the True Faith.'

Stephen had thought very little of this confidence of Nan's, but since his arrival at The Mote he had been aware of unpleasant incidents—the cruel beating of the scullery-maid, the killing of the puppy. He had expected some remorse, some mention of these during confession. There was none, and his tentative questions produced puzzled blankness. Stephen at last concluded that Emma Allen remembered nothing of her drunken lapses. The situation was new to him. He had often heard confessions from tipplers and toss-pots, but in a society where everyone drank fermented liquors—even his fellow Benedictines—occasional drunkenness was no mortal sin.

Stephen resolved to increase his efforts to regulate the spiritual behaviour of the household in his charge, and after saying the usual prayers climbed into his narrow bed. His thoughts were agreeable since the penances were over and he might hope for divine forgiveness. His disciplined mind forbade wonder about the mysterious gillyflowers tied with golden hair, yet the knowledge that they were in his coffer pleased him.

Celia awoke anxiously on the next morning and jumped out of the bed she shared with the other maids. She ran to the tiny latticed window.

'Wot's ado?' asked Alice yawning, though the chambermaid snored on.

'Naught,' said Celia. 'There's a fine golden sunrise poking through the mist.'

'Wot's that to thee, maidy?' asked Alice, shaking her tousled brown head, 'stuck all day i' the scullery.'

'I'm going a-walk,' said Celia. 'After Mass. I don't want it to rain. Alice—will my lady put you in the stocks today?'

The girl snorted. 'No fear. Master Charles's fond o' me. Besides, *she*'ll have forgot wot happened last night.'

'That's what I thought,' said Celia smiling.

She had lugged a tub of rainwater up to the attic, and Alice watched with growing interest while Celia washed her hair. 'It do come pretty,' she said. 'Yellow as buttercups, and so long. I didn't guess—allus a kerchief hiding it.'

Celia washed the rest of herself and then rubbed gillyflower essence on her skin. She put on a clean shift, and her other skirt which was of fine green wool and had been shortened from one of the Lincolnshire gowns. She laced her black bodice, hoping that Alice's sharp gaze would not notice that the ribbon was spread wider than usual at the waist.

Alice suddenly giggled. 'Who is he, Cissy, m'dear?' she asked. 'I hopes him worthy o' all this pother.'

'Oh, but aye ... that he be,' Celia laughed gaily. ' 'Tis a stout lad, merry as a cricket, a ploughboy in Ivy Hatch. We plan to wed come winter.'

'Fancy that, ye sly puss,' Alice laughed. 'I thought ye a stranger to these parts, where'd ye meet him? Must 've been some months back since I believe ye're breedin'! '

Celia reddened. '*Nay!*' she cried with convincing indignation. 'My belly's ever been plump since childhood, my mother used to lament it.'

Alice was dubious, but she said no more except, 'Have a care, Cissy, ye know what *she* did to t'last scullery-maid.'

'I know,' said Celia. 'Pray tell cook that I've the gripes, but

474

I'll be down to scullery i' time for the breakfast dishes.'

Alice nodded good-naturedly and buried her head in the pillow.

Celia had in the last days discovered Stephen's daily routine. After the quick early Mass for the servants he always went out to walk up the hill behind The Mote, towards a copse of beautiful beeches. Celia today skipped the Mass, and hurried in the direction she had seen him go, as she watched from the scullery window. She had no idea how far he went, so she waited in the first mossy glade, leaning against one of the smooth grey trunks, listening to the rustling leaves and a tapping woodpecker, watching little blue butterflies and then a red admiral.

When she saw Stephen's tall figure come up a grassy slope her palms began to sweat. She ran and hid behind a more distant beech to watch him. His face looked young, vibrant and thoughtful.

She watched as he suddenly leaned down and picked a purple mallow, holding it in his hand, touching the petals with his finger.

Celia took a deep breath and came around the tree. 'May I have the mallow, Stephen?' she asked softly. 'In return for the gillyflowers?'

His head jerked up. He stood as though turned to black marble, staring at Celia, at her face framed by loose curtains of golden hair.

'May I have the flower, my dearest?' she said, and coming near, took it from his hand. 'Now we've exchanged love tokens there should be another exchange.'

She lifted her face to his. He grabbed her to him with an inarticulate cry . . . and they kissed.

He had no preparation, no defence. He melted in the fire she kindled—nothing could now quell their avid desire for union.

On the moss, beneath the murmurous beeches they lay together in mindless joy—until a shepherd's horn blew from a pasture down the hill.

Stephen stirred. 'How can it be—how is it that you are here?' he asked in a dreaming voice. 'You were to wed Edwin Radcliffe.'

'Could you possibly think so?' She showered little kisses on his face, then nestled again on his shoulder. 'I've never loved any man but thee, Stephen.'

'Nor I any woman . . .' he said, and in the saying came the first realisation. 'How came you *here*?' he whispered.

She told him.

'You left all, you left Cowdray and your marriage—for me?'

'Aye, Stephen, for thee. And there is more . . .' She pushed up her skirts and put his hand on her belly. 'In there is your babe.'

He gasped, he pulled his hand away. 'God forgive me,' he whispered. 'God forgive us both.'

His eyes which had been full of love began to harden. He stood up. 'Holy Blessed Virgin . . .' he said. 'What can we do?'

She said quietly, 'You may take me—and the babe to the continent. Mayhap Germany? We could be . . .' she faltered, afraid of his expression. 'Priests can be married in Germany, Stephen—Martin Luther was once a monk . . . a priest.'

'*Martin Luther!* And would you damn me to heresy like that!'

'I don't ask it,' she said in a sad small voice, 'but if you love me . . .'

'I love thee . . .' he said slowly, 'above all human beings but that matters not.'

She sat very quiet on the moss, looking at him with heavy eyes.

'I must think . . . I must pray . . .' said Stephen. 'I'll make a Rosary to Our Lady. And Celia, be patient . . . God will grant us an answer.'

'Will He?' said Celia. 'Or your Blessed Virgin? I doubt they exist. Or if they do, that they concern Themselves with our kind of trouble. You and I must decide this, never mind *Them*.'

Stephen opened his mouth and shut it. He looked at her with horrified pity. And new guilt.

'So to my conscience I must add your loss of faith. Oh, my poor child. At least do this for me, Celia—pray to Our Lady in the chapel. Pray every day, as I will. I taught you the Ave. You have your beads still? Well, use them.'

Celia bowed her head. Suddenly she looked up at him. 'I'm afeared—frightened—something terrible is going to happen. I feel it. Can't we leave here together *now*. Today?'

'No,' he said. 'We must wait. I shall write to my Abbot for guidance. And surely, there's *no* babe. I've heard women are often mistaken. Queen Mary was twice wrong.'

'Alack . . .' She shook her head and was silent a moment. 'Stephen, there's a wise-woman in Ightham, I heard the maids speak of her—she sometimes can—can—stop the unwanted babes. She—she draws them out o' the womb. Would you have me go to her?'

Stephen stared at her. Her calm dry words conveyed nothing to him. He was unable to understand that there might be life within her for which he was responsible, inside that beautiful body which had given him ecstasy. The concept was so repugnant that it seemed ludicrous. 'I don't know what you mean,' he said. 'One can't murder a babe, its life is God's—but there can *be* no babe.'

'You want me to try?' she repeated woodenly. 'It's not wise to bring a priest's bastard into the world.'

Her eyes looked at him steadily, the long seductive eyes, which were the colour of a kingfisher's wing. The wide rosy mouth which he had so deeply kissed was drawn to a thin line.

'I—I cannot believe it. I know naught about these things—unless 'tis punishment for our . . . our odious love.'

'Odious love,' she repeated. 'Poor Stephen, and is it so odious, so hateful to you? Is this . . .?'

She reached up and put her arms around his neck and pressed her mouth on his. Again passion overwhelmed him. It was like a fiery cloud, it was like a lightning flash—no time for thought, for reason. Desire so long successfully quenched weakened his bones, and the world narrowed to one ecstatic moment.

Again they lay quiet on the moss looking up at the quivering ovate beech leaves, and he turned to her, whispering, 'My love . . .'

'Aye,' she said after a moment, 'and is *this* love not nearer to thee than the other— *Her*, in your picture. Can I not be first?'

He recoiled, wishing she had not questioned. How dared she question? Why must she speak?

'I can't answer,' he said at last. 'Leave be, Celia—I—it must be late. There's the next Mass—though I'm no longer worthy to celebrate it, may God forgive me . . . The sun is high, I'll be late. I must think and pray . . . my duty . . . my Order sent me to the Allens . . .'

Celia watched with angry eyes as he rose and smoothed his robes. She watched him tighten the knotted scourge around

477

his waist; the rosary was tangled and he jerked it into place.

'I can't think . . .' he repeated. 'Late for Mass, Jesu—why did you come here this morn? I thought it finished. I thought you happily wed.'

He ran from the copse and down the hill.

A great sob rose in Celia's throat. She picked up the purple mallow which had wilted, the petals were bruised and limp. Her anger gave way to sorrow. For the first time she began to comprehend her lover and the terrible dilemma he was in.

I'll go to the wise-woman, she thought, see what can be done. I'll go away. Then, with searing insight she thought, Or, if I make him go to Germany, break his vows to marry me—he'd truly *hate* me later. Master Julian said I did not understand Stephen, so I'll run away . . . but not yet. A few more days I can still be near him. Then I'll go. When—? A voice cut through her chaos, a stern voice, as distinct as though someone had spoken aloud in the quiet sun-dappled glade. The voice said, 'August eighth.' She looked around in fear. But there was nobody among the beeches. The voice was in her head, it did not sound real like the other voices she had fancied she heard, it simply said, 'August eighth.' Nay, not so soon, she thought, three days off. And I've no money. Stephen will have none, the Benedictines own nothing. Her hand went to the little pouch around her neck. There was her wedding ring —it could be sold, in London, maybe in Ightham—that kind Nancy at the George—or she could find more work some-where—but the babe—the wise-woman would want payment.

Stephen said to pray—*Ave Maria, Gratia plena*—and all she got as answer was Ursula's face, not as it was in the last weeks of illness, but strong, stern and remote.

Celia left the glade of beeches, she dragged herself back to the manor and crossed the moat into the servants' door.

Dickon was lounging outside the scullery. 'Been a jaunt?' he said winking. 'Ye look forespent. Ye're boy'll be a lusty one, eh?' It was evident Alice had been talking.

'He is,' said Celia managing a laugh. Already the scullery was piled high with pewter plates and tankards to be washed.

'Ye needn't go so far afield,' said Dickon, smirking at her. 'Me own cock robin's as able as the next, an'll be glad to oblige ye.'

'I thank 'ee,' said Celia, rolling up her sleeves, 'but I've no wish for it. I—I've plighted my troth.'

'Faugh . . . tarra diddle,' said Dickon. He grabbed her around the waist and fumbled her breasts.

Celia's disgust was too deep for action, as it had been at the King's Head. She spoke through her teeth with freezing venom. 'Don't you dare touch me, you mingy thieving little runt, you turn my stomach. You make me puke.'

Dickon's eyes narrowed. He stepped back. 'Thanks for that, your ladyship. I'll no forget it. Ye may be sure I'll no forget it.' He went to the Hall with a tray full of tankards. The family, having finished their Mass, were at breakfast.

Celia knew abstractedly that she had made an enemy. While she scoured and rinsed, her mind plodded in dreary little circles like an aged horse on a treadmill. Round and round, and no way to stop and rest. Leave now, leave now—I can't leave now, I can't leave now. I *must* see him. Pray then, as he said. I can't pray. Until finally a thick mist clouded her mind, and she did not think at all.

* * *

Sunday, August 6, was to be a Gaudy Day at Ightham Mote. It happened to be Emma Allen's forty-fourth birthday, and therefore a reason for inviting their tenantry to a modest feast. In the Catholic calendar it was also the Transfiguration of Our Lord on Mount Tabor.

It became clear to Stephen, when Emma came to his confessional on Saturday evening that she regarded this coincidence as a special mark of Divine favour, and had his soul been at peace, he might have found some amusement in her complacency. But after her confession, which was hurried and consisted of trivia—that she had not spoken sharply enough to little Charles when he was naughty, that she had forgotten to say the twelfth Pater Noster in her last penance, that possibly she had committed gluttony in savouring an extra cherry tart at supper—Emma received his equally hurried absolution, then suddenly lumbered up from her knees and sat on the other stool.

'We must chat a bit, Brother,' she said smiling at him in a way which jarred him out of his wretched preoccupation.

The confessional was tiny, squeezed behind the chapel, and like all those in private houses, had no grille. Stephen found that Emma was so close that her ample knees pressed against his. Her upper lip was faintly bedewed, her cheeks scarlet and she smelled of spirits. He had himself taken a little of the sack which was always served at supper, but this smell was different, and he suddenly identified it as being like the breath of a monk at Marmoutier who drank fiery white liquid from Cognac until he ended up as a raving lunatic and vanished from the Brotherhood. Stephen drew his knees away but his conscience forced him to question this soul who was still in his care.

'Lady Allen,' he said quietly, 'is it possible that—well, that you imbibe certain strong drink which may injure your health?'

'Oh, nay, indeed not,' she answered, looking at him tenderly. 'Yet, 'tis kind in you to consider my health. Ye know . . .' she put her hand over his, 'I believe you're like *Him*. On this eve o' the Transfiguration, I get visions. I see clear. White shining robes up on the mount—ye'll read the words out tomorrow, and I'll look at ye i' the chapel and think o' *Him*.'

Stephen violently removed his hand from under hers, and lifted his chin. 'I am in no way like *Him*, Lady Allen . . . and very shortly, I must leave Ightham Mote. I'll apply to—to my Abbot. He'll find you another chaplain.'

Emma smiled though not enough to disclose her jagged teeth. 'Nay, dear,' she said. 'Feckenham's gone. Mebbe to France. The Queen ousted him from Westminster last month. Ye've no master but *me*. I want ye here, and here ye'll bide.'

Her eyes darted sideways back and forth . . . she slowly held out her broad muscular beringed hands and clenched them. She opened her hands and stared at them as though they were strange objects. Then she laughed and said in a throaty voice which held a peculiar blend of menace and sweetness, 'My own kin Stephen! Tomorrow's the Feast o' my birth, and of Our Blessed Lord's a-shining on the mountain too. We'll greet Him together, Stephen. Your black robes'll turn white as snowdrops—pure, pure as snowflakes—you an' me . . . san . . . sanctified . . . you an' me.'

Stephen rose abruptly from his stool. 'Aye, well, Lady Allen. We need talk no more tonight. You must rest for your Feast Day. There's many of your household waiting in the chapel to make confession. *Benedicite!*'

He spoke with such authority, that though she wavered a second, and her under-lip shot out mutinously, she went.

Drunken, Stephen thought, surely no worse than that. Not madness, nor possession, yet for a second while she looked at her hands he had felt the presence of something besides Emma Allen in the confessional, something 'other' and most evil . . .

My own great sin has opened me to such fancies ... *misericorde* ... The woman is but drunk.

He shook himself and bowed gravely as the manor carpenter walked in and knelt. 'Bless me, Father, for I've sinned ...'

Stephen listened as they filed in—the manor servants, several of the tenants. Until midnight Stephen gave penances and granted absolutions. All the time, in a shut-off part of him he felt sickly longing for Celia.

*   *   *

Ightham Mote celebrated the Feast Day with unusual gaiety. Emma begrudged money spent on most festivities, even the Yuletide, but on this day she gave free rein to her husband's generosity and let him give orders to Larkin which resulted in an ox roasting over a bonfire beyond the moat, and a dozen kegs of ale to be swilled by the tenantry. Emma presided graciously at the long trestle table which had been set up in the courtyard. She was looking her most handsome in a new crimson satin gown made in London. Her headdress was edged with fresh-water pearls.

There were two fiddlers from Wrotham, and a piper, who scraped and tootled in their corner of the court. The day was fine, warm but not sultry, and though it was perfect for both hay-making and hop-picking, work was suspended in honour of Lady Allen's fortunate birth.

At Mass, earlier, when Stephen chanted the Epistle and came to 'shining robes' he had given Emma an apprehensive glance. She sat with Sir Christopher and Charles in the high canopied seats reserved for the manor lords, but her face remained bland, even vague. When she went first to the kneeling-pad at the altar to receive the Communion wafer, he thought that she looked up at him, but he was not sure and kept his own eyes on the pews at the back of the chapel.

Celia had come to neither Mass. Tomorrow, he thought. Tomorrow, I'll talk to her. After this is over. But his anxiety rose, until during the feasting he caught a glimpse of her piling mugs on a tray that Dickon was bringing out to the courtyard. Tentatively he rose, then sat down again. Sir Christopher had begun the toasts to his wife.

Emma responded to the fulsome compliments and cheers with little beaming nods, she even smiled broadly, disclosing the crooked teeth she usually hid, but her darting black eyes missed nothing, and she presently beckoned to Larkin.

'Where's the new scullery-wench, Cissy? I don't see her wi' the other housemaids.'

'I'll go see, my lady.' The steward bowed and scurried off.

He finally found Celia in the cool damp buttery which smelled of the sluggish moat which washed its outer walls. She was standing by the little barred window examining her wedding-ring, but the steward's blurred eye-sight could not discern what she held in her hand, and he was too flustered to note that her hair was hanging loose since she had not troubled to bind it.

'Cissy . . .?' he quavered uncertainly. 'Aye, I see 'tis. My lady wants ye i' the court wi' t' others. Hasten, then . . .'

Celia slipped the ring back in its pouch. 'I don't feel for merry-making.'

'Come on, do,' said Larkin, not having quite heard her, and thinking her shy. 'Just make ye're bob an' say I wish 'ee good health, long life, summat like that . . . an' there'll be dancing later. Why 'tis Ightham Mote's great Gaudy Day!'

'Aye?' said Celia. She threw back her head and burst into a peal of laughter, while the steward tugged impatiently at her arm.

'So be it,' said Celia. She gave her head a toss, then smoothed her loose hair, and came with Larkin through the passages into the courtyard.

Ursula or John Hutchinson, even Anthony, might have recognised the sparkle of defiance in her looks, the transformation from meek scullery-maid to something elfin and reckless. Julian might have said, 'Ah, the true Gemini—the other twin takes over'—but nobody at the Mote was prepared. Least of all Stephen, though he was painfully reminded of her behaviour on the night Sir Thomas Wyatt had sung, 'Celia the wanton and fair'.

She walked along past all those at the table, and with a flourish that was nearly insolent curtsied to Sir Christopher, curtsied to Stephen, curtsied again to Emma Allen. 'I would've come sooner, my lady,' she said, 'but I thought me forbidden outside servant quarters. May you enjoy many another Gaudy Day in your honour!'

Emma stared. This girl with her indecent wealth of golden hair, the wide turquoise eyes between dark lashes, something familiar? Something half remembered? . . . And the tone of that clear almost ironic voice, could that accent really be Lincolnshire? Emma's black brows drew together, she said coldly,

'Thank'ee, my gel, ye may go to the green and get some food.'
As Celia bobbed her head and went towards the gate tower
swinging her hips, Emma turned to Stephen. 'I'll have to get
rid o' *her*, she looks and acts a troublemaker. I believe she's
lewd. What's your thought, Brother Stephen?'

He could not answer, his throat was choked with longing
and apprehension.

Christopher said mildly, 'She's uncommon pretty, but she
don't seem *lewd*, I wouldn't say . . .'

Emma threw her husband an irritated glance which was
enough to silence him, and throughout the remainder of the
festivities, even during the country dances in which Emma
permitted herself to be led out by Sir Christopher, and then
Larkin, she was constantly aware of Celia. The tinder and the
spark had kindled, though neither of them knew it.

Celia danced with the carpenter and two stable-boys. Dickon
did not come near her. She ate and drank greedily. Tonight
she was hungry though she had not been so for days. When
the Mote clock struck eight she slipped away from the green,
and making occasion to pass near Stephen who stood silently
by the bridge, she looked up into his face.

'My love,' she whispered, 'I'll come to thee tonight. Leave
the door open.'

He flushed, started to speak, to say he knew not what, but
she was gone, flitting back across the courtyard.

Celia was apparently sound asleep in their lumpy bed when
Alice and the chambermaid staggered up from the festivities.
Lady Allen, it seemed, had cut these short with a sudden order
at nine, and both maids were resentful.

'Larst year *she* let us go on 'til midnight,' said the chambermaid. 'An' I was just bein' to dance out wi' blacksmith, too.'

'Lack-a-day,' agreed Alice who had not been at the Mote
last year. 'Still, we got our bellies filled fur a change, an'
there's no tellin' what *she*'ll do. I heard there might be a place
at Penshurst. I've a mind to go out fur it.' She yawned, and
flinging her clothes at a corner, dived into bed.

Celia judged it wise to stir and murmur crossly, 'Lay quiet,
do—I'm a-weary.'

Alice giggled. 'Ye didn't seem weary when ye was dancin'
—all the lads was eyin' ye, but then o' course ye're own boy
wan't there, poor chuck, so ye lost ye're vim.'

'Aye, that's right . . .' said Celia, and pulled over to her
edge of the bed. She lay very still while the other two bur-

rowed and wriggled on the crackling straw mattress. Presently they snored in concert, and Celia slid carefully out of bed.

Through the window she could see an orange slice of waning moon, and the hills around the Mote, undulating in the shadows.

She had kept on her shift, her best one, inherited from Ursula. It was made of imported linen, so old and delicate that it was soft as gauze, and over it she pulled her cramoisie mantle which looked black in the dim light and covered her down to her calves. She pulled the hood close around her head. The maids never stirred as Celia glided from the attic and down the wooden steps, testing each one for creaks before she rested her weight. She descended to the second storey, and reached The Solar.

Her young eyes had adjusted to the gloom, and she saw the vague shape of the squint which led to the disused chapel; therefore the door to the oriel room must be to her left. She waited, listening carefully.

There was no sound but the barking of a dog over by the stables. And then, for a moment, she thought she heard whispers, followed by a woman's voice, loud, bright and brisk. 'And now,' it said, 'we will proceed towards the Priest's Room and the Tudor Chapel. That chapel is a gem ... was built in 1521 during the reign of Henry the Eighth . . .'

Celia put her hand out for support against the panelling. The wood felt warm and reassuring. She held on to it, breathing fast. There was no more sound in The Solar, nor anything that she could hear in this part of the old manor except the scuttle of a mouse behind the wainscotting. Mice, to be sure . . . or maybe the ghosts, she thought. Poor Isabel in the nursery could not harm her, and this room was across the courtyard from the 'Cold Room' Larkin had mentioned. Celia was daunted only a second, then her love and purpose repossessed her.

She moved surely from The Solar into the long oriel room until she stood before the door at the end. It was ajar as she had known it would be. She edged inside and shut the door softly.

Stephen stood next to his cot. Neither of them spoke. He opened his arms and she went into them.

Eighteen

Emma Allen had ceased to enjoy her festival after Celia appeared with her curtsies and insolent beauty. Emma could not stop watching the girl, and she had not missed the instant when Celia paused by Brother Stephen and obviously spoke to him. Emma had been too far off to see clearly the expression on his face, but she knew that it was like none *she* had ever seen. And the way he bent tenderly down ... Suspicion was too monstrous, and yet Emma's unease grew until the stamping of feet, the scraping of fiddles were intolerable to her. She issued the command which stopped the Gaudy Day while ignoring Sir Christopher's startled protests: 'But, my dear, 'tis early ... and we always go on later ... They've not even finished up the ale ... They look forward to this day all year ...'

'I've had enough,' said Emma, and told Larkin to send all the manor folk back to their lodgings 'I feel the need for prayer,' said Emma, 'and I'll thank ye to let me be.'

'Aye,' said her husband, 'as ye wish. Ye don't feel poorly, my dear?' He spoke anxiously. He never understood his wife's moods, nor quite realised that during the past year they had been growing stranger, less predictable. He was fond of her, and proud of the son she had given him. He was indeed a contented man. He was pleased by the increased status his knighthood gave him, and knew that he owed it to Emma's pertinacity.

He enjoyed the possession of Ightham Mote, which his father, having prospered greatly as a London mercer, had been able to buy. Christopher wished to keep up the traditions of manor lord, and tried to do so, but his greatest interest lay in pottering around his estate. The success of the hopgrowing, additions to stables, dairies, the new dam below the fish pond, such concerns occupied his days. At night he slept soundly. He was a hale, wiry man of fifty-odd, and if he ever questioned Emma's divagations, he then thought with sympathy of her girlhood, and the outrageous way she had been evicted from her convent at Easebourne, despite a true vocation—as she often told him—and of the religious scruples from which she therefore suffered.

Sir Christopher went placidly to bed when the musicians left, and The Mote settled back to quiet.

Emma did not. She walked around the courtyard for a while, then went up to the chapel. It was, of course, empty. The two fat tapers on the altar sent out a steady glow. The sanctuary lamp burned like a tiny red eye above the crucifix.

Emma knelt, but her ears were alerted and she soon heard faint movement, footsteps, not twelve feet away from her at the priest's end of the chapel behind the altar. She waited another few minutes, then she rose stealthily. She crept through into Brother Stephen's parlour. She listened at the door of his bedroom. It seemed to her that there were murmurs inside. She opened the door a crack and heard Stephen's voice. It said, 'My dear love, we *will* leave here and fly to France.'

Stephen's room was dimly lit by the votive candle before the Virgin's picture; Emma could see naked limbs entwined on the bed. She could see long tresses of gleaming hair falling off it to the hay-strewn floor. She backed away silently.

Celia raised her head from Stephen's shoulder. 'The door's open,' she whispered. 'I saw a face.'

'Nay, darling.' He pulled her down close to him. 'That door ne'er shuts right unless 'tis bolted. There's nobody there.'

'I'm affrighted,' she whispered, shrinking against his chest.

'No reason,' he said. 'Everyone's asleep. We'll be gone tomorrow. To London. There'll be a ship sailing for France soon ... Mayhap Master Julian would help us—or, I'll think of someone ...'

'There's my ring,' she said, 'poor Sir John's ring. But he *gave* it me, 'tis mine. Stephen, put it on! It'll make a ... a kind of marriage between us, before we must sell it.'

She forced the ring, with some difficulty, on to his little finger.

'And what can I give to *you*, my love?' His voice roughened; there were tears in his eyes.

'Ye've given the babe inside me. Do you believe it now?'

'Aye,' he whispered. 'My child ... My poor child. Almighty God but I wish I were Tom—squire of the broad acres—Medfield ... But I thought I had a vocation ... I *did* have ...'

The votive candle flickered, and Celia sat up straight.

486

'There'll always be that between us, Stephen? Can you change your whole nature—for me? And I fed you the water witch's potion. Master Julian said that was wicked. 'Twas not *meant* for thee.'

'Hush,' he said. 'You babble.' He ran his hand down along her warm soft thigh. He kissed her, and she drew away.

'Something will punish us,' she said in a small dead voice.

'Rubbish, it is I should be talking thus, and I don't feel so now.' He kissed her breasts. 'My foolish one, hush. The morrow—after first Mass. When I walk to the beech wood as always, you need but follow. We'll soon be in London, and they'll never find us there—do they even search.'

'Aye,' she said, 'I know.' She leaned over and kissed him softly on the mouth. Then she gave an agonised sigh. 'Farewell,' she whispered.

He did not stir as she left; he lay drowsing until the Virgin's candle suddenly guttered and went out. He glanced towards the dim square which was Her picture, and turned away. Having decided on his course, and being filled with languor, he immediately slept.

Celia, no longer furtive, walked back through the oriel room. She observed without surprise that there was a light in The Solar where three people confronted her. She paused, holding her mantle tight around her. Emma Allen stood there flanked by Larkin and Dickon.

'Here's the priest's whore,' said Emma triumphantly. 'Ye know what must be done!'

The two men stood gaping. The steward made a feeble whimpering noise. Dickon said, 'Ah-h,' and licked his lips. But they did not move.

'Five noble apiece, men!' said Emma.

Still they did not move, both staring at Celia who stood very quietly just within the doorway.

'Very well, ye cowards,' Emma cried, her black eyes darted to the right, to the left, she made a low animal sound in her throat and lunged.

Her hands closed around Celia's neck and twisted, wrenching.

*   *   *

The next day, Stephen, after first Mass, went to the beech woods and waited until the time for family Mass. He was distressed, and yet partly relieved that Celia did not come. By

487

the chill grey light of a damp morning, the impracticality of his plan seemed obvious. He thought that they must wait a little.

It would be meet and right to consult with his Abbot, and he was sure that he could find Feckenham among the powerful Catholic families. Someone would have given the good old man asylum. He felt he must ask his superior about so drastic a step—one however, of a kind which had been taken before this. Feckenham would be greatly disturbed, but he understood England's changing conditions, and he was just. Stephen also thought of Master Julian who might have bracing advice. The doctor had probably left Cowdray by now, since news had filtered through that Lady Magdalen was safely delivered of a fine son, christened Philip—for the erstwhile King. Stephen looked long at the amethyst heart ring Celia had put on his finger, and was worldly enough to be able to assess its probable value—not sufficient to pay their passages to France and support them for long. Other means must be found.

He performed his priestly duties that morning with calm and precision. He was not astonished that Lady Allen did not come to Mass. Sir Christopher was there, and murmured that his lady was wearied by all the Gaudy Day festivities; that she was a-bed, somewhat ailing. Therefore she did not grace either the dinner or supper tables. Nor did the steward. It occurred to Stephen that Dickon, while serving, gave him some peculiar sideways glances, but he thought little of that either. The whole manor was disorganised by the excitements of the day before. They ate left-over beef and stale bread.

But in the evening Stephen's period of abeyance began to pass. He ceased to think that Celia was exhibiting only common sense and restraint and began to hunger for a sight of her. The hunger reached such a peak by nine o'clock that he went without excuse to the servants' quarters, and found Alice, the nursery-maid, angrily banging dishes in the scullery.

'Aye, Father?' she said bobbing.

'I was . . . well, wondering where . . .' he could not remember the name Celia had used, 'where the new scullery-maid was? Didn't see her at Mass this morning.'

'Oh, *her*,' said Alice. 'I suppose she's took off. Has a lover in Ivy Hatch she's hot for. A pleasin' maid she be, though flighty. Has left us short-handed, or I wouldn't be having to help the cook.'

'I see . . .' said Stephen. He felt a violent pang. 'She has a swain in Ivy Hatch?' His heavy black brows drew together in a frown resented by Alice who considered that there was far too much pother made about dalliance at The Mote.

'And why not?' she said, clashing a dish against the stone sink. 'She's young and comely, an' 'tis all in natur', an' I'm quittin' this house come Michaelmas. I'll find me a more agreeable place—no fear. I'm not bound arter Michaelmas.'

'I suppose not . . .' said Stephen. 'Are you *sure* that—that the scullery-maid is out? She might have been tired and gone to bed.'

Alice tossed her head; her flushed face went blank. She didn't hold with pryings, even from the priest. 'Mebbe so, mebbe not,' she said, 'and no doubt ye'll hear all about it when she goes to be shriven—if she do.'

Stephen left the scullery and wandered back to the tiny kitchen courtyard. He went out over the back bridge which spanned the moat. He wandered aimlessly up the path to the beeches.

The skids had cleared after the rainy day. He looked at the stars, and the crescent moon, silvery and remote. The dark wet woods were profoundly silent, hushed. Tomorrow, he thought, tomorrow, she'll be here. There *is* no man at Ivy Hatch, she but said that to quiet the other maid. She's asleep or readying her gear as we agreed.

Then, of a sudden, as he stood under the trees, near the mossy bank where they had lain together, an appalling doubt came to him; it clashed and clanged like cymbals, and evoked a memory from his boyhood at Battle Abbey. A Maundy Thursday, long ago—the Service, Tenebrae, the candles which were extinguished one by one, while the monks, pure and passionless, chanted the canticles, the dirge. At last no light was left within the abbey church and Stephen mourning—already dedicated—had wept for the blackness, for the betrayal and the death of Our Lord. Betrayal. '*I* have betrayed . . .' he whispered aloud, but could not voice the anguish of the next thought. Had *Celia*? What had she meant by her unheeded words, 'I gave you the water witch's potion.' Was it witchcraft that possessed him? He raised his crucifix to his lips, then dropped it. 'A lover in Ivy Hatch?' Impossible. And yet, the image of her allurement as she had listened to Sir Thomas Wyatt singing to her; the image of her last night at the Gaudy Day festival—provocative, dancing, laughing, hand in hand with those yokels. Was one of *them* from Ivy Hatch? The

489

wanton temptress—the monks had so often warned him. Nay, but could any woman feign the love he thought she had shown him?

It *is* my child . . . it *is* unless she lies, she has told other lies. Mad with jealousy he never knew existed, he began to pace back and forth among the tranquil beeches. A holly frond caught his robe, and he grasped the prickly leaves, rejoicing in the pain, watching the little drops of blood run down his palms, black droplets on his glimmering palm.

It was past midnight of that August eighth when Stephen walked back to the manor. The kitchen door to The Mote was still open, as it should not have been if the steward made his nightly round. Stephen groped his way through the unlit passages, determined to mount the servants' stairs and see if Celia were in the attic, though the open door could mean that she had arranged it so, to further her clandestine return. As she crept secretly to *me*, he thought, so may she creep to others, and why did she not see me today?

At the foot of the back stairs he paused, startled out of his furious pain. There was a strange noise in the Hall, a gritty rhythmic slapping sound, and there was a crack of light beneath the Hall door. Stephen held his breath. There should be no noise in the Hall at this hour, nor had he ever heard such a noise as this. He opened the door and saw Emma Allen sitting at the end of the table, her chin resting on her hands, gazing in his direction. She seemed to be chuckling—a low bubbling sound.

Stephen stood in the doorway staring. He was aware that there were men in the Hall, the lighted tapers showed them clearly. Larkin the steward cowered by the fireplace. It was Dickon who held a mason's trowel and made the slapping noise as he fitted a brick into the niche, then dipped into a bucket of mortar and plastered.

'What's this?' said Stephen, his voice unsteady. 'Lady Allen, 'tis an odd hour to be sealing up your strong-box!'

Emma stopped chuckling. Her massive face grew wary, as her eyes focused slowly on Stephen. 'And 'tis an odd hour for *you* to be abroad, my dear priest. Were ye seeking for your leman?'

Her speech was clear enough though there were pauses between the words. 'Near finished, Dickon,' she said. 'Only two, three more bricks.'

Dickon gave Stephen a look of stark terror. He dropped his trowel.

The steward began to whimper. 'I'd naught to do wi' it, sir—she was near dead anyways—the poor maidy. I didn't know ... what 'twas we carried up from the dungeon. 'Twas all bundled. I swear by God and the Blessed Virgin I didn't know.'

Emma turned and gave her steward a tolerant smile. 'O' course ye knew, an' so did Dickon. Ye knew that Christ in his shining robes'd want ye to wall up the priest's whore. 'Twas always done so. Leastways there was a nun bricked up at Easebourne i' the cloister, long time back. Maybe King Richard's time ... An' now ye'll not be tempted, dear,' she said to Stephen. 'We'll be easy together here at The Mote.'

Stephen stared at them for one more second, then he flung himself at the niche, tearing at the bricks and wet plaster, pulling down a great hole until he saw what was inside, crouched far below, shrouded in brown sacking.

'Stop him!' Emma screamed. 'She's near dead, he mustn't touch her!' She moved as she spoke and seizing the trowel, hit Stephen on the head just hard enough to stun him. He dropped prone on the rushes.

'Drag him away,' Emma said to her servants. 'Upstairs to his bed, bind him down wi' sheets—then Dickon, come back and finish the job.' She held up a purse full of gold coins and rattled them. 'Mind ye o' these, m'dear, ye can live like a lord, so ye can.'

Dickon looked down at the priest on the floor, and hunched his shoulders. 'As ye like, lady. Come on, old whiffler, gi'e me a hand wi' *him*.'

The steward trembled, he wheezed and gulped. 'What'll master say? What'll he say when he finds the cupboard plastered up?'

Emma's eyes wavered, they held a momentary bewilderment. She reached for the goblet at her elbow and drained it. 'He won't notice, he'll—he'll believe whatever I tell him. He —he don't—don't ...' She stopped and gaped at the hole in the wall. 'That must be filled!' she said in a tone of surprise. 'Naught there but a scullery-maid, a lustful scullery-maid ...' She picked up the trowel, and replacing a fallen brick began slapping on the mortar herself.

*   *   *

The next morning Stephen did not appear for the servants' Mass. It was Alice who later found him hanging from the beam over the fireplace, near the confessional, his knotted scourge around his neck.

*   *   *

On Michaelmas Day, September 29, Cowdray Castle celebrated the Feast with glorious profusion, for Anthony had returned from Spain and his new son, Philip, was to be christened that day. There were garlands of daisies and roses over every door. A white satin banner, embroidered in gilt, flew from the flagstaff above the buck's head pennant.

Hundreds of Michaelmas geese were a-roasting and their succulent odour mingled with that of baking apples, and of the crushed new herbs strewn on every floor. Outside the manor itself, the village of Easebourne, the town of Midhurst were decked as they had never been before. Those who did not bother with garlands, at least had ivy trailing from the door knockers. There was continuous music at the Spread Eagle and the Angel. There was singing in the streets and morris dances. The bell-ringers added to the joyous din, hand bells—but peals too from the church, and though there were some who wondered if such merrymaking might annoy the Protestant Queen, Anthony, who knew her better by now, and acquitted himself well on his brief mission to Spain, had no such qualms. Elizabeth approved of gaiety, and had sent a tiny gilt cup to the infant Philip as a christening present.

The Bishop arrived from Chichester to perform the ceremony and even young Anthony who was jealous of all this pomp and concentration on a baby brother, stopped sulking and played at Hoodman Blind with the children of the more aristocratic guests.

Julian alone among the Cowdray inhabitants did not share in the general rejoicing. Each day since the baby's birth he had started to think of plans for returning to Italy. And each day let them slide. He was given ample reward for his care of Magdalen while cynically aware that his presence was unnecessary. She had delivered with almost painless speed, and no more fuss than was made by a healthy Southdown ewe. He had been carelessly invited to stay on for the christening, so from an occasional prick of conscience he poulticed a burn or sewed up a cut among the manor folk. But he left routine blood-lettings to the Midhurst leech. He became increasingly bored and depressed. He dreaded the coming of another English winter, yet lacked the energy to leave. For his frequent joint pains he took poppy juice which dulled the aches.

On August 7 he had a dream entirely unlike the arid fantasies which followed after medications. It was a stifling nightmare in which he thought himself bound in a dark hole with Celia, struggling to escape, and heard her muffled voice moaning his name. The horror of this nightmare was tinged by guilt, and remained for some time after he woke.

He meditated awhile on the senseless folly of dreams. He had not thought of Celia since she had run away, possibly in lewd pursuit of her monk, though Brother Stephen was said to be at Ightham Mote with the Allens, and why should he dream of Celia with a literally suffocating remorse, almost as though he had wilfully wronged her? Celia, he thought, shaking himself impatiently—*ragazza testarda*—a headstrong girl who had thrown away a good marriage, loving friends, and even admitted to witchcraft, all for one obstinate and shameful desire. Though, the chances were that she had found herself a protector in London, and embarked on what seemed to be her inevitable career as a courtesan. Good fortune to her, he thought, and laughed dryly. *She*'d do well at that game in Italy where she might even have her precious monk on the side—or be a cardinal's mistress—*that* should suit her tastes! Julian was aware of anger that Celia had been the cause of such an unpleasant dream. All the same, when he finally got up he went down across the court to the kitchens and enquired for the page, Robin. When the lad came, Julian said, 'That foolish little dog of Lady Hutchinson's, are you caring for it properly?'

'Aye, sir,' Robin looked startled, then excited. 'Is my lady coming back? Have they heard aught?'

Julian shook his head. 'You were fond of her, weren't you?'

The boy blushed. 'Aye, sir. An' Taggle, he mopes. Last night he howled so much, horse-master himself wanted to gi'e him a beating. But I stopped it. I wouldn't let even Master Farrier harm Taggle.'

Julian patted Robin on the shoulder. 'Ah—you have a heart,' he said with a sigh. 'Mine has gone withered and sapless.'

Robin gaped at him; Julian, turning on his heel, left the boy abruptly.

Since then Julian had been troubled by no more nightmares,

and he had not asked again about the dog. He grew increasingly morose, and viewed the festivities today with a sour eye, though the weather was sunny and warm for a change. The instant the christening in the chapel ended he left to find a sunlit bench in some private place and bask. There *were* no private spots today. The manor grounds, the pleasuances, bowling green, tilting grounds, even the herb garden, all swarmed. Outside the great gate milled the beggars—they had come from as far as Southampton or Chichester to queue up for the generous dole dispensed by Lord Montagu's almoners—bread, beef, ale and christening pence. One tattered old man had an enormous growth on his neck, it was shiny red, pulsating and the size of a stool ball. What sort of tumour? Julian thought, wrong place for a goitre, doesn't look like a carbuncle—but his curiosity flickered out at once.

The stench of the beggars revolted him, he who had once ministered to countless foul-smelling mortals. The thought of the banquet which would soon start in the great Buck Hall also revolted him: Those lords and their ladies, the knights and the squires—silks, satins, velvets, laces—gorging and guzzling. They smelled somewhat sweeter than the beggar horde, but he felt no kinship with them either.

He had his staff, and he leaned on it heavily as he walked away from the gatehouse down the avenue of oaks towards the highway. He was heading for a bench near the water tower, which he knew would be sunny, and hopefully unoccupied, since it was far from the castle. As he limped along he drew irritably aside to make way for a party of galloping horsemen, and was astonished to have one of them draw rein and hail him. 'Master Julian, bigod. Good day ter ye!'

Julian looked up and recognised Wat Farrier's twinkling little eyes. Wat was a trifle drunk. He had been celebrating at the Spread Eagle in Midhurst.

'Good day, Wat,' Julian answered, and hobbled on.

But Wat dismounted and approached the doctor. 'Ye're the very man, now I think on it! I've the joustin' to arrange this arternoon, as m'lord has commanded—all the trappin's for the hosses, an' wouldn't want to plague m'lord on sech a day, noways. Ye can pick the right time.'

'What do you speak of?' said Julian scowling. 'I wish to be quite alone in the sunlight, while we *have* some.'

'Aye, sir, to be sure.' Wat did not question eccentricities. ''An' 'tis a smallish matter, though maught gi'e m'lord a pang, seein' how he used ter feel, even in Spain he mentioned the monk couple o' times.' Wat had accompanied his master on the quick journey to the Spanish Court.

'The monk? What monk?' Julian was exasperated. 'You're dithering—go see to your tournament!'

Wat nodded affably. 'I'll so do. Brother Stephen's the monk, o' course. He's dead, God rest him.' Wat crossed himself. 'His brother, Squire Marsdon's at the Eagle, an' wants m'lord's advice. Rid over from East Sussex. Didn't know about the christening, to be sure.'

Julian clenched his staff, his knees weakened. He had seen thousands of deaths, he expected his own before long, why then should the news of Stephen's death be a shock, and bring with it the return of the stifling miasma he had felt in his nightmare of Celia.

'When did he die?' asked Julian.

'Dunno. Last month, I think. Master Marsdon didn't say much, but I got the feel there's summat fishy. Leastways 'twas sudden.'

Julian compressed his lips, his knees stopped quivering. 'I'd better see Marsdon,' he said, and cast a sad glance at the sunny bench. 'May I have your horse?'

'Surely,' said Wat. 'Good idea. He's gentle, an' wearied from galloping. I'll give ye a hoist ... There ye be!' Wat strode vigorously towards the castle.

Julian rode towards Midhurst, wondering at this impulse and vexed by it.

In the once familiar stableyard at the Spread Eagle he found an ostler to help him down and look to the horse. He enquired from old Potts the landlord and soon located Tom Marsdon in the tap-room, sitting alone in a corner, grim-faced beside an untouched tankard.

Julian explained his presence, and Tom said, 'Aye—my poor brother mentioned ye when he came to Medfield last spring. When d'ye think it'll be seemly to see My Lord Montagu?'

'What for?' asked Julian gently enough. 'If Brother Stephen's dead—for which I'm sorry—he must be buried long since.'

'That's just it,' said Tom. 'He's not buried at Medfield wi' all the Marsdons. They've got the coffin at Ightham Mote, an' my sister-in-law, Emma Allen, won't give it up. Keeps it i' the chapel. I rode to The Mote when Sir Christopher notified us, had hired a hearse too, but I got no setisfaction. Emma 'ouldn't see me, an' old Kit, he didn't want her disturbed.

Said she was ill an' must be humoured. I can have the law on 'em, I believe, but don't rightly know, bein' 'tis not this county. I thought m'lord Montagu might write a word to Lord Cobham, who is Lord Lieutenant o' Kent.'

'I see . . .' said Julian slowly. 'What did your brother die of?'

Tom's face set, his hazel eyes, so like Stephen's, grew more sombre. 'I don't think Christopher knows. He just said 'twas unexpected . . . but I saw the nursery-maid who was watching the boy Charles while he caught frogs in the moat. I asked her, an' she gave a kind o' shriek, turned grey as glass, then had hysterics. She knows sompthin' ain't right, an' so do I. M' heart's heavy, an' Nan, m' wife, she weeps a lot an' won't be comforted. She had a fear o' Stephen's going as chaplain to her sister. Still an' all,' added Tom with an attempt at a smile, 'women's fancies don't mean much. Nan's breedin', too. On'y the whole business ain't *right* somehow, an' I want m' brother buried proper wi' his forefathers.'

'So he should be,' said Julian. Intuition, which had served him so well for diagnoses, seeped through his wall of inert resistance. He was certain that far more was wrong at Ightham Mote than a menopausal woman's idiotic refusal to part with a coffin.

'Was there any mention of a girl called Celia, or did your brother ever speak of her?' Julian asked quietly.

Tom blinked and frowned. 'Nay, never heard of such. What'd *she* have to do wi' Stephen? He was a godly monk, we was proud o' him. There'd *be* no girl in his life—an' by the Blood o' Christ I'd kill anybody who said so!' His heavy-boned face reddened, he grabbed his dagger hilt.

'Softly, softly,' said Julian with a faint smile, stepping back. 'Don't make mincemeat of *me*, my friend, I but asked.'

Tom's face cleared, he looked sheepishly at the gaunt dignified doctor with his grey beard, his gnarled hands. 'I be hotheaded,' he said apologetically. 'Us Marsdons 're proud, there's bin no slur on the family sence 'twas founded afore the Normans come.'

Julian inclined his head gravely. 'I understand, Master Marsdon, and will approach Lord Montagu for you tomorrow.'

He silently acknowledged Tom's thanks, and returned to Cowdray.

The next morning he waited until Anthony had recovered from the previous day's revels, and caught him in the privy

496

parlour, just before he set out stag-hunting with some of his guests.

'Will you spare me a moment, my lord?'

Anthony did not conceal impatience. The huntsmen had reported four fat stags running in the park, the hounds were already baying below, the horses were waiting, the horns a-winding. Indeed, he had forgotten that Master Julian was still at Cowdray, not having seen him in days. 'What is it?' he said, settling his big shoulders in the new sapphire velvet hunting costume, and pulling his plumed cap firmer on his head. Besides the blood sport there was other sport to pursue. The Fitz-Allans had brought with them an uncommon tooth-some young cousin who was to join the hunt. Anthony had enjoyed a few kisses last night when Magdalen had gone up-stairs to see how the baby did.

' 'Tis Brother Stephen, my lord—he's dead.'

Anthony, who had been motioning an usher to bring the quiver-full of yew arrows, let his hand drop, and after a second crossed himself. 'How—how can that be?'

Julian told him briefly of his talk with Tom Marsdon.

'Shocking . . .' said Anthony. 'Truly regrettable. Must've been plague for them to act that way at Ightham. I'll have Dr. Langdale say a Mass.'

Magdalen came out from the bedchamber. 'Did ye say "plague"?' she said in a whisper, her amber eyes rounded. '*Where?*'

She was dressed in a bed-gown—she did not care for hunt-ing, her coarse red hair hung in a plait, and her robe was milk-stained since she insisted on feeding the baby herself, despite the wet-nurse who had been hired. 'Not at *Cowdray?*' Her plump cheeks whitened.

Julian reassured her. 'And I do not believe it was plague, lady.'

'Weel, then . . .' she said, and accepted the silver mug of breakfast ale one of the hovering servitors offered her. ' 'Tis sorry news. He should niver ha' left My Lord when he was begged to stop on.'

'Aye,' said Anthony, his boot tapping as the horns let forth another blast below. 'He would've been useful to me i' Spain, yet I found other men to serve me . . . Oh,' he went on, in response to Julian's reproachful look, 'tell the secretary to write a line to Cobham. You'll know what to say, give it to

497

the Marsdon brother, tell him there'll be a Requiem Mass here soon, after all the guests've left.' He hurried from the parlour.

'Si, Excellenzia, como vuole,' said Julian under his breath. Magdalen did not understand the words, but she caught the bitterly sarcastic tone, and saw the look in the Italian doctor's eyes.

'I'll thank ye not ta mutter,' she said coldly. 'My lord ha' gr-ranted your r-request—an' iffen ye be discontent at Cowdray—Och, ye've altered, Doctor—last week I asked ye ta look at wee Mary's foot—ye didna coom nigh her, nor ha' ye been ta Mass lang time I hear-r.' Magdalen's northern burr got harsher when she was angry. Her anger now was straight-forward. Julian had brought a note of death into the house; he had seemed to reproach Anthony. Though well recompensed for his piddling services, he yet was malcontent and lazy.

Less clear to Magdalen was her resentment of Julian's presence during the time of Celia's wicked behaviour—her flight, her shameful treatment of poor Edwin Ratcliffe, for the unease she had felt about Anthony and Celia.

Julian bit his lips and shut his eyes a moment. 'You will no longer have to suffer me, lady,' he said. 'I regret—I regret—' He did not finish.

Magdalen stared after his departing back, which was slightly bowed under the furred doctoral robes. She noticed his limp. He was old. A momentary qualm of pity passed into relief. She had never much liked the Doctor. She went to the nursery to see her baby and give it suck.

*　　　*　　　*

A week later, Julian and Tom Marsdon descended the hill into the demesne of Ightham Mote. Tom was armed with an order from Lord Cobham, and the hearse, again hired in Ightham, rattled behind them.

They all drew up before the moat bridge. The porter lumbered out to enquire their names and wishes. Tom had expected the same vaguely hostile reception of his first visit but they were readily admitted.

Sir Christopher and Lady Allen were at supper, and would certainly be glad to receive anyone sent from Lord Cobham.

Julian, though stiff from days in the saddle, felt better than he had in months, while Tom had been glad of his company on the dreary mission.

They crossed the courtyard and entered the Hall which contained only the Allens and a lanky youth hired at Wrotham village by Sir Christopher himself, as servitor. Dickon had vanished weeks ago; the new scullery-maid—so briefly at The Mote after Lammas—had also disappeared. Doubtless they had gone together, Emma said. On top of that, old Larkin the steward had taken to muttering and weeping and soiling himself when he wasn't in sodden sleep. He had to be banished to a cottage near the blacksmith's, and tended by one of the dairymaids.

What with Brother Stephen's inexplicable death, and Emma's sullen refusal to leave her bed, or speak for days, except to demand another flask of the fiery-smelling drink brought up from the cellar, Christopher had been forced into command. He was now seeking a new steward, and expected one from London shortly.

He was pleased to receive the visitors, and relieved that Emma was greatly improved. 'Welcome—hearty welcome, my brother Tom,' he said to Marsdon as the two men entered. 'And—Doctor—? I remember ye kindly at the King's Head, was it?—time o' Queen Mary's Procession, and before that at Midhurst. Emma, m'dear, ye remember Master Julian, the Court physician?'

'Aye,' said Emma. She was dressed in black velvet, and much bejewelled. She had been cracking hazel nuts and eating them carefully, because they hurt her loosened crooked teeth. 'Pray sit down,' she said, and turned to the servitor. 'Bring sack.'

'Glad to see ye better, Sister Emma,' said Tom uncertainly. 'I fear I've returned on no pleasant errand. There's a hearse a-waitin' at the bridge—for Stephen's coffin. I—I've an order from Lord Cobham.'

Christopher looked anxiously at his wife, but she smiled the same bland half-smile with which she had greeted the visitors. 'Lack-a-day,' she said. 'To be sure. Ye needn't have troubled Lord Cobham. 'Tis natural, dear, ye'd want the poor priest buried at Medfield. How fares Nan—and the Babes?'

So reasonable a speech at once reassured Tom, but Julian looked at Emma and saw the tremor of her square muscular hands as she pried out a hazel nut with a silver pick. He saw the dilation of pupil in the strange eyes. And he felt an emanation of ancient evil, not entirely from her—though he felt her to be its focus.

The Hall was commonplace—small apple-wood fire burning pleasantly—the October night was chill—carved oak table and benches, the twin high chairs, the court cupboard—garish painted wall hangings, a greyhound curled up on the rushes near the fire, pewter plates and flagons on the board, the silver salt cellar—all details to be found in any well-to-do manor in England.

What then was wrong? His glance was drawn towards the south end of the Hall, near the entrance. There was a large rectangle of darker plaster there. He frowned at it, wondering, and Sir Christopher who was animated by company and wishful to be a good host, noticed the doctor's stare.

'That's where my lady keeps the strong-box,' he explained. 'Newly bricked in, and mars the Hall, but I've ordered a Flemish tapestry to cover it. Should arrive any day, but ye know how slow deliveries are from London.'

'I don't want it covered,' said Emma, 'I told ye, Kit, I like to keep an eye on it.'

'But my dear,' her husband expostulated, 'ye said 'twould be a safe place for Charles's inheritance. 'Twould take hours to chip through it again, no thief 'd try. 'Tis a fine device—but Hall 'd look better wi' a hanging there.'

Emma glanced at Tom, then at Julian. She turned to her husband. 'As ye like,' she said, and reached for another hazel nut.

The supper continued, though the fare provided was poor. Christopher apologised for it, and Julian, baffled, uneasy, could find no reason for the formless suspicions he had arrived with. The sack came and Julian allowed the sweet heady liquor to warm his stomach. They were invited to spend the night, and Tom who was naturally convivial and had begun to think he had made too much ado in running to Lord Montagu and then Lord Cobham, turned back to his natural hearty self. He was delighted when his brother-in-law said, 'Ye know, that long-faced youth I hired at Wrotham can play the fiddle, it seems. We'll have a round, something merry?'

'Why not,' said Emma, 'though too merry, 'd not be seemly, would it?—wi' our poor brother a-laying i' the chapel, struck down so sudden i' the very flower o' his manhood. 'Twas like a fit took him. Are the Marsdons given to fits, dear?' she asked Tom.

'Not as I know of.' Tom looked worried, and turned to Julian. 'Do they run in families, Doctor?'

'Seldom,' answered Julian slowly. 'Seizures may be caused by any disorder of the humours — or even a malign conjunction of the stars — if Saturn be trine to Mars . . .' He stopped. At that moment, while he was groping for a rational explanation of Stephen's death, inclined to agree with Tom that imagination and apprehension had bred a great deal of unnecessary worry, he felt a clap of certainty. There was death in the Hall, murder had been done, and that woman sitting there so complacent, so persuasive, was deluding them all.

'We'll sing the old riddle song,' said Emma, spitting out a piece of shell. 'We all know that an' I'm fond o' it. Get your fiddle,' she said to the serving-man. When he returned she led the singing in a hoarse grating voice. 'I gave my love a cherry wi'out a stone, I gave my love a chicken wi'out a bone —'

Julian did not sing. He felt the weight of tragedy enshrouding him like a sodden cloak, and the futility of trying to understand it. Whatever had happened could never be undone, nor might ever be known. The woman sang her silly riddle song, slyly, while her hands twitched, the jewels glimmered in her rings. She was evil, and would go unpunished. The Devil usually triumphed, much as true Christians tried to persuade themselves that he didn't. Julian's gaze passed again to the dark rectangle of plaster on the wall. From it emanated a blackness much darker than the patches of bricks and mortar, though as he looked the centre of the blackness glowed with a soft yellow light. In the midst appeared Nanak's face. The ugly froglike face of the man he had met in the flesh so many years ago in Padua. Julian saw the calm heavy-lidded eyes, the saffron eye-balls. There was both compassion and rebuke in the man's gaze.

'*Lascia!*' Julian said to it, in his head. 'Leave me alone! I'm tired of this coil — tired of frittering, tired of trouble. What would you have me do?'

The hallucination vanished. 'Tis the poppy juice and sack, and the days of riding. These people here are nothing to me. I'm cold. And, indeed, he began to shiver with an ague. It was the damp, he thought, the chilly damp and agues of this miserable country.

Emma and the two men finished the riddle song, then Tom burst out irrepressibly, 'But I know a better riddle song — we needn't be too glum—this 'un makes Nan laugh.' He began to bellow in a jovial baritone:

'What is a friar wi' a bald head? A staff to beat a cuckold dead?
What is a gun that shoots point blank, and hits between a maiden's flank?
Wi' a humble drum, drumble dum drumble down dee.'

Emma scraped her chair back and rose. 'Enough, Tom! I don't hold wi' bawdry in my house. Ye forget yourself!'

Tom collapsed at once. He mumbled an apology which Emma received coldly. The party broke up, and Tom, very subdued, went to say a prayer by Stephen's coffin which lay, properly guarded by tapers, in the chapel.

Emma went to the chapel much later, after everyone had gone to bed. She carried a candlestick through the upstairs passages, the flame wavered, died and leaped up again as her unsteady hand sheltered it from draughts. It flickered on her heavy face which was set with determination, though the slack mouth drooped at the corners like a mummer's mask.

In the chapel she went to the bier, and slapped her hand on the coffin. 'So,' she said to it. 'Now ye've brought danger to *me*, ye false-hearted monk. Not content wi' deserting me like this. Ye've brought threats to The Mote.'

She put her candlestick carefully down on the lectern, and tapped the coffin's oaken lid until she began to smile, the colour came back in her cheeks. 'Curse ye,' she said softly, and heaved a satisfied sigh. Her curses were unneeded, his unshriven soul would pay for its great crime, nor would find rest. There was a faint odour of corruption wafting from the coffin.

'Faugh,' she said. 'Ye stink now and I want no more part of ye. It shall be as though I'd never met ye.' She turned and picked up the candlestick. 'But, I'll keep an eye on your whore,' she added. 'She'll not escape.'

Emma returned through the passages to her chamber. She carefully removed her black velvet gown. 'I'll wear no more mourning,' she murmured, and putting on her night-shift clambered into bed next to her sleeping husband.

Early next morning the Medfield company left for Sussex. Emma did not come down, but as the men were sliding the coffin into the hearse, Christopher said to Tom, 'Emma, she

502

want's ye to take this ring. Seems 'twas found on Stephen's little finger, she says ye should have it.'

It was a heart-shaped amethyst ring held by two golden hands. Tom, completely mollified, relieved that his mission was so easily accomplished this time, took the ring with warm gratitude. He was thirsting to be home with his family, and back to the running of a manor which might soon be as impressive as The Mote.

'Look, Doctor,' he tendered the ring to Julian, ' 'tis a fine stone. I wonder how Stephen came by it—most unlike him to have such a bauble. I believe I'll send it to the goldsmith at Lewes, have our crest graved on it, an' the motto—Nan'll be comforted to wear it, she do like pretty trinkets, an' in memory of our poor brother.'

Julian stared down at the ring in Tom's horny palm. He knew what it was—Celia's wedding ring, the one put on her hand by Sir John Hutchinson at the Priory in Southwark five years ago, the one she had worn at Cowdray six months ago.

'I'm sure Mistress Marsdon will be pleased,' he said, and turned to the difficult business of mounting his horse. He had definitely caught an ague—chills and burning all night, bone aches as well as the familiar ones in his joints. Not fit for riding—but nothing would have induced him to stay another night at The Mote, and he tried to conceal his condition. When they picked up the Highway, he would ride eastward alone, must be an inn at Seven Oaks. Hold together until there. And rest . . . rest . . . forget . . .

Christopher stood punctiliously at the moat's bridge, his hand on his chest, his uncovered head bowed in respect for the hearse and its contents. The cortège plodded down the drive, while the manor folk who were not at work lined the way, hushed, murmuring, staring with thrilled awe at the four black horses and the shabby black ostrich plumes fixed to their bridles. Gape-mouthed they crossed themselves as the hearse passed them. There were a few 'God rest his souls' but many faces showed avid curiosity. Alice, the nursery-maid, was known to have found the priest dead, and though she wouldn't talk of it, there was that in her behaviour which caused conjecture. The girl had obviously been frightened—cowed—during her brief remaining stay at The Mote.

By the gate near the pond they turned on the lane to climb towards Ivy Hatch, where they would pick up the Highway and Tom was halted by an old man who had been sitting on a stump, mumbling a hunk of bread and honey. He came forward nimbly and tugged at Tom's foot.

'Ye got her in there?' He stabbed a bony finger towards the hearse. 'The poor fair maidy—so ye got her outa the wall?'

Tom looked down from his horse, saw the matted grey hair, milky white eyes peering up at him. 'Nay, nay, gaffer,' he said kindly but brisk. ' 'Tis my brother Stephen Marsdon's body I'm taking home.'

'I didn't do it, ye know,' said the old man earnestly. 'M'lady did. I swore I wouldn't speak on it, an' I haven't. I didn't know what we brought up from the old dungeon, 'twasn't hardly breathin' anyways, m'lady'd wrenched her good.'

Tom made an exasperated sound, but Julian behind him clutched his pommel.

'Loose my rein, gaffer,' said Tom, for the old man had now seized it. 'Go back to your stay-bite, we must hasten.'

The old man shook his head and held on tighter. 'I'm Steward Larkin,' he said with a trace of anger. 'An' sence ye've come to bring her home, I simply want ye to know *I* didn't do it. I never would e'en if she *was* the monk's whore.'

Tom started. Julian saw scarlet flame up on his neck.

'Ye're daft,' Tom growled. 'Whoever tends ye should *be* here.' He gave Larkin a mild kick in the chest. 'Loose rein or I'll hurt ye!'

'She were wi' child, too,' said Larkin, dropping his hand. 'Sech wickedness s'ld be punished. M'lady said so. But I didn't *do* it, mind ye, I didn't rightly know what we brought up from the dungeon that night and set i' the wall—but I'm glad she's gettin' *Christian burial* so her soul can rest. Was glad when I saw the hearse stop by to fetch her.'

'By God, ye're brains 're addled as a mashed egg, ye old turdy-gut!' Tom spurred his horse, and galloped far ahead of the funeral procession. Julian continued with it at a pace scarcely faster than oxen.

In a while he caught up with Tom who was waiting on the brow of the hill. The two men looked in each other's eyes. Julian gave a sad shrug. And said nothing.

'Did ye hear that old bustard, that madman?' cried Tom, whose face was still purple. 'The terrible things he said.'

Julian shrugged again. 'I heard, Master Marsdon. You must make what you like of it . . .' He paused a moment. 'After all, the man's senile, I suppose.' He saw that Tom did not understand, and simplified. 'In his dotage, maundering. I suggest that you give no weight to his words.'

Tom gazed hard for a moment at the Italian doctor whom he had come to respect. 'Aye, to be sure,' he said. 'Dotage . . . maunderings, is all.' He glanced down at The Mote, shimmering and calm in its hollow. He slapped the reins against his horse's neck. 'There'll be the tavern at Ivy Hatch—we'll stop an' get us a bit o' cheer, s'll we?'

'If you wish,' said Julian. ' 'Tis a long road ahead, a very long journey.' He glanced at the hearse which had also paused, while the black-plumed horses panted and wheezed on the hill-top.

'All the same,' he added softly, 'I believe there was truth in what the steward said.'

Tom heard him, and clamped shut his mind, as wooden shutters slammed against night-time windows to keep out the cold and fearsome dark. 'These hops,' he said, pointing to a field full of shrivelling vines, already stripped by the pickers, 'they do well here. I've a mind to plant 'em at Medfield, the soil's not so different. I vow they might make me a mint—'

'Da vero,' said Julian, 'we should all plan for our future comforts, nor permit disquiet to enter our lives.'

Nineteen

At eleven o'clock on the second June morning following Celia's admission to the London Clinic, Sir Arthur Moore swept past the tight-lipped Matron and nurses to Lady Marsdon's door. He banged on it thunderously. 'Open up, Doctor Akananda! This nonsense has gone on long enough!'

He was relieved to hear the lock turn, and have the door open at once, then startled to see that the Hindu's face had a grey tint under the dark skin, and there were furrows which had not been there before; the man had aged ten years.

'God, you look terrible!' said Sir Arthur. 'How's the patient? Whole bloody hospital's buzzing. Think I've gone mental m'self to permit these shenanigans.'

Akananda drew aside and pointed to the bed.

Sir Arthur went and gaped at Celia. 'I'll be damned! Brought her around, did you?' He bent over Celia, fingers on pulse. He put his hand on her chest which rose and fell slowly. He pinched her cheek and watched the blood flow back. 'She's alive all right,' he said, 'but what's the *brain* doing? You never know with these cataleptics.'

'Her mind . . . will gradually clear,' said Akananda. He swallowed, and poured himself a drink of water from the carafe. He swayed, clutched the bed rail, then collapsed into the arm-chair. 'It's been a struggle,' he said faintly.

Sir Arthur looked at his Hindu colleague with sudden sympathy. 'Don't know what you did, Jiddu, but the woman's come out of the grave. Good show. You'll have to teach *me* a thing or two.' He laughed. 'You got some secret pill — or was it hypnotism? Damn thing's coming back in fashion. Seems to work sometimes. Lot of mysteries, even now with all our scientific knowledge . . . You need a bracer, my boy.' He turned to the Matron who was hovering in the doorway. 'Lady Marsdon's much improved — get some brandy for Dr. Akananda. He deserves it.'

'No — thank you, Arthur,' said Akananda slowly. 'I'd like a cup of tea — *Indian*,' he added, smiling a little. 'And this one . . .' he indicated Celia with a motion of his slim brown hand, 'there's more to be done—not medically just now. Later we might try the H.C.G. test.'

'*What?*' said Sir Arthur. 'D'ye think the girl's pregnant?'

'Yes,' said Akananda.

'But the mother *said* . . .' Sir Arthur shrugged. 'Well, she's in a dither naturally, badgering me, and back and forth to Sussex where the husband's gone round the bend, I gather. Mrs. Taylor's waiting outside now, by the way, and so are an odd collection. Duchess of Drewton, Sir Harry something, and that "queer"—the dressmaker Igor—the rich women are crazy about.'

'So . . .' said Akananda thoughtfully. He leaned his head back, and sighed. 'They were all close to her once. Though I wouldn't have expected Igor. He was Simkin, I suppose—still he loved her in his way . . . and these things, we can't see clearly . . . the bonds of love and hate . . . the interplay . . . the compensations . . .'

'Look here, old boy,' said Sir Arthur, frowning. 'You've *had* it. Go home and sleep after you get your cuppa. Or shall I give you a shot—tranquilliser. I'll take over from here.'

'I shall be tranquillised,' said Akananda, 'when the divine spiral has ascended another coil, or, if you like, when I've finished achieving a balance for those to whom I owe it.'

Sir Arthur gave him a startled anxious glance. The man made no sense—well, different race after all, not quite—and whatever he'd done had apparently saved the patient. One wouldn't have believed forty-eight hours ago . . . Look at her—plenty colour which had been ashen, sleeping like a healthy baby. 'Dammit all,' said Sir Arthur, 'really a miracle. I'll write it up for *The Lancet*—give you full credit, of course, though hard to, when I don't know what you *did*.'

'Very,' said Akananda, his exhaustion was passing, and a gleam of humour returned to his eyes. 'You can hardly write that, with the help and guidance of my Master, who was once a Sufi named Nanak, Celia has just lived through a former life in Tudor times, and I with her.'

Sir Arthur cleared his throat and shifted uneasily. He tried to laugh, but there was something about the Hindu—a sureness, a composed detachment that was impressive. 'No,' he said, 'all that stuff. My wife used to dabble in it, and you were raised to it of course, but I don't see—medically speaking—no, I don't see at all.'

'Perhaps you will—some day,' said Akananda softly. 'And

though *she* will recover, freed from the past, the end is not yet, for the others—for redress, for redemption.'

Sir Arthur snorted. 'Those are very "pi" sentiments. Was a preacher in Staffordshire—I was raised chapel, though've tried to forget it—*he* talked that way . . . redemption and the lot.'

'Truth is naturally universal,' said Akananda, 'and shines into many different windows, though some of them are clouded. Arthur, we should summon Mrs. Taylor, poor lady —and I can see that the nurse is waiting to tend her patient and freshen the room.'

'Indeed, yes,' said the other doctor, thankfully abandoning metaphysics. 'Room smells queer, no air, of course—there's a flowery smell though—but something else. Patient begun to void again?'

Akananda nodded. 'Body functions returned to normal. Send for Mrs. Taylor, and reassure the others! She shouldn't see them for quite a while.'

Lily Taylor came in fearingly. She dared not believe Sir Arthur, who had gripped her hand and said, 'Trouble's all over. She'll do now.' But when Lily saw Celia—sleeping sweetly as she had in childhood, one hand cured under the pillow, the other cuddling a fold of sheet as it had once cuddled a little stuffed bear—Lily could not restrain a sobbing choke. She kissed her daughter on the cheek, then smoothed the matted, gummy curls.

Celia opened her eyes. 'Aunt Ursula?' she said. 'Have I been ill?'

'No, no, darling,' Lily cried. 'I'm your *mother* . . .'

Celia considered this, and nodded. 'Aye, to be sure—you almost were—you wanted to be . . . and I, too, starting at Cowdray. And Sir John, he was my father this time, and got what *he* wanted—riches—he died saying "silver", you know, but he *didn't* get the son, only me.'

Lily looked anxiously to Akananda who stood by the chest of drawers, sipping his tea; his eyes met hers with smiling sympathy.

'She seems—oh—she looks normal,' Lily whispered, 'but she's delirious. Oh, Doctor, will her mind be all right?'

He nodded. 'She has almost made the transition.'

'From what?' Lily asked sharply.

'From the far past and its evils.'

Lily, whose blue eyes were haggard, and who, like Akananda, had not slept for two nights, cried, 'The evil's *now*! I mean, I guess my baby's come through the worst, and I pray you're right. But Richard . . .'

Akananda put down his cup. He frowned. 'Yes, there's still Sir Richard who has a worse Karma to understand and expiate. I'll go to him tomorrow, after I've rested—and with God's help—regained my own strength.'

'Thank you . . .' Lily said, 'I don't understand, nor what makes you help us, except you're a doctor, and they *do* help people . . .'

'Usually,' said Akananda in a lighter tone. 'They *vow* to do so. Vows are important, Mrs. Taylor. I rather failed in mine four hundred years ago—failure all the worse, because in my soul I knew better. *Ignorance* can sometimes be excused. You know I died back then with only one desire. Sun, warmth . . . and I most certainly got it. I was reborn sixty-two years ago in Madras.' He gave a rueful laugh.

'Oh, were you . . .?' said Lily blankly. She was too harassed and tired to follow him. She jumped as there was a movement on the bed, a groping hand. She took it in hers, and felt the fingers cling. Lily put her cheek down on the little hand, and began to cry softly.

'Nor was *that* time I speak of in Tudor England, the first in which I failed you two,' said Akananda, but Lily did not hear him. He looked tenderly down on them both, and went to the door. He raised his voice. 'I'm sending a nurse in with a tablet I want you to take, Mrs. Taylor. You may stay with Celia for a time, but please don't talk. Let her rest.'

Lily nodded mutely.

*   *   *

Akananda's visit to Medfield next day was considerably delayed. He stopped at the Clinic to see his patient and found her sitting up in bed drinking beef broth, and wearing a pink satin bed-jacket her mother had brought her. Sister Kelly, the Irish nurse, was beside the bed, and greeted Akananda with a broad smile.

'Oh, we *do* feel better, Doctor! We'll be dangling this afternoon, and maybe take a step or two tomorrow—won't we, pet?'

Celia assented by a little nod, and a weak smile. 'I still get muddled—I had such strange dreams. You were in them, Doctor, only you had a beard, I think.' Her face puckered, her grey eyes grew confused. 'Something bad happened, something terrible . . .'

'Och,' said the nurse quickly, 'iverybody has nightmares. Finish your broth, dear, and a bite o' nice custard to follow.'

Celia obediently drank, while Akananda scrutinised her. They had brushed most of the electrode gum out of her hair, which lay around her face like a little dark cap. The colour was good under the rather sallow skin, but there were still signs of strain in the muscles around the grey eyes, and the bones were a trifle sharp, as was natural after the long fast. A pleasant little face, but it held none of the luring rose and gold beauty of Celia de Bohun, whose face he still distinctly remembered. *This* face would not inflame men, nor lead its owner towards wantonness and destruction.

He thought of the night at Medfield—Lord, only four days ago—when this Celia had suddenly merged with the other one—the wild sparkle she had shown, her reckless disappearance into the garden with Sir Harry—her defiance. Harry Jones—it was hard to believe that he had once been Anthony Browne, Lord Montagu—and yet Akananda thought so, and if the Law of Karma *could* be neatly explained he wondered what had happened during the rest of Lord Montagu's life, so that the soul this time chose for habitation a rather commonplace man, dedicated to womanising, and eloquent only on the subject of his war years. In his case religion, his Catholicism, had not carried over—probably because it was never a deep conviction. As for the Duchess—perhaps she had not altered much from the Lady Magdalen she had been except for a veneer of beauty and sophistication—both products of the present century. She had been a great lady, an aristocrat then, she was so still. She had again been born in a Cumberland castle; she had again moved south by marriage; and doubtless, might repeat the underlying pattern, having seen no reason to change it—as yet. Still, there was a change. While delving in the British Museum, Akananda had found a small seventeenth-century book purporting to be the biography of Lady Montagu. He had scanned it rapidly, and been repelled by the bigotry and smug prudery of Magdalen Dacre's later years. Whatever she was now did *not* include prudish bigotry.

Celia was dozing and Akananda sat down beside her for a moment, until her nurse should come back from an errand, while he briefly considered the vivid and painful experience he had lived through during the last days. It was not like watching a film—it *was* very like reading an absorbing novel in which the author dips at will into the mind of each protagonist. The difference lay in the purpose behind: Akananda's purpose, and that of the enlightened being who had directed it.

Most of the central characters had undoubtedly been brought together at the Marsdons' house party last week so that there might be a chance of resolving an ancient tragedy which was still producing tragedy.

Little Sue Blake, however, had not appeared in Tudor times. On the other hand there was no identification in the present with Wat Farrier, or indeed, the three Tudor monarchs of those bygone years.

At least, Akananda thought, cruelty is no longer condoned, when it occurs now. We have no ferocious religious persecutions, nobody in England is burned at the stake for their beliefs, nor is tortured, killed, according to the will of any single despot.

We have achieved instead a fuzzy general tolerance less exciting, but an upward climb on the spiral.

He was roused by Celia, who suddenly said, 'Where's Richard?' in a plaintive voice. 'Shouldn't he be here? I want him.'

Akananda started. The fascinating puzzles remaining from the past were not paramount. The central dilemma remained.

'Why, I'm sure Sir Richard will be up shortly,' he said. 'He too has been ill.'

'Oh, poor darling,' said Celia. 'Is it his back? Or maybe the flu. He was acting rather feverish before the'—she frowned, trying to remember—'the house party, when *I* got sick!'

'He'll be all right,' said Akananda, trying to impel a confidence he did not feel. 'Quite O.K.'

Nurse Kelly returned as Celia nodded. 'I'm longing to see him,' she broke off and looked at her left hand. 'Where's my ring ... the Marsdon ring? I had it over the wedding band. Somebody took it off!'

'Now, now, dear,' said the nurse quickly. 'Ye mustn't worrit yourself ... Is this it?' She took the amethyst ring from the bed table drawer. ' 'Twas on the washstand, we found it when we tidied ye up.'

Celia took the ring and smiled. She put it back on her finger. 'Of course. I seem to have forgotten a whole lot, but doesn't matter, I guess. I had a fall, didn't I? Or was it an accident? Somebody was talking about a car crash on the A27 and needing beds ... Richard wasn't hurt, was he?' Her pupils dilated, and she caught her lip.

'No,' said Akananda with such conviction that Celia relaxed. 'Sir Richard was *not* hurt. I want you to stop talking, eat what the Sister gives you and then sleep dreamlessly for three hours.' He raised his brown hand, moved it slowly in circles, then smoothed her forehead. 'Eat and then sleep, Celia. You will awaken refreshed. Tonight the same. Eat and then sleep. Awake refreshed.'

He had hypnotised many patients with varying results, but never so receptive a subject. He waited until she finished the tiny custard the nurse gave her, saw her eyelids droop, then said, 'Don't disturb her today, no dangling, or attempt to walk. I'll clear it with Sir Arthur.'

The nurse nodded. 'I've faith in ye, Doctor, God bless ye —no matter what matron thinks,' she added under her breath.

Akananda left Celia's room and went downstairs. As he passed the waiting room a small, grizzled man darted out, and clutched his arm.

'Doctor . . . *please* . . .' he said in a muffled squeak. 'I've been here an hour, they won't tell me anything!'

Akananda, whose mind was entirely set on the conflict ahead, had difficulty in placing the contorted face, the puckered eyes which were red with weeping. 'And what is it?' he said.

'You know me, Doctor—George Simpson. We met at Medfield. How's Lady Marsdon?'

'She's doing well.' The Hindu was puzzled, though an interior signal was alerted. 'No reason to be so distraught.' His own memories of the other lifetime experience in Celia's hospital room were beginning to fade, and except that George Simpson was connected with futility and terror—of which he had had quite enough—he barely remembered the man. 'No need to be so excited about Lady Marsdon,' he repeated coldly.

'Well, you see,' George Simpson chewed on his little grey moustache, ' 'tis Edna—she had an accident last night, bad, very bad. She's in hospital now—isolation—they won't let me near her. But the only thing she said before the pain got so bad was "Celia"—and knowing that was Lady Marsdon's Christian name, and *she* so ill, I thought I'd come to the Clinic and enquire.'

515

'Ah-h,' said Akananda. George Simpson had his full attention, and he drew the distracted husband into a small private consultation room. 'Sit down, sir. Tell me what happened to Mrs. Simpson.'

The little man made an effort. He fished out his pipe, tried to fill it, then gave up as the tobacco spilled all over his knees. 'She was burned,' he said with a gulp. 'When I got home from the office, they'd already smelled smoke and broken in — they heard her screams — people in the flat next us. They'd got the fire out — 'twasn't much except Edna's kimono caught, she was all in flames — they rolled her in the rug.' George made a dry noise and put his hands over his eyes. 'It's horrible,' he whispered. 'They doubt she'll live — third degree burns, her flesh was *charred* — her face —'

Akananda was silent for a moment, before he put his hand on the other man's shoulder. 'I'm deeply sorry. Can you tell me how it happened? It's better if you talk.'

'Must've been the spirit lamp,' answered George dully. 'Lit it to make a cup of tea ... She ... she liked to save the gas. And then ... she wasn't quite herself, maybe. Had a — a tincture the chemist gave her. When she'd take a lot ... she'd not be quite with it.'

'I see ...' said Akananda after a pause. 'A very sad accident. I feel for you, Mr. Simpson.' He had compassion in his voice, but he felt immense relief. In the end, the Karmic Law had worked, not quite as one might expect for the retribution of the murder and suicide once caused by Emma Allen, but in the great agony and purging of seemingly accidental fire. Yet, there was a link which only he could discern. Edna Simpson's accident had happened last night, probably at the hour that Celia had been reliving the moment of her own death at Ightham Mote.

'Shall I ring the hospital for you, and find out Mrs. Simpson's condition now?' he asked. 'They'll be more apt to give me information.'

George nodded, and mumbled the number.

Akananda reached for the telephone and spoke for some minutes. He put the receiver softly back on its cradle.

George lifted his wobbly little chin and stared at the Hindu doctor's face. 'She's gone ...' he said.

Akananda slowly bent his head. 'You should have someone with you. Children? Relatives?'

'We had no children, 'twas always a grief to her ... There's my brother, John Simpson—works in the City. Oh, Doctor, I can't believe it ... she's ... *was* often difficult—lots of people didn't like Edna, and she altered of late, so discontented and touchy, but I was fond of her ... and my God, what a ghastly death ... I can't believe it ... such a cruel death ... when I think of her screaming for help all alone in the flat ...'

Akananda sighed. 'In time you'll forget,' he said. 'Now, what is your brother's phone number?'

*   *   *

Jiddu Akananda and Lily Taylor arrived at Medfield Place that evening in the car-with-chauffeur Lily had hired in London.

They spoke but little on the ride, and Lily's apprehensions were gradually allayed by the Hindu's quiet presence. She felt strength flowing from him, and rested in it. A last-minute check on Celia had confirmed steady improvement, and a composure which was new. Though she was still weak there was left nothing of the childishness and confusion she had shown upon first waking from her trance.

She made no reference to her illness, nor to Richard. She had talked a little to Sister Kelly about Ireland, and then America, where the nurse had many relations. Just as Lily left, Celia asked for a Bible.

'A quite sane wish, Mother,' she had said, smiling at Lily's consternation. 'Don't be alarmed. You *did* send me to Sunday School in Lake Forest, you know! There's some verses I want to look up. It's funny, I used to hate the Bible classes, but some of it seems to have stuck.'

A Bible was found—not without difficulty—and when Lily left, Celia was quietly leafing through the pages and pausing to read now and then.

'You don't think that a sign of abnormality?' Lily said anxiously to Akananda in the hospital corridor. 'I mean, it's so unlike her to ask for the *Bible*, she's always been a little atheist.'

'I don't think it's abnormal,' said Akananda, 'and I think that you'll find Celia changed in many ways. Your own delvings and gropings and fundamental spirituality, probably caused her to rebel—this is natural, but not final.'

The hired Daimler purred through the twilight towards Sussex, and it wasn't until they approached Alfriston that Lily roused herself from an exhausted doze, and sighed. 'If Richard again refused all admittance, I suppose we'll have to put up at the Star. Telephone's not working at Medfield Place—Richard cut the wires. Perhaps we'd better book now?'

'It would be wise,' said the Hindu, 'in fact, I already did so before we left London.' He gave a faint almost boyish chuckle. 'I trust I'm improving in forethought and care for your comfort. There was need . . .'

Lily looked quickly around in the gloom of the back seat. 'How silly,' she said with an uncertain laugh. 'You've been wonderful through all this—this ghastly mess. And . . .' She paused, searching for the right words, embarrassed. 'You're a professional man, you've stood by, given a lot of your time . . . and I'm fortunately quite able to . . .'

'Recompense me with a generous stipend?' said Akananda softly. 'I know, my dear. But in this life, for me, money recompenses nothing. Later—perhaps—we can talk about specific ways in which you may help others.'

He put his hand suddenly over hers. She jumped with startled pleasure, then let her hand go limp under the tingling warmth.

'What do you see?' he asked very low.

Bewildered, she looked around at the Alfriston green, the church's thick squatty spire high on a mound against the dim-lit trees and the gabled roof lines of the old buildings. 'I see Alfriston,' she said, 'what else?'

'What do you feel then?' he asked, his grip tightened on her hand.

'Why . . .' said Lily slowly, 'it seems foolish, but I did have a flash just then—white columns like a temple, against a blue, blue sky—I felt love, desertion, sorrow . . . a man who abandoned me and—our little girl . . . grieving.'

'Yes, just so,' said Akananda.

They were silent again, while the hedgerows slipped by and the Downs—humped up darkly green and mysterious on their right.

Then Akananda spoke in a tender low voice. 'My love for you is still there—but in a higher form. You may trust it, now.'

Lily quivered. She caught her breath like a girl. From any other man she would have thought this an overture; she had received many since her widowhood, as what pretty, rich woman did not? She knew that from him, it could be nothing so crude, and that the melting and release she felt were not materialistic.

As they passed by a village church, he spoke again. 'While Celia was in great danger, you went to pray in Southwark Cathedral—do you know why you were drawn to that place?'

'No ...' she said after a moment, 'and it didn't seem to help. I sat for an hour in a pew as you told me, but I couldn't calm down. I kept having a feeling that there was something behind the church, buildings, unhappy buildings ... but when I went out to look, I didn't see anything but warehouses. I took a cab back to Claridge's.'

'There *was* unhappiness for you once where those buildings stand,' said Akananda, 'it was Lord Montagu's Priory four hundred years ago.'

'Did I live there?' asked Lily in a whisper. 'Do you *know* that I did?'

'Yes,' he said. 'But there's no need for you to puzzle over it. I was merely curious. Look!' he added on a brisker tone. 'Aren't those the gates to Medfield Place? They're shut, I wonder if they're locked. Will you ask the chauffeur to find out?'

Lily tapped on the dividing window, and complied in a hushed voice. The chauffeur nodded, touched his peak cap and presently flung the gates wide open for the Daimler to pass through.

The rhododendrons and the laurel were blooming along the short avenue, bunches of pale stars in the gloaming. Though it was past nine o'clock, the eerie glimmer of a late-June evening suffused the rambling house and its architectural mixture of periods.

Akananda retained some memory of the place as it had looked when he, as Julian, had stopped there briefly with Tom Marsdon on the way to Ightham Mote—much smaller then, lacking the Victorian wing, and even some Elizabethan rooms which Tom must have added himself. But the dovecote and huge tithe-barn seemed unaltered. And was that not another confirmation, he thought, of the many outward changes which a soul as well as a house might accrue without affecting its essential individuality?

The car drew up before the entrance steps; the chauffeur got out and opened the back-seat door. 'Seems to be nobody about, madam,' he said to Lily. 'Shall I ring?'

She said, 'Please,' and sat tautly, gripping her suede hand-bag, staring at the dark, silent house.

The chauffeur pushed the bell, then stood back and waited.

Nothing happened. He pushed again, and after a further wait came back to the car.

'Is there some staff, madam? I could go round to the back entrance. Front door's locked, I tried.'

'There *was* staff . . .' said Lily unhappily, 'at least Nanny was here Wednesday when I came to see Richard, though she acted very strange and scared, spoke through the crack, just said that Richard had given orders that *nobody* was to be admitted—especially not *me*.' Lily pressed her lace handkerchief to her mouth. 'Oh, Doctor . . . what *is* happening here?'

Akananda did not answer. He got out of the car and walked around to the garden, which was fragrant with roses, stock and carnations. Fireflies twinkled amidst the foliage, and over the swimming pool. He looked down at the pool. On the rectangle of water between tiny blue-glazed tiles a few brown petals floated, there was a slight scum. Incredible to realise that the scene beside this pool happened only a week ago— the apparently gay house party around the brink, the careless sunlight on bronzed bodies. The chatter, the banalities. And Richard's graceful, reckless diving . . .

Akananda walked to the coping and stared down into the cloudy water, seized by a frightening question. And was at once reassured. No. He knew that Richard was alive. Though the guidance was imperfect—or his reception of it—he *had* achieved a measure of certainties. Richard was alive somewhere in that dark cloistered house, but the next development could not be foreseen, and Akananda tried to gather together the golden forces into his body, into his brain, as he had been taught, while fighting weakness—an immense desire to be free from pressure, to rest again in his quiet isolated rooms in London, away from turmoil, misery, effort.

Even towards Lily, waiting in the car, he felt impatience. Let them all help themselves now, he thought, *Celia* is saved. Through whatever unorthodox measure I used, and suffered with her, expiation which would continue—for him. He had felt, since emerging from the ordeal in the London Clinic, a stricture in his chest, darting pains in his left arm, and knew very well what they meant. He had now sacrificed his splendid bodily health, the mechanism was impaired.

This beating on a closed door is stupid, he thought. There'll be comfortable rooms in Alfriston; I'll knock up the chemist, get some digitalin at least. But I want to be alone. I'll tell Lily Taylor, she'll do whatever I say. And nothing actually has to be done tonight. Arthur would think me mad ... perhaps I am hallucinating — self-hypnosis. At Guy's they thought I was cracked. 'Now, Mr. Akananda, will you kindly dissect for us the pineal gland, where you aver the soul ... has ... had ... but I admit *this* corpse is deader than mutton ...' and the sycophantic, jeering laughter.

Akananda turned sharply away from the swimming pool; he was aware of faint musical sounds from the house behind him. He listened, frowning, and walked towards the Elizabethan wing. The sound was unmistakably chanting ... men's voices ... the cadences ... the sliding mysterious harmonies — Gregorian — adoration ... to the Virgin ... to God ... as he had heard it in this house last week, as he had heard it many hundred years ago.

He sighed, bowed his head, and threw his arms out in front of him, palms up, in a gesture of weary surrender. Alien music, alien voices, but none the less compelling, and significant.

He walked to the door of the garden room and found it open. With sureness and resignation he followed the sound. Up the front stairs, down those passages, around a corner, down another small flight to the old schoolroom. Here, the din of men's voices from the speakers was garbled, deafening. The door was wide open, and Richard was kneeling in the tiny makeshift chapel, his head resting on his clasped hands. He jumped up when he saw the Hindu standing beside him.

'Get out of here!' he shouted. 'How dare you spy on me! How the hell did you get in?'

Akananda took a deep breath as the haggard, unshaven Baronet loomed over him. The hazel eyes were savage, the eyes of a trapped uncomprehending animal, and dangerous. Paranoid, Akananda thought. He had seen that look often enough.

Akananda gestured at the stereo. 'It's a bit loud,' he said mildly, 'though very beautiful — this old church music. I'd like to listen with you, but let's turn it down a little.'

Richard glared at the slight, elderly doctor in a well-cut brown suit. 'You were here when Celia died,' he cried. 'I remember you. Get out, you spy! I sacked the servants, and locked the doors.'

'Well, yes,' said Akananda smiling, 'I suppose you did, except the garden door — maybe the lock is defective.' He went to the record player and lowered the volume to a soothing murmur. 'My Latin is rusty,' he said, 'what are they singing?'

'A Salve Regina,' answered Richard warily after a moment. His eyes lost their dangerous glint and grew haunting and puzzled. 'I don't see what you're doing here.'

'Please sit down,' said Akananda. 'It's hard to listen to music standing, don't you think?' He sat himself on an old school bench, and waited, quietly watching, until Richard slowly followed suit.

'I've always wished I had a better knowledge of western religious music,' said Akananda casually. 'I heard some at Oxford, of course, but I didn't understand it, being reared among instruments so different, like the sitar, though our Indian chants struck me, even in my youth, as somewhat nasal. I'm afraid I don't have a very keen ear.'

'Oh, indeed?' Richard's eyes continued perplexed, but his fists relaxed. He swallowed once or twice.

'By the way,' said Akananda, 'your wife, Celia is *not* dead —I came down to tell you that she is at the London Clinic, and doing very well.'

Richard made a grimace. He jumped up. 'You're wrong . . . of course she's dead. I killed her, I and that Simpson woman. We killed her, you know, and by God, Celia deserved it. Celia the wanton and fair.'

'Edna Simpson *is* dead,' said Akananda, with inward trepidation. How far and how fast dared he go? 'She had a—an accident, fatally burned with a spirit lamp. *She* is dead, Celia is not,' he repeated in a slow, measured voice. 'Now, Sir Richard, I'd like you to go to bed and rest. We can hear the Gregorian chants in the morning.' He saw signs of renewed tension, and an angry spark in the Baronet's eyes. 'Is Nanny still here?' Akananda asked pleasantly. 'Or did you sack her too?'

Richard looked startled. 'Nanny? I don't know. She kept pestering me. I did make her clear out . . . I think.'

Akananda nodded. 'Nobody likes being pestered, though I expect she's around. Anyway, shall we go look? I gather she's always been devoted to you.'

'Devoted . . .' Richard repeated. He considered the word and shuddered. 'There *is* no devotion,' he said. 'There's always betrayal . . . soon or late, they betray. You, *too*!' He rounded on Akananda, his eyes slitted, his upper lip drawn up in a tiger snarl.

Akananda, for all his experience, felt a thrill of primitive fear. He *must* get the man from this room, and he must over-power with his will alone—there was no help to be had, no physical help.

'Go touch your crucifix, Stephen Marsdon!' cried Akan-anda in a loud voice so penetrating that Richard started. He shook his head like a goaded bull. 'What do you mean!' He glanced from the corner of his eyes to the altar.

'Do as I command you, Brother Stephen,' said Akananda. 'You vowed obedience to your Superior. *I* am your Superior!'

Richard wilted very slowly under the force behind the doc-tor's eyes, the concentrated beam of light. He licked his lips, and fumbled, breathing hard, at his brown leather Bond Street belt.

'Not the rosary on your scourge,' said Akananda. 'Touch the altar crucifix.'

Richard dragged himself to the altar and put his hand on the wooden shaft, below the nailed silver feet.

'Ecce Agnus Dei, ecce qui tollit peccata mundi ...' said Akananda, while the monks' voices murmured their imploring chant from the far corner which contained the speakers.

Richard stood rooted with his hand on the crucifix. 'Domine non sum dignus ut intres sub tectum meum,' he said in a muffled voice like a frightened child. He began to tremble.

Akananda walked three paces very quickly, and took Richard's other hand. 'Come,' he said. 'We'll find Nanny. She'll make us some tea and toast, I hope. I'm very fond of buttered toast.'

Richard followed the guiding hand out of the schoolroom.

*   *   *

Lily was admitted to Medfield Place over an hour later by Akananda. He stood in the doorway, smiling faintly, but she saw by the blaze of electricity in the entrance hall how tired he was.

'Is it bad?' she whispered. 'You *found* him, didn't you?'

He nodded. 'He'll do, I think. I'd brought a syringe of chlorpromazine in my pocket—in case. He's had it, and is sleeping. Nanny's with him. It *was* bad for a while.' Akananda gave a grim laugh.

He had no intention of telling Lily how bad it had been, though after leaving the schoolroom, Richard was docile long enough to permit Akananda to inject the powerful tranquil-liser, which had fortunately begun to take effect before, in the search for Nanny, Richard saw the slashed portrait of Celia in the stairwell, 'See—I told you she was dead, and I killed her!' he shouted furiously to the doctor. 'She betrayed me!'

Akananda looked at the ribbons of painted canvas hanging from the frame, and said nothing. He kept his charge on the move, while his anxiety mounted. What had happened to the little Scottish nurse? He dared not leave Richard alone to hunt on his own. By the time they had wandered through the great house, and Akananda had called out, 'Nanny, where are you?' in the silent passages, and even in the attic, he saw that his charge was flagging, and must be kept quiet, though he was as sure that Nanny was near by as he had been that Richard was, earlier. His intuition strengthened as they went downstairs and returned to the kitchen. Of course, and—with all his knowledge of the past which was so gruesomely inter-mingled with the present in Richard's disordered brain—he should have guessed.

'Did you put Nanny in the cellar?' he asked, maintaining the quiet, casual tone. Richard looked at him blankly. His lids were drooping. He yawned rendingly. Akananda pushed him down on a kitchen chair and debated summoning the chauffeur outside for help—the patient was probably beyond the danger of a sudden murderous spring, but any new stimulus was unwise.

'Sit there,' he repeated. 'Don't move! I *command* you!'

Akananda went down to the cellars, a labyrinth of coalholes, wine bins and storerooms. He switched on the lights, and found at the end, a cubby-hole with a little wooden door, bolted from the outside by a heavy iron bar.

This time in response to his call he heard a faint answer. Nanny was sitting in the dark on a pile of rusty household implements, thrust there long ago and forgotten by earlier Marsdons. The tiny resolute figure greeted Akananda with one sobbing cry, then said, 'God be thankit. I've been pr-ray-ing, pr-rayers I learned i' the kirk, as a bairn. How's Master Richard? Oh, but he fr-righted me, Doctor-r. He's gan daft, ye ken.'

Akananda wasted no words. 'How long've you been here?'

'Yester nicht,' she said. 'I'm a wee bit thir-rsty, but how's *him*?'

'In the kitchen. Hurry!'

Surprisingly nimble, Nanny pelted through the cellars and up the stairs ahead of him. She saw Richard hunched in a chair, and threw her arms around him. 'A naughty lad, ye are,' she said, 'playing tricks wi' ye're auld Nanny.'

Richard looked at her in a dazed way, then let his head fall on her round poplin-covered bosom. 'I'm sleepy ...' he said.

It crossed Akananda's mind to wonder from whence this love sprang. There was nobody in the Tudor life, as far as he knew, who might have been Nanny, nor did it matter. There had been other lives, or the attachment might have started in this one.

Between them they had got Richard to bed.

Lily's anxious blue eyes surveyed the Hindu. 'You look all in,' she said gently. 'Some supper, maybe? I take it the staff has bolted, but the fridge must be loaded. I'll scramble some eggs—and I guess I'll send the chauffeur into Alfriston. We won't want him, will we?'

Akananda said, 'No, I think not, and I've another syringe full of chlorpromazine in my kit—if he'll bring that in. Though I doubt if Sir Richard will need it. This psychotic break has passed, nor was it a typical one.'

*   *   *

The next morning Richard slept on heavily while Medfield Place rapidly returned to its normal appearance.

Lily, refreshed and competent, sent the hired chauffeur to the village to make phone calls and fetch a daily until she could get new staff from London. Before the woman arrived she and Akananda removed all traces of the destructive forces engendered by the week of violence and anguish.

Celia's slashed portrait came down from the stairwell, and being beyond salvage, they threw the fragments in the dustbin. Two photographs of Celia were unmarred except for smashed glass. Lily put them in her own bureau drawer until they could be reglazed. A telephone repair man came from Lewes, and was totally incurious as he mended the cut wires. When service was restored, an immediate ring to the London Clinic elicited the reassurance that Lady Marsdon was fine, had slept well and eaten a big breakfast.

'What about the schoolroom?' asked Lily. 'Should we change anything there? It seems to have been such a place of torment for him all these days he'd hardly leave it—poor man.'

Akananda frowned thoughtfully. 'Let's go and look.'

The bright June morning exposed nothing sinister in the

shabby room with its old coal grate, its battered desks and benches, the ink-stained drugget on the splintery floor.

'Mercy,' said Lily, 'look at the dust! This place certainly needs a good cleaning. What's that over there in that closet—could it be an *altar?*'

'Yes,' said Akananda. 'Sir Richard's chapel.'

Lily stared at the candles and crucifix. 'But he isn't Catholic, he always sort of sneered at religion. Any kind.'

'None the less, he *was* devoutly religious once—and the contents of that rather pathetic little cupboard saved him last night.'

Lily shivered, half in awe, half in joy, looking from Akananda's quiet face to the tarnished crucifix. 'Prayer ...' she said softly, 'the Redeeming Light?'

He smiled. 'You understand, my dear. I think we mustn't touch this room now. Let Sir Richard decide when he's able to.'

She nodded. 'You know, it's funny, but I remember hearing when Celia first came to Medfield, somebody said the Marsdons' old chapel, the one they used in early days—oh, long before the first baronet—it was built in this wing, do you think it was *here?*'

'Very probably. The Marsdons retain stronger links with the past than most, especially Sir Richard, though his haven't been quite conscious.'

'Yours *are*, aren't they?' she said wistfully. 'Oh, I wish I could remember.'

Akananda shook his head. 'Remembrance can cause great suffering. *Imperfect, uncomprehending* remembrance nearly killed Celia and Sir Richard, though it's a different and logical force of the Law which has punished Edna Simpson.'

Lily sighed deeply. 'I don't quite understand,' she said, and looked out through the smeared, diamond-pane window towards the garden and the old dove-cote. 'But I learned a poem once. I forget who wrote it—somebody Phillips—' She paused and went on in a groping voice:

> ' 'Twas the moment deep
>   When we are conscious of the secret dawn
>   Amid the darkness that we feel is green ...
>   Thy face remembered is from other worlds
>   It has been died for though I know not when
>   It has been sung of though I know not where ...'

526

She broke off, blushing a little. 'Awfully romantic,' she said with a rueful twist of her delicately rouged lips, 'but then I was romantic at fourteen, and I felt—felt—well, something *true* about it. It just came to my mind.'

Akananda joined her at the window. He put his arm around her shoulders, and kissed her cheek. 'There *is* something true about it, my dear, and *you*, at least, will always feel the hope of secret dawn.' He turned abruptly and added, 'I must go and check on Sir Richard. If he's awake, we'll have to get some food down him—the man hasn't eaten in days.'

Twenty

On July 4, Celia came home to Medfield Place, accompanied by Dr. Akananda and her mother. Sir Arthur Moore saw them off from the steps of the London Clinic; he was jovial and hurried. He was due at a Governors' Meeting, besides an appointment with a distraught countess whose son had suddenly and blatantly declared himself homosexual.

'Well, well,' said Sir Arthur beaming, 'you're fit as a fiddle, Lady Marsdon. I couldn't be more delighted. Good way to celebrate this day, eh? When you Yankees threw tea or something at us poor old fogies over here. Independence all the thing now, but your chaps thought of it first. Oh, I don't say you didn't have me scared for a while in hospital, but these episodes like yours — they pass — I've seen several — Dr. Akananda was most helpful.' He gave the Hindu a warm smile. 'Glad you're taking him back with you for a bit. Lucky fellow — I could do with some fresh Sussex air m'self.'

The Marsdons' Jaguar twisted deftly through the heavy London traffic. Akananda sat in front with the private chauffeur Lily had provisionally hired. She had, in fact, almost completely restaffed Medfield Place, and since the calamitous strain of the last weeks was lessened, had room for a moment of complacency. It was disturbed when Celia spoke.

'Why didn't Richard come for me?'

'But, darling,' said Lily, 'he isn't very strong yet, you know that. He was sick, too — but he's longing to see you.'

This was not strictly true. Richard was apathetic, detached. When Lily told him they were fetching Celia from the Clinic, he said, 'I suppose so, if she's well enough. I married her.'

'Much better ... has lost his delusions,' said Akananda later to Lily. 'But not completely recovered.' There would be an intermediate phase, but scant danger of acute paranoia again. 'Yet, there's a lot unresolved,' he added, and Lily, who felt that she now knew the Hindu doctor so well, had caught his uncertainty. She looked at her daughter.

Celia was dressed in a simple and very expensive violet linen frock, ornamented only by a white monogram. The colour became her clear, tawny skin, and the soft dark hair, shampooed in the hospital but not set, made her rumpled little head look boyish. Yet Lily again noted maturity in the grey eyes, and there were a few lines around the mouth which was tinted a faint iridescent pink. She looked older now than her twenty-three years, perhaps it was the hint of sadness, an other-worldliness. Perhaps it was the knowledge of pregnancy. The urine test had come back yesterday—strongly positive.

As they crossed to Southwark on London Bridge, Lily glanced at the Cathedral to their right, and said hesitantly, 'Does this locale, I mean the church and everything, bring back any—I mean, do you get impressions?'

'Why, no,' said Celia looking around at the blaring traffic, the jumble of ugly warehouses, the scurrying pedestrians. 'Just a tiresome bit of road to be endured. Should I feel something?' She gave her mother an indulgent smile.

Lily shook her head. 'I guess not, it's just that Dr. Akananda said . . .'

Celia interrupted frowning. 'I don't think I quite like that man. Oh, I know he worked hard on me at the Clinic, but . . .'

'He saved your life, Celia,' said Lily sternly. 'He's a good man and a good doctor!'

'Well, I know . . .' Celia was startled by her mother's vehemence, 'I know he tried something, but matron, and Sir Arthur, too, say I'd've come out of whatever it was anyway. They think his methods were arbitrary, unethical. I just feel that I can't entirely trust him, and don't want him long at Medfield.'

Lily controlled her spurt of anger as she stared hard out of the window at the rows of semi-detached villas sliding by.

'At least,' she said in a crisp authoritative tone she had seldom used to Celia, 'we need his exceptional skills for the treatment of Richard. And, my dear girl, you have fortunately no idea of the dangers already surmounted with *that man's* dedicated help. No matter what Sir Arthur and the nurses may have said during the last week, your life depended on Jiddu Akananda—and the life of the baby inside you.'

Conflict was so rare between this mother and daughter that it disturbed both of them. Lily at once changed the subject.

'Did you enjoy your Bible readings?' she asked smiling. 'Find what you wanted?'

'I found,' said Celia after a thoughtful moment, accepting the olive branch, 'many verses, especially in the New Testa-

ment, which had a new meaning and comfort I'd never seen
before.'

*   *   *

The meeting between Richard and Celia was like that of
polite strangers. Richard came out on the steps as the Jaguar
drew up, his mouth lifted a trifle at the corners when he saw
Celia.

'It's a pleasure to welcome you back to Medfield Place.
Sorry you were ill. I believe tea's laid on in the drawing room.
We've a whole new staff. Your mother's been most efficient.'
He nodded to Lily. 'And Doctor Akananda? So you came down
for a breather? Splendid. I expect Mrs. Taylor will show you to
your room, though I believe you've used it before?'

Akananda bowed gravely, but he was watching Celia, and
saw her eyes widen, heard her muffled gasp. She had held her
face up to be kissed, but deftly hid the motion by shifting her
handbag to the other arm.

'Some tea would be great,' she said. 'How are *you* feeling,
Richard? Funny we should both get sick at the same time,
but you look wonderful—except we've both lost our tan. We
must do some sunbathing tomorrow—between showers.'

She'll do, Akananda thought. She's handling this right. It
would be better if he and Lily Taylor cleared out, leaving them
alone here, but he did not dare. As they sat at tea he concentrated until he saw the emanations around Richard. There was
still danger in them. He saw with the third eye, the little organ
which he had been taught to use, but since the unhappy days
at Guy's Hospital was no longer so certain that it was located
in the pineal gland, or anywhere. Am I losing confidence? And
the girl—my Celia—his chest twinged and he felt sadly discouraged. As soon as they descended from the car he had felt
Celia's hostility. Justified hostility in view of the past lives, but
saddening.

The evening proceeded pleasantly enough—*if* Akananda,
Celia and Lily had been ordinary casual house guests of Sir
Richard Marsdon's.

They dined at eight, they watched a little television until
nine-thirty when Lily, whose own heart had grown heavy as
stone and who was barely able to endure some banal playlet
on the screen, said that a girl just out of hospital must go to
bed. Richard nodded agreeably, and said he believed that the
master bedroom was in order.

Celia held herself tight and spoke in a neutral voice. 'Where are *you* sleeping, Richard?'

'Why, in the red room as usual.' His heavy black brows rose, as though it were an impertinent question. 'There's some sort of maid to look after you, or perhaps Nanny will.'

'I see,' said Celia. 'Where *is* Nanny? I should've thought she'd greet me.'

'Oh, no,' said Richard. 'She never greets guests, always keeps to herself unless wanted. Have a night-cap?' he added politely to Akananda, who shook his head. 'Then off to bed with you all!' he gestured towards the stairs.

Lily gave a deep sigh, but began to ascend the steps.

'Are *you* going to bed, Richard?' said Celia quietly. 'Or what?'

He blinked. Her clear slow voice penetrated his private world, and he looked at her with more attention. Pleasant voice, no twang, but definitely not English. A small, chic, brown-haired foreigner who yet had some right to question.

'Might take a turn around the grounds,' he said reluctantly. 'Or spend a while in the library—I've been reading a lot. Fascinating batch of books my ancestors gathered through the years. Must get them catalogued.'

'And the most fascinating of all is the Marsdon Chronicle?' Celia spoke in the same neutral tone, but she flushed, remembering the last time she had been in the library, in her bikini, the last time he had shown her light-hearted warmth—or any real love. And after that—the visit to Ightham Mote—fear, darkness and a long void. A black tunnel.

'Well,' said Richard with an uneasy laugh, 'I do find the family archives quite interesting. I don't expect them to interest you. You had no part in them.'

'But she *did*!' said Akananda from the shadow at the foot of the stairs.

They had both forgotten him. Celia turned in some resentment. Richard, however, stared at the Hindu; his handsome face which had been closed, subtly hostile, showed the same perplexity it had shown in the schoolroom two weeks ago.

'Celia did what?' Richard said, trying to laugh. 'Except I suppose I entered our marriage date in the Chronicle last year —or intended to—I forget.'

Celia made a small choking sound. Her new strength began to crumble. She knew as surely as Akananda did, that Richard had not recorded their marriage in that damnable book which she hadn't known existed until she followed Richard to the library on the Saturday of the house party. A sea of desolation washed through her, and she clutched the banister.

Akananda looked at the small hand on the banister and said, 'Sir Richard, your wife wears the Marsdon bridal ring; you gave it to her, but she has also given it to *you* at a certain moment.'

'Nonsense,' said Richard, though he stared at the great amethyst heart set in massy gold. 'You make me uncomfortable, Doctor, you're a psychiatrist, aren't you? I suppose that dealing with crack-pots makes you . . . well . . .'

'A bit of a crack-pot, too?' said Akananda, nodding, while he thought, This is coming faster than I expected, and from a portion of his mind which was neither weary nor fearful he sent up a mantra for guidance. 'Lady Marsdon,' he said, 'as physician delegated by Sir Arthur for your care, and in view of the fact that you're just out of hospital, I wish you to go to bed. Your mother'll help you.'

Celia clutched the banister harder, her eyes flashed. 'I'm not a child, Dr. Akananda, I don't need either you or Mother to tell me what to do. Leave me alone with my husband!' But on the last word her voice wavered. What could she say to Richard? How could she approach the tall, indifferent stranger who had ceased even looking at her or the ring, and turned his back while he shifted, as though it were of great importance, a porcelain vaseful of glossophylia and carnations, pushing them sharply back on the polished walnut console.

'Courage, my child,' said Akananda so low that Celia did not quite hear, though she glanced at him, and felt through her distrust, a far-off comfort.

'See you tomorrow, Richard,' she said with all the lightness she could muster. 'I guess the Doctor's right. I am a bit wobbly.'

She slowly mounted the stairs.

'Lovely flowers — carnations,' said Akananda; he plucked a creamy pink hybrid from the vase which Richard had shoved. He sniffed it. 'Delicious fragrance of cloves, with a touch of jasmine. The gillyflower of centuries past, though of course they never grew them as big as this.'

'I hate the smell,' said Richard. 'Hate scents anyway, they give me hay fever. Are you going to turn in? I'm not up to chit-chat.'

Akananda nodded. 'I quite agree. But first, I wonder if

you'd be so good as to show me the library. I'm one of those who likes a book to go to bed with. Even a whodunnit, or don't you give them house-room?'

Richard smiled almost naturally. 'Lord, yes, my father had a shelf-full, Conan Doyle and the lot.'

He began to walk rather jerkily towards the Victorian wing, and the Hindu followed.

The long pseudo-gothic room, its varnished fumed oak stacks, its thousands of books, appeared as ordinary and homely as a loaf of bread when Richard switched on the lights. The windows depicting gaudy glass scenes from Tennyson's *Idylls of the King* were open to the sultry July air which felt thundery, breathless. There might well be a storm, Akananda thought, there was an odd yellow light over the Downs. He hoped there would be, hoped for any outside aid to explode the tension.

'Over here's the detective stories,' said Richard indicating a shelf in the bay nearest the courtyard. 'Take your pick.'

Akananda inhaled deeply and held his breath for a minute. He glanced along the rows of titles while Richard stood aside impatiently.

'Actual mysteries are perhaps more exciting, don't you think?' said Akananda moving into the next alcove which held the lectern and older books. 'I've heard so much about your Chronicle.' He paused. 'I mean,' he said carefully, 'I got some idea, possibly quite wrong, that there was a mystery in your own archives, some past puzzle not solved.'

Richard stiffened and his face grew black. 'Who said so?'

'Tonight . . . the way Lady Marsdon spoke, other ways too —and then you told me something when I was here a fort-night ago. Your unconscious mind remembers, I wish it to become conscious. *Sir Richard, sit down!*' said Akananda, indicating the armchair which stood by the window. 'You obeyed me in the schoolroom, though you've forgotten. You will obey me now, for my sole purpose is to help you.'

'You can't! I don't want help! Leave me alone!' Richard backed away.

'Oh, yes, you do—and you're not manic now, Sir Richard, you need no injections, no chemical restraints, you will sur-render to your hidden self and its true wishes—so if you won't sit—bring me the Chronicle! No, I'll get it. I know where it is.'

Akananda reached up for the great vellum-bound book and

thrust it into Richard's hands. 'Find the passage which has so long disturbed you. Ah, see it opens easily. Here—read it aloud to me. Quick!'

Though Richard looked down at the faded brown curlicues and flourishes, he spoke from memory in a flat, mechanical voice:

'All Hallows' Eve, the thirty-first year of her Majesty's reign, and a time of rejoicing since our fleet has sunk the wicked Spaniard . . .' He jerked back his head and glowered at Akananda. 'What's this tomfoolery you're doing? This is just a lot of stuff about some monk in the family—seems to have phil-andered, got a girl pregnant—wouldn't mean a thing nowa-days.'

'What happened to the girl, Richard?'

Both men jumped and gaped at Celia. She stood at the corner of the alcove, very still, wearing the shimmering yellow silk robe in which she had started to follow her bedtime routine.

'There's going to be a thunderstorm,' said Celia. 'You know they scare me.' She looked up into her husband's face and smiled with tenderness and pleading. 'I thought I'd find com-pany. I heard what you were saying . . . What happened to the girl . . . the pregnant girl?'

Richard winced and did not answer; he passed his hand over his forehead as though to brush away cobwebs.

Akananda moved quickly out of that alcove and back into the next one which held the mystery stories. There he stood, controlling his breath, immersed in a sustaining inner light. He listened with relief to a rumble of thunder, he also listened to the voices behind the bookstack.

'Let's read the whole entry,' said Celia, 'let me read it, too— if you'll help me, all those squiggles and "ye's" and funny spelling. Let's see.'

Akananda heard the duet of voices, Richard's slow and angrily reluctant, as he prompted Celia when she hesitated. Celia's voice alone finished the excerpt. 'Find the murdered girl for Christian burial.'

There was a long silence, while the thunder cracked nearer over Alfriston.

'Do you think you were once Stephen, and I that walled-up girl?' Celia's question was clear, gentle, assertive—yet tinged with sadness. The Hindu held himself tense, his body quivered. He waited.

'Yes, by God, I do!'

It was a strangled violent cry which shocked Akananda into immediate medical awareness. He touched the syringe he had in his pocket. One never knew, and with a case like this—a sudden breakthrough into realisation—and alone with the woman he had loved, hated, betrayed his vows for, and then ended his life by suicide on her account, believing that she might have betrayed *him*.

'But then,' said Celia, in the same calm dispassionate tones, 'you could hardly give those old bones of mine a Christian burial *now*. The guide at Ightham Mote said they'd been "dispersed"—I'd rather not try to find them, and what more would they mean, darling, than a dress I wore constantly in Chicago when I was twelve. Mama finally cut up the pretty sleeves for a rag-rug my aunt was making, and the rest went to the Salvation Army, I guess.'

Outside there was a thunderclap, Akananda saw a zigzag of lightning and quietly closed the window in his alcove. Rain began to spatter on the tiles but he could still hear Celia.

'Richard, my dear love, or Stephen, if you wish, that's all finished. *I* am carrying your child *now*, in the present—shall it not have welcome, and a father, as the other one did not?'

For a long time there was no answer. The lightning streaked again and there was thunder further to the south, then a lull, during which Akananda heard a different sound—that of a man's broken, barely audible sobbing.

*   *   *

On Thursday, August 8, at four o'clock, the village of Medfield, and certain guests who had been invited from London, gathered in the church for a ceremony which some of them thought bizarre, particularly holding a wedding on a Thursday, though the sentimental ladies of the parish agreed that it was all sweetly different. Sir Richard and Lady Marsdon had recently decided on a religious ceremony to supplement the registry marriage in London.

The rector was in his glory. It was always suspected that he had very High Church leanings, and Sir Richard who presented the living, of course, must have given the dear little man his head. The church reeked with incense, many candles were lit on the altar. Masses of flowers from the Medfield Place gardens were bunched along the aisles. The choir quavered raggedly through some old Latin chants—obviously requested.

The marriage ceremony followed the normal version and was, as usual, very brief, but a slight divergence before the final blessing startled a few. The congregation was politely, blankly waiting until they should be released and could go to the manor house where everyone had been invited to the reception.

The divergence consisted of prayers for the repose of the souls of Stephen Marsdon and Celia de Bohun.

'That's creepy,' whispered Myra, the Duchess, to Sir Harry Jones who was sitting next to her in a side pew. 'The padre's rung in a memorial service. And, look at this,' she put her hand on the old marble tomb in the niche beside her, then pointed to a shiny new brass inscription above it. ' "Stephen Marsdon. O.S.B. 1525–1559. Requiescat in pace, Misereatur tui omnipotens Deus, et dimissis peccatis tuis, perducat te ad vitam aeternam." Can he be doing an obit for *this* Stephen Marsdon?'

'Whole thing's peculiar,' Harry whispered back. 'Got a "Celia" in it, too. Wonder who *she* was—and a couple of R.I.P.s tacked on to a *wedding*! Could they have died the same day? But then, Richard always was an odd duck.'

'It's touching, somehow,' Myra murmured, her long green eyes misting. She knelt, bowing her auburn head which was swathed in a crisp of golden tulle, as the rector held up his plump hands and said, 'Let us pray—for the souls of Thy departed servants, Stephen and Celia, unto God's gracious mercy and protection we commit them. The Lord bless them and keep them. The Lord make His face to shine upon them and be gracious unto them. The Lord lift up the light of His countenance upon them and give them peace, both now and for evermore . . .' He lowered his hands majestically, and put them on the shoulders of the couple who were kneeling at the altar rail. He went on smoothly to finish the marriage service as Sir Richard had asked. 'God the Father, God the Son, God the Holy Ghost bless and preserve and keep you . . . that you may so live together in this life, that in the world to come you may have life everlasting . . . Amen.'

Richard and Celia Marsdon did not kiss when they arose. They looked long into each other's eyes, while the organ wheezed, blatted, then burst into Mendelssohn's triumphant march.

The Marsdons proceeded slowly down the aisle. Celia wore a long chiffon gown of a subtle cream colour which seemed

536

tinged with rose when it rippled. It made her look taller, as did the heart-shaped little silver headdress. Only Igor could have designed so flattering and lovely a creation, as indeed he had, and sent it from London two days ago as a wedding present.

Richard was magnificent in the conventional cut-away and a small white carnation in his buttonhole.

There were no attendants, but Lily and Akananda who had sat in the front pew followed the bridal couple some paces after. On the faces of the American mother and the Hindu doctor were expressions of quiet joy; though Lily had wept throughout the ceremonies she was now at peace and her soft blue picture hat hid any trace of tears.

The church bell clanged out with such congratulatory peals that they shook the little belfry, while the Marsdons paused between the churchyard and the lych-gate to greet their guests.

Myra rushed up first, and kissed Celia. 'Oh, my dear,' she said, 'so *sweet*, all of it, and *thank you* for asking us down!' She glanced at Harry, who stood beaming beside her. 'In this melting mood, I'm almost inspired to do likewise! May God bless you both,' she added seriously. 'You've had a rough time since the house party in June. I've worried a lot about you.' Myra's beautiful face looked surprised, for those words were not mere courtesy. She had enquired every day while Celia was in the Clinic, she had had two unhappy dreams about Celia. 'I'm very fond of you, hinny—as we say in the North.'

She moved back to let Nanny, resplendent in grey bombazine and a round flowered hat, extend her congratulations, and bridle happily as Richard bent to kiss her.

'That's a guid laddie,' she murmured, 'An' I bless the luik in ye're bonny face today.' She scurried off to help at the Manor.

The next to come up was Igor who was a gorgeous if startling sight in tight red velvet pants and a frilled white shirt. 'Too utterly charming,' he said, kissing Celia's hand. 'The quaintness—touch of Merry England as it was—do we now have dancing on the green? I'd simply adore to trip the light fantastic in your honour—though actually I'd not live back in *those days* for anything. I'm satisfied with the present.'

'So am I,' said Richard. He put his arm around Celia and smiled down at her. She leaned against his arm, her face quietly radiant.

Akananda stood apart and watched. Though his soul was full of gratitude, he was staving off physical exhaustion. Even the walk out of the church was an effort, and he leaned against a buttress. He saw George Simpson hanging around the outskirts of the crowd, noted the mourning band on his sleeve and his puckered anxious face. The Hindu smiled a greeting and George came over to him.

'Nice wedding,' he said. 'Church looked pretty—Edna'd have liked it—she used to like to go to weddings, that is, way back when we were first married ourselves. The last years, she'd hardly go anywhere. But she'd've liked this one at Medfield. She was so partial to Sir Richard.'

'Ah, yes,' said Akananda. He was almost drained of emotion, yet still capable of feeling pity for the good, bewildered little man who grieved for a woman who had caused so much suffering. No blacks, no whites were painted on the spokes of the eternally revolving wheel. In the Light of evolution they all became grey, and eventually—*eventually*—transparent, when they merged with the Light.

'Are you ill, Doctor?' cried George, putting his hand under Akananda's elbow. 'You look very seedy. Come and sit on that bench. We're not as young as we were, are we? And all that incense in the church . . . stifling . . . don't hold with that muck myself.' He propelled Akananda to the bench in the lych-gate.

'Thanks,' whispered Akananda, collapsing, 'I do have these —these spells, lately. It'll pass.' He reached in his breast pocket for a capsule of nitroglycerine, bit it, and put it under his tongue.

The wedding guests were leaving the churchyard, many on foot since it was less than a mile to Medfield Place. The Marsdons had gone ahead in the Jaguar, Myra and Harry in her Bentley, Igor in his new Isotta-Fraschini, though he had good-naturedly given lifts to first-comers.

The church bells pealed on, a joyous Epithalamium.

Akananda sat on the bench beside George Simpson who gnawed at his moustache and said in his squeaky voice, 'Do you feel better? I've got my old Rover parked way down the lane . . . if you can make it? No, wait here—crowd's thinned out, I'll bring it up.' He trotted off.

Akananda sat huddled on the stone bench which had been built six hundred years ago for the resting of coffins before they were carried into church for burial rites. The stricture in his chest, the lancinating pain down his left arm began to ebb.

I sat here *then*, he thought, while Tom Marsdon was inside the church bullying the sexton about Stephen's tomb, before we left for Ightham Mote. I was near to death then, too, but it was pneumonia that time. How very strange. His thoughts slid together, though he could watch them with some objectivity. The lych-gate had not changed much in structure, new posts, a tiled roof instead of the thatch he remembered. Would the lych-gate still be here after another four hundred years? Undoubtedly not. But something would—he looked out across the Cuckmere to the Downs. Would they be different? Engulfed, perhaps, in some unimaginable catastrophe? Eroded? Bombed? He thought not. There would still be the land, and wild flowers blooming on those quiet chalk hills, despite man's violence and blind encroachments, despite pessimism, confusion and wars.

He raised his head at a touch on his shoulder. Lily Taylor stood beside him peering down anxiously. 'You don't feel well?' she said. 'I thought you'd gone with the Duchess. There's some mix-up. I came back—Celia missed you. She's going to cut the bride-cake—all the old customs Richard wouldn't have in London. Celia won't start until you come.'

He said nothing for several seconds while she waited, much distressed.

'Here let me take your arm,' said Lily gently. 'I'm sure you can manage. You wouldn't want to disappoint Celia. She's so happy today, and she wants you beside her—so does Richard.'

Akananda rose from the lych-gate bench, he took Lily's arm. 'They and you *shall* be happy today,' he said, 'I too. No matter what human errors may occur in the future, several tragic wrongs *have* been redressed by love, by knowledge, and by the Grace of God in whatever form we envisage the Supreme Being.'

He paused and smiled at her. 'These particular lingering debts from the past are finally paid.'

Katherine

Katherine was born the daughter of a humble herald, was betrothed to an obscure knight but was loved by a prince. She became the mistress of John of Gaunt, then his wife and the ancestress of the Tudor Kings of England. The dramatic and brilliantly told story of her life and love is set against the superbly recreated pageant of fourteenth century England.

'Miss Seton's enthusiasm for both character and period is infectious. Katherine emerges a glowing, vital figure who played no minor part in one of the significant periods of English history.' *The Daily Telegraph.*

Devil Water

Conflict, courage and loyalty, recreated in the lives of people who chose their course and kept to it—a stubborn perhaps misguided loyalty, but given to a cause as poignant as any of the lost causes with which history is studded.

'Brilliant historical construction.' *Evening News.*

'Tremendously readable.' *Punch.*

My Theodosia

The eighteenth-century life story of Theodosia, daughter of America's famous politician, Aaron Burr.

Her arranged marriage to a Carolinian aristocrat, her perpetual love and loyalty to her father, her child, her emotions, and her love for a man she never sees: all described with a wealth of passionate feeling.

Foxfire

This is the story of Foxfire, that luminous glow as fake as any mirage. It is a story about love that started inexplicably and learned to be real. It is a story of adventure that ended in discovery.

'Perhaps the best gifts Anya Seton brings to her historical novels are the zest of her narrative, the life she breathes into the most insignificant characters, and the atmosphere of the era she evokes around them.' *Books and Bookmen.*

ORDER THESE BEST SELLING NOVELS
BY ANYA SETON ON THIS FORM
OR THROUGH YOUR BOOKSELLER

☐	15699 6	THE HEARTH AND EAGLE	35p
☐	15693 7	DEVIL WATER	40p
☐	01401 6	MY THEODOSIA	35p
☐	15700 3	THE TURQUOISE	35p
☐	01951 4	THE WINTHROP WOMAN	40p
☐	02469 0	DRAGONWYCK	35p
☐	02488 7	FOXFIRE	35p
☐	02713 4	AVALON	35p
☐	15701 1	KATHERINE	40p
☐	15683 X	THE MISTLETOE AND SWORD	30p

All these books are available at your bookshop or newsagent, or can be ordered direct from the publisher. Just tick the titles you want and fill in the form below.

CORONET BOOKS, P.O. Box 11, Falmouth, Cornwall.

Please send cheque or postal order. No currency, and allow the following for postage and packing:

1 book – 10p, 2 books – 15p, 3 books – 20p, 4–5 books – 25p, 6–9 books – 4p per copy, 10–15 books – 2½p per copy, over 30 books free within the U.K.

Overseas – please allow 10p for the first book and 5p per copy for each additional book.

Name...

Address..